THE STEWARDESS'S DIARY

S.M. PRATT

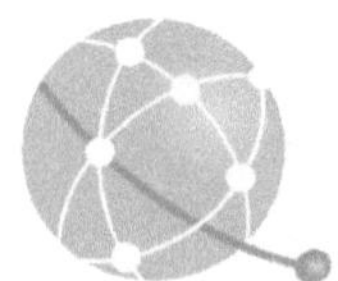

PRAISE FOR S.M. PRATT'S ONGOING SERIES

LIST OF EPISODES

The Stewardess's Diary contains ten episodes:

Part 1: Canada introduces the mystery stewardess as a woman who's heartbroken following a disastrous weekend getaway. Alex, a fellow flight attendant on a red-eye flight to Toronto, recommends she stop looking for relationships and instead focus on enjoying the moment, trying out one-night stands. Will the stewardess quiet down her mind and pull it off?

In *Part 2: Mexico*, the stewardess is stranded in Cancun, once again let down by another man. Finding herself without plans at the last minute, she joins two young, beautiful blonde women on their yacht for a quiet afternoon... Or so she thought.

Part 3: Costa Rica sees the stewardess come out of her shell, actively putting herself out there to try and enjoy herself. During a weekend getaway on her own, she signs up for a surf lesson with a handsome instructor. But a surprise awaits them when a cop finds them naked on the beach and makes demands of his own.

In *Part 4: USA*, while in Los Angeles, the stewardess and one of her friends decide to interview for a publicity campaign promoting an aviation school. They discover what it's like to get screwed—both literally and figuratively—by manipulative, cunning, and good-looking men in L.A.

In *Part 5: Ireland*, the stewardess heads out on a romantic weekend getaway at an Irish castle with her current boy-toy. But she has no idea that the castle offers such unique 'amenities' to their patrons. Butlers, maids, and even guests seem to be at everyone's beck and call.

In *Part 6: Thailand*, the stewardess explores Bangkok with a fellow flight attendant. While at a spa, she and her coworker experience sensations that most tourists visiting Thailand will never experience. She crosses boundaries that even the captain would never dare touch. Will the captain manage to get closer to the stewardess by tracking down her unique Thai coworker?

In **Part 7: France**, the stewardess goes through a roller-coaster of emotions after learning of her aunt's passing. Her past gets dug up, and she exposes some of her painful romantic memories. Will the identifying details she slipped in her journal be enough for the captain to discover who she is?

In **Part 8: Holland**, the stewardess and one of her coworkers go cycling through the Netherlands and entertain themselves with the handsome men they encounter. The captain believes he may have found her. But did he?

In **Part 9: Japan**, the stewardess participates in a unique Japanese game show. The captain, while trying to track down a copy of that recording, gets himself in deep trouble. Can he find a way to protect his reputation? And will the risk he takes prove to be worthwhile?

In **Part 10: Spain**, the stewardess comes to terms with her sexual desires and leaves a clue behind for the captain to find. Will it be enough for him to finally uncover her identity and meet her?

PROLOGUE

I'm Charlie, a veteran pilot for a major international airline that shall remain nameless for reasons you'll soon come to understand.

A year ago, while waiting for my flight to London in the airline's lounge at one of America's largest hubs, I discovered a special and highly personal journal among my belongings. How it happened, I'll never know, but the beautiful brown leather notebook nonetheless appeared in my carry-on at some point between the time I left my New York penthouse apartment and arrived at the airport lounge.

Perhaps it was a mix-up at security, or some devious stewardess with sly hand skills, but I've since become obsessed with the person who wrote that diary, her stories, and—to be blunt—her unconventional sex life.

My best friend—let's call him Bob—is one of my regular co-pilots. Bob advised me to forget about the journal and ignore my hunch to track down its rightful owner. After my initial reading of her hand-written accounts, the part of me who's loyal to the airline and wants the best for our passengers certainly needed to find that stewardess and expel her from our company—or whatever airline she's with. This woman is surely a threat to any crew with her irreverent disregard for our uniforms, her sexual behavior with passengers and airline employees, and the way she ignores regulations. She should clearly be punished for her conduct...

But after reading and re-reading each one of her journal entries, another, more animal part of me has grown fond of her complete lack of boundaries, her willingness to experiment, and her ravenous sexual appetite.

I've had my fair share of illicit affairs with female flight attendants and co-pilots, but none of them were interesting enough to be granted a second fuck by yours truly, let alone be courted or considered for a long-term relationship. But the woman who's filled so many pages with delicate calligraphy and salacious words deserves my full attention. She's certainly maintained it well past the time I closed the cover of her journal—again and again.

Imagining how her naiveté was gradually—and most willingly—robbed from her was simply... enthralling. She's been haunting my wet dreams.

Now, every time I see an unknown stewardess, I wonder if *she*'s the one.

After many conversations with Bob over the past months during our overseas flights, I've come to share some of her journal entries with him. He agrees that I need to locate her. If not for the airline's sake or to satisfy my personal curiosity, then for the mere reason that I could stop obsessing about her and resume paying attention to my actual job: piloting giant aircrafts and safely getting passengers from point A to point B.

The following short stories record my obsession toward her. There are ten in total. Each installment contains my mystery stewardess's original journal entries for a specific location, followed by my own experiences in trying to track her down. You'll discover what (and whom) I did in an effort to identify and locate my stewardess based on the clues she's left in her diary. You can read the episodes in any order, but they'll probably make more sense if you start from the beginning and follow along as I attempt to find her.

And, just to be clear, these stories should *not* land in the hands of any prude or underage person. Some are just romantic, sensual, or highly erotic, while others are immoral, perverse, and possibly even illegal in some parts of the world.

Ah, the things I'll do to this mystery stewardess when I finally encounter her in the flesh!

I'm hard just thinking about it...

Yours truly,

Capt. Charlie
Undisclosed Airline

PART I

CANADA

THE STEWARDESS'S ENTRIES
CANADA

2:29 a.m.

AT LAST, I got to take a break from walking up and down the aisle. Most of the passengers in economy class were asleep and giving their service button a break. Most except for a workaholic in 8A and a musty-mustached man in 14D who kept winking at me.

How stupid was I to wear brand new heels on a red-eye flight? My feet and legs are killing me! If I don't have blisters yet, they're coming. That's for sure.

But these black babies look fantastic, and I enjoy being a little taller.

Maybe I shouldn't have bought into the marketing hype, but high heels did make me feel sexier... and happier. And after my disastrous weekend getaway with Stupid-Self-Centered-Sam, I needed to take any emotional, mental, or shoe-related compensation I could get.

My sense of self-worth had to rise from this muddy bottom, and it had recently gone up by exactly three inches.

2:48 a.m.

Argh!

Musty-Mustached-Man-in-14D suggested (for the second time) that his ticket included entry to the mile-high club.

It was the only part of the job I didn't like.

Having a hottie flirt with me was always enjoyable, of course. But being hit on by a man who physically grossed me out and made me want to Febreze the heck out of the entire plane... Forcing myself to be polite and smile at him was just...

But thankfully, Alex, a tall red-headed stewardess I'd flown with before, graciously took him off my hands a minute ago.

I stayed within earshot while she chit-chatted with him.

Her exact words were impossible to recall, but she was nice and thoughtful. She certainly knew how to serve shit on a tray with a smile. She even got thanked for it.

Incredible.

I headed toward the back of the plane, a large smile on my face, shaking my head.

"Alex, I owe you one," I told her when she joined me back in the galley.

"No worries. I know how to handle those guys," she said. Alex lifted her eyebrows before continuing. "Not to toot my own horn, but I know how to manipulate most men to get what I want."

3:05 a.m.

I busied myself seeing if there was trash or empty water bottles to get rid of, but my thoughts kept spinning back to Self-Centered-Sam.

"If only I had your ways with men," I told Alex. "Maybe I wouldn't be stuck spending my next over-nighter alone in a hotel room."

"Stop whining and move on with your life," she said, pouring herself a cup of coffee.

"But I thought he was the right guy for me. I liked him. I actually thought we were going somewhere, you know?"

Her big green eyes wide open, Alex stayed motionless for a second before shaking her head. She sipped more of her coffee, staring down the aisle, then at me. She sighed, shook her head again, then finally spoke. "What the heck happened? You might as well get it off your chest."

"I don't know," I said, mentally debating whether talking about it would help or make things worse.

"Come on," she persisted in-between sips. "Might as well pour your little heart out because I'll never ask about your love life again. You know me." Alex paused, raised her palm as if to stop the words she'd just let out, and then continued. "I'll never ask about your romantic life, but I reserve the right to ask about your sexual adventures."

I could feel my cheeks flush.

Talk about my sex life with her?

Then again, I needed to vent. Plus, we had a few hours to kill before landing.

She nudged me, her eyebrows raised, then walked away for a second to get rid of her empty coffee cup.

My inner debate continued, with logic taking the upper hand over my shyness and need for privacy.

Alex has politely offered her kind ear. It's now or never. Who knows? Maybe she can help me understand where I went wrong?

She came back and leaned against the bulkhead, her eyes locked on me.

"I don't even know where to begin..." I started, then let out a long breath. *How can I summarize it all?* "To make a long story short—"

She flicked her fingers against my shoulder. "No way. I want all the details. Especially the juicy bits."

"Not sure about that. We'll see. It all started when we arrived at the campground near Banff."

"Which one?" she asked.

"You've probably never heard of it. It's not even posted on any of the maps I've seen."

She tilted her head. "Try me."

"Slanted Pine Roads, I think."

Alex twisted her face for a second.

Is she trying to pinpoint that campsite on the map of her mental atlas?

"You're right: no idea. Never heard of that one. Continue."

"Doesn't matter anyway. Sam knew where it was, so he headed directly to the little building at the entrance so he could check in and pay for one of the sites where his pickup truck would fit."

"You guys weren't camping in an RV?"

"No, just the back of his truck. Believe me, I'd have preferred a tent. At least the ground wouldn't have been so hard. Anyway, he stayed in there for a few minutes. I remained outside and hung around the truck, trying to get cellphone reception—which was impossible. He finally walked out of the building and returned to our vehicle, then we drove and parked at one of the campsites. There weren't many. Maybe twenty-five or so—"

"But please tell me there were showers, right? Regular toilets and showers with running water?"

"Of course. He knew better than to take me camping without the basic necessities. He was an ass in many ways, but he was still a gentleman... Well, at that point he hadn't proven otherwise yet."

"So, what happened?"

I stopped as I noticed a tired-looking passenger walking toward us. *Probably wants to use the bathroom at the back of the plane.*

Alex frowned, her palms flipped upward in a silent WTF. I pointed my chin at the man.

She turned around. "Ah," she said.

We stayed quiet for a couple of minutes. Out of boredom, I yet again tidied up the food preparation area.

A loud flushing sound echoed from the nearby toilet, and I waited for the passenger to exit and return to his seat, out of earshot, before finally continuing. "So, it was all fine and good. We went for a walk around the site. It was nice. The smell of the forest, the quietness of it all, the chirping sounds and everything... We hiked up some random path. Must have been on it for about an hour before we reached a small river. Beautiful, but holy cow was the water cold!"

"You swam in it?"

"Hell no! But Sam did. I don't know why. Anyway, after he came out, he was freezing. Obviously. So I... warmed him up again," I said, tilting my head to the side.

"I said I wanted to hear all the juicy bits," she whispered, although her expression was silently yelling at me, ordering me to divulge everything.

I popped my eyes at her. "I promise to give you some, the important ones, but let's just say that we had a... quickie by the river and some body heat got transferred where it mattered."

"Seriously, you've got to work on that. If that's as exciting as your story gets, I don't want to hear any more."

"Alex, just be patient!" I exclaimed in a hushed tone. "So, about an hour and a half later, we were back in the truck. It was already getting pretty cool by then. He told me he was going to start a fire, so I got changed into my jeans and sweater. He said he was heading out to buy a pack of logs. That was all fine and good. The chilly mountain air was getting to me, so after waiting for him for what felt like an eternity—or at least thirty minutes—I made my way to the reception building to see what was taking him so long. I walked in on him flirting with a cute twenty-something girl wearing a large sweater and possibly shorts, although I couldn't tell. Long legs, wool socks, and hiking boots were all I could see. I guess she was the campsite employee."

"Ooh la la!" Alex said.

"Yes. I think that's when our romantic getaway took a left turn. I greeted them both. He picked up the stack of fire wood and said he'd be right out, but I saw him lean toward her and whisper something in her ear. I should have known something was up, but I didn't want to see it. Anyway, we headed back to our campsite together. He then carried on explaining himself. Telling me some bullshit about how they grew up in the same town."

"What? In Canada?"

"Yeah! I thought he was American. Tells you how much I knew about him. Not that his nationality mattered, but I simply didn't know anything about this guy. So we started drinking beer (he had brought a cooler full). He got busy cooking potatoes and steaks on the fire. That girl from the registration building kept patrolling around the path that connected all campsites. Every time she drove by in her pickup truck, she'd smile and wave at us, although I suspected she mostly waved at him."

"So... Are you telling me that smiles and hand gestures were the only things that happened? That's lame."

"No, no! Patience, Alex. Don't get your panties in a big wet knot! So, we were cuddling by the fire, trying to stay warm, but I was exhausted and wanted to go to bed. We moved to the back of his truck, made love, then I fell asleep."

"Why am I listening to you? You don't stand a chance in Top-Sexy-Weekend contenders. You must be boring as hell in the sack."

Who is she to insinuate what I'm like in bed?

I did my best to ignore her insult and continued with my story. "That night was pretty dull. Had to stick to missionary position so the truck wouldn't rock too much and bother nearby campers. I woke up a little later and realized he wasn't in his sleeping bag. So, since I had to pee anyway—those nights are damn cool in the mountains—I put on a sweater and jeans and headed out of the truck. My eyes took a second to acclimate to the dark night sky, but then a cloud moved out of the way and the full moon lit my path. I was heading toward the bathroom when I noticed the campground vehicle a few feet from our site, on the main path. I wouldn't have thought anything of it, except that it was moving... to a certain cadence, if you catch my drift."

"Someone was fucking the campsite employee in there?" Alex asked, looking like saliva was about to come out of her mouth.

"Yeah. So, putting two and two together, Sam not being asleep next to me and the rocking motion of the pickup truck... I felt an urge to go and see. The windows were fogged up and a woman's moans were becoming less and less discreet. Then a hand reached toward the window and landed flat on it before slowly dropping down, clearing enough of the condensation and letting enough moonlight in for me to see inside."

Alex's green eyes were glued on me. "And?" she asked.

"It was the campsite employee alright, and I would have recognized that tight ass and left-slanted cock in any line-up. It was *my* Sam, going at her, just a few feet from where he'd left me to sleep after making love to me."

"Oh no! What did you do?"

"What do you think I did?"

"Oooh!" A large grin appeared on Alex's face. Her eyes had never been rounder. "You slammed a baseball bat on the windshield? Smashed the head lights? Did you call her supervisor? Oh, I know! You did something much, much better..." She paused and grabbed me by the arm before whispering her last guess in my ear. "Did you join them?"

I pulled away from her and shook my head. "What's wrong with you?"

A throat-clearing sound made me turn around. A teenage kid was standing there, wanting some water. Based on his glazed-over eyes, he hadn't heard a word of what I'd been saying. *Good.*

I grabbed a plastic glass and filled it with water, then handed it to him. "Here you go, dear," I said, and then waited until he was seated again to turn and look at Alex once more.

"No. None of that," I answered. "I went back to the truck and pretended to be sleeping when he snuck back in."

She flipped her hands up. "Seriously. What the fuck is wrong with you?"

"Nothing. I was upset. I was really upset—and I still am to be honest—but I needed to first process the information in my head before confronting him. I don't believe we need to dramatize everything."

"Well, your life would be a lot more interesting, at least sexually speaking, if you were a bit more dramatic—"

A light sound chimed in the galley, indicating that someone had pressed the service button. I used it as my cue to walk away from Alex and her uncomfortable statements for a minute.

Would my sexual life be more exciting with more drama?

4:05 a.m.

"Anyway," I continued when I returned to the galley at the back of the plane a few minutes later. "I'm over him now. Well... I'm trying to be. I realize he wasn't right for me. We ended it when he drove me to the airport."

"Way to go, that's my girl," Alex told me with a smile. "You can't end up with a cheating bastard if you never commit, and you can't be hurt by someone who doesn't belong to you. At least, that's my take on relationships."

I let her words marinate for a few minutes. She and I certainly viewed things differently... Not that she was right or wrong.

"And to think I was considering leaving my job to spend more time with him," I said.

"Whoa. Hold your horses. Men who expect women like us to give up traveling to exotic destinations... Men who want us to stop meeting new people from all over the world... They're simply not for us! You know that, right?"

Alex shook her head at me, probably recollecting a similar conversation we'd had a few months ago. She didn't share my love ideals and definitely didn't believe in 'finding the one.'

Can she be right? Have romantic movies ruined me? Are my expectations unrealistic?

I let my eyes stare into nothingness for a while, trying to forget about the whole thing.

When reality kicked back in, Alex was looking at herself in her powder case, fixing her makeup before spilling out more of her wise pearls.

"If you stop expecting things from men—or from anyone for that matter—

you'll be a lot happier." She smacked her bright red lips before continuing. "For example: I don't seek relationships; I only want to find my next fling with a handsome man who can make me come like the princess that I am. Just let yourself be. Enjoy the physical company of another human being for once! One-night stands are so liberating. You should really give them a try sometime."

"Don't you have a new boyfriend? That black guy from Seattle?" I asked.

"A boyfriend? That's... way more than a stretch. But I guess I could call him a multiple-night stand. I'm seeing him again tomorrow..." She looked at her watch. "Or tonight, I should say. It'll be his first time in Toronto. Doubt he'll see more than the four walls of my hotel room, though."

I smiled at Alex.

Should I take cues from her? Should I stop caring so much about trying to find men who displayed decent relationship potential?

What I'm doing is certainly not working.

What harm is there in trying something new?

I decided to find out.

"Any tips on how to become more like you?" I asked her.

"Listen. You follow my lead and I gua-ran-tee you'll have a guy sharing that hotel room with you tonight. You up for it?"

What? Now? Here?

A wave of fear came over me.

Definitely out of my comfort zone. But then again, why not?

I raised my shoulders and nodded silently, trying to hide the fact that my heart was beating way too fast.

"That's my girl," she said before taking off her uniform jacket. "Is it just me or is it hot in here tonight?"

I nodded again. The plane *was* really warm right now, probably because whoever had set the temperature knew we didn't have enough blankets onboard for everyone.

"I've got an idea," she said before unbuttoning her shirt a little. "Seriously, follow my lead. We'll offer the passengers who are still awake an extra snack and drink service. Watch and learn."

She reached behind her back and undid her strapless bra, then pulled it out of her shirt from the front. After tucking it in the inner pocket of the jacket she'd just hung in the storage area, she pinched her nipples until they became firm and started poking through the fabric of her white shirt.

"Your turn," Alex said. I hesitated for a second and she tried to reassure me. "Hardly anyone's awake! What are you afraid of?"

Turning around to peek at the passengers, I saw that most of them were deep asleep, just like she'd said. I took off my jacket, but my bra wasn't strapless. I stepped in the bathroom for a second to take my top and bra off, then I put my long-sleeve shirt back on.

"You've got nice tits!" she said, grabbing them with both hands through the fabric of my shirt.

I was a little surprised by her lack of boundaries, but hey... I obviously needed to be more audacious.

"Let's go down the aisle. There's a cutie near the front who's still awake," she said.

We got the cart ready and I followed her, pushing our collection of overpriced airline snacks and drinks.

After picking up various pillows and items that littered our path, we finally made it to the front. Alex was all smiles, her partly unbuttoned shirt gaining the attention of Cutie-Blondie. He looked like he was around twenty-five or twenty-six years old.

"Would you like a beverage, sir?" she asked, her hand stroking her collarbone and pulling her shirt open more, allowing her forearm to push her loose breasts against each other.

"Hmm, sure. Coke?" the man asked.

"Let me see if I have any left," Alex said, maintaining eye contact with him for a couple of seconds, then bending down and letting him peer into her shirt while she was retrieving a can from the drawer. A Coca-Cola in hand, she stood back up and then popped open the can before talking to him some more. "It's so hot in here tonight," she said, moving her shirt to supposedly let some air in, but obviously letting him see more of her. "Would you like some ice with that?"

The man stirred in his seat, closed the magazine he was reading, and placed it in his lap before nodding.

Alex poured his drink slowly over a few ice cubes in a plastic cup. "Anything else?" she asked.

"Hmmm," was all Cutie-Blondie said.

"I'll be back later if you need anything."

She nodded at me, and I pulled the cart back.

We offered a quick, non-flirty service to another couple of passengers who were awake near the middle of the plane.

"Can't believe what you did," I whispered. "So smooth!"

"Now's your turn," she said. "Behind you on your left," she continued while pushing the cart.

I finally understood who she meant when I saw a brown-haired man with a pronounced 5 o'clock shadow. He was sitting alone in the second-last row, wearing jeans and a light-blue shirt. A sitcom was airing on his monitor, but he was watching us, a twinkle in his eyes.

From his aisle seat, did he see Alex's little game?

"Good evening, sir," I greeted him, flashing my biggest smile and rubbing the back of my neck, giving myself a chance to push out my breasts without being too obvious about it. I saw his eyes divert that way for a second before meeting mine.

He had a large grin on his face. "Good evening," he said.

"May I interest you in a drink?"

"Don't know. Kind of late for coffee," he said, still smiling at me.

"Well, we also have soda, beer, hard liquor, and wine. Alcohol prices are listed here," I said, grabbing a brochure and leaning way closer than necessary to offer him the pamphlet. I swear I heard him take a whiff of my scent. *Good sign?*

He took the onboard menu and inspected the listed offerings. "It's hot in here; maybe I'll have a beer, but only if it's cold," he said.

I bent down to reach into the drawer where we kept the cans. I made sure to pick the coldest beer I could find, then brought it to my cleavage, letting the chilled aluminum exterior cool me off for a second, enjoying its refreshing effect, and smiling at him.

"Yes, definitely cold," I finally replied.

He motioned for me to lean in, and I did.

"Two tips are telling me you're not lying," he whispered before brushing one of my nipples with the back of his hand.

A shiver ran down my spine.

"I'm John by the way," he said, now in a normal tone, as I returned to my cart. He handed me the brochure back, and I turned to face Alex for a second.

She winked at me, then nodded toward Cutie-Blondie and walked away, leaving me alone with John.

"Nice to meet you, John," I said.

"You accept credit cards, right?" he asked, his brown eyes meeting mine.

I smiled and nodded.

He undid his seat belt before digging in his back pocket for his wallet. While he was doing that, I grabbed the payment machine and had it ready by the time he handed me his card.

I dealt with the transaction with half my attention on him and the other automatically processing the purchase, something I could do in my sleep. I returned his card along with a printed receipt before popping open the can for him. "Glass?"

"Yes, please," he said, once again smiling at me, a devious expression in his eyes.

I poured some of the beer into the cup, then handed him the plastic container and the half-empty aluminum can. "Enjoy!" I said before pulling the cart back to its storage location.

Alex stepped into the galley a minute later.

"So?" she asked.

Is it going well? Probably.

I answered with just a smile.

"Wait for it. There's a part two," she said before glancing at the passengers and ensuring no one was looking back toward us. She rode her skirt up, pulled down her lacy white panties, and then placed them in one of the duty-free magazines that were stored in the nearby wall holder. "Here's something he can't resist." She smoothed down her skirt and walked down the aisle toward Cutie-Blondie, her loaded magazine in hand.

I stayed back and watched from a distance.

A few steps later, she leaned forward, offering him once again a good view of her cleavage. She said something, winked at him, and then handed him the magazine before coming back toward me, beaming.

"What did you tell him?"

"There's a special offer on page 24," she said, once again flashing me her white teeth. "Okay, now's your turn, lady. Handsome brown-haired guy's looking at us right now."

John was making the 'come-here' motion with his fingers, so I walked up to him.

"Sorry to bother you," he said without a word more.

"Not at all." I smiled.

He motioned for me to lean forward again. "What magazine did your colleague hand the man up front?" he asked.

"A copy of our duty-free magazine."

"I believe I might also be interested in that special offer you ladies appear to have at the moment..." His fingers, which had previously been positioned on the armrest, now grazed the side of my leg. I could feel blood rushing to my cheeks.

Jeez, he overheard that?

"Any chance you could hand me your copy of the magazine?" I didn't know what to say to that. I moved my shirt a little, not trying to expose myself, but honestly trying to ventilate so I could think more clearly.

Is it just hot or is he having an effect on me? Or both?

"Hey," he said before undoing his seat belt and moving over to the empty seat next to him. He tapped on the cushioned chair he'd occupied only a second ago. "Sit for a second."

I looked back at Alex, who'd been watching me from the nearby galley. She nodded.

Why not?

I sat next to him, and he reached up to turn on the air and direct it at me, right at my décolletage. The cooler air felt really nice. I moved my shirt to let more air in.

"So, what do you think?" he prompted again, his fingers still discreetly moving up my side. "Looks like you're feeling cooler now." The back of his hand barely touched my left breast as he spoke. My nipples were hard.

I turned to face him. He was obviously intent on getting his request fulfilled.

"So, those duty-free specials?" he asked again.

I took a deep breath and mustered all the courage I had before looking into his brown eyes and divulging the truth in a quiet whisper, "You're quite the looker... I'd love to share those specials with you... but it's just that..."

"What? Are you too shy now?" he asked, his hand now grabbing my knee firmly enough to double my heartbeat.

I licked my lips before leaning in to whisper in his ear, "No, it's just that I'm not wearing panties right now."

Yeah, stupid me.

In my rush to end things with Self-Centered-Sam, I had left behind some of my clothes, including all my panties, except for the pair I'd had on, which reeked of campfire smoke. I'd stowed them away, sealing its stench in a plastic bag in my carry-on luggage.

His eyes brightened up and he tilted his head. "Is that so? Now, that's surprising."

He now looked at me with a provocative gaze, then he leaned closer and whispered in my ear, "Any chance you could give me a quick glance?"

After asking me, he leaned back into his seat, his eyes glued on mine with the expression of the cat who'd gotten the cream. He looked around before continuing. "Not right here, of course. But if you were to grab me a snack from that bottom drawer... over there," he said, pointing to the far corner of the galley. "I'd really appreciate it."

What he'd requested was definitely not in my nature, but my competitive spirit had been challenged. By him and by Alex. "And what would I get in exchange?" I asked.

"And look who's talking now!" He eyed me up and down and leaned closer to me again, his lips a mere inch from my left ear. "Show me yours, and I'll show you mine."

I got up, stared him down, and then nodded. "Deal."

I headed to the corner of the galley, where no one but John could glance at me. Alex was nowhere to be seen, but a quick look forward confirmed she'd taken a seat next to Cutie-Blondie.

I teasingly raised the hem of my skirt, a little bit at a time, until the lacy top of my black self-adhesive stockings became visible.

John sent me a smile of approval.

I hiked my skirt up some more, front and back, until it reached the perfect height, then turned around, bent down at the hip, and then opened up one of the drawers where we kept the extra cookies and napkins. I shook my bootie a little, raising my tailbone as high as I could and spreading my legs for just a second, then turned around and lowered my skirt again.

When I looked at John, his mouth was agape. Then he joined his hands repeatedly in a silent clap.

I walked back toward him and handed the cookies and napkin I'd just got. I was about to sit down next to him when another passenger across the aisle saw the offering and requested cookies as well.

"Of course, just a second," I said to the man, feeling my cheeks redden as I walked away.

When I reached the galley, I turned around, John was looking at me, a large smirk on his face, his eyebrows raised.

Is he expecting a second show?

I shook my head. Playtime was over. More and more passengers were waking up, so I put on my jacket, hiding my unsupported breasts for now until I could put my bra back on later.

Now looking—and acting—more professional, I brought the requested treat to the other passenger then discreetly addressed my flirty brown-haired man. "And I believe you owe me something, Mr. John."

"Of course," he said before getting up and taking his phone into the unoccupied washroom next to the galley.

In the mean time, Alex returned to the back, put on her jacket, and we both started getting ready for the final drink service.

"So, how's it going with 48C?" she asked.

"I think you'd be proud of me."

She leaned in, brimming. "Tell me more!"

"Later—he's in the washroom," I whispered, pointing at the door a mere two feet away from us.

"Ooh la la, can't wait."

5:35 a.m.

I didn't see my handsome John come out of the lavatory until the final service had started.

By the time I reached his row at the back of the plane, he'd returned to his assigned seat. He had his phone ready, as if paying in kind for the abysmal cup of coffee I was about to pour for him.

"It's unlocked. Just look at the last photo," he said, handing me the device. I took it, placed it in my jacket pocket, and then finished serving the other seats across the aisle before pushing the cart away, finally able to view my reward.

"Wow!" I couldn't help but gasp when I saw his large cock on the screen. Alex came over, and I hid the phone, but John was looking at me and had seen me react. By the way his shoulders lifted, I understood he didn't care whether or not the image was kept private. I showed Alex the photo and she smiled, sending flirty eyes toward John. A polite nod later, he turned his gaze toward me. I mimicked his previous silent clapping motion.

John got up from his seat and walked toward me. Alex stepped away and headed to help a passenger who'd just pressed the assistance button.

What now? This was brand new territory for me, so I didn't know what to expect.

I extended the hand with which I was holding his phone. He was probably coming here to get it back.

"It's a little late for me to suggest we join a certain club, but maybe we could... grab a coffee when this plane lands? What do you think?" he asked.

Alex's previous remarks about my need to have a one-night stand still echoed in my mind. "Why not?" I finally replied.

He scribbled his number on the corner of a nearby in-flight magazine and ripped it off before handing it to me.

"Call me, gorgeous! I'll be in Toronto for a few days."

"Maybe," was all I said, and he returned to his seat just as the captain turned on the seat belt sign and announced that we'd be landing shortly.

7:00 p.m.

I donned a classy yet simple black skirt with a silky white blouse and slipped on my new heels over the Band-Aid covered blisters I'd gotten earlier in the day.

After taking one last look in the mirror, I spritzed a dash of jasmine on my neck and left my room to head to the place that Alex had recommended.

Once seated in the contemporary-fusion restaurant, I ordered myself a steak and french fries with a glass of Bordeaux. Meeting her down here was somewhat unlikely—with her quasi-boyfriend being in town tonight—but who knew. Maybe I'd find a kind soul to converse with over a drink.

The short, curly-haired bartender was cute. I smiled at him, but he showed no interest in me. A handsome man came and sat a few bar stools away from me. My efforts to make eye contact with him proved futile.

Fifteen minutes of light background jazz music later, a short brunette joined him. His wife. Good for him.

Fed, alone, lonely, and without any sign of Alex—she was probably getting laid now—I returned to my hotel room, anxious to watch a movie or do something to once again get my mind off Self-Centered-Sam and his cheating ways.

Why am I still thinking about him?

I was toying with the idea of calling John but somehow couldn't bring myself to do it. Was it too romantic of me to want something more than a one-night stand with a stranger? Even a good-looking one with a nice cock?

After unlocking my door with the magnetic card, I flipped on the lights and kicked my heels off. It was incredibly hot in my room. I walked over to the air conditioning unit by the window.

Just as I was about to cut off what was left of daylight outside and block out the bright lampposts that already illuminated the inside courtyard of my hotel—yes, I had a crappy view of other people's suites—I found the perfect distraction for me. It was exactly what I needed this very minute: a naked couple going at it two floors down, across the courtyard from me.

Their lights were on, their blinds wide open. It was an open invitation for all voyeurs out there, and I was certainly one of them. However, not being of the exhibitionist variety, I decided to turn off my lights before sliding the large padded chair directly in front of the window, where I could get a good view of the action without being seen. It was like watching my neighbor's porn channel through my bedroom curtains. I couldn't make out their exact facial expressions or even their traits, but sometimes these things were best left to the imagination.

A tall and slender woman was on all fours, naked on the bed, her head facing the headboard, ankles and feet dangling off the end of the mattress. Her red hair draped and hid her face. Behind her, a black, muscular man was doing her doggy style. His large hands contrasted against her ivory body, like two huge ink spots. Her breasts bounced forward and back, almost hitting her in the face. The visual intrusion on their actions felt so real and close, I could almost hear the flapping noises of their skin. She put her face down on the comforter, resting her breasts against the bed and lifting her ass to change the man's penetration angle.

I couldn't resist. My view would be so much more entertaining and enjoyable as an interactive experience. To add to that, the various scenarios my mind had imagined since my encounter with John hadn't done anything to suppress my horniness.

Without hesitation, I stood up and took off my skirt and the new panties I'd bought to replace the pairs I'd left behind, then sat back down, resting my feet on the air conditioning unit in front of me. I adjusted the knobs to the coolest setting and let the powerful breeze tease my trimmed pussy. I undid the top three buttons of my shirt and slid one hand into my bra to get a hold of one of my breasts. The other hand joined the breeze in caressing my exposed lips.

Just as I got comfortable, the couple changed position. The woman pulled away from the man and stood up before walking toward the window. The man followed. He stood about a foot taller than her. As they passed the writing desk, he grabbed her by the hips and sat her down on the solid piece of furniture.

Wonderful. Perfect viewing point.

They were probably a foot from the window, the entire desk visible and their beautiful bodies exposed for the world—or at least the whole courtyard—to see.

He pulled up her legs one at a time and rested them against his strong shoulders, then his black shaft entered her. He slid her toward him, letting her head and back rest on the desk while he held her ass in his large hands, banging her with ardor.

I inserted a finger inside me, then two, imagining his large black cock fucking me. I matched my rhythm to his, my other hand caressing my breasts, then moving down to my clit.

The woman lifted her arms up, and he slowed down. She reached up to wrap her arms around his neck. While still inside her, he lifted her from the desk and pressed her back and ass against the window. Each of his pushes flattened the woman's exposed bottom and lifted her up slightly.

I finger-fucked myself harder, faster.

I pinched my nipples, making them erect, then returned to my clit. I couldn't help but arch my back, moving closer to the window as if the couple across from me were magnetically attracting me, supporting my orgasm, increasing my heartbeat along with theirs. My body approached the quivering point.

As the first wave of pleasure exploded from within me, I saw the man peer out the window, over his partner's shoulder, in my direction, as if he'd seen me. Then I recognized Alex. They were both looking out the window in my direction, probably in their own post-orgasmic euphoria.

But they can't see me. No, that can't be. My lights are off.

I nonetheless closed the curtains.

And who cares if they saw me.

Alex certainly wouldn't care. In fact, she'd probably be happy about it. And I'd just had a great show, free of charge, shame, and guilt. Well, mostly. I now knew what Alex's layovers were like.

Feeling a little less bored, I took a shower to cool off and return to reality. Maybe I'd find myself a hot lover like Alex had. Actually... maybe I had this lover's number in my purse.

Is it just a matter of picking up the phone and finding out?

9:15 p.m.

He picked up on the second ring.

"John?" I started, "It's—"

He started talking before I could introduce myself. "Hi, gorgeous. I was hoping you'd call. Do you want to meet?"

His sexy voice made what was left of my hesitation evaporate.

"Join me at Korimate?" I offered.

"Sure, I know where it is. Thirty minutes?"

I felt an irrepressible smile appear on my face. "Perfect. I'm already here, sitting at the bar."

After hanging up, I rested my phone on the marble countertop. I got the attention of the bartender. *Work shifts must have changed.* A blonde woman with her hair neatly tied up in a ponytail now manned the bar. I asked for a glass of Chardonnay.

Excitement and a little bit of apprehension entered my mind. I stared at my nails and resisted the urge to bite them and ruin my manicure. My reflection in the large mirror behind the bar guided me in readjusting how my red necklace fell into my cleavage. I still had that healthy, rosy glow that resulted from having come just a little while ago.

I told myself that I looked okay, as attractive as I could be with what nature had granted me. I was staring at the bottom of my empty wine glass when I heard John's sexy voice behind me.

"Hey, there!" he said, placing his hand on my waist and kissing me on the left cheek, but ever so close to my lips. I inhaled his cologne. *Aqua Blue?* I once dated a guy who wore that delicious scent all the time. Before I could go down memory lane and remember who that was, he started talking.

"What's your poison?" he asked, noticing the empty glass in front of me.

"Cave Spring Estate Bottled Chardonnay Musqué," I replied.

He got the bartender's attention and ordered our drinks while I took the opportunity to have a good look at him. I had found him quite handsome on the plane, but now he was quite simply a tall, dark, and handsome stud in his jeans and crisp white shirt.

How I loved men with cufflinks... *Fairly wealthy?*

A few minutes later, drinks in hand, we headed toward an empty booth near the back of the bar.

"You've kept me waiting a long time," he said after we sat down next to each other on the crescent-shaped red leather seat. "But I'm really glad you called."

"Well—"

"And I really have to consider making your airline my preferred choice if that's how you ladies serve your passengers," he continued, sliding his finger along my lower arm.

I felt my cheeks redden. "That's not regular service," I said, smiling. "Doubt you'll have the same experience again on one of our flights."

"That's too bad, but I'm glad I did."

He slid closer to me in the booth.

"So where did we leave off?" he asked, one of his arms wrapped around my shoulders while the other slid down to my leg.

"About there, I guess." I had goose bumps and could feel myself getting wet already. Half of me couldn't believe I was actually capable of meeting a quasi-stranger in a bar, going through with a one-night stand. But my body was clearly fine with the idea. I ordered my mind to shut up and just enjoy it.

"Are you still lacking a certain piece of clothing?" he asked with a crooked smile.

I thought about how much I had stressed out earlier about whether or not to wear my new panties for him. "Actually, I had a chance to go shopping this afternoon... But I left those in my hotel room."

"I don't believe you. Mind if I check?"

His fingers moved to outline the hem of my skirt, which sat about four inches below my pussy. I looked down, the table wasn't draped with a tablecloth, but the lights were low. Chances were that none of the people in the bar would notice anything. I parted my legs slightly in agreement.

His digits slid up my inner thighs and stopped just short for a second, his eyes locked onto mine. My slight annoyance at his stopping must have shown on my face because his smile became a little more crooked when he resumed and finally reached my pussy.

At first, his fingertips just tickled me. But I wanted more.

I lowered myself to get closer to his hand by an inch or two, hiking my skirt in the process. He leaned in to brush his lips against my neck. His kisses were ocean-scented whispers that only served to crank up my horniness. But his fingers were more eager. His thumb teased my clit while the tip of two of his fingers circled my pussy, pinched my lips, then finally entered me just a tad.

His mouth met mine in a fervent kiss. Our tongues intertwined, his passion apparently as high as mine. His hand was still busy with my pussy, but he pulled his mouth away from my lips and moved on to kiss my ear.

"You're so wet. I love it," he whispered before nibbling on my earlobe.

Two of his fingers were now fully inside me, and I swear I could hear how lubricated my pussy was. I wanted him. I couldn't wait any longer.

"I want you to fuck me," I whispered in his ear.

"Right here in this booth?" he asked, pulling away from me, a big smirk on his face.

By now, all I could think of was finding the closest private—or semi-private— location. My hotel room was way too far. I wanted him this minute.

A quick glance around provided the answer I needed.

"The bathroom. Join me in the ladies' in thirty seconds," I ordered while grabbing a napkin from the table, pushing his hand out of the way, and then quickly wiping my inner legs. I awkwardly pulled down on my skirt just as I exited the booth.

After grabbing my purse, I headed to the washroom.

On my way there, I saw my reflection in the mirror behind the bar: my cheeks were red—blame it on the wine or him?—and my hair was a little out of place. I drew my hand through it to smooth it out a bit. I was so turned on by John that I could almost feel my heartbeat in my genitals.

A few steps later, I turned into a hallway and pushed open the door to the ladies' room. A fifty-something woman stood in front of the mirror reapplying lipstick.

Damn. Is she almost done? Staying?

Unsure, I washed my hands in the sink next to hers. We shared a silent smile across the mirror; then she headed into a stall.

Shit!

I quickly dried my hands and then walked out just as John arrived at the door.

"Occupied," I said discreetly, then I noticed the large handicapped bathroom a few steps away. I nodded in that direction, and we both headed that way.

A few seconds later, we arrived at the large door. He checked it, and it opened right away.

"Ladies first," he gallantly offered. I snuck in and he joined me in the industrial-cleaner-scented room before locking the door behind us.

I made my way to the sink and rested my small black, silky handbag against the mirror. My heart pounded in my chest.

Am I really going to go through with this? Can I be that kind of woman?

His voice brought me back to the here and now.

"A bit larger than an airplane's washroom, but it still works for me," he said, moving toward me before framing my head in his hands, and then kissing me.

I backed up until my back hit the tiled wall partition that separated the toilet from the sink area. He lifted me up and sat me next to the low, wheelchair-accessible wash basin. He unbuttoned my blouse, digging in to expose my bra and feel my breasts. After helping me get the blouse off, his hands reached behind my back and released my breasts from their lacy prison. I pulled my arms out of the bra straps and tossed my undergarment to join my blouse in the sink next to me.

"Ah, those gorgeous tits!" he said, moving away from me slightly as if wanting to take in the view. "You know you were driving me mad, the way you were moving that beer can in your cleavage on the plane? I just wanted to suck on your tits, squeeze them, pinch those nipples."

I could feel my cheeks flush.

Being so blatantly seen as the object of a hot guy's sexual desires was a first for me. Cloud nine—or maybe nine hundred—was my emotional address at that exact moment.

John neared me again and began massaging my breasts. I reached for his silver belt buckle and unfastened it. He wore button-up jeans, and I undid the metal fasteners one at a time, very aware of his erect cock ready to pop out. Halfway done, I squeezed one hand into his jeans and grabbed his firm ass, pleasantly surprised to realize he was commando. I undid the last few buttons and finally exposed his glorious cock. I brought him closer to me and kissed him.

Our mouths were hungry, demanding, but my pussy was the horniest of all. Two of his fingers fucked me while I stroked him with my hand. I pulled out of his embrace for a second to reach into my purse for a condom.

He used this opportunity to go down on me. Spreading my legs wider and licking my inner thighs, then the tip of his tongue teased my lips, my clit... I pulsated with desire. I needed to have his hard cock in me now.

I tore open the condom wrapper. "I like what you're doing, but I want you to fuck me. Now."

He came back up, kissed me, and I unrolled the ultra-thin latex on his glorious cock.

The counter was not suitable for intercourse with me sitting by the sink: he was tall and the counter was ridiculously low for that purpose. He lifted me up, my skirt now hiked to my waist, and then pushed me against the cold tiled wall in the corner. I didn't care. I just wanted him inside of me. Now.

His eyes locked on mine; the tip of his cock penetrated me. I let out a sigh. I felt my insides parting to make way for his glorious appendage.

Finally!

I wrapped my legs around his ass and my arms around his neck and back. He started to fuck me, hard. He was grunting quietly, and I tried to keep quiet although my instincts were to moan. I almost lost my breath as my heartbeat kept increasing.

"Fuck me harder!" I whispered in his ear.

"I want to take you from behind," he said, pulling out of me.

I unwrapped my legs and put them down. He held me up for a second as I got on my feet, feeling a little uneasy on my heels.

My blood must have concentrated in my pussy.

A couple of seconds later, having regained my balance, I moved to face the mirror, with him standing behind me. He grabbed one of my exposed breasts in his hand and looked at our reflection above the sink: him standing behind me, kissing my neck, my skirt bunched up at my waist, my pussy and tits exposed, wanting his attention. With my heels on, it looked as though I was the perfect height for him to take me from behind.

His lips left my neck, and he bent me forward. I leaned to rest my hands against the low counter. He thrust his cock in my pussy again, and his hands grabbed a hold of my hips. John started pounding into me, my breasts bouncing with each push. I let go of the counter and reached to grab a hold of them. I pinched my nipples and locked eyes with him through the mirror as he penetrated me, over and over. His eyes then looked down toward his cock.

For a second, I wished I'd taken off his shirt earlier. I could only imagine how chiseled his abs would be. I released one of my breasts and brought my hand to my clit to rub it.

"You like it?" he asked, his eyes once again meeting mine through the mirror.

"Hell, yeah! Fuck me, John." I arched my back, enjoying the new angle his cock took inside of me. It was now hitting me exactly where I wanted it. I felt my legs getting weak. A first wave of tremors took me over, and he pounded me harder, deeper. I bit my lips, then sighed. I couldn't help but quiver. A second wave flooded over me when he gave me his final push, accompanied by an animal grunt.

"Fuck, yeah," he finally said, folding his body over mine. "You're everything I imagined you'd be," he whispered in my ear.

"And so are you," I said. "And more," I continued after I felt him pull his cock out.

I turned around to face the gorgeous man who'd just made me come. John was holding the condom with one hand, carefully keeping its contents inside. He was biting his lips. For a second, I wondered what life with him would be like; but then I realized I didn't know anything about John, and that was probably better.

I felt my own juices running down my legs and reached for a paper towel. He grabbed my breasts again and kissed them.

A knock on the locked door followed by a brisk attempt at opening it terminated the moment.

"Occupied," John said aloud. "Give me a few more minutes."

I grabbed my bra and put it back on. I lowered my skirt, donned my blouse, and then fixed my hair.

"Wanna go out first?" he asked in a whisper.

There was no way we'd be able to leave this room discreetly. I raised my shoulders.

What would be less embarrassing?

"Don't know," I said, finally.

"You go first. I'll deal with whoever it is."

After grabbing my purse and giving a final glance at my reflection to make sure all of my clothes were back on and I hadn't left anything behind, I kissed him.

"Thanks for calling me. Maybe we can do that again?" he offered after ending our kiss.

I walked away from him and crossed the short distance that separated me from the door. He stayed back, leaning against the sink.

"Maybe," I said before blowing him a kiss and unlocking the door.

As I exited into the hallway, the frowning face of the blonde ponytailed bartender greeted me. I shot her a fake smile and walked away as fast as my heels would let me, mortification adding to my already orgasmically blushed cheeks.

I walked out of the bar and headed back to my hotel room.

11:34 p.m.

Alone, lying in the comfortable queen-sized hotel bed, just as I was about to set the alarm on my phone, a flashback of John's brown eyes and fantastic cock came to mind.

A wave of something went through my body, and I felt my cheeks flush for the umpteenth time today.

Is it delight? Embarrassment? Excitement? Shame? A sexual craving for more?

How can my actions over the past few hours feel so wrong yet so right at the same time?

Getting out of my head for a second, I flipped through my phone contacts until I came across the one labeled 'Toronto John.'

I stared at it for a second.

Could be nice to see him again... He could be my Toronto fling. Maybe more?

Damn it! Why can't I turn this relationship-seeking instinct off?

I hit the 'delete' button before I could talk myself into keeping his number.

I'll never know what his last name is and it doesn't matter. I'll always have the memory of meeting Toronto John on that flight and sharing one special experience with him.

Alex's probably right.

Could I enjoy men without feeling the need to have a relationship with them?

Maybe.

Hmmm. I think a new and much more exciting phase of my life has just begun.

MY XXX EXPERIENCE
CANADA

THE PLAN

MY MYSTERY STEWARDESS left me three options:

OPTION 1: Canvass all airlines that fly into Toronto, Canada, and find a red-headed flight attendant named Alex who could potentially identify my mystery stewardess.

I'm a positive guy and I like a good challenge, but considering that at least sixty-five airlines fly into YYZ/Pearson, and that each has a drove of flight attendants (not to mention high personnel turn-over)... I don't have enough contacts in high places to pull the right strings to get all the confidential information I'd need.
Likelihood of success: Close to nil.

OPTION 2: Go to the campground near Banff and potentially run into the employee who could then lead me to the stewardess's ex-boyfriend, who could direct me to her.

At least I have the campground's name. The rest would depend on luck. Small campgrounds can't have that many employees, right? Worst case, I could stay there a few extra days or kindly ask whoever is working at the time to get the right employee's phone number. Would her ex have kept her contact information? Possibly.

Likelihood of success: Average.

OPTION 3: Find Toronto John.

I don't even think that guy lives in Toronto. And even if I were to randomly bump into the right brown-haired, brown-eyed man named John out of sheer luck, I don't think she gave him her details. Does he even know her name? But then again, maybe the blonde ponytailed waitress could be bribed into looking at old credit card receipts? But I have no idea *when* the stewardess was in that restaurant/bar... Last month? Last year? Five years ago?
Likelihood of success: Sliver of hope.

The campground/ex-boyfriend route is definitely the best plan of attack.

WHAT HAPPENED

After a few well-placed calls, I managed to locate the campground the stewardess had mentioned in her journal. Wasn't easy, but an old colleague who'd turned bush pilot had access to detailed cartographic maps of southern British Columbia and Alberta, and he pinpointed it for me.

Taking advantage of a few scheduled days off, I flew to nearby YYC/Calgary airport on a Tuesday morning with a small carry-on bag full of outdoor clothes. I then rented an SUV and made my way to a sports rental store to find the camping gear I'd need.

Another short trip followed, this time to the grocery store to fill my cooler with ice, beer, and camping food, and then I was good to go.

Here's how it went down.

11:30 a.m.

The Slanted Pine Roads campground was located in an idyllic sequestered spot in the large pine forests of the Rocky Mountains, quite a few miles from the Trans-Canada Highway.

After veering off onto a dirt road, I drove about a mile before passing under a carved wooden sign welcoming me to the site. I immediately spotted the reception building and parked my rental vehicle in front of the small rustic shack.

I turned off the ignition and stepped out, inhaling the fresh air. What real pine-scent was like.
Refreshing.
I walked into the reception area that obviously doubled as a small camping

supply store. Piles of firewood for sale were stacked on the left side of the door, and a large electric ice cooler occupied the other side. After walking up a couple of steps, I opened the squeaky door and entered, triggering a bell in the process.

Inside the building, behind a small counter, a freckled twenty-something girl with frizzy reddish-blonde hair and a hunter-like red and black plaid flannel shirt was seated on a stool, book in hand. But the bell had made her look up toward me, and she greeted me with a smile.

"Hi there," I said, wondering if she was the one who'd gotten frisky with the ex-boyfriend.

"Hey!" she replied, placing her Harlequin romance down on the counter and jumping to her feet.

"Do you have a spot available for tonight?"

"Of course," she said before walking around the counter to join me on the customer side.

I couldn't help but notice how large her boobs were for her petite frame. They brought her shirt up in the front, exposing a little bit of jean fabric past the flaps of her flannel shirt. Otherwise, her barely tanned legs were exposed all the way down to her rolled gray wool socks and brown leather hiking boots.

The barely visible skirt, the socks, the boots... She has to be the woman the stewardess described in her journal.

I decided to ask the campground employee what I had come here to find out.

"This is going to sound a little strange, but I'm trying to find a friend of a friend who comes camping here," I said.

She tilted her head and stared at me with a strange look in her eyes, her eyebrows angled. "I'm not sure I can be much help. Lots of people come here."

"His name's Sam."

"Sam who?"

"That, I don't know."

A few seconds went by. She turned her palms up. "You'll have to give me a little bit more than that."

"He's Canadian. You may have gone to school with him."

"How would you know that?" she asked, but I remained silent, hopeful that she'd still answer my out-of-the-left-field question. Her eyes veered toward the top left corner, *accessing her memory bank?* "Most people who know about this campground are Canadians. For some reason, we've never quite made the official campground maps. And I've gone to school with a few Sams. I need a bit more."

"Okay," I leaned closer to her and put my hand on her shoulder. "I know one more detail."

She didn't seem bothered by me touching her. "Shoot," she said, a smile on her face.

I hesitated for a second, then voiced the awkward words I had been hoping I wouldn't have to say aloud, "His dick leans to the left."

Her eyes were now wide open. "What? Now, that's a detail I didn't expect! Didn't peg you as a player for the other team," she said, placing her hand flat on my six-pack abs, just above my belt.

I shook my head sharply. "I'm not gay!"

Being mistaken for a gay guy's a first. But my question certainly didn't help my case.

"Are you a cop or P.I.?" she asked.

I didn't understand what was going on in this woman's brain. "Do I look like a cop or private eye?"

"Maybe you're more of a *Privates' Inspector* then?" she asked with a wink and a smile.

Is she flirting with me?

"Well, tell you what," she said, getting back to business. "Most spots are open for tonight."

She looked out the window at my parked vehicle before addressing me again.

"Sleeping in a tent or in the back of your Cherokee?" she asked.

"Haven't decided yet. Got a tent in there."

"Well, why don't you go and set yourself up at number 12 over here," she said, circling a number on a photocopied map of the site. She marked two other icons: the bathroom and garbage area. "Don't keep any food outside of your vehicle. We had bear sightings a few days ago."

"That settles the tent question. I'll sleep in the back of my SUV!"

"As you wish," she replied in a nonchalant way, obviously not as scared of bears as I was. "So it's fifteen dollars for the night."

"Okay," I said, then took my wallet out and retrieved one purple and one blue bill. "So, do you know the Sam I'm talking about?" I asked as I handed her the exact change.

"Maybe..." she said, taking my money and then handing me the map.

"Any way you could help me track him down?"

"Depends."

"Depends on what?"

"Meet me in the bathroom in a few minutes. I'll show you how to work the shower and I'll decide then. Maybe," she repeated, eyeing me down.

I bid my goodbye for now then turned around, my black-and-white map in hand, before stepping outside to return to my vehicle.

11:55 a.m.

Having driven around the whole campground to reach my spot, I now knew that the place was near vacant. There was one RV parked a few sites down, but otherwise it was empty.

Guess nobody goes camping in the middle of nowhere on a Tuesday, even on a sunny day.

I backed the Cherokee to fit into the limits of my campsite, making sure it was on even ground so I could get a good night's sleep. Vehicle in place, I then made my way to the bathroom, hoping the campground attendant would be able to help me track down Sam.

It was a basic concrete-block structure painted white with green metal doors and a matching green roof, but it had electricity and running water. Everything I had imagined. Nothing more, nothing less.

"Hello?" I said aloud, wondering if the friendly young woman was already in here.

No reply. The building was empty.

I took the opportunity to empty my bladder. The wall in front of the urinals was plastered with graffiti. I let my wandering eyes read some:

"Don't ruin a good thing by divulging our little secret!"
"Some things are better kept out of guide books."

What are those making reference to?
Bladder relieved, I headed to the other side of the room to wash my hands. I was admiring my two-day beard in the mirror, trying to see if any grays had started to appear among my light-brown stubble, when the employee burst into the men's room.

"Good. You found the place," she said, a big smile on her face.

I looked at her again, pretty certain that she'd unbuttoned her shirt some more since I'd last seen her. I could now see her cleavage line. A couple of fleshy, natural-looking breasts sat under there.

"Hard to miss. There aren't that many buildings around here," I replied.

"Well, that's the way we like it here, mister."

"Call me Charlie," I said, walking to her to shake her hand.

"I'm Tiffany." She shook my hand briefly then took an impromptu seat on the counter next to the sink, just a few inches from me. Her skirt barely reached the fold of her hips. Her legs were spread apart ever so slightly. I was willing to bet that if I stepped back by a few feet, with a furtive glance, I'd be able to see her panties. But before I could move, she started talking again.

"About the shower. See that machine next to the knob?" she asked, pointing at the wall in front of her.

Perfect opportunity for me to change my point of view.
I turned and took five steps toward it, then pivoted once more to look at her again.

Before making eye contact, I took a peek at her groin.

No panties? Is she aware I can totally see her bush?
I looked up, and a large grin adorned her face.

"It works with loonies. Do you have any?" she asked as she spread her legs open some more. However, she immediately rested both of her palms in between, blocking my view of her pussy but leaning forward and framing her boobs between her arms and making her cleavage crevice more inviting than ever.

I cleared my throat and shook my head. "Your dollar coins? No. Don't have any," I answered.

"If you're interested in giving me a hand, I can show you how to get three minutes of hot water for free."

A hand?

A little confused by her request and exhibitionism, I raised my shoulders. I needed to get the information I came here to get. "And what about Sam? Can you tell me something about him?"

"Well..." she started before pausing. Her hands went to the topmost button that was still done up on her plaid shirt. She slowly undid it, then repeated the process with every button while staring at me with her green eyes.

The last one undone, she took her flannel layer off, and then threw it on the floor. Surprisingly, under her lumberjack shirt, she had on a beautiful black laced bra. She pulled one of her huge breasts out of its classy cup, pushing down the unexpectedly stretchy fabric, and then repeated with the other before caressing their curves and squeezing them together.

"So the Sam you were asking about earlier..." she said, continuing to give me a show while getting my brain's attention back to why I was here in the first place.

"Yeah?"

She remained quiet, eyeing me up and down.

I stood still and silent, save for my eyes—they were busy taking in her performance. Increased blood flow rushed below my belt, causing a bulge in my jeans.

"Thing is, I have a lot in common with him," she continued. "Some people say our libido is just too high. I say these folks can't appreciate a good thing when they have it in front of them."

And with those last words, she parted her legs even more before bringing one of her feet to the edge of the counter. Her pussy was now fully displayed. Below the bushy mat, her fingers parted her thick pink lips. I could hear how wet she was from where I stood. She fingered herself, then brought the guilty digit to her lips and licked it.

"I've got needs. Some call me a nympho. Some call me a slut. As long as they give me the attention I want, as long as they fuck me, I don't care what label I get." She returned her hand to her pussy, while the other toyed with one of her huge breasts. "You need a written invitation?" she asked.

Still stunned by her behavior and revelation, I was unsure if the annoyed tone of her voice was for real or not, but it didn't matter. No living-and-breathing man would let an opportunity like that slip by.

I moved toward her, my hands instantly going for her tits. I kneaded her natural, fleshy mounds for a few delicious seconds. Squeezing them, I appreciated what talents Mother Nature had granted her. My hands were nowhere big enough to grab all of their plump goodness. My cock pushed hard against the fabric of my jeans, indicating its desire to participate sooner rather than later. I was about to bend down to kiss her nipples when she reached for my belt and started undoing it. "No, wait," I hesitated before continuing.

With that kind of sexual history, I should probably take precautions.

"I don't have condoms on me. They're in my vehicle," I said.

She stopped me before I could move away by tugging on my collar. She then nodded toward a wall dispenser a few feet away from us.

"No need to put money in it. Just pop the side latch," she whispered in my ear. "So, what's it going to be, Mr. Charlie? Can you give me a hand or not?"

I couldn't think or talk.

All of my blood—and common sense—had already left my mind and reached my groin. I let her finish undoing my belt, then the zipper of my jeans. With her expert hands, she reached into my underwear and let my engorged member out for air before lowering my boxer briefs and jeans and letting them fall around my ankles.

Finally comfortable.

"Well, look at what we've got here," she said, a luscious smile appearing on her pink lips. "You may be quiet, but you sure make up for it in size, shall we say?"

She jumped off of the counter and knelt in front of me, her bare knees on the concrete floor. She immediately swallowed the tip of my dick.

"Oh," I let out, feeling the warmth of her moist mouth.

She tightened her lips around my shaft, and I pulled her head closer, letting her swallow another six inches or so, but then I felt the back of her throat. Tiffany readjusted herself, and then, as if by magic, she continued to take more of my length into her mouth.

My eyes rolled back. With my hands wrapped around her frizzy hair, I increased her cadence, pulling her head toward me. I fucked her hungry mouth. Faster, faster... but then she pulled away before standing up.

"What?" I let out.

"I want you to fuck me. I want your big dick in my cunt. I need to feel you in me."

She walked toward the wall, her barely supported boobs bouncing with every step. When she reached the condom dispenser, with a flick of her fingers, she unlatched the side of the machine. She grabbed a handful of rubbers and walked back to me, placing her newly acquired goods on the counter next to us.

I unwrapped the closest wrapper and covered my cock with the thin, lubricated latex. She faced the mirror and bent forward over the counter, letting her huge breasts hang to rest against the stainless steel counter. Her mini-skirt was pulled up; her white ass and bushy pussy were winking at me, desperately waiting to be filled.

I pushed myself into her dripping, engorged opening. She was surprisingly tight considering what she'd just told me about herself. She felt goddamn awesome. Her salty and lightly musky scent filled the air.

I pounded into her, slow at first, but deep.

She moaned.

She roared.

Through the mirror, I saw her biting her lower lip. Her eyes were closed. With every one of my motions, her roars echoed in the empty building. Her outspoken behavior was turning me on a lot more than I'd expected.

"Put your finger in my ass," she ordered.

The sight of her bouncing boobs in the mirror was hypnotizing, but I obeyed. I lubricated my middle finger inside her, and then took my digit out of her pussy to circle her anus briefly before pushing my fingertip into her ass. Her roars got louder and louder.

"Faster! Deeper!" she yelled. Through the mirror, I saw one of her hands frantically rubbing her clit, then I felt her reaching for my balls.

I twisted my finger in her anus, then squeezed my index in beside it. I fucked her hard and fast while fingering her ass. Her moans had turned into howler-monkey-like noises after she'd arched her back, making herself feel even tighter. This was too much stimulation. I was about to come.

"Fuck me, Charlie. Fuck me, hard!" she ordered before I gave her my all.

A minute or so later, having caught my breath and my heartbeat now back to normal, I pulled out of her, carefully holding the semen-filled condom. I pulled up the clothes from around my ankles to my thighs so I could walk over to the garbage can and dispose of the used latex, then returned to her.

She'd already turned around and was once again sitting on the counter. I allowed my fingers to circle her large, pink areolae.

"Anything else you want to know about Sam?" she asked. Her cheeks were rosy and her eyes seemed more peaceful, as if I had somehow tamed something inside of her.

"I'm trying to find one of his ex-girlfriends," I said.

Tiffany almost choked on a giggle. "Well, good luck with that!"

"What do you mean?" I asked her, taking my hands off of her.

She reinserted her tits into her bra while replying, "He's brought many here over the years, but he stopped coming last fall. I think his wife finally found out about this place... and me, I guess. Haven't seen him since. I don't have his number anymore. He's changed it."

"Damn it."

I tucked my deflated dick back in my boxer briefs before doing up my jeans.

Well. It was worth a shot.

"But if you stick around and come see me at the front when you're bored, I may remember a few more details," she said before jumping down from the counter and stealing a kiss from me. She lowered her skirt, grabbed the flannel shirt that was laying on the concrete floor, and then walked to the shower knob.

"Crank it two full rotations clockwise and you'll get about three minutes of hot water," she said before smiling at me and heading out of the men's room in her bra, shirt in hand.

And just like that, I think I finally understood some people's fascination with camping.

9:30 p.m.

With a long spike, I poked the red coals from my amateur campfire.

Although it had been years since I'd had to build a fire of any kind, my memories and experiences from the Boy Scouts decades ago came in handy.

The coals' intense heat combined with the lack of high flames would be perfect for cooking my steak now. I carefully flipped the foil-wrapped potato I'd added onto the metal grill about five minutes ago, and then threw my one-inch-thick slab of meat next to it. I didn't have any spices, but that was alright. Smoke would work just fine as a flavor-enhancer. And Alberta beef should be pretty darn good to start with.

How perfectly the day turned out!

A smile drew on my face just thinking back about the afternoon. I dug a hand in my jeans and readjusted my junk. I couldn't recall having been this raw in years. Turned out that Tiffany had no useful information for me, but she was definitely worth a fuck or two... or four. That hot—albeit hairy—Canadian pussy was insatiable.

Flannel and wool will never be the same again; they've suddenly gained a new sexual connotation. *Maybe the same goes for pine-scented objects as well?*

I flipped my meat on the grill and gulped down another swig of beer.

Stronger than our American varieties. Good stuff. Or is it the lingering pussy taste in my mouth that's affecting the flavor? Either-or.

In the distance, I saw headlights making the rounds around the site. *Must be Tiffany, checking up on things.* The headlights stopped by the RV a few sites down, then the roaring engine grew quiet and the headlights turned off.

By the time my steak felt firm (about medium doneness) and ready to eat, I heard the roar of her engine again.

Her doctor's visit to the neighbor is over?

Tiffany's headlights turned back on and headed my way; she was continuing her rounds.

I transferred my steak onto my plate and started cutting away. I was chewing on my first tasty bite when I saw her silhouette appear by the light of the fire.

"Hey, stranger," she greeted me. "Everything good?"

I smiled at her, nodding and still chewing. I stabbed another piece of meat on my fork and pointed it at her. "Want a bite?"

"Why not?" she said before taking the fork from my hand and eating my offering. "Tasty," she said after swallowing it.

"Want a beer?" I offered.

"I'm still working for another thirty minutes. Later?"

"Sure."

She nodded and turned around to return to her vehicle.

I watched her tight ass walk away from me for a few steps before the light of the fire no longer shone on her.

It's okay to fuck on the job, but she can't drink? Is that part of Canadian laws?

I smiled and shook my head before cracking open another can of beer. I leaned my head back for a minute to stare at the sky above; a shooting star crossed the sky.

I couldn't think of anything to wish for other than to find my mystery stewardess... And for the Yankees to win the World Series?

10:15 p.m.

The crackling sounds of the fire had me hypnotized. Sitting on a large log, wrapped in a wool blanket, I was lost in my own thoughts. I didn't hear Tiffany's footsteps until she was right there next to me, her hand on my shoulder.

"Hey," she said. "Looks like you're ready for bed." She leaned in and kissed me. She was still wearing that same flannel shirt and the near-inexistent skirt.

"Aren't you cold?" I asked, opening my blanket and expecting her to sit on my lap. But instead, she pulled her miniskirt up—exposing her pussy as if it were a body part like any other—then opened her legs and got on mine, facing me.

After wrapping her arms around me, she locked her lips onto mine. I readjusted my blanket to envelop the both of us the best I could. She was already untying my belt.

"Again?"

I've never said that before and never thought that moment would come, I found myself thinking as soon as I said it aloud.

Her puppy eyes were begging me. "My pussy's aching," she said. "Your big dick is—"

My lips met hers, and I let go of the blanket to wrap my hands around her face. *Let the damn blanket fall as it may.*

I reached under her shirt and untied her bra. As excited as she made me, my cock was not ready for action yet. I motioned for her to stand up, and I did the same before reaching down for the blanket.

After shaking the dirt and leaf debris from it, I placed it flat next to the fire. She followed my cue, leaning back on it. She unbuttoned her shirt and I knelt in between her legs. With her skirt around her waist, I was free to open her legs as wide as I needed them to be. The fire and its shadows turned her already beautiful body into a work of art. Her pussy was glistening wet, again. I licked her inner thighs, worked my way to her clit. I glanced up for a second. She was massaging her tits with one hand, the other arm was folded to prop her head up like a pillow.

I dug in, her pussy juice the perfect dessert to my camping meal. It also turned out to be the cue my cock needed to harden again. I savored her, lightly pinching her labia, then fucking her gently with my tongue and my fingers until she grabbed me by the hair and pulled me back up. I licked her flat stomach on my way to her humongous tits, attending to each as a gentleman should. Then I moved up to her neck and made my way to her mouth, leaving my tongue's wet trail behind.

She kissed me briefly and held my face a couple of inches away from hers, just enough for us to make eye contact.

"Fuck me quietly under the stars," she whispered.

NEXT STEPS

After leaving the campground, I returned my camping equipment, and then dropped off the rental vehicle at the airport.

When Wednesday evening rolled around, I was glad to be boarding a plane again.

Now, don't get me wrong. I'm not complaining. It was a fun camping experience, but my dick needs a break!

I had to say that the past couple of days were one of my best layovers to date.

Even though I didn't get any closer to finding my mystery stewardess, that Tiffany woman proved much more entertaining than most of the random girls I've picked up at bars in the past.

———

Now comfortably seated in business class, a cold beer in my hand, I try to think of nothing. You could call that my way of meditating, I guess.

I try and resist the urge to pull out the diary, here on the plane. I succeed for now, but my other brain still appears to be controlling the show. I can't help but imagine what each of the female attendants on this flight is like in the sack.

Is one of them *my* stewardess?

I don't even know if she's White, Asian, Black... Maybe she's Hispanic?

Well, at least I know she speaks English.

I change my mind; the temptation is too strong. I can't just sit here and wonder. I dig into my carry-on to retrieve her leather-bound journal.

Maybe if I re-read it one more time I'll find a clue I missed before?

The in-flight blanket carefully placed to cover the large bulge I know will soon appear in my pants, I start studying her detailed account of the all-girl threesome she had with the two hot blondes in Mexico.

They left evidence behind: a sex tape.

Could I potentially get my hands on it?

Would it hold the key that would allow me to uncover her identity?

PART II

MEXICO

THE STEWARDESS'S ENTRIES
MEXICO

12:15 p.m.

CONFIRMED passenger list printed and walkie-talkie in hand, I stood by the glass door a few feet away from the counter, waiting for the crew to report that our Cancun-bound plane was ready for boarding.

Can't wait to get there.

Kate and I had spent the past thirty minutes at the gate, reassuring an incessant stream of pasty-white passengers concerned about possible delays.

Don't think I'm the only one who's anxious to get my feet in the sand and body under the hot sun.

But my plans for this three-day-weekend included a few more extra-curricular activities with Matt—my friend with benefits. Lazy mornings, sex, brunch, swimming... Did I mention lots of sex? Or *good rolls in the sack* as he calls them...

Gosh, I can't believe it's already been a month since we met, during his very short stint as a flight attendant.

We shared a few pleasant evenings here and there, mostly when our schedules happened to coincide. Nothing serious, conversation over wine and cheese, and lots of hot sex.

He's soooo frigging handsome.

And I'd managed to keep thinking of him as something other than boyfriend material. Not quite the string of one-night stands my friend Alex had recommended, but still...

I'd made progress. My disillusion about *finding the one* was hibernating. My sexual life was headed in the right direction.

Hanging out with Matt for three delicious long nights and two full days would be so nice. I missed his hands on my body, his tongue on my—

My cellphone vibrated in my pocket, interrupting my daydream.

I dug it out, and the small pop-up showed I'd received a text message from Matt.

With butterflies in my stomach and a big grin on my face, I swiped my way past the password protection screen to read his words:

Sorry
Have to cancel weekend plans
Back with ex
Will explain later
Sorry, babe
:(

12:20 p.m.

What the fuck?

Ten minutes to boarding. And *now* I learned I was about to spend three days alone in a party town during the busy season *without* a hotel reservation... or any plans, really.

Shit.

What can I reply to that?

I shook my head for a few seconds, letting all the things I really wanted to say escape my mind, then I settled on sending the plain and politically-correct "ok."

I returned my phone to my jacket pocket, trying to don a happy face and push my anger and worries down my throat. The walkie-talkie finally screeched the report I'd been waiting for, so I acknowledged it and then returned to Kate at the counter.

I placed a hand on her elbow. "Time to make the announcement," I told her.

She nodded, flipped her brown hair behind her ear, and then picked up the handset.

While listening to her read the pre-written script in English then in Spanish to announce we'd soon start boarding families with young children and those who needed special assistance, I glanced at the crowd. A couple of families were getting their things together and coming our way. I didn't have much time, but maybe Kate could help.

When she hung up, I used the couple of minutes we still had to talk to her. I knew it would become impossible once the actual boarding process began.

"Kate, are you staying in Cancun?"

She shook her head. "No, I'm deadheading to San Francisco a couple of hours after we land. Are you?"

"I was planning to, but my... *friend* canceled on me." It still felt funny whenever I had to refer to him. He wasn't my *boyfriend*. *Fuck-buddy* just seemed flat-out rude, and I wasn't sure if *fucker* would have been a better label right now.

Then again, Matt didn't owe me anything. I couldn't be mad at him for canceling on me.

But it still sucked.

Her answer brought me back to reality. "That's too bad, but I'm sure you'll have fun anyway. Weather's supposed to be great!"

She started walking, covering the few feet that separated the counter from where she'd be checking our passengers' tickets.

"Do you have friends in Cancun?" I asked. "Someone who may have a couch or bedroom where I could crash?"

"No. Why do you ask? Don't you have a reservation?"

"No, unfortunately."

Her mouth made an upside-down U and she raised her eyebrows. "Good luck with that. Hotels near the beach are gonna be packed. You'll pay through the nose... if you find something!"

I'll be fine. I'll figure something out, I told myself while smiling at the tired-looking father of three standing in front of me with his offspring. I greeted him and took the boarding passes he was handing me.

1:20 p.m.

A handful of straggling and slightly inebriated last-minute passengers having joined us, we finally closed the gate.

Kate and I quickly walked around economy class, closing all overhead bins and ensuring our complete planeload of excited passengers was accounted for and seated in a full upright position, with their seat belts on. As ordered by the captain, we put the doors on automatic, cross-checked them, and then reported back.

Once we pushed away from the gate, the safety video started airing.

I love these modern planes with individual monitors that take away the need for our in-person safety demonstrations. Only ten percent of passengers paid attention to those anyway. I don't know if more people are watching the video, but I hope so.

I headed to my seat, which faced the front row in economy class. It was the most socially-awkward seat in the plane.

Most passengers probably feel like I'm just staring at them, especially those trying to make a quick call after we make it clear their phones have to be put on airplane mode.

I decided to smile my way through the uncomfortable minutes spent facing the passengers.

Won't be long until I can get up again.

Let's see, maybe I know someone on this flight. Someone I can hang out with this weekend...

1:25 p.m.

No, I don't know anyone. Damn it.

The intercom crackled overhead. "Hi there, folks. Captain speaking. Due to a fairly long line of planes taxiing to take off on the runway in front of us, we expect a slight delay. We're... seventh in line. Please sit tight, keep your seat belt on, and refrain from using the washroom. We should be leaving the tarmac in about ten minutes. Thanks for your patience and sorry for the delay."

Oh goody.

1:30 p.m.

My cheeks were getting a little sore from fake-smiling and I'd run out of things and people to look at without staring. I obviously couldn't check my phone while facing everyone; that'd be a sure way to get our passengers upset.

Instead, I opted to start listening in to the conversation people sitting directly in front of me, close to the window, were having. Two beautiful, twenty-something blondes with perfect tans, long legs, and barely any clothes on were chatting and giggling. Next to them, in the aisle seat, a thirty-something, rugged, muscular Latino man with a crew cut introduced himself to the blonde sitting closest to him.

Military? Police?

The man who'd called himself Sebastian spoke English with a Spanish accent.

The ponytailed woman sitting next to him in the middle seat introduced herself as Isabel, then turned her attention back to her wavy-haired friend sitting by the window.

"Tracy, you'll love the birthday present I got you," Isabel said.

"You got me something? You didn't have to, Sweetie," the woman in the mini-skirt replied before kissing her friend on the lips.

Ah, they're together. Good for them.

...And less competition for the rest of us, plain-looking, mere-mortal, older straight women.

Tracy, the birthday girl sitting by the window, turned to her girlfriend to whisper something in her ear. I didn't want to make it obvious I had been listening, so I looked down. However, my eyes stopped on their path when I saw that, in leaning toward her girlfriend, the birthday girl had parted her knees by about a foot and, with her mini-skirt being so short, I currently had full-frontal view of her blonde pussy.

Trying not to react or stare was hard.

I've looked too long already.

I glanced up again. The birthday girl had moved her attention to me, and she sent a slight smile and a wink my way.

Blood rushed to my cheeks.

Totally not appropriate! Need to think about something else, fast. Small talk.

"So, where are you all going? Home?" I asked, mostly directing my question at Sebastian to avoid the women's stares.

"Back to work for me," he said.

"What kind of work do you do?" I continued, pleased to have succeeded in my attempt at distraction.

"Search and rescue, but I mainly patrol the coast on a boat."

"Neat. Must be nice to spend time on the water instead of in the air!" I replied.

"We love spending time on the water, too," Tracy, the pussy-exhibitionist, started before placing her hand on her girlfriend's lap. "Isn't that the best thing in the world, Isa?"

"Love it. My family has a nice yacht that we take out. This weekend, it'll just be the two of us, to celebrate Tracy's birthday."

Isabel had a melodious voice. She smiled at the coastguard, myself, and then her girlfriend while she replied, then she squeezed Tracy's knee, moving it once more to expose her girlfriend's pussy.

I swallowed hard. *I've stared at it twice now. Get a grip, girl!*

I wasn't playing for that team, but somehow I couldn't help looking.

Curiosity? Probably.

Both women were now grinning at me. They were obviously doing it on purpose.

What did they whisper to each other earlier?

"Tracy and Isabel," the coastguard started before his face turned stern. "Be careful out there. We've recently had reports of a few pirates boarding unsuspecting sailors and stealing their boats."

"Pirates? Like Johnny Depp? You've gotta be kidding." The two blondes giggled.

"I wish I was. But I'm serious. Don't go too far off the coast without other boats around you."

Isabel was shaking her head. "Really? Nah."

"This *is* important, girls. I'm not joking." He shifted on his seat and grabbed the wallet from his cargo pant pocket. He opened it and dug a business card out of it, which he then handed to Isabel. "Here's my number. If you intend on sailing out alone, keep contact with me via text messages and send me your location."

Isabel took his card and thanked him. "Maybe you can come over for dessert if you're in the area," she offered with her velvety voice.

Maybe it was her friend's exposed pussy that had my mind down the gutter, but I'm pretty sure Isabel was flirting with Sebastian.

"That could be interesting. You girls like to party a lot?"

I'm not crazy. He got the same vibe.

The loud roar of the airplane's turbines suddenly filled the air. The passengers sunk in their seats while I purposely pushed my back into mine, trying to compensate for the inertia and acceleration that wanted to throw me face first toward the back.

We were powering up and taking off, finally.

4:55 p.m.

I spent the entire flight on my feet, attending to hungry and excited passengers who didn't want to waste a second of their vacations. The lesbian couple in the front row, along with most of the young adults flying in economy class, were partaking in a fair amount of onboard drinking. Overpriced beers were a hot commodity.

Each time I answered one of the blondes' service calls, they greeted me with large grins. They even tried to tip me on their sparkling wine purchases, but I couldn't accept.

"Why don't you get yourself a drink then? On us?" Isabel suggested.

I thought about it for a second. *It's against regulations, but who'd know?*

"Sure, why not? I'd like one of those mini wine bottles to wind down after work. Thanks, ladies," I said handing them each their unopened mini-bottles that Isabel had just purchased. I made a mental note to sneak one of those tasty —and now paid-for—bottles into my purse before leaving the aircraft in an hour or so.

The coastguard was drinking beer, keeping up with the party girls next to him with his eyes blatantly surveying Isabel's cleavage.

"And you, would you like another one?" I asked him.

His eyes glanced away from Isabel's breasts and met mine. He ordered another beer and reached for his wallet. I entered the transaction in the payment processing apparatus while he was pulling out his card.

As I reached out to take his Visa, unexpected turbulence sent me crashing into him. Like the arm of a mother instinctually reaching out to protect a child sitting in the passenger seat of a car, Isabel's arms instantly stretched out to protect both Tracy and Sebastian. But her hand—conveniently?—cupped my left breast in the process. She nonetheless prevented my shoulder from landing square in Sebastian's jaw, and I was grateful for that.

Frantic commotion echoed all around us in the plane, followed by an announcement from the captain: "Sorry about that little bump, folks. Looks like we'll be flying through a small turbulent area for a few more minutes. Please return to your seats and fasten your seat belts."

Isabel winked at me, gave my breast a gentle squeeze, and then lowered her arm back to her lap. Tracy bent down to grab the sparkling wine bottles that had rolled onto the floor, thankfully still unopened. I apologized to Sebastian, but he would hear nothing of it.

"Maybe you need to get your feet on a boat for a change," Tracy suggested. "What do you think, babe?" she asked her girlfriend.

Isabel nodded. "That's a great idea. Are you staying in Cancun for a few days, or are you taking off to another exciting destination right away?"

"I'm sticking around for the weekend," I replied, finally feeling hopeful that I may have found some people to hang out with.

"Would you like to join us?" Tracy asked.

I looked at Tracy, then Isabel. Both had genuine smiles on. *What else am I going to do? Could be good fun: beautiful women, a boat, the ocean, drinks, maybe the handsome coastguard would be invited too?*

"Sure, why not?" I said.

"Wonderful. You'll sit here again during landing?" Isabel asked, pointing at the vacant seat facing them.

"Yep," I said, nodding. "Best seat in the house." The words left my mouth without thinking, out of habit as it had become a running joke among my flight attendant friends. None of us liked sitting in front of the passengers, facing them. Isabel's eyes illuminated, and both she and her girlfriend burst out giggling.

I could once again feel blood rushing to my face. "If you'll excuse me, I have to continue my garbage run. We'll chat later," I said before pushing my cart down the aisle and collecting an empty water bottle from the young woman sitting behind them.

5:30 p.m.

I returned to my front-row seat after checking that all passengers' belongings had been properly stowed, seats in their upright positions, and seat belts fastened. The blondes and the coastguard were pretty happily drunk by now, and several passengers had their passports in hand, custom forms filled out and at the ready. A few were fidgeting, but most had a big smile on their faces.

After fastening my own seat belt, I noticed that Tracy and Isabel had traded seats. Tracy, the birthday girl, now sat next to Sebastian, her lap covered by a sweatshirt. *Good! Won't be caught inadvertently staring at her naked pussy one more time.*

A beep echoed in the main cabin, preceding the captain's final announcement. "We're now approaching our final descent. We should be at the gate in about five minutes." While he continued with the standard *thank-you-for-choosing-us* bit, Sebastian leaned in to Tracy and then whispered something in her ear. I took another glance at the other rows. Many passengers were looking into the closest portholes to see the ocean and coast below, alternating between the port and starboard sides depending on which way the plane was leaning.

When the plane started veering to starboard again, bringing clouds into view on our side of the plane, the passengers' stares went to the portholes on the opposite side.

I saw Isabel slide her hand under the sweatshirt that rested on her girlfriend's lap.

A second later, a grin appeared on Tracy's face. Sebastian was still whispering sweet nothings into Tracy's ear, none the wiser.

Probably too tipsy to notice.

I felt Isabel's stare and turned to look at her. She smiled at me before speaking. "I'm sure we'll have a lot of fun this weekend when you join us on the boat."

Tracy giggled and sent a furtive glance my way before returning her attention to Sebastian. A couple of minutes later, Tracy's hand launched toward Isabel, grabbing her firmly by the knee. Tracy then turned to stare at me, biting her lip, her eyes starting to go up in a pre-orgasmic stare, but she closed them again, her cheeks brightening, her chest raising higher—lifting her cropped top higher and exposing more of her flat stomach. Then, a few seconds later, Tracy let out a loud sigh, turned to face Isabel, and then kissed her.

"Thank you, baby. I needed that," she said to her girlfriend. Their eyes stayed locked for a few more seconds, and then they both turned and smiled at me. I swallowed hard. I felt the heat on my cheeks, but I had nowhere I could flee to. I was stuck in my discomfort zone between voyeurism and guilt.

The aircraft's wheels hit the tarmac, creating a vibration that reverberated through the cabin, and the plane steadied its course after dealing with a split second of cross-wind on the landing strip. Some of the passengers clapped. Sebastian crossed himself. *Superstitious or religious?* Either way, I was certainly happy that today's oddly sensual work shift was nearly over.

"So, you'll meet us at *La Esperanza Marina* around 10 a.m. tomorrow morning?" Tracy asked, her cheeks flushed.

I nodded. I hadn't been on a boat in so long, and it definitely hadn't been part of my original weekend plans, but I had no doubt it would be filled with surprises.

"Should I bring anything?" I asked.

Isabel shook her head. "Your bikini... or nothing really. We've got everything we need. Look for *Delicious Sunset*. We'll be expecting you."

6:30 p.m.

My over-worrying about not finding a hotel room turned out to have been pointless.

I managed to find a comfortable room in a hotel close to the airport. Sure, it wasn't the Ritz-Carlton and it wasn't on the beach, but at least it was a place to leave my belongings, kick off my shoes, and crack open that tiny sparkling wine bottle.

I opened the patio door and let the warm tropical air into my room. Songs of piña coladas and sailing with Captain Morgan echoed in my mind as I leaned on the guard rail, watching the last pink and orange hues color the evening sky while sipping the now barely-cool, bubbly liquid.

Tomorrow should be interesting.

10:00 a.m.

I found the *Delicious Sunset* without problems. It was one of the nicest yachts at *La Esperanza*, and everyone around seemed to know the two luscious blondes.

After I crossed the small walkway to step onboard, Tracy welcomed me wearing the tiniest of bikinis and a matching hot pink hair clip in her shoulder-length, wavy hair. 'Weirdly-knotted-strings-with-three-tiny-triangles-of-hot-pink-fabric' would have been a better name for her outfit, but she pulled it off. At least her pussy was covered with one of those triangles. That was already a big change from her airplane apparel.

"Isabel, our guest is here," she yelled out after hugging me for a solid ten seconds.

Her girlfriend came up from below deck wearing a similar bikini, except that hers was white. Just like Tracy's, her entire body was tanned—with the possible exception of what the three tiny triangles covered, but I highly doubted it. Women with such bodies and access to a boat had all the reasons in the world to bare it all and get a full-body tan.

Tracy grabbed my overnight bag and headed to wherever her girlfriend had come from.

Isabel walked toward me, arms open and at the ready for a hug. We embraced. After a few seconds, she pulled away from me, her hands on my elbows and a large smile on her freckled face. "Come on, I'll give you the grand tour," Isabel said, grabbing my hand and pulling me. Then she suddenly stopped, turned, and took a second glance at me, my light-blue summer dress seemingly the cause of her concerns. "You brought a bikini, right?"

"I've got a swimsuit and towel in my bag," I replied, pointing in the direction Tracy had disappeared with my belongings.

She nodded and then began her quick tour of the upper deck. The stern featured a nice patio-like space with cushions lining the U-shaped sitting area, a table, and large speakers attached to the bulkhead. Ten to twelve people could comfortably sit there and party all day.

We then headed toward the bow. After showing me the helm and various other controls, we made our way down to see the bedroom, galley, and heads. The passageway was narrow and quite short.

"It's not overly spacious, but it's perfect for what we use it for," she said before opening the bedroom door. A large queen-sized bed occupied the majority of the room. There was standing room next to the bunk, and a little more than sitting room above the mattress itself. The overnight bag I'd brought rested at the foot of the bed. By the door, a flat screen TV was mounted, with red, white, and yellow cables dangling from it, as if someone had recently unhooked a DVD player.

After showing me how to use the marine toilet, Isabel headed to the galley, and I followed. A hint of garlic butter filled the air. Tracy was standing in front of a small stove, stirring something in a medium pot. She smiled at us when we walked in. Isabel wrapped her arms around her, then kissed her neck.

"I'm almost done," Tracy said.

Isabel let go of her girlfriend, slapped her ass, and then smiled. "Tracy's quite a cook, and she's got a whole brunch menu planned for us. It's gonna be tasty! How about something to drink?" she asked me.

"Sure. What do you have?"

Tracy turned to face us and chimed in, "Champagne Mimosa?"

"Wonderful," I said, really looking forward to a refreshing drink. Although quite a few hours separated us from the midday heat, I could already feel the humid, salty air on my skin. Being in a small enclosed galley—with the stove on —certainly didn't help either.

I watched Isabel pour the champagne and orange juice into three delicate champagne flutes. She handed me one, then brought one over to Tracy.

"Here's to a fun day at sea!" she offered, raising her glass. The three of us clinked. I repeated her toast and then had a sip. The refreshing bubbly drink was delicious, and I was thirsty, so I emptied my glass in less than a minute.

"We'll get going shortly," Isabel said, taking away my flute. "Why don't you go and change in the bedroom? Tracy's nearly done in here. Come and join us back on the upper deck when you've changed clothes, okay?"

"Perfect," I said before heading to the bedroom she'd shown me a few minutes earlier. Alone, I dug into my bag. I took off my dress and underwear, then slipped on my black and white Ralph Lauren one-piece suit. I tied the white strap into a bow behind my neck. I certainly felt overdressed compared to them, but I didn't own a bikini.

A couple of seconds later, I heard the engine start.

I put my dress in my bag, then left the bedroom to join Tracy at the stern just as the boat was pulling off. A handful of young, handsome men in surfers' shorts —probably those who'd let go of the ropes that kept the yacht attached to the jetty—were waving us goodbye.

"Is this what you wear at the beach?" Tracy asked as I slid next to her onto the cushions that surrounded the table. She offered me another Mimosa.

I accepted the flute as I replied, "I don't go to the beach very often."

"You're so..." she started, then tilted her head, "...interesting," she finally settled on.

Other people had never voiced their opinions about me aloud—except for a few ex-boyfriends who never hesitated to point out my flaws. I wasn't sure how to feel about Tracy's comment, so I disregarded it.

"I think you take life too seriously, but deep down you like to have fun, no?" Tracy asked, her hand grabbing mine. "Would that be a fair assessment?"

"You're probably right," I said with a shrug.

"Stay right here," she said, squeezing my hand, then letting go of it before getting up. "I've got something that will make you relax. We're here to enjoy ourselves, right?"

I smiled and nodded. She went away, leaving me alone with my second Champagne Mimosa, which I quickly finished.

She returned a couple of minutes later with a freshly rolled joint and a silver Zippo lighter.

"This will do the trick, I promise," she said, winking at me. She lit it, then took a few puffs before passing it to me.

I can't recall the last time I smoked pot, but why not? I have to let loose, relax, and forget about my worries. Live in the moment, right?

I took her offering, brought it to my lips, and inhaled, coughing my way through the first puff. But then it got easier. Smoking was a little like riding a bike. Although my latest smoke-free cycle had lasted years—including regular cigarettes—my body hadn't really forgotten how to smoke. Or the thrill of it. The rush it inevitably brought on.

We smoked the whole thing between the two of us, and I didn't feel anything for a few minutes. Then it hit me.

As I turned my head to watch the harbor sail by on our way out of the marina, I felt as though I'd drunk a full bottle of wine in one sitting but without the headache, the blue lips, or the slurred speech. I just felt dizzy. No, dizzy wasn't it. I felt relaxed and a little dazed. Comfortable. Happy. Really happy. Happier than I'd been in a long time.

I looked at Tracy. Her face was adorned by a large, relaxed smile; her pupils wide open even though bright sunlight reflected on the calm harbor water all around us.

"Good, right?" she asked me.

"Strong!"

She reached for the pair of black oversized sunglasses that rested on the table and put them on before returning her attention to me. "Best way to wind down!" She exhaled loudly and wrapped her arm around my shoulders and brought me closer to her. "You're really pretty, you know that, right?"

I felt my skin blush. "Thank you. And you're gorgeous."

"Ah, I wasn't saying it to receive a compliment, but thanks." She suddenly removed her arm from around me and both of her hands cupped my breasts.

I froze. *What?*

Without flinching and totally ignoring the surprised look that had to have been on my face, she asked, "You're what, a C?"

Still taken by surprise, I nodded, and she removed her hands before smiling. "Wait here. I've got something much better for you to wear." She jumped to her feet and went down below, leaving me alone and a little confused. I enjoyed my high while awaiting her return. I decided to step away from the table for a little while. I got up and leaned against the bulkhead, letting the cool ocean breeze caress my skin. The passing scenery kept my attention: lots of sailboats, speedboats, Sea-Doos, and fishing boats near us, but their numbers dwindled as we sped out to sea.

Some moments later, I was taken by surprise again when Tracy appeared next to me and reached behind my neck to untie the back of my suit. Then without any sort of warning, she took a hold of the front and pulled it down, like she was ripping a Band-Aid, exposing my breasts.

"Hey!" I yelped, instinctively crossing my arms over my chest to cover myself.

"Don't be a prude. Come on, try this on," she said, handing me a non-padded but wired, white bikini top. "It's Isabel's. I think it will work for you."

Our boat was passing near other boats, and I saw people pointing our way. *Better cover up.*

I unfolded my arms and picked up the bikini top she was offering me, concealing my breasts with the material. After adjusting the underwire to be comfortable, Tracy spun me around to tie it in the back.

"Let me have a look," she said, once again spinning me around, then taking a step back.

She clapped and jumped like a teenage girl, her small breasts bouncing up and down with a split-second delay. "Much better! Let me grab the bottom. I'll be right back."

A minute later, as promised, she returned with a tiny piece of fabric. So tiny, in fact, I didn't even know which was the front and which was the back. Tracy probably saw the hesitation on my face and flipped the piece of clothing 180-degrees in my hands before pulling down the rest of my swimsuit, leaving me standing butt—and pussy—naked in front of her.

"Trimmed and tidy, ah!" she said. "Good, but put it on before those fishermen decide to board us," she continued, a large smile on her face as she nodded toward the left.

I turned to see what she was pointing at then gasped. We were not even one hundred feet away from the fishing boat in question. I kicked off the one-piece from around my ankles and slid on the new bottom before adjusting it into place.

"We'll have to work on your tan, girl," she said before slapping my mostly exposed ass. "You're pale as hell! But don't worry. Lots of time for that later today, and no fishermen where we're going. You won't have to be so prudish anymore." She winked at me.

Something tingled deep in me, then spread outward, warming my entire body from within. *Arousal?*

"I'll check with Isabel, but I think it's time I set this table up for brunch. Are you hungry?" Tracy asked.

"Starving," I said, not sure if I meant for food, sex, or both.

1:00 p.m.

After a sumptuous brunch—Tracy could certainly cook some mean eggs Benedict —we headed another twenty or thirty miles farther out to sea, away from shipping lanes and pleasure boats.

The engine noise faded out. I lay down on the deck and closed my eyes, letting the calm sea rock me gently while the sun rays and light breeze caressed my skin. My straggling fears and doubts about what would likely happen today on this boat had somehow disappeared from my mind, jettisoning themselves into the chasm marijuana and alcohol had temporarily carved into my head. Life was great. I was opening myself up to new experiences.

The pop of a champagne cork took me out of my daze. When I looked up, Isabel was giggling, a large Dom Pérignon bottle in hand, trying to pour the foaming liquid into the flutes sitting on the table in front of her while Tracy was tickling her flat stomach with kisses.

"Okay, okay," Isabel said as her giggles wound down. "Drinks are ready! Come and join us," she said to me.

I stood up and took the remaining glass from the table. The girls already had theirs in hand.

Isabel turned to her girlfriend and began singing, "Happy Birthday, Tracy..." I joined in.

Tracy's cheeks were pink. A childlike quality decorated her smile. When we finished singing the last words, she clapped and jumped up. We clinked glasses and returned to the cushioned seating area.

"How old are you?" I asked the birthday girl after we sat down.

"Twenty-two," she replied. *Nearly a dozen years my junior.*

Isabel stood up and folded one section of the table before walking away. She returned with three pails half-filled with ice cubes. After tossing some of the cushions covering the seats a few feet from us, she opened a couple of hidden storage areas. She reached in to transfer water bottles into the first ice bucket, and then beer cans into the second one. After closing the storage bins and covering them with their waterproof cushions, she placed the magnum she'd opened just minutes ago into the third bucket.

"Be right back," Isabel said after moving the ice-filled containers closer to us. *Definitely won't go thirsty here.*

A couple of minutes later, Isabel came back and sat on my right. She'd brought back another joint, which she lit, smoked a little, and then passed over to me.

"I want to have some fun," Tracy said on my left while I was taking a puff.

"A little later, I think," Isabel replied. I turned to look at her; her crooked smile greeted my glance.

Wow. I'm really going to go through with this?

I was pretty buzzed. Happily inebriated, not drunk—yet—but definitely high and relaxed.

"How about that cute coastguard?" I asked Tracy. "He gave you his number, right?"

She nodded. "Yes, I have it on my phone. Wanna send him some pics?"

"Sure, we could have some fun with him," Isabel said. "But let's warm him up nice first. Okay?"

Tracy agreed, stood up, handed me the lit joint, and then left.

I took another puff and felt Isabel's eyes on me. She said, "We like to tease good-looking men. Sometimes we do more than tease... It depends. We'll see how it goes."

Tracy returned, phone in hand, already typing something onto her screen.

"I wrote, 'Hi, handsome. I'm one of the cute blondes from the plane'," she said.

Just as she finished her sentence, her phone beeped with a reply.

"'Hi,' he wrote, with three exclamation points," Tracy reported before lifting her index finger. "He's typing something else." A pause followed. "'You girls having a good time?'"

"Tell him, 'Of course.' Let's send him a picture," Isabel suggested.

I was getting a little dizzy, turning left and right to follow along with their conversation. I passed the joint to Isabel.

"Of what?" Tracy asked excitedly.

"Let's all sit together and do a selfie of just our tops," Isabel suggested, her eyebrows raised, a sparkle in her eyes.

"Good start," Tracy replied before pushing me closer to Isabel and aiming the phone camera at our chests. She looked at the result: champagne flutes and barely covered breasts. She smiled in approval then sent it off.

"I bet you we get a dic-pic under five," Isabel said.

"Dic-pic under five?" I asked.

"Nah, I say seven," Tracy said before turning to me. "We'll keep exposing more and more of ourselves until we get a photo of his dick. The trick is to do it without incriminating evidence or without exposing our pussies first. That's too desperate."

I laughed. *Desperate is probably right, but incriminating?* "That's not illegal..." I said, confused.

"Of course not. But we don't want too many naked pictures of ourselves on the wrong people's phones, you know? Best to leave our heads out of—" Before she could finish her train of thought, her phone beeped with a reply.

We all looked at her screen. It was a picture of his Coast Guard ship, clearly at sea, a few uniformed men standing in the shot, facing away from the camera.

"Oh, he's working," Isabel said. "We may not get the money shot from him while he's at work."

"Nah, he's a guy," I said. Maybe it was the alcohol, maybe it was the pot. Or perhaps it was intuition, but I agreed with Isabel's initial guess. "Five pics, but we have to choose them wisely. How about a picture of the two of you in bed, in bikinis, heads out of the shot?"

"Sure. Why not?" Tracy said.

2:00 p.m.

A very short bedroom photo shoot later, Tracy had about a dozen pictures to select from. I handed Tracy her phone back on the way up to the stern, and she picked the photo she liked best, then sent it off, along with the caption: 'What's missing here?'

Sebastian replied with a picture of the gun mounted at the front of his ship.

"Either he's violent or the gun's representative of his dick!" Isabel snorted.

"Come on, girls," Tracy said, getting up as though someone had lit a firecracker under her small, round ass. "What gets a guy really excited?" Her doe-eyed stare alternated between me and Isabel. We both remained silent. "Come on... A wet T-shirt contest! I'll grab the video camera." She left running.

"Video camera? I thought you said pictures could be incriminating. Wouldn't videos be worse?" I asked, confused.

Isabel shook her head while finishing the last bit of our latest joint. "We use an old-fashioned mini-camcorder with tapes. There's only one copy of the tape and we control it. We're fine with that."

"Okay. But I don't have a white T-shirt."

"No need. That top you've got on, it gets really transparent when wet. It's not lined at all. In fact, I can already see your nipples through it. You have nice tits," she said, gently cupping them, caressing them through the fabric of the borrowed bikini top. A muted thrill came over me. She let go of me for a second to dip her right hand in the bucket closest to us. She then brought a half-melted ice cube to my left breast.

I instantly felt the chill of it, my flesh reacting instantly to the frozen surface, hardening. She made circular motions with the cube around my nipple, the ice quickly melting to expose my areola through the now transparent fabric.

"See? What did I tell you," Isabel said.

I grabbed my own breast, staring at it as though I'd never seen it before.

And come to think of it, I've probably never seen it like that, in broad day light, in the middle of the ocean.

Tracy came back, having traded her hot-pink bikini top for a cropped, white tank top. Her small nipples perked through the fabric. She frowned at Isabel after seeing what she had done to the top I was wearing.

"Don't worry, I wouldn't start without you here, baby," Isabel said, her words bringing Tracy's angled eyebrows back to their regular, softer positions. "It will dry before we get started, I promise. I'm going to have a beer and maybe smoke another one." She bent to grab a can from the bucket and handed me one.

Although I was really tipsy and pretty high as well, I couldn't resist. It was just too hot. I grabbed the can she offered.

2:15 p.m.

Ten minutes, a happy smoke, and a beer later, my bikini top was dry, as promised.

Isabel even rubbed my nipple to prove it to Tracy. "See? Fabric's solid white again. Just like before. No harm, no foul."

Save for my arousal, which was still climbing.

It was weird hanging out with two women who were so comfortable with their sexuality. Touching a stranger's most private body parts seemed... natural to them.

And to be fair, taking part in their game has certainly been enjoyable so far. I've always liked men that's for sure, but a little part of me's very curious. These two women here are wonderful specimens. Young, firm bodies, sensual, and... very open-minded.

After grabbing my empty can out of my hand, Isabel broke the silence. "Who's first?" she asked. "I vote for our new friend," she said, nodding in my direction.

She paused briefly, but Tracy and I stayed quiet.

"Tracy, why don't you hook up the camera on the post, and then we'll be able to record all three of us doing it together. Okay, baby?"

Tracy lifted her thumb, got up, and then proceeded to attach their camera to the existing tripod.

How many videos do they record out here?

Tracy walked away for a few minutes, then came back with a new ice bucket. She knelt down by the other pails and moved the empty magnum, water bottles, and beer cans out of the old ice buckets, transferring the ones that were still full to a fourth bucket, filled with fresh ice, that she'd just brought out.

The birthday girl then relocated behind the camera and adjusted the direction in which it pointed. As ordered by Tracy, Isabel and I carried the older, waterier buckets to the exact spots they needed to go.

I'd never done a wet T-shirt contest before, but had nothing against them. Prize or not, the idea of it was exciting, and I could definitely cool off.

"Perfect. We've got the sun behind the camera," Tracy said. "Not another boat in sight. Just us girls. What do you say we have ourselves some fun?" Tracy's pitch had increased so much over the past few sentences I could have believed she was leading a pot legalization rally.

Isabel and I hooted in unison. "Anything for the birthday girl!" I added.

"I hope so," Tracy said, grazing my waist with a finger just as she passed behind me to grab the ice bucket. A shiver ran through me. "Stand right here," she ordered, pointing me to a spot in front of her, just a foot away from where I currently was.

I obeyed and she continued. "Now, both of you look at that camera and flirt with it, tease it with everything you've got. Shake those girls."

I joined Isabel's hoots and screams. We cheered like we were two teenage girls at a boy-band concert. Isabel was standing next to me, raising her breasts toward the sky, feeling them, letting her fingers slip underneath the tiny triangles of fabric that covered her nipples. I did the same.

We were just girls, having fun, acting a little crazy and not hurting anyone.

Then... I felt it.

Tracy, who had been standing behind us the entire time—letting the tripod take care of the recording for her—poured the entire ice-cold slushy mixture over my head, the top of my chest getting the bulk of it, my top totally transparent. I was so frozen—from both the shock and temperature—that my shoulders automatically recoiled forward. Tracy's hands came from behind and pulled my shoulders back, then massaged my breasts.

"Let us see your magnificent tits, girl," she ordered. "And smile, you're on camera!"

2:30 p.m.

Tracy's hands gave my breasts a final squeeze, then Isabel slapped my and her girlfriend's ass at the same time.

"Your turn, Tracy," Isabel ordered.

I moved aside and Tracy took front stage. Isabel stood behind her, ice bucket at the ready.

Tracy was playing her part, flirting with the camera, zigzagging the bottom edge of her tiny top upward and downward sensually, at times exposing the curvature at the base of her breasts, but never her nipples—or at least not for longer than a split second. She then pulled the fabric downward to stretch it and arched her back. Isabel dumped the bucket's contents on her. Tracy let out a high-pitch squeal and Isabel's hands joined hers in exposing what her tiny T-shirt had previously kept hidden from the naked eye.

After a minute or so of stroking, Tracy turned her head to steal a kiss from Isabel, and then they traded spots. "Your turn, baby."

Tracy turned to me. "Why don't you do the honors this time," she asked, winking. "You've seen how we do it. Easy, right?"

"Sure," I said, eager to reciprocate the painfully delicious sensations I'd just experienced, and... partly curious to see which of Isabel or Tracy had the best rack.

Isabel started her performance as if she were teasing an invisible cameraman—or woman. Just as she raised her chest in anticipation for the cold shower, I dumped the melted ice cubes all over her. She screeched and then backed onto me, her hands grabbing mine and forcing me to touch her, to knead her breasts, some of my fingers over and others under the little triangles of fabric. Then, she grabbed one of my hands and moved it down to her pussy. I was in unchartered territory; the only pussy I'd ever known was mine, but I let my fingers graze the fabric of her bikini bottom.

Tracy joined us. She kissed Isabel, sandwiching her between us. Tracy's arms then reached down my back, and she grabbed a handful of my ass, pulling me closer to Isabel, but making her lose footing. We crashed together on the deck, laughing.

Although such a fall on an epoxy surface should have been at least a little painful, I suspect our level of intoxication softened it. Our high certainly made it hard for us to stop laughing or groping each other.

"That's perfect for number three! Hold on," Tracy said, springing back to her feet to snatch her phone from the nearby table and then crashing back down next to us. She extended her arm in the air for another selfie, then showed us the results: a beautiful mid-chest shot—no heads in sight—with six hardened nipples, five of which were covered by transparent fabric, plus one of Isabel's magnificent, natural C-cups fully exposed. Our fall—or my hands?—must have pushed the puny triangle out of position.

"What will you say to that, Sebastian?" Tracy asked rhetorically just after she hit the SEND button.

Her phone beeped a couple of seconds later. "Ah! He's asking, 'Who's the third?'"

"Hot flight at-ten-dant," Tracy replied, saying the syllables aloud as she typed the letters into her phone. She then sent it off.

The next beep had the three of us staring at Tracy's screen: 'Can I come over for dessert?'

"Now we're talking!" Isabel said, a large smile on her face. Her hand had somehow moved and was now rubbing my groin. "Dic-pic in no time," she said, her eyes locked onto mine. Isabel's touch was far more gentle than that of most men who'd rubbed my pussy before, yet it was precise and firm. I didn't know if the pot had anything to do with how aroused I was, but Isabel was turning me on, making me wet my bottom.

"'De-pends on what you're bring-ing'," Tracy was once again saying the words aloud as she typed them.

"Oh! That's good, baby," Isabel said before kissing her.

A few minutes elapsed. The girls couldn't stop giggling. They had come up with various 'salami' variations he could have replied with, but since his answer had yet to arrive, they were convinced that Sebastian was now busy making himself hard in the heads somewhere on his ship. *Of course, he'd have to send us a picture he was proud of!*

Once our giggling wound down, Isabel returned to caressing my pussy, but her fingers had now slid under the fabric. She was kissing her girlfriend, her finger tickling my clit, when the phone beeped again: 'Where are you?' was his reply.

"Guess he's coming!" Tracy squealed. "Where are we, baby?" she asked her girlfriend, tapping her on the chest like an excited kid tugging on his mother's sleeve. Isabel spurted out a latitude and a longitude and Tracy typed the numbers in, and then sent them off.

Tracy sat up. "I'm so excited. I haven't seen a dick in so long!" She turned to me and added, "I bet his is nice and big, you know?" She bit her lips. Her hands flew in the air, and she held them about nine inches apart, just to clarify her expectations.

Isabel sat up as well, taking her hand out of my bikini bottom. "Come on, Tracy. Don't exaggerate. Remember that firefighter I found for you a few months ago? He had a nice, big cock, right? You liked him."

"Ooooh, I'd forgotten about him." Tracy smiled, jumping to her feet. She pulled Isabel, then me up from the deck. "Let's go. I want to watch him again. He's hot."

"Whatever you want, birthday girl!" Isabel said. She then walked to the video camera, turned off the recording, and detached the device. "Let's go."

Isabel grabbed my hand and escorted me below deck to their bedroom.

"Make yourself comfortable. I just have to attach this to the TV and find the right tape," she said indicating to the camera she was still holding. "You want to smoke some more? Tracy's out back, having a few more puffs."

"No, I'm good," I said, probably with a stupid, happy smile on my face. I hadn't felt that relaxed in... forever. I brushed my hand against my own skin. It felt different, almost as if someone else was touching me. I caressed my own stomach, letting my hand slip down to my bikini bottom. With my other hand, I brought my hair up behind my head, leaving it in a messed-up chignon that would fall the second I moved, but it freed up my neck. My own fingers on the nape of my neck felt oh-so-delicious right now, even though I knew they were mine.

If getting high could be measured in terms of floors, I had reached my penthouse; nothing too crazy, nothing too plain... And I was *so* horny.

I kept touching myself, waiting for Isabel to find the right tape. She finally did. She paused it and then joined me on the bed while we waited for Tracy to return. We kept ourselves occupied with light kisses and caresses, but when I turned my back to her, asking her to undo the intricately knotted strings in the back, she stopped me.

"No, Tracy would kill me. You're her birthday present. You know that, right?" Isabel paused. I raised my shoulders, then she continued, "She has to unwrap you, even if there isn't much left to the imagination," she said, winking. "I'm looking forward to the official unwrapping," she told me before leaning onto me, her lips firm and demanding.

"Hey! Don't start without me!" Tracy said from the foot of the bed a second later.

"Don't worry, baby. Just hit PLAY on the camera. It's ready to go."

Tracy did just as ordered and squeezed herself between me and Isabel, her hands on each of our laps.

The girls were pretty good actresses, it turned out.

In this brief recording, Tracy—while cooking in nothing but an old, cropped T-shirt—had inadvertently left the burner on, and a small galley fire had erupted. (To be clear, there was no actual fire involved in the movie.) The brave firefighter came in, uniform and all, to save the day, and take off her burning clothes, of course! And once the day had been saved, the good Samaritan had to be paid off for his services, but it was overtime for him, so he'd required double payment— i.e., double pussy. And so, Isabel had then joined them in front of the camera.

They were right.

That firefighter's cock was splendid. And he also knew what to do with it.

I felt myself getting wet just watching him fuck Tracy on TV. His large dick thrusting into her pussy, the same pussy that had distracted me and made me blush at work yesterday.

Then, my attention got sidetracked.

Tracy's fingers had slid their way past the lining of my soaking-wet bikini bottom.

With one of her hands in her own bikini and the other stroking my pussy, Tracy sat on top of my lap. She then retrieved both of her hands from our clothing and motioned for Isabel to do something with the camera. Tracy brought her hands to my face. She leaned toward me, then kissed me on the lips, biting me gently, her tongue licking mine. Then, her appetite increased. She moved down to my neck, whispering something I couldn't quite make out, but the feel of her breath against my neck was inebriating. She sat back up then let her fingertips dance around my breasts for a while, teasing but never quite grasping them the way I wanted... yet.

Her lips then returned to my chest. This time, they were more demanding. Her hands pulled the fabric up, exposing my breasts, which were heaving with insatiable hunger. She nibbled on one of my nipples while squeezing the other with the exact pressure I wanted to feel. I let out a moan. I reached for her top and pulled it down. She abandoned me for just a few seconds while she untied her top. Tracy then tossed the unwanted clothing away toward Isabel, who was busy filming us. I gently cupped Tracy's small, beautiful breasts, then sat up so I could kiss them and grant them the attention they deserved. I felt her arms reach behind me, and suddenly my bikini top fell lose between us.

Tracy pushed me back down. My back landed on the mattress, my breasts bouncing for a couple of seconds from the unexpected movement. I then watched her walk backwards on all fours, her eyes locked on me, her hanging breasts gently swaying as she backed toward my legs, taking with her the only piece of clothing I was still wearing. She brushed a gentle kiss on my pussy on the way down, her breath tickling me. However, once the bottom cleared my ankles, Tracy came back with a serious appetite. Her pointy tongue and agile fingers knew exactly what to do with my womanhood.

I couldn't help but let her.

I felt a little lazy lying there, unable to do anything but thoroughly enjoy her licking me, fucking me with her tongue, then with her fingers. Every now and then, I'd manage to open my eyes, my own chest surprising me in how much it was moving. I was breathing hard, moaning, enjoying every lick, every prick, every kiss from the woman laying between my legs. I reached down to brush her hair, massaging her scalp, not knowing how to return the pleasure she was filling me with when she looked up, and her eyes met mine.

Her tongue circled her lips, then she made her way toward my chest, still straddling me. I reached to pull down her bottoms. The familiar blonde landing strip was just a foot away from my face. She briefly rolled over to one side, letting one leg out of her bikini bottom, then returned to the straddling position, inching her pussy toward my mouth. I grabbed a second pillow and placed it under my neck and let her lower herself onto my face. For the first time ever, my tongue explored the most secretive part of another woman. Her moans became more frequent and louder as I learned what she liked. I suckled. I licked. I poked her with my tongue. I gently nibbled on her lips then brought along my hands on this inaugural, explorative experience.

A few minutes later, I felt a weight near the foot of the mattress. I came up for air and looked past Tracy's narrow hips. Isabel had put down the camera on the corner by the TV, its small light still flashing red. It seemed like Isabel had decided to partake in the birthday festivities and was now making her way up to me, licking and caressing my inner thighs. Just as she was getting seriously busy with my genitals, Tracy called out her name.

Isabel abandoned my pussy and straddled my stomach, kneeling behind Tracy. One of Isabel's hands grabbed her girlfriend's breasts from behind and brought her body closer to hers, pressing Tracy's back against her chest. Isabel's other hand went to Tracy's ass an inch from my face. I saw her thrust a couple of fingers up Tracy's ass just as she was about to come.

I teased her pussy with my tongue for a few seconds longer, but her muscles contracted and she pulled up, then sat just below my breasts. She exhaled loudly, a large grin on her rosy face. After pressing her hands firmly onto my tits, Tracy said, "Best. Birthday. Ever," each of her words accentuated by a push of her hands.

"Can we make this an annual tradition?" she asked. She wasn't addressing me, but Isabel, who was still kneeling behind her.

"We'll see, babe," Isabel said, slapping Tracy's ass.

Tracy lifted her right leg then pivoted away from me before jumping out of bed. "I'm going to dive in the ocean to cool off for just a second. Be right back," she said before running up to the main deck, butt naked.

"You don't mind if I have your leftovers then?" Isabel shouted out toward the bedroom door.

A few seconds later, not having heard a bleep from Tracy, Isabel turned to me and said, "I guess she doesn't mind." Then she leaned over me and pressed her lips against mine.

After a delicious kiss, she licked her way down my body, back to her previous position, her tanned ass now perked up in the air. She spread my legs wide, then lowered herself to sit on one of my knees, her wet pussy rubbing onto me as she fingered me with one, then two digits. I lowered my hand and started playing with my clit. Her hips were riding my knee at the same cadence as her fingers were fucking me. I started flicking my clit more rapidly, about to come when Tracy came back into the bedroom.

"Girls?" she said. It took a minute for my mind to register the strange tone in Tracy's voice. I ignored the distraction until I finished quivering.

Clapping sounds then echoed through the small bedroom. Multiple sets of hands. Multiple people were clapping.

"What the...?" Isabel asked, turning around as I sat up to look at Tracy, curious as to how she could have made those noises by herself.

I gasped when I saw five skinny Afro-Hispanic men, with rifles, standing behind Tracy, whose arms were raised above her head. Her entire naked body was shivering.

The coastguard's warning echoed in my mind, but the hard reality prevented noises from escaping my mouth. *Pirates? What now?*

"Money. Key. For boat. Now!" the man standing in front of them said before the butt of his rifle pushed Tracy's back, and she fell onto the bed with us.

"One minute," Isabel said, her hands covering herself the best she could. I did the same with whatever portion of the bedsheets I could grab. Tracy just sat there, as though frozen.

Images of my own body floating in the deep blue ocean, a bullet hole through the chest, flooded my mind. I started thinking about my past. I had begun my last stroll down memory lane when a loud horn sounded in the distance.

The man who had asked for the money and keys turned to face his crew and ordered the man at the back to do something in a language I didn't recognize. If it was Spanish, it was a dialect I didn't know. The man furthest back ran toward the upper deck, then returned a couple of seconds later, screaming. All five men left right then and there, without our money, without the boat's keys, and—thankfully—without killing any of us.

"What scared them?" Isabel asked, making her way toward the tiny porthole on one side of the bed, then the other.

I wrapped my arms around Tracy, who had come out of her trance and who was now crying her heart out.

"Worst... birthday... ever," she said in between sobs.

"Did they touch you?" I asked her. She shook her head. I wrapped my arms around her shivering body and rocked her gently. "It will be fine. We'll all be fine, Tracy."

"The fucking coastguard's here!" Isabel exclaimed. "Sebastian sent us something much better than a dic-pic. We should probably get dressed before another group of men sees us naked," she said.

I laughed. Maybe it was my nerves, maybe I was still high. One thing was for sure: I was glad to be alive.

Less than two minutes later, we were dressed again and back on the upper deck, watching none other than Sebastian himself coming up to our yacht in a small boat that had likely been dispatched by the larger ship we could see a few miles away.

He came onboard and inquired if we were alright.

"Thanks to you," Tracy said. "They came onboard, with weapons. I thought they were going to kill us."

"I know. That's what I was warning you about on the plane. But you're okay?"

We all nodded and he was about to step back into his boat when Tracy stopped him. "Hold on a sec, will you?"

Sebastian shook his head, then pointed at the pirates' speedboat that was dashing away, soon to disappear off of the horizon. "I don't have much time; we need to go after them."

"It will just take a sec, I swear. It'll be worth it."

She came back about ten seconds later, a small video tape in hand. "You'll have to rewind it and find an old camcorder to play it in, but consider that your *dessert* and thank-you present," Tracy said before giving him a big hug and kissing him on the cheek.

After letting go of her embrace, he sent a curious smile her way, then toward Isabel. He tucked away the tape into one of his uniform pockets and stepped back into his boat.

We thanked him again and waved at our savior as his boat sped away.

11:00 p.m.

Back in the safety of my airport hotel room, my marijuana-induced mental fog now fully dissipated, I couldn't help but reflect on what had happened yesterday and today.

Sure, I hadn't been able to meet with Matt, my friend-with-benefits, but the weekend had nonetheless included sex and had offered... a transformative experience.

I'd never thought I'd ever have a threesome, let alone a lesbian encounter in my lifetime. But those two women... They were so sensual, so comfortable with their bodies, so beautiful.

But what does it mean?

Am I gay, now?

No. Definitely not.

I didn't think a pussy could ever fulfill me as much as a glorious cock could, but today's experience... It was something I'd like to try again (aside from the pirate part).

Exhausted, I put down my journal and closed my eyes.

Images of pirates, sexy coastguards, and beautiful blonde women started to populate my emerging dreams...

MY XXX EXPERIENCE
MEXICO

THE PLAN

FOR THE RECORD, let's just state that I don't want to risk getting caught by modern seafaring thieves who call themselves pirates, but I would sure as hell like to get my hands on that video tape. In order to do that, I have to pick my approach among the three trails left behind by my mystery stewardess:

OPTION 1: Canvass all airlines that fly into Cancun, Mexico, and find either an ex-flight attendant called Matt or a female one called Kate, either of which could identify my stewardess.

I've got nothing to go on here. CUN/Cancun is the second busiest airport in all of Mexico. Too many airlines and chartered flights to count. Worse odds than finding red-headed Alex in Toronto.
Likelihood of success: Nil.

OPTION 2: Go to Cancun and find the hot blondes who could direct me to my mystery woman.

At least I have a name for both the boat and the marina. But boats can easily be relocated to another port or stay out in international waters. That being said, those blondes don't strike me as survivalists who would go out to sea for months at a time and brave tropical storms. I'm hoping they haven't slipped to another marina yet. And if they have, I could try and follow the trail left behind by various utility or jetty receipts associated with their yacht.

Likelihood of success: Average to high.

OPTION 3: Find coastguard Sebastian.

I looked up various organizations in charge of patrolling Mexican waters. Sebastian must be with the *Búsqueda y Rescate Marítimo*, the Mexican Search and Rescue organization. Unfortunately, I don't have many contacts south of the border who could help me with that. But maybe the two hot blondes still have his cellphone number? Possibly. Wouldn't they want to stay in touch with the guy who saved their lives (and who could maybe do it again?)

Likelihood of success: Average, but I'd have to succeed with Option 2 first.

This time, I should have enough to find her. I know the name of the boat, the marina, and the town. All I have to do is take a short flight to Cancun and track them down. Easy peasy. Mystery solved.

...Or so I thought.

WHAT HAPPENED

CAN/Cancun is one of my regular stops, so I figured I could track down the girls on any of my layovers. I could deadhead home a few hours after getting the information I'm looking for. No need to take extra time off.

I landed in Cancun on a sunny Monday afternoon. After clearing customs, I stopped by the currency exchange booth, then rented a convertible from one of the car companies operating out of the airport.

A large smile on my face, still wearing my pilot's uniform, and quite a few *pesos* in my wallet, I made my way to *La Esperanza Marina*. Nothing like breathing in the salty, humid Caribbean air with the top down to get my hopes up.

Here's how my Mexican adventure unfolded.

6:16 p.m.

Finding the marina and the *Delicious Sunset* was easy.

Although it wasn't the largest motorboat in this harbor, the beautiful yacht appeared luxurious alongside its neighboring, smaller pleasure boats.

Isabel's family has to be fairly wealthy.

I turned a few heads walking on the jetty in my pilot's uniform, but I didn't care. I certainly would have been a little more comfortable in shorts, like most of the people I saw hanging around here, but I only expected to drop in, get the info I needed, then head back out. The sun was about to set anyway, so the heat should go away soon.

Now standing in front of their boat, I called out from the jetty, but no one answered. I walked alongside the boat, heading toward the stern and then tried again. "Hi there, Isabel? Tracy? Are you onboard?"

The boat was tidied up. I could see the patio-area where the girls had partied, but no sign of life. I decided to turn around and make my way back toward the bow and the boat's walkway.

Is it appropriate for me to step onboard?

I had my hand on the guardrail, about to step forward on the walkway when a balding man in his fifties wearing plaid shorts and an oversized tank top draping over a beer belly walked up to me.

"Hey there. Where you going?" he asked.

I stepped back onto the public jetty, let go of the guardrail, and then brought my right hand in the air. "Hey, man. I'm just looking for Isabel and Tracy. Is this their boat?" I asked, pointing at the yacht.

"Ya. That's the one. But the ladies ain't here." The man crossed his tattooed arms on his chest, then stepped closer to me, blocking my path to the walkway.

I backed off some more, waving my hands in the air like two white flags. Although I was in better shape than him, there was no telling if he was crazy. I didn't want to risk getting into a fight. "No worries, man! I'm not gonna go onboard if they're not here."

The man stood still, his expressionless eyes riveted on my face. I glanced around for a few seconds and realized we had attracted quite a few stares from nearby boaters.

"I'm gonna get going, but any idea where I could find them?"

The fat man remained silent. I gave up and turned around, ready to walk away when a woman's voice addressed me from a nearby boat. "The girls headed out to a bar about an hour ago to celebrate one thing or another," she said.

I released a breath I hadn't realized I was holding, then headed, smiling, toward the elderly, red-headed woman in the flowery sundress.

"Thank you, ma'am. Do you, by any chance, happen to know the name of that bar?" I asked her.

"*Pacifico,* I think," said a seventy-odd-year-old man who'd suddenly appeared from behind the red-headed woman.

I decided to push my luck just a tad more. "I'm not from 'round here. Would you happen to know where this *Pacifico* place is?"

He scratched his head, worsening the messy state of his gray hair. "Roughly, sure. Exactly, no."

"I'll take rough directions," I said, pleasantly surprised.

He turned to face the town, and then pointed at the church. "About four blocks that way," he started, then he moved his hand toward the right before continuing, "Then two or three that way, I think."

Mental note made of the bar's rough location, I thanked the helpful neighbors, and then left the marina.

6:58 p.m.

Salsa music resonated past the entrance.

I pulled open the door to *Pacifico* and the volume tripled. *Who goes out dancing this early?* On my way in, I walked past a large Mexican man who stood, arms crossed, blocking a large wooden door. Next to him was what seemed to be a coat check counter where a young Latina worked, tagging empty coat hangers. She smiled at me as I walked by. I'd left my hat in the trunk of the car. No need for her services. The bouncer/doorman eyed me up and down but otherwise stayed motionless. I kept going.

No cover, I guess.

A few steps later, the room opened up in front of me. Flashing red, green, and blue lights bounced on the mirrored walls that surrounded a dance floor at the back of the room. A DJ sat in the far left corner, behind two large speakers that acted as supports for the flat plank that held his equipment. On the far right corner was a small bar. A tall and skinny man dressed in black stood behind it, wiping its surface. Half the stools were occupied by Latinos who were scoping out the local dance talent. A few round tables dotted the area surrounding the dance floor, where women of various skin shades sat, heads bobbing to the rhythm, sipping colorful drinks that came with umbrellas. Oddly enough, the majority of them were blondes. Bleached blondes.

I decided to join the male-occupied bar as it offered the best vantage point. I sat myself on the left-most stool, leaving some breathing room between me and a perfume-deluged, curly-haired Latino in ripped jean shorts and a fluorescent yellow top.

Once seated, the bartender acknowledged my presence with a nod. I yelled out my order, trying to overbear the loud music, "Gin tonic, *por favor.*"

The barman nodded again, then turned to grab a bottle of gin with a label I'd never seen before. He returned to me a minute later, placed my mixed drink on a small, square, white paper napkin, and then voiced the amount I owed him, which I didn't understand. I sat up from my stool, reached for my wallet, then took out a two-hundred-peso bill and handed it to him. He walked to his register, then came back with some change. I dropped a few coins in the prominent tip jar—the establishment had obviously integrated their northern neighbor's capitalist ways—then put the rest of the change in my wallet before sitting again, this time facing the dance floor.

Picking out two lesbian blondes shouldn't be too hard, right? Just have to wait for them to kiss each other on the mouth, and I'll know who to approach. Patience is all I need here. Patience, Charlie.

A busty blonde shook her hips and generous booty a few feet from me. She was dancing with a skinny man half her size. Her skin rolled underneath her leopard-print top, even though her legs were slender. I took a sip of my drink, then continued scoping the dance floor. I spotted a couple of decent-looking twenty-something blondes dancing together, close to the DJ. Not as breathtaking or as gorgeous as I expected them to be based on my stewardess's diary entry, but hey... Maybe they'd put on weight since meeting my mystery woman. Maybe encountering pirates on the high-seas had had some sort of post-traumatic effect whose only cure turned out to have been ice cream and cake.

I pivoted on my stool, intent on ordering them drinks: a great way to break the ice. I had another two-hundred-peso bill in my hand and was waiting for the barman's attention when a velvety voice sounded behind me, *"Hola, capitán."*

I got up from my stool and turned around. A gorgeous, young, petite woman with bright-blue hair was staring at me. She had on a very short red dress with a scoop neck exposing something I wanted to see more of. I racked my brain for a second. *Is this someone I've met before?* I was a little lost for words—interrupted in my plan to approach the blonde lesbians—so I settled for the obvious.

"Do I know you?" I yelled out over the song that was finally winding down.

"No. I wanted to ask if you were a pilot, but..." she said before extending her arm and then patting the left side of my jacket, where my wings were pinned down, "...I see that you are," she finished with a smile, a little shrug, and a few too many flicks of those mascara-covered eyelashes to mean nothing.

I sat back down on my seat, lowering myself so I wouldn't tower so much over her short height. I leaned forward toward her, partly so she could hear me over the latest song that had just come on, partly because I wanted an excuse to bring my face closer to her, to catch a drift of her scent, and, of course, to peek down that cleavage without her knowing a thing about it.

"You... like pilots?" I asked her, taking in her tit-town scenery from above.

The blue-haired girl moved in closer, then her finger slowly traced the crease in the middle of my pant leg, from my knee all the way to the fold of my thigh. "Yes. You could say that... But I'm not here for me. My... friend *really* likes pilots, but she's shy. I thought I could invite you to our table and introduce you to her. If you don't mind. I can buy you a drink for your trouble," she said before moving away from my ear, her lashes batting again to accentuate her bright blue eyes.

I leaned in. "Where's your friend?" I asked.

She somehow squeezed herself between my partially parted legs, then gently turned my neck toward the back of the room. With her index finger, she pointed to an athletic-looking blonde in tight, shiny red pants and a black tank top sitting alone at a table in the back.

I thought about it for a second.

Should I join two hot chicks who dig pilots—an option which would probably result in a very happy ending for me—or should I approach the average-looking lesbians who hold the information I need? It's not like they're sailing away this minute. I can go and meet them on their boat first thing tomorrow morning...

I smiled at the blue-haired woman. "Why not?"

I stuffed my money back in my wallet, then got up from my stool. She smiled then grabbed my hand and pulled me away from my seat. My near-empty drink in my other hand, I ogled her long legs and red heels as I followed her to her friend's table.

7:15 p.m.

The girl in the red dress walked over to her seated friend and said something to her that the loud music made impossible for me to overhear.

Her blonde friend stood up, then reached her hand out toward me, her lips moving but the words not reaching my ears. The DJ's decibel output was over-the-top, especially considering the time of day and how empty the bar was.

I could ask her to repeat herself, but chances are I still wouldn't hear it over the loud music.

My hand met hers in a shake. "I'm Charlie, airline pilot. Nice to meet you," I shouted.

The blonde girl had a wide smile on her face. She motioned for me to sit down. I grabbed a chair from a nearby table and moved it next to her before taking a seat.

The blue-haired woman lifted the Modelo bottle in front of her friend, then shook it, meeting her eyes. The blonde nodded. The blue-haired woman then tapped me on the arm before leaning in and then pointing at my glass. "What is it?" she yelled near my ear.

"Gin Tonic," I replied loudly.

She nodded, then walked away.

Part of me felt awkward letting a woman buy me a drink. Not typical for me. I made too much money to let that happen. But then again, perhaps women who dyed their hair bright blue liked to take charge and buy men drinks?

I could always return the favor on the next round. Gives me an excuse for chatting them up longer if my natural charms don't melt away their resistance as quickly as they should.

The blonde woman moved her chair closer to mine, then placed her hand on my arm before leaning in and voicing something inaudible, yet again.

I cupped my ear with my hand, and then raised my shoulders.

"Want to dance?" she asked, this time, over-articulating her words and yelling loud enough to cover the rhythmic music.

I frowned and shook my head.

I'd rather admit defeat now than make myself look like a fool. At least the uniform gives me a pretty-good chance at nailing one of them tonight. That hope would dissipate if they saw my lack of coordination on the dance floor. I can dance, kind of. But next to Latino men? Not a chance in hell.

The following minute was a tad awkward.

What can you do in a bar when you can't talk or dance?

The blonde tilted her head, staring at me, possibly sizing me up. Out of nowhere, she grabbed my left hand and pinched my naked ring finger. I looked up at her. I believe her lips motioned, "Not married?"

I shook my head.

Her smile got bigger, then she bit her lower lip. Blondie got up, then sat on my lap. Wrapping her arms around my neck, she engulfed me with her sweet, fruity scent. Her lips touched my ear. "No girlfriend or otherwise engaged for this evening?" she asked before pulling back to make eye contact with me.

I shook my head slowly and watched a strange hunger swell in her eyes.

Too easy. I love women who fantasize about pilots.

Just then, the hot, blue-haired fox in the red dress came back to the table, holding two beer bottles in one hand and my clear drink in the other.

"Here you go," her lips appeared to say while handing me the drink. I thanked her and she shrugged. She then handed her friend one of the bottles and held hers up in the air. Her lips moved again, but I didn't catch what she'd said. I nonetheless raised and clanked my glass against their bottles.

To a fun evening...

The blue-haired woman sat and looked at the blonde and me. Her friend was now kissing my ear, her fingers massaging my scalp. I met the blue-haired woman's eyes. She too had that hunger in her eyes.

Are they both into me? Could this lead to...?

Just as the thought entered my mind, the current song came to an end and the blonde sitting on my lap asked, "Want to come with us elsewhere?"

Hell, yeah!

I nodded. My last threesome was probably a decade ago. And I don't recall the willing parties being that hot. The blue-haired woman downed her beer, her eyes locked onto mine. Blondie got up from my lap and did the same.

I normally enjoyed sipping my gin, but I didn't want to risk having them change their mind. I quickly swallowed what was left of my gifted booze. As I put my empty glass down on the table, Blondie gripped my hand and pulled me up. I followed Blondie's hurried step away from the table, the blue-haired fox in tow.

When we reached the lobby, the bouncer's previous blank expression turned into a crooked smile and a nod my way.

Does he know these two?

He stepped sideways, clearing the door behind him. The Latina in the coat check buzzed it open.

What the fuck?

Blondie pushed the door and a tall staircase appeared in front of us. She hurried upstairs. I watched her small ass in those shiny red pants and felt my cock nod in approval. I kept going up, following her booty like a horse racing for its carrot.

When I reached the top of the stairs, Blondie turned around and the blue-haired fox grabbed my ass.

"Wanna have some fun?" Blondie asked. This time the music was muffled by the door one floor below. It must have closed on its own. I was able to hear her silky, sensual voice. The bass still reverberated loudly through the floor, but it only served to turn me on even more.

"Who's first?" I asked.

7:55 p.m.

Blondie dug a silver key out of her red pant pocket, then unlocked one of the two doors that stood at the top of the staircase.

What kind of cheap hotel is this? Do they live here?

She pushed the door open, then her hand blindly felt the inside wall. A light turned on a second later to illuminate a bare room with a double mattress lying in the middle of it. The unmade bed was covered with white sheets, albeit stained ones. Tethered paisley wallpaper adorned the wall in front of me. Blondie held the door open while I stepped in. On the right side was nothing but a bare window protected by rusty steel bars; across from it was a crooked painting of a bad landscape faded by years of exposure to direct sunlight. I blinked and wasn't sure if I saw cockroaches running along the seam where the wall met the orange, cigarette-burn-scarred carpet. A lingering aroma of incense filled the air.

But just when the gloomy surroundings were starting to downgrade my excitement, Blondie took her top off and tossed it on the bed behind her. She started dancing to the salsa rhythm that was permeating the room from underneath. She didn't wear a bra under her top; she didn't need one. Her small, firm breasts were perky, naturally. Blue-haired girl joined her and started dancing behind her, her hands all over Blondie's newly exposed, cute little breasts and flat stomach. Blondie was shaking her tits, tossing them to the intoxicating rhythm, her skinny but muscular arms up in the air while the other woman's hands reached from behind her and undid her red pants: first unbuttoning the silver clip, then unzipping the fastener. Blue-Hair let her hands slide down her friend's pants, caressing her ass, her pussy. My mind was flying at a thousand miles a minute; my cock was hard, pushing against my uniform.

I didn't know if it was Ricky Martin, Enrique Iglesias, or some other Latino pop artist who was responsible for these beats, but I would have given him my future first-born right now, no questions asked.

Blue-Hair slowly pulled down her friend's pants, revealing the tiniest of red-stringed panties. I could no longer stand still. I started walking toward the blonde beauty dancing in front of me. But her friend left her stripping-duty-post behind Blondie when she saw me move. She ran to me and stopped me in my path. She brought her arms to my neck and loosened my tie, then danced slowly backwards, still holding on to the ends of it. When I returned my attention to her friend, the red pants had come off. She was now facing away from me, shaking her tiny booty to the music, her firm butt cheeks, barely separated by a red string, calling my name.

Blue-Hair joined Blondie, then it was Blondie's turn to help get her friend naked. She moved behind Blue-Hair and got a hold of the bottom of her red dress, shaking it, tossing it upward and downward with the salsa rhythm. I saw a flash of blonde pussy.

I started moving forward again, as if guided by where my hardened cock wanted to point, but both women shook their heads, sending me disapproving looks. I stayed put but started unbuttoning my jacket. Their frowns flipped upward. Blondie's hands left the bottom of the red dress and instead, dove into the front of her friend's scoop neck and dug out one of her tits.

Natural. Round. Perky.

I tossed my jacket on the floor, then loosened my tie some more before pulling it off fully. I was now undoing my white uniform shirt, my finger quickly unfastening each of the buttons while Blondie's hand brought out her friend's other tit.

It was too much for me.

I threw my shirt onto the carpet, then crossed the few steps that were separating us in a split second, not caring whether or not they wanted to keep that tease cycle going.

I pushed both of them onto the bed. I undid my belt, unzipped my pants, and then dug out my swollen cock. A quick glance at their faces indicated they were as eager as I was. Blue-Hair had landed with her legs spread open, her blonde pussy winking at me, so I went for it. But Blondie intercepted me, wrapping her lips on my cock before I could dip it into her friend. Blue-Hair's hands reached for my face and she kissed me.

The rest was too much of a heavenly blur to be described in a coherent sequence.

I licked their tight pussies, I kissed them, I fucked them. I was sandwiched between tits. I didn't have enough fingers to touch everything I wanted to feel at once. My cock went from one to another while they kissed each other, kneading each other's breasts, rubbing each other's sensitive clits. I kissed and was kissed. I watched them eat each other. I swear, for a few minutes, I thought I'd died and gone to X-rated heaven. And then, just as Blondie was about to come, just as I was about to give her my all, Blue-Hair inserted a couple of fingers into her ass. I gushed into her as she yelped. I felt her wet pussy spasm onto my shaft and let out a groan, my heart matching the salsa rhythm still resonating below us.

But when my senses came back to me, they were accompanied by a long list of realizations:

Bright-blue hair, but a blonde landing strip. Two hot, beach-looking babes with full-body tans. Fingers in the ass just before coming.

Fuck.

Are these two the blonde lesbians I was looking for?

9:25 p.m.

I got out of bed and started dressing myself.

"May be a little late to ask, but I didn't catch your names earlier, with the loud music and all," I asked, bringing up my pants.

"I'm Isabel," Blue-Hair said.

"And I'm Tracy," Blondie said.

I pulled up my pants' zipper, snickering. "I can't fucking believe it."

"What?" Tracy asked with round eyes.

I shook my head. "I came to Cancun looking for the both of you. I was at your boat a few hours ago, but you weren't there. Obviously. Some older couple said I might be able to find you in this bar."

"What?" Tracy asked again. "Why were you looking for us?"

I let out a long sigh then began telling the tale of the mysterious diary that had come to be in my possession. Once I divulged what I knew of their encounter with the stewardess, large smiles appeared on their faces. Tracy moved to sit behind Isabel, then wrapped her arms around her waist.

"She wrote about us in her journal?" Isabel asked.

I nodded.

"Good things?" Tracy asked before gently kissing her girlfriend on the neck.

"Better than you could ever imagine," I replied. "Do you know her name?"

Isabel turned her head to look at Tracy. They stared at each other for a second, squinting. Isabel then turned to face me again. "Don't think we even asked... I was so pleased to have reeled in a hottie onto our boat for Tracy's birthday."

"So, that's what I am? Another prey that you reeled in for some celebration or another?" I asked, intrigued by their behavior.

"I guess you could see it that way... But didn't you have fun?"

"What are you celebrating?"

"Our one-year wedding anniversary," Isabel said before stealing a kiss from her wife.

I snickered again. "Congrats! Glad you opted to fuck me instead of buying each other flowers. But why didn't we just head back to your nice boat instead of this..."

"Dump?" Isabel finished.

I nodded, glad she'd said it and not me.

Both of them grinned. "Rocking the boat isn't good for our reputation," Isabel said. "We try to avoid it whenever we can."

"But that yacht. Aren't you rich? Can't you afford something a little less... dodgy?"

Isabel got up and walked up to me, her nipples still erect. Her hands buttoned up the shirt that I'd just picked up from the floor and donned. "It may surprise you," she started, "but there are many freaks out there. It's not like we do this every day or every week. But maybe once a month or so. We don't want the random men or women we hook up with to know that we're wealthy. We're not looking for anything serious, and we definitely don't want someone to start blackmailing us or start begging us for money. Coming here is safe. Nacho downstairs knows us, and he keeps things... private, if you know what I mean."

Isabel had finished doing up my shirt. She bent down to grab my tie, and I couldn't help but slap her beautiful ass.

"Hey!" she yelped with fake outrage.

"So, that flight attendant. You wouldn't happen to remember what airline she was with, would you?"

Tracy and Isabel looked at each other again, then shook their heads. "We fly with whichever airline has the most convenient flights for where we're going. Anything else you need to know?" Isabel asked, now doing up my tie for me.

"I have no idea what she even looks like. Any chance you have a picture?"

"Of her face? No," Isabel replied.

"But we have another you may want to see," Tracy said before rolling out of bed. She dug a phone out of the red pants that lay about a foot from her. She unlocked her device, then flicked her finger through several screens. I walked toward her.

While she was rummaging through her pictures, I asked Isabel about the sex tape they'd given the coastguard.

"That? He loved it," she said before pausing for a few seconds. "We saw him a few months later, and he asked if we had made a copy of it. Turns out that his wife found him masturbating to it in their bedroom one day, so she went at it with a hammer and destroyed it."

"And? Did you have a copy of it?"

Isabel shook her head.

"I found the photo!" Tracy exclaimed, bouncing to her feet, her perky, small breasts barely bouncing around. She moved the screen closer to me. I looked at the two naked women standing next to me and compared their tits with the selfie in front of me. The other two nipples were those of my mystery woman.

"Nice breasts, no?" Tracy asked rhetorically.

"All of you have gorgeous tits," I answered, handing Tracy back her phone then grabbing a breast from each of the naked women and giving them a good squeeze.

"Stop it," Isabel said, swatting my hand. I let go of their breasts to pick up my uniform jacket.

"How would you describe her?"

"Brunette, curvy, a bit taller than us I think," Isabel started. "She's beautiful but doesn't know it. A bit of a girl-next-door you could say? I wasn't sure if she'd be up for it, but believe me... she didn't disappoint."

Tracy let out a sigh. "Hell no!"

NEXT STEPS

I arrived at the airport an hour after leaving my gorgeous lesbians. I returned my rented convertible, and then got myself a seat on the red-eye flight to New York.

These two blonde beauties had taught me something: I had no idea lesbians could crave cocks from time to time... Interesting... Or maybe they're bi. Anyway, I was glad to have shared that experience with them, prey or not.

While waiting for my plane to board, I observed women strolling by, especially the stewardesses. One of them could be her. Just as the thought crossed my mind, a brunette walked by, her airline carry-on rolling behind her. Her high-heels and slender calves enticed my eyes to continue their upward scan of her body, albeit covered by her uniform. She was great looking, with a curvy hip-to-waist ratio, but her tits were B-cups at best.

Not my gal.

I didn't know what I expected my stewardess to look like physically, but I was glad to now know that she was an attractive, tall, curvy brunette with solid C-cup tits. I didn't have a preference in terms of ethnicity, but knowing that she was Caucasian certainly didn't simplify my quest.

Damn it! I should have asked the girls to forward me that wet T-shirt selfie. Well, I got distracted by those blonde lesbian beauties. That's okay, though. I think I've got her gorgeous tits and large nipples engrained in my head now.

Knowing these physical details about her will make my next reading of her Costa Rica entry a lot more lively. I'll be able to imagine my mysterious brunette on the surf board, then on the beach... Those glorious tits...

I gotta book myself some free time to fly down there so I can try to find her surf instructor. If I describe her to him—and mention what they did in his van and on the beach —he should remember my mysterious brunette.

He could even have her name written down on a surf lesson receipt...

PART III

COSTA RICA

THE STEWARDESS'S ENTRIES
COSTA RICA

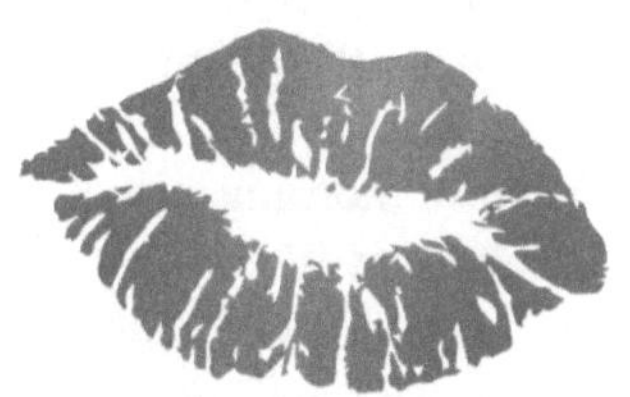

4:15 p.m.

FINALLY, some real time off.

I flew into Liberia and booked myself a long weekend alone, on purpose, as a way to kill my loneliness demon. *Ugh...* It would have been more accurate to say that I didn't resent loneliness as much as I was afraid to end up alone for the rest of my life.

Happiness was part luck and part planning, no?

I had to put myself in situations where I could entertain myself, solo or otherwise. Maybe it was true that we were more open to new experiences when traveling alone.

With that reasoning guiding my steps, I traveled to a tiny coastal town in Costa Rica. I didn't have any plans, but an hour ago, when I arrived at my Airbnb, the owner recommended I try surf lessons.

Why not?

It would give me a chance to wear the brand new bikini I'd bought after my splendid weekend in Cancun with the gorgeous blondes. They had certainly given my self-esteem a boost.

But now, looking at the tiny red pieces of fabric in front of me, on the bed, I doubted myself. *Can I pull it off?* My eyes went from the business card the *Tico* owner had left me an hour ago to my brand new bikini. *Yeah, I can do it. I can do it!*

I grabbed the business card and sat down on the bed before getting a hold of the corded phone. I punched in the numbers to the local surf school. The line started ringing at the other end.

"*¿Hola?*" a male voice answered.

"*¡Hola! ¿Habla inglés?*" I asked, half-expecting the man to speak English. Costa Rica had become so commercialized over the past few decades. It only made sense for them to cater to English-speaking tourists, especially surf shops.

"Yes, of course. How may I help you?"

"I'd like to sign up for surf lessons. Do you have anything for tomorrow?"

"Private or group lessons?"

"I'm by myself, but I've never surfed before. A group lesson for beginners would be ideal if you still have spots available."

"Let me have a look," the man said before going silent. I could hear women giggling in the store, not too far from the phone.

He came back to the phone a minute later. "Yeah, I've got room with a group that heads out of town tomorrow morning. It's a half-day lesson, but out-of-town, so you'd be gone for the full day. Would that work for you?"

"Sure," I replied, hoping it wasn't just going to be couples on a romantic getaway together. He relayed the price and meeting-point information I needed, and I agreed to show up the following morning at 8 a.m. sharp.

7:35 a.m.

Beach bag packed with my sunscreen, a book, towel, T-shirt, banana, bottle of water, ham and cheese sandwich, and just enough *colones*, their local currency, to pay for my surf lesson, I left my rental apartment and headed into town, large sunglasses protecting my eyes from the already bright and hot sun. I wore my red bikini, covered by a sarong I'd purchased in Thailand a few months ago.

The flip-flopping sounds of my sandals scared a few large lizards as I headed down my quiet side street to meet the main road that would lead me to town. Although the main road itself was paved, its asphalt surface ended sharply just as the road slanted into deep dirt ditches on both sides. Cars with miscellaneous, miss-matched colored parts and hanging bumpers whizzed by me, often honking first. *Good thing I've got less than a mile to walk.* I watched my step, avoiding broken Imperial beer bottle fragments and other trash that lined the ditch while still taking in the beauty of the large fuchsia flowers that dotted nearby trees.

I arrived at the meeting point ten minutes early, which was good, but I didn't have anything other than my book to keep me occupied. I'd left my phone along with all of my valuables in my apartment.

A white minibus with worn-out surfboards strapped to the top finally arrived at 8:05 a.m. A tanned and short *Tico* got off and greeted the group of foreigners that had gathered near me.

"*¡Hola Mae!* Hi, guys! *Soy José,*" he said. "Ready for your surf lesson?" Excited cheers resonated around me.

I let the other passengers board first, then gave my name along with my payment to the young man. When I walked onto the bus, I counted eight other passengers, ranging from late teens to mid-thirties, all seated in pairs.

Couples. Argh.

I nonetheless smiled at those who made eye contact with me, then found a seat at the back of the bus.

10:15 a.m.

A couple of hours of a bumpy ride later—and quite a few chapters read in the police thriller I'd taken with me—the minibus finally came to a halt.

I looked out of the window and a majestic beach, lined with palm trees, greeted me. Waves rolled in, crashing loudly into the two-mile-long semi-circle of beige sand. The other passengers got off the bus and I followed them.

I stood facing the ocean, inhaling the warm salty air with a smile on my face. This place was so peaceful, yet there was some inner rage built up in those waves. For a second, I doubted my decision to try surfing.

José, our *Tico* bus driver, brought me back to reality when he instructed all of us to make a line so we could unload the boards and take them to the beach. José climbed onto the top of the bus, and then asked one of the male students to grab the hard plastic boards as he lowered each of them to our level.

About ten minutes later, a row of 9 boards lay on the beach. I was already sweaty from this light physical task under the hot sun. José then informed us that the instructor would be here shortly and asked us to meet him again at this same spot for pick-up at exactly 5 p.m., then headed back onto the bus, leaving our group of nine foreigners alone on the beach.

"This beach's amazing," a brunette said to the short muscular man standing next to her, holding her hand.

A skinny African woman wearing shorts and a tank top dropped her bag by her friend's feet and ran all the way to the waves. She stopped when the water was up to her knees, then turned around to look at her friend. "The water's nice! Come! Eeeeh," she screeched as a wave came up from behind her and soaked her shirt and shorts. She nonetheless managed to stay on her feet.

"Hi, guys!" a voice said from the line of palm trees behind us. I turned around and our little group started paying attention to the tall, sun-tanned, long-haired blond man with an eight-pack stomach walking toward us.

Dang! He's more than dreamy. If learning to surf sucks, at least I'll have good eye candy to look at all day!

"Lati! Come back," a Latino man exclaimed, his arms motioning to his now-soaked friend.

The good-looking beach bum waited for her to get out of the water and join us before beginning his speech.

"*Pura vida.* Welcome to the beach. You all speak English, right?" he asked, his white teeth contrasting against his tanned face.

Everyone in the group nodded.

He cleared his throat before continuing. "My name's Ian. I'll be your surf instructor today. With a show of hands, how many of you have taken surf lessons before?"

The group remained motionless.

"How many have tried surfing on their own or with a friend?"

Lati's boyfriend raised his hand. He was the only one.

Ian addressed him. "Did you manage to stand up?"

The man shook his head. "Nope. That's why I'm here."

"Well then. Looks like we'll need to start with the basics. Perfect."

10:30 a.m.

"Leave your bags here and let's form a semi-circle over there so we can start with some stretches," Ian instructed us, pointing to a spot closer to the water. Our group rearranged itself around him after piling our bags under a tree.

For about ten minutes, we stretched our body in various yoga-inspired positions a few feet from where the foam of the surf sizzled, spitting thousands of droplets into the air.

I enjoyed watching Ian stretch and arch his muscular back. The other women in the group had their eyes glued on our instructor's firm glutes. I couldn't judge them, as I was doing the same.

"Now, ladies, I see that some of you have some really pretty bikinis on today," he said, nodding in my direction as he said it. I felt my cheeks burn. "But I recommend you cover up with one of the shirts I've got in the back of my van. Gents, same goes for you if you want to avoid board rash on your chest or nasty sunburns. Follow me," he said before heading toward an old BMW minivan that was parked by the tree line.

We followed him, then we each picked a blue, short-sleeve, neoprene top that best suited us among the three available sizes. Once everyone was dressed, we walked toward the boards we'd lined up on the beach earlier.

Ian grabbed one of the boards and educated us on it. "Now, this won't come as a surprise, but here's the nose, the body, and the tail," he said, pointing at the respective parts of the board. "You'll need to put an ankle in that tether so you don't lose your board. As to which ankle, we'll determine that now." His blue eyes then scanned our group. "Damien, right?" he said, nodding his head toward Lati's boyfriend. "Come here. Stand in front of me, facing away, relaxed. I'm going to push you, but it's not to pick a fight."

Damien nodded, ready.

Ian then pushed Damien, who caught himself by placing his right foot forward. "You're goofy," Ian said. "Easy as that to find out. So pair up, and find out if you're regular or goofy. Regular is if your left foot goes forward. Goofy's right foot first."

The couples around me paired up, leaving me alone.

"You came without friends?" Ian asked me once everyone else had paired up with their partner.

"Yep."

"No worries. Come, stand in front of me here," he ordered, then placed his big, tanned hands around my waist. Before the thoughts of his hands on other parts of my body had reached my brain and made me blush, he'd pushed me. "Regular footed," he said.

He returned his attention to the group. "Everybody's sorted? Now, that's the leg that will go forward when you pop up, so the other leg is the one you'll wrap the tether on, alright?" Once again, our group nodded in understanding.

"Now, let's practice the four basic steps. Everybody grab a board and lay it flat in the sand in front of you."

We obeyed, each grabbing our own piece of hard plastic.

"Now watch. I'll explain each of the four steps and demo them, then we'll practice them one at a time until we're comfortable enough to hit the water."

He moved his board in front of our group. The roar of the waves in the background, I listened to the handsome instructor's demonstration.

"Step 1: Lie belly-down on your board so your body is lined up with the middle of the board and paddle with your hands cupped." He moved his strong arms for a few seconds, demonstrating this easy step. "Step 2: Once you're just at the right spot on the wave, not too early and not too late, place your hands palm-flat just under your chest on the board and lift your torso," he continued, his back arched, delineating his muscles and making me want to see what was under those shorts. *Is his ass tanned or white?* "Now, for the tricky part. Step 3: In one swift motion, bring your knees together, extending your dominant foot to the middle of the space between your hands. And step 4: The fun bit. Stand in a crouched position with your knees bent. Fix your eyes on the shore. Keep your feet firmly planted and spaced out in the middle of your board."

His demo over, Ian stepped down from his board and back onto the sand. A couple of people clapped. He looked surprised by the applause, and then curtsied.

"I know this may seem like a lot, so let's all lie flat and practice these one step at a time. Everyone, belly-down on your board, face toward the front. Paddle with your arms like fish out of the water."

11:30 a.m.

After spending a solid thirty minutes mastering those four steps on the sand, we were granted permission to hit the water.

"Okay, guys," Ian started. "No need to worry. The beach here's all sand at the bottom, so you won't crack your head open on some hidden rock. But you still need to pay attention to your surroundings, especially the other surfers around you."

Other surfers? The beach is deserted. There's only our group of beginners to worry about.

I reapplied sunscreen on my face and arms, then got a hold of my board and joined the rest of the students in the warm sea. Ian was standing there, waist-deep in the water, his bronzed, hairless chest taking in more of the rays. He ordered us to get on our boards and start paddling.

He swam toward me, instructing me to catch the next wave that was coming my way. He turned my board to face the beach, and I started paddling as fast as I could, my hands pushing away at the turquoise waters.

"Up, up, up!" Ian yelled at me. I somehow managed to get my knees together, I sprung my foot forward, twisted up, then realized I was actually standing! *I'm surfing!* I tried to keep my knees bent and look toward the beach, but I crashed into the water a mere second later, my first-time exploit ending with a splash.

12:15 p.m.

We broke for lunch.

After leaving my board on the beach, next to the other students' boards, I got my bag, and then sat myself in the shade of a tree along the beach, a fair distance from the other couples. I spread my towel on the sand and sat down. Saying that I enjoyed my sandwich would be a lie; I gulped it down in less than ten seconds. The banana had the same fate. I cracked open my water bottle and drank half of it in one large swig.

Now what?

Ian had given us an hour to relax and eat, recommending we take full advantage of it because he wouldn't be in the water to help us if anything happened. *Might as well work on my tan and read my book... Unless I can find that cute surfer and flirt with him a little bit.*

I got up, took off the neoprene layer, and then hung it on a nearby tree branch. I looked at the other students sitting about a hundred feet down the beach. I couldn't see the instructor's blond hair among the group.

Just as I was about to sit down again, I saw Ian a few feet away from me, walking toward his van.

"Ian?" I called out, a smile on my face.

He stopped in his steps and looked my way.

"Would you mind giving me a hand?" I asked him, sunscreen bottle in hand.

He smiled. "Not at all," he said before walking toward me.

I handed him the bottle and lay on my towel, face down. He straddled me. I heard a squirt of liquid ooze out of the bottle, then a slap of hands. Next thing I knew, he was lathering the cool lotion on my shoulders, his firm hands massaging my skin in the process.

"So how come you didn't bring your boyfriend with you?" he asked.

"No boyfriend," I said.

"That's surprising," he replied, his hands moving down my back, sliding under my bikini string. He then worked his way down, adding a bit more lotion, and covering my lower back. His fingers slipped into the top inch of my bikini bottom. I stayed quiet. A few seconds later, his hands returned to my waist, and then worked their way up, applying lotion to my sides.

"It feels good," I said, enjoying his firm hands on my skin.

"What do you think of Costa Rica?" he asked, a little too business-like for my taste.

"It's nice," I said. "Warm, lots of birds and interesting animals."

His hands continued massaging my skin. "And don't forget about the beautiful beaches!"

"Of course! How long have you been here?" I asked.

"Came here six years ago for a short holiday. Haven't left since, other than a short trip to Nicaragua every three months to renew my visa. How long are you staying?"

"Just the weekend," I said.

"The country or the people you've met haven't convinced you to stick around a little longer?" he said, this time his fingers sliding under the string of my bikini top and then digging their way into the flesh on the sides of my flattened breasts.

Now's the time girl, say something sexy! But nothing came to mind.

"Want me to do your legs, too?" he asked as he moved off of me.

"Sure, if you don't mind," I replied, somewhat saddened that he hadn't lingered on my breasts.

"You've got a very nice bikini," he said, tracing where the fabric ended on my ass before stepping away from me.

"Thank you," I replied, still raking my brain as to how I could flirt with him. *I have to get better at this.*

A couple of seconds later, his hands were on one of my feet, lifting it up in the air. He massaged it, then moved up to my calf, rubbing sunscreen front and back. He repeated the action with the other foot and calf, then parted my legs so he could sit between them. He applied lotion to my left thigh and rubbed it in from my knee to my ass, then repeated with my other thigh.

"Maybe you haven't seen enough of Costa Rica to be swayed by its charms yet," he said, rubbing more lotion between my thighs, working his way up. His thumbs kneading my skin, they made their way between the towel and the front of my thighs until he reached my groin. His fingers were now groping my ass, his thumbs feeling the fabric over my pussy.

I didn't mind what he was doing at all, but I didn't know what to do or say. I finally settled on asking, "What would you recommend then?"

"For starters," he said before his left thumb crept so faintly and discreetly under the fabric of my bikini. "You should hang out with some local people and relax. *Pura vida*, you know?" His other hand was massaging the exposed portion of my ass, but his thumb was in exploration mode around my pussy.

I swallowed hard. "You think so?" I asked.

A man's voice echoed in the distance, calling out Ian's name.

"Gotta go," he said before getting up and running away, leaving me hot and bothered with nowhere to go.

5:00 p.m.

The rest of the afternoon was spent in the water; no more inappropriate groping from Ian, unfortunately.

After helping José load the boards on top of the bus again, we got on the shuttle and headed back into town. I let the passing coastline scenery lull me to a peaceful sense of calm until we headed inland again. Beaches and palm trees were replaced by lush vegetation everywhere around us.

Damien and Lati were seated across the aisle from me, chatting about the day and whining about their sore muscles. I didn't feel like reading anymore. I was exhausted, so I listened to their conversation. They were excited about their evening plans, something about celebrating a job promotion. I was leaning my head back, stretching my neck, when I felt a tap on my shoulder. I turned my head. It was Lati.

"Want some of that?" she asked, handing me a clear glass bottle.

"What is it?" I asked, reading the label: *Guaro*.

Damien answered, "It's the *Tica* version of vodka, but made with sugar cane."

Why not? Two hours to kill on this bus. I accepted the bottle and took a good swig, which forced a grimace on my face.

"Ugh. Potent!" I said before thanking Lati and returning the bottle.

Damien and Lati told me about their month-long trip in Costa Rica and what they'd seen to date. Between colorful descriptions of the micro-climates they'd experienced and unbelievable stories about the crazy people they'd met, the bottle kept getting passed around between us. It didn't take much of it for me to start feeling inebriated.

About forty-five minutes after leaving the beach, just as Lati's bottle went dry, the bus's engine gave up.

José pulled over. Much of the fading sunlight was hidden behind the lush green hills on both sides of the road. He got up and instructed us to leave the vehicle and attempt to stop drivers if we saw any cars, trucks, or buses. He then stepped out of the shuttle and opened up the hood to try and figure out what went wrong.

Two of the men joined the driver in his effort to pinpoint the mechanical problem while the rest of us got off and hung out behind the shuttle bus, its flashers on. After about fifteen minutes, a car came our way, and an Italian ex-pat driver with a bright yellow Imperial tank top pulled over when he saw our group wave at him.

After a short exchange between José and the Italian man driving the 1990 Mazda, some money changed hands and two couples left in that stranger's car.

Damien, Lati, an Australian couple, José, and I were the only ones left.

Another twenty minutes went by before we saw the next vehicle. The same money-exchange occurred, and the Australian couple went away with a family of three. *No room for the rest of us.*

6:30 p.m.

The sun had now set, the last of its rays tinting what we could see of the sky above us with orange and purple shades.

"So much for our reservation at the Argentinian grill tonight," Lati told Damien.

"Well... I'm sure we can postpone it some. We might still get there in time, if another driver comes by soon," he said.

I didn't have anywhere to go tonight, but I certainly didn't want to spend my night on the side of a road. There were no street lights here. It'd be pitch black very soon.

As if he could sense the growing apprehension in me and in his girlfriend, Damien spoke again. "I have just the thing to help us relax," he said, digging into the fanny pack hanging in front of him. He dug out his wallet, then opened it before retrieving a joint that was hidden in the crease of the leather. He returned the wallet to his bag, then pulled out his lighter and lit it.

A few puffs later, he passed it on to his girlfriend. "That's good stuff," he said, grinning.

The metal clunk of a hood being slammed shut reverberated around us.

José, having obviously given up on the idea of fixing the engine, came and joined what was left of our group. The four of us sat against the back of the shuttle, and the joint got passed around until it was gone. With the Guaro still in my system and the happy smoke added to the mix, I was no longer annoyed by the mosquitoes that had come out, nor worried about the increasingly loud and unknown noises coming from the tangled vegetation on both sides of the road.

Headlights veered past a bend in the distance in front of us.

José got up and walked toward the vehicle, waving his arms in the air. It slowed down and came to a stop about twenty feet behind the shuttle. A red sports car. A two-seater. José talked to the driver while we pondered our options.

"There's only the one seat," Lati said. "You should go with this guy."

I raised my shoulders. "I have nowhere to go. You two have a dinner reservation to make. You're tiny. I'm sure the two of you can sit together on that passenger seat."

Lati's eyes brightened up. She turned to Damien. He shrugged. "Are you sure?" she asked me.

"Of course, go ahead!"

They got up, we exchanged a hug, and I watched them leave, José and I remaining the only human flesh around for the mosquitos to feast on.

7:20 p.m.

"I told the first driver to contact my boss and get us another vehicle," José said. "It should be here soon."

"Can't you just call your office from here?" I asked him.

He shook his head. "I tried, but no reception."

José and I exchanged small talk in Spanish for the next little while, until another set of headlights came toward us. Once the vehicle got close enough for me to not be blinded by its lights, I recognized the surf instructor's van.

Ian got out of his vehicle, leaving it running, with the emergency flashers on.

"What happened?" he asked.

"The engine died on me," José answered.

"Want me to have a look?" Ian offered.

José shrugged, and they headed toward the hood. I tagged along, not really interested but bored and a little curious. José popped it open. A few vain pricks, pokes, and dipstick pulls later, José slammed the hood down again.

"Want a ride?" Ian offered.

I nodded and followed him, my beach bag on my shoulder. After bidding José goodbye, I boarded the surf instructor's van. I dropped my bag at my feet in the passenger's seat.

Ian turned off the flashers and merged onto the road again, waving at José and his stranded bus as we slowly passed him. Both my hands fumbled around, digging in-between the back rest and the padded seat, trying to find a seat belt. Just as I was about to ask, he spoke. "No seat belt, sorry."

"Why are you driving back this late?" I asked, unsure how to go from small-talk to flirting with the man who'd populated my daydreams all afternoon.

"I wanted to do some actual surfing," he said.

"Did you have a good time?"

"Always," he said.

He then briefly tapped my lap, letting his eyes off the road for a second to meet mine. "So, how much are you going to pay me for this emergency ride home?"

Seriously? ...or is he flirting with me? His hand moved up on my thigh and gave me the answer I was looking for. "I'm so sorry, but I don't have any money on me," I replied before biting my lower lip.

His smile widened. "That's fine. I accept payments in-kind," he said, his eyebrows raised.

I felt my cheeks warm, glad there was hardly any light around for him to see me blush.

"Show me your tits?" he asked. "Flash me and we'll call it even."

My high having increased my confidence and not wanting to seem uninterested, I sat sideways on my seat, my back to the door, facing him. When he took his eyes of the road to look my way, I pulled the triangles of my bikini off to the sides and gave my breasts a good shake.

"Now, that's what I'm talking about," he said, smiling and then returning his attention to the road in front of us. "So, did you have fun today?"

"I sure did! I had no idea surfing was going to be such a full-body experience, though. I'm exhausted," I said.

"Yeah, I get that a lot from newbies."

"It gets easier with time?"

He lifted his shoulders and tilted his head. "People build up muscles with practice, but it's always a good workout."

His defined body's proof. My eyes had adjusted to the dark cabin, and I could now see his bare, ripped chest. He was still wearing his surf shorts.

Ian's hand reached into a storage case where the radio would normally be in a more recent vehicle, then dug out a yellow and black striped pipe, a small plastic tub, and a lighter, then placed it all on his lap. "Wanna smoke?" he asked.

"Not right now but go ahead," I shrugged.

All the while driving, Ian opened up the small container; skunk aroma filled the cabin. He placed a small dried flower bud into the pipe, then screwed his container shut again before returning it to the storage space in his dash. He then steered with his knees for a few seconds while holding the pipe with one hand and lighting up with the other. A pungent puff of smoke filled the cabin, thickening the air.

"Now, that's *pura vida*," he smiled before starting to stroke my leg.

Although I didn't smoke it directly, about ten minutes later, I felt buzzed. Buzzed and hot.

I had my hand on the window handle, ready to roll down the tinted glass when he stopped me.

"No, no," he said. "That's expensive smoke. Don't let it out."

I shifted in my seat, a little uncomfortable and possibly motion sick. *Is the Guaro not agreeing with me now?* "I'm hot," I said.

"I'll turn on the air conditioning instead." He did, and then pointed the vents toward me, the settings cranked to maximum.

A few minutes later, the aromatic cloud had dissipated. The air had cooled off. I was still focusing on taking deep breaths, trying to settle my stomach, when I felt a brush on my left breast.

His fingers were grazing my erect nipple. "Just checking if you're cooler now," he said, then grinned.

"Definitely, thank you," I said.

He continued caressing me. He groped the flesh of my breast, then his hand slid under the fabric, where he gently squeezed my nipple. His touch magically made me forget about my upset stomach.

Probably out of years of practice as my previous uptight-prude self, I instinctually pushed his hand down, then regretted it. I wanted him to touch me, to feel me up some more. I looked at him, his eyes glued on the dark road in front of us, only the next fifty feet made visible by the van's headlights. His hand was back in his lap. *He let me push him away just like that?*

I grabbed his hand and returned it to my breast, my eyes fixed on his profile, his pointy nose, his slanted jaw. A smile once again appeared on his face. My eyes went down to his chest and stomach, then I saw a bulge form in his shorts. His hand left my breast for a second to dig down inside his shorts, to adjust himself and bring the bulge upward toward his waist. Then he returned to my breast, squeezing it harder, pushing the fabric aside.

Then, out of nowhere, a car appeared in our lane, just a few feet in front of us, without tail lights or headlights on. Ian instantly retracted his hand, brought it to the wheel, and steered us into the passing lane just in time to avoid a collision.

He honked at the driver and yelled something in a language I didn't understand. *German?*

I adjusted my bikini top to cover myself again.

My heart galloped in my chest.

That was close!

8:20 p.m.

My stress level had lowered back to normal just as we reached an intersection a few minutes later. My libido, however, was on the rise. We were in the middle of nowhere. There were no traffic lights, just one wooden sign with an arrow on it pointing to the nearest village.

Ian pulled up on the side of the road, put the van into park, then turned to face me, his expression as stern as a pope's. "I'm heading a different direction. But you should be able to catch a ride into town from here."

"What?" My hands flew up in the air. "Are you kidding me? It's dark outside. I don't know what could happen to me here, left alone in the middle of nowhere. I don't even have a flashlight!"

"Well," he started, leaning back in his seat, bringing his elbows up behind his head. "You may be able to convince me to make a detour and take you back to your place..."

His eyes were set on me, letting me imagine how I could finish his suggestion. Ian certainly knew how to push my buttons... and make me want him even more. "You've already seen my breasts..." I said, feigning innocence. "Are you open to a different payment plan?"

His hand slid down into my lap, then up, lifting my sarong and making its way up to caress my pussy through the moist fabric of my bikini bottom.

My heartbeat increased. I was ready to fuck him right here, right now. I undid the knot that tied my sarong around my hips and opened up the fabric. I then grabbed his hands and brought them to the strings on either side of my bottom.

"Go ahead, undo me... then do me if you want."

He pulled on the strings and untied the knots, his eyes locked on mine. "Goddamnit, you're hot," he whispered once he pulled on the now unattached triangle and exposed my pussy.

Without much of a warning, he thrust his middle finger into me. I gasped in surprise, but then smiled as he twisted his digit in me, soaking it with my fluids. Ian then brought his finger to his lips and took a whiff before sucking on it.

"Hell yeah. I know just the spot. But first, I want you to blow me on our way there," he said. He pulled down his shorts to his mid-thigh, letting his cock rise free, then he moved his seat back a notch.

He put the car into first gear, and then merged back on the road before making a left toward the village onto a smaller paved road. He shifted up a gear again, then again. I couldn't take my eyes off of his cock. His flat abs, the line of hairs leading down to his manhood. No tan lines—all of his hard flesh had been kissed by the sun. I wanted to be one of the sun rays for a second. I spit on my palm then reached for his cock. "Give me a sec," he said, just before shifting into top gear. "Good now. Come and wrap those sexy lips on my cock," he ordered, his right arm reaching for the back of my head, gently but firmly pushing me down, closer to his erect member.

At first, I licked the tip of his cock, circling my tongue around it, then I swallowed it. I bobbed on his shaft, hungry for it. I felt his hand on my back, fumbling to untie the knot of my bikini top with one hand while the other steered. I felt the top coming undone, my breasts hanging free below me. I swallowed him as deep as I could, allowing his member to fill my mouth while he groped my loose breasts. I came back up, brought a hand to the base of his shaft, and kept going.

His right hand lifted my neck up just as my hunger approached its pinnacle.

"What?" I asked. He'd taken my lollipop away without explanation. His hand reached for the gear stick, he downshifted, and then the vehicle turned off onto a dirt road. He allowed my hand to return to him, stroking him while he maneuvered the potholes. My breasts bounced around and he had a good look, then he returned his finger to my pussy briefly between shifts.

The dirt road finally opened up. The ocean was in front of us, in all of its peaceful glory.

"Back-road access to another beach," he said.

He turned off the engine but left the headlights on. The sky was littered with stars but no moon. The soothing sounds of the waves rumbling to shore reverberated around us.

8:45 p.m.

"Come with me. We'll go skinny dipping," Ian said before fully taking off his shorts, and then stepping out of the driver's seat.

He didn't wait for me. He started running toward the ocean.

I decided to take my time. I stepped out of the van, slipping my neck out of the top string of my bikini, the only thing that was still knotted together, then left all of my clothing on the passenger seat and walked toward the water. I looked at him, the headlights illuminating his strong back, his epic sun-kissed ass, his muscular legs, his defined calves, then he turned around, and his engorged dick called out to me.

My groin twitched with desire when he spoke again. "Come on!"

I hesitated. I'd never gone skinny dipping before.

Tonight certainly sounds like the best time to try: beautiful night, handsome man with a delightful cock, no one else around...

I made up my mind and ran toward him, my breasts bouncing with every step, and I swear I felt pussy juice running down my legs. He was already in the water by the time I reached the shore.

The water wasn't cold, but it didn't feel as warm as it had been earlier today when the sun was shining.

I walked toward him, enjoying the massaging effect of the breaking waves over my skin. His head disappeared below the water, and I finally dove head first into the next wave before standing up on my feet again. I turned around looking for Ian but couldn't find him. Then I felt his hands grabbing my legs below the water, behind me. He surfaced, then pivoted me around.

We were now waist-deep, facing each other, the vehicle's headlights shining straight at us, the tip of his erect cock poking me in the stomach. He traced the outline of my breasts, moving my wet hair out of the way before locking his lips onto mine. My pussy was aching for him. The moving water around us caressed me while his tongue explored my mouth. He grabbed my waist and then moved me back a little, lowering himself about eight inches in the water. I grabbed a hold of his dick and he pulled me in as I guided him to the itch I wanted scratched.

With my feet wrapped around his back, I let him fuck me like he meant it. I moaned, enjoying his girth inside me. I let my back float on the surface while he pounded me hard. He was keeping an eye on the waves, lifting me up before the next one arrived, then lowering me down again. His hands hung on tight to my hips, moving me back and forth faster and harder. Stargazing had never been so enjoyable.

When he lifted me up in anticipation of the next wave, he brought my torso closer to him. He kissed me, his tongue eager. Then I felt him walking us back to the shore, his dick still in me but no longer moving. I squeezed the muscles in my genitals, enjoying feeling him there, then he pulled out of me and laid me flat on my back at the water's edge, just where the waves finished caressing the sand. He placed one knee between my parted legs, then guided his cock back into me.

"Fuck me," I ordered, squeezing his butt cheeks and forcing him deeper into me. "Fuck me hard."

He was breathing heavily, only serving to increase my arousal. I brought one of my hands to my clit, flicking it closer to orgasm while I squeezed my breast with the other. I looked at the sky again, where a million stars peppered the night. I swear I saw a shooting star just as I reached nirvana.

Ian came after me, grunting and pulling out just in time to spill his warm juices over my stomach and chest. I delighted in smearing it all over my breasts, making them glisten under the headlights that were shining on us.

Without a single kiss or a peck on the cheek, he got up to his feet, then returned to his van, leaving me alone on the sand, legs and arms now spread apart like a starfish. A very ecstatic starfish.

After a minute, though, I felt the urge to go and rinse off. I stood up then made my way back to the water. While I let the waves wash off his come, I started hearing Bob Marley's music resonating from the beach, then saw him return to where we had been lying a few minutes ago. He sat down, his movements still illuminated by his vehicle's headlights. I saw him place a bottle of water and his portable radio next to him, then he lit up his pipe. His long legs folded in front of him, his junk resting limply between them. I dove in one last time before joining him on the beach.

Once seated a few inches from him, he passed his pipe my way and showed me how to block the small hole with my finger while setting alight the marijuana bud with the lighter in my other hand. We sat and smoked for a few minutes, enjoying the beautiful night, my pussy still throbbing from having had him inside of me. I let my back fall into the wet sand, and he leaned sideways next to me. With his finger, he traced imaginary lines on my chest, then he approached me and started licking and sucking on my nipples.

He pulled away from them, his gaze still locked on my chest, his hands massaging my breasts. "Your tits are out-of-this-world," he said. "I could sleep on those fleshy mounds of pleasure."

I smiled but said nothing, letting my high and his words strike my ego, enjoying this *pura vida* moment.

Redemption Song accompanied the continuous rumble of the sea just feet away from us. Ian's lips moved down to my stomach, I could feel the wetness of his tongue moving toward my belly button, then past it. His fingertips glided past my trimmed bush and he started teasing my other, still engorged, lips. My heartbeat still pounded in my pussy.

I let a sigh leave my lips, then raised myself up a bit, resting on my elbows. I saw that Ian had also sat up, his dick once again erect and ready for action. He rolled me around, then started slapping the sand away from my naked ass. I giggled, the pot making this much funnier than it really was, but I stopped abruptly when I saw blue lights flashing and lighting up the trees behind Ian's van. I stayed quiet but squeezed Ian's knee, digging my nails into his flesh, then pointed at the lights.

"Shit!" Ian said. He bounced to grab his pipe and pot canister, and then tossed them on the beach, as far away from us as he could.

A second later, the beam of a flashlight started making its way toward us, a few feet from where the vehicle's headlight's coverage ended.

Then, in Spanish, a man's voice ordered us to turn off the music and return to the vehicle, hands up.

We obeyed, walking toward the van, stark naked, hands in the air. Unsolicited thoughts flashed through my mind. They ranged from, 'This is the most embarrassing moment of my life,' all the way to, 'Fuck, I'm going to jail,' and every shade in between.

Once we reached the van, the officer requested to see the vehicle's papers, which Ian grabbed from the glove compartment, then he ordered us both to place our hands against the vehicle and spread our legs. I didn't dare go to the passenger side of the van. I needed to stay next to Ian. Who knew what could happen if the patrol officer had me all to himself, in my birthday suit, legs spread?

Being seen naked by a police officer is one thing. I may get a ticket for indecent exposure... But I don't want to get raped by a power-hungry cop or get arrested because Ian's got weed—or possibly more potent drugs.

A few excruciatingly long minutes went by, during which the patrol officer reviewed the papers, then searched through the vehicle, moving and tossing neoprene shirts and surf boards in the back. The good news was that nobody else appeared to be with him. The officer then inspected the both of us with his flashlight, spending most of his time lighting up my ass and tits. I wanted to protest, but refrained from it, not due to a language barrier, but because I didn't want to worsen the situation.

His inspection finally over, he handed Ian his papers again. But as Ian reached to pull open the glove compartment, the patrol officer lit up the inside of the cabin and spotted a loose baggie filled with weed.

"¡No es mío!" Ian exclaimed in Spanish, informing the patrol officer that it wasn't his, but the man ordered Ian to once again lean on the vehicle with his hands against it.

"I swear, that's not mine," Ian said to me quietly. "Damn cop must have planted it earlier when he searched the freaking van. They're all corrupt!"

"I... I don't know," I said, the heaviness of the situation taking my high away. I was suddenly no longer enjoying the evening breeze on my naked body. "Do you think we can talk our way out of it? I don't have any money to bribe him. Do you?"

"I've got my pay from today's lesson. I'll see what I can do," he whispered to me before slowly moving away from the vehicle, his hands still up in the air.

"Mae, dime. Podemos hablar y ver... ¿No?" Ian said to the officer, hoping to open negotiations.

I couldn't see or hear the rest of it, but based on how long Ian stayed away, it was either looking very good or very bad. But the longer I remained by myself, the more scared I got. I brought my legs back together, as though I could regain some of my composure with that action alone.

It didn't work.

I finally heard the police officer's voice behind me, ordering me in Spanish to spread my legs open again and to keep my arms up against the vehicle. The flashlight beam was once again aimed at my ass. The only thing I could see was my own shadow on the van a foot from my face. I closed my eyes.

Then, I felt two hands wrapping themselves on my right ankle, slowly going up my leg, but stopping short of my pussy.

Searching me? As if I physically could hide anything while naked!

The hands then moved to the other leg and repeated, this time, examining my ass. I was being treated like cattle; my butt cheeks got pushed apart, the flashlight probably lighting all of it up. I didn't want to open my eyes to find out.

I winced, imagining the police officer's hands on me. Tears were at the brink of my eyes, but something felt... odd. The hands were touching me in a kind, almost loving manner. They moved to my pussy, caressing it. In fact, it felt like when Ian was touching me a little while back. When the hands grabbed my breasts a few seconds later, I re-opened my eyes and saw Ian's big, strong hands pinching my nipples. He leaned and whispered in my ear, "It's me. He'll let us go without arresting us for indecent exposure and weed possession in exchange for a show. I tried offering him money, but he wasn't interested. Don't know about you, but I figured having sex is better than going to jail, right?"

I froze. *Fuck in front of him?* I didn't know if I could... But then, what other option did I have? "Okay," I finally told Ian, nodding while I mustered my courage.

"Take a few steps back and keep your hands on the vehicle," Ian said. I obeyed, ending up in an L-position. I tried to forget the police officer was there, but it was hard since his flashlight was now aiming at my hanging breasts. *As long as he keeps his distance and only watches us.* I closed my eyes again and focused on my lover's hands and on his kisses caressing my back. Then he slapped my ass, hard. The smacking sound against my flesh surprised me, but not as much as what followed.

Ian then parted my butt cheeks and circled the tip of a wet finger around my anus.

"Relax," he said once again, close to my ear. "We have a special request."

Shit. I did my best to relax, but I'd never been penetrated from behind before, and I certainly wasn't ready for his finger. "Take a deep breath," he said. As I did, he pressed not his finger, but his large cock into my ass. After inserting the head of his cock, I felt my sphincter tighten around his shaft. He brushed his hand in circles on my back. "Relax, breathe..."

He moved one of his arms around my hip, and with his hand, started teasing my clit. I looked down and saw Ian bring his other hand to my pussy, pinching my lips and then finger fucking it. The police officer was a few feet away, his flashlight illuminating everything. I closed my eyes again, breathing deeply, trying to forget about the cock that had barely entered my anus, focusing on what Ian's fingers were doing to my pussy instead. It worked. A few seconds later, I manage to relax my muscles, but then he pushed into my ass some more. He kept finger fucking my pussy while pushing his large cock deeper and deeper into my ass, until I felt his balls bounce against my butt cheeks.

Ian then pulled out, but not completely. I had time for one deep breath before he fully pushed himself in me again.

He moved both of his hands to my hips. He repeated the motion, thrusting himself into my ass faster and faster, deeper and deeper. Ian's cock had felt big in my pussy, but he really felt huge in my ass. I brought one hand to my clit, flicking it to try and distract myself from the pain. But then it turned into some sort of pleasure. The discomfort hadn't disappeared, but it had somehow morphed into excitement, as if it had added another layer of sensation.

Each time Ian pounded me in the ass, he grunted, louder and louder. While my right hand was still rubbing my clit, I brought my other hand to my pussy, letting go of the vehicle completely and unfolding my torso half-way. I slid two digits in my pussy while he continued fucking me in the ass. Another man's moan sounded just a few feet away from us. I reopened my eyes and saw the police officer looking at us, his small dick in hand, beating off to us. I did my best to ignore him, return my attention to the hottie that was fucking me, the one I had fantasized about all afternoon. The one who'd made me come an hour earlier. I could hear his breathing getting louder behind me. I finger fucked myself faster, rubbing my clit as though I needed to start a fire. He grunted, gave me a few final pokes with all of his might, and I came just as I felt him ooze into my ass.

Ian folded his body over mine, grabbed my breasts, and pressed me against him.

"Fuck for freedom," he whispered. "Thanks for playing along," he said.

And just like that, the police officer turned off his flashlight and retreated to his car.

I heard the roar of an engine, then the flashing blue lights gradually backed away from us, out to the main road.

Ian dug for a flashlight in his van, then ran to the beach to collect the smoking paraphernalia he'd tossed earlier.

I slowly made my way to the water to rinse myself off, letting his come ooze out of my very sore anus. I stood in the waves for a few minutes while he tried to locate the items he'd tossed. Once I saw him move back toward his vehicle, I walked out of the water and met him by the driver's door. He wrapped his hands around me and hugged me.

"I know, that was... weird," he said.

I was still confused, so I stayed quiet. He tapped me on the shoulder and dropped his arms. "I'm going to rinse off, then we'll get going?"

"Sounds good," I said before walking around to the passenger side to find my towel.

A few minutes later, we had both dried off and gotten dressed. Ian drove us back to the main road and then headed into town. The rest of the drive was done in silence. We were probably both lost in our thoughts—or at least I was.

10:00 p.m.

Forty minutes later, Ian dropped me off in front of my rental apartment. I hugged him, then we exchanged one last passionate kiss. I watched my gorgeous blond-haired man get into his van and drive away.

After unlocking the metal gate and the wooden door to my apartment, I walked in, closed the door, and then let my body drop onto the floor, my back leaning on the closed wooden partition.

Today had seen the first of many new things: first surf lesson, first skinny dipping session, first 'sex on the beach' that didn't come in a glass at a fancy bar, first anal sex, and first time having sex in front of a stranger. I guess it was better to be part of a corrupt policeman's fantasy than being stuck in jail in a foreign country because of indecent exposure or drug-related charges...

I got the easy way out. But did I get a thrill from it?

Nah. It was probably just Ian's touch.

Or was it more?

I showered to rid myself of the grains of sand that had gone up every crack and crevice within my body, letting the warm water wash away the last of the day's stress. I then rolled into bed and cranked up the A/C. My sore muscles—and sore ass—ready for a good night's sleep.

Enough excitement for one day.

Tomorrow's all about relaxation.

I should probably start the day off with a massage... I wonder if I can get one from a hottie with wandering hands?

MY XXX EXPERIENCE
COSTA RICA

THE PLAN

THIS TIME, my stewardess really didn't leave me much to go on. My three options are slimmer than ever:

OPTION 1: Access flight records and try to find her among thousands of passengers and flight attendants who flew into Liberia.

I don't know the date she flew in and... the obvious: I don't know her name! I've got no idea if she was working that flight or just a passenger. I know nothing. This is a dead end.
Likelihood of success: Nil.

OPTION 2: Go to Liberia, then try and find the right surf instructor.

The problem with this is that LIR/Liberia isn't anywhere near the coast. She could have flown there, then gone to any of the dozens of beach towns that litter the Pacific Coast. Sure, I can probably safely eliminate the Caribbean side since she would have probably flown into San José for that. But still... Playa Hermosa? Jaco? Tamarindo? Sámara? Where the heck do I even start? Contact the Nicaraguan immigration services and look for someone named Ian who crosses the border every three months? Not going to do me any good. Best bet—and a really bad one—is to try and find a school that has a blond instructor named Ian... If he's still around.

Likelihood of success: Close to nil.

OPTION 3: Scope out all Airbnb places in small Costa Rican towns.

Airbnb, a website where people can rent apartments from locals is fortunately—or unfortunately?—growing in popularity. Plus, what's there now may not have been what was there when she went. If finding the surf instructor doesn't pan out, I may have to sit myself in front of a computer for hours and contact a bunch of owners, asking them if they rented their apartment to a brunette. I have yet to think of a way to ask without sounding like a stalker and being reported as acting inappropriately. I could also spend hours reading reviews and hope she's left one, but I don't know what her face looks like...

Likelihood of success: Nil.

This time, my hopes aren't high. But I do have a week off coming up.

Should I spend my holiday in Costa Rica, hoping that I could somehow find another clue?

I don't know if it's worth it.

A FRIEND'S HELP

A little abashed at my abysmal odds of tracking her down or learning anything new from replicating her Costa Rican experience, I sought advice from my best friend Bob.

"Doesn't sound too promising, Charlie," he started, pausing to sip his beer. "But I know you're a hard-headed bastard. Based on how obsessed you've been with her over the past... What now? Feels like it's been close to a year of you going on and on about this broad... I know you'll head down there, no matter what. Heck, you'd fly down there in the hope of tracking her scent if I told you she'd farted in the wind."

I let Bob's comments marinate for a second, then washed them down with a swig of my drink. "But what would *you* do?" I asked him.

"Other than burn that damn diary and erase those memories?"

I stared him down. We'd been over this a million times. He knew I'd already invested too much. I was addicted, unable to let go of the chase. I simply *had* to find her.

After taking another sip, he continued. "Tell you what. Stacy and I actually have a timeshare in Costa Rica—"

"What? How come I've never heard of it?"

Bob's eyebrows went up, his eyes round. "Do you think I'm proud to have been roped into buying one?" He shook his head. "Anyway, it was Stacy's idea.

We've only been there once. Let's just say that timing hardly ever works out for us. No clue if it'd be convenient to use as a home base for your research."

"Tell me more," I said.

"It's in Guanacaste. West Coast, just south of Nicaragua. Lots of beaches around. If you want, I could look into what weeks are available. See if it meshes with your time off?" he offered.

"Certainly sounds like a good option... But am I going to have to suffer through one of those pesky, time-sucking timeshare sales spiels?"

Bob shook his head and let out a muffled laugh. "No, they don't have a sales team on site, but... what they do have on site, though..." A weird grin appeared on his lips. "I think you'd appreciate the... amenities there," he finally said, finishing his thought.

"Amenities? You mean there's a pool?"

"Oh, Charlie," Bob said, shaking his head at me. "There's a lot more than that. Sure, there's a communal pool, a beach within walking distance, a phone, TV, A/C in the bedroom... Everything you need."

But his smirk told me he had yet to divulge the best part. "And?" I asked before tilting my vodka glass to see if there was anything left other than the ice cubes.

"If you're lucky—and I know you're a lucky son-of-a-bitch—you may meet Henrietta." His grin was now that of a Cheshire cat.

"And who's Henrietta...?"

Bob stood up, downed the last gulp of his beer, then placed a ten dollar bill on the bar. "Oh, you'll find out," he finally said.

WHAT HAPPENED

As luck would have it—yes, I may have been born with a four-leaf clover embedded in my ass—Bob's Costa Rican timeshare condo was available during my days off.

I took him up on his offer and packed my suitcase with a bit more than a pair of swim trunks and my toothbrush. I included everything a single guy would need: condoms, sunscreen, a bad print shirt featuring brightly colored palm trees (a great conversation starter), a hat, sunglasses and more condoms. I booked myself a flight to LIR/Liberia, and purchased a phrase book to brush up on my Spanish, especially my pick-up lines.

If this trip didn't bring me closer to finding her, at least I could catch up on my tan, learn to surf, and maybe encounter some beautiful beach babes looking for a good time under the sun... or moonlight.

And maybe I could figure out who the heck Henrietta is.

Here's what happened during my week-long Costa Rican retreat.

4:16 p.m.

After clearing customs, my small checked luggage in hand, I made my way past a series of men holding signs until I reached the one that read "Charlie."

The man introduced himself as Alejandro and offered to take my small, wheeled suitcase to his car.

"*¿Hay un lugar donde puedo comprar una cerveza?*" I asked him in my heavily-accented Spanish.

"Yes, Mr. Charlie," the man said, obviously intent on practicing his English. "The store over there," he said, pointing to a small kiosk about fifty feet in front of us.

"Wait for me a minute?" I asked and he nodded.

I headed to the store, purchased an ice-cold Imperial, which the employee kindly opened up for me, then returned to my driver.

"Good choice. Best beer," Alejandro said, smiling. "Ready?"

I nodded, took a cold, refreshing sip, then followed him out to the parking lot.

6:10 p.m.

Nearly two hours later, Alejandro dropped me off at Bob's timeshare complex. The ride and chit-chat with the driver had proved enlightening on two fronts:

First, although Costa Rica is a small country, I had no idea covering such a short distance would take me so long. That meant I'd have to pick my destinations carefully, and I may not be able to come back to Bob's place every night.

Second, Alejandro gave me a list of activities I could occupy myself with, including one surfing school in town, whose address I noted on the back of Alejandro's business card.

Really pleased with his professional behavior and his wealth of knowledge, I left him a hefty tip before getting out of his cab, suitcase in hand.

Alejandro's car sped away, spitting a few bits of loose dirt and gravel around my feet. I stood still for a second, adjusting from the change in temperature from the air-conditioned cabin to the hot, humid environment that now surrounded me, and admiring the neatly trimmed, lush trees that bordered the entire complex where I was to sojourn for a week. In the middle, right in front of me, a large, ornate, metal gate stood, closed. Through its iron bars, I could see a dozen clay-roofed condo units peppering a well-manicured lawn, with a large pool in the center of it all. My airport beer long gone, the pool looked really enticing right about now.

I made my way to the gate. A security guard in uniform—complete with a rifle—greeted me and asked for my name. I gave it to him. For a second, I wondered if Bob had arranged for everything, but my slight worry evaporated when the guard nodded, checking his watch then writing down the time next to my name.

The man stepped aside and reached into the small security shack. A light sound buzzed and the locked gate clicked open. The armed man walked to the center of the gate and then widened its opening, letting me in and welcoming me, *"Bienvenidas, señor Charlie."*

I followed the dirt path into the complex. I wasn't sure how this whole 'timeshare' thing worked, but I spotted a building on my right marked *Recepción*. It seemed like the best place to find out.

I left my bag by the wooden door, knocked, then let myself in. A Latino man dressed in a white shirt and black pants greeted me by name, in English. *How did he know?* A walkie-talkie on the counter behind him gave me a good clue.

"Welcome to our complex," the man said, his hand motioning for me to join him at a nearby table laden with a large pitcher of water, condensation beading off its side. "I'm Juanito, the on-duty concierge today. Please sit down and I'll give you an overview of our residential area," he said, indicating one of the chairs placed around the table.

I sat, then wiped my face with my forearm. As if he'd read my mind, he poured a glass of water and handed it to me.

"So," he started, pulling out a map from a file folder sitting at the far edge of the table. "We are here," he said, circling a building. "You'll be staying in unit number seven, which is here." He circled another building.

"Sweet, close to the pool!" I exclaimed, seeing the large freeform shape on the map.

"Indeed," the man said, smiling, then checking his watch. "Unfortunately, we have rules concerning the pool. Our guests can only use it during the daytime. Right now, pool hours are from 7 a.m. until 6 p.m."

I looked at my watch: 6:15 p.m.

"Really? No 15-minute exception for a tired, hot, and jet-lagged guest?" I asked. The jet-lagged part was an over-statement. There was just an hour difference, but I really wanted to dive into that pool now.

"Sorry, sir. It's for safety and liability reasons."

I listened to him go on with the rest of the rules, covering laundry, loud noises, how to dial out, etc. I nodded, hoping to speed up the process so I could go and shower—second best way to cool off—then head into town for a few refreshing drinks.

The introduction over, we got up, left the reception building, and then Juanito walked me over to Unit 7. He unlocked the front door, then handed me the key. "Dial 1 if you have any problems. Someone is always on call at the reception," he said.

I thanked him, then dug for a small bill in my pocket to hand to him. He was obviously waiting for a tip of some sort, standing next to me, a large but contrived smile on his face. After rolling my bag into the building, I closed the door and gave myself the grand tour. The two-level building featured three bedrooms, the largest of which was on the top floor, with a full en-suite bathroom. The entire room was tiled; the oversized shower occupied half of it. A regular toilet, sink, and other standard bathroom fixtures made up the rest. I emptied my bladder, then decided to assess the view.

I looked through both bedroom windows. Through the first one, the setting sun colored the sky over the ocean a few miles away; through the other, the unoccupied turquoise pool surrounded by a dozen or so unoccupied pool chairs.

7:00 p.m.

Showered and dressed in my tacky shirt and shorts, I headed out of the timeshare complex on a beer errand, briefly stopping by the security shack to inquire about the location of the nearest store and town. The same guard was still on duty and, after a few too many attempts—I really had to brush up on my *español*—I finally understood that I had to head down to the right and walk 100 meters, then turn right again and follow the main road into town for about 500 meters—about a third of a mile in total.

I followed the directions I'd been given. The state of the paved road I was walking on (deep ditches, broken glass bottles, and fuchsia flowers) made my chest swell with hope. This could possibly be the same one that my stewardess had walked on... Passing cars kept honking: some slowing down to yell, "Taxi!" out of their rolled-down windows, some totally dashing by me, forcing me to take my walking path into the ditch. It was dark, other than when passing cars lit my way. Good thing I'd brought a flashlight with me. Didn't want to step on a snake or something.

I finally arrived at a cluster of small buildings, the first one lit by a large Pilsen sign—another Costa Rican beer.

I stepped inside, eager to quench my thirst. I headed to the large branded refrigerator, opened the see-through door, then grabbed a six pack of tall cans. There was absolutely no line. I paid the man at the till, opened the first can, then gulped half of it down as soon as I stepped back outside.

I stood in front of the store for a second, looking right toward the town, then left to where I'd come from.

The surf shop would be closed by now.

What could I gain from heading into town now? Possibly some fresh pussy? But I've got a lot of planning to do and just one week to visit these surf shops.

After finishing the first can of beer, I'd made up my mind. I tossed my empty in the garbage bin, then headed back to the apartment with my remaining beers in hand, still sealed.

9:00 a.m.

The following morning, I headed into town to find out if the local surf shop knew of an instructor called Ian. A short Latina woman in a bright orange bikini greeted me as I entered the store.

"Hi there," I said, taking a good look at the goods—both hers and the store's.

Continuing my way through the shop, I saw a tall Caucasian man behind the counter and walked up to him.

"What can I help you with?" the young man in his twenties asked me.

"Well, this may sound a little strange, but I'm trying to track down a blond-haired man, possibly German, whose name is Ian. Surf instructor. Does that ring a bell?"

"Holy shit man. Are you a friend of his?"

I frowned then shook my head. "No, never met the guy. I'm just hoping he can help me find someone else I'm looking for."

The young man's cheeks turned bright red, as if I'd triggered a spike in his blood pressure. "The fucker lived a few miles out of here. He was just bad news," he said, shaking his head. "But don't take my word for it. Hold on a sec." He flashed his index finger up in the air, then brought it to his phone screen, flipping through his contacts before dialing a number. He brought the same finger back up, looking at me.

"Yeah, Lucy? ...Dan here. I've got an American guy here in the shop, and you won't believe who he's trying to track down... Yeah! Do you have time to meet with him? ...Can I give him your number and you guys can work out the details? ...Yeah, sorry... I've got other folks to attend to here... Okay. Take care. Bye."

He hung up, then grabbed a business card from the nearby holder, flipped it, and copied down Lucy's number on it.

"Give her a call. She'll fill you in on the shitty stuff this guy's done."

"Okay, thanks, man!" I said, grabbing the card from his hand.

I stepped out of the shop and hailed the first cab that came by, happy with the day's developments so far. Maybe I wouldn't have to travel all across Costa Rica to find this Ian.

9:30 a.m.

Back in Bob's apartment, I sat by the phone, Lucy's number in hand. I also had a piece of paper and a pen at the ready.

Maybe I can get his name, his shop's address... Then the rest is easy!

I crossed my fingers for a second, then started dialing.

"*¿Hola?*" a female voice answered.

"Hi, is this Lucy?"

"Speaking."

"Hi, I'm Charlie. I was at your friend's surf shop about thirty minutes ago, and he gave me your number."

"Argh! Yeah, I remember." She let out a loud breath. "You're the one looking for *Fuckface?*" The increased volume of her voice made me pull the receiver away from my ear.

"Is this his legal name?" I asked, hoping my humor would calm her down.

"Argh. I just wish I could—"

"Listen, he's not a friend of mine or anything. I'm just trying to track down one of the women who took a surf lesson from him."

A cacophony of snorts and laughter echoed at the other end of the line. When the odd noises finally stopped, she continued. "Man. Let me guess: *Fuckface* had sex with her? The asshole left town. No forwarding address. He fucking burned down the shop that hired him in the first place."

"Whoa! Hmm..." I dropped my pen and stayed quiet.

"Sorry, man. I'm just upset. Not at you. And this freaking heat... I just wish I had a pool I could dive in."

I paused, weighing the odds: although she was an emotional train wreck, she knew my guy and could help me track him down. I had a pool. *Win-win, right?*

"I have access to a pool... Would you like to come over?" I asked.

"You shitting me?" Her voice had now reached teenage-girl excitement levels.

"No, I'm serious."

I gave her the address; we agreed to meet at the gate in an hour, then I hung up.

Maybe I'll get at least one useful bit of information from her once the cool water calms her nerves.

10:30 a.m.

I waited for Lucy at the gate, as agreed. A cab arrived exactly on time. A pretty twenty-something blonde popped her head out of the rear door, but I was taken aback when I saw the rest of her body come out.

"Lucy?" I asked, walking toward the very pregnant woman who had exited the cab.

"Yes. Charlie?" she said.

I nodded, then walked to her and kissed her on the cheek as was customary down here.

"You're pregnant?"

"And ding, ding, ding!" she said, her fist up in the air. "That's the number one reason why I hate that asshole."

Holy shit.

"Well, come, come," I motioned to her. "Let's head to the pool and cool off."

The guard opened the gate for us and we headed to the swimming area.

"You don't know how much I've been dreaming about soaking my body into fresh water lately. This heat, it's pretty unbearable normally, but... as a pregnant woman... You wouldn't believe it."

I looked at her again, shaking my head.

When we arrived at the pool a few minutes later. She took off her dress, exposing two very swollen breasts, barely covered by a bikini top, and a ready-to-pop belly.

"We're supposed to shower first," I told her when I saw her dipping her toes in the pool. She turned toward me, and I pointed toward the protruding shower head a few feet away from her.

She turned on the water, and I watched her soak her very pregnant body under the light, cool stream. She leaned her head back, then slid her hands through her wet hair, smoothing it. Her swollen breasts were now receiving the full spray of the water. *Was I getting aroused by her?* Her yellow top soon showed her dark areolae through it. Her nipples slowly became erect, pushing their big, long tips against the fabric. I felt a twitch in my shorts. I had to think about something else.

"Listen, Lucy. I brought down beer, but obviously, that may not be the ideal beverage for you... considering. Go ahead and dive in, make yourself comfortable, and I'll be right back with some cool water."

"Awesome," she said, raising her thumb at me.

I turned around and headed to my unit.

What's wrong with you, man? She could pop any minute.

11:15 a.m.

I placed a tall plastic glass of water on the side of the pool for Lucy, along with a beer can for me. After a quick shower, I jumped in the water, splashing my pregnant guest in the process. She screeched and smiled.

"Thanks again for letting me come over like that, out of the blue, to use your pool."

"No worries. Listen, I know you don't want to talk about... *Fuckface*, but I just wanted to ask you one more question. Do you know his last name or something I could use to track him down?"

She shook her head. "Nah." Her shoulders went up, then she frowned and scrunched her face. She turned away from me. "I guess I'm the type of woman who sleeps with a guy without knowing his last name," she said, the words having sprinted out of her mouth in one fell swoop. Her shoulders trembled as she started sobbing.

Oh shit. What now?

I looked around. There wasn't anybody else near the pool.

I can't just stand here, but I can't leave either; she's my guest.

I swam toward her, then lifted her chin with my finger. "No, no. Don't cry. It's all good," I said. I hesitated, then reached behind her and patted her lightly on the back.

What did I say?

She stretched her arms and pulled me in, hugging me. Her pregnant belly pushing against my stomach, her tits moving up and down very close to my face. I swallowed hard, sending a telepathic message to my cock to stay put.

A few minutes later, her emotional roller-coaster appeared to have reached a plateau. She released me then looked at me, her green eyes red with tears. "Let's just talk about something else and have fun, okay?"

"Sounds like a plan," I said, smiling at her.

"You have a girlfriend?" she asked, stepping back from me but keeping her eyes locked onto mine.

I shook my head. "Nope."

She was now walking around in the pool, letting her body bounce with every step. "Interesting," she said. My eyes couldn't help but go to her bobbing yellow top, her two erect nipples coming and going past the surface level with every step, pointing directly at me.

Get a grip, man!

"When are you due?" I asked her, hoping to get my mind out of the gutter.

"Last week," she replied, still bouncing. She spun around. When she faced me again, the fabric of her yellow top had somehow shifted, half of her large areola was no longer covered. That was too much for my cock. The last few days had been dry, and it knew it.

"Have you ever been with a pregnant woman?" she asked, bouncing her way toward me.

I shook my head. My cock was pushing hard against the fabric of my trunks. "No, at least not that I know of." *And definitely never with someone who would have been so far along.*

She finally put an end to her hypnotizing motion, and was now standing a foot in front of me, her humongous breasts finally submerged.

I let out a breath. Maybe my mind could take the upper hand and convince my cock that fucking a woman who was about to pop—no matter how hot she looked—wasn't the best idea.

But no! Lucy arched her back to soak her hair in the water behind her. Her two large tits came out of the water, the partly visible nipple now fully exposed. Her pregnant belly pushed forward and received a full-frontal poke from my trunk-covered cock.

It was too late to back up now. She straightened her back again, her hungry eyes meeting mine.

Guess she felt that.

She closed the gap between us, looking down below my waist. She then saw the exposed nipple that had caused me quite a bit of grief.

"Oops," she said, bringing a finger to her pink lips. "Didn't mean to spill out." She pressed her tits together, an action that caused me to struggle with what should have been a natural swallowing reflex. "It's just that my tits have gotten so big. Nothing fits anymore."

She reached below the water, grabbing one of my hands and placing it on her exposed tit. "What do you think? Are they too big?" she asked.

I raised my eyebrows, bringing up my other hand to make a fair assessment of the situation. "Don't know, really." I squeezed them. Her hands dove into my trunks, going directly for my cock, which she released from the fabric. "They look perfect to me."

She let go of my cock to wrap her hands around the back of my neck, then her legs floated up around my hips. I was glad to have buoyancy on my side here, helping me support her pregnant weight. She moved her ass back and forth, lowering and raising it until my cock was perfectly aimed at her bikini-covered pussy. A slight movement of the fabric and I'd be in, freely. My eyes went from her tits to her pink mouth, to her eyes, back to her mouth. She was now licking her lips.

A man cleared his throat nearby. We both turned around and saw Juanito standing there, smiling. "Mr. Charlie?" he asked.

"Yes?" I said.

He looked at me, then pointed at the video camera I hadn't realized was there. "Pool rules are not optional."

"I understand," I said, donning a fake smile and ordering my cock at ease. It didn't listen quite yet. I moved Lucy's bikini top back in position and she unwrapped her limbs from around me, allowing me to tuck my erect cock into my trunks.

"How about a drink?" I suggested, swim-walking toward the glass of water and the beer can I'd left on the side of the pool earlier.

"How about we go to your place?" she offered, reaching for the waist of my trunks, pulling it back toward her.

I looked at Lucy. That hungry flame was still in her eyes, possibly more ardent than before. I tilted my head. "Give me a second to... wind down before I step out of the pool."

"As long as it'll be easy to get... wound up again," she said with a pout.

"That won't be a problem," I said before letting the cool bubbles quench my thirst—at least the thirst in my mouth.

12:08 p.m.

Five minutes later, we were upstairs in my bedroom.

"Listen," I started while looking at the beautiful but extremely pregnant young woman in front of me. "I—"

"Charlie, I can't force you to do anything. But you've got me all hot and bothered now. I need to use your shower. If you change your mind, I'll be in there, masturbating."

She pivoted and headed into the en-suite. The water started gushing.

Is this wrong? Isn't there a rule about fucking pregnant chicks?

I walked toward the door, which she'd conveniently left ajar. Lucy was sitting in the shower, naked. Her legs were wide open, one hand was aiming the shower head at her pussy; with the other, she fingered herself. She was breathing heavily, her swollen tits now fully exposed, resting on her firm, pregnant belly. Her long nipples were going up and down with her breath.

My dick won the battle against my mind.

I walked to her. As soon as I was within arms reach, she stopped what she was doing and pulled down my shorts. I cringed when my erect cock met the sudden drop of my waist band past it, but no permanent damage was done.

She reached for my manhood. "Come to mama!"

I knelt, part of me a little scared by the hungry/crazy look in her eyes.

"You wouldn't freaking believe how horny I've been..."

For the first time in my life, I felt the need to pause. "But... uh... How do I... I don't want to hurt the baby."

"Don't worry about that. Just do me. Fuck me from behind," she said, moving and turning so that she was on all fours on the tiled shower floor.

I moved behind her and guided my cock into her pink pussy. She moaned loudly as I gently parted her pussy. I pulled back, then pushed back in, still cautious.

"I'm not a virgin... obviously! Fuck me. Fuck me hard," she ordered.

I thrust my hip forward, pounding into her. I saw the shower head move then felt some of the water pressure reflected back toward my balls.

"Harder, Charlie," she said between moans. I could hear the noises of the pulsating water jet she was aiming at her pussy. I pushed harder into her, letting my hips bounce against her ass, parting her butt cheeks, then slapping them. My grunts got louder along with her screams. She suddenly arched her back, dropping the shower head and grabbing both of her tits, groaning in ecstasy.

I felt her pussy pulsate just as I came inside her.

10:00 a.m.

The next day, I was sitting by the pool in my swim trunks, enjoying a fresh cup of local, organic coffee I'd picked up from the reception area a few minutes ago, when Juanito called out my name.

"Mr. Charlie?"

I turned around to look at him. He was walking my way, a piece of paper in hand. "Ms. Lucy called and left you a message," he said before handing me the yellow note.

"Thank you," I said, taking it from him. He once again stood there with a smile. I raised my hands in the air. "Juanito, I don't have my wallet here with me. Let's just make this easy on ourselves and I'll leave a large tip when I leave, okay?"

"Very well, Mr. Charlie," he said.

Now alone, I unfolded the piece of paper and read the handwritten note:

Lucy called.
She had a healthy baby boy late last night.
She's at the Playa Grande Hospital.

I folded the note again, then finished my coffee while staring at the pool in front of me.

What kind of gift should I get her and the baby?

3:00 a.m.

My eyes popped open in the middle of the night.

Did I hear something?

I twisted my naked body out of bed, then slowly stood up. Both of my windows were open, a skunkie smell filling the air. Somehow, over the loud buzzing of cicadas in the background, I could hear water noises. I made my way to the large window that faced the swimming area.

The freeform pool was lit from under the water, the bright turquoise bottom making the still surface look pristine and inviting from here. The stench of pot was definitely coming from the pool area. Then I saw movement in the water: those mini waves that reverberated from something or someone moving in the part of the pool that was hidden from me by the building next door. Curious, I stayed there, leaning against the window frame, enjoying what little night breeze there was.

A minute later, I was rewarded for my patience.

A tall brunette was swimming her way to my side of the pool, doing the breast stroke, her long hair flowing over her back. Her ass bobbing as she opened and closed her legs like a frog. When she reached the side of the pool, she paused for a little while, letting her body float still. That's when my mind—and my cock—registered that she didn't have a swimsuit on. Her bare ass reflected the soft moonlight from above. I let my cock rise, then spat in my hand and started stroking it.

That should cure my insomnia.

I watched her, imagining what she would look like up close. I thought about heading down to the pool to find out, but I didn't know if she was alone.

Why risk ruining a good thing?

Her ass wiggled in the water, then she turned around, and stood in the fairly shallow water, resting her elbows against the side of the pool. Her back was arched, her tits pointing at the moon.

I increased the pressure on my cock. My other hand reached for my ball sack. I tightened my grip, I pumped harder, faster, but I needed moisture. I let go of my cock for a second, spat in my hand again, and then resumed pumping. Harder. Faster. The woman in the pool was caressing her own breasts. I imagined my hands on those tits. Then, without warning, she disappeared, lowering herself into the water for a second... two... three... four... five... six... Then she popped back out, her tits jumping and bouncing out after her. That was all I needed to reach the point of no-return. I brought my other hand to the tip of my cock, trying to catch my own jism instead of letting it splash onto the mosquito screen in front of me.

I let out a faint grunt.

She dove back under the water, then disappeared again, this time behind the other building.

6:20 p.m.

I spent my last Costa Rican sunset sitting at a bar on the beach, my feet in the sand, a cold beer in my hand.

As I watched the fading sun rays stream out from behind a cloud, coloring the rest of the sky in various pink and orange tones, I couldn't help but reflect on my short holiday in the sun. *I'll be back in New York this time tomorrow.*

I did take a surf lesson, and I'm glad to report that my experience was uneventful. I managed to stand up on the board. I even had a few good runs. Unfortunately, no luck with the cute *Tica* surf instructor. And... very fortunately, no incidents involving the police.

Lucy's little boy, Stewart she called him, is very cute. I did go and visit with her a couple of times. She said she'd like to keep in touch. I think I'd like that. As a friend, maybe.

The rest of my time was spent in the pool or strolling the beach. My evenings were spent in the company of my mystery stewardess through her diary.

As to Bob's Henrietta, I have no clue. Could she have been the woman skinny dipping in the pool the other night?

Or did I dream that whole thing up?

NEXT STEPS

Well, even though this particular trip proved fruitless in terms of discovering something new about my stewardess, I still had a great time. I'm still intent on tracking my mystery woman down. If anything, her diary's always given me the opportunity for sexual encounters I wouldn't have had otherwise.

Her next journal entry is all about Tinseltown.

Believe it or not, my mysterious stewardess and one of her girl friends got roped into auditioning for an advertisement spot for a flying school... But like many young, aspiring actresses have discovered, quite a few casting directors have X-rated plans in mind instead.

Maybe I'll track down her casting tape and finally see her face... and the rest of her beautiful body.

Next stop: Hollywood.

PART IV

USA

THE STEWARDESS'S ENTRIES

USA

11:15 a.m.

AFTER HANDING the woman sitting in 5A her mini-bottle of Chardonnay and the chicken-breast sandwich she'd purchased, I peeked out of the porthole. Absolutely no clouds here. The same was expected for Los Angeles this weekend. In a few hours, I'd be seeing my friend Katrina, whom I haven't seen in ages... 13... 15 years already? I was looking forward to catching up with her over a couple of days.

I continued with the in-flight service, turning my attention to a distinct-looking blond man with shoulder-length wavy hair. He was quite handsome, save for his oddly crooked nose, but it added to his charm. I interrupted his chat with the young exotic woman sitting next to him. I couldn't tell her ethnicity, but she could have been the love child of an Asian-Brazilian couple. Long silky black hair draped over her shoulders, some of it falling over her large breasts. Her eyes were not almond-shaped to match her hair; they were round and light-colored. She reminded me of a National Geographic cover I'd seen years ago.

I smiled at them. "Sorry to interrupt, but what would you like to drink?" I asked the lady first, handing them both a paper napkin while waiting for her reply.

A shy smile preceded her words. Her green eyes met mine when she spoke. "Diet Pepsi, if you have it?"

"Diet Coke, okay?"

She nodded. I then turned my attention to the rugged man seated next to her.

"One second," he told me, his finger in the air while he turned to the woman. "Why don't I buy you a drink, to celebrate. After all, you're on your way to Hollywood." The woman's eyebrows slanted and so did her mouth. "Come on... One drink. On me. You may become a big star one day. I'd love to brag that I bought you a drink once."

She nodded, her cheeks registering a slight change toward pink.

The blond man turned toward me. "Let's make that two sparkling wines," he said while digging his wallet out.

"No problem. That will be eighteen dollars, sir."

I processed the payment and handed them the mini-bottles while reflecting on my friend Katrina, who, just like that young woman, had come to L.A. to make it. As far as I knew, Katrina still hadn't. The city was filled with young women like them, with big dreams and varying levels of acting talent.

I continued with the rest of the service, greeting people and serving them. Most were excited to be headed to sunny California: a family of seven was on their way to Disneyland; some were headed home for family reunions, and others were traveling for business purposes. Overall, the mood was definitely festive.

11:45 a.m.

By the time I reached the back of economy, a bell chimed. I secured the trolley then walked toward the lit indicator. Blondie and Exotic-Girl were the ones who had requested my attention.

I arrived while he was finishing a sentence, "...And that's how I became a casting director."

"So, you hire actors?" she asked, her doe eyes fountains of innocence and hope.

"Of course," he replied before turning his attention to me.

"Hi, could you get us another two sparkling wines, please," he asked, a wide smile on his face, his hand now on the girl's knee.

"No problem, sir," I said. "I'll be right back."

Once in the galley, I grabbed the drinks then returned to Blondie's seat with my payment processing machine in hand. As I walked toward him, I noticed his head sticking out in the aisle. He was watching me come toward him, eyeing me up and down as though inspecting prey in a bar.

I tried to keep my skin from blushing, but I could feel heat rushing to my cheeks. *Is this shyness or arousal?* I didn't mind being ogled by a hottie, but I was working after all, and he was clearly hitting on Exotic-Girl sitting next to him. *What kind of man acts like this?* He pulled his head out of the aisle once I got within a couple of feet from him.

"Here you go, sir," I said, handing him the drinks.

We repeated the payment routine. I handed him the receipt along with the processed credit card, but he paused, his hands almost picking up the items but stopping short by an inch.

"This may sound a little strange, but my company is running auditions tomorrow, hoping to cast the role of a female flight attendant. I realize you've already got a job, but your work experience makes you the ideal candidate. The campaign is aimed at female flight attendants, just like you, who want to become pilots."

I frowned at him, confused. "You'd like me to participate in a movie?"

"No, no." He shook his head. "It's a publicity campaign. Short videos, pictures, posters, that sort of stuff."

"But I'm not based out of L.A.," I said, pushing the card and receipt toward him, hoping he'd grab them this time.

He did. "We're casting tomorrow and filming on Sunday. Very short-term gig. Possibly extra money if you get the part. Are you staying in town for the weekend?" he asked, his eyes now focusing on putting the credit card into its rightful slot in the black-leather wallet he was holding.

Is he serious? Maybe I'd get a chance to hook up with him... Then again, hard to compete with Exotic-Girl... but why not? Then I thought of Katrina. "Is this open to anyone?"

"Yeah, of course," he replied, now digging for something else in his wallet.

"I've got an acting friend who may be interested. Can she come, too?"

"The more the merrier," he said, pulling out a business card. "Tomorrow morning at 10 o'clock. This address," he said, pointing to the text that was printed on the front of the card.

"Thanks," I said, taking it from his hand.

"Hey! And me?" Exotic-Girl asked, apparently offended.

"Oh, of course you should come too! I was just about to mention it to you," I heard him say as I walked away, heading back toward the galley at the back of the plane.

1:45 p.m.

I almost didn't recognize Katrina when I saw her at the airport.

If it hadn't been for her jumping up and down and yelling out my name, I would have passed right by the silicone-breasted blonde woman in a mini-skirt and tank top.

"Katrina? What happened to you?"

Of course, I'd expected her to have changed. I'd seen some of her pictures on Facebook. I knew that she now flattened her naturally red and curly hair and that she'd dyed it blonde. But that body?

We hugged. She smelled of strawberries and cream. I pulled back, my hands holding hers, and had a good look at my friend.

"You look amazing!" I said while shaking my head in disbelief.

"Does that mean I looked awful before?" she asked. If I didn't know her, I would've worried about having offended her, but I knew it wasn't the case. She let go of my hands, her fake frown turned right-side up, and she finally explained. "Gotta put all the odds in my favor. Hollywood wants skinny blondes with big breasts. Here I am!" she exclaimed, hands on her hips, twisting her shoulders and posing à la Marilyn Monroe, her lips pursed in a sexy smooch.

"Wow. Good for you!"

"I gotta say that my tips at the bar have tripled since. Although I struggled to scrape the money I needed for the surgery, these babies have paid for themselves a couple of times over! But enough about that. Welcome to L.A. I'm so glad you'll be able to hang out with me. My boss gave me a couple of days off—don't ask what I had to do to get them—but I wanted to be around so we could catch up."

I wondered what she had to do to get time off. *Flash him her new breasts? Let him have a feel? Something else?*

"I thought we could relax and I could show you around town a bit. Are you hungry?" she asked.

I shrugged. "Sure, I could eat."

"Good, I've got a reservation at a raw-vegan bistro. You'll love it."

She started walking. I grabbed my wheeled bag and followed her toward the exit. I didn't know how she thought I would enjoy anything raw and vegan, considering we used to go out and share large plates of chicken wings, but I went along with her suggestion. If eating raw vegan food had helped shape her new body and rid her of a few pounds, it couldn't be bad.

After we crossed the automated doors and were greeted by a blended wave of warm air, exhaust, and smog, I announced my news to Katrina. "You won't believe it, but I've got us an audition for a publicity campaign tomorrow, if you're interested."

Her blue eyes went round. "Really? Awesome! What is it? And how did you..."

Cars driving by us made it hard for me to hear her. "Long story. I'll fill you in on the details on the way to the restaurant," I suggested as we crossed the road.

She nodded. "Awesome," she repeated.

7:30 a.m.

The warmth of the sun rays streaming in from the bare window woke me up. I opened my eyes. For a few seconds, I couldn't remember where I was, but then I saw Katrina lying next to me on the bed.

I rolled out of the pilled cotton sheets and placed my feet on the cracked tile floor on which the mattress rested. In front of me was a doorless, built-in closet where an assortment of plastic hangers were crammed, holding bright, colorful outfits. Piles of underwear, socks, and other clothes that weren't meant to be hung rested on the floor in a semi-organized fashion. Next to it, a large, unframed mirror leaned against the wall.

I heard water running in the room next door. *One of her two roommates taking a shower?*

"Hey," Katrina grunted in a raspy voice.

"Good morning," I said, turning to face her. "Did you sleep well?"

She nodded, her eyes blinking away her sleepiness. She cleared her throat then asked, "What time is it?"

I scanned the rest of her bedroom. No dresser or nightstand to support an alarm clock. I reached over to my purse, which I'd left against the wall next to my opened suitcase. I found my phone and looked at the screen. "7:30," I replied.

Katrina rubbed her face. "What time is that audition again?"

"Starts at 10 the man said."

As if someone had injected her with caffeine, Katrina jumped out of bed and rushed from the room. A second later, I heard banging on a door.

"Bunny! Hurry up and get out already. I've got an audition."

"You're not the only one. Wait your freaking turn, Kat!" a voice yelled over the running water.

Katrina came back and sat next to me on the bed, a defeated look on her face.

I tried to offer a comforting smile. "Not the best roommate relationship?"

"Nah," she said, raising her shoulders. "We're all trying to catch our big break. Jealousy gets the best of us at times. But it's okay."

She got back up and exhaled loudly and slowly, three times in a row. "I'll pick my clothing and do other things to get ready anyway."

8:15 a.m.

I put on a pair of jean shorts and a white T-shirt after taking a very short shower —Bunny had graciously used up all the hot water.

I was blow-drying my hair when Katrina walked back in, her hair wrapped in a pink cotton turban and her body barely covered by a matching towel, the corners of which she held under her armpit in an effort to keep her enlarged breasts from bursting out of it. I saw her lips move, so I turned off the hair-dryer.

"Is this what you're wearing to the audition?" she asked, pointing at my outfit with her free hand.

I took a glance at what I was wearing. "I didn't bring much clothing. Mostly shorts and T-shirts... and a bikini since I thought we might go to the beach."

"Believe me, from the hundreds of mostly unsuccessful auditions I've been to, you have to look sexier than that if you want to even stand a chance at getting the part. Why don't you pick something from my closet?" A smile grew on her face. "Now that I've got bigger boobs, my clothes will probably fit you."

9:15 a.m.

Dressed in a very short hot pink summer dress with spaghetti straps, I finally received Katrina's approval. She had donned a bright green tube dress that barely reached mid-thigh. My friend and I headed to the audition in the same Toyota she had owned since high school, many, many moons ago.

While driving and swerving her way through side roads and avoiding grid-locked streets, Katrina shared how her career was coming along—or not. She'd landed a few commercials and one-time appearances as a side-character in various TV shows, none of which I'd heard of. But her unrelenting enthusiasm and positivity were nothing short of impressive. *I'm happy she's got a part-time job to cover her living expenses.*

After a short detour caused by slightly inaccurate instructions provided by my phone's GPS app, we finally arrived at the address shown on the business card five minutes before the auditions were to start.

9:55 a.m.

A large cardboard sign stapled to a wooden post read "Capt. Dick Harding Flying School - Casting Auditions." The hand-written words were followed by an arrow. We headed in the direction indicated, then saw a few more smaller signs until we found ourselves on the third floor of a large office building.

We knew we'd reached our final destination when we walked into a sizable reception area where about fifty women, most of whom were dressed provocatively, sat on black plastic chairs filling out forms. *Guess Katrina was right about my outfit.* A strong aroma of mixed perfumes filled the air. Light background music sounded from a speaker in the corner next to us. I glanced around the room and recognized Exotic-Girl from the plane. She wore a mini-skirt and tank top. Before I could walk over to say, "Hi," a young woman in jeans and a Capt. Dick Harding Flying School T-shirt greeted us and handed each of us our own stack of forms and a pen. "Please take a seat and fill these out," she said.

We sat together near the back of the room and started filling out the forms. At first, it was nothing out of the ordinary: name, date of birth, social security number, previous acting experience, etc. But then, a few fields appeared odd to me.

"Why are they asking for my ethnicity, bra size, weight, and height?" I asked Katrina.

She shrugged. "That's common. Could be because the part calls for a particular body type, or maybe their outfits need to be tailored, so they're just saving themselves some back and forth, collecting the data they need now."

Makes sense, I guess.

Once we'd filled out all required information, we handed our paperwork to the same woman. She informed us that we could use one of the lockers to store our purses and other valuables if we so desired. The idea of lugging it all morning didn't really appeal to me, so I did and Katrina did the same. Then, we sat down to wait, our locker keys attached to our wrists.

I tried to make eye contact with Exotic-Girl, but sensed that she was avoiding my glance. I didn't want to bother her, so I gave up on the idea. I turned my attention to the other women in the room: some of them were repeating some tongue twisters, others were nonchalantly scooping their hands in their tops to adjust their breasts in their outfits, a couple of very young girls were fixing their make-up. I looked at Katrina: she was biting her nails.

"It'll be fine," I said, winking and tapping her on the knee.

"Do you know how much the part pays?" she asked me.

I shook my head. "No idea."

And just then, the lady we'd handed our forms to called for everyone's attention. "I'm going to read a list of names. If you hear yours, please proceed through the door behind me. If not, we thank you for your time and you're free to go home."

"Already?" I asked, surprised.

Katrina lifted her shoulders. "They're probably looking for a specific age group or ethnicity," she whispered to me.

The woman started listing names and Katrina grabbed my hand, squeezing it as though it would increase our odds.

10:40 a.m.

Having successfully made it past their pre-selection filter, Katrina and I joined the other lucky women behind the door, which opened onto a long and bare hallway painted light gray.

At the end of the corridor, just before another door, sat a short & skinny bald man who also wore a white Capt. Dick Harding Flying School T-shirt. He turned out to be responsible for the second part of the selection process. With a nod or a shake of the head, he picked which of us could go past the next door.

The woman in front of Katrina and me, a tall, strong and athletic brunette with a *don't-mess-with-me* attitude was turned away. Her traits immediately morphed into the same saddened expression that had colored the faces of the women who had been eliminated just a few minutes ago.

Thankfully, Katrina and I got the nod and proceeded into what appeared to be a large change room.

Hot pink flight attendant skirts as well as white short-sleeved shirts filled two large racks, and rows of black high-heeled shoes were neatly lined below them.

Katrina high-fived me. "We're doing great," she whispered in my ear.

No wonder it's hard to make it as an actress. We haven't even said a word yet! I counted the women in the room. We'd already dropped from the approximate fifty that had shown up to twenty-five. Exotic-Girl had also made it.

Another woman dressed in the flying school's T-shirt measured us around the breast, waist, and ass. She then yelled out our measurements to a young, effeminate man standing by the rack of clothes who, a minute later, would hand us the exact sizes we'd each need. We were ordered to change into the outfits.

About a dozen staff members, men and women, all in the same uniforms, were roaming the room, notepads in hand and talking to each other. I turned to Katrina, unsure about the procedure to follow. "Are there change rooms?"

"Probably not," she said after glimpsing the room.

The increased confidence and improved self-image I'd gained over the past few months proved worthwhile. Not that long ago, I would've been very, very uncomfortable getting undressed in front of that many men and women. But I was much more comfortable with my body now; the idea of changing in front of people even made a slight thrill go up my spine.

I started undoing the first of the many delicate buttons on the sexy summer dress I'd borrowed from Katrina while glancing around the room. Katrina pulled down her green dress in one swift motion before stepping out of it. Her large, perky silicone implants and white panties were soon covered by the white cotton shirt. About half-way done with my buttons, I met the glance of another woman for a second, but she kept scanning the room before shaking her head. She then walked out the way we'd come in.

The last of my tiny buttons undone—there must have been about twenty-five of those—I finally slipped out of my dress and put on the uniform I'd been handed. The pink polyester skirt ended three inches above my knees. The waist and hips fitted nicely enough. The white shirt, however, was a bit tight. The two chest-height buttons threatened to pop and fly across the room. I looked at Exotic-Girl, who stood a few feet away from me. Her breasts also pushed the confines of her shirt; the embroidered details of her red bra pushed through the fabric enough for a blind person to read their Braille-like contours.

"Okay, ladies. Once you're dressed, go find a pair of shoes that fits, then stand in line, ready for inspection," a man said.

The voice sounded familiar. I turned to see who it was, and I recognized the blond man from the plane.

"That's the casting director who told me about this," I whispered to Katrina.

She leaned toward me. "He's cute. Tall. Blond. Totally your type!"

He walked slowly in front of us, reminding me of a military official inspecting troops in a movie, except that his nod or shake meant whether or not we'd proceed to the next step in the audition.

"Hey, you made it," he said when he reached me in the line.

I smiled. "And I brought my friend Katrina," I said, pointing to her standing next to me.

"Katrina," he said, eyeing her up and down. "Nice."

Katrina and I both got the nod, and he continued his inspection of the other women past us. I overheard him greet Exotic-Girl. She was standing a few women down the line from us, giggling and grinning at the casting director. *Oh dear. That's the look of an infatuated young girl. She probably slept with him last night... Good for her. And it doesn't necessarily mean my odds are nil. It's not as though I'd want him for the rest of my life. I just want to experience him a little... And it's not as though I could have called him up yesterday anyway. What kind of a friend shows up, then says she's got other plans and heads out to meet a man instead of hanging out with the friend who's invited her?*

A few minutes later, the third round of the selection process was over and our count had officially dropped to twenty, including Katrina, Exotic-Girl and me.

The unsuccessful candidates were stripping out of their uniforms and donning their own clothes when the casting director told us to gather up around him.

11:00 a.m.

"Good morning, ladies," the director started. "First of all, thank you for coming to this audition and for looking so lovely. We're casting the role of a flight attendant this morning. It's for a print and video advertising campaign targeting female flight attendants who want to become pilots. Capt. Dick Harding Flying School is no regular aviation program. They're passionate about what they do. They hand-pick those who join their ranks. Only select women that meet very stringent entry criteria and who truly feel destined to become pilots are invited to join their school. Your performance here today will have to reflect that aching passion in your heart," he said, tapping on his chest. "You'll have to perform; you'll have to show us that you'd do a-ny-thing to join their ranks. A-ny-thing," he repeated, accentuating the syllables once more. "Are you ready to do that today?" he asked our group, his voice that of a coach trying to psych his football team up for a big game.

A few heads nodded, including mine.

The casting director frowned and shook his head. "Are you ready to act passionately and do anything for this part?" he repeated, this time yelling.

A resounding, "Yes," echoed from my mouth and that of the other women around me.

"Good," he said, grinning and nodding. "Now, please line up next to each other behind the tracks here." He pointed to an area of the floor near us. "Stand about two feet away from each other."

Once we were positioned in our appropriate spots, the casting director continued with his speech. "Our artistic vision for this campaign is very emotional and avant-garde. To visually represent your inner desire to become a pilot, we will tattoo wings on your heart, where the real pilot wings that you want will hopefully be pinned one day. So, please undo your shirt, and one of our assistants will apply a temporary tattoo above your left breast," he said before turning around to face the people who were standing behind him. He snapped his fingers.

A small group of men and women headed our way, each with a small pail, a rag, and a few other things in hand. A cameraman moved and started recording, a red light blinking from his gear.

We're being filmed now?

The short bald man who'd previously manned the hallway door stood in front of me, waiting for me to undress so he could apply the wing tattoo. I undid five buttons and opened my shirt to clear my left breast, then moved my bra strap out of the way.

"I gotta clean the skin first," he said before unwrapping an alcohol wipe from its envelope.

I nodded.

He unfolded a small rectangular tissue then brought it to the top of my breast to wipe the area. A faint smell of lemon reached my nose. He then placed the wet, used tissue in his short pocket. A second later, he grabbed the temporary tattoo, peeled off the plastic sheet covering the image, and then placed the wings against my skin, just above my breast. While he held the tattoo on me with one hand, he dipped the other into a small bucket and then pressed the cold wet rag on the tattoo area, patting the paper lining. A few drips dropped into my white bra.

"I gotta keep the paper wet for about thirty seconds," he said, patting some more, then soaking the rag into the pail. Once again, he brought it back to my chest and repeated the patting. I looked at his balding head, a few drips of sweat beaded on his forehead and a light musky smell mixed with a Cheetos aroma emanated from him. More cold water dripped into my bra. Every few seconds, just when the rag would start getting a little warmer—less freezing would be more accurate—the man would dip it into his pail again. *Really? Again? Does tattoo application require frigid water?*

I turned to look at Katrina, standing a couple of feet from me, receiving a similar treatment from a young woman. We exchanged smiles. Then the cold rag moved away from the tattoo area.

What the heck?

I looked down at my left breast. The man was now pressing his wet cold rag directly onto the center of my breast, making that part of my white bra transparent and forcing my nipple to harden even more. The bald man's eyes were glued on my breast. He had a slanted grin on his face, exposing a few yellow teeth. A tented bulge formed in his loose shorts. Although the thought of slapping the man crossed my mind, I didn't. Why risk ruining Katrina's odds... or mine? *The poor man isn't the handsomest. It may have been a while since he last saw a nipple that wasn't on his computer screen...*

"How are those tattoos coming along?" the casting director asked loudly in the background.

The man in front of me returned his wet rag up to the tattoo area.

"I'm gonna peel it off now," he said after licking his lips and bringing his eyes up by a few inches. He tugged on one edge of the paper and removed it, revealing a large set of beautiful golden pilot wings. "And now I have to keep the area wet for a little while, to make sure it won't peel off," he said before re-dipping the rag into the icy water pail.

Once again, his rag started in the tattoo area, but explored further south than it had to. His hand then went for an unrequested, full-hand squeeze of my breast.

"Hey!" I discreetly uttered. *What's going on in this guy's mind?*

He shrugged, then winked at me and told me I could button up my shirt again. He grabbed his things then walked away, still erect in his shorts.

I shook my head and brought my bra strap up then buttoned my blouse while glancing around me at the other women.

Am I the only one who got the creepy perverted treatment?

Hard to tell, but most had gotten their tattoo and were standing still, many braless with perky nipples poking through their tight white shirts. Very few wore bras.

Surely this isn't normal for an audition, right?

A couple of girls still had an assistant standing in front of them, but they appeared to be nearly done.

Dead center in front of our line of hopeful candidates, the casting director sat in a movie-director chair, a large monitor at his feet. The man I'd seen earlier, the one walking with a camera on his shoulder, had now relocated his gear to the dolly at one end of the rails.

A few minutes later, his camera anchored to the dolly, the cameraman started filming the first woman on the far right, about a dozen feet away from me.

"Dave, zoom in," the casting director ordered.

The cameraman moved his hand on his apparatus.

"No, I can't see the tattoo," the casting director started, shaking his head. He got up. "Ladies," he continued, now in a louder voice, "unbutton your shirts some more, so the camera can capture your new tattoo."

I obeyed, undoing two buttons and pulling the fabric away toward my shoulder. Women around me did the same.

"No, this won't do," the director said, his eyes still glued on the monitor in front of him. "I still can't see the full tattoo. Take off your shirts," he ordered.

I turned to Katrina. "This is normal?" I asked her while undoing the rest of my shirt's buttons.

She raised her shoulders and nodded.

Strange.

Katrina's enlarged breasts were fully exposed, her small nipples pointing straight forward. I looked around the room and less than half of us in hot-pink skirts and high heels had bras on.

Were women once again going through a revolution of sorts? Did I miss a social media campaign about women giving up wearing bras for one reason or another?

"Much better," the casting director said, still looking at the monitor in front of him. The cameraman crept his way along the tracks. About three women later, the casting director spoke again. "No, no, no." He shook his head. "Those with bra straps, we can't see the full tattoo. Take your bras off."

A couple of women walked out, this last request probably proving to be too much.

Katrina looked at me, and we both shrugged.

She leaned toward me and whispered, "Exposed breasts aren't a big deal. Common in auditions, really. And it's for the director's creative vision."

I obeyed, undoing the back clasp, then tossing my white bra at my feet, along with the shirt I'd removed earlier. I saw the man who had put on my tattoo standing a few feet behind the director. He was staring at me, another creepy grin on his face, a hand in his pocket. The fabric of his shorts may have been covering his erect dick, but it didn't hide the fact that he was touching himself right now. *Does his pocket have a big hole in it, allowing his hand to stroke his cock like that?*

I felt a shiver go up my spine, not from the bald, creepy man touching himself but from the cold breeze that had suddenly started blowing on us. I rubbed my goose-bump-covered arms in an effort to warm up.

"Stand tall, ladies," the casting director said, still looking at the monitor in front of him. "Bring those shoulders back. Imagine you're already a pilot. Your dream's come true! Show us how delighted you are to have gotten those pilot wings. Place your hands on your hips. Look up. Be proud!"

The cameraman kept moving slowly on the tracks in front of us.

"Now, that's what I'm talking about! Good work, ladies. Keep that position," the casting director said, now taking his eyes off of the monitor to look at us directly.

He stood up and, with two fingers, motioned for a Latino man with a Canon hung around his neck to come toward him.

"These tattoos are looking good, ladies. Pedro and I will now take your mug-shot to see how photogenic you are," the director said.

While the cameraman continued filming us from the dolly rig—he was about three-quarters done now—the casting director and Pedro headed to the first woman standing on the far right.

They spent a couple minutes in front of her. Being out of the cameraman's vision field, I turned my attention to what the cute director was doing. He was looking at the man's camera screen after the shots were taken, then he addressed the brunette in front of him. "Thank you for coming out. You're lovely, but it won't work for our campaign." The woman let out a loud sigh, then bent down to grab her bra and shirt from the floor in front of her. "Please return the uniform on your way out," he said with a large smile as she stormed away.

What was the deciding factor?

I turned to Katrina and kept silent. She too had seen that woman walk away. She raised her shoulders.

Once the photographer and casting director arrived in front of me. I returned to the pose, standing proud, pushing my breasts out, hands on my hips, looking at the camera. At first, the photographer was taking a picture of my face, then it was obvious most of his 'mug-shots' were in fact 'jug-shots.' The Latino man wasn't just taking a picture of the tattoo. He was aiming his Canon way too low for that, but the blonde lesbians I'd met in Mexico did tell me my breasts were awesome. Who better than them to know? *Let them have great shots of my beautiful girls.* I pushed my shoulders back even more, making eye contact with the blond hottie. He quietly nodded, a spark appearing in his eyes before winking at me. A sense of pride entered my mind. No... *Not pride. Probably lust.*

A minute later, the two men moved to Katrina. She was looking up, her tits bulging forward. I admired her enhanced breasts for a moment. I was glad she'd gotten a good boob job. With all of the horror stories I'd seen on TV with one nipple pointing left and the other down, or weird bumps deforming the natural drop-shaped breasts... The photographer took several shots—of her face but mostly her breasts—then the two men moved on to the next woman.

"Yeah!" she quietly said to me, exposing all of her whitened teeth in a smile and jumping up and down, her silicone twins bouncing in an unnatural rhythm. "We both still stand a chance!"

I smiled.

While I was a little baffled that my friend hadn't realized these men were just taking advantage of us—creative vision my ass—I decided there was no real harm being done.

I might as well enjoy myself in the process. Who knows, maybe this could turn into a date or one-night stand with the cute blond director?

The thought of seeing him naked moistened my panties.

12:15 p.m.

Pedro and Dave now done with the latest phase of the auditioning process, the remaining twelve of us—including Exotic-Girl, Katrina, and me—were once again ordered to gather around.

"Okay, ladies. You're doing fantastic," the casting director said, his large encouraging smile still decorating his rugged, handsome face. His crooked nose was really growing on me. "All of you still stand a very good chance at being hired for this publicity campaign. But we need to see your walking stroll so that we know if you can really portray the way a proud captain would walk to the departure gate, ready to pilot a large Boeing 747 to some exciting destination. Of course, the flight attendant's uniforms won't do for that. You'll have to change into a captain's jacket."

He snapped his fingers and the effeminate man rolled a new rack of clothing toward us. This time, it was filled with navy-blue uniforms.

The jackets were one-sized: men's small. We each grabbed one from the rack, then I stepped away from the crowd to strip and don the new outfit. Katrina joined me a few seconds later.

"I'm so excited," she whispered as she unzipped her skirt. "I rarely make it this far! There's only twelve of us. We stand a really good chance," she said, her eyes exploding with hope.

I smiled at her, putting on the pilot's jacket. *I can't crush her hopes. But maybe I'm just wrong. Who am I to tell, really... It could be a legit audition?*

"No pink skirts," the casting director yelled out.

The rack in front of us was now empty. No skirts therefore meant no bottoms at all.

"Keep those bras off as well," the director yelled out. Exotic-Girl dropped down the red lacy bra she'd picked up from the floor in front of her. "Nothing wrong with your lacy undergarments, ladies. But we don't want the color of them distracting us from the professional look of the uniform. You don't want to lower your odds at being selected for this role, right?"

I buttoned the double-breasted jacket and pulled on the front, trying to make it drape as best as possible on me, but it was all in vain. The jacket ended a couple of inches below my white panties. The V-opening of the flaps showed a good forty percent of my cleavage, but it wasn't supported by my underwire bra. *I can't say that my girls look as sexy now as they do when supported...*

"Okay, ladies," the casting director continued once all of us had donned the new uniform. "This next phase is really simple. All you have to do is walk in front of the green screen, rolling a carry-on bag behind you. Simple, right? But remember to smile and look proud. Any questions?" he asked.

I glanced around. The other women were shaking their heads, some trying to pull down the jacket a bit more, some trying to close the deep opening in the front to cover their breasts. The one-sized jacket appeared particularly short on one red-headed woman with a long torso; her blue boy-cut panties were half visible below it. One young and extremely large-breasted woman couldn't even cover her dark brown nipples with the lapels of her jacket.

Katrina and I stood sixth and seventh in line, just behind Exotic-Girl. The director sat a few feet away from the line of women waiting for their turn. The effeminate man brought a pilot's hat and a black wheeled suitcase to the first woman in line.

She strolled in front of the director a couple of times, following his orders, then passed the props to the next woman, who was eliminated right away. So was the one in front of Exotic-Girl. No reasons were voiced aloud, but the two women certainly didn't have the slenderest legs among our group.

On Exotic-Girl's first attempt at strolling past the screen, she was stopped by the director.

"No. Go back and try again," he said, pointing her back to our side of the screen. "Chin up, smile, look proud, but walk a little slower, please."

She repeated her stroll. "Good, but do it again, this time, running toward the gate as if you're urgently making your way to save a passenger's life."

I frowned at the unlikely suggestion, then took a few steps back to peek at the monitor sitting in front of the director to get an idea of what he was focusing his attention on. Exotic-Girl began her stroll again, the camera zoomed to frame her from neck to mid-thigh. We couldn't even see her face. Her bouncing tits and the barely covered red panties were the stars here.

"Great," the casting director said. "Pass the hat and luggage to the next woman."

It was now Katrina's turn. I returned to her just as she received the luggage prop. "Go for it, Kat. Be confident and proud," I whispered in her ear before squeezing her shoulder.

Katrina walked away toward the fake airport gate, black suitcase in tow, her blonde hair tucked under the captain's hat. She repeated the walk a couple of times, then the director announced it was my turn.

After a few strolls at varying speeds, I joined Katrina with the rest of the women who had passed the latest audition stage. To congratulate me, my friend high-fived me, which didn't go unnoticed by the director.

"Hey, girls. Do that again, but can you jump up in the air this time?"

Katrina and I looked at each other and nodded. I took a few steps back and we ran toward each other. We both jumped before our hands met in mid-air. I turned to look at the director and noticed a cameraman aiming his camera our way.

"That's wonderful, ladies," the director said. "Very representative of how it'd feel to graduate from the aviation school."

He called out louder this time, getting the attention of all of the women still auditioning.

"Ladies, you saw what these two just did? Pair up, then you'll run up to each other, jump up in the air, and high five each other, large smiles on your face. You've graduated. All of your hard, hard work has paid off."

Running up in high heels and then jumping up to high-five another person turned out to be quite a difficult task to do for many of us, but the cameraman and director were patient. After Katrina and I had redone the feat once more, I discreetly repositioned myself behind the cameraman, just to see what he was recording. As I suspected, he was zooming in on the edges of our jackets. Jumping with an arm raised was making them lift up, exposing our panties, and in this particular case, one woman's shaved pussy, since she didn't have any underwear on. Just the captain's jacket.

Katrina was standing a few feet from me, beaming and looking at the other contestants, apparently still clueless as to what was really going on. I walked over to her to chat while the last pair of women got ready for their camera time.

"So, this... audition," I started whispering in her ear. "Does it follow a similar process to what you've been through before?"

She raised her shoulders and eyebrows. "So far, most of it seems quite common. I've had to do similar things in previous interviews. Not always in group settings, though. Directors always have a creative vision, and they must ensure the actors they hire will properly portray their vision. Makes sense, no?"

I nodded.

Why shatter my friend's hopes? What's the harm in letting her think she still stands a chance at being hired? She obviously doesn't mind being objectified... It could even boost her self-confidence for future auditions? After all, she and I are now part of the top ten finalists for this "advertising gig"... if we can call it that.

1:45 p.m.

After a brief lunch break—they'd provided their crew and us, the ten remaining candidates, with an assortment of pastries, mini-sandwiches, raw veggies, and dips—we were ordered to change back into our flight attendant's pink uniforms and gather around the casting director yet again.

"Hope you enjoyed your free meal. Now, we'll record a demo lesson. Please take a seat in the classroom next door." He motioned for us to head toward the back of the lunch room.

The classroom setting was reminiscent of one of those mini university auditoriums, as I'd seen them in movies, with rows of chairs, each higher than the other. A muscular man stood behind a large wooden stand that occupied the middle of the floor in front of an immaculate white board that read *AVIATION 101* in bold black letters. The tanned, crew-cut, brown-haired man wore a tight white, short-sleeved shirt that almost ripped on his carved biceps. Pilot wings were pinned above his left breast pocket.

We each took a seat.

"He's cute," Katrina whispered in my ear as the director walked to chat with the instructor. "I wouldn't mind getting private lessons from him!"

I smiled in agreement. He was definitely handsome, although a little too young for me.

The cameraman stood with his gear on his shoulder; he was focusing on the instructor. Upon hearing the director's cue, the hot instructor smiled, welcomed us, then started his lesson about the four forces acting on planes: lift, weight, thrust, and drag. The instructor read long-winded definitions from a teleprompter in front of him.

"...When the thrust becomes greater than the drag, the plane accelerates forward, which is best explained by Newton's Second Law of Motion..."

I was trying to pay attention to his lesson, but his physique was more interesting than his words. I could only imagine how defined his abdominals had to be. *Does he have a six- or an eight-pack? He probably spends the rest of his waking hours lifting weights at the gym... or doing whatever woman throws herself at him.*

That had to happen quite often for such a stud. And he even sounded intelligent while reading those lines. I was unsure if he was as smart as he sounded, but I gave him the benefit of the doubt. My eyes veered toward the blond director, now sitting in the front row. He was more my type. Probably very intelligent, although he was clearly a manipulative man who excelled at fooling women and getting them naked in front of a camera... not the most respectful of men... but just looking at him made me tingle and got me wet where it mattered. *Unsure why exactly. Maybe it's his air of power... or something about his crooked nose... Is it the result of some well-deserved punch in the face by one of his lovers' husbands?*

"...Newton's Laws and Bernoulli's Principle explain how lift is generated..." the instructor continued. I returned my focus to him. His lips moved, but I didn't want to pay attention to his words.

Then, as if he'd realized how much of a bore he was, he grabbed a pile of papers from the stand in front of him and waved them in the air.

"I hope you've been listening because it's now time for a pop quiz!" he said, finally moving from behind the lectern, where he'd remained since the beginning of his lecture, which had started about ten minutes ago.

What I saw surprised me. I had expected him to wear the traditional navy-blue or black pants that pilots normally wore, but instead, he had on tight white shorts, probably made of a mix of Spandex, rayon, or similar. His mini shorts clung to his every curve and groove, leaving nothing to the imagination. His shirt was tucked in, a silver buckle differentiating where the shirt ended and where the shorts began, but something else hadn't quite been tucked all the way in: his flaccid penis was running down his right thigh, and its surprising length—even at rest—meant that its tip was protruding, as if to say hello.

Quiet giggles and whispers echoed around me. It appeared we were all staring at the same part of his beautiful anatomy, but the instructor managed to keep his concentration and walked toward us to hand out quizzes, along with pencils.

"What the...?" Katrina asked as she poked me in the ribs.

"Still think this is a regular audition?" I asked her in a whisper.

She rolled her eyes before shaking her head. "...But he's so hot!"

Hot (and well-hung) actors are probably a requirement if the director wants his porn movies to be popular.

"Cut!" the director called out.

A tall Asian woman used the director's word as her cue to stand up and leave. "I'm out," she said before exiting the room. The brunette sitting next to her hesitated for a few seconds, then got up and followed her out.

I looked at Katrina, wondering if she was still interested. She raised her shoulders. "Some famous actresses had their break in porn," she whispered. "Are you still in? I'd understand if you wanted out."

"Why not," I said just as the hot guy handed me a piece of paper, his eyes glued on Katrina next to me. Katrina's pop quiz was delivered with a smile and a wink, then the hot instructor continued handing his sheets to the remaining women. "I'm curious to see how far they'll go... And so far, the experience has been... entertaining to say the least," I whispered to Katrina.

"Awesome. And maybe one of us will get the part... And maybe I can get this hot guy's phone number." Katrina's eyes were now focused on the instructor's firm glutes as he headed back to his stand.

While I was pretty sure there wasn't going to be a *part* other than what we were currently doing for free (or, to be more accurate, in exchange for a free lunch), I had no doubt she'd be able to get that man's number.

"Okay, ladies," the director, who had moved and now stood in front of the podium, called out. "You've each received a sheet of paper. On it are script lines, questions for you to ask the instructor. Take a few minutes now to familiarize yourself with your question and be ready to ask it aloud without reading from the paper. Remember, we're looking for passionate students! We'll record your performance to see how you come across on video."

I looked at mine:

I'm a woman who dreams to become a pilot.
Can I do it in such a men's world?

It wasn't going to be too hard to memorize. I concentrated on my lines and mentally repeated them for a few minutes until I no longer needed my piece of paper.

The casting director walked around the classroom while we were preparing. Some women were rehearsing aloud, and he was giving them feedback if and when asked.

No point in practicing aloud. I'll just wait my turn and do it live.

A few more minutes went by, then the classroom got quiet again. The eight of us that remained were ready for this next part. My cute crooked-nosed crush got up and stood next to the instructor before addressing us again.

"So, there's a number in the top-right corner of your sheet. We'll use this number to determine the order. Whoever has number one can come down here and stand next to the instructor."

Exotic-Girl stood up and, in her four-inch heels, slowly walked down the steps that separated her from the two handsome men. The director had returned to his seat by the time she arrived next to the instructor. She fluffed her ebony hair over her shoulders, straightened her back, pushing her breasts out in the process, then smacked her bright red luscious lips.

"Ready?" the director asked her.

"Yes," she replied, all smiles.

"Are you ready, Nick?" the director asked the instructor.

He inhaled deeply, then nodded.

The director turned his attention to Exotic-Girl again. "Okay, stand next to him, both of you facing the camera, and touch him on the forearm when you ask your question. Clear?"

Exotic-Girl nodded.

"And... Action!"

She flicked her eyelashes at the instructor, then her delicate hand grabbed his tanned, muscular forearm.

"But learning to be a pilot... it's hard, right?" she asked with puppy eyes.

He wrapped his arm around her waist as he replied, his eyes locked on her breasts, which heaved noticeably as she breathed. Maybe the wave-like motion of her chest was caused by the stress of the audition. Or it could have been a natural reflex based on her innate feminine sex appeal or the pheromone effect of standing next to a hottie in tight white shorts.

"A lot of things are hard here," he said before pausing, as though concentrating on something. His other hand went to the side of his own waist, in a Mr.-Clean-esque pose. My own eyes diverted to what was happening in his shorts: his dick elongated and widened in girth. A few glorious inches were now fully exposed out of his shorts, the fabric barely able to keep it from going up. I realized my jaw had dropped a second later, just as he pulled on the waist of his shorts and the fabric ripped, letting his full manhood bounce up, exposing his clean-shaven genitals.

The cameraman was recording all of it: the half-naked man ready for action, Exotic-Girl's surprised expression, the audience's whispers and utters, as well as three of the remaining candidates leaving the group, clearly offended.

"Cut!" the director said. "Great job. On to number two. Please come down."

A bleached-blonde girl who couldn't be older than eighteen or nineteen walked down and stood next to the erect instructor. She blushed, then turned and focused her attention on the director.

"Ready?" the director asked both parties.

She nodded and so did he.

"And... Action!"

She turned to look at the instructor, her eyes locked with his. "How's Capt. Dick Harding Flying School different from the other aviation schools in town?" she asked.

He turned to the cameraman. "We stand behind our students, all the way," he said before taking a couple of steps to reposition himself behind the tall blonde woman, his hands grabbing her by the hips. Her innocent eyes suddenly widened and her already blushing cheeks somehow cranked up to crimson; his erect dick had clearly poked her somewhere. From where I sat, I couldn't quite tell if any direct skin contact had occurred, but the cameraman was moving around to record the best angle.

"Cut, great job. Great reaction," the director said to the young girl. "It's good when actors express their emotions like that. You can go back to your seat." He turned to face the rest of us. "Who's number three?"

Nobody moved, except to look around.

The director raised his shoulders. "She must have left already. Better odds for those who remain! Number four?"

Katrina stood up and squeezed behind me on the way to the aisle.

"You go, girl," I whispered to her as she walked by. I didn't know what her question was going to be, but I was excited. I was about to experience the first real acting part of the audition for my childhood friend.

Katrina stood next to the hot instructor, who whispered something in her ear. She pulled back to make eye contact with him and nodded, a large grin on her face.

Did he ask her out on a date? When she started unbuttoning her shirt, I realized his question had to have been different. The last button undone, she removed her shirt and tossed it on the ground. Her exposed tits had the effect of scaring away one more candidate, who left quietly through the back door. *The erect dick hadn't clued her in?* Only four of us remained.

The director addressed Katrina. "You stand over there and look my way. For number four, you'll ask me your question, and the instructor will be behind you, off camera, until he replies. Are you ready?"

They both positioned themselves according to the director's instructions, then the recording began.

"What can I expect from Capt. Dick Harding Flying School?" Katrina asked.

"Cut!"

Katrina sent the scared glance of a hunted bunny my way. *What? What did she do wrong? Her question sounded natural.* The director explained himself immediately.

"It'd be better if you raised your hand to ask your question. You did well, just raise your hand first, then repeat the question the way you did it a second ago. It was great."

A sigh of relief came out of both her mouth and mine. I turned my attention to the monitor at the director's feet. It showed the cameraman's live output. Katrina's entire body was framed in the shot, alone. The instructor was standing just out of view. When the director called "Action!" she raised her hand, making one of her augmented breasts go higher than the other, then she repeated her question. "What can I expect from the Capt. Dick Harding Flying School?"

She lowered her arm and a second passed. Still hard, Hot-Instructor walked into the shot. He stood behind her, cupped Katrina's breasts and answered, looking directly at the cameraman. "We offer one-on-one support. With us, you'll be in good hands." He gave her breasts a gentle squeeze.

The camera zoomed in on the both of them: her breasts and his hands now the only visible body parts.

"Cut! Good work, both of you."

Katrina smiled and bent down to grab her shirt. Hot-Instructor slapped her on the ass and she jumped back up. "Hey!"

"Couldn't resist," he said.

She smiled at him, then whispered something in his ear as she buttoned up her shirt. He nodded, then she walked back up the steps and returned to her seat, squeezing my shoulder when she passed behind me.

"Got a date with him tonight!" she said.

I smiled at her. *At least one good thing will come out of this for Katrina!*

"Okay," the director said after standing up and turning to face us. He scanned the room, as though counting how many gullible want-to-be-actresses were still present. "Looks like we have one left to go. Number five or whatever your number is."

I got up and walked down to center stage, next to Hot-Instructor. I wondered what sexual innuendo they had planned for my particular question. I looked at the instructor's erect member and felt my pussy twitch. I turned my attention to the other hottie, my crooked-nose director, to await his instructions.

"What question do you have?" he asked.

"Seven," I said.

He flipped through the flash cards he held and read some hand-written notes. He looked back up at me, a large grin on this face and a sparkle in his eye. "Perfect. Looking forward to this. Same as your friend. Address the camera, and the instructor will come in later."

I nodded.

"Ready? And... Action!"

I looked directly at the camera and asked my question: "I'm a woman who dreams to become a pilot—"

"Cut!"

"No, if you really dream to be a pilot, you need to have that desperate desire in your eyes. I need more passion. Show me you're CRAVING it. Imagine that huge airplane in the air. You want to be in control, you want to be the one in charge. You want to be a pilot!"

He got up and walked toward me. His hands pushed my shoulders back, and I pushed my breasts forward. *More confidence, more pride.* As I did so, however, my top button gave up—the tightness of the shirt proved to be too much for the poor piece of thread that had held the button in place for so long already.

"Ah!" the director said as the button hit him on the chest. "Call that a sign. Let's unbutton your shirt and expose your tattoo. That will help convey your inner drive to become a pilot."

His fingers unbuttoned my shirt, his eyes locked onto mine, his smile crooked. Electric currents flooded the small space between us. I wanted him and he knew it. The last button undone, he peeled off my shirt, his fingers brushing against my arms and FedExing a thrill all the way down to my pussy.

He took a step back and eyed me from head to toe. "Great. Now keep those shoulders back and repeat your question. Move your feet shoulder-width apart, you'll look more confident. Do it again... with passion this time!"

I inhaled deeply and spread my legs as he said, although that wasn't a natural pose. Who stands with their feet shoulder apart in a mini-skirt? I shook the idea out of my head, rolled my shoulders back, then inhaled deeply again before staring at the camera.

"I'm a woman who dreams to become a pilot. Can I do it in such a men's world?"

The instructor walked toward me, and I turned my head to face him.

"You're definitely a woman, and I can see how much you want to be a pilot," he said, lowering my bra strap to expose my tattoo. He slowly moved behind me, walking away from the cameraman, who was repositioning himself. The instructor undid my bra and helped it slide down my arms. It dropped on the floor with a light noise, but my own breathing was now getting louder, deeper. My heart started racing.

"It's also a men's world, that's for sure," the instructor said as he hiked up my skirt. Then, he placed his hands on my hips and thrust his pelvis forward, pushing his erect member between my legs, poking my warm, wet panties. "I'll personally stand behind you and make all your dreams come true," he said. His dick twitched, and I couldn't prevent cock-hungry moans from leaving my lips. He bent me forward, pushing my body into a fold, letting my breasts hang loose. "You can do it in a men's world, and we'll do it together," he said, thrusting his erect member back and forth, rubbing it against my underwear.

"Cut! Wonderful!" the director said, bringing me back to reality. The instructor let go of me and walked away. I lowered my skirt to its normal height, then picked up my clothing from the floor. After putting on my bra, I walked back to my seat, shirt in hand.

"Whoa, girl! What happened to the shy, reserved girl I used to know? I never thought you'd be comfortable doing that! What happened to you?"

I buttoned my shirt, trying to think of a way to answer my friend's question when the hot director stood up and addressed us again.

"Good job girls. The four of you who are still here have done a fantastic job in this audition so far. We only have one more scenario to go through with you before we elect the lucky one who will be representing Capt. Dick Harding Flying School for their next publicity campaign. We're talking about television, printed brochures, the whole works... and it pays well! This could be your stepping stone to a great acting career."

Katrina looked at me, her eyes spilling with optimism and unfulfilled dreams, her smile larger than ever. "One in four!"

Seriously? Katrina's this naive?

"Let's take a short break and meet again in the lunch room in fifteen," the director said before exiting the room.

3:45 p.m.

"Now, for the last part of the interview, we'll take you to a simulator. Obviously, we couldn't bring the real one here, but we've got a fairly large device in a private room and we'll have to do this last part of the interview individually so we can finally select the best candidate to represent the school."

The casting director pointed at Katrina.

"We'll start with you." He turned to the rest of us before continuing. "Please return to the waiting room in the mean time. Someone will come and get you."

I watched Katrina go past a door, then I headed back as instructed.

Using the key that was still wrapped around my wrist, I retrieved my purse, then took a seat and read a few pages of an e-book on my phone.

Two chapters later, Katrina's voice broke the spell my crime thriller had put me under. I looked up. Her cheeks were blushed, her hair a little jumbled.

"Your turn," she said, pointing her hand toward the hallway.

I wanted to ask how it went, but she interrupted me before I even began. "Don't make them wait!"

I placed my phone back in my purse and handed it to her before making my way to the private room I'd seen Katrina disappear into thirty minutes ago.

4:15 p.m.

I knocked and let myself in. After pushing the door open midway, my eyes couldn't help but focus on the large red plane sitting in the middle of the small room, surrounded by bright lights and reflective screens. The plane was reminiscent of one of those kid rides in shopping malls, but adult-sized and mounted on a much higher pole. A small step-ladder had been placed next to it. *Am I supposed to climb on this thing now?*

I scanned the rest of the room. My crooked-nose crush was sitting in his director chair, and near him were two cameramen and the instructor, in a bathrobe this time. All of them appeared ready for recording this last part of my interview, whatever it entailed.

Why am I doing this again? I have no real desire to get the part, since there is no part to be had anyway. But my genitals certainly wanted a piece of that director.

"Are you ready?" he asked, flashing a big smile at me.

Now's my chance.

"Listen, could we chat for a second?"

He shrugged then nodded.

"In private?" I asked.

After frowning for half a second, he requested that his crew get out, including Creepy Guy, who had been hiding, standing in a dark corner of the room until now.

Once all of them had gone, I walked up to the cute blond director. He got up before I reached his chair.

"Listen, I know this isn't real," I said.

"What do you mean?"

I lifted my fingers to wrap the rest of my words in air quotes. "Your audition for the—"

"Come on, you're so close. One in four! All you have to do is ride that plane. It's actually a lot of fun, like a carnival ride."

Curiosity had the best of me. "Really?"

He pressed a button on the small remote he held and the thing started moving. It went up and down, slowly at first, in a wave-like motion. It tilted a little to the left, then to the right... Then the speed increased, along with the sound of hydraulics or whatever was powering the contraption. The now jerky motion clued me in as to what it really was: a disguised mechanical bull like those used in country bars to test out the patrons' bull-riding skills.

"All you have to do is ride it—naked—smile and say one line: "Join me at Capt. Dick Harding Flying School, where fun is part of every lesson.""

I could imagine what the recorded video would be like. *Nothing but bouncing breasts. How uncomfortable would it be?*

"Listen, if you want to see me fully naked, all you have to do is ask," I said, my eyes fixed on his as I slowly undid my shirt, then tossed it on the floor. I took a step forward to close the gap between us then looked down to his waist. I undid his belt; he let me. I could hear his breathing getting louder and I could feel its warmth on my right cheek. I undid the metal button then slid down his zipper, the familiar sound only serving to increase my horniness. I couldn't wait to see what he kept hidden in his trousers, underneath the now visible black underpants.

"Is that so?" he finally said, his finger lifting my chin and forcing me to look at him again. His eyes were calculating. "So you really won't ride the plane? You're so close to getting the part."

Unbelievable. He's sticking to his story, still?

"I'd rather let my friend Katrina get the part, but..." I traced a finger down his chest from his collarbone to his waist. "I'd be satisfied with you doing me instead. Right here, right now. What do you say?"

His hands reached behind my back and undid my bra.

Finally!

Moments later, after having disrobed each other fully, he bent down to the floor to reach into his pant pocket and retrieve a condom. His erect and soon-to-be-covered cock was at the ready, strangely showing a slight bent comparable with the crook in his nose.

His lips swallowed mine without much of a prelude, as though he shared the same urges I felt toward him. My hungry lust, fueled by a full-day of partial nudity and tacky porn lines, could have lit a forest on fire.

I don't recall how we made it to the wall, but I clearly remember having my legs wrapped around his waist when he thrust his swollen cock into me. A loud groan escaped my lips as my insides parted to welcome his large cock.

"You're so fucking wet," he whispered between two grunts. "And tight... Holy shit..."

Squeezed between him and the wall behind me, my back couldn't arch the way I wanted it to, but it didn't matter. I dug my finger in his tanned, hairless pecks. He was looking down, between my tits, staring at his own cock coming in and out of me.

His breath smelled of onion and curry, but it didn't matter. All I could think of was how to maximize my pleasure. I was already so close to the edge.

I let go of him and attacked my clit with frenzy, allowing myself to reach an orgasm before it was too late. I could hear the cadence of his breathing and grunts change. He too was about to come. My other hand squeezed one of my nipples just as he gave me the final push, my pussy throbbing with pleasure.

5:45 p.m.

When I returned to the waiting room a few minutes later, once again dressed, fully satisfied and most likely rosy-cheeked, I headed toward Katrina. She was chatting with the instructor, who was still wearing his bathrobe. Katrina whispered something in his ear, then got up and walked out with me.

As we were about to leave the room, the young woman who had welcomed us earlier in the day addressed us again.

"Ladies, thanks for your time. We'll contact the lucky one by phone at 9 a.m. tomorrow morning."

Katrina sent a hopeful smile my way before turning quickly to wave goodbye to the instructor, who winked at her.

10:05 a.m.

Staring at myself in the airport bathroom mirror, dressed in my real flight attendant's uniform, I couldn't help but mentally review what my relaxed getaway weekend had turned into.

Katrina and I never got a call—no surprise there. Lesson learned in getting screwed—both literally and figuratively—by manipulative, cunning... and good-looking men from L.A.

I was unsure if Katrina'd gotten any wiser from it...

Deep down, I knew she'd find success in this industry one way or another. Next time I'd see her could be on the big screen... or online porn. She had the body for it. I wouldn't judge her for making money using the talents given to her at birth... and those added by that skilled plastic surgeon.

Yeah, this past weekend had definitely offered entertainment in ways I hadn't imagined it would.

MY XXX EXPERIENCE

USA

THE PLAN

I GOTTA SAY that re-reading this particular entry always gets me hard. And she's into tall blond men? She'll love doing me when I finally find her! This time, she's at least left a few decent clues behind. I know she's not based out of L.A., which isn't the most useful bit of information, but it's a start. My options for tracking her down are as follows:

OPTION 1: Use Facebook to find an L.A. actress named Katrina.

If I find one of her friends on Facebook, I could then go through her list of friends to find her (although I still don't know what she looks like). Facebook's search functionality to 'Find a woman named Katrina who lives in Los Angeles' may work, but would entail hours—if not days—of research. And what if her friend goes by Kate, Katie, Kat or some other nickname on Facebook?
Likelihood of success: Close to nil.

OPTION 2: Go to Los Angeles and find the aviation school.

I've got a name, I've got a town. An Internet search didn't bring up anything, though. Probably not a real school, just a scam made up by the casting agency.
Likelihood of success: Low.

OPTION 3: Go to L.A. and find the casting director.

Once again, I don't have much to go on, but I do have a description of the blond director. Feet on the ground and a few questions to the right people may work.

Likelihood of success: Low to average.

City of Angels, here I come.

You know my mysterious stewardess's identity. Get ready to share that secret with me!

WHAT HAPPENED

Since I fly to LAX fairly regularly, I looked at my upcoming schedule and booked myself a nice hotel room for three days and two nights at the next available opportunity.

Sunny weather, palm trees, and beautiful people welcomed my gaze the minute I exited the airport. Sun rays—albeit hindered by the layer of haze—warmed my exposed skin. I put on my sunglasses and soon realized I should get out of my pilot's uniform and put on something more comfortable so I could blend in a bit more with the crowd.

I drove down to my Santa Monica hotel in the convertible I'd rented. While waiting for a traffic light to change near my destination, I smiled at a gorgeous brunette standing on a street corner. She wore the tiniest bikini top, sexy torn-up jean shorts, and a pair of rollerblades. Her toned skin had been kissed by weeks (or months?) of sunshine. *How I'd like to have a lick and taste her sweet goodness* L.A. certainly had more than its fair share of sexy residents I'd like to get acquainted with.

But my luck may have ended there, right at that traffic light.

After checking in at my hotel and donning a pair of white cotton shorts and a light blue polo shirt, I headed into town to visit my first of several talent agencies. Finding the right casting director in L.A. was more difficult than finding a needle in the proverbial haystack, even though I thought I had a good metal detector to help me with my task. How many casting directors could meet the exact physical description I had? I doubted crooked noses had become a fashionable item among the list of plastic surgeons' offerings in the area.

I did my best.

My first two days were spent digging, calling, visiting. I met with casting directors, talent agents, actors... I talked with anyone and everyone who could have possibly known the devious, crooked-nosed casting director.

My evenings were spent planning my days, scanning the local newspapers and online bulletins for shady casting calls and re-reading my stewardess's journal for clues I might have missed.

But my L.A. trip finally got interesting when I least expected it.

Here's what happened on my last day in Los Angeles.

12:16 p.m.

With less than twenty hours left in this town, I was nearly ready to give up. While meandering to my parked car after yet another fruitless chat with an agent, an airplane-themed diner captured my attention.

Should I have another look at today's classifieds? I needed something. Another possible lead... Caffeine and food would certainly not hurt either.

I crossed the road and pulled open the diner's glass door, triggering a chime. Despite the deep-fried fish aroma tinted with burnt coffee that instantly reached my nostrils, the restaurant seemed popular: most tables were occupied, but two spots were available at the counter. So I walked in and sat on one of the old-fashioned stainless-steel stools padded with scratched up red leather.

A short and chubby waitress with a fraying gray chignon and dark wrinkly bags under her eyes came to me, coffee in hand. She wore a stained white apron over a black uniform.

"Coffee? Menu?" she asked, as expressive as the pot she was holding.

"Yes to both," I replied, smiling at her, hoping for a hint of amiability. It was in vain.

She reached across the counter, then underneath it, before pulling up a one-page laminated menu, which she handed to me. She flipped the empty mug that rested upside down on my paper placemat and poured me a steaming cup of coffee, then walked away, leaving me alone to browse the diner's slim food offerings. Most of the items were deep-fried.

I looked to my left and saw the remains of a burger and fries on the next patron's plate. Their fries appeared to be home-made and crisp. It had been a while since I'd indulged. *Why not?*

I placed my order when the waitress came back. Then I pivoted on my stool, taking in the aviation-themed decorations that included an antique wooden propeller, a wing stripped of its skin and paneling, showing the exposed ribs and stringers, and a dozen old picture frames filled with black and white images of the Wright brothers, an Antonov biplane picture, and lots of warplane photographs. I left my stool for a minute to go and grab one of the newspapers resting on a ledge by the door.

I returned to my seat with the mangled paper. It took me a few seconds to find the classifieds section, which I scanned. It was the same ads I'd already looked at this morning. I'd already talked to those people today. Nothing I'd missed. *Damn it.*

The waitress arrived with my plate just as I folded the useless newspaper. I thanked the emotionless woman, but she ignored me, obviously not keen on getting a tip. The burger did look juicy though. I lifted the top bun to include the side pickle I'd been given and then pressed all of the juicy bits with both my hands as I raised it to my mouth. The first bite was as tasty as expected, leaving a trail of greasy liquid dripping down my chin. I was chewing and enjoying every morsel while I let my eyes settle on the wall in front of me, which was littered with over a hundred business cards. I took my second bite when I saw something that nearly made me choke. Among the cards that were displayed in exchange for a free slice of pie and the right to be contacted by the diner for future promotions (according to a large sign on the same board) was pinned an exposed breast with tattooed wings above it, just like the photo shots that my stewardess had described.

I called up my waitress, and she immediately refilled my cup of coffee, at first ignoring my question, but then I begged her to let me see one of the business cards.

"No can do."

I slid her a twenty-dollar bill and asked again.

"The tit?" she asked.

I nodded.

She walked behind the counter, put down her pot of coffee, and then let out a sigh. She reached up and unpinned the card I wanted from the board then handed it to me. "I need it back," she said, holding the card between us, her eyes threatening me with shrouded, thunderous anger.

I nodded some more, trying to appease her, and she finally let go of the card.

I brought it closer and beamed as I recognized the beautiful breast I'd seen in the Mexico group selfie the hot lesbians had taken. The erect nipple, the subtle shades of light burgundy coloring her areola before the lightly tanned fleshy breast. It was tear-shaped, the perfect breast. A perfect C-cup, indeed. I took a picture of both the front and back of the Capt. Jack Harding Flying School business card and handed it back to the waitress. She sighed again, shook her head, and pinned it back where it had been minutes before.

She's probably made more money from showing that card than from her tips.

I finished and paid for my meal while trying to plan my next move. I had a phone number (no address), but I was pretty sure it wasn't going to be of any use.

After leaving the diner, I dialed the L.A. number and waited, pacing the sidewalk. Seconds later, I got my answer: an automated phone greeting announced the number had been disconnected. *Big surprise there.*

But two things were for sure: 1- It could have been the casting director or any one of his employees, but someone with that casting crew had been around this part of town in person; and 2- The photos taken that day had been published.

Could the video footage have ended up on the porn market? I didn't know how the other three finalists had finished their private audition, but I wouldn't be surprised if actual fucking had taken place. Based on the stewardess's journal entries, they'd recorded enough tacky lines for the movie intro. The instructor had been present for the final bit, ready for action in a robe... Published video footage could very well exist!

I decided to investigate this neighborhood more thoroughly. Google maps activated on my phone, I looked at my current location then searched for the nearest porn store.

1:40 p.m.

About fifteen minutes later, I saw XXX in bright red neon above a tinted glass door. I opened the metal-bar protected door and walked into the shop.

The store was much larger than it looked from the street. Dozens of shelves were staggered at various heights on the walls, displaying dildos, whips, and other adult toys. Five clothing racks held various latex, leather, and old-fashioned lace outfits for men and women. On the right, three aisles of movie cases covered the entire depth of the store, and on the left stood a Goth-looking cashier with pearl-like skin and long ebony hair. She stood behind the counter, surrounded by locked glass enclosures that displayed higher priced items. She wore a black leather top with a built-in girdle that pushed her fleshy breasts up. She deserved a closer look.

I walked to the counter and inquired if they carried porn movies featuring flight attendants.

"If that's what you're into. Of course," she said, her bright, luscious red lips moving and making me fantasize about having them wrapped around my cock. She winked, then folded her body over the counter, granting me the best possible view of her pushed-up breasts. She then pointed to the shelves where I could find everything I needed. "End of second aisle."

I took my eyes away from her tits and smiled, thanking her. I then walked away toward the videos.

I stood in the section she'd indicated and examined the tape and DVD covers that lined the shelves. It seemed both options were mixed together. Themes were obviously more important to them than movie format. I tried to find a cover with the school logo or an image I'd recognize, but couldn't, so I resorted to reading the descriptions at the backs of the cases.

About five minutes later, I noticed another man slowly approaching my section. He wore a long trench coat and sunglasses. Was he one of those perverts who flashed people in public? Why else would he wear a trench coat in 85-degree weather, on a bright sunny day? I didn't want to stay long enough to find out, so I scooped out every one of the tapes and DVDs that were related to my needs and headed to the cashier.

I didn't recall having seen a VCR or DVD player in my hotel room, but the Goth-cashier was kind enough to offer VCR/DVD player rentals as well, which I gladly accepted and paid for. Necessary wires and all.

She placed the items in a large canvass bag—thankfully unbranded—then winked at me as she handed me my rented goods.

"Thanks and enjoy!" she said.

3:00 p.m.

Call it excitement, anticipation, or whatever else, but once in my hotel room, after rushing to hook up the rented DVD player, I froze.

Is today the day I finally uncover her identity? Will I finally get to see her body and look at her face on video?

I lined up all of my rented cases on top of my bed. There were twelve of them: eight DVDs and four tapes. Although none of the covers seemed to have been produced by the Capt. Jack Harding Aviation School, it was worth a try. (Not that I ever needed a reason to watch porn, but it was nice to actually *have* one.)

So I came up with a plan: I'd start with the less likely videos (i.e., the more professional looking covers), then work my way to the shadiest/crappiest covers. Yes, I was potentially keeping the best—or the very worst—for last.

I got in a quick shower, donned the fluffy robe that the hotel had provided, and inserted the first DVD in the machine. After navigating my way through the menu, I pressed play, then turned down the volume before sitting on the edge of my bed, remote in hand.

I watched the first two on 4X speed, resisting the instinct to beat off. The bouncing images were exciting enough, but my mind hadn't yet seen anything close to what the stewardess had described in her journal. Sure, lots of beautiful tits, inviting pussies, tight asses, and luscious lips, but nothing close to the images I was looking for.

I continued working my way through the other DVDs, limiting myself to the first ten minutes of each video. I set aside one that featured a blonde with a tiny ass and humongous tits as my back-up plan. If the stewardess didn't turn up, I'd sure love to give her a mental go.

Ninety minutes later, my pile of DVDs was all checked: no lucky winner. I headed to the bathroom and splashed myself in the face with cold water. Doing so, I realized seeing all of those hungry pussies had somehow made me thirsty (horny's a given here, of course). I returned to the bedroom and called room service to ask for a couple of cold beers to be brought up to my room.

While waiting for my refreshments, I unhooked the DVD player and plugged in the VCR in its place. I decided to also ditch my initial plan. I picked up the worst tape cover. My patience definitely had limits, and I'd reached them. The words 'Welcome to the Aviation School' had been printed on a white sheet of paper in large, bold black letters, then slid into the transparent lining of the case cover. Could be promising... But no image and no description on the back. I opened the case to find a tape with a blank TDK label—the type that came with new VHS tapes, something I hadn't seen in decades. That certainly didn't bode well.

"Here's to nothing... probably some dude's home video," I said aloud while sliding the tape into the VCR slot. The mechanism swallowed it loudly just as a knock resonated on the door.

"Room service," a male voice said.

I opened the door and let him in with his serving tray. Along with the two bottles I'd ordered, he'd also brought bags of peanuts, chips, and chocolate, one of which I purchased as well. *Clever up-sell tactic.* Eager to return to my unknown tape, I tipped him and sent him on his way.

Door now closed and back in my private porn-viewing universe, I cracked open my first beer, took a couple of swigs, then sat at the end of my bed, VCR remote in one hand and my beer in the other. I pressed PLAY and heard the old gears do their thing. Then, a couple of seconds later, a logo popped on the black screen: the same that was on the business card I'd photographed a couple hours ago.

"Holy shit! This can't be! I'm the luckiest bastard on Earth!"

Someone banged on the wall next door. I shut up but kept gloating on the inside. I took another swallow of my beer to celebrate.

As the Capt. Dick Harding Flying School logo faded, long legs in high heels took over the screen. Twenty or so women were lined up; the cameraman had captured their profiles, very slowly working its way upward, going from high-heels and calves, to thighs, and now bringing hot pink skirts into view. After showing the profiles of busty women in white blouses, the camera focused on the first woman, finally showing a face along with her torso: a tall, thin blonde girl with her hair tied in a ponytail smiled at the camera, hands on hips, her nipples poking through a shirt that was clearly two-sizes too small.

"Come on, come on. Show me the other girls. My naughty stewardess is on TV tonight!" I whispered to myself, feeling my cock grow. I rested my beer on the nearest flat surface, untied my robe, grabbed my shaft in my hand, and began thrusting into my open palm while watching the movie.

Transitions were unprofessional at best. Next, I saw a pair of long legs wheeling a suitcase. Then, another long pair of legs going up to a redhead in a Captain's jacket. Another crappy transition, then the shot moved to a panoramic view of several women, all tall and long-legged, seen from behind. Blondes, brunettes, red heads were within the group. Skin shades varied from very white to ebony black, probably a few Hispanic or Asian women in the lot. I couldn't tell which of the brunettes was my stewardess, but I remained hopeful I'd see her tits and would be able to place a face on her soon enough. Then, a snarling sound followed by a clipping noise echoed from the VCR. The TV screen flashed and froze on a distorted, twisted image of the line-up.

"Noooo!" I screamed.

Someone once again pounded on the wall. I shut up.

"Fuck, fuck, fuck!" I mumbled to myself.

I jumped from the bed and rushed to the machine. I pressed the EJECT button. Nothing. I pressed STOP, REWIND, POWER. Nothing.

I unplugged the damn VCR, then plugged it back in again. Each time the device emitted a mechanical gurgling sound, as though it was trying to spit out the tape, but to no avail.

The fucking VCR didn't just eat my only link to the stewardess. That can't fucking be! I have to break it open.

I looked around, trying to find a screwdriver-shaped object I could use to prop open the VCR and retrieve what was left of the tape. But then, smoke started oozing out of the slot, accompanied by a strong burned plastic smell, and, seconds later, the loud ringing sound of the fire alarm went off in my room.

Shit.

7:05 p.m.

After getting dressed and dealing with very unhappy hotel staff (thankfully, I stopped the events from escalating before the fire department arrived), I tossed my rented videos and equipment in the canvas bag and returned to the store, ready to give them hell.

When I arrived, the hot Goth cashier no longer worked the counter. She'd been replaced by a skinny little thing with blonde hair, half of it shaved, the other side tied up in a side braid, the tip of which rested on her barely covered breasts. Large blue eyes and a big smile decorated her face. Our eyes met, then she walked around the counter.

I headed toward her. I couldn't help but notice her long legs half-covered with black diagonal nylons. The rest of her toned body was covered by two stretchy pieces of yellow fabric: one that barely hid her tits and the other, about the same size, that barely concealed her ass. Her flat stomach and metal-pierced navel were exposed. After taking a few more steps toward her, I was willing to bet she also had a ring through her left nipple, or one heck of a mole that was poking through the fabric of her top. There was no way I could be upset at that woman, especially since she wasn't the one who'd rented me the faulty VCR, so I let my built-up anger evaporate.

"Hi, I'm here to return the videos I rented earlier today, along with a faulty VCR," I said, placing my bag on the counter, letting the stench of burnt plastic fill the void between us.

"That's too bad. Did it swallow one of the tapes?" she asked, walking back behind the counter.

"You could say that," I replied. "But I would like to get another copy of the tape it destroyed," I requested.

"Let's see," she said before entering a code in her computer, then comparing my pile of tapes and DVDs with what her screen read. "Welcome to the Aviation School?" she asked.

"Yes, that's the one," I said, nodding and letting a flicker of hope raise in my chest.

She smiled and punched in a few more key strokes. "You have a thing for flight attendants?" she asked with a wink.

"Maybe I do. I'm a pilot."

"Really? You're a pilot?" She grinned at me, then returned her attention to her screen. "No, sorry, this was a one-off."

"What? No copies on DVD either?"

She looked at the screen again before continuing. "No, only this VCR tape. We bought it from a private seller. That was the only copy."

"Do you have his contact information?"

She hit a few more keys and looked at a few more screens. "No. I'm sorry, we don't."

What now. To come so close and to leave empty-handed?

"Could you try to retrieve it from the VCR?" I asked her.

"Our technician can try, but..." she waved her hand in the air. "Based on this awful smell, I doubt there's anything usable left." She returned her attention to the screen. "It will be an extra $25 for the destroyed tape and $250 for the broken VCR."

"What? You gotta be kidding... I can buy a brand new DVD player for less than $50."

"I know..." She looked around the store then bent over the counter to whisper the rest. "Listen, I go on a break in five minutes. What do you say you pay off that debt in kind? Think you can get me off and fly me to cloud number nine, Mr. Pilot?"

After the quantity of porn I'd sped-watched during the afternoon without coming, my cock made the decision without consulting with my brain. I nodded and smiled.

"Meet me around back. Go through the alley. You'll see a back door, just around a large red-brick wall.

I left her with my rented goods and headed out.

Having come so close to seeing my mystery woman to then find out I was once again helpless made me crave a cigarette. I hadn't smoked in years. I walked across the street to a nearby convenience store to buy a pack and lighter, then headed down the alley. I saw the brick wall, went around, then saw the blonde cashier leaning against it, a lit cigarette in her mouth.

I realized it wasn't tobacco once I got within a few feet.

She offered a puff of her nearly-gone joint, but I turned her down.

"I don't have much time," she said as I came within ear's reach. She flicked the crutch of her joint on the bare asphalt next to us. Without any other warning, she dug her fingers behind my belt buckle and pulled me closer to her. Her lips swallowed mine while her hands fumbled to undo my belt.

Talk about going right down to business.

I reached for her top and brought it down, letting her firm tits hang loose and exposing a small ring piercing on her left nipple. I gave them both a squeeze, feeling myself harden. Her hand had already dug down my pants, grabbing out my cock, pulling me in toward her. I let go of her tits and lifted her skirt. No panties. A green lantern greeted me. *Leave it to L.A. stylists to groom your bush with a super-hero logo.* I lifted her by the waist. She wrapped her legs around my back, and I pressed her against the brick wall. Seemingly out of nowhere, she pulled a condom, opened it, and unrolled it over my erect shaft. Within seconds, I was pounding her, watching her implants barely shake from my rhythmic thrusting. She was caressing her tits, pressing them one against the other, hypnotizing me in the process.

"Fuck me hard, Mr. Pilot," she said, now biting her lower lip. "Get me off!"

I spat on a couple of my fingers and brought them to her clit. I massaged it as I increased my cadence, pushing my cock into her harder, deeper.

"That's the spot," she said. What were you doing when you broke that VCR?" she asked.

"What?" *Why is she talking?* I looked up at her. A tease sparkled in her eyes.

"Tell me. What were you doing when the VCR swallowed your tape?"

Guess words turn her on.

"You know, pleasing myself," I said.

"No, you're a pervert. Tell me what you were doing with your hard cock while watching those stewardesses get naked?"

Oh, she wants me to be graphic? I can play that game.

"I was looking at her pussy, wanting to lick it, but all I could do was grab my cock and give myself a good beating."

"Oh, you were a bad boy. You deserve a good beating." She unwrapped her legs from around me and pushed me off, making my dick come out of her. "Show me how you beat yourself off," she ordered, her own hand getting busy with her clit, her other still playing with her exposed breasts.

I obeyed, gliding my hand up and down my shaft, the other tickling my balls. "Do you like it?" I asked.

"Yeah, I want to suck it. I want to lick your hard cock. I want you to beat yourself off in my mouth."

She knelt in front of me and pulled the condom off my cock. She stuck her tongue out, exposing yet another piercing. I moved my hand closer to the base of my shaft and dipped myself into her mouth. She closed her full lips around my cock, then reached for my balls, squeezing them together with her palm while the tip of her fingers caressed my anus. She brought her head forward, taking half of my cock into it. I felt it pound against the back of her mouth. She pulled back a little, then came back in. Faster and faster, her other hand pinching her nipples, pulling on her piercing.

A few garbled moans came out of her mouth in between swallows and licks. It was clear this wasn't her first blow job. I could feel myself close to the brink.

"I'm gonna come," I said.

"I want to swallow. Come in my mouth," she ordered.

I obeyed, and she locked her mascaraed eyes with mine. I came, pulled out, and the last drip of come fell onto her chin. She wiped it with a finger, then licked it off.

Then, just as if nothing had happened, she lifted her top back up, and pulled down her skirt. I tucked my cock back into my pants and did up my belt. That's when I noticed the security camera above the door.

I lifted my chin toward it. "Is this all on camera?"

"Of course, but don't worry. This is solely for the owner's private collection. She's a bit of a voyeur, and it's a way for customers to pay off certain debts. It's a win-win, really, right?"

"You do this often?"

"Not so much lately, fewer and fewer tapes get caught in VCRs these days, but we also have a 'service fee' for those who want to return or exchange a defective sex toy. You could buy one and try to return it tomorrow," she said, smirking, her hand tingling my cock through the fabric of my shorts. "Amelia's working tomorrow. She's hot. Listen, I'll ask the technician to recover whatever tape may still be in there, but I highly doubt he'll get anything out."

Based on the noise and amount of smoke that had come out of it hours earlier, I shared her opinion.

A part of me was curious as to what hot Amelia could do to me in the alley tomorrow, but a larger part of me needed to get back to work. I had a flight to catch in a few hours. I also needed to plan my next excursion to find my stewardess.

NEXT STEPS

I never heard back from the L.A. porn shop lady.

No doubt the sex tape from Capt. Dick Harding Flying School got destroyed.

Damn it, I was so close to seeing her face, but no cigar. I did toss that pack of cigarettes I'd bought in a moment of weakness the second I left L.A., and I'm proud to report it was still sealed.

At least I discovered how tall my mystery woman was, relatively. *I love long legs. Legs are my weakness (but come to think of it, so are asses... and tits...). I guess every part of a woman's body does the trick for me.*

I'm a weak man, what can I say?

You won't believe what my stewardess got up to next. She's managed to find a very, very special castle in Ireland. An "all-inclusive" resort. They offer every service you could dream of, and everything is included. *Everything.*

Best part?

I know the castle's name and I've made a reservation.

Now, I just have to find a very open-minded lady to accompany me as I try and track down any clues left by my mystery stewardess in Ireland.

PART V

IRELAND

THE STEWARDESS'S ENTRIES
IRELAND

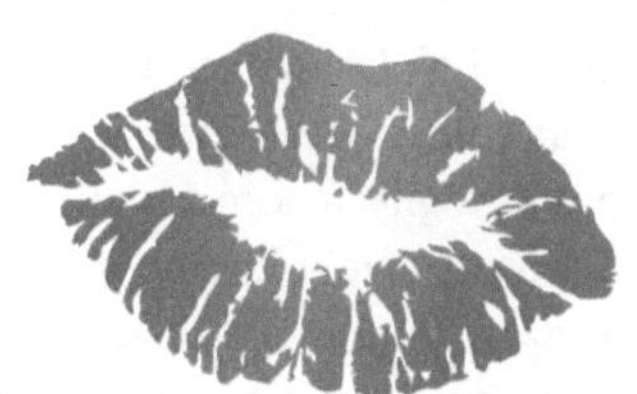

10:30 a.m.

I SMILED at my boy-toy Matt when I pulled my duty-free cart next to row 44.

I reached up and toggled the call button off. Sitting next to Matt, an older gentleman held the in-flight magazine opened on the perfume page. He was clearly the one who'd pressed the service button.

"Do you think my wife will like this sample box?" he asked me, pointing at a Dior variety boxset.

"I don't know your wife and her taste in perfumes, but this particular assortment's quite popular. And I'm sure she'll absolutely love the thoughtful gesture."

The silver-haired man smiled at me. "Perfect, I'll take it. Now let me find my credit card," he said before digging through the seat pocket in front of him. A few seconds later, he unbuckled and got up, so I moved my cart forward to clear the aisle. It seemed the man had placed his wallet in the overhead compartment.

While waiting, I glanced at Matt, who was tucking a strand of his long brown hair behind his ear. He winked at me, his chocolate eyes disrobing me from within. I couldn't believe how handsome he looked... and how lucky I was to have him with me right now. But maybe it wasn't all luck. I'd learned from our planned Mexican getaway. This time, I'd made sure Matt wasn't going to cancel on me: I'd gotten him a seat on *my* flight. But our plane wasn't going fast enough. We'd be landing in Dublin in less than an hour. But still, that was too long. Couldn't I already be naked next to him? Hell... *over* and *under* him as well? The more positions, the better.

"

"Ah, there it is," the older man said, a brown leather wallet in hand.

I opened the cart drawer where the perfumes were stored and found what he wanted. After taking the credit card he offered, I processed the transaction, then handed the gentleman his card back along with a duty-free bag that contained his wife's gift. *How thoughtful of him. Can't say anyone's ever bought me duty-free souvenirs, but I can buy my own. Come to think of it, pretty little trinkets and perfume bottles are at the bottom of my wish list. I'd much rather enjoy a sensual getaway with a tall hottie like Matt. Collecting experiences is much better than accumulating objects.* Especially when these experiences brought me to the brink of earthly pleasures.

I smiled at the elderly passenger and Matt before making my way back to stow the duty-free cart in its rightful location, lost in my own thoughts. When Matt contacted me to say that things were through with his ex, I couldn't have been more pleased. If there was a guy whom I wouldn't mind having a string of one-night stands with, it was Matt. We'd known each other for over six months now, since his brief stint as a flight attendant. I always knew he wasn't relationship material, but that aspect of his personality was fine with me now; I wasn't looking for love anymore—*at least, I think I've convinced myself of it.*

I couldn't think of anyone better to share a long weekend with at a secluded, one-of-a-kind Irish castle—according to the online reviews I'd found. I'm sure our free time will be spent having sex more than taking in the scenery.

And I was fine with that.

I could enjoy the beautiful Irish landscape some other time.

12:00 p.m.

Customs cleared and our small overnight bags duly stashed in our rental car, Matt closed the trunk—or the boot, as he called it.

"Want to drive?" he asked, keys in hand.

I had no issues driving in general, but couldn't say I felt super comfortable doing it on the left side of the road.

"I can if you want to close your eyes and rest, but—"

"Rest? I was asking to be polite. I'd much rather drive! It's been a while since I drove on the *correct* side of the road," he said, a sarcastic smile on his lips. "This little sports car should be great craic to maneuver around winding roads."

I got on my tip-toes and kissed him. *How I loved Irish accents... Or any accent for that matter.* "It's all yours!"

Being spoiled and letting men treat me like a princess was quite a pleasant change. *I should have started years ago.*

As we headed west out of Dublin, embarking on our three-hour drive toward the secluded castle, we finally left the urban scenery and the green rolling hills gradually began to expand in all directions. The odd rock wall or herd of sheep broke the emerald color scheme every now and then. The gray sky hung low, threatening to rip open, but it appeared that good ole Irish luck was on our side.

3:05 p.m.

After veering off the road and following the signage, we finally made it to the castle. The large stone building was well kept, at least judging by the beautiful edges and trimmed trees lining the driveway. Lush climbing plants covered the castle's tallest tower; they'd almost successfully camouflaged the gray stones to match their surrounding green environment.

Matt kept driving until we reached a sign that identified the main entrance. Thunder roared the instant he turned off the ignition. We got out of the car and grabbed our carry-on bags, leaving our vehicle parked in front of the entrance. Although we both ran to the door, our excitement to get out of the rain came to a halt when we saw the sign telling us to knock and wait.

My boy-toy rapped the heavy iron knocker, whose ring must have been nearly a foot wide and about an inch thick. We waited. Like a true gentleman, Matt left me standing under the deep, pointed doorway made of stones while he got soaked; his beautiful hair was no longer flowing and wavy, but now dripping wet.

"Don't be silly, there's room for the two of us," I said.

"No, best keep you and our bags dry." His head nodded toward the two carry-on bags stacked next to me on the threshold. A smile then grew on his lips. "I'll get out of these wet clothes the second we're in the room—"

With a creaky squeal, the heavy wooden door opened behind me. A tuxedoed butler let us in. While his clothes reminded me of Michael Caine's outfit in *Batman*, the young lad's face looked a lot more like Liam Hemsworth from *The Hunger Games*. *How strange to see a real live manservant, especially one that was in his early twenties and sexy.*

Matt finally left the rain and joined me as I walked into the building.

"Welcome to our castle," the butler said while I looked up and around, taking in the vast entrance hall. The stone walls had been painted in white, and beautiful large tapestries hung to cover most of the available space. Above our heads, dark wooden beams met in pointed arcs at least three stories higher than our level. A large electrical chandelier hung about ten feet above our heads in the center of the room. Around us, a few pieces of humongous wooden furniture sparsely decorated with wild flowers adorned the space.

"Wow!" I couldn't help but say aloud.

"First time?" the butler asked.

I nodded and so did Matt, who was now holding both of our bags, looking toward the reception desk.

"I'm sure you'll have a wonderful stay," the manservant said, looking at the both of us. "Do you have any luggage you'd like me to take care of?"

"No, we're good, thank you. But what should I do with the car?" Matt asked, holding the keys in the air.

"I'll take care of it for you, then I'll leave the keys with Jessica. Why don't you go ahead and check yourselves in?" The butler said, his hand pointing toward the reception area that Matt had been staring at. "She'll take great care of you."

"Thank you," I said before following Matt.

The second I set eyes on Jessica, I understood why Matt had so intently been staring that way. The beautiful red-headed woman wore her hair in a ponytail tied on one side, reminding me of 80s fashion, but her green eyes, pale skin, and bright red lips screamed *cougar in bed*. Her outfit certainly supported that theory. She wore what would best be described as a French maid outfit, with a very, very deep scoop neck. Her breasts were pushed up, their white flesh bulging out of the outfit. So much of her chest was exposed that her nipples had to start less than half an inch from where the lacy white border ended. A little bit of black fabric puffed around her tiny shoulders. The short sleeves ended on her slender arms in a lacy border that echoed the pattern of the tiny white apron that hung around her waist. I couldn't see her legs from where we stood, but I was willing to bet the bottom of her body matched the top. So far, the castle staff could have been picked right out of an issue of GQ magazine.

"Hello, *Dia dhuit!* Welcome to the ███████████ Castle."

3:10 p.m.

Once Jessica had registered us and upgraded us from the *breakfast-only* to the *full-meal plan*, which she highly recommended—the same recommendation that had been made by every online reviewer—she assigned us our room for the weekend. Our old-fashioned metal keys in hand, we stepped off of the thick *Welcome* mat we were standing on and turned around before heading toward the metal spiral staircase located at the back of the room.

At the foot of the stairs, next to a brass luggage trolley, stood two beautiful women, one tall blonde and one curvy brunette, also wearing matching French maid outfits. The bottoms of their uniforms left as little to the imagination as the top did. The puffy black fabric flared out for about a foot from the waist down. Then a couple of inches of white crinoline poked out all around the hem. Sheer black stockings covered their legs, the darker band at the top was visible just below the end of the crinoline. "Hello, my name's Kate," said the brunette closest to the luggage trolley as we got within about three feet of them. "I'll take your bags and bring them to your room if that's alright?"

Matt, who was holding his bag over his left shoulder and rolling my carry-on behind him, seemed to consider it for a second, but the narrowness of the staircase probably made him change his mind. He placed both of our bags on the trolley, which Kate then pushed out of the room. The clicks of her high heels and the thumping noises of the wheels as they rolled over the ceramic tiles faded out as we watched her disappear with our bags into a small hallway.

The blonde woman then addressed us. "I'm Chloe. If you'll follow me, I'll take you to your room now."

I nodded. She turned around, then started her way up the stairs.

"After you," said Matt with a fake curtsy.

I grabbed a hold of the black metal railway and started climbing, then looked up to see where I was going. Chloe was already ten steps ahead of me, her puffy crinoline bottom swaying as she made her way up, forcing my eyes to inadvertently turn into heat-seeking missiles aiming for her lacy white panties. They covered less than a third of her butt cheeks. I looked down at Matt, who met my eyes. He had a wide grin on his lips. He nodded toward the maid above us. I smiled and raised my shoulders at him, then resumed climbing. I wouldn't be giving him a show of my own since I'd changed into jeans and a light V-neck sweater after landing. *Too bad for him.* And I was certainly happy to be wearing flat shoes. I don't know how these maids could walk all day on uneven tiles and narrow metal staircases in that kind of footwear!

Once the three of us had finished climbing, Chloe smiled at us and headed to the right, down a wide hallway lined with large oil paintings.

"Feel free to explore every nook and cranny of this castle," she said as I admired the work of the artists.

The first painting was of a large woman eating grapes in a deep green garden, naked, lying on her side. The second one displayed a man with a woman kneeling in front a him while he kissed another woman standing next to him, all of them naked, save for the top hat worn by the man. *Hmmm. Am I just horny, or is this place 'one-of-a-kind' for a specific reason?*

Matt wrapped his arm around my waist and whispered in my ear, "My, my! What kind of place did you book for us? They certainly know how to put people in the mood. Can't wait to get you naked—"

"Consider this castle your home for the entire weekend," Chloe said as she veered left into a smaller corridor. "Ab-so-lu-tely nothing is out of bounds here."

A light beep sounded and I turned to look in the direction the noise had come from. An elevator door opened and out came Kate with the luggage trolley.

"Just in time," said Chloe.

I turned to face her, and she walked into the tall wooden door she'd just opened. Matt and I followed her into the room.

Chloe smiled at the both of us. "This is your bedroom. Remember that the entire staff is at your beck and call, for any and all of your needs." She pointed to a phone on one of the nightstands. "Press 0 and you'll reach Jessica or whoever is manning the front desk."

Just as she finished speaking, Kate rolled our luggage into the room, then placed each of the bags on a large wooden bench at the end of the four-post, king-sized bed, which could have come from a princess story with its sheer burgundy curtains. They covered the top of the bed then had been loosely tied around the posts.

"Should I unpack your bags for you?" she offered.

I shook my head. "No, there's no need. But thank you."

Matt dug into his pant pocket to retrieve his wallet then walked toward Kate.

"Fine," she said. "I won't unpack your bags, but I'll light a fire. We wouldn't want the two of you to catch a cold." Kate reached up to place a strand of Matt's wet hair behind his ear. She smiled and winked at him before turning away and heading toward the sizable fireplace across the room from the bed.

Am I imagining things or was she flirting with him?

Matt turned to look at me, his face scrunched up. *Guess I'm not the only confused one here.*

A creak then sounded on my right. The other maid had opened up the large wardrobe on the outside wall. "We offer an assortment of dresses and tuxedos for our guests in the event they forgot to pack formal evening wear. Based on the size of your bags, I assume you may need to borrow from what you'll find in here. Like I said, feel free to open drawers, wardrobes, and whatever you find. Poke around. Everything here is clean and ready for our guests." Her right hand motioned toward the fireplace as she finished speaking.

I turned to see what she was pointing at. Her words suddenly took on an entirely new meaning.

Kate's body was folded in half at the hips, her arms were busy arranging the firewood in the fireplace, but what drew my focus—and probably Matt's as well—was Kate's naked ass and pussy, exposed in the midst of her crinoline.

Matt's arm wrapped around my waist, and he bent down to whisper in my ear. "Is this an early birthday present for me?"

I looked at him. His chocolate eyes simmered with hope. I shook my head. "No idea what's happening."

And with that, the faint sounds of small branches lighting up reached my ears, followed by the clicks of Kate's heels. She was heading our way with a large, innocent smile on her face.

Matt unwrapped his arm from me and handed Kate a five-euro bill he'd previously retrieved from his wallet. "Thank you," he said.

Kate took the money and waved it in the air toward Chloe, who walked over and took it from her hand.

"We're sorry," said Kate. She turned her attention to Matt and brought one finger down the center of his wet shirt. "We... don't... accept... tips..." Her hand was still going down, slowly but definitely. She passed his leather belt. "Not in cash, anyway..." Her sliding finger turned into a full-hand grab of Matt's genitals.

I was about to protest, but felt something slide into the front of my V-neck. I looked down. Matt's folded five-euro bill was resting in the tight groove of my pushed-up cleavage.

"What the—"

Chloe locked her lips onto mine, one of her hands behind the nape of my neck and the other wrapped around my left hand, which she brought to her own breast. She pulled down her scoop neck and pushed my hand onto one of her soft, squishy but firm breasts. No bra. I felt the built-in wire in the dress's stretchy fabric on the back of my hand. Chloe pushed me onto the bed, her lips hungrier than a starving porn actress. Her tongue parted my lips before exploring my mouth. I let her but couldn't return the enthusiasm. I turned to look at Matt, which forced Chloe to move her kisses to my neck, then to the exposed skin of my cleavage.

Matt's head tilted back, his eyes locked on the ceiling, his mouth agape. His pants were crumbled around his ankles, his hands wrapped around the brunette's head. She had knelt in front of him and had gotten busy sucking his dick. He started moaning. His hips began moving back and forth toward Kate, forcing her to take all of him inside her mouth.

"We don't accept tips in Euros," Chloe said to me as she sat up on my hips, her legs folded around me. "Kate likes full-lengths, and I... like other types of tips," she said before lifting my sweater.

I'd come here for a sensual weekend. I hadn't planned for it to involve people other than Matt... *but why not?*

I raised my arms and lifted my back off from the dark burgundy comforter, letting her pull my sweater above my head. She tossed it to the side. Her hands then reached behind my back and unclasped my bra. A second later, with my arms cleared of the straps, she tossed the unneeded lacy garment toward my sweater. Chloe's hands brought my breasts together, massaging them forcefully before focusing her attention on my nipples. She twisted and squeezed them before getting closer to me and sucking on one of them. She moaned, the sound partially obstructed by my breast as her lips gently nibbled on my nipple.

Matt's groans started getting louder. I knew him well enough to know he was about to come.

I looked at him; his gaze had turned to Chloe and me. My eyes met his as he reached orgasm. His hips jerked forward and he pulled Kate's head closer, not even giving her the option to retract.

He let out a loud grunt and closed his eyes. Kate forced her head back a few seconds later, then slowly got up. She smiled at him before wiping some of Matt's come from her chin with her index finger.

"Welcome to our castle. I hope you'll enjoy your stay," Kate said.

And just like that, Chloe got off of me and left me half-naked on the bed as I watched both maids walk away. But just before they reached the door, Chloe turned around and said, "Dinner will be served at seven in the main dining hall. Formalwear, please. You may want to get some rest before then. You'll need it."

The door creaked as they closed it behind them.

Matt took off his shoes, then kicked off his pants and underwear before walking my way. In a swift motion, he removed his wet shirt, exposing his six-pack abs just as he reached the bed.

"How did a five-euro note lead to this?" my gorgeous, naked Adonis asked me as he approached the bed.

I sat up. "Disappointed?"

Matt raised his shoulders. A half-smile on his lips, he asked, "What would twenty euros have gotten me you think?"

I slapped him on the ass. "Probably the same..." I inhaled deeply as I pulled him closer to me. "Matt, I didn't get my happy ending... Would you mind giving me a hand?"

He pushed me back onto the bed and undid my pants.

"Can I give you a tongue instead?"

3:55 p.m.

My cheeks rosy with post-orgasm glee, I walked butt naked toward the en-suite bath.

"I think I'll do like they said and relax. I feel like taking a bath," I said to Matt as I opened the en-suite door.

Whoever had decorated the room had done so with women patrons in mind. Heavy flowery curtains decorated the window. Three beautiful ceramic vases were overflowing with fresh-cut white roses, baby's breath, and assorted green leaves. Two sets of plush white towels hung on a rack in front of the window. Other than the thickness of the window frame—which had to be at least a foot deep—there were no signs of being in a stone castle. The walls were flat, flawless, and had been painted in a light shade of salmon. A large and ornate gold mirror decorated the main wall. This bathroom had everything one would expect and more: a modern pedestal sink, a four-legged bathtub with brass fittings, a large corner shower, a vanity table with a small mirror and a padded, armless Victorian chair upholstered in a flowery pattern that matched the curtains, a modern low-flow toilet, and even a bidet! Behind the bathroom door had been hung two soft bathrobes. I reached and touched the fabric. *Decadently soft.*

I wrapped myself in one of them then stepped out of the room to look at Matt.

He was sitting up in bed, remote in hand, his naked lower body tucked under the covers.

"The tub's huge. You want to have a bath with me?" I asked.

"Nah, I found a game I'd like to watch: Republic of Ireland's playing Belarus."

"Aren't you cold from getting soaked earlier?"

He shrugged. "I'm good. The fire's hot and the sheets are keeping me warm."

"Enjoy the game then," I said as I returned to the bathroom.

I turned on the faucets, adjusted the temperature, and filled the tub with warm water. An assortment of bath products had been stacked on the vanity table. I opted for the jasmine-scented bath salts.

Once my bath was ready, I lowered my body into the perfumed water and rested my back against the slanted end of the tub. I closed my eyes and relaxed, inhaling the delicious aroma and letting the fizzy salts caress my thighs as they dissolved.

4:45 p.m.

"Ireland won," Matt whispered in my ear, waking me up.

He was sitting on the vanity chair that he'd pulled closer to the tub. Seemed he'd also given in to the temptation to wrap himself in a soft, plush bathrobe. One of his arms was immersed in the tub. I smiled at him as I felt his finger tease me from under the water.

He bent toward me and kissed me. His mouth nibbled my lips, then his tongue probed and twisted in my mouth. I wrapped one of my hands around the back of his neck. His hair had dried up.

A few seconds later, he pulled away.

"Your water's cooled off," he said. "Want me to give you a massage?" His eyebrows lifted and he smiled. "I found massage oil in the nightstand drawer... among other things."

I was unsure what else he'd discovered, but Matt's expert hands on my skin sounded divine right now. And he could continue tickling my pussy anywhere.

I kissed him again. "Sounds like a great idea."

After he pulled his arm out of the water, I got up, then stepped out of the tub. Matt stood up as well, then extended his arms to offer the bathrobe I'd left resting on the back of the chair.

4:55 p.m.

Lying flat on my stomach on the very comfortable bed, my head facing the TV and fireplace, I asked Matt to pass me the remote. The sports channel didn't offer the most relaxing soundtrack—at least not for me. I flipped through the channels, trying to find one with soft music. I felt Matt's weight on my butt, the warmth of his naked thighs against my hips. He squirted massage oil in his hands then rubbed them together before touching my back. I continued flipping through the channels, glancing at various options along the way: news, movies, cartoons, more sports, porn... Seemed the castle had opted for the most complete cable package.

Matt's hands rubbed my neck and shoulders, loosening knots I didn't realize I had. I stopped my channel flicking for a second to enjoy his handy work. It seemed I had reached a black and white channel. The footage moved sideways slowly, displaying stone walls with strings of garlic; pots and pans hung from various hooks. Then, a tall wooden shelving unit came into view. It held four large old fashioned clay containers, three Italian coffee makers, and a bunch of larger pots. Half a dozen French maids seemed hard at work, chopping vegetables and tenderizing meat on an oversized island in the center of the room. *A security camera in the kitchen?*

A few feet from the busy maids, a tuxedoed man was stabbing a large brick of ice with a pick to break it into small chunks. The camera kept rotating. It now showcased another French maid stirring a large pot on a stove. *Soup for dinner tonight?* Then, as the kitchen camera reached the end of its wide angle, another French maid appeared—a patisserie chef based on the rolling pin and the amount of flour spread out on the surface in front of her. But her humongous breasts were no longer confined by her uniform; they bounced and brushed back and forth against the flour while a tall, dark, short-curly-haired man in jeans and T-shirt pounded her from behind, his hands on her hips, the bottom of her dress bunched up in front of him.

The camera kept rotating and slowly returned to the maid who was stirring soup then headed back the other way.

Once my agape mouth returned to its normal position, I turned to Matt. "Did you see this?"

"Hell yeah! They weren't kidding about doing what the fuck we wanted." He grabbed the remote from my hands. "I wonder what else... or *whom* else we can see on camera..."

"You think it's live? Or pre-recorded?"

Matt raised his shoulders, his mouth turned upside down. He flipped to the next channel.

More black and white footage populated the screen, but this time, various straps, shackles, whips, and other assorted tools hung from the stone walls. A large chandelier with lit candle sticks dangled low in the room. So low in fact that a six-foot tall person like Matt could easily reach up and replace the candles... Or use them to do whatever. As the camera rotated, I wondered what I'd see in this room. *A woman with one of these ball-thingies in her mouth? A man wearing a leather outfit with metal spikes?* But no, the room was empty.

"I wonder where this is?" Matt asked before flipping to the next channel.

This time, the shot was fixed, the security camera wasn't moving at all since there was no need. It was a small laundry room featuring a modern washer, a dryer, and a half-dozen laundry baskets in front of the machines. In the far corner, several drying lines had been strung, currently covered by uniforms, underwear, and other items of clothing. Yet another gorgeous French maid sat on the top-loading washer. Hard to tell with the black and white image, but her hair was either blonde or light red, tied up in a braid whose tip rested on her breast. Her eyes were beady and dark. But what was obvious was her enjoyment of the spin cycle. Her entire body vibrated along with the machine. One of her legs hung nonchalantly in front of her while the other was folded, her foot resting on the top of the washer. Her panties had gone AWOL but she'd replaced them with a dildo whose full length she slowly pushed and pulled out of her. Her other hand was resting on the top of her thigh, two of her fingers busily rubbing her clit.

"We need laundry done?" Matt asked. "Maybe I can go and help that poor maid."

I took my attention away from the TV screen and turned to look at my boy-toy. He'd already begun stroking his erect shaft. "Seems like someone's ready for action," I said.

I pushed my ass up in the air, nudging him to get his hips off of me and start poking me where I wanted: deep down into my wet pussy.

"Can I do you in the ass, babe?"

6:55 p.m.

After browsing through the selection of evening dresses offered in the armoire, I opted for one that fit me best: a long, one-shoulder black dress with embroidered details. The main part of the dress was made of solid, silky black fabric with detailed lace patterns on the shoulder and down the front. It contained vertical and semi-circular wires like a built-in corset of sort, serving to keep the dress in position, slim my appearance, and push up my breasts. Exactly what I wanted from an evening gown. Once the dress got to mini-skirt length, the solid fabric turned into a sheer lacy pattern that matched the flowers on the top. That see-through section was slit down the left leg in the front, allowing for a comfortable stroll. I picked a three-inch black sandal from the armoire's selection and put on my set of silver looped earrings to finish my outfit.

I looked at myself in the full-length mirror lining the inside of the wardrobe. I pivoted and noticed the unsightly lines my panties made through the bottom of the dress. I took them off and looked at my reflection again.

What a dress! I should ask if I can buy it when we check out.

"You look hot!" said Matt as he came out of the bathroom, his ocean-scented cologne reaching my nostrils before I even turned to look at him. His tuxedo fit him impeccably; his hair brushed the shoulders of his jacket, making him look like an actor on Oscar night. He walked toward me, hunger in his eyes.

"You think we have time for a quickie?" he asked, one of his hands reaching into the slit of my dress and exploring my groin. "A lady commando! Now that's exciting."

A quick glance at his tented pants proved he meant what he'd just said.

The hands of the gold-framed clock on the wall indicated it was already 6:55 p.m.

I was unzipping Matt's pants just as a man's deep voice echoed above us: "Ladies and gents. This announcement is for all patrons who are joining us for dinner. The first service will commence in five minutes. Please join us in the great hall. We appreciate your punctuality."

"Guess that means no?" Matt said before letting out a sigh.

"Come on, we don't want to be rude and show up late."

He looked down at his pants. "Give me a minute. I can't walk out like this..."

I giggled. "Really?"

His eyes sent question marks my way.

"Come on... Given what we've seen so far in this place, nobody will mind." I wrapped my hands around his shoulders and stole a kiss from him.

A few seconds later, we headed out of the room and descended to the main floor in the elevator I'd seen Kate use a few hours earlier.

7:00 p.m.

A muscular, crew-cut blond man in a tuxedo offered us each a flute of champagne as we entered the great hall.

The room had to be at least one hundred feet across. A dozen couples mingled, creating a light background of high-pitched giggles, laughter, and chit-chat that echoed in the three-story-tall space. Some couples stood by the large lit-up fireplace while others sat on the oversized leather furniture that lined the gray stone walls. Although a vast diversity of skin tones and body types were portrayed, one thing was common among all: everyone was dressed to the nines, as though attending a glamorous event reserved for the rich and famous.

Draped in white linen at the center of the hall, a large rectangular dining table commanded the room, raised on a platform along with its chairs. *How did they manage to place the ornate floral arrangements in the middle of such a large table?* Someone had had to walk on top of the table cloth to do so. I counted sixteen chairs at the table.

"Look at this guy," Matt whispered in my ear, pointing to a brown-haired man chatting with a petite, strawberry-blonde woman.

I finished my sip and lowered my glass. "You know him?"

"No, but wasn't he the guy?"

"What guy?"

He lifted his eyebrows. "In the kitchen? Security footage?"

I looked at the hair on his nape: little curls that kinked out.

"You're right!"

Matt pulled me by the elbow and we walked over to introduce ourselves.

I recognized French when we got within ear shot.

"*Bonsoir*, good evening," the petite woman said to us as we approached. Her thin lips framed the cutest smile. She wore a burgundy, spaghetti-strapped dress that embraced her miniature curves. The large nipples of her tiny perky breasts poked in the front. The hem of her dress ended diagonally, showcasing her athletic calves. *One would be hard-pressed to find fat on her body.* The man accompanying her—Jean-Michel he called himself—was already conversing with Matt. His charismatic smile complemented his clean-shaven, square jaw. He winked at me as he wrapped his arm around his wife's waist.

"It is our second time here. And you?" Jean-Michel asked Matt.

"First-time," he replied.

"Ah, I remember our first hour here last time." Jean-Michel inhaled deeply, his eyes looking up as though he was reminiscing. "Surprising place, no?"

While Matt and the handsome Frenchman got to know each other, I conversed in French with the woman whose name turned out to be Lucie. She and her husband of twenty years had come here to celebrate their wedding anniversary this weekend. *They don't look their age at all!* Not a speck of gray could be seen in Jean-Michel's lush dark hair and not even a hint of crow's feet registered around the corners of Lucie's eyes. *How can people married for twenty years still look like they're in their early thirties at most? White lies? Or do they take great care of their bodies?*

Once our social niceties were over with, Lucie grabbed my elbow and dragged me away from Matt and her husband, toward the closest waiter.

She grabbed my empty glass and placed it on the waiter's tray before helping herself to two new flutes of champagne. She handed me one. "*Après le repas, tu verras, les gens vont bien s'amuser.*" She raised her glass and offered a cheers. "*Santé!*"

"*Santé!*" I repeated before clinking my glass against hers, wondering what she meant by the expected after-dinner fun.

"*Tu pourrais venir nous rejoindre plus tard? Moi et mon mari? Chambre numéro 6?*"

While I pondered her offer for me to join her and her husband in room 6 after dinner tonight, she motioned for me to follow her.

We headed toward a towering David-esque ice sculpture on a long table. It was similar to the famous Michelangelo's stone sculpture, except that the ice artist responsible for this piece of art had given David a large boner. Next to him, on a bed of crushed ice rested fresh oysters and a three-tiered platform overflowing with pink prawns. A row of condiments were at the ready: salt, a bottle of Tabasco, fresh lime quarters, and a small bowl filled with red, chunky sauce.

I thought about her offer while enjoying another bubbly sip. *"Avec ou sans Matt?"* I asked her, wondering if she also wanted Matt to come along.

She grabbed a juicy oyster and brought it up to her lips. *"Toi seulement,"* she replied, her frank eyes steady, almost as though a mental duel was about to begin. She tilted her unadulterated oyster, maintaining eye contact with me before noisily slurping all of its content. With her pointy tongue, she licked her lips to suck up some of the liquid that had escaped before tossing the empty shell on the platter where other empty ones had already been piled. *Looks like it's not just her husband who's looking for an extra woman?*

A light bell chimed, and I turned to look at yet another tuxedoed man. This one was bald and tall, his skin as dark as the night. He cranked *handsome* to a whole new level. He cleared his throat before addressing us. "Ladies and gents, please have a seat. Make new friends and mingle."

I recognized his voice from the earlier announcement.

"Et puis?" Lucie asked me, prompting me to provide a response.

I looked at her handsome husband in the distance, still chatting with Matt. *A threesome with one handsome Frenchman and another woman? That would be a new experience. Maybe figure out if French people were the best lovers as some of them claimed.* "Why not? *Oui.*"

After telling me she had to share the news with her husband, she excused herself and walked away, leaving me standing alone. Everyone around me had started making their way to the table. I looked at Matt across the room. A short cappuccino-skinned woman whose long black hair reached her waist was already dragging my Matt to the table, her arm intertwined with his at the elbow. Matt lifted his free hand in the air and pulsed his shoulders up while looking at me.

Guess I'm on my own for dinner.

And just as the thought occurred to me, a pale-skinned, red-headed man approached me.

"I'm Kenny. Would ya like to chat with me over dinner?"

7:15 p.m.

I joined Kenny at the dining room table. He chose a seat to my right. Before I could sit myself down, a tuxedoed waiter gentlemanly approached the chair for me. On my left sat a plump black woman in a beautiful pearly-white gown. She smiled and nodded at me before turning her attention to the guest on her left, a tall brunette with her hair wrapped in a chignon.

I looked at Kenny just as one of the gorgeous maids was placing a small bowl of pale green liquid in front of me. The castle's staff worked in perfect unison, serving all guests within seconds of each other.

"Dig in!" Kenny said as he covered his lap with a white napkin.

I dipped my silverware into the steamy liquid and brought a spoonful to my lips: delicious cream of broccoli. I was starving and hadn't realized it.

"So, ya like our castle here?" Kenny asked between spoonfuls.

"Gotta say, I didn't quite know what I was getting myself into..."

He nodded, a large smile on his lips, which created two cute dimples on his freckled cheeks. "When did ya arrive?"

"This afternoon." I dipped my spoon into what remained of my soup.

"Ya're in for a whale of a time," he said, his red bushy eyebrows going up a couple of times.

"So, you're from around here?" I asked him after finishing my soup and tapping my napkin on my lips.

"Sure look it. What about ya? What's the story?"

We continued on with social niceties and chit-chatted about nothing of importance while the perfectly-choreographed service continued. The next courses consisted of poached salmon with a side of baby potatoes then a small tossed salad with a raspberry vinaigrette. Two tuxedoed men constantly circled the table as we ate, ensuring every guest's wine glass remained full throughout the meal.

By the time the plates of lamb cutlets had been cleared from the table, the conversation had gotten pretty loud, which wasn't unexpected considering the amount of alcohol everyone was ingesting.

After a quick and polite apology, my dinner friend turned his attention to the lady on his right, a short, spiked-hair blonde, therefore freeing me to look around without guilt. I saw Matt six seats away from me, chatting up the cappuccino-skinned woman. The whiteness of her teeth contrasted vividly against her thick red lips. Just as I was trying to guess her age, her eyes widened and her entire body jolted, her back straightened, and her hands reached below the table. Then, a second later, Matt's body pulsed up; his eyes lurched down at his groin. A groan from Kenny on my right brought my attention to him. But he didn't appear surprised at all, his dimples had reappeared on both sides of his wide smile. His eyes were closed.

What the heck is going on here?

Then, I felt it too.

I looked down at my hips and saw a bulge form from under the table cloth in front of me. A hand with bright red nails brushed up my lap, coming out from underneath the cloth for a few seconds as it pushed the bottom of my dress out of the way, bunching up the fabric and pushing it off to the side. I lifted my ass for a second, just so I'd be more comfortable, then I slid myself down, closer to the mystery woman below the table in front of me.

I looked around me once more. The waiting staff had all disappeared. The room had gotten quiet, all conversations having abruptly ended. My mystery woman proceeded to part my legs wide enough to lodge herself between my thighs. Soft silky hair brushed against my skin, two hands and a tongue slowly made their way up my inner thighs. A warm breath blew onto my genitals. Wet fingers slid down my pussy, then back up, stroking my lips without poking me... at first.

Then, the warm and moist air of her breath blew harder onto my clit, her wet tongue twirled around it before the woman's mouth nuzzled into my pussy, forcing my thighs to part even more. Her agile tongue licked and sucked on my clit, her fingers still stroked my lips, faster and faster, squeezing my folds tighter. Then her wet finger slid into my pussy. Another finger soon joined it. They rubbed and tapped upward, as though feeling their way toward the right spot. A few delicious seconds later, they found it.

A moan escaped my lips. Then another... and another. I couldn't control myself. Her tongue and lips left my clit, then she tongue-fucked me as her fingers polished my wet button. I brought one of my hands down to keep my lips parted. My other hand went to my heart, as though its presence there could prevent it from exploding out of my chest. Her expert tongue kept going. Then it was again replaced by her fingers. I could hear my own moisture as she thrust her digits in and out, quickly. She poked at the exact right spot where I needed to be prodded. My legs quivered. My back arched. My neck fell backward onto the back of my chair as I came. My thighs framed the mystery woman squarely in place as my drenched pussy pulsed out of control around her fingers.

I reopened my eyes once the orgasmic tsunami finished washing over me.

The dinner conversations had morphed into a cacophony of moans, groans, and calls to diverse deities. Everybody was receiving or had just finished receiving premium head, at least based on every patrons' facial expressions. Some were grabbing on to the table, a woman had pushed down her dress and was twisting her bare nipples, another pushed over her wine glass, which landed in a clang over her empty tea cup and plate.

I looked down at Kenny's lap just as the black-haired woman who was sucking his cock came out for air. I got to see his masterpiece: his bright white dick had to be at least ten inches long. And who knew if there was another inch or two that remained hidden within his Irish red carpet.

My dishes slid to the left, along with the table cloth. I couldn't catch my plate before it crashed on the stone floor, breaking into a thousand pieces. The black woman next to me had—probably inadvertently—pulled on the table cloth. Her mouth was agape. Her hands were wrapped around a dark-haired person nuzzled in her groin.

"God, yeeesss!" she screamed.

8:15 p.m.

The waiting staff trickled back in the room in the moments that followed.

While a tuxedoed waiter refilled my wine glass, a French maid appeared out of thin air with a broom and tray. The red-headed woman bent down to sweep away my broken dishes, her panty-less, bold crotch staring at me a mere six inches from my face. Her light musky scent reached my nostrils, and she shook her booty, as though inviting my fingers to tease her while she worked. Blame it on the wine, or blame it on the fabulous head I'd just gotten, but I couldn't resist. I reached to touch her. She moaned the instant my fingers came in contact with her wet labia. She was warm. She was dripping wet. She backed up ever so slightly, pushing herself onto my fingers, as though urging me to move them, to probe her, and explore her inner folds. My digits made circular motions around her wet opening before dipping into her. Her juices dripped down my hand. She backed up some more, forcing my fingers deeper into her. The black woman on my left got up, walked up to the cleanup maid, and started kissing her. The maid's body unfolded as she straightened up. The maid let go of her broom and tray, her hands reaching up to the black woman's face as their kiss increased in intensity.

I hesitated for a second. Unsure what to do.

"Keep going," I heard Kenny's voice say from behind me.

I turned and saw him looking at the three of us. He had moved his chair sideways. He was now facing us, stroking his humongous naked shaft. A few feet behind him, the spiked-hair lady was kneeling, sucking on one of the waiters. The whole room had seemingly agreed upon a free-form orgy of sorts.

I resumed finger-fucking the maid's pussy. I brought my face to her soft and firm butt cheeks. I kissed their plush roundness, I caressed their contours. My cadence increased, following the maid's hips' rocking motions. Her hand then suddenly lurched to her ass, parting her cheeks and exposing her anus. I let the tip of my tongue go down her crevice until I could tickle her opening.

I felt another hand come near her pussy, touching my fingers, then retracting back toward the maid's clit. The maid's moans got louder. Her inner walls were clenching around my fingers. I thrust deeper and deeper into her. Her wetness lubricated my fingers so much that I felt the need to insert a third one, then a fourth one so I could fill her soaked and slippery pussy. And just with that, she came, squirting a jet of liquid that streamed down my arm and dripped off of my elbow, onto the stones below.

"Fuck yeah!" Kenny groaned.

8:40 p.m.

One of Mozart's concertos played in the background while patrons and staff finished up their *activities*—for lack of a more encompassing term. The maid resumed her clean-up duties and walked away with the broken dishes in her tray, as if nothing had happened, save for her own juices running down her leg.

A minute later, I watched Kenny squirt onto the floor about a foot away from me. I felt my pussy twitch. This fuck-fest had yet to include a dick in my pussy. Matt's or someone else's. It didn't matter whose. I just needed to be filled right now. I sipped more wine as I looked around to see whose dick was still at the ready and available.

Unfortunately, my quest terminated abruptly as the handsome black butler rang his bell and announced that dessert would be served in a few minutes.

He would do. That hot, bald butler would certainly have a great dick.

I took a few more sips and waited patiently for the hot butler to announce what 'dessert' would consist of. I looked toward the French couple who had invited me for an after-dinner session. Was their offer still on? Or would 'dinner' have done the trick for them? As though they were reading my mind, both Lucie and Jean-Michel were staring at me. Jean-Michel lifted his wine glass toward me, nodded, then winked. Lucie was biting her lower lip. Her hand went from her mouth to her neck, down to her right breast, which she squeezed while locking eyes with me.

The hot butler rang his bell again before clearing his throat. "Tonight, dessert will be picked at random from this hat. Alternatively, you can grab whatever you like and eat it here or anywhere else, as usual. I will be walking around the table for dessert selection."

And with that, the hot bald butler started with Lucie. She dipped her hand into the hat and retrieved a piece of paper. The butler walked over to the next patron and offered her the hat. The routine continued until he reached me. I smiled at him as I plunged my hand into the hat.

The butler walked away before I could even say a thing.

Gotta work on my pick-up lines. Guess I could have just grabbed him without a word?

I unfolded my mystery dessert, which read:

Treasure hunt: A collection of golden cocks has been hidden in the castle. Find at least three and bring them to the butler or maid of your choice to claim your prize.

I smiled. *Here you go. Butler selected. His dick will be my prize, golden or not.*

"What did ya get?" asked Kenny.

"A treasure hunt. You?"

He nodded with a smile before handing me his sliver of paper, which read:

Jello fight: Pick two staff members and join them in a jello boxing match.

I overheard other people around me mentioning a "spa evening," "kitchen raid," and "chocolate fondue." Seemed every dessert had its appeal.

The light ring of the bell echoed again in the dining room and the hot butler addressed us again. "Please proceed to claim your dessert, as directed by your slip of paper. Enjoy the rest of your evening."

I pushed my chair back, then slowly got up, realizing that I had drenched my chair. I adjusted my dress, grabbed a last swig of my wine, and headed down the hall on my quest to find golden dicks. I decided to start with the kitchen.

9:05 p.m.

After looking in vain from one cupboard to the next, I headed out through a small door in the back of the kitchen to explore the rest of the castle.

I followed the narrow, sparsely decorated stone hallway. A minute later, displayed under a glass dome in the center of a small wall alcove, I found my first golden dick. A golden vibrator really. It even had an on/off switch. A small push of the button indicated the batteries were charged and ready. My aching pussy urged me to think it over for a second. The girth and length of the golden shaft was enticing, but with so many real live dicks around, it seemed worth my while to do as instructed and claim my preferred butler's real appendage once I collected two more golden dildos.

First prize in hand, I continued down the hallway until I reached a staircase that spiraled down below the ground floor. A few electrical lights illuminated my way. A spa-like aroma of mineral salts grew stronger the deeper I went. The humidity level also kept increasing.

Thirty steps later, I ended up in Shangri-La—at least the way the legendary place presented itself in my mind. The colossal, irregular-shaped room appeared to have been carved out of a natural cave, then enhanced by technology and molded to fit the needs of the castle. A beautiful narrow waterfall gushed out from ground level and fell into the back of the larger basin in front of me. Its surface was calm, save for the waves made by Jessica, the red-headed receptionist, who was swimming out of it. The woman had started to make her way out, each step exposing more of her white skin, her fleshy, hard-nippled breasts, her flat stomach, her trimmed red mons, her long legs... Once fully out of the basin, she turned and headed toward a smaller pond that was already occupied by two of the waiters—Liam-Hemsworth-look-alike was one of them.

He smiled at me as I walked by the smaller pond they sat in, feeling the warmth of the nebulous layer that was evaporating from the water. "Want to join us?" he asked.

A hot tub with two hot butlers... Enticing... But I've got another mission. "Maybe later," I said, waving my golden cock in the air. "I'm collecting my dessert."

"Good luck!" he said with a wink.

If I can't find the hot black butler, I'll come back here.

10:00 p.m.

I followed the asymmetrical pathway that outlined the circumference of the room until I found a large wooden door. It opened onto yet another stone passageway, this one lit with flickering candles whose molten white wax dripped along the walls and floor below.

Screams and grunts echoed from farther down the hall. I walked toward the noises. The snap of a whip. A woman's cry. The orders of a man's voice: "Shut up and take it!"

I know this voice.

I hurried my pace, my heart pounding against my chest.

Matt? What are you doing?

I reached the door from which the sounds emanated just as the cries morphed into moans of pleasure and worship.

What the heck?

I peeked through the small barred opening that provided just enough of a tease for voyeurs like myself. *The torture room from the security footage!* Matt was standing in the center of the chamber. He'd donned black leather chaps and a studded leather collar. His head was tilted back, his eyes closed. Like a piston, his hips repeatedly and violently rammed into a cappuccino-skinned woman's ass. Her face was fully covered by a red mask, but her long black hair extruded into a ponytail from an opening in the back of the mask. She rested on all fours, her wrists and ankles bound by large black straps tied to the floor. Her stomach rested on a padded stool, but her breasts hung in front of it, with clips that looked like large clothespins attached to her nipples.

Her moans intensified. She arched her back, her buttocks gyrating in front of him. He slapped her ass then gripped her hips to force himself deeper into her anus, impaling her repeatedly, faster and faster until he pulled out and ejaculated all over her bare, creamed-coffee back.

She yelped, begging for more, but I walked away before finding out what would follow.

Guess I don't really know Matt...

I continued my walk down the dim passageway, shaking my head to repress the recently acquired memories.

Hoping to see something a little less distressing (and hopefully find another golden dick), I pushed open the next door, which had been left slightly ajar.

This room was different and dead quiet. Its decoration stood on the opposite end of the spectrum from what I'd just seen. It reminded me of a British tea house. Small round tables were peppered around the room, covered with lacy white tablecloths and fresh-cut flowers. Each table was surrounded by two or three padded Victorian chairs for guests to sit on and chit-chat. A large fireplace reigned at the center of the wall in front of me. Around it were displayed gorgeous, gold-framed paintings, but instead of the Victorian or medieval portraits I would have expected to find here, each chef-d'oeuvre featured bigger-than-life, overly-detailed genitalia of both varieties. The first one I looked at featured a gargantuan erect cock. The artist had made the skin appear velvety soft and inviting, with shadows that made the huge member appear to come out of the painting. I looked at the next one: a large set of engorged labia upon which reigned a stubby clit. This time, the finish wasn't velvety soft; the paint glistened with the flickers of the fireplace. And just then, as I was about to look at the next large painting, a woman cleared her throat.

I turned around and saw one of the maids standing next to a blank canvas.

"Would you like to become part of our collection?" she asked.

This place keeps on surprising...

"Hmm, I think I'll pass for now," I said before once again waving my gold cock in the air. "I'm looking for a few more of these."

"Ah... Well I had taken one, in the event the evening got boring, but you can have it. I'm sure I'll find someone else to occupy myself with," she said with a smile. Her hand reached down among her painting supplies. She retrieved the golden dick and handed it to me.

After thanking her, I left the room and continued on my quest.

A short stroll down the passageway later, I found another alcove built in the stone wall. I retrieved my final piece of the puzzle from underneath its protective dome. At the base of the glass holder were engraved the following words:

May your hungry pussy eat up my entire weight in gold.
Again and again.

My third and final dildo in hand, and a grin brought on to my lips by the castle's attention to prose, I opened the last door at the end of the passageway and found another set of stairs, this one leading up. But strangely, the more steps I climbed, the darker it got. I slowed down, letting my eyes adjust to the darkness. A light feeling of claustrophobia rolled over me the higher I got, as though I was climbing to a dead end.

But no. It wasn't the case.

After my eyes finally adjusted to the darkness I found a square opening at the top of the stairs. The ceiling was really low though, I could touch the wooden surface. *No, not a ceiling,* I realized. A faint light came in all around me. I walked toward it and reached a layer padded with plush cushions. Then a step, then a cloth draping from above.

I crawled out from underneath the surface and saw that I had found the waiters' secret passageway to the "head course" of the meal. The diners had long gone though. I was alone in the great hall and had absolutely no idea where I could find my hot butler so I could claim my prize.

Security camera!

With a plan in mind, I went back to my room. I knew Matt was probably still down in the torture room, inflicting pain to the cappuccino woman, whose cries still resonated in my mind. *She found pleasure in that?*

Once I got in my bedroom, I flicked through the security channels: laundry room, torture room—Matt was still at it, but another woman had joined them, this one with a studded leather outfit. *Argh, that's too much for me.* I continued flicking: the kitchen, the dining room, the reception... *There he is!* He was alone, watching something on a screen.

But I realized all of this running back and forth had kind of dried me up... *Maybe I should warm myself up again.*

I turned on one of my dildos. Its soft burr roared gently in my otherwise quiet room. I sat on the bench at the foot of the bed, looking at my bald black man on TV. He had a remote in hand. Whatever he was watching had probably dulled his interest. I looked at his dark beady eyes on the screen. His tongue moistened his lips, exposing his bright white teeth for a second. He changed the channel again. I brought up my dress slightly, parted my legs, and brought the purring device to caress my inner folds. The gentle vibration of the device sent soothing Barry-Manilow-like low frequencies onto my pussy and beyond.

I returned my full attention to the TV screen. My bald butler raised his eyebrows and readjusted the way he sat in his chair. He placed the remote down in front of him, then unzipped his pants. With his right hand, he pulled out his humongous black cock and started taming it, slowly. I felt an uncontrollable smile grow on my face.

Seems we're both playing the same one-player game.

The tip of my golden dildo fell into my pussy, tingling my opening as I pushed it in a little more. I looked down at myself, spreading open my lips as I watched the golden apparatus come out of me, wet from my own juices. I cranked the speed up a notch and prodded myself some more, trying to find just the right spot. I adjusted my hips on the seat. With a fling of my fingers, I undid the strap of my left sandal and brought my naked foot up onto the bench. My dildo had found just the spot. I cranked up the speed some more, both on the device and on my own prodding motions.

I stared at my bald man giving himself a beating. His own speed increasing as well... until he stopped. He let go off himself, then stared right at the camera and made a "come here" motion with his fingers before pointing at his erect cock.

Poor thing. He shouldn't leave that huge cock standing there, all alone!

Without thinking, I reached down to undo my other sandal then rushed to the reception area—bare feet and pussy dripping wet— before someone else could claim my large, erect prize.

10:30 p.m.

The tall, bald butler got up from behind the desk as I approached.

"You were watching me, weren't you?"

"Maybe," I said between hurried breaths. My chest heaved as my breathing returned to normal. From where I stood, I couldn't tell if he'd hidden his cock or if it was still out in the open. I wanted that wooden reception desk to dissipate instantly so I could jump his bones already.

"No need to pretend," he said with a smile. "From here I can see what channel everyone's room is tuned on."

"Interesting," I said before biting my lips. I looked down and realized I was still holding on to my purring vibrator.

"And...," he started before walking away from me along the counter. He pushed an access panel that allowed him to join me on my side of the counter. "I could see that you were enjoying that golden dick," he said while taking it away from my hand. He turned it off and stuck it upright on the counter next to us. "Would you like to trade it in for a black one?"

I looked at him. There it was. His bare, glorious shaft pointed upward at a 45-degree angle, out of his pants' zipper opening as he walked closer toward me. I swallowed hard to prevent my own saliva from dripping out of my mouth. It certainly wasn't golden, but its shape and foreskin made me appreciate that some men really do look like their cocks... Big, huge, and bald. But right now, I wanted his humongous shaft more than anything—as long as it didn't come with a whip and restraints.

He kept walking but stopped within a foot of me. He pushed my hair back behind my shoulders and looked down at me.

"Beautiful dress. Looks great on you," he said while sliding the back of his hand along my neck, then along the skin of my exposed chest. His hand kept gliding down. He lowered himself and rested his knees on the *Welcome* mat on which I had stood during check-in earlier today. His hand found its way to the slit of my dress while his other hand lifted up and bunched the fabric off to the side. He blew onto my pussy as he approached it, his warm breath feeling delicious among the cool air of the castle. His adept tongue traced my lips and tickled my clit, but it wasn't what I needed.

"Enough foreplay," I said between moans. "I need you inside of me now!"

He pulled his head away from my pussy and looked at me, his fiery eyes in agreement with my request. He dug in his pant pocket and retrieved a condom, which he quickly donned.

"Come down," he said, his hands on my hips, pulling me down toward him. He sat on the mat. I hiked up my dress and parted my legs so I could position myself around him. My knees on both sides of his hips, I lowered my pussy onto his huge shaft. I delighted when my insides parted, swallowing almost all of his length. I was so wet that even his huge girth slid into me like it belonged there. I rocked my hips toward the front for a second, wanting my clit to rub against him, then pulled myself up again. Slowly. Until he almost came out of me. Then, I slid down that pleasure pole, again and again. Each time faster. His hands dug my breasts out of my dress and I let them bounce away as my hungry pussy feasted on his large cock. Out of habit, one of my hands reached down to my clit. I had to flick it. I had to build up the pleasure. I had to come before him.

He moaned. He grunted. Then an orgasm enveloped my senses, forcing me to become still, save for the uncontrollable shivers. He took over the motions, thrusting his hips upward into me as my insides kept convulsing. He kept ravishing me as my entire insides pulsated in pleasure. My yelps of joy echoed in the large entrance hall, then his climax joined my chorus. I let myself fall on my side, the tiled floor cooling my quivering body. His hips had followed my fall, turning slightly. My hands went to my exposed breast. My ecstasy and pounding heart were making them heave out of control, but it was nothing compared to my throbbing pussy. I could feel it kneading convulsively onto the butler's cock, which it still held hostage.

"How I love my job!" said the butler, bursting my orgasmic bubble.

11:00 p.m.

After doing up my dress, my pussy finally satisfied, I agreed to partake in the champagne the butler offered. How grateful was I for that enormous itch to have been scratched!

"Fancy seeing what people are up to? Or what they're watching?" he asked.

Curiosity had the best of me. "Sure," I said.

He sat on the chair behind the desk, then tapped on his lap to invite me to join him.

I did, wrapping an arm around his muscular shoulders.

He flipped through the channels of the small TV screen that had been installed on the desk below the computer monitor. With a click of a mouse followed by a swift flight of fingers across the keyboard, he made tabulated data appear on the monitor.

"See? I can see your room is still tuned to the reception area, but nobody's in your room now," he said after flicking to the video camera in my bedroom. I hadn't seen a camera in there, but based on the angle, it had to be located just above the fireplace.

"Looks like two rooms are watching the dungeon and another is watching the spa."

He grabbed the remote again, flipping through more channels.

"Stop," I said as I recognized Lucie and her husband. The two of them were sitting at the foot of their bed, a bucket of champagne next to them, with three flutes.

"Shoot! I was supposed to join them after dinner," I said.

"There's still time."

I got up, and he slapped my ass. My golden dildo stared at me from the desk. I hesitated for a second then grabbed it before rushing away.

"Mind if I watch?" his words echoed unanswered as I climbed up the stairs, feeling my juices dripping out of my slightly sore pussy.

11:20 p.m.

I went down the main hallway, but continued past my bedroom until I saw number 6. I approached the door and brought up my hand to knock, but the first tap of my fist pushed the door open. The wooden door squeaked as I opened it some more.

"Lucie?" I asked.

"*Entre ma chère!*" she said, inviting me to come in.

I walked in and closed the door behind me. Their room was similar to ours, furnished with oversized, hand-carved, wooden pieces but decorated in shades of forest green instead of burgundy. As I'd seen on the security footage, Lucie and Jean-Michel were sitting in front of their bed. They'd tossed a dozen cushions on the carpet in front of the fireplace. He'd taken off his tuxedo jacket, bow tie, shoes, and socks. I looked around the room in search of clues to see if this couple was into pain or had objects similar to those I'd seen in the dungeon a.k.a. torture room. I let out a discreet sigh once I realized I couldn't see such items here.

Lucie, still wearing the same burgundy dress, got up and walked toward me, a large smile on her face. The room was obviously warmer here, her nipples hiding quietly underneath the fabric of her gown.

"Welcome, please come and join us," she said, taking my golden dildo out of my hand.

What I was about to do came with a ton of questions that piled up in my head faster than I could answer them.

How is this supposed to work? Should I approach her? Him? How does protection work here? Oooh... I should probably clean up first. Couldn't say that I'd had sex with different people so soon one after another before, but I knew I should definitely clean up. *Isn't this what bidets are for?*

I suddenly realized Lucie had addressed me in English, so I asked her why while she led me to the cushions in front of the fireplace, holding me by the hand.

"Because that's part of Jean-Michel's fantasy. He wants to have a threesome with a gorgeous foreigner."

I could feel my cheeks warm up. Guess I'd never learn to take a compliment without blushing.

Fingers grazing against my arm made me realize that Jean-Michel was now standing behind me.

"Very gorgeous foreigner..." He walked slowly around me, his touch a soft breeze on my skin. He approached my neck; I heard him inhale my scent. He brushed a hand through my hair, then brought it all to rest in front of me on one shoulder. His fingers traced my neck then slid down below my nape. His hand kept lowering until it reached the small of my back. He twirled me in front of him. After the slow revolution was over, his light brown eyes sparkled, his lips parted slightly, and he took in another deep breath, making me feel like a fine bottle of wine he was assessing for an award. He pulled me in closer, and his free hand traced the outline of the dress's fabric, caressing the exposed portion of my breasts.

His eyes were questioning me, but his mouth remained quiet. His gaze went from my eyes, to my lips, to my cleavage, then back to my lips. He smelled like a temple in exotic Bali.

He approached, his mouth closer to mine. I could hear his heavy breathing, the warm air of his exhalations brushing against my skin.

I finally came out of my paralyzed state. "Listen, Jean-Michel," I said. "I think I should clean up first. You know..."

It took him a second to register my words, but then his eyebrows went up. "*Oui*, of course! Why don't you take a bath? I'm sure Lucie can pour one for you."

She grabbed me by the hand and led me into their bathroom. Instead of being peach-colored, theirs was light green, but the same attention had been given to the exquisite, luxurious decor.

"Let's pour you a bubble bath. Don't you think that would be nice?" Without waiting for my reply, she grabbed a few bottles from the vanity and return to the bathtub. She bent down to the center of the tub where the knobs and drain were located. She adjusted the water temperature, then plugged the tub and let the water run. Once about an inch of water filled the tub, she emptied the small bottle of light green liquid and it foamed instantly.

Lucie turned around and approached me. Her hands came up and framed my face.

"You're so pretty. A true, natural beauty," she said before letting go of me.

She then felt up the sides of my dress until she found the small zipper. With an expert hand, she undid it and released my breasts from my gown's corset-like restraints. I pushed down the dress past my hips and stepped out of it. Lucie picked it up and draped it over the back of the vanity chair as I stepped into the tub. The water was exquisite, but the expansive foam was already reaching the edges of the tub. I turned off the water. An aroma of freshly baked apples filled the air. I let my body sink into the water, which was not as deep as I'd expected it to be. The water barely reached my hips. The rest was all light, foamy, scented bubbles.

Lucie came back toward me, a large hair clip in hand. She expertly wrapped my hair and clipped it in a loose chignon to prevent it from getting wet. Then she undid her dress, her eyes locked onto mine as she disrobed. Her cute breasts were perkier than a teenager's. Her dark nipples came out to greet the cooler air of the bathroom. Like most of the European women I'd seen on various beaches, her upper body displayed no tan lines. With a flick of her hips, she pushed down the stretchy dress and stepped out of it, leaving me a full frontal view of her narrow, blonde landing strip.

Just as she'd done with my dress, she bent down to take her gown then draped it on top of mine on the back of the chair.

She walked up to the tub and stepped into the opposite end. "Mind if I join you?" she asked after the fact.

I heard footsteps and turned around. Jean-Michel had walked in. He headed to the vanity and moved our dresses onto the small desk to clear the chair onto which he sat, facing us.

Lucie turned on the water once more and grabbed the flexible shower head and released it from its holder. She turned the brass fitting around the head and adjusted the water to a wide pattern, which she then sprayed on my chest, destroying some of my bubbly cover until she exposed my left breast. Then my right. She let go of the shower head, which fell somewhere among our limbs. Her hands reached up and cupped my breasts.

"I'd love to have breasts like those," she said as she gently kneaded them. She adjusted her position, going up on her knees, which both fit between my parted legs. She bent down toward me and licked some of the foam off of me. She backed up after a few licks, once again looking at me. The water level increased slowly, pushing more foam onto my chest and covering me once more. Lucie's hand dove underneath the surface and I felt one hand graze my pussy for a split second. Then she retrieved the shower head and adjusted the spray, this time to a pulsating jet.

"My favorite setting," she said, straightening up on her knees and bringing the jet toward her. The foam that had previously covered her groin disappeared instantly. She aimed the jet right at her pussy with one hand. With the other, she parted her thin pink folds. She was a miniature woman even in the smallest details. She closed her eyes, then took in a deep breath, her small breast moving, her nipples even perkier than before. She sighed as she exhaled, her mouth wide open.

"Don't be selfish now, Lucie," Jean-Michel ordered from his corner.

Lucie smiled and reopened her eyes. "Of course not." She redirected the shower head at me. The strong jet first hit my stomach, then she lowered it. The deeper it had to go into the depth of the water, the weaker the jet got. I reached my hand toward the drain. I pulled on the chain and waited, feeling the strength of the jet getting stronger as the water level dropped. The foam however, had remained attached to both of our bodies, except for where the jet was aimed.

I closed my eyes, enjoying the pulsating jet expertly being guided by Lucie. I felt her delicate fingers circling my outer lips, cleaning me up. Then, a demanding mouth suckled on my left breast. The roughness of the skin and the exotic smell told me it wasn't Lucie who was nibbling on my upper body. I reopened my eyes and saw Jean-Michel bent over the edge of the tub. His large hands tightened their grip around my breasts, squeezing them while Lucie had started probing my pussy with her digits.

The pulsating jet, the probing fingers, the nibbling of my nipples... It was all too much. With my body still blushed from my very recent orgasm, the experience overwhelmed my senses in a flash.

I screamed as I convulsed. "Oh myyyy goooddd!"

I pushed away the jet and Lucie's hand before cupping my pussy to protect my sensitive, engorged clit and lips. I moaned in pleasure as I tried to gain control of my breathing again. When I opened my eyes, Lucie's cute, tiny ass was stepping out of the tub. Jean-Michel backed away and got up. His cock tented his black pants as he bent his arms into what was left of the apple-scented foam. One arm under my knees and the other around my back, he lifted me out of the tub and brought my drained body over to the cushions in front of the fireplace.

He unbuttoned his shirt and tossed it aside. His pants and underwear soon followed suit. While Jean-Michel was getting naked, Lucie was busy picking up after him. She hung his clothes on a hanger. *I guess there are no rules to threesomes, OCD cleaning routines included.* I returned my attention to Jean-Michel who straddled me on my stomach, although his weight—thankfully—rested on his own legs. He cradled his cock between my breasts, then squirted sandalwood-scented oil all over my chest. The coolness of the oil surprised me, but his hands soon massaged my skin and warmed me back up. He then buried his cock deep in my cleavage before starting to drive himself back and forth between my breasts. He squeezed them together, tightening the gap and probably enhancing his experience. Among the slurping noises of his back-and-forth motions between my oil-covered breasts, I heard the gentle roar of my golden dildo getting closer. I glanced to my left and saw Lucie playing with the device as she knelt and approached me.

A few seconds later, I felt the familiar poke of the golden device fill my pussy. I brought my hand to Jean-Michel's bare chest, my fingers skimming the light layer of hair between his pecks as he kept tit-fucking me. He suddenly let go of me and slapped my left breast. Hard. "Whoa!" I yelped, watching it bounce from his slap.

"Sorry," he said before squeezing my breasts even tighter together and grinding himself into them faster. With each deep push, I saw his pink, glistening head poking toward my face. I stuck my tongue out and stretched it, as though I could tickle it if only I timed it right. Then, without notice, he gushed out onto my face and into my open mouth. He grunted and kneaded my breasts some more while I licked his salty, gooey treasure off of my face.

And just then, Lucie cranked up the speed on my golden device, while she suckled on my clit, bringing on yet another tidal orgasmic wave to wash over my body.

3:00 p.m.

I hugged Matt prior to him boarding his flight, a light pinch stinging my chest.

Matt had been a great partner for several encounters, but it was probably time to call it quits. I was unsure if I could keep seeing him without feeling like I was preventing him from fully experiencing all of the things he truly enjoyed... Or perhaps I'd risk getting attached to his good looks and fall back to my past, needy behaviors.

I watched his firm ass walk away and join the file of passengers that trickled through the flight attendants' check. His tall body, his broad shoulders, his ocean-scented hair, his fantastic cock, his skilled tongue... I'd miss him, that was for sure.

I smiled and waved at him just as he looked my way after having his ID checked by the flight attendant.

I let out a sigh. That was that. *Goodbye, Matt.*

I turned around and flicked a piece of lint from my uniform.

Time to get ready for work. My own flight would depart in four hours.

As I walked away toward the shops and restaurants in search of a decent cup of coffee, I thought about what I'd seen and done this weekend. I'd made some progress with my sexual life (and definitely kept up with my higher self-esteem), but I also felt like I'd only seen the tip of the iceberg, like I was a virgin of sorts when it came to certain sexual acts.

There were so many new experiences I still had to try.

Multiple partners at once I think I could really enjoy, but S&M and bondage... Can't knock it until I try... But I'm definitely not ready for that yet.

A hot British Airways pilot smiled at me as we crossed paths. I'd never seen him before, but I felt my pussy twitch just thinking about the fun I could have with him in bed. It wasn't the first uniformed man who had me fantasizing at first glance.

Guess I have a weakness for airline captains?

I had to figure out a way to scratch that itch without making a reputation for myself. After all, captains were at the top of the hierarchy once in the air. *Is having sex with authority figures my fetish? Or is it the captain's uniform that turns me on? Or something else?*

I'm sure Freud would have something clever to say about it.

MY XXX EXPERIENCE

IRELAND

THE PLAN

MY STEWARDESS'S last entry puzzled me, especially her having a thing for airline captains. *Does she know me? Have our paths crossed before? Did she purposefully drop her diary in* my *bag?*

If only time travel existed... I could simply turn around and look at her face (and the rest of her...) But it's impossible, so it leaves me with the following options for now:

OPTION 1: Determine which airline employs my stewardess by reviewing their onboard duty-free offerings and eliminating those that don't offer a Dior perfume set.

First, that would be a lot of airlines to check (not to mention tedious work); and second, current airline offers may not be the same as last month's, last year's, or those of whenever she wrote that journal entry.
Likelihood of success: Close to nil.

OPTION 2: Deduce her employer by eliminating airlines that don't fly into Dublin/DUB and other airports she's flown to based on her journal entries.

Theoretically, that *could* help, but with shared flight codes and airline partners... It would still be useful to know if she was part of Star Alliance, SkyTeam, or Oneworld, though. The task of determining her exact airline (and her identity) would then be a little easier. But I can't do much with the information I have to date. And what if she's changed airlines for some reason?

Likelihood of success: Close to nil.

OPTION 3: Go to the one-of-a-kind castle in Ireland and track her down.

Jackpot! I know the name of this unusual castle. As to whether or not I'll be able to retrieve any useful information from the staff... Who knows? But definitely worth a try. Can't wait to ravish all of these hot maids. Is there a better way to retrieve information?

Likelihood of success: Average to high.

I can't wait to get to the Emerald Isle and start my all-inclusive fuck fest.

WHAT HAPPENED

I did find that special Irish castle, but I've since redacted its name from her diary (should it ever fall into the wrong person's hands). Last thing I'd want is for this place to become popular with butt-ugly, lame-in-bed tourists. That would destroy one of the last few, true, remaining Wonders of the World.

I was planning to travel alone so I could take advantage of all the amenities on my own time, but when I called to book a room for a long weekend that coincided with one of my scheduled layovers, the receptionist informed me in her velvety Irish-accented voice that it was a very romantic hotel, so the castle only catered to couples. Hearing her words (and imagining the red-headed body that came with it) got me hard in seconds. Couldn't wait to get there.

But that meant that I had to find myself a woman to accompany me on the trip, a great-looking one if at all possible. Since I don't have a stand-by, go-to woman I haven't discarded after the initial go, I figured I'd wait to see what my crew had in store for me and then pick the best looking of the bunch, at least of those who were into the *Pilot-Stewardess Mentoring Program* as I liked to call it. I needed to be careful though. The lawyers who provided our mandatory annual harassment training had scared me enough that I now only approached the cute ones who smiled at me. Normally, the ones who brought me lunch were a good bet.

And if not, I'm sure I could hire a good-looking escort once I set foot in Ireland.

12:00 p.m.

It seemed the universe had received my request loud and clear (or at least, my lucky star still shone bright from above.)

A couple of hours into our flight, after getting a call that my meal would be served shortly, a knock was heard on the cockpit door.

Bob, my co-pilot, pressed the toggle switch to open the door then got up, letting the lunch-holding stewardess in. "Enjoy your meal," he told me. "I'm gonna stretch and take a long bathroom break. I'll be back in about fifteen."

He squeezed passed the tall brunette in the tight space and addressed her, "Can you keep my lunch warm and bring it to me in half an hour?"

She nodded and I invited the brunette to sit down on Bob's seat. As per airline policy (to avoid hijacking and other security breaches), I was not allowed to be alone in the cockpit, and the door always had to be locked.

So, there we were: a hot brunette with me in a small, locked space. But I had to be careful with my words. After all, the voice recorder was always active.

We chit-chatted about nothing for a few minutes while I ate. Between bites, I asked her about her plans: if she was going to stay for a few days, or if she was heading back right away. She said she had the weekend off.

Perfect.

"Do you have an itinerary? A place to stay, things you want to see?" I asked.

Her mouth went up in a frown as she shook her head. "Nah, I like to wing it. I'd like to visit the Guinness Brewery. Maybe go to that bar that U2 owns..."

I finished my last bite then wiped my mouth with my napkin. "Are you staying somewhere special?"

"Haven't booked anything. But it's low-season. I'm sure I'll find a room." She smiled at me in a way that could mean something.

Just so I'd have the benefit of the doubt should someone listen to the in-flight recording, I crumbled the aluminum foil that previously covered my meal as I spoke again. "I have reservations at a unique castle. I'm sure they could accommodate the both of us." I tossed the aluminum mess I'd created into my empty glass.

Ball's in her court.

"Accommodate the both of us," she repeated, a smirk on her face. "If you're inviting me to your bed, I hope you're a more straight-forward lover than that," she said, standing up then letting her hands graze up my pants.

I pulled on her arms to force her to bend toward me, then planted my lips onto hers, one of my hands reaching to squeeze her breast through her shirt.

Solid C-cup.

Her tongue blazed into my mouth. Her hand grabbed the nape of my neck. Then, without a reason that I could tell, she pushed me away and backed off.

"That's more like it," she said before winking at me. "I'll see you at the car rental desk?"

And just like that, she unlocked the door and exited the cockpit, leaving me wanting more.

But now was not the time or place. My co-pilot was coming back in.

12:15 p.m.

"She's alright," Bob said, his hand pointing toward the cockpit door that the stewardess had just closed on her way out. He took back his seat and buckled up.

I nodded and gave him the thumbs up while I chewed on the last bite of my dessert.

"And she's a brunette. Hey, you think she could be *the* woman you're looking for?"

"What?" I asked him while glancing at the console to ensure gauges and displays all read as they should.

"Your gal from the diary. Or have you given up?"

I shook my head. "Can't give up. You think she could be the one?" I paused to think it over, remembering her exact appearance. Hair color and breast size were correct. She was fairly tall. *Really curvy ass, though. Unsure about that. The girls in Mexico would have mentioned that detail, no?*

"Still don't know her name?" Bob asked, interrupting my reflection.

"Sometimes I call her Stefanie, or Samantha, or Suzy..."

Bob's eyebrows went up. "You found out her name starts with an S?"

"No." I shook my head, wondering how I'd come up with those. *Mental association with the word stewardess...?* "Could be Julia, Barbara... Her name's not important. It's her body I care about... and her—"

Bob chuckled. "Her name could be George..."

I flicked the back of my hand against his shoulder.

He lifted his chin. "Serious man! What if some guy played a prank on you?"

I looked at him squarely: his face was stern, his eyes steady.

"How much money are you going to waste looking for her?" he asked.

"Come on, Bob! A prank *that* elaborate? The hand-writing's too pretty to be a man's. And the girls I spoke to in Mexico, the video I found in L.A... She exists."

"Well... I still think you're wasting your time. You're chasing a ghost."

2:30 p.m.

As promised, the tall brunette met me at the car rental desk.

She arrived right after I'd finished reviewing and signing the rental agreement. I watched her stroll toward me, carry-on in tow. *Could she be the stewardess?* I didn't remember ever crossing paths with her before today's flight. But maybe an even more attractive woman had distracted me at the time. She was pretty. And obviously open to having a good time. I eyed her slender legs as she quickly bridged the gap that separated us. She hadn't changed out of her uniform yet and neither had I. *What's another three hours in my work clothes?* I couldn't wait to get to my special castle. I could undress her to find out if her tits matched those of the picture I'd seen in Mexico. *Or would she just tell me if I asked? Or would she lie and stretch the mystery as far as she could?*

Keys in hand, I headed toward the car I'd been assigned. She followed.

"This is the one," I said, pointing at the silver Corolla a few feet in front of us. "What's your name by the way?" I asked her, turning around to look at her.

"Crystal," she said, flashing me her pearly whites.

Memories of a very special Crystal sliding around a brass pole in Florida flashed in my mind. *A name with potential.* I unlocked the car doors and popped the trunk with the keychain remote.

"It was my grandmother's name," she continued while pushing her bag's handle to retract it into its slot. "She died just before I was born, so my mom insisted on naming me after her."

So much for the mental image of my pole-dancing Crystal. It'd irreversibly been replaced by a gray-haired lady dusting her crystalware.

"And you?" she asked while I placed her bag in the trunk next to mine.

"I'm Charlie," I said with a smile. "Nice to officially meet you."

I took off my hat and jacket, which I then lay on top of our small suitcases in the trunk before closing it.

Once in the driver's seat, I oriented myself with the somewhat awkward positioning of the control, while she chitchatted some more about her grandma. I turned on the GPS and entered the castle's coordinates while her verbal deluge of useless information continued.

I started the engine, which granted me her silence, followed by a strange outburst of teenage-like excitement that came complete with clapping and bouncing up and down.

"Can't believe we're going to a castle!"

"Never been to one?" I asked, happy that the topic had moved away from her family.

"No, I've never been anywhere else in Ireland outside of Dublin."

Strike One. Or is she just lying?

We managed to stay on a semi-interesting topic for a while, but about twenty minutes later, she reverted back to her family.

"It's funny, my new brother-in-law, the one who now owns the farm I grew up on, was asking me—"

"At junction 9, use the left three lanes to take the N7 exit to Limerick/Cork/Waterford/N8/N9," said my GPS. I ignored what Crystal said next, focusing my attention on the unfamiliar road signs and ensuring I kept focused on reversing everything I knew about lane directions and driving behavior.

Amid the flat, suburban scenery that started filling my view on both sides of the motorway, I overheard bits and pieces of my guest's never-ending verbal diarrhea. If only I could plug that mouth with a piece of myself and shut her up. Hard to do while driving... *Should I ask her to blow me right this minute?*

"Do you keep a journal?" I asked her, opting for a different tactic and abruptly interrupting the tale of her second cousin's wedding.

She paused for a few seconds, so I turned to look at her. Confusion—or was it resentment?—lurched from her eyes. I returned my attention to the road.

"You mean like a blog?" she asked.

I shook my head. "No. Journaling. Writing stuff down on paper. Do you keep a personal diary?"

She scuffed. "Hell no! Who has time for that?"

If you were to shut up once in a while, hours would magically appear.

Strike Two. Well there goes that theory. She's not my stewardess... and actually, I'm relieved she isn't.

"So... other than family farms and weddings, what are you into?" I asked.

A solid two hours of celebrity gossip and fashion tips followed, save for the much-appreciated interruptions provided by my GPS. Its computerized voice was a delight to my ears. I couldn't care less about whatever that Kardashian woman that Crystal kept talking about had done or was doing unless she was sitting on my face—and doing so in total silence.

The following goes without saying: I was relieved beyond belief when we finally arrived at our destination.

"Wow! You weren't kidding. It's a real castle!"

She clapped again. *Argh.* Then she undid her seat belt and opened the door. I appraised her ass as she got out of the car. On a scale of 1 to 10, she deserved a solid 8 for hotness but got a -6 penalty for not knowing when to shut up or act like a grown woman.

I can ditch her soon enough, though. I'm sure the staff here will keep me entertained.

5:55 p.m.

A tall blond butler opened the door for us and led us into the expansive entrance hall, which matched to a T what the stewardess had described in her journal. *So this place does exist...* A part of me had remained skeptical, but I'm an optimist and was hoping for the best.

Unfortunately, the butler didn't look anything like Liam Hemsworth. He obviously wasn't a tall, bald, black man either. But based on my guest's googly eyes, he was attractive.

I scanned the vast space, hoping to find someone I could recognize from the stewardess's diary. The woman behind the reception desk wasn't the red-headed woman I'd fantasized about. *Too bad.* But the strawberry-blonde little thing standing there was very hot nonetheless. *Her luscious bubble-gum colored lips would look stunning around my cock, her doe eyes looking up at me...* Her French-maid outfit was even better than the one I'd been picturing in my mind. With so little fabric, nip-slips had to be common workplace hazards.

While I admired the receptionist, my guest once again clapped like a stupid thirteen-year-old. I turned to look at her. She was twirling, her arms stretched out to her sides, her head tilted back to look up at the ceiling.

"Helloooo!" she called out, listening to her own voice bouncing and echoing against the stone walls.

Seriously?

I let her be and proceeded to greet the hot receptionist and check ourselves in.

6:00 p.m.

Once again, my hopes that Kate and/or Chloe would be the ones to bring up our bags got dashed.

Is my good luck gone?

The maids who'd been assigned to us were definitely hot and fuckable, though: Victoria was tall and skinny, her hair pitch black; Sharla was shorter, very curvy, and slightly oversized. *They wouldn't know my stewardess or be able to help me track her down. Guess I'll just have to get on with the program and make the most of my stay.*

We left our luggage with Victoria and were led up the stairs by the shapely Sharla.

Crystal's childish excitement kept growing the deeper we got in the entrance of the castle. She oohed and aahed at the tapestries hung by the staircase while going up. I admired the bare crotch above my head instead. She giggled like a young girl when she saw the large oil paintings lining the upstairs hallway. I mentally prepared myself for the tipping routine instead. *Will I get Victoria or Sharla?* Sharla's pussy sure looked inviting a few seconds ago.

Victoria arrived just on time with the luggage trolley. She met us in our room, then offered to unpack our bags.

I declined, but Crystal took her up on her offer. "And could you also pour me a bath, please?" she asked the tall and skinny maid.

"Of course, I'll run the bath," said Victoria, leaving our bags on the brass trolley. I watched the rounder maid grab Crystal's suitcase and place it on the bench at the end of the bed. I felt a little ungentlemanly to not offer to lift the carry-on bag, but, having taken it out of the trunk a few minutes earlier, I knew it was light, and I wanted to watch her bend down and contort her body in the tiny outfit. She proceeded with a smile, first unzipping the navy blue suitcase, then carefully unfolding the neatly folded shirts, skirts, and black underwear my guest had brought. Sharla then walked to the wardrobe to open it and retrieve a few hangers, stretched up to reach the pole, and then down, and... *Ding, ding ding! First nip-slip!* And a big one at that! By the time she had finished hanging all of Crystal's clothes, the maid's entire beautiful left tit hung loose.

"Um..." Chrystal said before clearing her throat.

"Anything else I can help you with?" Sharla asked Crystal.

Crystal's hand flew up in the air, rotating around her own breast. "You're... You're... showing," she finally said.

The rounder maid looked down at her breasts, then her eyebrows went up. "It'd probably be better if I evened things out, don't you think?" she said before pulling out her other round tit from her dress.

"That's not what I meant!" Crystal said, her eyes going from Sharla to me, then back to Sharla who was walking toward Crystal while massaging her swollen, natural globes.

"You don't like them?" Sharla asked. "Why don't you show me yours so your captain friend here can tell us if our bodies are beautiful."

Crystal was now more confused than ever.

"I want to play, too!" said Victoria as she came back in the room. I turned toward her as she pulled down her top, exposing her small, perky breasts.

"What kind of place is this?" Crystal asked, her face red, her voice approaching the boiling point.

"First time I guess." Victoria frowned, then covered her small boobs. She walked over to one of the nightstands and retrieved a black leather binder, which she handed to Crystal.

Sharla's hand placed most of her left tit back in her dress, and she was about to cover her other large, pink nipple. "No!" I said, taking a few steps toward her so I could caress her fleshy mountains of natural goodness before it was too late.

"Ah, I see the captain may be interested in our services." Sharla smiled at me, her hand pulling down her dress and re-exposing her beautiful mounds. I kneaded them and pinched her nipples.

From the corner of my eye, I saw Crystal march into the bathroom, binder in hand. The door slammed shut behind her. I couldn't see where Victoria had gone to, but it didn't matter. Those gorgeous DDD-cups were out of this world. I was about to bend down to suckle on them when Sharla pulled on my tie and backed up toward the bed, taking me along with her. She landed on her back. I landed on top of her, on the world's most comfortable pair of cushions. My erect shaft pushed against the fabric of my pants, but Victoria suddenly reappeared, her hand reaching between me and Sharla, undoing my belt, then pulling down my zipper.

I lifted myself off from the beautiful tits and brought up the bottom of her crinoline dress. There it was, the pussy I'd seen while climbing the stairs, in all of its bare glory. I heard a drawer sliding nearby. I turned and saw Victoria reach into the nightstand and retrieve a handful of condoms, which she placed next to Sharla on the bed. Victoria then climbed onto the bed. She placed a pillow underneath Sharla's head, then knelt herself squarely above Sharla's face before lifting her dress up in the front and exposing herself to me. Her black stockings were held up by black garters. Her matching black bush had been trimmed into a small V, or perhaps an arrow pointing down. Sharla was looking up, her fingers grazing Victoria's pussy while another hand was groping her own exposed breasts. Sharla's bald pussy was spread open for me to inspect or do as I wish with.

Best Irish scenery ever.

The bed was at the perfect height for me. I suited up my cock with one of the condoms, then gently pulled Sharla's pussy closer to the edge of the bed. Victoria took care of repositioning the pillow, then herself while the tip of my cock made a recon move into Sharla. I probed her gently and slowly at first, taking in the view and pacing myself. I let my hands seize her humongous tits while my hips began their regular thrusting rhythm. Her tunnel was tight, slippery, and wet. I brought my hands back to her legs and pussy, parting her thighs some more, bringing one of her legs to rest on my shoulder, then parting her folds. I licked my fingers before bringing them to her clit. I teased it while looking at my cock sliding in and out of her. Sharla started moaning. I increased my cadence. I started pounding her harder and harder, watching her huge boobs bounce out of control while she sloppily ate her counterpart's pussy.

In between slurping and sucking noises, whenever Sharla came up for air, juices glistened on her cheeks and chin. Above her face, Victoria started squealing like an ambulance siren. One hand rubbed at her own clit while she twisted one of her nipples. I throttled Sharla's clit with my thumb while ramming her. I felt Sharla's pussy clench around my cock. Her head pulled away from Victoria's pussy. Her back arched, bringing her tits up, even though they still spilled over to her sides. She squeezed them together as she came in a loud scream. That was all I could take. I gave her my all and came into her pulsating pussy.

While my heartbeat returned to normal, my senses came back to reality. Sharla's mouth had returned to her friend's pussy. Victoria's squeals had reached new levels. She closed her eyes and her cries stopped suddenly. I watched her face contort in silence as her hips quivered above Sharla's head.

I wonder if turndown service will be the same?

6:30 p.m.

After the maids reminded me of the upcoming dinner that started at 7 p.m. sharp, they left me—fully satisfied.

I did up my pants and decided to check on Crystal.

I walked over to the bathroom door and gently rapped on it. "Crystal, can I come in?" I asked.

A few seconds elapsed, making me wonder if she'd left the room unnoticed while I was doing the maids.

"Yes," she said, finally.

I pushed open the door and saw her coming out of the tub, butt naked, a few clouds of foam still attached to her firm, young, and beautiful body. For a few seconds, I admired her curves, her tan, her tits, and her pussy. She actually deserved higher than an 8, especially now that her mouth was closed. Her tits, although beautiful, confirmed that she wasn't my stewardess.

"Like what you see?" she asked while reaching toward a large white towel than hung nearby. Her C-cups had yet to display the damages of gravity.

I smiled at her. "Indeed."

She wrapped her body into the towel, forcing me to look away from it and notice her stern face. Her stare was icy. Her lips flat.

"You're mad?" I asked.

Her hands flew up as she shook her head, her eyes now perfect circles, her mouth agape. "You brought me to a whorehouse and you don't expect me to be mad?"

"Last I checked, I'm the one paying the bill. You accepted my invitation, and you seemed eager to get to know me better..."

She snorted. "I was looking forward to having sex with *you*, Charlie. Not the maids!"

"Well... this place is an open-bar," I said. "Me, maids, butlers, other guests... You can have whoever your cute little pussy fancies."

"So I read," she said, her head pointing at the binder sitting on the vanity.

Her comment had me curious. I headed toward the vanity and picked up the leather binder. The cover was soft. On it were engraved, in gold letters, the words *Rules of Conduct*.

I flicked past the first few pages, then stopped on a numbered list:

1- Have the decency to protect yourself and our staff. A large supply of condoms is provided free of charge in all rooms.
2- If someone doesn't want you, be respectful and walk away.
3- Open your mind. Try new things and new people.
4- We will not be held liable for unwanted pregnancies or medical claims.
5- For emergencies that are not related to your being horny, dial 1-1-2.

I put the binder down, not wanting to read anything that would remove the mystique from what I was so eager to experience.

"By the way, dinner starts in..." I paused to look at my watch, "...twenty minutes. There are evening gowns in the wardrobe. Formalwear is required."

She grunted as she stepped out of the bathroom.

I took it as a sign that she had registered the information, then undressed and stepped in the shower.

I needed to freshen up for dinner.

6:55 p.m.

Dressed in a tuxedo, and with a slightly angry but thankfully-still mute guest on my arm, I headed down to the great hall.

Classical music aired in the room that bore its name extremely well: it *was* great. Twenty or so people—all dressed in penguin suits or sexy gowns—were mingling, champagne flutes in hands.

I grabbed two glasses at the first opportunity, temporarily stepping away from my guest to do so. When I backtracked to offer her a drink, she was gone. A quick scan of the room told me she was headed toward a blond, muscular man whose neck was as wide as his square face. He was sitting on the arm of a large leather chair, chatting with another champagne-holding man.

Good riddance.

Now... What lovely lady will have the pleasure of getting to know me better tonight? The options were numerous, but I had to pick an open-minded woman. *I don't want another Crystal.* A wild-haired brunette reached me before I had made a decision.

"Are you going to drink them both?" she asked, her head pointing at my extra champagne flute. Below the tangled mess of her curls, the twinkle in her mascaraed eyes and her thick bright lips screamed *good time.*

"This one's for you," I said, handing her a glass. "I'm Charlie, by the way."

"Heather. Nice to meet you." She picked up the flute I was offering then clinked it against mine. A sip later, she licked her lips. "First-time?"

I nodded. "You?"

"I'm a convert. I come here every three months or so."

I eyed her up and down. Her ivory skin hadn't seen much sun. She wore a navy blue dress that consisted of two small bunches of fabric going from her shoulders to her hips, where they merged and widened to continue as the bottom of her dress. I couldn't see her legs at all, the flowing fabric reached the floor, but those two small bunches of fabric left an expansive V-neck that sank all the way down to her pierced navel. The fabric barely covered the center of her breasts, leaving the curvatures of her natural, perky, drop-shaped tits hanging visibly on both sides.

Although the only thing I wanted was to dig those breasts out, I restrained myself. After all, I had to act the part: I was wearing a tux. "Any tips for a first-timer?"

"Go with the flow. And... Actually, during the meal, if anything happens, just close your eyes and enjoy. You won't believe how heightened your other senses are when you—"

"Ladies and gents," said a deep voice a few feet away from me. I turned and saw a red-headed butler. "Please have a seat. We will begin with the first course shortly."

"Shall we?" I asked my new friend Heather, sliding my arm between her arm and body, grazing her soft white skin in the process.

I led her to the table and helped her with her seat, taking the opportunity to get an aerial view of her cleavage as I pushed her chair forward. Her stomach was totally flat, her piercing twinkled in the distance past her breasts. I inhaled to take in her scent: fresh-cut flowers.

I then sat myself on my guest's left. A man had taken the seat to my left.

A few seconds later, a dozen French maids came into the room, steaming bowls in hand. A petite blonde with huge breasts that reminded me of Pamela Anderson's brought my bowl with a large smile, and, as I looked at Heather's maid, I realized she too was being served by a petite, big-breasted, blonde maid. *Twins? That can't be!*

"New staff, again!" I heard Heather say.

I brought my attention back to the crazy-haired brunette. "High personnel turn-over?" I asked her.

"Seems like it. Unsure if unwanted pregnancies could be to blame," she said.

"Since you like this place so much, have you ever considered... working here?" I asked, making small talk, but mostly trying to gauge if she'd want to join me later for some after-dinner treats.

She pursed her lips, her eyebrows went up. She looked excited about the idea.

"There are certain... perks that are only available here, so it would be nice. But clients would keep me busy most of the time, so I wouldn't be able to enjoy what I like as often as I want."

Intriguing. "Does this particular perk have a name?" I asked.

I swear, her skin changed color as though the temperature had risen fifty degrees all at once. She fanned her hand in front of her. "Dustin," she finally said.

I looked around the room. There had to be a dozen menservants. I lowered my voice and asked, "Is he here right now?"

Her eyes widened. "In this room? God no!"

Her breasts were now heaving rapidly. Her hand moved faster to cool herself off, making the fabric of her dress sway... but not enough for my taste. *What is so special about this guy? How can he have that effect on a woman?*

I needed to know, if only so I could replicate his results. I kept probing. "So he's here at the castle but not in this room?"

As though a shiver had gone down her spine, her entire body shuddered. She inhaled deeply, once again forcing me to stare at her breasts as they rose. "I hope he still is." She dipped her spoon in her bowl, putting an end to my questions. At least for now.

A minute or so later, I finished my cream of vegetables and the same blonde waitress (or her twin sister?) picked up my empty bowl, brushing her large breast against my arm while she did.

Heather's obviously planning to hook up with that Dustin after dinner. Might as well work on my Plan B.

About a minute later, the tiny blonde waitress (or her twin) came back with a small plate of antipasto. This time, I allowed myself to grab a feel. Very firm, too firm to be natural, but I wasn't a judgmental guy. She winked at me when our eyes met.

Gotta love this kind of service.

A few plates later, the most anticipated course finally arrived.

I saw Heather's body jerk first, then she said, "Remember to close your eyes."

I did.

I felt my legs slowly being parted, then a body squeezed between them. The sound of my zipper getting undone seemed louder than it should have been. I instinctively coughed to cover it up. An expert hand quickly brought me up to speed. Then, the warmth of a hungry mouth swallowed my cock. A tongue flickered. A hand held the base of my shaft as the open mouth feasted on me. *Is it one of the blonde twins?* Skillful fingers circled and clamped my balls with the exact pressure I needed. The lips and tongue kept at it, their warm embrace sometimes spiraling around me, sometimes deep-throating me. I had kept my hands on the table in front of me until now, but could no longer resist. The stimulation—or perhaps my heightened senses—had grown my excitement much faster than it normally did. I was about to come. I wanted to grab the woman's head and hold on to her hair. *Best head I've ever received in my life.* I let go of the table and reached for the head in my crotch just as I came, squirting my juices into the mouth of my...

I froze when I felt the short hair. I opened my eyes and saw large rectangular hands—one of which was still wrapped around my cock. A young, brown-haired, baby-faced man pulled away from me. Some of my come must have overflowed out of his mouth. It was dripping off of his chin. He smiled at me before disappearing under the table cloth and away from my legs.

What the fuck?

Heather's exalted cries made me turn to look at her. I swallowed hard. She had parted the front of her dress, her back was arched, and her hands were cupping her beautiful, now fully exposed breasts. Her small nipples pointed to the sky. That sight should have delighted me, hell it should have made me want to stand up and grab them. Eat them. But I couldn't move right now. I blinked. Repeatedly. My heartbeat was still racing. Was it just from my orgasm? *What the heck has just happened?* I looked to the man sitting on my left. He was still busy, couldn't care less about what had just happened to me. The head that bobbed on his lap had long brown hair. *Lucky.* I kept swallowing harder and harder, as though it would make me feel better. But it didn't.

Was it the certainty of my heterosexuality I could no longer swallow?

8:25 p.m.

I missed most of what happened during the fifteen minutes that followed. If any of the kinky stuff that my stewardess had described occurred, I totally missed it, dealing with accepting the fact that I'd just had my first male-to-male encounter... and it had felt good? Better than good, actually... I pushed those thoughts down past my brain's non-return valve.

I came back to my senses as the butler was reaching Heather's seat, hat in hand.

"Is Dustin available?" she asked him.

"Yes, he is. Ready as usual in the stable."

In the stable? Was Dustin a farmhand?

"Good. He'll be my dessert, then." Heather's chest once again started heaving profusely. This time, she brought one of her hands into her dress, squeezing her breast. She closed her eyes. I could hear her heavy breathing from my seat.

What the heck is so special about this guy?

The butler walked toward me and offered his hat. I was glad he was red-headed and therefore not the guy who'd given me the best blow job I'd ever had. I retrieved my dessert:

Spa treatment: Pick one (or more) of the staff and enjoy an all-inclusive spa treatment of your choice.

A few minutes later, people started pulling away from the table. I stood up and headed toward the first twin I found to make sure nobody else was going to claim her.

I handed her my paper slip. "Would you and your sister be interested in joining me at the spa?" I asked.

She smiled at me, exposing her white teeth for the first time this evening.

"We'd love to. We've been chatting about you all evening. Meet us down by the pool in about twenty minutes?"

She gave me instructions on how to find the pool, then I looked at my watch. I had some time to kill.

Why not find out what was so special about that Dustin? I'd love for women to get flustered like that just by thinking about me.

9:05 p.m.

I left the great hall via a door that led to the courtyard.

Once outside, I noticed a faint smell of manure indicating that farm animals did live near the castle. I looked around and saw the silhouettes of a few buildings against the falling dusk. A horse neighed in the distance. The noise had to have come from the stable, so I headed in that direction.

The closer I got, the louder and more frequent the neighs occurred. Then, Heather's moans joined suit. When she screamed to god a split second before the horse neighed and hoofed again, I froze.

Shit. I suddenly understood who Dustin was.

I turned around and hurried back toward the castle as though the farther I got from the stable, the faster the unthinkable mental image I was seeing would disappear.

I don't know for sure. I didn't see anything. But wouldn't it rip her open? Is it even feasible?

I shook my head. For all I knew, she could have been playing with herself while looking at its cock. Or maybe there was a farmhand called Dustin and a horse just happened to be neighing while the two people were going at it.

Yeah. Let's just leave it at that. I didn't want to think about this a second more.

9:20 p.m.

I was beginning to regret coming to this castle, but once I got to the pool and saw my blonde twins wearing tiny red bikinis, I changed my mind.

Their four ballooned-breasts were near perfect spheres, with puny nipples poking through the undersized fabric. They were sitting on the side of the hot-tub, their legs dangling into the water. Their arms extended behind their backs, holding their torsos up, their breasts out. They were smiling at me.

I greeted them while trying to spot a trait that I could use to differentiate them, but I couldn't find anything. Both had soft green eyes, their long blonde hair was exactly the same length. The one's lips were just as luscious as the other's. Their tits were equally humongous and fake.

"I'm Deidre," said the one on the left.

"And I'm Cassandra," said the other.

"I'm Charlie," I said, taking off my jacket, then bow tie. "I don't want to be rude, but how can I tell who's who. You are both beautiful and... identical?"

"There's a very easy way," Cassandra said while pulling on the string of her sister's bottom. Deidre pulled on the other, then pushed down the fabric before spreading her legs open. "Deidre's got a bush," said Cassandra before pulling on both of her strings and sliding down her own bottom. "I don't."

"That will work. But seems like I've got some catching up to do," I said, hurrying my pace as I took off the rest of my clothes.

"Good! Join us when you're ready." Cassandra said before letting her body sink into the steamy tub.

Deidre slipped in beside her, then fully immersed herself in the water before coming back out. She then slicked her wet hair back, her back arched.

I looked away from them for a second, then smiled as I read a safety notice next to me advising patrons that birthday suits were not only allowed, but recommended.

When I turned to look at them again, the twins' beautiful faces were just out of the water. They were floating on their backs. What drew my attention were the floatation devices on their chest. Although still covered by their tops, the red fabric had shifted slightly, partly exposing a couple of their burnt-pink areolae. Their implants were just incredible. They could possibly save a drowning man's life. And with that view, I stepped into the tub, my cock at the ready.

I was glad to feel the warm water on my skin, but couldn't wait to feel their skin against mine. Their mouths, their gorgeous floatation devices, their warm pussies... Their *female* parts. Maybe the past two hours had somehow emasculated me... but I was determined to once again prove my heterosexual identity.

I stepped down once, then twice. After the third step, my dangling balls felt the warmth of the water, my cock seemingly floating toward them. I went further toward the center of the oversized tub—it was really more of a small pool with jets—reaching a deeper level.

The twins straightened up and circled me, bouncing up and down slightly as they stepped around me. One after the other, I undid the knots that kept their farces-of-a-top on. I tossed the wet fabric onto the edge, then stuffed my face into Deirdre's chest. I could feel Cassandra's boobs pressed against my back while she wrapped her arms around my waist. She started feathering my cock with her fingers.

I came out of Deirdre's cleavage, then climbed up a couple of steps and lifted her out of the water to bring her ass onto the edge. She sat upright and I parted her legs and looked at her overgrown blonde pussy as it dripped. Cassandra moved to follow me. The light strokes of her fingers had morphed into a full fist around my shaft. I bent forward, bringing my mouth to Deirdre's hairy pussy. Blowing on it while one of my hands irrepressibly went for one of her knockers.

My tongue twitched there for a second, right at the opening of the wild jungle, ready to part its thick bush and clear the trail to Come Town.

"But what about me?" Cassandra whined behind me.

"Come out with me," I told her. Like a gentleman, I let her go first and watched her ass as she climbed out of the tub. As part of an uncontrollable reflex, my hand slapped her ass. She giggled.

I spotted towels rolled up on a side table and grabbed a few, which I unfolded and laid flat by the side of the tub. Condoms had also been thoughtfully placed here. After suiting up my cock, I took Cassandra by the hips and brought her onto the towel with me. I lay down on my back, holding her by the hand and then guiding her to sit on my erect shaft. She slowly made her way onto my pole in a squatting position. One move after another, she found her rhythm, sliding up and down my shaft like I was a carnival ride. I motioned to Deirdre to join us. She knelt down next to me, then stepped one knee over my face before lowering her Amazonian blonde jungle onto my hungry mouth.

I could no longer see their humongous boobs, but that was alright. I closed my eyes again, letting my other senses intensify the experience. Deirdre's juices salted my mouth while her musky scent inebriated me. I suckled on her. I flicked my tongue against her. I managed to squeeze up one of my arms from between her legs and bring it up to her pussy, parting her folds and then teasing her clit with my fingers. Her sister was still riding my shaft, but was no longer doing it in silence. Slowly but surely both sisters started moaning and groaning. Their quiet groans turned into pre-orgasmic sighs, gaining both in pitch and volume. Cassandra changed position. I felt cool air around my naked cock for a few seconds, then it was once again swallowed by her pussy. But she'd definitely changed my penetration angle. Her breasts brushed against my legs as she rode me downward in a potentially dangerous slant. But she rode me to the finish line with flying colors a minute after her sister came into my mouth.

Isn't it nice when sisters share everything?

5:30 a.m.

Thankfully, I didn't have to deal with Crystal much more over the rest of our stay at the castle. She spent both of her nights in some other bedroom. She even managed to hitch a ride back to the airport with that muscular guy, which made me the happiest guy on earth (especially after a few more successful encounters with the female staff).

I was all packed up now, relaxing a little before checking myself out of this amazing castle.

As I looked out of the bedroom window, putting my thoughts down on paper to keep a record of my Irish experience, I let my gaze settle on a nearby church. The rising sun was shining its pink light just right to emphasize the church's large Celtic cross. In an odd way, the cross's shape represented the perfect woman for me: the intersection of intelligence with sex-appeal, combined with a little circle of craziness. Crystal was lacking in the first; Heather was overly gifted in the third. My stewardess appeared to have just the right balance for me. I'm certainly glad her journal didn't include any mention of Dustin. I'm well hung, but two-legged men can't compete with *that*.

I didn't learn anything new about my stewardess, which sucked.

But I'm glad to know she's obviously not the jealous kind like Crystal. A woman willing to share her man with other women had some sort of je-ne-sais-quoi.

Was it just me, or was it every man's fantasy? Such women seemed to be very few and far between... Of course, the castle's employees appeared to all share that rare quality.

But that stewardess... I couldn't wait to find her. I needed to put my obsession to rest. Maybe I'd get to know her a little first. Or not... But I definitely couldn't wait to thrust my cock in her warm pussy...

And this could happen very soon if I keep at it... If I keep following the clues from her diary.

NEXT STEPS

I re-read her next journal entry, and I'm still impressed by her ability to push her own boundaries and explore hidden territories.

It's hard to believe what the innocent woman who went camping with her boyfriend has turned into... Her layover in Thailand proves that she's certainly changed a lot since that camping trip. Her Thai spa experience is definitely... unique. At least I can't say that I've experienced that kind of massage in the past (in Thailand or in any other country). And, to be honest, I'm not sure if I'd want to experience *all* of it.

But I still have some data processing to do with respect to my own experiences. I'll deal with it some other time. I've gone beyond a line I didn't believe I'd ever cross. I don't think there's any possibility of going back after this... But for now, this fact is filed away, labeled as uncomfortable and raw data, into a different part of my brain.

My mystery stewardess has left me a few decent clues that should hopefully help me learn more about her identity. I think I'm getting closer to my goal: figuring out who she is so I can fuck her until my obsession disappears for good.

Better stock up on antacid as I'm planning on having quite a few spicy Thai meals in the near future.

PART VI
THAILAND

THE STEWARDESS'S ENTRIES
THAILAND

6:12 a.m.

AFTER TURNING on the lights and making the morning announcements in both Thai and English, Ellie came to chat with me in the galley at the back of the plane.

It was my first time working with her. She was the living incarnation of sweetness, politeness, and cordiality with every guest and flight attendant. Since I'd discovered (during our pre-flight meeting) we'd both be spending a few days in Bangkok, we'd been using our few minutes of downtime here and there to get to know each other a bit more. She didn't talk about herself much, though. And it's not like I loved talking about myself either... but not answering her questions would have been impolite. So we ended up mostly chatting about me, then about nothing and everything, except her.

Maybe she's just shy.

However, I wanted to ask her one specific question, but I'd yet to find a way to phrase it without sounding strange or rude. Ellie looked like a mini Thai Barbie (if such a thing existed). She had that weird big-breast to small-waist/small-hip ratio that the famous doll portrayed. I couldn't say that I'd come across many big-breasted Asian women before.

She has to have had a boob job, no?

6:50 a.m.

Ready for the flight's final food service, I followed Ellie with the cart down the port aisle. She looked as fresh and energetic as someone who'd just woken up from a ten-hour sleep in the world's most comfortable bed.

As she walked backward to the front of the economy section, pulling the cart while I pushed it, I couldn't help but stare at her pale—probably cosmetically-bleached—skin, her shiny, silky black hair, and her impressively large breasts for such narrow hips. The short-sleeved white uniform blouse she wore had to have been tailored especially for her.

Ellie and I began offering hot breakfast to the economy folks sitting on our side of the plane, starting with those at the front. We slowly handed out small plastic trays to our sleepy, red-eyed passengers. They got to choose between a tomato-and-cheese omelet or French toast, and both were accompanied by yogurt, orange juice, and a two-bite fruit salad. We then offered hot coffee or tea prior to moving our attention to the next row. Slowly but surely, we made our way toward the back of the plane. Ellie served those in the front while I attended to the rows behind the cart.

After taking 34A's drink order, Ellie called out to me, so I turned my attention to her. She gave a slight head nudge toward the man sitting right next to where she stood while pouring hot coffee into a disposable cup.

Curious, I paused my service and looked at the blond man. I couldn't see much from where I stood, but his medium-length hair and the profile of his nose and jaw made me realize who he was. I'd spotted him when he'd boarded. Handsome would have been an under qualifier for this man. I looked at Ellie again.

She stretched her upper body across the other two passengers sitting between her and the woman who was sitting by the window. "Here you go, ma'am," said Ellie, her large breasts coming less than an inch from handsome 34C's face as she delivered the woman's drink.

She moved out of the passengers' way and smiled at 34C. "Sorry for my reach," she said.

"No problem at all," said the blond man before pushing the button on his armrest to straighten the back of his seat, which made his upper body move forward a bit. *Is he hoping for seconds with 34B's upcoming drink delivery?*

"Green tea?" asked 34B, an older Asian man who looked up from his food tray just long enough to make his request.

Ellie made 34B's drink, then winked at 34C while she served 34B his tea. No boob contact, but I swear she overfilled 34B's cup just so she could deliver it super slowly to grant 34C more time to stare at her breasts. *Man, she's smooth!*

Drink delivered without a drip, she looked at the handsome blond man again. He cleared his throat then asked, "Black coffee, and do you have any salty snacks left-over from the previous service?"

Ellie looked at me with a large smile before replying, "Let me check." She motioned for me to back the cart a bit, then adjusted her scarf to clear the front of her cleavage.

I backed the cart as she'd requested, even though we didn't have anything but breakfast trays in the slots and hot drinks on top. *What is she doing?*

She bent down and rummaged through the trays, looking for snacks that both she and I knew were not there. But 34C's eyes were glued on her cleavage. She was obviously taking her sweet time and enjoying the man's attention.

36A cleared her throat next to me, so I turned to her and handed her the breakfast tray I'd been holding in the air for nearly a minute now.

8:52 a.m.

Ellie and I helped the last passenger off the plane: an elderly American woman who'd told us she was traveling on her own, hoping to visit as many countries as possible before kicking her ultimate bucket. *Is this what I'll become? Is she a future version of me?*

She wore a loose-fitting, flowing dress with a paisley pattern, which gave her a hippy look. Her long gray hair was tied in a braid; she didn't seem to wear any make up, save for a pale shade of shiny pink on her lips. *Traveling the world solo as an elderly woman would certainly beat sitting around in a retirement home and playing bingo with a bunch of grumpy, bitchy women with white-blue hair who do nothing but compete to get the attention of one of the rare few remaining men. Traveling would open the door to a lot more options...*

A few minutes later, having tidied up the plane and ensured nothing had been left behind by the passengers, Ellie and I headed toward customs, chit-chatting about Bangkok, our carry-ons in tow. She'd grown up in the capital and was excited to have the opportunity to share her knowledge of the city with me.

"Why don't you follow me to my favorite hotel? It's clean and inexpensive. Maybe we can have a short nap and then you can put on something pretty? I can take you out this afternoon and show you around town?"

"Sounds like a plan!" I said, looking forward to resting for a couple of hours.

12:00 p.m.

The air in Bangkok was heavy and smoggy. Much muggier than I had remembered and anticipated.

Thankfully, the hotel Ellie and I went to offered air-conditioned rooms. After a short nap, I felt re-energized, at least enough to dig through my carry-on and remind myself of the clothes I had packed. I didn't have many options, but since

Ellie said to wear something pretty, I skipped my jeans—it was way too hot for those anyway—and settled on my burnt-orange, button-down sundress with a pair of comfortable yet feminine sandals.

I had a quick look at myself in the mirror. The chiffon-nylon fabric ended about an inch lower than the middle of my thighs, which was a good length for me. However, my bra straps showed, clashing with the outfit. *Should I go braless?* I took it off, then looked at myself again. *Much better, but will I attract too much attention?*

I took a few steps back, then walked forward toward the mirror, paying attention to my chest as I advanced. Sure, my breasts were not hanging by my belly button—I had to admit they were still quite perky, especially in this air-conditioned room—but the light, flowing fabric of my dress followed my breasts as they swayed unrestricted with each step. *Don't breast tissues benefit when women go braless? Or will it offend local people?* I definitely didn't want to cause any cultural discomfort if it could be avoided by wearing a bra, even though the straps were unsightly at best.

I put my bra back on and opened my bedroom door to head out into the hallway when I saw Ellie standing in front of me, her arm raised as though she was about to knock. She wore an outfit that reminded me of a Japanese school girl. She'd donned a white shirt tied in a knot around her tiny waist, exposing her flat stomach. Her belly button was decorated by a silver ring. Her breasts pushed the blouse's semi-sheer fabric to the extreme; two buttons barely kept the blouse closed over her bright, lime-green bra. She'd kept her stewardess neck scarf and had added a short pleated skirt and long white socks to her look. *Most men would probably want a piece of that!*

"Hi," I said.

She lowered her arm and smiled at me. "Ready?" she asked.

I pointed at my shoulders. "I'm unsure about my straps."

She looked at me. A tiny vertical line appeared between her brows as she shook her head. "It's a really pretty dress, but those straps..."

"Okay," I said, relieved that my initial guess was right. *Better fix my outfit now.* I invited her to come in, then closed the door behind her.

I unclasped my bra through the fabric of my dress before taking it off. After contorting my arms around the dress's spaghetti straps, I tossed the unneeded garment on my bed, then readjusted the dress's straps before looking at myself in the mirror again. *Much better.*

I turned to face Ellie. "But do you think it's too much if I walk around like this?" I asked her while trotting around the room, probably a little faster than I'd be walking anyway, but my breasts really bouncing with each step.

She shook her head. "No problem." The large smile she'd displayed throughout the entire flight had reappeared. "You're much prettier without the ugly straps."

"But this won't offend anyone?" I asked.

She raised her shoulders. "If they're offended, they can look elsewhere. We're not going to visit a temple. What really offends Thai people is tourists who point their feet at them or at monks... or at Buddha statues. You're ready now?"

I nodded.

"Let's go," she said, walking out of my room. "We're going to have fun today, right?"

"Sure," I said, looking forward to being led by this exotic little thing on our upcoming tour of her native Bangkok.

I locked my door, then followed her into the hallway, my small purse in hand.

"Are you hungry?" she asked as we stepped into the elevator.

"A little," I replied, surprised by my stomach, which growled in agreement.

"First we feed your belly, then your mind. After that? Party time!"

"Why not? Let's do it!" I had no idea what she meant by *feeding my mind* since she'd already said we weren't going to visit a temple, but it didn't matter anyway. I was certain Ellie would show me a good time.

We stepped out of the elevator, then left the hotel and hit the streets.

Ellie hailed a *tuk-tuk*. She said something to the driver in Thai, then we got in the three-wheeled motorcycle taxi, which soon merged into traffic, sputtering loudly as the driver weaved his way to our destination, whatever it was.

I couldn't read (or speak) Thai, so I relied on what Ellie told me, especially since she'd promised we'd head out, away from the popular tourist traps.

1:10 p.m.

We spent an hour at a food market. The smells were out of this world. *I wish I could just bottle this sweet and spicy aroma and bring it back with me in my suitcase.* There was something about Thai food I'd always loved. Some vendors grilled fish, others offered roasted duck and chicken. Of course, there were lots of soups, noodles, and curries to pick from as well. After our initial stroll through the market, Ellie and I settled on eating a green mango salad, *moo ping* (grilled pork skewers), shrimp pad thai, and a little bit of fresh (and very stinky) durian for dessert.

"Are you thirsty?" Ellie asked while getting rid of our empty food containers.

"Yes, quite a bit actually."

"I know a very special tea room. It's just around the corner from here."

I would have settled for a stop at the nearest shop or vendor stand to pick up an ice-cold bottle of *Est* Cola, but tea was probably healthier. "Sounds good."

I readjusted my sandal strap, then followed Ellie down the busy street. Her tiny school-girl outfit had certainly caught the eyes of more than a handful of men as she strolled away, a few feet ahead of me.

1:40 p.m.

A wall lined with various glass jars stood behind the man at the counter in the shop we'd just walked in. Some were nearly full, others nearly empty. They all contained loose tea leaves, herbs, roots, dried mushrooms, or dried fruit. The shop attendant exchanged a few words with Ellie, then she winked at him and leaned on the high counter, her huge breasts resting on it. The Thai man did not even bother being discreet about eying her oversized cleavage. After whispering something to him, she slipped him a few bills. He grabbed them so quickly I wasn't able to see how many *bahts* she'd spent. He stuffed the money in the till, then headed to the back, leaving us and the other customers waiting.

Two minutes later, he came back with a steaming teapot and two cups on a tray.

"Now, let's go and get ourselves seated," Ellie said, walking toward the back of the shop, where a couple was just leaving.

The hot beverage was a little strange tasting. More bitter than green tea, yet fruitier at the same time. It quenched my thirst, but it also made me feel more rested, more open-minded, and more curious about the world around me. An irrepressible need to examine the painting that hung close to my head came over me. A super-fat, super-happy Buddha had been hand-painted in shades of yellow, pink, and green. Once I'd taken in all the gorgeous details and paint strokes, I returned my attention to Ellie and suddenly noticed the tiny freckles on her cheeks.

"How are you doing?" she asked just as a man poured more steamy water into our teapot.

"Very relaxed yet energized. Isn't it strange? I'm normally exhausted after a fifteen-hour flight, but I'm... full of energy," I said.

"Excellent, your mind has been fed! Let's finish this teapot, then we'll head out for a spa treatment and massage. How does that sound?"

"Like pure heaven," I replied, suddenly realizing how much I was craving physical contact. Even the feel of my own fingers mindlessly brushing my forearm was amazing right now. I could imagine 34C's hands on my shoulders, rubbing away the pain of a long day. He could rub me elsewhere, too, and maybe prod me a little... or a lot... My insides twitched in agreement. I closed my eyes for a few seconds, imagining what 34C would feel like in me... But when I felt blood rush to my face, I suddenly became afraid that I'd just let out a loud moan for the entire tea room to hear.

I looked around. Nobody was staring at me. *Good!*

Ellie pushed her chair away from the table, then got up.

"You're ready now! Let's go."

I'm ready? How would she know if I no longer wanted any more tea? But I was certainly craving that massage now. It had been a while since I'd splurged.

I downed what was left of my cup, got up, and then followed Ellie out of the tea shop.

2:30 p.m.

Ellie hailed another *tuk-tuk*. About fifteen minutes later, we once again left the hot and humid air of Bangkok's streets behind us. But this time, it was to enter a spa.

A small two-tiered fountain gurgled in the middle of the entrance, and the sounds of singing monks filled the incense-laden air. A handsome, young man stood behind the front desk, and a short woman with silky black hair wearing a matching white linen uniform was escorting a thin, gray-haired client to another section of the building, past the fountain.

"Ellie!" the man exclaimed before running around the counter, wrapping his arms around her, and then lifting her up in the air.

"Chakrii," she said once he finally let her down, "this is my friend. She needs... a special spa treatment. Can you arrange this for us?"

The man eyed me up and down, as though his black eyes could read my mind and figure out if I wanted a facial or a body wrap. But I swear he paused for a second or two on my breasts. I looked down. A big, wet horizontal line was visible on the orange fabric, just below my breasts. *Probably from sitting and sweating in the* tuk-tuk *too long...* Back home, I would have been a little embarrassed, but it was freaking hot and humid in this country. *Can't blame myself for perspiring!*

"May I see your list of services?" I asked him, wiping sweat off my brow. My own hand felt a little foreign on my face. *Am I getting heat stroke? No... Just a little buzzed. But from what?*

"Of course," he said before walking back toward the counter.

When he returned, he handed me a one-page leaflet with a list of spa treatments offered by the *Shave, Massage, and Beyond Spa,* along with their respective prices. He then added, "And we offer whatever other services you may need." As he finished his sentence in perfect, near-unaccented English, his hand wiped a drop of sweat that was making its way down my cleavage. A small tattoo of a flower adorned his index finger, which was a tad delicate for a man's, but his touch sent a tingling ripple down my spine nonetheless.

I smiled and let out a nervous laugh. Chakrii was probably one of the better-looking Thai men I'd seen to date. Tall, tanned, his hair neatly kept, a charming smile, and black eyes that were currently locked onto mine. I almost dared undoing the top two or three buttons of my dress just so I could feel more of his touch. I was sure more and more sweat would trickle down, but I restrained myself. I had to put my horniness aside for now. "Let me have a look," I finally said, looking at the leaflet and feeling a wave of arousal engulf me.

The full Brazilian wax and full-body massage seemed quite appealing at this very moment. I'd never had a Brazilian wax before, but why not give it a try? If I didn't like it, I could just keep my bald pussy to myself until I could grow my regular narrow strip again.

"I want the Brazilian wax and full-body massage," I told Chakrii.

"Sounds like fun," said Ellie. "I'll get the same. Can you book us together?" she asked.

Although she hadn't checked with me first, I was fine with it.

"Of course, Ellie. Anything for you, you know that." Chakrii turned his attention to me. "Please wait here," he said, pointing to a couple of chairs facing the fountain, "and someone will be right with the both of you."

"Exciting," Ellie said, grabbing my hand and pulling me to the waiting area. "You'll love him... it," she corrected herself before winking at me. "I just know it."

2:50 p.m.

A short but muscular man who wore the spa's white linen uniform bowed at us with the symbolic *wai*. "Please follow me to the shower and change room," he said.

Ellie and I got up. He led us into a wide-open, circular area surrounded by thin white linen curtains that danced in an invisible breeze. A huge fan hung high in the center of the ceiling. The humongous device was responsible for the delightful breeze that was now cooling my overheated body. Right below the ceiling fan stood a tall and wide pillar with a few shower heads peppered around its circumference. Water currently spurted out of them like rain showers. The room itself looked like an oversized water fountain. The shower's circular floor was tiled with tiny black and white squares and enclosed within a foot-high rim, which served to keep some water in the lower basin.

"Please wash up, then put on a robe," he said, first pointing at the pillar in front of us, then moving his hand to indicate the rack of towels and silk robes that hung in various sizes across the room from us. "You can leave your clothes and valuables in one of the lockers on your right. Don't worry, your things will be safe here."

Taking a communal shower was new to me, but I was hot and sweaty. And I'd grown quite comfortable with my body over the past months. Plus, the only other person in the room was Ellie. If she saw me in the buff, that would mean I'd get to see her naked, too. I'd finally know the answer to the question that had puzzled me since I first saw her. I looked around and the muscular man seemed to have quietly disappeared. He was nowhere to be seen.

Ellie stored her purse in one of the small lockers, then took off her shoes and socks. I followed her lead. She then jumped into the fountain-style shower without even removing her scarf, blouse, or skirt. She let me finish taking off my sandals, but then ran back up to me and dragged me under the stream of water with my dress still on.

"Isn't this fun?" she asked.

I had to agree. It was as though we'd backtracked in time; we'd morphed into two younger girls who were now doing what adults claimed was not appropriate. Ellie let go of my hands, then leaned her head back, letting the stream of water wash over her sheer white blouse, making it even more transparent. She pulled back her long, shiny, black hair, letting the water soak it, then flipped it repeatedly like a dog shaking itself dry, except that it was her huge boobs bouncing left and right that got my attention, not her long, wet hair that had sprayed me in the process. She untied the knot in her shirt below her breasts and undid her buttons. The fabric finally got a rest from its overextension. She slowly pulled the wet blouse away from her body, as if she was giving a show to a large audience at a strip club.

She was freaking sexy in that lacy green bra. I envied her breasts and how much sensuality oozed out of her.

After throwing her blouse on the floor a few feet away from us, out of the basin, she came toward me, then brought me back with her under the fountain's lukewarm stream.

"Close your eyes," she ordered before lifting up my chin, removing my hair clip, and then running her fingers through my wet hair. "Doesn't this feel good?" she asked.

All I could do was smile. The water hit me at just the perfect temperature and pressure: it cooled me off and teased me at the same time. Ellie's fingers went down from the crown of my head to my face to my neck. After pausing for a second, she slowly unbuttoned the front of my dress, as if she was enjoying every titillating second.

When I opened my eyes, all of my buttons were undone. Ellie was kneeling in front of me, her head aligned with my crotch. She wrapped her hands around my knees then slid them up along the outside of my thighs, grabbing a feel of my ass quickly thereafter. Her soft touch was just what I craved this minute. I couldn't wait to enjoy what the upcoming whole-body massage would feel like. Ellie pulled her hands away from me before standing up.

"Let's have a look at you," she said before peeling off one side of my dress and exposing my left breast.

"Even more beautiful than I imagined," she said. She traced the shape of my exposed breast with her finger then looked down at my wet panties. "White, just like I thought."

"Why?" I asked.

"You come across as a very... innocent woman," she said, smiling at me before peeling off the other side of my dress. "What's the expression? The girl next door?"

I let her rhetorical question be while she turned me around. She pulled off my drenched orange dress before tossing it near her blouse, outside of the basin.

Now wearing nothing but my panties, I arched my back and enjoyed the way each water droplet landed on my exposed breasts. I was definitely buzzed on something. Didn't know what, though. I hadn't smoked anything. And I don't think food poisoning had ever had that kind of pleasant effect... It had to have been the tea. Each water droplet from the shower felt like it had been imbued with some sort of super power to both cool me and caress me. But it wasn't just that. It was as though every single thing that touched my skin sent a large ripple that reverberated all the way down to my pussy. I was horny as hell. I craved physical contact. And there I was... showering next to a beautiful, big-breasted woman who still wore a few more layers than me. I wanted Ellie as much as any man I could get my hands on. *34C would be so useful right about now...*

Ellie reached behind her back and undid her bra. Her perky, globular girls bounced out in the world just inches from my eyes. They were simply too round to be true. I finally let out the question I'd been meaning to ask ever since I saw her. "Are they natural?"

"Are you kidding? Hell no!" Ellie grabbed both of my hands and placed them right on her breasts, forcing me to squeeze them tight. "Do you like them?"

As though my brain no longer controlled my limbs, I kept touching them, squeezing them, kneading them. They were so firm, yet so soft; her dark nipples were so small, yet the amount of soft, light flesh around them was unbelievable.

"Got them last year. A gift to myself, along with my new hair extensions. What do you think?" she asked, pushing her chest out even more while I kept fondling her.

"Wow," is all I got out.

She reached for my natural breasts. Her hands were much more gentle with mine than I was with hers. She rolled one of my nipples between her fingers. My breathing sped up and my chest started moving up and down much more rapidly. I closed my eyes for a few delightful seconds, then opened them again, feeling as though someone was spying on us. I looked toward the curtains in front of me: a pair of feet was visible at their base. When the fan-induced breeze once again lifted the light fabric, I recognized the short muscular man.

"I think he's waiting for us," Ellie said. She took her hands away from my breasts. "One more thing, and you'll be ready to go."

What now?

She once again knelt in front of me, but this time, her fingers slid into the sides of my panties. She pushed them down to my ankles with her face not even an inch from my wet pussy. I lifted my feet to step out of my underwear, then she tossed it out of the basin.

"And let's not forget to get you clean, too. The massage will feel so much nicer, I swear," she said before getting up, turning around, and then walking toward the soap dispenser on the center pillar.

A few seconds later, Ellie came back to me with a handful of light blue liquid. Still wearing her scarf and her skirt, she made the soap foam in her hands before washing my hair, massaging my scalp, and then rinsing my hair. I grabbed some of the soap to wash my face. Removing a layer of pollution from my skin had never felt so good.

While I closed my eyes to rinse away the suds from my face, I felt Ellie's hands on my breasts. I stepped away from the stream, and she got more soap. A moment later, she started lathering my womanhood, my trimmed pussy hair helping to create more foam. And—I had to be honest—hair had started to regrow around my landing strip. Maintaining my pubic 'do seemed like a full-time job at times. Ellie stood in front of me and let her hand slip down between my legs. Her breasts were against mine, her soapy fingers sliding slowly up and down around my private folds. Without warning, she slapped me on the ass before pushing me down to sit in the shallow water. A second later, she joined me on the floor. Her fingers brushed back and forth between my lips, quickly and firmly. Then, as though nothing but mechanical tasks had happened, she stared at me right in the eyes and said, "Good to go."

She stood up and helped me get on my feet. A second later, she playfully pushed me away from her, toward the towels and robes. "Dry yourself up and follow him. I'll be right with you," she said, a large smile on her face.

By the time she'd finished her sentence, the short, muscular spa employee had stepped up next to me. He extended a towel like a barrier between the two of us. I turned 180 degrees and he wrapped the thick, luscious fabric around me before patting me dry. He wasn't feeling me up per se, but it still felt good.

A couple of minutes later, he let my towel drop to the floor. He then handed me a short white robe that I would have described as a silk kimono. Nothing like the plush robes normally used in spas. The fabric felt so smooth and soft against my skin. I almost felt naked with the robe on since the fabric was so thin and so short; it ended just an inch or so below my pussy.

I turned around and saw Ellie, still enjoying the shower, her hands soaping her huge breasts sensually.

Right now, I wouldn't mind doing her.

3:10 p.m.

I followed the short man into another circular room, which was also surrounded by linen curtains.

No fan hung from the ceiling this time, but a large one was resting on a low stand on the floor next to two strange-looking massage chairs. They were angled away from each other and looked as though the makers had incorporated features from a dentist's chair, a massage table, and a gynecologist's exam area. The chairs had the regular padded hole where the patrons' faces could rest when lying on their stomach, but they were currently angled, and they each had two foot rests like an ob-gyn's exam table. With the number of sticks and levers below the center of the chairs, they could probably be repositioned to be flat like regular massage tables when needed.

"We'll start with the Brazilian wax," he said. With his hand, he indicated the first chair. "Do you want a mild analgesic to dull the pain?"

Because I was unsure of what would follow—having never had the wax procedure done before but having heard horror tales—I agreed to his analgesic offer. I sat down with my legs together, hanging between the foot rests.

He acknowledged my reply, then exited the room, leaving me alone to think.

Where's Ellie? Still cleaning herself up in the shower?

Wasn't it strange that seeing her exposed breasts—and imagining her under the shower right now—could turn me on so much?

...And it wasn't the first time a hot woman had had that effect on me. I often thought about those two blondes in Mexico...

Does this mean I'm officially bi?

When my short masseur came back about a minute later, he rolled a low stool in front of my dangling legs. He wrapped one hand around my left ankle and lifted it to the closest foot rest before tying it in place with a piece of pink silk fabric. He repeated with my other ankle, leaving my legs parted like a woman who was about to deliver a baby. I looked at myself: the short silk kimono no longer covered anything below my loosely-tied belt. I saw that the short man had brought along a small tray with him. My legs were parted wide enough for him to roam free between the tray and my pussy.

After warning me that the cream may feel a little cool, his gloved hand spread a thick layer of it over anything and everything that had hair down there. "It will take a few minutes to work," he said with a smile. "Would you like a cup of tea while we wait?"

"Why not," I replied, realizing I was indeed thirsty.

He left me alone once more. It was strange to just sit there, with my legs wide open and pussy exposed, but it wasn't like I was going to undo my ankle ties and make him re-tie them again. My inner prude forced me to bring my knees closer together for a few seconds, but the new position was uncomfortable, so I let my thighs drop to their previous positions. My pussy was again wide open for business. Images of handsome 34C floated on my mental canvas, and I wondered what he'd do to me if he were to walk in here and see me in this inviting position.

3:20 p.m.

My short spa attendant came back a few minutes later, tea tray in hand, and Ellie in tow.

She too wore the same white, short-sleeved, silk robe, although hers looked a little longer on her shorter body. Her soaking wet hair rested on her right shoulder, making her beautiful dark nipple greet anyone glancing her way.

"More tea. Great!" she said, taking two cups and handing me one. She then walked toward the second chair and sat down. The way the chairs were positioned, my head was close to hers, but her legs dangled away from my sight. We were near enough to chat, yet our intimate parts were hidden from each other.

The short woman I'd seen before came in and greeted her. "Wax?"

"Yes, please. Take everything off," Ellie ordered the woman who took a seat on a rolling stool.

"No pain killer?" the woman asked Ellie.

"No need. I'm used to it," Ellie replied.

The man between my legs suddenly asked, "Do you feel this?"

"No. What?" I looked down between my legs. He was pinching one of my outer lips.

"Perfect," he said. "I'll get started."

"They use a very strong numbing cream. You won't feel a thing," Ellie said, reassuring me.

I watched the man dip a small wooden stick into a hot container of wax. He applied it to a small area before posing a strip of muslin paper over it. He rolled out of the way, then moved the fan so it now aimed directly at my wide-open legs, saying it helped cool the wax faster.

A few seconds later, he sat back between my legs and snatched the strip of fabric off. As promised, I didn't feel anything down below, even though the ripping sound I'd heard made me believe I should be in a lot of pain. The only thing I could feel was the breeze against my silk robe, my erect nipples announcing the cooler temperature to the world. I slowly sipped my tea while the short muscular man worked his painless magic and bared my groin of hair one strip at a time.

"Do you want your armpits done as well?" the man asked me once he was done with my Brazilian wax, which took a lot less time than I had anticipated.

I had shaved my legs in the shower yesterday before work, but I'd obviously missed my armpits. Suddenly embarrassed that I had unknowingly let my hair grow for a few days—and walked around like that—I agreed.

He took away my empty teacup then tied both of my wrists together with a silk pink ribbon above my head. I could no longer move my arms. I didn't know what he'd tied them to, but I looked at Ellie's chair next to me and saw a small piece of rounded metal that stuck out past the head of her chair. Mine probably had one, too.

"I've applied numbing cream there as well. Let me know when you stop feeling the breeze on your armpits," he said before getting up and walking away from me. The short but very wide sleeves of my kimono had dropped and piled on my shoulders. The ample sleeve gaps had granted lots of room for him to cover my armpits with his pain-numbing cream. I suddenly felt the fan's direction being changed and aimed at my side. The strong breeze forced one side of my kimono to open and flap loosely.

Five minutes later, my armpits were numb—not to mention how cool and perky my exposed right breast was. The same short masseur rolled next to me again and waxed my left armpit clear of hair, then he rolled to the other side and repeated the procedure.

"You're good to go," he said right after he finished. "We'll just wait for the numbing sensation to dissipate before starting your massage. We wouldn't want you to miss any of it." A large smile decorated his face. "I've applied another cream to speed up recovery."

He rolled away from me, leaving me tied up and unable to do anything, save for watching him move the fan back to its previous position. Its strong breeze was once again aimed at my bare pussy, which pushed the other side of my robe away from my body, exposing my other breast.

"I'm all done," I heard Ellie say from the chair next to me. "I'll wait until you're ready, and we'll get our massages at the same time."

"Okay," I said.

I waited. There wasn't much else I could do right now. The light breeze caressed my chest and stomach like a kiss from heaven. Looking at my own body made me feel very sexy. I was a sitting duck—and a horny one at that. My wrists and ankles were tied, my legs wide open, my breasts and pussy exposed. With the fan aimed straight at me, I closed my eyes and imagined 34C gently blowing on my pussy, his fingers reaching for my inner thighs, touching me. I could picture his digits gliding between my folds. I could feel myself getting wet. I spent the next few minutes imagining what he'd do to me and how he'd caress my body, paying particular attention to my pussy.

Then I realized I was not just imagining it. Someone was actually touching me down there. I opened my eyes just as a piece of dark silk approached my face and blindfolded me.

"Are you feeling this?" I heard Ellie ask from somewhere in front of me while a few fingers caressed my slit. *Were they hers?*

"Yes, I feel it," I said before letting out a long sigh.

"Does it feel good?"

"Yes!" My breath sped up. My body demanded more.

"Later," Ellie said. "It's now time for your massage."

The fingers disappeared and a smell of sandalwood started to envelop me. The sounds of oil squirting out of a bottle and being slapped on skin echoed all around me, then two sets of hands began their work: a person massaged my hands and arms above my head while another massaged my left foot.

I soon felt another pair of hands: this third person caressed my breasts. At first the person's touch was soft, but it quickly became a bit more forceful. A set of wet lips smacked themselves onto mine. A pointy tongue demanded immediate entry, and I parted my mouth. The kisser kindled an urge in me. I didn't know who it was, I could only feel the softness of the skin, the long hair brushing against my face, then the humongous, firm breasts pressed against mine.

It has to be Ellie.

She moved her kisses downward, taking her time around my neck, letting her pointy tongue slide down and tease my nipples as her fingers kneaded my flesh. She made her way to my stomach, then went past it. She traced my newly shaved area with the tip of her fingers. A moan escaped my lips. A little left-over pain from my hair having been pulled stung my flesh, but the cooling cream and the breeze had certainly helped reduce the soreness I expected to feel. For a few seconds, she went away, then her touch resumed. She teased me more and more with her warm breath blowing on my pussy, her tongue licking my folds. All of a sudden, a fingertip prodded my slick opening. The silkiness of someone's long hair brushed against one of my open legs. Other than my guessing that Ellie was the one teasing my pussy, I wasn't sure who was where. However, what they were doing, and the way they were touching me felt marvelous like I was a queen whose every need had to be attended to. Ellie's delightful finger suddenly changed gears and blazed into my wet opening. She pushed it in fully, then slid in another one. Her warm palm cupped below my opening as she stroked my insides with her digits.

And then yet another set of hands joined the party. That fourth person began working my breasts. The person massaging my foot undid my left ankle, lifted it up in the air, and then started kneading my calf. That person was slowly working up toward my thigh. The one massaging my arms had worked his or her way down to my shoulders. The one who'd been massaging my breasts now suckled on my nipples. The person toying with my pussy—likely Ellie?—was becoming more and more demanding and my body craved it equally. All of it. A hand pushed up my skin to make it taut, announcing my clit as the sole sovereign of my womanhood, then the lick of an agile tongue—a freezing one at that —teased it.

"You like icy kisses?" a woman asked. It was Ellie's voice, and it came from somewhere in front of me.

She's definitely the one between my legs. "I love what you're doing," I said.

"Do you want more?" she asked between licks.

I couldn't resist. "Please!"

She continued licking me and teasing my clit while finger-fucking me. I could feel her entire mouth being buried between my legs, her tongue swirling and exploring my innermost secrets.

"You like that?" she asked.

A moan was all I could muster.

The person who'd been massaging my left leg moved away from me, but a few seconds later, my other ankle was untied and the massage process began again with my right leg. The person who'd been kneading my breasts and suckling on my nipples was now kissing me. I could feel that person's skin being a little rougher than Ellie's lips. I wondered if it was the short muscular masseur or Chakrii, the taller one who had manned the reception earlier. *Or someone else?* Then again, it didn't matter. I had four people caressing me, sending me to cloud nine with their hands, their lips... But, just as Ellie's fingers, tongue, and lips were irreversibly reaching my excitement threshold, she pulled away.

A few seconds later, the soft silky hair that had been brushing against my inner thighs was replaced by the warmth of someone's skin. And then... I felt it.

It was just a poke at first, then more of the man's length slid inside my wet entrance. The hungry mouth that was kissing me swallowed up any moans that escaped my lips as I relished in the filling sensation. While I was blindfolded and couldn't see what was happening, I discarded the idea of a dildo. A warm member filled my hollow and a set of balls slapped my ass as the man buried the full length of his shaft in me. He was kind and slow at first. He gently thrust himself, as if testing the waters or the depth of my womb. Soon thereafter, the cadence increased. I delighted in the feeling of being kissed and massaged and having my breasts caressed while being fucked.

But my wonderful earthly pleasures all stopped at once.

"No!" I yelped like a kid robbed of her ice cream.

"Give us a sec," Ellie's voice replied from in front of me. I heard footsteps nearing my chair. All four of the people had let go of my body. No matter how much I arched my back on the chair, no matter if my pussy was dripping wet, no one appeared to be coming back.

"Come on... Please!" I begged.

A few seconds later, someone walked up to me, finally.

The soft lips that kissed mine along with the ultra-firm, large breasts brushing against my side told me it was Ellie.

She stroked my face gently then untied my wrists. I wanted to pull down my blindfold, but she grabbed my wrists and brought my freed hands to her breasts instead. "Keep your blindfold on for a little while longer," she said before once again locking lips with me and letting her greedy tongue wander in my mouth. A few seconds later, Ellie pulled away from me.

"Now stand up, keep your blindfold on, and I'll guide you."

She pulled me up from the massage chair and dragged me away, very slowly.

The curtains brushed against my skin as she led me out of the room and into another.

4:30 p.m.

"Watch your step," said Ellie.

I slowed down, expecting an obstacle. A second later, my bare foot bumped against a low but fairly soft object in front of me.

"Sit on the mattress," she ordered as she guided me down to a sitting position with both hands.

I once again attempted to remove my blindfold, but Ellie—or someone else— got a hold of my hands and brought them behind my back. I couldn't see anything, but the silky fabric of my open kimono brushed my arms as someone disrobed me. A person started caressing my breasts.

Once my hands were released, I moved them forward, and found Ellie's ultra-firm, naked breasts in front of me. I brought my hands up to her neck and pulled her head closer to mine until our lips met. Her hands gently pushed me over to the left until we both landed sideways, facing each other. We devoured each other's mouth with our heads resting on soft cushions. One of her hands reached down and nudged itself just above my pussy, one of her fingers perfectly positioned to tickle my clit.

I attempted to do the same to her, but she pulled her hips away from me.

"Why?" I asked, wanting once again to pull down my blindfold.

She stopped me. "Not yet," she said, squeezing my hands into hers.

Then something hard and warm poked my ass, successfully distracting me from Ellie. While the person behind me caressed my bum, Ellie repositioned her body away from me—at least it was my best guess since I could no longer feel her body heat—but her lips moved down and started kissing my breasts. I let my hands run through her long silky hair.

Someone squeezed my butt cheeks and then parted them before tracing my crevice all the way to my anus. Ever so gently, something small entered me from behind. But it wasn't a cock, though. I could feel that body part still poking the back of my thigh. *His finger?* Someone circled my inner ring for a while, then probed deeper, slowly, a little bit at a time.

A third person lifted up my right leg and placed my right foot in front of my left knee, turning me into an open oyster ready for the picking. Ellie was still caressing my breasts, and a warm and soft body nudged itself between Ellie and my legs. Unidentified fingers proceeded to look for a hidden pearl in my pussy. That person's touch was delicate, too delicate to be a man's. Then a small breast rubbed against my leg.

Is it the woman who waxed Ellie earlier?

What is this? A foursome? Counting the number of hands touching me was hard with so many delightful sensations ebbing through my body.

The man behind me spoke up. "You feel warm and ready. Take a deep breath," he ordered.

I did. And just then, he pulled out his finger and replaced it with his cock. He must have lubed the hell out of his member because it slid in without any pain. The sound of his lower abdomen slapping against my ass surprised me, but not as much as the feeling inside of me. I hadn't felt so full since... my Costa Rican surf experience. *No, make that the last time I had sex with Matt in Ireland.*

The man behind me stayed still in me for a few seconds while I felt the weight of people shifting in front of me on the mattress. It seemed the man in my ass was the only person left touching me.

But soon, my breasts began to once again receive gentle caresses, and fingers got busy again, entering my wet pussy and tapping me on that oh-so-very-sweet inner spot. The man had set into a rhythm behind me while the unknown fingers fucked my pussy. My right leg started to quiver. I was unable to restrain the movement of my foot; my whole body knew that an orgasm was just around the corner.

Then, the fingers pulled out and a cock took their place. Another one. If I thought I'd been full before, I now knew otherwise. For a few seconds, I was the inner part of a delightful sideway sandwich. But it didn't last long. The man behind me pulled out and spoke up.

"Sit up and ride that cock," he ordered.

Being blindfolded didn't make things easy, but the man in front of me pulled out, and I sat up. Two hands grabbed my shoulders and directed me as I walked on my knees toward the other, whomever that was. My hands helped guide me and I lifted my leg once I felt hips and an erect cock in front of me. Someone guided my right knee to land on the other side of the man's hip. Using only my sense of touch, I lined myself up above his latex-covered dick and slowly lowered myself onto him. At first I rode him slowly, controlling the movement of my hips as my pussy clutched onto his shaft. But then my motions became hastier, driven by my pussy's insatiable hunger.

Moments later, I felt the man behind me caress my ass again, parting a way to return to his previous position, pushing me against the one I was riding. His dick forced his way back into my anus just as I was reaching the threshold of pleasure. Caught off balance and in reaction mode, I moved my hands in front of me to slow down my fall onto the man's chest. But what my hands reached left me flabbergasted.

Large breasts softened my landing just as I came, my insides pulsating out of control.

I let myself rest onto the ultra-firm breasts I'd gotten to know very well over the past few hours. Her lips eagerly found mine while the man behind me kept at it, his balls bouncing against my engorged genitals. The man behind me kept plunging his hard shaft in and out of my ass while my mind was too high on orgasmic chills to deal with what it had just discovered. I lifted up the blindfold and met Ellie's eyes. I kissed her ever so briefly. I pushed away from her with one hand while the other reached down, first to caress her breasts, then to make its way to the base of her shaft, still in me.

"I'm not fully a woman, yet. I just wanted to have one last go with a woman before they performed the other surgery," she said, as if she needed to explain herself.

All of a sudden, Ellie's new breast implants, her hair extensions, and her comfort level with men made sense. Her hand reached down to my clit and she played with it before slowly resuming her cadence with her dick. The man behind me moved one of his hands from my hip to my waist, then grabbed one of my breasts, bringing my back up a bit, against his warm, bare chest. I was a few inches away from Ellie's breasts. I could feel him breathing next to my ear. *Chakrii*, I realized when I saw the small tattoo on his hand. *All 100% man that one.*

I closed my eyes and let myself ride high on the delightful sensations that enveloped my entire body. Chakrii changed his rhythm and depth. He squeezed one of my breasts tighter, then pinched my nipple just a tad too tightly, making my whole body flinch. Then, after a final thrust deep in my ass, he suddenly stopped moving. Ellie's fingers were still busy with my clit while she continued to pound me like it was her cock's last meal, for that it may very well be.

I reopened my eyes and took a hold of Chakrii's hand, which was still firmly squeezing my breast. I brought it down toward my hip again. He slowly pulled himself out of my ass, then stepped away from me, leaving me and Ellie alone in our continuing embrace.

A minute later, Ellie rolled me onto my back, her cock still inside of me. I turned my head and saw other people next to us, naked. The woman who'd waxed Ellie earlier was on her knees, sucking the short, muscular masseur's dick. He was standing up, staring at Ellie and me, his hands on the woman's head, controlling her cadence. Chakrii, who had left me moments ago, had now joined them. He was laying on his back and had squeezed his head between the woman's leg. His hand went up and he began finger-fucking her.

My head dizzy with whatever drugs had been added to my tea, I kept staring at the threesome, hypnotized by the short man's increasingly loud groans. He was about to come, and Ellie's moans above me made it clear she too was approaching that point. Ellie's hand squeezed my cheeks and turned my face forward again, forcing me to make eye contact with her. I stopped looking at the threesome next to us and returned my attention to her. My needs had already been fulfilled, but a faint quiver was telling me I was about to feel another orgasm. With one hand, I reached to squeeze one of her nipples, and with the other, I played with my own clit, making myself quiver more and more until Ellie and I came simultaneously.

She fell forward onto me, our breasts became cushions against which my heart beat out of control. I closed my eyes and relaxed with Ellie still in me.

A moment later, I heard the muscular man grunt as he came. I opened my eyes and looked at them again. The woman, now sitting on Chakrii's face with her throat clear of the short man's dick, soon followed suit and moaned to her heart's content.

5:22 p.m.

I lay next to Ellie on the mattress after she pulled out of me, a condom securely keeping her come contained.

"Don't worry, we all use protection," Ellie said, as if she'd read my mind. "And he's used the numbing cream on you, so you will likely feel sore tomorrow."

Tomorrow...

Good thing I have an extra day in Bangkok to recover from this new experience, physically and emotionally.

Having had a small orgy with a transgender woman while high on some weird drug-infused tea was certainly a new checkmark on my list (and definitely not one I was planning on ever experiencing in my lifetime).

The past few hours didn't settle my self-questioning about being bisexual.

Am I more of a pansexual?

My pussy didn't seem to care whether it was touched by a man or a woman —or someone in the process of becoming one. Some men got me aroused. Some not. Same was true for women. And then there was Ellie... She definitely got me aroused...

Who knows what label I should assign myself... But does it matter?

It's probably best to step back, turn off my mind, and let my heart and emotions guide me when it comes to intimate encounters and relationships...

MY XXX EXPERIENCE

THAILAND

THE PLAN

MY STEWARDESS IS DEFINITELY MORE open-minded than I'll ever be. But
if she went through what she described in her diary, it just proves that she could
be the one to satisfy ALL of my fantasies, even the nasty ones I don't admit to
having... even to myself.

But first, I have to find her.

And for that, I'll have to track down Ellie so she can give me more
information about the last woman she fucked. She has to remember that, no?

Here are my options:

OPTION 1: Canvass the airlines for transgender employees.

If only airlines kept those personal details on file, life would be easy... But
that would breach some privacy rights and other politically-correct bullshit.
Asking around could backfire and instigate a reputation I don't care to have.

Likelihood of success: Close to nil.

OPTION 2: Find Ellie using her language credentials.

Airlines keep records of their employees' language proficiency for obvious
reasons, but I'm not sure if *Ellie* is her real name. Doesn't sound Thai to me.
And she could have easily changed her name after her final surgery. Too many
unknowns to risk wasting my time on this.

Likelihood of success: Low.

OPTION 3: Track down Ellie by talking to the spa employees.

She appears to be a regular at that spa. How many transgender Ellies could be regular clients? And from there, Ellie could hopefully give me my stewardess's name. Sounds like the stewardess shared some personal information with her, so it's not that much of a stretch.
Likelihood of success: Average.

Now, let's just hope my trip to Bangkok doesn't include a tucked-away pig-in-a-blanket.
I'm not interested in that. At all.

WHAT HAPPENED

Armed with her journal, a healthy sexual appetite, some curiosity (but not too much), and a whole lot of hope, I took advantage of a two-day layover in BKK/Bangkok to try and track down Ellie, who could hopefully point me to my mystery stewardess.

Bangkok is a large city. Smelly but intriguing. Finding one's way around can be tricky, though. Especially for a non-Thai speaking tourist like me who needs to find a specific location in a city of over eight million inhabitants. However, thanks to a very helpful concierge at my hotel, I did manage to locate the *Shave, Massage, and Beyond Spa.*

About an hour after my initial inquiry, the short Thai man who was fully fluent in English came back to me with some information. He reported that he'd found it, but that it was a *special spa with full services,* if I was looking for that.

I didn't know if *special spa with full services* was international code for *transgender sex* or simply *massages with happy endings,* but I was hoping for the latter.

The address in hand and a large smile on my face, I hailed a *tuk-tuk* and made my way to the spa with a thick pile of *bahts* in my wallet.

3:20 p.m.

About thirty minutes of loud, heavy, and stinky traffic later, I stepped out of the *tuk-tuk* and paid my fearless driver. He nodded at my generous tip and showed me the largest smile I'd seen in a long time, complete with a couple of gaps where teeth had gone missing. I returned my wallet in the pocket of my khaki shorts, which were damp with sweat and probably saturated with pollution. The same was true for my gray T-shirt. But a nearby food stand offered an aroma that made me salivate and instantly forget about the humid climate. There was food everywhere in this city, but I wasn't here to eat. Food could wait. I was here on a mission. An important recon mission.

I looked up to the big white sign my driver had pointed to before leaving. The name of the spa wasn't written in English, but the squiggly Thai characters on the oasis-themed signage matched what my hotel concierge had scribbled on the piece of paper I held.

"Here's to nothing," I said to myself as I opened the dark glass door and stepped into the much cooler reception area, triggering a chime in the process.

An overpowering smell of incense made me sneeze just as a short man welcomed me in. I missed his first name, but it wasn't Chakrii. *Could he be the short muscular man who had taken part in the orgy with my stewardess?* I couldn't really ask him that question right now, but I wouldn't have described him as muscular. I was probably twice as heavy as he was. But then again, I spent a fair amount of time at the pool and at the gym, and I was definitely built on a bigger frame than he was.

He smiled at me and offered me a list of services printed in English on a narrow sheet of white paper. From my limited experience with spas, everything offered on their leaflet seemed legit. No extra-curricular services there, but that was no surprise. As expected, there was a Thai massage on the list of services, but from what I'd learned before while researching Thai spas online (hoping to find the right one), those massages were normally done with your clothes on. After a few more seconds, I settled on the deep-tissue, therapeutic massage, claiming that my back and neck hurt from spending too much time in front of a computer. Then, realizing I wasn't necessarily targeting anything physically close to a happy ending, I added that my legs also hurt from running.

"Do you want a man or a woman to give you your massage?" he asked.

"A woman, if at all possible," I said, hoping that it could possibly be the short, small-breasted woman who'd taken part in the orgy. Or that she could end the massage on a happy note.

He nodded and then guided me to the waiting area before returning to his reception desk.

I sat quietly while observing the rest of the entrance. There was a fountain in the center of the hall, just like my mystery stewardess had described. I looked at my sweaty T-shirt and hoped to be taken to the communal shower next...

Maybe a couple of women would already be in there?

3:30 p.m.

Just as my brain finished adding intricate details to the imaginary tall, beautiful, naked women in the shower I was looking forward to seeing, I was taken out of my daydream by someone addressing me.

I turned to look at the short but very busty woman who had come to greet me. She was in her late twenties or early thirties. *So much for randomly finding the woman from the orgy! Guess it wasn't in the cards for today.*

The woman in front of me wore a very short white uniform, just as the stewardess had described in her journal. However, I was surprised at the amount of cleavage she showed. Sure, a nip-slip wasn't just waiting to happen—like with the maids' uniforms in my special Irish castle—but the visible portions of her cappuccino-colored mounds were still very pleasant to the eye. Her outfit reminded me of a slutty nurse uniform a woman-friend had once worn (very briefly) for Halloween. I don't think we'd made it to the party that night. The memory of what had ensued was enough to make my dick twitch in my shorts. *But that was then and I'm here now.*

I got up and followed the tiny-assed woman past some long curtains and we arrived in the shower room that looked just like what I had imagined (save for the naked women—those were missing). Not much had changed since my stewardess's journal entry. That was probably a good sign. At least she hadn't written her entries decades ago...

I followed the short woman's instructions the instant she left.

I stripped down to nothing, placed my wallet and clothes in one of the small lockers, then hopped under the stream of running water. While I showered, a couple of people took a passing peek. But I could care less. I had nothing to hide. In fact, my cock, even when flaccid, normally appreciated all of the attention it could get.

Once all of the sweat and pollution had come off my skin, I stepped out of the shower and dried myself off before picking one of the longer silk robes hanging from the rack.

3:35 p.m.

The woman who'd brought me to the shower magically reappeared the instant I tied the robe around my waist.

Guess she was hiding somewhere and looking at me the entire time? Good for her.

She took me to a small circular room with only one massage table and one large fan on a pedestal. There were no walls per se, only curtains. The massage table looked normal to me, nothing like the weird contraption the stewardess had described in her diary. But it had a pedal underneath it, probably a hydraulic jack.

"Please. Lie naked with face down," the woman said in a staccato with her strong Thai accent before exiting the room.

After looking around for a place to hang my robe and finding nothing—not even a hook—I dropped it on the floor. I lay down and placed my face in the wide, barely padded opening. It wasn't like that of the regular massage tables I'd been on before. My head hung lower than normal. I'd barely lost any of my vision field, save for what was behind me and above the table, obviously. But the weird hole was still comfortable, and it was all that mattered.

A few seconds later, some strange, soothing, Enya-like music speckled with the rings of singing bowls began to air just loud enough to cover the sound of the oscillating fan near me. The woman returned to the room shortly thereafter, rolling a small tray in front of her.

"Your neck and back hurt?" she asked while placing a towel over my ass.

"Yes, and my legs, too," I replied.

My vantage point was odd, but I quickly got used to it. I could see her standing next to the tray. Based on the odor that tickled my nose and made me want to sneeze, she had lit a stick of incense. Her bare foot then came toward me, and she pumped up the pedal to lift the table.

For a split second, I thought I got a glance at her pussy, but then she walked away and returned to her tray.

She picked up a brown bottle and squirted out some of its aromatic oil. After rubbing her hands together, she walked closer to me, bringing her tray along. With another squirt, she spilled the cool oil directly onto my back, then she traced circles on my skin to spread it. She slowly made her way around the table. It was so high—and her uniform was so short—that every now and then, whenever she reached out across my body, her white uniform would ride up, exposing her shaved pussy. No landing strip on display there, nothing at all. I could have been fooled and assumed I was looking at a very young girl, but I clearly remembered seeing the face of a woman who was at least in her late twenties.

A guy could never be blamed for looking at naked female parts while in plain view, but getting a hard-on while lying face down wasn't the most comfortable thing in the world. I lifted my hips and used one hand to nudge my erect dick into a more bearable position as discreetly as I could.

"You like?" she asked, untangling knots in my back with her vigorous hand motions.

Guess my readjustment wasn't as smooth and swift as I thought...

Considering I likely wasn't the first man who'd been turned on by her intermittently exposed pussy, I played along, wondering how this scenario would unfold.

"Yes, of course," I said. "You're good. How long have you been giving massages?"

She returned closer to my head, once again offering me a good vantage point of her pussy as she worked on the knots I really did have at the base of my neck. "Few years..."

Asking for a precise number probably fell in that large basket of inappropriate questions women didn't like to be asked, like their age, weight, or number of sexual partners. "Do you mainly massage women or men?"

"Men and women," she said, not expanding any more on the topic.

And people who are simultaneously a man and a woman? Or transitioning from one to the other? My thoughts alone took care of my erection, so I was once again lying comfortably on the table.

After undoing all of the knots in my back, she moved to my arms. She worked her way from my shoulders down to my fingers. At first, my hand rested on her shoulder, but she gradually moved backward and my fingers landed on the exposed part of her breasts. I hesitated for a second, then figured it was worth a shot. I wiggled my fingers lightly, brushing them against her exposed flesh. A second later, she popped a button off her dress and asked again, "You like?"

So, this is how happy endings were offered?

I twisted my elbow around and flat out grabbed one of her breasts out of her bra before giving it a good squeeze.

"I see you like this, mister," she said. "Do you want more?" she asked, moving out of my reach.

"Sure," I said, my dick once again reaffirming its uncomfortable enthusiasm.

A second later, she moved to the front of the table, then knelt below my head. My masseuse unbuttoned her top and let both of her gorgeous cappuccino breasts pop out of her bra.

Too firm and perky to be real, but glorious for sure.

"You like?" she asked again. Her delicate hands decorated with hot-red fingernails started caressing her exposed breasts. I couldn't see her eyes, but her smile was that of an innocent young girl. However, I didn't let myself be fooled by it. She was an experienced sex trade worker who knew how to get a big tip.

"What else can you do to relax me?" I asked, curious as to how far massage parlors took it in Thailand.

She stopped caressing her tits, then unbuttoned her uniform some more. Although my view point was perfect, my erection made the whole thing near painful to watch laying face down. So I turned around on the table and my erection bounced to celebrate its newfound freedom. I sat in the middle of the table, then swung my legs off to the side while she stood up and repositioned herself in front of me.

With one of her delicate fingers, she slowly traced the sensitive underside of my cock. "I see you like this," she repeated again.

"What kind of... services do you offer?" I asked.

She winked and her smile grew even bigger. "Anything you want, big mister. If you pay, I give you."

"What about orgies?"

She let out a giggle and feigned being offended. "Orgies? A lot of money, mister."

"But they happen here? Sometimes?"

"No say," she said before literally not being able to say a word as she bent forward and swallowed my dick in her mouth.

I parted my thighs and slid to the edge of the table.

She was good. Just the right amount of pressure, just the right tempo.

Damn. Can't think. Must continue asking. Must track Ellie down.

When she slid her mouth off of my dick for a second, I finally mustered enough concentration and blood flow to my brain to ask, "Do you know Ellie?"

"Ellie? What Ellie?" she said, her eyes locking onto mine as she massaged my balls with one hand and gave me a hand-job with the other.

"I don't know her last name. A *he-she*. Used to be a man, now a woman."

She squeezed my balls upon hearing my words.

"Ow!" I yelped.

She released her grasp. "Sorry... No news from Ellie in long time."

"So you know her?"

She nodded. "Why you look for her?"

"I'm trying to track down a friend of hers."

"Maybe I help," she said, tilting her head and stepping back.

"What do you know?"

"Ten times the price, I tell you everything."

I pondered for a second. The massage wasn't that expensive anyway. Her offer seemed fair, but I knew bartering was part of the way people did business here.

"Here's what: Happy ending with you and another woman in the shower, and you tell me everything you know. Then I'll pay ten times the price."

She started buttoning up her uniform again. "Fifteen times and it's deal."

"Twelve times with a guarantee that I'll make you come."

She pursed her lips for a few seconds. Her stare went from my eyes to my cock, then back to my eyes.

"Okay, big mister. Deal. I go get Anong."

She tucked her breasts in her bra before disappearing behind the curtain and leaving me alone to contemplate my situation for a second.

Not a bad deal. She could know enough to help me. And if not, I'll get a threesome with two small Asian pussies. Can't be bad, right?

4:12 p.m.

When I saw my short masseuse return with a gorgeous, slender, and slightly taller woman by her side, I knew I'd made the right call.

This other woman must be Anong.

She too wore a uniform that was two sizes too small, leaving two-thirds of her small breasts a secret to be uncovered and her pussy a stretch from being exposed. Unfortunately, I also had to rule her out of being the other woman who had taken part in the orgy. She was too tall for that. But that didn't matter. I had two gorgeous Thai women at my mercy, and I was going to make the most of it, no doubt about it!

I jumped down from where I sat and walked toward the two women. "We're done with the massage part of the program," I said before wrapping my hands around their waists. "Let's hit the shower."

My erection led the way to the room on the other side of the curtains.

The water was still running although no one was using the shower, and an urge to see what the stewardess had experienced came over me. I wanted to see these beautiful women get wet with their clothes on. I wanted them to soap themselves up in front of me and then explore each other's body.

I brought my gorgeous ladies to the outer rim of the shower basin and they both started to unbutton their uniform dresses. "No, with your clothes on," I said, which made them stop disrobing immediately. "Come with me."

Without arguing, protesting, or even displaying a hint of a frown, they followed me to the nearest stream of water.

I sure love women who play along.

After a few seconds under the stream, it became clear that the taller woman was braless. The dark circles of her areolae and her tiny, pointy nipples poked through the white fabric of her wet uniform. *Small, perky, young, natural breasts.* It had been a while since I'd seen a pair of those.

The older, shorter woman pulled a long metal pin out of her hair, which she then flung behind her. She shook her head, tossing her now-free, long black hair sideways a couple of times before leaning backward to wet it. Once it was drenched, she took a step back and let the stream of water hit her on the chest. She undid the rest of the uniform buttons that covered her bra and then pulled her augmented breasts out in the open.

Saying she was a sight for sore eyes—not that my eyes were sore at all— would have been an understatement. But just when I thought the view couldn't get better, my short and busty masseuse bunched the bottom of her dress around her waist, exposing her bald pussy. Anong took a few steps back, away from the water stream. A wide smile illuminated her face as her stare repeatedly went up and down, eyeing her coworker's body.

Anong closed the one-foot gap that stood between her and my short masseuse, and they kissed under the running water. But it wasn't just a peck. They devoured each other's lips and mouth. Anong's hands were all over my short masseuse's fake tits. I took a few steps to the left, taking in the view while I grabbed a hold of my cock. The masseuse's hands went for Anong's ass and lifted the bottom of her uniform to expose her bum before grabbing it. Seemed Anong too had skipped putting on panties this morning. Her small, round ass was as beautiful as they came. From where I stood right at that moment, her pussy still remained a mystery.

I made my way to them, my hand gently pumping my cock, while I pondered how to best play this threesome. I had promised the older woman an orgasm, and I wasn't one to make empty promises. She was going to get it, but... Anong's young ass tempted me more than anything right now. It was a perfect peach, ripe for my poking.

I walked to them and moved the masseuse's hands away from my plump prize. It was as firm as I'd imagined it would be. I massaged and parted her cheeks. I squeezed the hell out of her flesh. I was about to poke her when the masseuse broke away from Anong and knelt down in front of me.

The older woman took hold of my wild beast and started licking it. Her mouth was truly gifted, so I let her warm me up.

I released Anong's ass, then spun her around. Her dark brown eyes looked down the instant I tried to make eye contact. I lifted her chin, hoping she'd look at me, but she didn't. Instead, she pulled down her uniform, hiding her pussy before I could even glimpse at it. Her eyes went to my cock next. Or was she staring at the older woman sucking me?

First time she's seen a cock this size? Shy? Or does she prefer women?

I traced an imaginary line that followed the water's path as it streamed down Anong's uniform, from her neck to the hem of her skirt, just past her still mysterious pussy. I started unbuttoning her dress slowly. She let me, her arms hanging by her sides while she watched my masseuse repeatedly guzzle my cock. Anong wasn't pushing me away, but she wasn't encouraging me either. I grabbed her breasts through the soaking wet fabric and squeezed their natural goodness. I reached down to grab the hem of her skirt, and I lifted it to see if her pussy was as gorgeous as her ass. A lightning bolt greeted my stare. *That's different.* I reached out to the soap dispenser and pumped out a handful of the aromatic gel. I rubbed my hands together to create foam before taking them to Anong's breasts. Then, as though I couldn't help myself, my hands erred south to tickle the tip of that lightning rod.

At that precise moment, as though my touching her clit had activated a switch in her brain, Anong started to participate. She pulled her soaking wet uniform over her head and tossed it away from us. The beautiful Anong now stood butt naked next to me and the one who was blowing me. I wasn't going to last long if the older woman continued to use her mouth like that.

I looked around the room and realized the edge of the tiled shower area could be wide enough to fuck on. I gently pushed away the head of the one blowing me, and like the true gentleman that I am, I offered her my hand so she could get up and off of her knees.

A second later, once on her feet, she took off her uniform as well. I pointed toward the rim and the two naked women looked at each other.

"One minute," the older one said before walking away.

She came back three seconds later with a towel and a bunch of condoms. She spread the towel on the wide ledge, then lay her bare back on it. The younger woman came and squatted over her face, at the perfect height to be licked by the other woman. They definitely offered a nice, electrifying view for me. *Her southern lightning 'do sure is nice, but her ass...*

"Turn around," I ordered Anong.

She obeyed. After straightening her legs and stepping over the ledge to turn away from me, she realigned herself with the other woman's face. I stared at her sublime ass as she lowered her pussy over her friend's mouth.

While she licked Anong, the older woman touched herself, her fingers swarming and circling her clit like hyperactive bees. Her legs fell on both sides of the wall, her pussy rested wide open for the world to see. I unwrapped the first condom and protected myself before making my way to her. She obviously knew how to warm herself up. Her implants pointed to the sky and I squeezed their perfect semi-spherical shapes while admiring the most perfect ass hovering a mere foot away. That visual simulation was like dumping gas on my already blazing libido, so I sat on the ledge in front of the masseuse's pussy.

The older woman sure had good balancing skills to keep herself from falling off on either side of the eight-inch-wide rim. To ensure I wouldn't mess up her balancing act, I carefully lifted, then rested the older woman's legs over mine one at a time. Her calves dangled past my thighs as I moved forward and brought my knees to the floor. Carefully—I didn't want her to fall off—I plunged my cock into her bare pussy. It glided inside her like butter on steaming bread. Either she was really loose or really turned on. *Maybe she has a thing for blond-haired Caucasian men? Or Anong?* I increased my pounding slowly, ensuring I wasn't going to throw her off balance, then my hands reached out to Anong's ass. I parted her firm, fleshy cheeks and caressed her crack. The masseuse's tongue was taking care of Anong's pussy, so I moved my attention to her taint. *It ain't quite pussy, t'ain't quite ass.* I dipped a finger in the water that had accumulated in the basin, then brought it to the rim of her ass. I circled it, then poked the tip of my finger into her dark hole.

Anong yelped. I took it out, then slowly pushed it back in, this time, deeper. As I shoved it in farther, she moaned and straightened her back. *Guess you like ass-play, dear? Coming right up.*

The third time around, she moaned even louder, this time twisting at the hip in an attempt to look my way.

"More!" Anong ordered. "Give me more fingers!"

I'm a man who gives women what they want—at least while doing them—so I added a second finger. I finger-fucked Anong's ass while I cock-fucked her friend's pussy, watching the large implants bounce between Anong's beautiful ass and me.

A few seconds later, Anong's moans skipped a few notches on the Richter's scale, and her screams became that of a winding ambulance siren. She bent her body forward, away from me. She landed flat on the ledge, past her friend's head. So I had to let go of her ass and concentrate on the older woman.

She, too, appeared to have had enough stimulation to reach her pleasure threshold. Now that her mouth was free from Anong's pussy, I started hearing her groans. Her left knee bucked a second before her entire body started convulsing into waves of pleasure, contracting against my shaft as I stayed inside her.

I paused there for a few seconds, feeling her heartbeat through her engorged genitals before pulling out. I still had a few minutes in me, so I carefully detangled my legs from the masseuse's limbs then got up. Anong's glorious ass was right there. So I quickly washed my hands and traded my condom for a new one before walking toward her. This time, she looked me in the eyes. Then she looked at my cock and smiled. Without saying a word, she looked back toward her ass and parted her cheeks.

Clear enough!

Her friend had since gotten up, so I now had room to sit behind Anong. I rode the ledge just behind her ass and, after parting her cheeks, pushed my dick into her plumpness. Her ass was tight. She squealed—joyfully of course—as I finally plunged my full length into her. I bent forward and wrapped my body behind her, getting a hold of her small breasts. The older woman had already made her come, so I didn't worry too much whether or not I would. Although I would never admit to this aloud, at forty-two, I no longer had the endurance I used to have. Pleasing two women in one go now involved a lot more strategy, but I wasn't one to give up so easily. I lifted my hips to ensure I wouldn't put extra weight on her tiny body, then let go of one of her tits to reach for her clit. Seemed she'd beat me to it. Instead, I dipped one finger then two into her wet pussy. She rubbed herself so quickly and forcefully that her wrists forced my fingers out of her. Her moans began to get louder and I knew I wasn't going to last a minute. A few more deep thrust into her ass and we both came. Her high-pitch squeals nearly deafened me—and most certainly covered up my own ecstatic grunts.

Once my bliss came to an end, I pulled out of Anong's fantastic ass and remembered that these women possibly held useful information about my mysterious woman, or at least her friend Ellie.

4:50 p.m.

I slapped Anong's gorgeous ass as she got up, and she flashed me a shy smile. Her cheeks were bright red.

I turned to my masseuse, who was busy picking up their wet uniforms from the floor a few feet away from me.

"So, you promised me information about Ellie," I said as I walked closer to her. "I'm looking for a friend Ellie brought here. She had sex with her and other people here."

The masseuse raised her brows. "Ellie has lots of friends and lots of sex."

"It was while she still had a dick," I clarified. "She was with a Caucasian woman."

The older woman's eyes went up, "Ah! I know who you mean."

"Do you know her name?"

"No. No name," she said while shaking her head.

"Do you know what she looks like?"

"You say she your friend and you no know how she looks?"

"I found something that belongs to her, and I'm trying to find her so I can return it, okay?"

"More than we agreed. Fifteen times the price."

"Fifteen times and you answer all my questions about that woman and Ellie?"

"Okay, mister," she said before turning away to Anong. "You go now, prepare for next client."

And just like that, Anong left. I looked at her gorgeous ass as she walked away, out of the room.

"Anong no knows Ellie. She starts working here after," she explained.

"So, describe that other woman for me. Tall? Short? Fat? Pretty? Ugly?"

"Taller than me and Anong. Pretty. Brown wavy hair. Medium breasts, large ass. All white women have large asses."

At least the descriptions remained fairly consistent, but a large ass? Could I really have been obsessed by a woman who may not be that attractive? I tried to clarify how large her ass was by putting my hands about two feet apart. She moved them closer by about three-quarters of a foot.

Definitely not the tiny Asian ass that had just left the room, but it wasn't that bad, assuming she had the right curves to match. But trying to find an average looking, brown-haired woman among the sea of stewardesses out there would be difficult. Red hair or huge breasts would have stood out a bit more. But at least she was sexy enough to have sex with other women... and open-minded enough to do it with a transgender woman as well. That had to count for something.

"Did she speak with an accent of any kind?"

"American, like you."

"From the South?" I asked, hopeful to narrow it down a little.

"Don't know. I do massage. I'm not language teacher."

"Fair enough. What else can you tell me about her, or about Ellie?"

"You get dressed, I go get a picture of Ellie."

A few minutes later, I had hopped in the shower again, dried myself off, gotten dressed, and then returned to the reception area to wait for my masseuse and her photo. Because she still had to appear, I also dug out my wallet and pulled out the agreed-upon money to settle my bill.

I had just double-counted my pile of *bahts* when my masseuse appeared with a worn out photo of her and Ellie, both sporting large smiles and sexy tops that put on display their large implants.

"After my surgery," she said, pointing at her breasts.

"Can I keep this?" I asked, pointing at the photo she held.

She shook her head and sent angry looks at me. "No, my photo." She brought it against her chest, hiding it from me.

"Could I snap a picture of your photo with my phone?"

She raised her shoulders and tilted her head.

I took a few more bills out of my wallet and added them to the pile I was about to hand her.

"Okay," she said, taking my money then handing me her photo.

I dug out my phone and accessed the right app. "Do you know which airline Ellie works for?" I asked as I photographed her old picture.

"No more information," she said, shaking her head. Her smile had disappeared from her face. She was busy counting my money.

I knew when to stop pushing my luck and other people's patience. I gave her back her photograph, thanked her, and then headed back to my hotel room, unsure where to go from here.

6:00 p.m.

Back in the comfort of my air-conditioned room, after a stop by a food stand to pick up the most delicious pad thai I'd ever eaten, I threw myself on the bed.

What a day!

I lifted my hip from the mattress, then dug out my phone from my back pocket. I made my way to my photos and then looked at Ellie with my masseuse. Ellie sure was a good-looking transgender woman. Delicate nose, beautiful eyes, luscious lips... And those tits! She could have easily fooled me. Unsure how I would have reacted to seeing her dick, though. *Anger? Confusion? Repulsion? All of the above?*

No one could ever convince me to trade in my cock, no matter the price tag. For Ellie—or anyone else born as a male—to be willing to go through that sort of life-altering surgery, there had to be a monumental reason behind it. I doubt any man would be willing to lose his dick just to get a thrill. Or to be able to grab boobs 24/7. *What was it? Tremendous discomfort in one's skin?*

I shook my head, not wanting to waste a second more on this topic. It didn't matter anyway. What mattered was that I now had Ellie's headshot.

How can I try to track her down? Through company records?

But which airline does she work for?

All major airlines flew to Bangkok or had a partner airline that did.

Maybe I'll encounter her in person one day, in a random airport, by sheer luck...

Talk about the slimmest of odds...

My eyes went to the masseuse that accompanied Ellie on the photo. She had said something about her surgery. Could it be that *she* was the small-breasted woman who'd taken part in the stewardess's orgy?

And with that thought, I closed my eyes and mentally relived my afternoon shower adventures, but turning it into a foursome that included my mystery stewardess.

NEXT STEPS

I re-read her next journal entry, and what she wrote about her experience in France just proves to me that she's a woman. *Take that, Bob, for your idea that it's a man playing an elaborate prank on me!* Even if a man had somehow forged the experiences I was able to track down so far (by paying off the people I spoke to for example), no man would have ever gone through such a roller-coaster of emotions and then written about it.

Messed up shit? Don't know, but it's definitely not what I'd consider to be a regular fun trip to France.

Can't judge her, though. Everyone has their ups and downs.

Who's to say that her way of dealing with them wasn't the best under her circumstances?

But maybe she made a mistake by blabbing so much in her diary.

Maybe she left me enough clues to track her down this time...

PART VII

FRANCE

THE STEWARDESS'S ENTRIES
FRANCE

6:03 a.m.

I WAS LYING CURLED up in the middle of my queen-sized bed, lost in my own fantasy, when a buzz reached my ear.

Go away.

I grabbed my spare pillow and squashed it on top of my exposed ear to muffle the annoying rhythmic noise, but it persisted and pierced my sleepy veil.

Opening my eyes, I looked at the alarm clock on my nightstand: 6:03 a.m.

Who calls this freaking early?

I stretched out for my phone; the number had too many digits to be local. *What the heck?* I cleared my throat in a moot attempt to sound semi-awake. "Hello?"

"*Bonjour, mademoiselle. Je suis Maître Lancelot, le notaire en charge de la succession de Mademoiselle Gabriella Andrews.*"

"What?" I sat up in bed and rubbed my eyes.

Why would some French lawyer call me to talk about my aunt's succession?

"I am sorry. My file says you speak French. We can continue in English."

"I do. Either language is fine. It's just that... it's early here... Are you telling me my aunt Gabriella's dead?"

The line went silent.

"Hello? Are you still there?" I asked.

"I'm so sorry for your loss, miss. I thought you knew. I did not mean to announce such bad news to you in that awful manner."

Now it makes sense... The numerous missed calls from my mom. The email asking me to call her as soon as possible...

"It's alright," I said. "I wasn't very close to her. Barely knew her really."

"Well, it seems she liked you very much because she's left you her French property and business."

"What? Is this a joke?"

"I'm not known for having a sense of humor. So, no. *Mademoiselle* Gabriella's business was quite... particular, and I was calling to see if you could travel to Paris in the near future so I can show it to you. Then you could decide whether or not you want it, or if I should give it to the second person in line."

"Would that be my mother?"

"I'm afraid not. Your mother will be receiving a check for her share of *Mademoiselle* Gabriella's inheritance."

"Can't you just send me a check as well?" The idea of receiving money— whatever the amount—sure sounded good.

"I'm afraid I cannot discuss this matter over the phone. We need to meet in person."

"Is my mother expected to go to Paris as well?" I asked, trying to wrap my head around my schedule, but nothing came to mind. I got up and walked over to my daily planner.

"No, and this phone conversation as well as our upcoming meeting need to remain a secret. *Mademoiselle* Gabriella specifically requested that you be the only person to know about her business. Her sister, your mother, is in no way to be made aware of it. Under no circumstances. Do I make myself clear?"

As if I could tell her anything based on what he's told me...

"Well, I've got a few free days at the end of next week. Would that work for you?" I asked, my fingers tapping on my agenda.

"*Oui, bien sûr.* I'll let you make flight and accommodation arrangements, then please inform me of your date of arrival so I can clear my schedule and meet with you."

"Give me a second," I said while reaching out for a pen. I hated trying to add a new contact to my phone while talking on it.

I wrote his number down, then hung up after he once again shared his condolences for my loss.

Holy shit. What a way to start the freaking day!

6:40 a.m.

Now wide awake, I made a mental note to return my mother's calls. She probably needed a few words of comfort. *Her only sister...* I looked at the clock. *Too early to call her now.*

I headed to the shower and reflected on what I'd just learned while the water droplets massaged my back.

I wasn't particularly close to Gabriella—I hadn't seen her or spoken to her in at least two or three months.

How did she die? Was she sick? Or the victim of a freak accident? Why did she choose me as the one to inherit her business?

Gabriella never married, at least as far as I knew. She didn't have children of her own, but why not give her business to my mother?

Come to think of it, I don't even know what she did for a living.

I racked my brain while lathering my body with jasmine-scented soap.

I'd last seen Gabriella in a fancy restaurant somewhere in New York City.

What was the occasion? I couldn't recall.

She always dressed in the latest trends. She incarnated modern-day fashion, except for her retro, super long and narrow cigarette holder she always had at the ready... Well as soon as she was outside restaurants and other non-smoking areas.

Maybe she worked in the fashion industry?

She had an air of superiority, but that could have been from her decade-long French immersion. Her cigarette holder didn't help with that either. *Who still used those nowadays?* But it fit with her Audrey Hepburn wannabe look. She'd picked up the typical *Parisian Pretentiousness* syndrome, as I liked to call it. Not every Parisian had it, but I'd encountered enough throughout the years to start naming it.

But, if I have to travel across the globe to deal with this, Paris is probably a good place to do it.

Hair washed, skin exfoliated and squeaky clean, I got out of the shower, patted myself dry, and wrapped my hair in a towel turban before heading to my computer to plan my upcoming trip.

Twenty minutes later, I had booked my flight and hotel. I'd spend three days in the City of Lights. Too bad I couldn't think of a boy-toy to bring along with me. Paris was so romantic. But maybe I could hang out with some old friends I knew who had settled there?

Who is it again? Renée and Luc? And there's also Mark and...what's-her-name...?

I decided to check Facebook to see if they were still there. And if so, maybe they'd be around next week?

After some online-stalking and catching up on these friends' lives (at least the parts they shared publicly), I learned that Mark had left town, but Renée was still there. I sent her a private message. Seemed she and Luc no longer were an item (at least based on her relationship status... and he was nowhere to be found on her pictures).

Too bad.

I hated breakups. I loathed having to choose sides. *But do I really have to? Luc was a nice guy. Maybe I should find out what he's been up to?*

I finally found his profile, then saw the photo of someone I hadn't expected to see. Right there, near the top of Luc's timeline, was a post by the man who'd broken my heart over a decade ago. The post, which had 255 likes, announced his upcoming wedding in Paris. I swear my heart winced in my chest. Or maybe it was left-over heartburn from last-night's extra spicy pizza.

Ady... My beloved Ady...

I had cut ties with him long ago. Actually, *he* had cut ties with *me*.

Before Facebook existed, he'd broken up with me via email—what would be a jerky move nowadays—but his work had him gone for months, unable to access phones, so email was probably better than waiting to do it in person.

But obviously, I hadn't become friends with him online—that would have brought on too many painful memories—but it seemed our common friends from back in the day had connected with him on the social platform and were sharing and spreading his good news, and, of course, congratulating him.

I pushed that new information past the precipice of my consciousness.

At least, I tried to.

6:45 p.m.

So here I was now, a week after learning the bad news, looking out my porthole and mindlessly watching the ground crew wrap up their tasks: bags were being loaded and food resupplied; around me, the voices of friendly flight attendants helped people board and stow their bags.

Not working the flight had left me with nothing better to do than be lost in my own thoughts about my impending sweet-and-sour trip to Paris.

Having to deal with my estranged aunt's inheritance didn't make me happy, but I could use a little extra money, and inheriting a business would surely involve a little of that, right?

The past few days had flown by. I talked to my mom, to try and console her, but there wasn't much I could do. I tried to learn more about my mysterious aunt, but my mom didn't know much about her own sister either.

I did find myself thinking of my ex, though. A lot. After all those years...

What is wrong with me? Am I afraid of running into him with his new bride while in Paris?

I didn't know the date of their wedding, and I'd been hard on myself, shutting down my computer or phone every time the thought of looking him up arose. I didn't even want to write anything in my journal, afraid it would stir up even more damaging emotions.

The odds of somehow encountering them are slim, especially since I don't know where or when they'll tie the knot.

The stabbing sensation reappeared in my chest again as I buckled up.

What am I really afraid of?

Was it that I could still love him and that seeing him in the flesh would bring up the pain I had somehow managed to put behind me after all those years? Was I afraid that my heart would implode from too much unrequited love?

Then again, maybe one glance at him would be enough to know that my lips no longer craved his, that my heart no longer longed to be his, and that my pussy no longer craved his cock.

He had quite a good one, though… If I recall.

As the plane finally taxied to the runway for takeoff, I realized that pinpointing the root of my fears was hard, but ignoring them was much, much harder.

So I let my emotions fill my heart with angst and negativity just as the plane's powerful acceleration pushed me into my seat.

7:05 p.m.

The plane ride didn't do much to cheer me up.

The woman sitting next to me appeared to be around my age, but dressed to the nines, and with makeup thick enough to completely hide her true skin color.

About ten minutes into the flight, she interrupted the twirling negativity of my inner chatter.

"Can't believe we'll land in Paris tomorrow morning. I'm so excited!" she said.

I politely smiled and nodded, careful not to say anything that could indicate I wanted to chat with her.

"I'm going to visit my oldest daughter. I haven't seen her in nearly a year!"

Guess she isn't a great mind reader. "That's nice," I said with a fake smile.

"Don't think I've ever been this excited in my life… Not recently anyways. Too bad my husband couldn't fly with me today," she said while bringing up the large purse she'd stored below the seat in front of her.

Making small talk with passengers while working is one thing, but don't I deserve the right to enjoy a plane ride in silence when riding as a passenger?

"He couldn't?" I asked, feigning interest forced upon me by my inner courteous self.

"No, he had a deadline to meet. His boss wouldn't let him leave the country before his documents had been handed in. But he told me he was nearly done. A couple of days max. Then he'll be able to join me and our daughter. This is SO exciting!"

I smiled at her, then turned my attention to the buttons on my armrest.

If this woman intends on keeping up her undue exuberance for any extended period, alcohol will certainly help in making her more bearable and less annoying.

I pressed the service button then returned my attention to the woman, unsure if she was done with her overly happy jabber.

She was now digging through her purse. She pulled a small paperback from it before returning the bag to its temporary home at her feet.

Great! She won't be able to talk while reading, right?

Then I saw the cheesy cover of a bare-chested man with an oiled-up six pack and a few tattoos.

Argh. One of those impossible happily-ever-after romance novels.

God, did I hate how unrealistic their endings were. Then again... Once in my life, I did enjoy those books. But the only true happy endings I'd ever gotten had been purely physical. Real-life relationships that made both people happy didn't exist. I'd long looked for one, but I had since seen the light.

Damn it, girl. Why are you so freaking annoyed by this woman and her choice in books right now? Is my period about to start?

But no calendar check was required. My heart screamed that it was all related to Ady's upcoming wedding. Did a tiny part of me still long for him, my one perfect guy?

Unfortunately, I forgot to look away from her book while lost in my thoughts.

"This book is amazing. Have you read it?" she asked, her light brown eyes meeting mine when I finally looked away from the cover.

I put on the largest fake smile I could muster and shook my head. "Can't say that I have..."

"I highly recommend it. SO hot! Can't put it down!"

The flight attendant reached my seat and depressed my service button. "What can I help you with?" she asked.

"Glass of white wine, please."

"Of course," she said before walking away toward the back of the plane.

I grabbed my headset from the seat pocket in front of me and plugged it in, hoping that my behavior would clue the woman in.

"So why are you going to Paris?" she asked just as I was putting the first earbud in.

I turned to face her. "Someone died."

Her smile dropped. I looked at the screen in front of me and donned my other earbud while my other hand touched the screen.

Good. I should have mentioned it earlier.

Now, what non-romantic movie can I watch?

8:35 p.m.

I patiently waited for Renée, who had agreed to meet me for dinner on my first evening out in Paris. She'd sent me a Facebook message to say she was running late.

While I sipped my glass of wine, the fashionably-dressed French patrons around me in the bistro offered a good distraction (and so did the few young, loud-mouthed Americans who were enjoying inexpensive local wines).

I let out a yawn.

Jet-lagged, my body wasn't ready for bedtime, but my mind was totally dead from all its mental and emotional juggling over the past week. The afternoon nap I'd taken earlier today didn't help in resetting my internal clock.

And then, just as I blinked away my tiredness, I saw Renée.

My friend was as gorgeous as ever. Highlighted shades of browns and blondes cascaded from the top of her head in a decadent chignon. She wore capri pants and a light blouse, topped by a bright scarf that had too many colors to count. She didn't appear to have any makeup on, save for a smear of peach on her lips. She opened her arms wide and let out a small yelp when she saw me.

I stood up and then closed the gap between us before diving into her open embrace.

"Can't believe it's been so long... It's soooo good to see you!" she said as she held me tight against her Chanel-No.5-scented chest.

"So happy to see you, too!" I said before pulling away. "Come. Sit with me and let's catch up over wine, like in the good ole days."

She smiled at me and nodded, then I turned around and returned to my seat.

A waiter appeared out of nowhere to help my friend take a seat at our table.

"So, how have you been? We have so much to catch up on... It's been way too long," I said, shaking my head.

She inhaled loudly, then tilted her head while draping the white napkin over her lap. "Life's had its ups and downs. Luc and I broke up. But work has been fantastic."

Talk about getting the Cliff's Notes!

The waiter lifted my already broached bottle of *Le Duc de Belmont* from the table. It was a tasty and inexpensive *Coteaux Bourguignons* vintage he'd recommended about thirty minutes earlier when I'd arrived. He looked at my friend and asked her, *"Un verre de vin, mademoiselle?"*

"Oui, s'il vous plaît. Merci."

I waited until he was done pouring and left us alone before continuing. "Well, that sucks. But let's first toast and then you can tell me all about it—or not—whatever. What do you say?"

She raised her glass and smiled. "To old friends!"

"To old friends," I repeated. "And may we not lose touch for so long again."

We clinked and had a sip.

How amazing were those inexpensive French wines? Even with the bistro markups, they were still very affordable. Once the rich, fruity sip had left my mouth, I returned to the conversation where we'd left it. "I'm so sorry to hear about you and Luc. No chance of getting back with him?"

Renée was downing her glass like she hadn't drunk anything in days. She quickly placed her glass down, empty. She reached for the bottle to refill it before replying to me.

"Once a cheater, always a cheater. No chance in hell."

I was taken aback and almost choked on my current sip. "Luc? A cheater? I would have never guessed."

"Me neither... but I caught him red-handed with the young neighbor, in our bed."

"Well, good riddance, then," I said as I lifted my glass to clink it against hers, hoping her current glassful wouldn't have the same fate as the previous, or else I'd be dragging my friend out on all fours very shortly.

She chuckled then repeated, "Good riddance."

A sigh of relief inadvertently left my lips when she put her glass down after one sip. I tried to cover it up with another question. "Are you dating someone else?"

"No, it's hard to find men now. I mean men who are interesting enough to have a long-term relationship with."

I smiled in agreement. "I know what you mean. I've given up on that."

She frowned while taking another sip. Once her glass returned to the table, she asked, "What do you mean? Are you into women now?"

I shook my head at my friend. *If only she knew... But I doubt she'd understand.* "I've given up on trying to find 'the one'."

She shrugged. "Don't think I could give up on that." She raised her glass and emptied it again. "And what about your Ady's upcoming wedding? How do you feel about that?"

"I haven't seen him or spoken to him in over a decade."

"Wasn't he 'your one' though?"

"Hard to be someone's 'one' when he doesn't love you back. I guess I was just a fun pastime for him. Nothing more than a two-year hobby... or something like that. My love for him was... inconsequential."

"So, him getting married is not bothering you?"

My heart stung in my chest, but I lied through my teeth. "Guess not." I waved at the waiter and got his attention before pointing to the empty bottle of wine on our table. He circled his finger in the air while his lips seemed to silently voice *"Une autre?"* I nodded. If we were going to be talking about him, I'd definitely need more alcohol in my system.

"Then you won't mind being my plus one at the wedding?"

"What?" I turned to stare at my friend.

"Hey! You said it didn't bother you. Prove it. Plus, I've RSVP'd with plus one and I haven't found anyone to accompany me to the event."

"I'm just here for a few days. I'll likely be gone by then."

"Are you here tomorrow?"

"He's getting married tomorrow?"

"Yep."

I took a long sip, drinking the rest of my glass to appease my competitive side. I couldn't tell my old friend the truth and admit my emotional weakness. I just had to come up with an excuse instead. "But I have a meeting with my aunt's succession lawyer."

"What time?" she asked without losing a beat.

"At 10 a.m."

"That's fine, the ceremony is at 4 p.m. And then the reception is at a hotel right after that."

"Who gets married at 4 p.m. on a Friday?"

"Technically, they're already married. Got married in the UK a couple of weeks ago. They're just doing a ceremonial wedding here by Notre-Dame, where they met."

I pushed back the pain that was growing in my chest.

Is this jealousy? Or just the cheesy romantic gesture? But, most importantly, can't I talk my way out of this?

"But I don't have an evening gown, or anything fancy to wear." I finally said in a last attempt to be excused from that ceremony.

"Are you kidding me? We're in Paris. There are loads of shops with beautiful dresses. That's not an excuse. More like a good reason to pick up a nice dress and bring it home."

Fuck.

I inhaled deeply, then shook my head. "Then you're coming with me either early tomorrow morning or right after my meeting, and you'll have to help me find something to wear. And help me do up my hair, too!"

10:00 a.m.

"Please, *mademoiselle*. Come in," said a tall, bald man in a light-gray linen suit.

His shirt was bright blue with white cuffs and collar. Fashion at its finest, and it brought out his matching blue eyes. Even if it weren't for his good looks, his outfit alone would have given any man a three-point hotness bonus. Eleven out of ten.

Not bad for a bald French guy.

"*Croissant? Café?*" he offered after inviting me to sit on the empty chair in front of his massive desk.

"Black coffee would be wonderful, *Maître Lancelot*," I said while taking a seat in the leather chair.

"Please, call me Nicholas," he said with a smile too white to be that of a smoker.

The chair's breadth left plenty of room for me to rest my purse against my hip. I felt tiny compared to everything in his office. His desk had to be eight-feet wide, covered with piles of papers and a very large computer monitor. The glass-paned balcony doors that lined an entire wall had to be twelve-feet high. One of the oil paintings that decorated the other walls was big enough to cover my largest wall back in my apartment.

"Very nice office," I said, forcefully pushing down my stress about the upcoming events. In a weird way, I was grateful for the distraction Gabriella's inheritance was causing... Then again, if she hadn't died, I wouldn't be here in the first place. I would have never heard news related to Ady. He would have stayed in my mental oubliettes where he belonged, along with the painful memories that had swum back to the surface.

"*Oui, merci*," Nicholas said as he handed me a cup of espresso on a tiny saucer. "I like it."

He took a hold of the other cup and saucer, then headed behind his massive cherry desk.

I waited until he was comfortably seated before talking. "So... Now that I've flown all the way to Paris, will you tell me what this mystery business is all about?"

"Of course." He brought his cup to his lips. After two brief sips, he put it down then exhaled loudly. "I'll tell you everything you want to know, but it's simply not something we could have discussed over the phone."

In one gulp, I emptied my drink then placed the empty cup on his desk, between two tall stacks of important-looking papers. "Enough of the mystery, please. I'm here now, so what is it?"

He straightened his back before aiming his blue eyes at me. "Your aunt—may she rest in peace—ran a very successful, high-priced *maison close*."

I moved forward on my chair. "*Maison close*?" I repeated, wondering what the hell he meant by a closed house.

"*Une maison de plaisirs érotiques*. A fancy brothel. A whorehouse, if you wish, but with class. Expensive carnal luxury for the local elite."

"What?" My eyes must have been the size of two beignets. "Aunt Gabriella?"

He leaned back in his leather chair. His growing smile dug dimples in his clean-shaven cheeks. "She was quite a woman."

I still couldn't believe it. "Gabriella ran a whorehouse? *That* was her job? ...That has to be illegal, no?"

"Well..." he said, tilting his head repeatedly, "Technically speaking, yes. Brothels are illegal in France. But hers was... and still is... within the confines of the law. Let's just say that my job is to make sure everything's above board. I was Gabriella's private slave when it came to her legal needs," he finished with a glare that made me wonder if he meant it in more ways than one. He rested his elbows on his desk, cupped his manicured hands, and rested his chin on them. "Your aunt was very special, in many ways." A dark cloud passed through his eyes.

I didn't want to think about this hot specimen getting it on with my now deceased aunt (though I wasn't sure if I was misreading him), so I moved the conversation along. "On the phone, you said there was a second person in line to inherit her business. Who would that be?"

He got up. In a few steps, he was standing by the tall windows, looking out toward the street below. His silence tested the limits of my patience.

"Who?" I asked again.

He turned around and his stare met mine. "Me," he finally said.

I cleared my throat and readjusted in my chair. "Isn't it unethical for you to represent my aunt's final wishes when you stand to benefit?"

"*Bien sûr!* Of course!" he exclaimed before lowering his voice. "This entire business is... in the grayest area of the law... But the fewer people in the know, the better. Gabriella arranged it all, and she trusted me to make the best decision at the end of the day. And I hope you can trust me, too."

I tucked a strand of loose hair behind my ear while trying to make sense of it all.

A few seconds passed and I still couldn't. "If you know everything about her business, why didn't she simply give it to you? Why involve me?"

"She knew you'd ask." He returned to his desk. "If you don't mind, I'd like to show you the video she recorded a couple of months ago."

I swallowed hard.

Oh no. A video from beyond? I've barely accepted that she's dead. Am I ready for that?

As though Nicholas could sense my reluctance, he opened his bottom drawer, then pulled out a bottle of whiskey and two tumblers.

"I think we could both use a bit of this," he said, his head nodding toward the golden liquid. "What do you think?"

I let out a sigh while glancing at the expensive Irish bottle. "It's early..." *But then again, seeing my dead aunt on video and later, in just a few hours, watching the love of my life get married?* "Probably wouldn't hurt, considering..."

He smiled at me and poured half an inch in each of the tumblers before handing me one. "To Gabriella, an extraordinary woman who left us too early."

We clinked glasses, then he changed the angle of his monitor so I could see if from my seat. He opened a file on his computer and then enlarged the video player so it occupied the entire screen.

And there she was: Gabriella in a chic baby pink *tailleur*, probably from a well-known designer, as always. Her lit cigarette in her long, slender holder hung from her delicate fingers, its twirling smoke forever frozen in time until Nicholas clicked the play button.

I took a sip. The liquid warmed my dry mouth.

"Dear, if you're watching this," she said before taking a puff and exhaling, "...you and I both know what that means... Which is something more unsettling to me than it is to you now. Well, I hope so anyway... Hell, you have no fucking idea what's been happening with me..."

She took another puff, then extended her arm to set aside her cigarette on what I presumed would be an ashtray just out of the frame. "Anyway, you're probably confused as to why you're in a French lawyer's office, watching a video featuring yours truly."

She paused again, her eyes looking in the direction where she'd left her cigarette.

"Okay, here goes. I realize you and I didn't really know each other. In fact, we were barely more than acquaintances, and I'm sorry about that. I really am... The thing is... I never got close to anybody in our family. Not you. Not your mom. Not even my own parents. But that doesn't matter." She shook her head. "Anyway, last time I saw you, you were different. Somewhere, below that innocent layer you've always impersonated so well, I sensed something... Something that had been awakened... Something we somehow shared. Maybe I was mistaken, but that's unlikely. My instincts are normally right."

She uncrossed her legs, then crossed them opposite (without exposing herself *à la* Sharon Stone in *Basic Instinct,* thankfully.)

"See, I have a somewhat unique business. A certain... personality is required to run it... and to understand its existence in the first place. My intuition has always served me right, in business and in life, and I trust it still can, even though I'm on my last burst of steam."

Gabriella looked away from the camera for a minute, but not toward her cigarette. Her stare was directed up and to the side. When she returned her attention back toward the lens a few seconds later, her eyes glistened with contained tears.

"I've lived a full life. I've got no regrets. But the bulk of it was kept private because society doesn't see my lifestyle and the path I chose as socially appropriate... Maybe things will change in your lifetime? ...I hope so... For your sake."

She brought her right hand to the corner of her right eye, then, with a tissue I hadn't realized she'd been holding, dabbed the tears that were on the verge of running down her face.

"See, I believe that people—men and women—have urges that need to be taken care of. Satisfying carnal needs isn't just a tick in a box, or a dick in a cunt. People are so much more than fleshy orifices. We're curious beings. We all have fantasies. Our urges are much more complex; they run much deeper than our mere physical, raw animal desires. Many people repress them, but some—like me and you—understand that life can be a lot more interesting, pleasurable, and entertaining when we give in to those urges. I see them as a gateway to learning more about ourselves, about what matters in life. I'd even go as far as saying that these urges can help us accept others the way they are... Races, sexual orientations, fetishes, and all the rest..." She chuckled and raised her shoulders. "Maybe my approach would be a great first step toward world peace... But I digress. People who don't repress their urges need a safe place to explore their needs and sexuality. Somewhere where they won't get judged... or where they won't be put in jail for being who they are..."

I brought the glass to my lips. I took a second sip, now that my initial shock had passed.

Aunt Gabriella... Quite a secret keeper that one.

"The thing is," she continued before pausing again with what had to be an impromptu speech. She was rambling way too much for all of this to have been planned. "France is a little ahead of other countries in some ways. Prostitution here has remained legal, but lawmakers have begun a process that I fear is unstoppable. I trust our advantage may soon disappear. So, I expect things will soon get much harder for me and my business... But I'm certain Nicholas will be clever enough to navigate these hurdles for me... or you, if you're up for it. That legislation may very well happen after I pass." She smiled to an invisible person above the screen, as if trying to get the cameraman's approval to continue.

Was Nicholas there? Was he the one recording?

"But as much as I care and respect him, as a man, as a magic-worker with French laws, and in many, many other ways, I believe I need a woman to run my business. I'm sure Nicholas will help and support you, with whatever you need. He'll teach you the ropes, introduce you to the right people, and lead you so you can become a great business person." A light chuckle escaped her lips. "There's quite a gap between being a flight attendant and a businesswoman... But you've got the goods, the brains, and I'm pretty sure you've also got the curiosity and personality required to do this job well... However, it would involve quite a change. You'd have to move to Paris for one. I'm afraid this isn't a job that can be done remotely, if you know what I mean. But you could transition gradually. I'll let Nicholas fill you in on the details. I hope he can convince you."

She got up, then sat down again.

"There's one more thing... I'd hate myself if I'd forget to mention this... My business, the one I want to hand over to you after I pass, is the best 'job' I've ever had," she said with air quotes. "If you can find a way to make money doing what you like best in the world, you can't ignore that opportunity. For me, this was it. Maybe it can be for you, too. If you decide to knit sweaters for a living, and if it makes you happy, so be it. But I think you may be better fulfilled by doing something along the same lines as what I've done with my life. So please, I urge you to take your time and think it through. Seriously."

She once again turned her attention to that invisible person behind the camera. "Nicholas, please give her plenty of time."

Her gaze then returned to the camera. She leaned forward and pointed her index right at it. "And please... don't ever mention this to your mother." Her eyes were those of an angry parent about to yell at a kid, but then her gaze softened as she once again leaned back on her seat. "She and I have had our differences over the years, probably like most siblings. But from the few attempts I've made at broaching the topic, I know for a fact that she isn't as open-minded as I am, so... Knowing what my real job was could crush her. I'd rather she keeps a fond memory of me, without knowing anything about this part of my life. I hope you understand and can do me this great favor."

After a final pause, she brought her right hand and tapped her heart. "I love you, *sobrinita*. Please pass on my love and best wishes to your mom as well."

3:45 p.m.

The hours following my meeting with Nicholas had been a blur, though a strangely efficient one.

Renée had flocked to the indigo dress in the second shop we'd walked in, saying its cap-sleeves, V-neck, and V-back had been designed for my body shape. A quick change of clothes followed by a twirl in front of the mirror had me agreeing with her. The store attendant recommended a matching pair of shoes and bracelet, both of which they carried in my size. The ensemble was perfect. Never had one of my shopping excursions been so fast and effective. (Nor that expensive.)

So, here we were: two old maids sitting in a cab, heading to my first and only true love's wedding ceremony, Renée in her burgundy sleeveless dress and me in my new faux-wrap satin gown. She had done up her hair and mine in nonchalant yet formal 'dos. She was the only woman I knew capable of making partially undone chignons look chic. But even knowing that my dress was flattering didn't do a thing to tame my stomach butterflies. Yes, I'd manage to set aside my thoughts about potentially quitting my job and becoming a full-time Parisian businesswoman, which could possibly enable me to afford designer couture like the dress I was wearing on a regular basis. That decision could wait.

But seeing Ady after all those years was no longer avoidable.

Right now, I had to focus on preparing my reaction. I had to muster enough strength and composure to act graciously in front of my ex and his new bride... Or at least stand still without the urge to run away, cry, or scream.

I was taken back to reality when Renée addressed the driver. "*Vous pouvez nous déposer ici, s'il vous plaît.*"

She paid the fare while I exited the cab, carefully holding the satin fabric of my dress so it wouldn't drag on the ground in the process. Once out, I realized we weren't anywhere near a wedding ceremony.

Are we too early and first to arrive? Why did Renée ask the driver to drop us off here? Is the ceremony held in an area where vehicles aren't allowed in? Who knows... And who the fuck cares. I can't believe I'm about to see him after so many years... On his freaking wedding day of all days, ceremonial or not.

Random people walked nearby, chatting in various languages. Some had cameras strapped around their necks, some just appeared to be local people going about their business, taking a stroll in their city. A svelte effeminate man walked with four tiny dogs on pink leashes, followed by a couple holding hands.

Renée squeezed her right arm in the crease of my left elbow.

"Come on," she said.

I lifted the bottom of my dress so it cleared my heels and Renée led me around the majestic Notre-Dame cathedral, whose view helped calm my nerves. At least a little.

A short stroll later, we entered the gardens at the back of cathedral. Thankfully, Renée's cadence had been slow. I hadn't broken a sweat, although each step I'd taken had somehow increased the sense of dread that floated above my head, like a false dark cloud that would mess up this otherwise beautiful day. Sunny days in Paris seemed so rare to me. Most of my visits had been under gray weather or drizzle. Today wasn't hot. It wasn't cold. The temperature was ideal. Above us stretched a solid blue sky, save for a few scattered, puffy white clouds. Seemed luck was on Ady's side. *Hasn't it always been?*

Renée stopped suddenly.

I turned my eyes away from the magnificent cathedral and followed the direction of her gaze.

At first, I saw a mime in a striped white and navy shirt, with white gloves and a black beret crowning his painted-white face. I watched him for a few seconds, but he was immobile. *Crappy mime.* Immobile, save for his eyes, which were locked on something... or someone.

I followed the mime's stare.

And there was Ady, a hundred feet away from Renée and me. A handful of well-dressed people stood around him and his bride. He wore his formal Navy uniform, and the petite woman next to him was dressed in an understated ivory gown. He was still as tall and handsome as I remembered him to be, at least from a distance.

The sight stung my eyes, then my heart.

That could have been me. Why hadn't he loved me as much as I had loved him?

My heart thumped in my chest, its irregular beats fueled by unrecognizable emotions. I concentrated on my breath for a few seconds, trying to keep my eyes dry while doing my best to analyze the mixture of sensations brewing in my gut. Pain, hurt, anger, and disappointment seemed to win over love and lust.

"Want to get closer?" asked Renée.

I swallowed hard, then replied without looking at her, "No."

"Good. Cause the ceremony itself is just for close family."

I turned to face her. "What the fuck? What's wrong with you, Renée? Why are we here then?"

"There's nothing preventing us from witnessing it from a distance! Then, we can follow them to the hotel when they're done."

My hand flew and slapped her shoulder before I could restrain myself.

She smiled at me with the expression of a teenage girl trying to bully her way through life. "I just wanted to see your face while Ady voiced his vows aloud. I don't believe you've forgotten about him like you claim."

"So that's why we're here?" My voice came out louder than I'd hoped. I turned to look at the ceremony and saw a few guests turn our way. I leaned closer to her and whispered, "You want us to crash their ceremony just so you can rub it in my face and prove me wrong?"

She raised her shoulders, but her expression remained cool as steel. "I've run out of ways to entertain myself."

"Quite bitchy of you," I said, staring into her brown eyes. I couldn't recall her ever being that mean to me or anyone in the past.

Her eyes held up my stare, then her eyebrows popped up and she broke eye contact. "Fair enough. Yeah... Probably wasn't cool to force you to come here. Let's head to the hotel and grab a drink instead."

I froze for a second, unsure if I wanted to go through with this. *Why am I doing her this favor? A favor that's inflicting me pain?*

"Come on, my treat. To apologize."

6:50 p.m.

The number of people at the reception must have hovered around a hundred.

Among the fashionably dressed guests, I spotted a few acquaintances from way back when. Most appeared to be here with their significant others. Everyone save for Renée, me, and that weird mime from the ceremony. I spotted Luc among the guests, but didn't want to mention it to Renée. He was accompanied by a girl half his age. *Was she the one he cheated on Renée with? Guess it didn't really matter.*

"Why is there a mime here? Is this some sort of French custom?" I asked Renée, hoping to take her attention away from her ex and his guest.

She laughed. "No, silly. What do you think?"

I slowly shook my head at her. "I wouldn't be asking if I knew."

"That's how they met. Looking at the same mime, and then their eyes met. They went for coffee... and the rest is history."

I sighed as my eyes inadvertently rolled.

They even had their meet-cute moment when they fell in love at first sight? Fuck.

What is wrong with the world? ...Or is something wrong with me instead?

My wine glass stared at me, its emptiness unable to solve my inner conundrum.

"I'll go get myself another glass. Want one?" I asked Renée.

"Sure, why not," she replied, not even making eye contact with me. She appeared enthralled by the mime's motions.

As I parted the crowd to make my way back to the bar, I saw a handful of old familiar faces. *Do they remember me?* Then again, it had been so long ago... If they did, they probably wondered why the heck I would have been invited. They probably felt sorry for me or didn't care at all. At least nobody dared to say anything aloud about my presence here.

A few minutes later, I was once again standing next to my only friend in the room, sipping a crisp Chardonnay, letting its effects smooth out my edgy feelings. Seeing him up close with his new bride when they had entered the room, with guests cheering and clapping loudly, had pinched my heart, but not as much as I thought it would have.

He was still as handsome as I remembered him to be. Sure, maybe his hair had thinned out a bit, but his smile hadn't lost an ounce of charisma. And, I'm slightly ashamed to say, I checked out his ass. Nothing seemed to have changed there. It even brought back a few memories that made me blush.

The bride, Heather, was pretty. Really pretty. Way prettier than Renée had described her to be. And she was quite an intellectual as well. *Good looks and smart. Fuck.* I wish I could have recorded her speech. It was perfect: beautiful, funny, touching... almost sickeningly so.

They say we shouldn't compare ourselves to our exes' new girls, but seriously. Who can resist?

I finished my glass and stared at its bottom before heading back to the bar to get myself another one.

8:23 p.m.

While at the bar, a couple of wine glasses later, a familiar, deep English voice greeted me. "Fancy seeing you here today... After all these years," he said.

I turned around.

It took a second for my drunken eyes to settle on him. Ady was standing less than a foot away from me, champagne flute in hand. So handsome... especially *without* his new petite bride by his side.

"Hi, Ady... Sorry for showing up unannounced. I swear I'm not here to crash your wedding. I'm Renée's last-minute plus one."

"Ah..." was all he said as he nodded.

In a split second, his dark brown eyes dug their way through my protective layer and pierced my soul, just like they used to.

"Well, I guess congratulations are in order," I said, putting on the biggest smile I could muster and raising my glass, which I realized was empty, yet again. "Toasting with an empty glass is bad luck. Let me rectify that."

I turned to the bartender and ordered another drink. Contradictory feelings fought to the death in the pit of my stomach while I patiently watched the waiter uncork a new bottle for me.

"Still looking good, though. You haven't changed a bit," he said while my attention was focused on the waiter.

I must have reflected on his words for a few seconds too long because by the time I turned around to deliver the smart-ass reply that was on the tip of my tongue, he was gone.

9:30 p.m.

I was inebriated enough to withstand the events around me without tipping over, but since I had long lost count of the number of drinks I'd consumed (and I hadn't seen Renée in quite a while), my blacking out point was surely fast approaching.

Did she hook up with someone and leave?

A nagging feeling in the back of my neck made me turn away from the bar. A tall and muscular man was walking toward me. Around forty-five or fifty years old, with long sideburns going all the way to his jaw bone. I'd seen his face before.

What's his name? Kevin?

Whoever he was, he headed my way with puzzled eyes locked on me as if I was about to save the world with toothpicks or do something significant.

"Here's a bird I hadn't expected to see here. Or ever again, really."

Has to be Cousin Kevin, or another member of Ady's large family I saw once or twice, a long time ago.

"*Votre vin, mademoiselle,*" the waiter said from behind the bar.

I pivoted just enough to grab my drink, then raised my glass at that quasi-stranger who stood in front of me, now with a large smile on his rugged face. "Hear, hear. To miracles and unicorns," I said, smirking at my drunken muse's wit.

He clinked his high-ball glass against mine. "To running into you. Miracle or not."

I downed half of my drink. "I know it's super weird for me to be here... today... at his wedding. Renée roped me into it."

He was shaking his head at me. "Then I'll have to thank her for that."

"Thank her?"

He bridged the small gap between us and squeezed himself sideways next to me along the bar, increasing my level of confusion.

"Why?" I asked as I pressed my hand against his tuxedo, hoping to push him out of my personal space, but I felt his firm, muscular pecs instead. I reconsidered my instincts. *Hmmm. Cousin Kevin or Whatever-his-name has beefed up.* "Sorry, I'm not sure I remember your name."

"Keith."

"Keith! Of course." *Damn you, girl. You're definitely drunk now.*

He put his drink down on the bar and then his index finger traced my arm. "So, you forgot about me?"

"No, I haven't forgotten about you," I said, taking another sip to try and comprehend what was happening. "I remembered your face. Just forgot your name. Can you blame me, after all these years?"

"Well... I still remember your name," he said as his hand landed on my waist.

I looked down at his arm, then looked back up to meet his gaze. "Really?"

He leaned in and whispered in my ear. "My cousin may have tossed you out, but you've retained a starring role in one of my fantasies," he said, his warm breath caressing my ear and sending quivering waves down my body.

Maybe it was my drunken stupor, but I pulled away and stared him in the eyes. "What?"

He brought me back closer. "I won't repeat myself. Come meet me in the coat check in five, and I'll show you... Or... Miss the opportunity and forever wonder," he said before walking away from the bar.

I watched his large, tall body part the crowd and head out of the room. For a brief second, he turned and made eye contact with me, then he was gone.

What the fuck?

And why the fuck not?

It's not as if I owe anything to Ady. He's freaking married now. Who cares if I fuck his hot cousin?

I scanned the rest of the room. Older relatives I didn't want to talk to. Couples. Couples. And more boring couples. *And... come to think of it, why shouldn't I enjoy my singlehood—being at my ex's wedding or not—and fuck whatever handsome quasi-stranger that presents himself to me?*

Sure, coat check wasn't the most romantic spot, but it could be hot.

Why fucking not?

9:45 p.m.

Keith was leaning against the wall in the hall just outside the unattended coat check, seemingly waiting for me.

The door had been left wide open. Today having been such a lovely day, it made sense that hardly anyone had brought in—let alone checked—a coat. But a couple of hats had been left on the top shelf.

I walked in and grabbed the nearest one. I put it on and turned around to look at him as he locked us in, leaving the lights on.

"What do you think? Can I pull this look off?"

"Oh... You can leave your hat on, baby," Keith said before closing the gap that separated us.

His lips devoured mine. He smelled and tasted of Old Spice and rum. He forced his body against mine, his hands reaching for my chest, and I stumbled backward. The proximity of the wall prevented me from tumbling on my ass (along with him), but resulted in my head banging against the hard surface. The hat I wore dropped to the floor.

My colliding against the wall had hurt like hell, but I was unsure if I yelped or not. If I did, his hungry lips swallowed any sound that may have left my body. Next thing I knew, my bare breasts hung out of my dress and his erect dick poked through whatever fabric stood between us.

The cocky bastard's fast.

My heart pounded as his thick tongue left my mouth then traced its way down my neck. He moaned while nibbling on my left nipple. I brought my hand up against the back of my head, wondering if I'd cracked it open. I sighed in relief when I saw that my fingers weren't covered in blood. He bit my nipple, then one of his hands reached down toward the bottom of my dress.

"Easy..." I whispered. "Don't bite."

He grunted as he came back to my mouth. He grabbed a hold of my dress and lifted it up around my waist before undoing his pants. "I like it rough—"

"Keith! Keeeiiith! Where are you?" yelled a woman in the hallway. Sounds of high heels rapidly clicking on the marble floor got louder. Her steps were getting closer.

"Fuck," he swore under his breath.

The whiny, nasal-pitched screaming continued. "Keeiiith? Honeeyy, are you here?"

The woman's voice seemed familiar... Then it came back to me. I could picture her face now. I had met her... with Keith... at their house. *That's Keith's wife!*

I pushed him away. "You're married, aren't you?"

He grabbed my ass. "Yeah, so? You knew that. You met me here—"

I slapped him in the face and pushed him again, more forcefully this time. He lost his balance and crashed into the adjacent wall.

"What the fuck? You seemed into it?"

"Sorry, Keith," I said while pulling the fabric of my dress over my breasts and covering myself up again. "Totally forgot you were married. Can't do that. Won't do that. I'm not going to ruin your marriage."

He chuckled. "Who says it's not ruined already? Come on..." he begged, his bare dick pointing at me through the flaps of his shirt, his pants had dropped down to his ankles.

"Not me," I said.

I lowered my dress and ensured my ass wasn't hanging out before storming out of the coat check, leaving him there alone.

Thankfully, his wife seemed to have moved on to another section of the hotel and didn't see me, but I knew my hair had to be a jumbled mess. Seeing a few guests heading my way, I rushed to the ladies' room two doors down from the coat check.

I needed to have a hard stare at myself in the mirror.

A cold-water splash wouldn't hurt either.

10:00 p.m.

God, am I glad to have stopped in time!

Well... I guess that depends on one's definition of cheating... But I can't blame myself. I did the right thing. I stopped as soon as I realized.

I inhaled deeply, then exhaled. I repeated the process for a few minutes, my eyes locked on my own reflection.

Who is that woman looking back at me in the mirror?

Who have I become?

Those questions were too deep and too meaningful to be answered now.

Am I already too drunk?

Probably. Nah, most definitely.

I just had to fix my outward self and move on.

At least, my mascara and eye liner had remained intact. My lipstick was long gone, probably transferred onto one of my countless wine glasses. I didn't bring any make up with me to touch it up, so who cared. But my hair was a mess.

After three attempts, I finally remembered how to tie a chignon the way Renée had shown me hours earlier today.

Renée... Where the heck is she?

It's time to find her and go home.

10:20 p.m.

Back in the reception hall, after ensuring I was presentable and didn't show any signs of my quasi-extra-marital, coat-check interlude, I ordered myself yet another drink.

Unsure why.

I didn't *need* any more alcohol. Maybe it was just more liquid courage. But it was probably just a habit. It was something to hold on to while I looked for my friend.

I've undoubtably put a fine dent on his open-bar tab. Call it pay back for dumping me by email years ago.

I scoured the room again. Couples, couples, and more couples. *Where did Renée go? Did she leave without telling me?*

I let my eyes settle on the mime doing his 'stuck in a box' routine. It all seemed so ironic to me. 'Marriage and commitment' sure looked like a real box.

...It's a life sentence.

Better hope you pick the right person... or else...

Guess there's always divorce: today's get-out-of-jail-free card.

The mime finally came out of his box and people clapped.

Hmmm, that mime is actually pretty good... Or am I too drunk to notice he sucks?

And come to think of it, he may be cute under that layer of white make-up...

I spotted an empty table closer to him, so I relocated, carefully avoiding familiar faces among the crowd. I paid special attention in avoiding Keith and his wife, but thankfully both were nowhere to be seen.

But not running into them didn't help with the fact that my body had been aroused and left to hang without payoff. I had to release that sexual tension... I scanned the room for men standing alone, away from their lady counterparts and without wedding rings on.

Nobody fit that description.

I returned my attention to the mime.

Maybe he'll do... I can't tell if he's wearing a ring under his white gloves...

Hard to tell what he looks like under all that makeup and those overly expressive faces... but his body certainly shows potential. Tall, not muscular, but not scrawny... He'll do.

So, how do I get his attention?

6:45 a.m.

My eyes first recognized my open suitcase on the desk in front of the bed where I lay.

Bright light shone through the window, hurting my sleepy eyes, but I couldn't muster the strength to get up and close them.

Fuck! Why didn't I do that when I went to bed last night?

When did I go to bed?

And how the fuck did I get back to my hotel room?

I lifted my head from the pillow but felt a sharp sting on the back of my head. My hand swung to the sore spot. I pressed on it. "Ouch!"

How did I get that fucking bruise?

The coat check incident flashed in my short-term memory. But trying to recall anything else beyond that only served to increase the pinging pain in my cranium.

I rolled over to my side to minimize the light reaching my pupils. But before closing my eyes again, I saw black smudges smeared all over the ivory fabric of the spare pillow next to me.

"What the fuck?"

Sure, I probably forgot to take off my makeup—wouldn't be the first time—but no way my mascara could have stained the pillow case that badly.

In an effort to figure out a logical explanation, I tried to sit up, but at least a minute elapsed before I found my balance. After rubbing my eyes in a last-ditch effort to stop the room from spinning, I spotted my new (and expensive) indigo dress on the carpet. My panties hung on the back of the chair.

"What the fuck?" I repeated, as if the walls could talk and fill me in.

I looked down at my body. *Naked breasts.* I tossed the sheet away from my lower body. *Completely naked... and dirty as hell.*

"Seriously! What the fuck???"

My inner legs were smeared with white and black, and so was the contour sheet under me.

I covered my eyes with my hand, trying to recall the previous night.

Fuck. Black and white make-up. Did I bring the mime home last night?

I could not recall a damn thing.

Maybe this is just a nightmare and it will all make sense when I wake up in a few hours.

9:00 a.m.

Somewhere in the distance, my phone rang. The familiar ringtone blasted through my ear drums as though a nuclear alarm had gone off.

"Shut up!" I yelled at the device, knowing fair well that it wouldn't do anything to stop it, but it somehow made me feel a little better.

Maybe Siri has a command for that?

I flapped the sheet away from my body, exposing my white-painted thighs and confirming my earlier memories were real, then walked over to the damned device.

"Hello?" I said after finally quieting it down.

"*Bonjour, c'est Nicholas.* Are you ready to go visit your aunt's business? I could pick you up in about fifteen minutes?"

"Oh... Fuck... Sorry... *Désolée*... I totally forgot about it. Hmm... Any way to reschedule for a little later today?"

"Ah! Did you have a nice evening out on the town last night? I understand. Why don't you call me when you feel rested and ready to go?"

"Will do."

"*Au revoir... et bonne nuit, ma chère! Faites de beaux rêves.*" I heard him say just as I pressed the button to hang up.

Yeah, yeah...

I turned off my ringer and all notifications.

Doubt my dreams will be sweet, but I'll definitely try to get some sleep.

Maybe some of last night's blacked-out events will have reinserted themselves in my memory by the time I get up again.

I closed the curtains in one fell swoop, then crashed back on my bed, this time in total obscurity.

5:00 p.m.

"I was beginning to think you'd forgotten about me," he said in a tone that had me wondering if I'd totally messed up and if he'd be sending me an invoice for a full day's worth of work.

"I'm so sorry," I repeated. "I swear this is not typical behavior on my part. It's just..." Weighing the pros and cons of divulging the truth was too difficult for my hung-over mind. *Fuck it. Truth is nearly always better.* "Last night, the long-lost love of my life got married. I over-indulged, if you know what I mean..."

"Ah? Well, glad you're finally awake then. One would assume this situation will only present itself once. So... You're forgiven. Don't worry about it."

A wave of relief came over me. "Thank you for understanding."

"That being said, we've got a slight problem with our new timeline. We can still tour your aunt's business, but by the time we'll get there, some patrons will have arrived, so we'll both need to blend in as to not break the illusion of—"

"What?"

"You'll understand when we get there. Would it be fair for me to assume that *Mademoiselle* Gabriella's body size and shape is similar to yours? I could pick up one of her outfits for you to wear?"

I had to think about it for a second. "We're probably about the same size, but I'm a few inches taller, if that matters."

"Perfect. I'll swing by your hotel in about fifty minutes."

After hanging up with Nicholas, I checked my messages. Renée had left me five of them, all of which were long-winded and apologetic.

The gist? She'd left early without telling me because she'd hooked up with Luc. Again. She was sorry for having dragged me back into Ady's life. Not cool of her. She should have given me a heads-up before she left... *Blah, blah, blah.*

Well, she'd have to wait for me to get over my hangover (and to get over how bitchy she acted) before she'd get a phone call back from me. She didn't need to know the sad end to my evening... And she'd be unable to fill me in on the details I still couldn't—and probably never would—recall.

After taking something for what was left of my hangover headache, I showered and tidied my room the best I could to hide the evidence of my shameful behavior.

Then, I changed into my jeans and T-shirt and dried my hair.

I was grateful Nicholas had offered to bring me an outfit—whatever it was going to be—but I was curious to learn why I needed to wear something special.

5:55 p.m.

First the reception called to confirm I was expecting a guest, then he was at my door two minutes later, dressed in a full tuxedo, one of those opaque suit protector cases in one hand and a square box in the other.

"Wow! You sure clean up nice!" I said. "Come in."

"Here's something your aunt loved wearing, along with a coat," he said, handing me the thick but light case.

"A coat? Is it cold out today?" I asked.

He shook his head, and I took a few steps toward the bed to lay the case flat on the comforter before unzipping the cover. Two hangers. The first held a very long charcoal-gray trench coat. I pulled it out of the case, exposing the second item: a semi-sheer black outfit that would likely be sold in the lingerie section of a very expensive boutique. I pulled it out and held it up against the light.

Well, at least there were some *opaque parts to it.*

"I see..."

"You're fine with wearing it?" he asked. "Cause if you're not, then there's no pressure. And there's probably no point in visiting your aunt's business if the outfit alone makes you uncomfortable."

"I'll go and put it on," I said with a smile before heading to the bathroom.

A few minutes later, after realizing the outfit didn't leave room for any underwear to be worn with it, I came out and twirled in front of my lawyer in his penguin suit.

"You actually pull this off. I'm impressed," he said, quietly clapping his hands. "Now, *la pièce de résistance...*" He opened the box he'd dropped on the corner of my desk and walked toward me.

The white fabric box contained two golden masks with jewels embedded in them. I lifted the first one. Heavier than I had expected.

"They're not real stones, are they?" I asked while bringing it to my face and wrapping the three sturdy elastic bands around the back of my head.

"Real precious stones and three types of gold, but it's only dipped in gold. Otherwise it would be too heavy to wear."

"Really? How much is it worth?"

"Much less than your aunt's business," he said before taking out a second mask from the box, this one more masculine. In doing so, he exposed another object previously hidden underneath it. "And this is for you as well."

Resting on the black velvet was a gorgeous golden necklace with stones matching those of the mask I was wearing.

"Let me," he said after placing his own mask on the comforter and extracting the necklace from the box.

He dropped the box on the bed, then lifted my hair away from my neck and placed it on my right shoulder, then dropped the heavy necklace around my neck and clasped it behind my back. "Now, go and have a look at yourself with the complete outfit on," he said, pointing me toward the full-length mirror on the back of my bathroom door.

I walked the short distance to the mirror, the long slit that went up to my hip along one side of the dress allowed for long, unrestricted strides. I was stunned by the woman I saw in front of me. The baroque mask only covered my eyes and nose. My mouth was unobstructed. And this necklace...

"*Magnifique. Mademoiselle Gabriella serait ravie de vous voir ainsi,*" he said.

I turned to face him just in time to see a familiar black cloud return to his eyes.

"Nicholas, I've been meaning to ask you..."

He looked at me "What?"

"A few things really... But how did she die?"

"She was really sick—"

"But I didn't know anything. My mother never told me she was sick."

"I don't believe she told anyone. Gabriella was a very private person."

I let that sink in for a few seconds. Maybe that's where I got that trait from. "Sick with what?"

"Lung cancer that remained undiagnosed for too long. It spread to other organs. Her odds were meek."

"But didn't she want to do chemo? Or wasn't there a treatment she could have done to stop it?"

He shook his head. "It was too little too late for her. She wanted to live life to the fullest until the end."

"So, when I last saw her, she knew she was dying..."

He nodded, then looked away, but not before I noticed the tears forming in his eyes. I wanted to ask him if there'd been something between him and her. There had to have been something. Something quite special really...

"Let's get going," he said before removing the trench coat from the hanger and holding it up for me to slip into.

6:20 p.m.

Nicholas drove a luxurious BMW. Gray and practical as opposed to something red and loud he could have probably purchased for the same price. *Or maybe he owns one of those as well?*

He gave me a little bit of history about Gabriella's business on our way there, but I couldn't seem to focus on any of what he was saying; my mind was still vainly trying to piece together my previous evening.

I don't even know—or recall—that mime's name!

On my lap, the weight of the box that contained our masks brought me back to the moment.

"Should I be worried about someone stealing my mask?" I asked him as he turned off from a main street and headed down a tree-lined, narrow, cobbled-stoned road.

"No. Our patrons are wealthy. We run thorough security checks on them. Criminal records, financial statements, medical screening, the whole lot."

"Isn't it illegal to request all of that information?"

"And aren't brothels illegal?" he asked rhetorically. "Our employees are run through the same checks, and they are paid very well, especially for their silence. Our patrons appreciate the peace of mind and confidentiality of our business. They pay very good money to be members of our establishment, and if our rules don't work for them, they're not allowed in."

"And how much money are we talking about? How much does the business make?"

He grinned and kept quiet.

As he turned into a small driveway, a black metal gate appeared before us. He stopped the car, rolled down his window, and pressed a button before saying his name aloud.

The gate's mechanism clicked loudly, then the doors opened slowly in front of us. He rolled in, and I watched the gates close behind us through the passenger's mirror while Nicholas kept going forward. The moment they were closed, I returned my attention to the road in front of us. What I saw made me gasp.

"The business could probably afford one of these buildings every year," he said as I almost drooled watching more and more of the beautiful architecture appear in front of my eyes. It was three stories high, built in a style reminiscent of the *Château de Versailles*. My eyes continued their inspection of the property until they reached a wall.

The gardens aren't as extensive though, but who cares! I doubt people come here to take a stroll in the garden. Or do they?

"Holy shit!" I couldn't help myself.

"Yes. Serious money. I can show you financial figures later if you want. But first, I'll give you a tour of the property. Please put on your mask and hand me mine when I stop the car," he said as he drove around to the front of the property. Once our wheels stopped, a valet instantly walked to the car and opened my door to let me out. Then, after holding my hand as I stepped out in my high heels, he closed my door and guided me up the steps before going back to the car and taking a seat in the driver's side.

By then, Nicholas had already joined me by the front door.

As if someone had been monitoring our entrance, the heavy wooden door opened for us and a man's voice welcomed us: "*Bonsoir Monsieur Nicholas.*" He turned to me, then added, "*Mademoiselle.*"

"*Bonsoir,*" Nicholas said with a head nod.

I followed suit and greeted the man. Nicholas then turned to me, and I understood it was time to take off my trench coat. One arm at a time, he helped me peel away my only opaque layer, then he handed my coat to the man who had opened the door for us.

"Let's begin our grand tour!" he said.

I followed him down the marble entrance hall; our footsteps echoed against the tall, intricately carved wooden walls.

A few moments later, we began our ascent on the wide marble stairs. I kept a hand on the balustrade to avoid falling off while looking around me. Then, I saw her: dead center in front of us on the first landing, a large oil painting of what seemed to be Gabriella surrounded by a handful of women, all wearing beautiful masks, scant clothing, and stilettos.

6:50 p.m.

The first room we stopped in, which Nicholas called *le salon*, reminded me of the British tea room I'd seen in that very special Irish castle a while back. Except that it was probably three times as spacious.

According to my lawyer-turned-official-tour-guide, this room was meant as a mingling room for guests to interact with the staff shortly after they arrived. But right now, it was empty, save for Nicholas, me, and a couple of men in white shirts with simple black masks standing behind an ornate wooden bar that occupied half of the back wall. I recognized several premium brands among the large selection of bottles held on the shelves behind them. The rest of the room was expansive enough for about twenty or thirty people to sit comfortably in various, fairly isolated areas. There were couches, love seats, and even mattresses surrounded by sheer curtains. A few sizable plants, vases, and other decorative elements offered some added privacy, at least from certain angles.

"Let's try and show you more of the property before the first guests arrive," Nicholas said before wrapping his arm around my waist and leading me out of the room, greeting the bartenders on the way.

He pushed a swinging door and we ended up in a narrow hall, which winded a few times then went up two steps before opening into a wider passageway. A dozen doors lined each side.

"And here are some of the bedrooms for our guests to use as they see fit," he said. "There's also another level, which can be reached if you go all the way to the end of the hallway. There's another wide staircase there."

But it seemed we weren't going to go there. Nicholas had stopped in front of the first door on our left then opened it. He walked in, and I followed him.

I imagined that's how one of the rooms at the Ritz would look like, having never stayed at one of their hotels. Luxury oozed from every detail. Thick, velvety embroidered fabric hung in decadent loops over the tall windows, which sheer curtains currently covered. Another layer of thick burgundy fabric was nested on the outer edges, ready to enclose the room into obscurity should the guests want it. A Victorian-era settee, two padded chairs, a long coffee table, and a large fireplace occupied half the room while the other half was presided over by a king-size bed whose ornate and massive foot had seemingly been painted with gold. At the head of the bed, a luxuriously padded oval reigned, crowned with a thickset gold seal. The same fabric that had been used to upholster the headboard hung in loose hoops several feet above the bed, its edges decorated with golden trim and ending with two large tassels, one on each side. A dozen decorative pillows of assorted shapes and sizes had been piled on the bed. But the details that I liked most were the intricate moldings on the wall. A light baby blue covered the larger, plainer areas, but the trims had been painted white and some of the detailed carvings, in gold.

"Are all the rooms just like this one?"

He looked around before replying. "More or less. We can visit a few more later if you'd like. But first, let me show you something." He headed back toward the open door so I followed, but I was taken by surprise when he closed then locked the door instead.

"Sorry!" I said as I walked into him. "What are you doing? Didn't you say you wanted to show me something?"

He turned around and faced me. "In here, but I don't want anyone else to know," he said before proceeding to the wall next to the fireplace. He pulled a small table away from the wall, then pressed one of the wooden carvings in the dado railing about a third of the way up the wall. A section of the wall panel receded. He pushed it in further.

"Won't people get suspicious when they see the door is locked?"

"What do you think? They'll assume we got *busy*." He smiled. "Come and follow me," he said before sliding into the small space.

At first I hesitated. Confined spaces didn't scare me per se, but this gap didn't appear to be any deeper than a foot, and it seemed pitch-black in there... But this secret passageway had aroused my curiosity.

First having to wear masks, then this...

Gabriella sure had lots of secrets in her life.

I stepped in on the plush carpeted floor, and then Nicholas's arm brushed against my chest as he moved the entrance panel to close it again.

All of a sudden, a series of very small lights brightened up the edges of the floor, just like the emergency aisle-lighting system I was familiar with on planes.

"Follow me," he repeated.

And I did.

7:05 p.m.

I was sure glad *not* to suffer from claustrophobia.

What felt like fifteen-minutes later, after he had pointed to several hidden panels and sliding openings along the narrow passageway, Nicholas stopped.

The lights along the edges of the floor indicated we'd reached a dead-end. But a soft beeping sound made me look up. My tour guide was punching numbers in a backlit keypad on the wall.

Shortly after pressing the last digit, a latch came undone, its click partly muffled by the plush carpet.

Nicholas pushed the wall in front of us.

Another hidden door.

Light once again reached my pupils, making me squint while my eyesight adjusted. It wasn't daylight. More like that blue light that TV sets emitted in a dark room at night. But I nonetheless felt a wave of relief as I left the confined hallway and followed Nicholas into the larger space.

More than a dozen monitors had been tiled on one of the walls. *Is this a control room?*

I turned around and realized it couldn't be—or at least it couldn't be *just* that.

There was an entire bedroom in here, with a king-sized bed covered by a dozen pillows, a tall wardrobe, a dresser, a few closed doors leading to who knows where. Heavy curtains that went from floor to ceiling covered the wall next to the control monitors.

Nicholas walked toward the bed while taking off his mask, which he then dropped on top of the ivory comforter. "This was Gabriella's bedroom." He continued his trajectory and crossed the room to reach the curtains. With a light screeching sound, he pushed a set open, and a stream of what remained of the sun's rays poured in. He unlocked the clasp on the large windows and pushed them open, then looked at me. "Come and have a look."

I obeyed and dropped my mask on the bed as well. A light breeze caressed my face and brushed the light fabric of my outfit against my body. The view was stunning. A couple of acres of beautifully tended gardens expanded in front of the balcony onto which Nicholas and I stood. Sure, in the distance the city continued its sprawl, but I felt like we were in a private oasis, just out of the city.

The size of the land alone has to be worth a fortune... Then the luxurious building on top of it. No wonder Gabriella was always dressed in the latest trends!

"Beautiful, no?" Nicholas asked.

I let out a long sigh. "Incredible is more like it. Did she live here full-time?"

"No. But she spent most weekends here. And some weeknights when special events were hosted."

"Where did she live the rest of the time?"

His eyebrows lifted and his Adam's apple jerked as he swallowed. "You know... Here, there... Other people's apartments..." His gaze then settled on the garden in front of us.

"You mean she regularly hooked up with... clients?"

He nodded slowly, his silence seemingly burdened by a secret that had become too heavy to bear.

"Were you one of her lovers?" I asked.

He turned to face me, tears in his eyes. "Yes. I loved her very much."

I wrapped my arm around his waist and rested my head against his chest, carefully avoiding my sore spot. "I'm sorry you lost her so soon," I said to him.

He reciprocated, wrapping his arm around my shoulders.

A few minutes elapsed while we stayed in a comforting embrace on the balcony.

Guess he's like my uncle or something...

We watched the last stream of light disappear and he tapped me on the shoulders before dropping his arm away from my body.

"Anyway. Let's finish the tour so you get a sense of what happens here."

He walked back in the room, and I followed him.

He closed the curtains then locked the doors behind me.

"Security monitors don't cover every part of the property, but as you saw through the multiple sliding panels in the secret passageway we came in from, Gabriella could peek on pretty much every room in this place. The employees don't know how to reach this room, and it needs to stay this way. Our guests sign a release form. They're aware nothing is private here; they know video cameras or similar equipment are used to monitor the premises, but they know none of it will ever be released, unless we're legally obligated to. That's why I asked you to wear a mask. Since you haven't officially accepted the... job... if you want to call it that... Or ownership of the business? ...Anyway, I didn't want you to be connected to it in the event someone decides to shut us down and come after those who knew of the business's existence."

"So how many employees are we talking about, and what kind?"

He walked toward the monitors. "A few cooks, bartenders, and gardeners, but most of our staff consists of our very special women," he said while pointing at a specific screen which displayed about twenty women in outfits similar to the one I wore. They were pampering themselves up, applying makeup and straightening their hair in what appeared to be a large change room complete with those mirrors outlined with large light bulbs I imagined famous actors used in their dressing rooms.

I moved my eyes to the next screen. On it, a handful of women had already taken seats in the *salon*, their colorful masks also secured by strings around the backs of their heads. The women weren't positioned near each other, though. Instead, they were peppered throughout the room, a cocktail in hand, as if socializing among themselves wasn't permitted. A man dressed in a tuxedo appeared into the frame and joined one of the ladies. He too wore a mask, not just hiding his eyes, but obscuring his entire face.

"A customer," Nicholas said, noticing what I was looking at.

Over the next few minutes, more and more men appeared in the *salon*, where most employees had moved to. Only a handful of women were left in the change room, based on the security footage we were watching.

"That's all live?" I asked.

"Of course."

"What kind of people come here? I mean are they locals?"

"Most live in Paris, at least part-time. We have several high executives in the fashion industry, politicians, entrepreneurs, self-made millionaires..."

I scanned the rest of the monitors so I'd get a better understanding of his business proposition. "So where are the male employees?"

He laughed at my question, then cocked his head at me when I repeated myself.

"Men are our target market. Straight men," he said.

My arms flung up. "So? You mean you've never thought of including women customers and men employees? And what about homosexual guests?"

"We've had special evenings with a few hand-selected men... But those were rare occurrences."

A groan escaped my lips before I could restrain myself. "What about women patrons?"

One of his eyebrows went up, then he frowned and shook his head. "Not many women openly cheat on their husbands like that. At least not here."

"What do you mean? All of these men..." I said, pointing at the monitor showing them flirting with the female employees. "*All* of them are married?"

"Well, no. But many of them are."

"What?" I brought my hand to my forehead but kept staring at the monitors in front of me.

Why does everything have to do with marriage and cheating bastards these days?

Is it just me who's so behind and old-fashioned about this? Have marriage vows become meaningless to everyone?

I'm not opposed to people exploring their sexuality and trying out new things, new people... But it must be done in all honesty, especially if it involves consequences with a mate, someone you've made a promise to.

Sure, I'm not sharing any of that information with my family. I totally understand and agree with Gabriella's request about keeping this from my mom. And my lifestyle is definitely not something I'd like to share with my dad either. His little girl would be forever tainted in his mind.

If I were married, though... I'd like to think I'd have married an open-minded person who'd accompany me in this adventure.

Yeah, an open-marriage of sorts... Could such a marriage work?

"Should we continue the tour?" Nicholas asked, taking me out of my head.

I sighed. "I guess so. Where do these other doors lead to?" I asked while pointing to the opposite wall.

"The passageway we came through only grants us access to some of the rooms. There are other passageways that lead to the other side of the hallway, and another that grants us access to the rooms upstairs, but they both involve climbing up and down ladders, so I thought it'd be better for us to come through the one we used. If you decide to take over the business, you'd be welcome to explore all of them as you wish, whenever you want."

He walked to one of the doors and opened it. "But this one is the bathroom, should you need to use it."

I shook my head.

"Well, what do you say we go and mingle. Experience the business for yourself?" he asked. "But no obligation. You could interact with a few guests so you understand if they're happy with the services here?"

"You mean run a customer satisfaction survey?" I asked.

He grabbed both of our masks from the bed then handed me mine. "As long as you promise not to give out questionnaires. That would kill the mood."

"And you say you don't have a sense of humor," I said, jabbing two fingers in his stomach. Its firmness took me by surprise. *Hmmm. Gabriella probably had some good times with him.* I followed him back out of the room, and the door locked automatically behind me.

Somehow, the passageway didn't seem so intimidating on the way back. The walls were not paper-thin, but they were certainly not insulated enough to hide the rooms' occupancy status. I stopped in my tracks when I heard a woman's longing moans on my right. I felt the wall, hoping to find one of those sliding panels Nicholas had pointed to earlier.

A few seconds later, I did.

I slid it open and lined my eyes behind the two peepholes.

At first, I only saw an empty bed and thought I hadn't found the right room, but then a hand flew up about two feet from my observation point in the wall. I readjusted—or at least I tried. The guests seemed either too low or too close to the wall for me to see anything. Then something—more likely someone—rammed into the wall, making the whole passageway shake. The grunts that ensued clarified that I'd see nothing from that peephole since that couple was obviously fucking against my wall.

Nicholas tapped me on the shoulder then, through the faint light, I saw his fingers motion to follow him.

A moment later, we were back in the original bedroom we'd walked in before I'd found out about my aunt's voyeurism fetish.

"So, again. Please keep that secret room and passageway to yourself. Guests and employees are in no way to be privileged to that information."

"Of course!"

"Now, what do you want to do? We can mingle and have fun, or I can show you the books and employee roster... Or we can put an end to this tour if you're not interested."

He continued his path toward the door, and I thought about my options while following him.

I couldn't say I wasn't interested *at all*, but the thing that bothered me most wouldn't be resolved by looking at some books. Unless my aunt was also involved in some illegal drug trafficking, it was clear from the property alone that she made a lot of money. I needed to talk to the guests and find out if they were all married men looking for a way to cheat on their wives without getting caught, or if there was more to it. Or maybe I wanted to find reassurance that my new way of living had a potential future with a man... *Whatever.* If I found a handsome single man back in the *salon*, then what harm would there be in spending a few minutes toward the pursuit of some mutual, heavenly carnal fun?

After all, I was all dressed up for the part. Having nowhere to go—or come—was certainly not the most wanted outcome here.

"First option would be better," I said a few steps after we'd returned to the main passageway.

"To the *salon*, then," he said before elegantly pointing me back the way we'd come from.

8:30 p.m.

Back in the *salon*, I scoped out my options.

It was obviously a one-way menu where women sat pretty and waited until a man approached them. I decided to challenge that approach. Instead of looking for an empty seat, I glanced around and looked for unmarried men. (Not that rings couldn't be removed, but at least I narrowed down my choices to a handful of men without rings—or tan lines—on their fourth fingers.)

I settled on a blond, pony-tailed man with a charming smile. It was hard to gage a man's age when he had a mask on, but as I walked toward him, I saw no obvious crow's feet around his bright emerald-green eyes. He was probably 25 or 30 years old.

"*Bonsoir,*" he said, smiling back at me.

It suddenly dawned on me I had to pretend to be French. "*Bonsoir,*" I said with my best accent.

"*Vous êtes nouvelle, non?*" he asked, wondering if I was a new girl.

"*Oui. Vous êtes un régulier?*" I tried to keep my smile on while mentally rolling my eyes at my bad conversation skills. *Of course, he's a regular client... It's not like I was standing in a neighborhood bar where anyone and everyone could walk in.*

"*Lorsqu'une chose nous plaît, il faut revenir,*" he said, referring to how much he liked the place, so that's why he kept coming back. "*Alors pourquoi n'aprennons-nous pas à mieux nous connaître?*" he asked, pointing to the door leading out of the room, toward the main hallway I'd accessed earlier with Nicholas.

His invitation to get to know each other certainly was a polite way to present his intentions... But once again, no surprise considering where we were standing... and how I was dressed.

I looked down at my sheer outfit once more.

Aunt Gabriella's outfit.

This whole thing's surreal.

He placed his hand on the small of my back and led me out of the room. Just as we passed the bar, he asked, "*Vous voulez un verre de champagne?*"

"*Pourquoi pas?*" I replied, not seeing a reason to turn down a drink right now. After all, they say it's the best cure to a hangover, and I had to try the full experience.

"*Attendez-moi ici. Je reviens tout de suite.*"

I waited where I stood. Just as he'd promised, he came back ten seconds later with two flutes of champagne. He hadn't paid or tipped the tall bartender.

Guess this is an 'all-inclusive' private club... With lightning-fast service!

I wonder if those bartenders offer services in addition to drinks? Or maybe they entertain themselves with some of the hostesses during slow times?

My Frenchman handed me my drink and we clinked glasses. "Santé!" we said simultaneously.

I took a sip, and he grabbed me by the waist. "*Allons boire notre verre sur un balcon. Ça vous plairait?*"

I smiled and nodded, agreeing to his offer to go and drink on a balcony somewhere.

We left the room and headed toward the familiar main hallway where the rooms were located. On our way there, we crossed another couple. They were clearly done for now: him with his bowtie untied around his neck, his shirt not fully done; her with her rosy cheeks and ruffled hair. Polite nods were exchanged in silence.

We walked past the bedroom I had visited earlier with Nicholas, and I followed my guy through another door that had been left ajar. The room was empty, and the bed was still made.

Are there maids who take care of changing linen throughout the night?

Or are people assigned their own room?

So many questions to ask Nicholas, but I forced myself to return to the present moment, to be mindful.

My emerald-eyed man placed his drink on a small table, then took off his tuxedo jacket and hung it on the back of a chair. He then walked over to the curtains and opened them up. His ass certainly appeared round and firm, his shoulders broad.

I couldn't wait to have a feel.

He opened the tall doors, grabbed his drink again, finished it, and then put the empty glass down. He stepped onto the balcony. *"Venez. La vue est magnifique,"* he said, ordering me to join him and enjoy the beautiful scenery.

I walked toward him after taking another sip and getting rid of my empty glass.

This room's balcony was smaller than the one in my aunt's bedroom, and it faced a different side of the property, but he was right. The view was stunning, both when I looked out of the balcony and after, when I turned around and faced my mysterious masked man. We were so close; I could feel the warmth of his mint-scented breath on my cheeks.

Who is he? A fashion designer? A banker? ...But does it matter and do I really want to know?

With a lone finger, he slipped one of my straps down my shoulder and traced my shoulder bone a few times before diving down into my cleavage. He moved in closer, pushing his tall and firm body against mine. My lower back rested against the top of the guardrail. His excitement transcended the layers of clothing that separated us.

I undid his belt, then his zipper before scooping a hand down his soft underwear. A firm, thick dick twitched in my hand as my fingers wrapped themselves around his girth.

He let out a deep breath, blowing warm air onto my neck. While one of his hands was still exploring my breasts, his other hand flicked my hair behind my neck and he bent down to kiss my ear. He nibbled on my earlobe, and I let my head go backward a little, enough for me to see the large moon above us. Its light brightened up the sky for a few seconds before it got partly covered by clouds.

He spun me around to face the guardrail and lifted the back of my dress.

"*Ah, mais quel cul!*" he said before slapping my ass.

I felt my cheeks warm up from the compliment. "*Merci,*" I said, shaking my praised booty a little.

I readjusted my mask and rested my hands on the guardrail while he massaged my ass and then parted my cheeks. He let out a groan then let go of me. A ripping sound followed. *Unwrapping a condom?*

A few seconds later, I felt the tip of his cock slide back and forth below my pussy. I raised my ass and arched my back to grant him a better angle, which he accepted in one slow and highly lubricated swoop. *The vibe in this place leaves very little need for foreplay, well at least when it comes to me and my hormones.*

A yelp escaped my lips as his long shaft bumped against the back of my insides, but it didn't stop him. Instead, he pulled out and reinserted himself a little faster, but thankfully not as deeply this time.

I delighted in our bodies meshing so perfectly, my breathing loud and slow at first. Then he added a few sharp slaps on my ass, each time taking me by surprise, forcing my insides to inadvertently clench against his shaft. And each time, it took me a little closer to my finish line.

He was the silent type, save for his breathing and the clapping sounds he made on my ass. But his cadence was also speeding up and his thrusts were getting deeper. Except for the odd slaps, he had mostly kept his hands on my hips. When he let go of me again, I half expected to get slapped, and even clenched my insides, but instead his warm breath brushed my back, and then I felt his hands on my breasts. He pressed them, forcing me to unfold my upper body and stand up more. I did, at least as much as I could while keeping him inside of me.

A loud male groan made me turn my head to the right.

Two balconies down, others were enjoying the peaceful night sky. At first I only saw a woman standing next to a man, kissing him. *But this doesn't make sense. How can he groan so loudly while his mouth's busy?* Then I looked down and saw another woman, this one bent in half at the hip. She held on to the kissing man's hip as her head bobbed forward and back in front of his crotch. Then, I looked behind that woman. Standing on the balcony, in the doorway to the room was another man, fucking that woman in the ass.

Guess this maison close *is a little more flexible than I thought. It's not limited to one-on-one action...*

But my emerald-eyed man had noticed my distraction. He slapped me on the ass again, then pulled away from me before spinning me around to face him. He grunted at me, his eyes now displaying a fiercer, predatory quality.

A wave of disappointment surged through me. My pussy wanted his cock back as much as I needed air to breathe.

"I need you to fuck me hard!" I ordered.

"*Quoi?*" he asked, reminding me I was in France.

I shook my head, trying to recall my French sex talk, but the only thing that came was *"Prends-moi."*

His strong hands got a hold of my ass and he lifted me up. I wrapped my legs around his hips.

Another spin and a few steps later, he had me pinned against the outside wall. His dick finished me off within a few delicious, powerful thrusts. He came a few seconds later, loudly exhaling into my ear while I was still quivering from my own bliss, looking out toward Paris's beautiful skyline.

9:30 p.m.

The car ride back was spent in silence.

Nicholas had fulfilled the promise he'd made to Gabriella. He'd shown me her business, books, finances, etc. He'd answered all my questions. It all seemed very appealing... Very appealing indeed, if it weren't for one important flaw: it catered almost exclusively to married men who wanted to cheat on their wives.

And right now, that one flaw went against my core beliefs.

"So, what do you think?" he asked as he double-parked his car in front of my hotel, its blinkers gently ticking away the seconds I needed to make up my mind for good.

I undid my seatbelt and turned to face him.

"Very enticing..." I opened my door and stepped out before putting down the box containing both of our masks on the passenger seat. "But I think I'll have to pass."

His eyes remained still, but he swallowed hard.

"Very well then. Keep the dress, necklace, and coat. Have a good night and a safe flight back tomorrow."

"Thank you, Nicholas. Have a good night, too," I said before closing the door.

And just like that, he was gone, his tail lights quickly disappearing.

A cloud of dread and guilt began to occupy the void his offer—Gabriella's final wishes—had created.

10:25 a.m.

Phone in hand, I couldn't bring myself to remove my French SIM card and replace it with my regular Virgin Mobile one. All I could do was stare at my screen.

For a brief instant, I made eye contact with the man sitting across from me at the departure gate. Beautiful green eyes. But it couldn't be my guy from the night before. His hair was short and brown.

We broke eye contact when he turned to kiss the woman sitting next to him. I looked down at his fingers.

Wedding ring.

Marriage can't help but fuck with one's mind. Watching happy people tie the knot surrounded by their closest friends and family was hardly a sore predicament, but getting married was just one day. One happy party-like event (with or without religious baggage). But when those first-day celebrations ended, a long life together began where nothing else in the world had changed. Getting married only meant getting on the ramp to a long and repetitive life where routine and boredom undoubtedly ended up murdering whatever passion and lust may have existed in the first place.

...Is this what leads married people to cheat?

Then again, people who aren't married also cheat on their partners...

My current way of living, of experiencing men (and sometimes women), was probably more exciting in the long run. Probably easier to find carnal happiness than find "true love" (if that even existed). *Fulfilling? Physically: yes, most times. Emotionally: it certainly has its fair share of highs and lows.*

But everything does.

The perfect relationship—marriage, boyfriend, one-night stand, regular sex buddy—didn't exist. After questioning myself over the past few months, I'd settled on the following perfect arrangement:

Finding a hot guy who was open-minded enough to let me explore my sexual horizons, possibly accompanying me along the way, but not exclusively. But that person could also be there for me at times, to fill needs other than my sexual ones. We could discuss things, intelligently. I didn't know if that man even existed and knew even less about how to find him. Putting this up on an online profile would certainly attract a herd of creeps, from horny teenagers wanting a cougar, to never-leave-their-mom's-basement porn addicts... And describing my needs as anything else would be misleading men and attracting those vanilla-types who want to start a family and get on the regular program that now seemed so boring to me.

It was unthinkable for me to settle for that now.

I should really thank Alex for broadening my horizons on that Toronto flight way back when. Thinking back about the past few months warmed my cheeks.

Will I ever stop blushing for no reason?

Who cares? I've certainly come a long way.

The tall French stewardess boarding my upcoming flight began her pre-departure announcement, inviting families traveling with children to line up. I didn't know her. I couldn't tell if she led an exciting life, but I was certainly fond of the work we shared. It was quite a job really. *Lots of perks. Could I give it up?*

Would living in Paris be as exciting?

Maybe...

Would running an already successful business and making loads of money be appealing? Certainly.

But supporting a business where only rich men could cheat on their wives seemed wrong...

But what if the odds were evened out. What if the business could be turned into something I'd be able to support with my heart and soul? Something where everyone stands to win...

I unlocked my screen, then looked at my list of recent calls before dialing Nicholas's number. The call rang without answer, but I left a voicemail:

"Nicholas, c'est moi. S'il vous plaît, oubliez ce que je vous ai dit hier soir. J'ai besoin d'un peu plus de temps pour y penser. Je vous rappelle dès que j'aurai pris ma décision finale, d'accord? À très bientôt j'espère."

MY XXX EXPERIENCE

FRANCE

THE PLAN

AFTER CAREFULLY COPYING HER WORDS—WEIRD accents and all—into Google Translate, I discovered that she asked Nicolas to give her more time to think it through.

My stewardess could one day leave her job to become a whorehouse manager—or whatever they call those people—but I've already read her remaining three journal entries. She traveled to other countries after Paris, so I'm obviously getting outdated news through her journal.

That being said, I believe my luck is about to change. She left me too many leads, too many details. One of them has to bear fruit this time. Here are my options:

OPTION 1: Track down Gabriella Andrews's obituary.

Determining the date of her death will give me a timeline of sorts. I should be able to figure out at least the month and year her Paris journal entry was written. As for getting my stewardess's name, the woman's related to her on her mother's side, so that probably means shit for last names. Unless she took on her mother's maiden name instead of her father's?

Likelihood of success: Worth a shot, at least for the timeline information.

OPTION 2: Meet with *Maître Lancelot.*

I can't speak French to save my life, so tracking him down in Paris would be a little difficult… But if I can get to talk to him in person (he obviously speaks English), I could ask to join that high-class whorehouse so I can have a look for myself. Maybe she'll be there in flesh and blood?

Likelihood of success: Worth a shot.

OPTION 3: Uncover more information about Ady's wedding.

If I can figure out Gabriella's death information, I could look for Paris weddings that occurred shortly thereafter. Tracking down Ady (or whatever Ady would be short for) could lead me to his ex-girlfriend/my stewardess's name, but seriously… Too many unknowns, and my other two options are more promising.

Likelihood of success: Low to nil.

I've got a bit of research to do before getting on my flight to Paris.

And I'll need some help.

A FRIEND'S HELP

A rare bottle of Knappogue Castle 1951 whiskey was enough to convince Bob to once again help me track down my mystery stewardess, starting with a real translation of her last entry:

> Nicholas, it's me. Please forget about what I told you last night.
> I need more time to think about it. I'll call you as soon as I've made my final decision. Very soon I hope.

Yeah for me. Google's translated grammar and sentence structure sucked ass, but I had gotten the gist.

I looked at the large calendar on Bob's home office wall. Had she taken the job by now? That, I didn't know.

"And what about that obituary I asked you to track down? Anything?" I asked.

"Found something alright, but you've got to spill the beans," he said before typing something on his keyboard, then turning the monitor so I could see it from my side of his desk.

Eight gorgeous, tall, and slender women in colorful bikinis, masks obscuring half of their faces, occupied his large screen. I enjoyed the sight for a few seconds before noticing the elegant woman standing in the center of the group, a fur jacket on and a cigarette holder in her right hand.

"That's her. Right there in the middle of Gorgeousville's finest. Who the fuck was she? Your stewardess? Can we now celebrate the end of your ridiculous quest?"

"No. And I'm so close to finding her. That was her aunt."

His eyebrows went up. "Well, the gene pool certainly seems decent... Even surrounded by those top-notch babes, she still looks attractive. But who are these fine specimens? And what is up with the masks? The article didn't say anything about them. Are they models?"

"Have you checked centerfolds lately?" I asked Bob.

He squinted, as though weighing the odds I was lying to him. "You've got naked pix of them?"

"Fuck, no," I had another look at the big-breasted blonde whose wavy hair flowed down all the way to her tiny waist. "I wish... But there might be a way to get your hands on them for real... if you can afford it."

Bob's eyes widened. "They're whores?"

"That'd be my guess. But high-class ones," I said.

He minimized the image and then returned the monitor to face him. "What the fuck have you gotten yourself into? And how is the dead aunt going to help you find your mystery woman?"

"I was hoping you'd help me find out! Heck, that's what that expensive bottle was for. Tell me you got something."

Bob let out a sigh before turning off his monitor. "All I dug up was that she died a year and a half ago. No cause of death."

I rested my back in my chair. "Did it mention her age?"

"61." Bob got up and walked around his desk. "Now, shall we join Stacy in the dining room? Dinner's probably ready by now. Don't want to get in trouble for keeping her waiting..."

"Wouldn't have guessed based on that picture," I said, getting up. I followed him out of his office while reflecting on that number. It didn't matter really. The stewardess had mentioned something about being in her early-thirties when she went to Mexico. Assuming her entries were written relatively close to each other, she should be in her mid- or late-thirties at most... Guess I'd be fine with that.

But more than a year has passed since her Paris entry?

A lot can happen in a year... Including, perhaps, a career change?

WHAT HAPPENED

While Bob and I were out on his deck digesting the delicious ham dinner Stacy had prepared for us—and smoking a couple of Cuban cigars—I tried to entice him to take a few days off and come to Paris with me to act as my interpreter. But by the time I left that night, I hadn't received an official answer.

That was a week ago, but he finally sent me his answer today via text message:

I'll go, but only if Stacy comes with.

I shook my head as I pressed the button to dial his number. He picked up on the second ring.

"Come on, man!" I said without greeting him. "You really want her to know what we'll be up to?"

"It's my only condition. That, and you're still covering my expenses, as you said you would."

"Why? I like your wife, but this... This is a gentlemen's errand."

"Don't worry," Bob said. "She wants to shop. She'll do her own thing, I swear."

I paused for a second, hoping I'd think of a clever way to convince him. "I can't be held responsible if she sees or hears something she shouldn't."

"What? Are you planning on killing someone?"

"Bob, I don't know how things are between Stacy and you, but let's just say that she could catch you in... a compromising position... or at least in a place that wouldn't be suitable for her."

"You mean we'll go and visit that whorehouse?"

"Possibly."

"Awesome. Don't worry about Stacy. She's cool."

"Fine, let's coordinate our schedules. I'll text you my free dates. Pick those that work for the both of you then."

And this is how and why the three of us ended up traveling to Paris together.

Not according to plan, but I had to roll with the punches.

But wouldn't you know... I got to learn an interesting thing or two I'd have never known—and would have never guessed—about Bob and Stacy while we were in Paris...

Here's how our French adventure unfolded.

6:40 p.m.

With the Wi-Fi password added to his tablet, Bob began his online search for *Maître Lancelot*. "Sure hope your guy isn't on holiday right now..."

"Doubt his entire office would be closed if that's the case. Someone in his team will help me find her this time."

"Got one here," Bob said as he scrolled down the results page. "Christophe Lancelot."

"Not him. His first name's Nicholas."

He groaned. "And you tell me *now*?"

"Sorry, I thought I'd mentioned it," I said, scanning the room for the nearest waiter.

Seems the staff is in no rush to swing by our table to offer us menus or anything…

"I'll go get us drinks." I got up and headed to the bar. Luckily for me, the waiter spoke English.

Maybe everyone in the French capital speaks it, at least to some extent?

I ordered two beers and returned to the table where Bob sat, his eyes glued to his device.

I handed him a glass. "Here you go."

"Thanks." He took a sip. "Ahhhh. Just what I needed." He took another swig, then rested his drink on the table. "I found two possibilities."

He handed me his tablet and pointed to the open tabs in his browser window. "You know what he looks like?"

I traded my glass for his electronic device, then swiped down the page until I saw a photo of the first Nicholas Lancelot. I couldn't read French, but I spotted his name in one of the captions. The man in question had curly blond hair and a large smile. "Not him." I tapped on the X to close the tab and the other one came into view. Stern, tall, and bald. "That's the one," I said, handing Bob his tablet back. "Can you find out their business hours and address?"

He took another swig, then tapped his way to a different page on their website. "Yup. They should be open tomorrow at 10 a.m. Do you want me to email them, or should I call and see if anyone picks up so I can request an appointment?"

"Doubt they'd be able to book us tomorrow anyway. Why don't we just show up unannounced? Maybe we'll catch him off guard, and he'll divulge something he wouldn't have otherwise?"

He raised his shoulders. "Why not? And I'll make sure Stacy's all set with her shopping plans for the day."

"Now that's a good friend. Hope she won't max out your credit card. Cheers!" I said, clinking my half-empty glass against Bob's.

He shook his head. "I better get my hands on one of those hot babes like you promised."

"No… I'll do everything to try and make it happen. But I never promised *that*."

Bob tilted his head from side to side a few times before taking another swig. "Still worth it. And with your never-ending luck, my odds are probably good."

10:00 a.m.

Architecturally speaking, the facade looked like a regular Parisian residential building. No visible sign that we were at the correct address.

Bob was the first to spot the intercom panel and its multiple buttons in the entranceway, partly hidden behind the glass doors in front of us.

He pulled open the outside door and went in. I followed. I tried the second door, but it was locked.

"Hold on," he said.

I turned and saw him squint at the list of names on the panel. A few seconds later, he pressed a button.

After a minute of waiting, I asked Bob to try again. "Maybe hold it and speak. See if they can hear you," I said.

He did, and we once again waited for nothing.

But then, just as I was about to give up, a woman unlocked the door from the inside. A young boy was with her. They politely left the door open for us (or I may have squeezed my shoe in the doorway just as it was closing).

Once the woman and her kid were out of sight, I pulled the door opened for Bob to lead the way.

"What floor is it on?" I asked him as we climbed the narrow stairway.

He replied without turning around. "The panel said fourth, but I don't know if it means three or four floors up from here. You know... Ground floor sometimes being first floor and all... Can't remember how French buildings work."

And we could have gotten our answer soon enough, but I didn't care nor keep track of the number of flights we'd climbed before finally seeing the business sign we were looking for.

"Bonjour," a female voice said to us as we stepped in the large lobby. I looked around and saw a young, twenty-something carrot-head behind a desk. Then, after looking at both of us, a long string of incomprehensible blabber spilled out of her mouth, in a tone that was far from the friendliest I'd heard.

Bob took over, seemingly trying to appease the young thing, and I followed him to the reception desk behind which she stood.

That young secretary was cute, in an austere and angry librarian kind of way. Her bright orange hair had been tied into a braid, and she wore glasses with a dark-brown frame that made her skin seem like it'd never been exposed to a single sunbeam. Ever. Her pink lips were bunched as she shook her head at Bob. The line between her brows deepened. She was pointing at the door through which we'd entered.

Shit.

A large brass plate sat on the corner of her desk: *Amélie Desmoines.*

"Amélie," I said, interrupting my friend half-sentence through his French gibberish. "Do you speak English by any chance?"

Her stern face turned to me. "Yes, of course," she said with a thick accent, rolled Rs and all.

"Great. I'm Charlie. I love those glasses, by the way," I said before flashing her my most charming smile.

Her left hand flew to the thick arm of her eyewear. She blinked a few times, brought up her glasses ever so slightly, then looked at me, this time without that line between her orange brows. Her eyes' shade of brown was so dark, it almost seemed black. *How rare on a red-head. Contacts?*

"Listen. We're so sorry to show up here unannounced... But see, we came all the way from America to see *Maître Lancelot,* and we're only in Paris for a couple of days—"

"That is *not* how it works," she said, shaking her head at me and making her brow line reappear. "You need to book an appointment. *Maître Lancelot* is a very busy man."

"I realize that. And I'm so sorry to inconvenience you." I stepped closer to her, pushing Bob aside, then rested my elbows on the marble surface and leaned toward her. "This is a gorgeous office, by the way. I love the leather furniture, the marble top here," I said, sliding my fingers toward her on the surface that separated us. "Even the staff has that classic look of beauty that never goes out of style."

Her cheeks flushed.

Got her.

"Did you know that my friend and I are airline pilots? I assure you that we can more than cover any inconvenience caused by our unexpected visit." I paused and looked at her, gauging what my next move should be. "Maybe I can take you out to dinner tonight? Fancy place... Your pick... What do you say?" I asked.

Her hand flung to her collarbone, and she played with the tip of her braid.

My trusty pilot card never fails. Today won't be any different.

She squinted at me before replying. "I can't tonight."

"How's tomorrow night? My last night in town... My friend Bob here is nice and all, but I certainly would prefer spending my last night in Paris in great company..."

She let out a long sigh. "Okay, I'll see what I can do. Please take a seat," she said, pointing to the oversized chairs in the waiting area.

A few seconds later, we had both taken a very comfortable seat out of earshot —at least if we whispered.

Bob shook his head at me. "What kind of black magic do you work on women?"

I raised my shoulders. "Natural charm."

"Whatever," he said, picking up a magazine from the coffee table in front of us.

I looked around the lobby once more. Other than a W.C. door in front of us, there was only one more door, and it was closed. It had to be the lawyer's office.

"Did the website mention any other lawyers working here?" I asked Bob.

"Nope. You better hope your magic works. Do you plan on getting her to spill the beans over a pillow?"

The thought made me smile. "That's not a bad idea... But I don't know if she knows anything about my stewardess." I turned to the reception area. The redhead was on the phone, presumably talking with *Maître Lancelot*.

"Hey," I said, tapping on Bob's magazine to get his attention. "What if I tried to get her to step away from her computer..." I whispered to Bob. "...Long enough for you to go and see if she's got some information about that Gabriella Andrews. There've gotta be some records. Her niece's name and number, an address, something, don't you think?" I sat back in my seat and looked at my friend.

He frowned then leaned toward me. "You realize you're asking me to do something ill—" he mumbled quietly before straightening up and donning a large smile.

I looked up and realized the secretary had walked up to us.

Damned Turkish rug must have silenced the clicks of her stilettos. Quite the legs on that one...

Unfortunately, she forced me to skip my more detailed appraisal of her goods by addressing us too quickly.

"I just got off the phone with *Maître Lancelot*. He cannot make it today, but he said he is willing to spare 15 minutes of his time tomorrow at 11 o'clock. Would that work for you gentlemen?"

"Sure," Bob said as he got up.

Shit. That leaves us with nothing to go on.

"Then, if you'll accompany me, I'll walk you down to the front door and let you out," she said, pointing at that damned door again. "I'll grab my keys, and I'll be right back."

Quick, Charlie. Think of something.

But nothing had come to mind by the time she joined us again.

She asked us to follow her out of the main office door, her purse strapped around her shoulder. I watched her tiny round ass lead us down that narrow staircase. Her short tailored skirt and the back seams on her nylons that lined up perfectly with those pencil heels didn't help me think straight either.

We'd gone down a full flight of stairs when I suddenly stopped and turned around to face Bob, who was following me—thankfully quite a few steps behind.

"Hey, didn't you say you needed to use the bathroom?" I asked Bob with one of my hands directly in front of my chest, wiggling my fingers to mime typing the best I could without Amélie seeing any of it, hoping he'd understand my plan.

He cleared his throat while his eyes sent daggers flying my way. He was shaking his head.

I opened my eyes as big as I could. "Are you sure?"

A second passed before he folded. "Yeah, you're probably right. I don't think I'll be able to make it back to the hotel in time." He moved his head so he could make eye contact with the receptionist a few steps below me. "I saw you had a washroom in there. Would it be alright if I quickly ran back up and used it?"

I turned to watch her reaction and silently prayed.

That line reappeared between her brows. After letting out a loud sigh, she finally gave him permission. But she also started climbing back up the stairs.

I threw my arm up to block her path, brushing her small breasts in the process.

She frowned at me.

"Amélie," I started while lowering my arm. "Why don't you and I head down and wait for him by the front door? Get some fresh air, get to know each other..."

She shook her head and squeezed next to me as she passed me on the stairs. "No, I left my comp—"

"Okay, I didn't want to embarrass Bob but..."

She stopped, turned around, then looked at me. "But what?"

"He's got a bad case of diarrhea. I'm sure he'd appreciate a little privacy... And you probably wouldn't want to hear the noises that come out of him either."

She rolled her eyes. "Fine. But I need to smoke. You are pushing my limits."

"Fine by me!" I said, bringing my back against the wall to clear her path down. "Lead the way, beautiful."

10:35 a.m.

It was only after we hailed a cab and both slid onto the backseat that Bob lashed out at me.

"Are you fucking out of your mind?" he yelled, his fist tightly wound up and aiming at me, his nostrils flaring.

I raised my hands as though they were a peace barrier between us. "Man, I get it. Not cool at all. I'm sorry." Bob wasn't moving, but I could see him clench his jaw. "Come on. You *had* to take one for the team. I couldn't leave you alone with her. From what I saw, she hates you. Did you get anything?"

He dropped his fist, but I could tell he was still fuming. He kept shaking his head, looking at his feet, his mouth turned upside down.

Shit. He got nothing? How else will I get information then? Pillow talk tomorrow night? Nah... Not his fault, though.

"Man, don't worry about it. Nothing bad happened; you didn't get caught."

"Nothing? NOTHING?" he repeated, screaming at me, making the cabbie turn and yell something at us in French.

Bob lowered his voice, but his facial expression made it clear he was pissed. Sweat was beginning to pearl on his forehead. "What if they have security cameras? What if I forgot to close a tab. What if—"

"Relax, Bob!" I slapped him on the shoulder. "Hey, look at me!" I waited until I got his full attention. "She's got absolutely NO REASON to even think that you've looked at her computer. I told her you had diarrhea. A bad case of it. Doubt they have a security camera in there. And even if they do, she doesn't know your last name. How many American Bobs do you know? Absolutely no worries, man!"

But my words didn't seem to reach my friend's ears. His entire body was shaking, something I'd never witnessed once since meeting him, decades ago.

"What about fingerprints?" he asked.

"What? Come on! This is real life. Not fucking CSI. Did you steal something while you were in there?"

He swallowed hard while shaking his head rapidly.

"Then there's nothing to worry about. By now, she's back to work, none the wiser. Her own fingers have already covered and smudged whatever print you may have left on her keyboard. NOTHING to worry about, man!"

He was now breathing deeply. Inhaling and exhaling while moving his hands up and down in front of him.

"Okay. Okay," he said.

"Sorry. I promise I won't ask you to do anything like that again. Drinks on me."

He exhaled loudly, wiped his forehead, then dug his phone out of his pant pocket. "You're right. I'm freaking out for nothing. She's got nothing on me."

I watched him unlocked his screen and I finally relaxed a bit.

Fuck. No idea Bob could turn into such a nervous wreck.

"So, you want to see what I found?" he asked.

10:50 a.m.

I grabbed my phone, then opened my navigation app to enter the address shown in the photo Bob had taken of Gabriella's business data sheet.

Sure, he hadn't found anything about her niece, but an address could be useful... Assuming it was what I hoped it was.

After pressing the *Search* button, I crossed my fingers and waited.

And there it was: a large acreage within driving distance from here.

"Fuck yes!" I said. I wrapped my arm around Bob's shoulders. "You did it, man! This is the place!"

"What place?"

I looked toward the cabbie and my eyes met his in the rearview mirror.

"I'll tell you as soon as we sit ourselves in that hotel bar. You're gonna like this." After the freak-out Bob had just put me through. I simply couldn't believe it. "You're the man," I said, feeling a smile grow on my face.

11:30 a.m.

I filled Bob in on the details I knew as soon as we got ourselves a couple of cold ones.

"But if there's a gate, and you have to say your name to get past it, what the fuck is your plan?" he asked.

"Well... We can wear mask to hide who we are... but you got a point." I stared at the condensation that started to drip down my bottle. "I have no freaking idea, unless you're willing to shave your head and pretend to be that lawyer? That's the only name I know, and I don't know how tall the fucker is, so... I don't have a plan."

Shit. Why did I get my hopes up so fast?

"Do you think we could somehow climb over the fence without having to give our names?" Bob asked.

I thought about it for a second. "No idea. Maybe, but there's a guy at the front door who does valet parking. Showing up without a car would be strange."

Bob took a swig, and so did I.

"Is there a side door we could use?" he asked.

"Shit, I think they have cameras outside. And they definitely do inside."

Bob waved his hand in the air. "So all of this stress for nothing? Really?"

"What do you suggest?" I asked. "We attach ourselves to another vehicle that's going in? Right under the axle, James Bond style? Then somehow distract the driver and sneak our way in? Don't think that would be good for your stress level..."

We finished our beers in silence and ordered another round.

An idea sparked in my head the moment the cold liquid of the next beer hit my mouth. "We don't get in. We wait until one of them gets out, then we follow her."

Bob furrowed his brow. "Her who? Your mystery woman?"

"That would be fantastic, but unlikely. We follow one of the whores, then question her once she's out of the brothel."

"We stalk her?" He took another sip, seemingly pondering the idea. "What time do they finish working?"

"No idea."

"And what if it's a live-in brothel?"

"From what I read, it seems they only offer *evening services*. The ladies must go home at some point..."

"So, we're going to follow some random beautiful woman back home?"

I tilted my head while bringing the bottle to my lips again.

It could possibly get us in trouble... But let's hope my lucky star stays on my side a bit longer.

"That's the plan, unless you have a better idea," I said.

"And it could be one of the gorgeous girls in that photo with the dead woman?"

"Possibly," I said, my shoulders raising on their own.

"Well... The risk would be worth it then... I'll need to take a nap this afternoon if we're going to spend the night staring at a gate."

"And I guess I'll go rent us a car. A cab won't do for tonight."

I finished my beer, then took out my wallet. After retrieving a few bills, I flagged our waiter over. Bob too was done and getting up from his chair.

"Meet down here at 8," I told him. "And wear something nice. We don't want her to think we're regular creeps. I'll go buy some binoculars, too. They could be handy."

10:50 p.m.

"I wonder how much this one costs..." Bob said, his eyes glued to the binoculars.

I poured myself another cup of coffee from the Thermos we'd brought. Even with the overhead light near the security camera, I couldn't see much without binoculars. Bob had parked too far for that, but any closer would have been suspicious. "What is it?" I asked.

"Mercedes. Convertible."

"Probably a small fortune... like a membership to this whorehouse."

He lowered his binoculars and looked at me. "Mercedes, MG, Rolls-Royce, Maserati... Everyone here's loaded."

I sipped the hot liquid, letting it warm my throat and help keep my eyes open. "We're not poor ourselves," I reminded Bob.

"No. But I don't spend frivolously on cars..."

I muffled a laugh. "Cause Stacy gets to your money first," I said.

He laughed. "Yeah. She's a big spender."

Another vehicle had turned onto our deserted street. Its lights first pointing toward us, then toward the metal gate when it turned into the entrance. Bob brought his binoculars up again.

12:20 a.m.

"Hey, remember when I stayed at your place in Costa Rica?" I asked.

"Yeah?" Bob nodded.

"I forgot to ask you. Henrietta, who is she?"

"You saw her?" He dropped his binoculars and looked at me. "What did you think?"

"I saw a woman, but I don't know if it was Henrietta. You didn't tell me anything about her."

"She could compete with those brothel ladies in terms of looks, but maybe a bit rounder..."

"Would she swim naked in the pool?"

"Ah! That's the one. You did her, you dog?"

"No, I didn't even talk to her. But what's her deal?"

"Let's just say that she spices up my Costa Rican getaways."

I watched yet another car turn into the entrance. "With Stacy there?"

He let out a long sigh. "We have an arrangement. We've been married so long..."

I frowned and looked at him, unsure if I'd misheard.

"Remember when things weren't great between me and Stacy? A while back?"

I nodded. Of course I did. His *dog house* had been my couch for a few weeks.

"We met with a therapist, and turns out we both craved more variety. So we quit going to that overqualified bitch and started seeing other people instead. Henrietta is my other person in Costa Rica."

"But how can you have an affair with her when Stacy's right there with you? That complex isn't that big."

"No, not an affair. Stacy knows about her. She knows Henrietta *very well.*"

"What the..." I stared at my friend in the dim moonlight. No spark in his eyes. No hint of a smile. *He's serious.* "Well, hats off to you... And to Stacy." And then I had my light bulb moment. "Ahhhh! *That*'s why you thought Stacy wouldn't be in the way if she came with us to Paris? Did you tell her what we're up to tonight?"

He raised his left hand. "Whoa! She doesn't know—or need to know—everything. She's got no clue about your obsession with this mystery stewardess. I told her we were going to a *special establishment*, and that maybe I'd bring back some late-night entertainment for us."

The words that came out of Bob's mouth were blowing my fucking mind.

"You have trios with your wife?" I asked.

He nodded and smiled. "Yeah. I still love her. She's hot. And that way we can add variety without the guilt, shame, and paranoia that come with cheating."

I realized my head had been shaking. Unsure for how long, though.

Incredible.

"But, your wife is into other women... or... Do you..." My hands started moving as though they could express what I wasn't going to say aloud.

"Do we sometimes have the *Devil's three way?*"

"Yeah. That." I swallowed hard.

"She deserves variety, too," Bob said.

No, he didn't! Shit just got weird.

I could no longer move or speak. I didn't want to ask nor know if there was any touching between him and the other men with whom he shared his wife. And then, just when my discomfort had seemingly reached its apex, memories of that amazing blow job under the table in Ireland flashed back in my mind... A homophobic shiver traversed my body. *The best blow job I've ever gotten.*

"Come on, man. Nothing weird there, I swear." He chuckled. "If you want bizarro, here's something: a couple of years ago, Stacy suggested we add *you* to one of our 'variety evenings'." He punched me on the shoulder. "I like you, man. But that's where I drew the line. *That* would have been fucking weird."

My stare froze somewhere in the darkness in front of the car. Stacy looked like Jennifer Aniston, but even hotter. The Bro Code had always kept her out of bounds, so discovering this little bit of information was weird indeed. "Yeah," I said, nodding.

"But don't tell her I told you—or anyone for that matter. The only reason our arrangement works is because we keep it a secret from the world... And because we respect and love each other. The other people are just a means to an end. Purely physical. That's it."

I swallowed hard and forced myself out of my stupor.

Am I that old-fashioned?

I started nodding. "Your secret's safe with me."

"Thanks. Appreciate it. So, are you gonna become a member of this place?" Bob asked.

"I'll for sure attempt to tomorrow." I looked at my watch. It was already past midnight. "Who knows when we'll get home. I'll have to set up a couple of back-up alarms. But then again, we'll have a car."

"We? Am I going with you again?"

I turned to look at Bob. "I assumed you would, but the lawyer speaks English. And that receptionist really didn't like your face or something."

"Yeah... It's hit and miss with me and women."

1:30 a.m.

A string of twenty cars had trickled out of the gates over the past hour.

Our Thermos long empty, my caffeine levels were beginning to dwindle, but I knew our luck was about to turn. If men were leaving, the girls were also likely to start heading home soon.

"Here's another one," I said to Bob.

I waited until the perfect spot where the beams from the car's lights were blocked by the nearby bushes and where the light from the security camera shone directly into the car, illuminating the silhouette of the driver. I saw a ponytail with a long, delicate neck.

"It's a woman," I said. "Finally!"

The boring surveillance task was coming to an end.

"Are we stopping her right here?" Bob asked.

"That would be creepy. Let's follow her and see. Maybe she'll stop at a gas station or something."

"And *that* wouldn't be creepy?" Bob started the engine, letting his rhetorical question die unanswered.

2:15 a.m.

About forty-five minutes later, she stopped and parallel parked her small Renault, leaving us too close to noticeably do the same without her seeing us.

"What now?" Bob asked as he slowed down.

"Keep driving and go around the block," I said.

We passed her vehicle as she finished backing into her spot. Her head was looking behind her so I couldn't see her face but it was clear her hair was long and blonde.

By the time we came around again, she was nowhere to be seen, but another parking spot was available nearby.

"Park here," I ordered Bob.

He did.

"Now what? Unless you saw something I missed earlier, we've lost her. Smart move, Charlie," Bob said with a smirk after turning off the engine.

I leaned forward and looked out of the windshield. Very few windows had their lights turned on. Most of the people in the neighborhood appeared to be fast asleep.

"Either she lives around here, or she went for a night cap some place. Can you think of another reason why she'd have parked here?"

"You want to start buzzing doorbells and asking around? At this time of night?" Bob asked.

"Of course not! But do you think you'd be able to get straight home after a night doing what she does? I'm going for a walk. Come on."

We exited the vehicle and Bob locked it, its single but loud beep probably annoying a few insomniacs and waking up others. Then we started walking down the deserted streets of Paris. But at least we were doing it in style with our dark suits, although quite a bit wrinkled from a night spent sitting in the car.

The first street was nothing but residential, save for a few shops on the ground level, all with their metal doors rolled down to the ground and locked.

We continued our walk around the block, heading back to our starting point when I saw a small neon sign on a street corner one block away. I recognized one of the beer brands we'd been drinking.

"There?" I asked Bob.

"Fine. You're buying," he said, not bothering to hide a yawn.

Why are yawns contagious? I followed suit then rubbed my face in an effort to wake up a bit.

Two minutes later, we walked into the establishment, which was near empty.

No blonde ponytailed lady anywhere.

"Shit," I muttered under my breath, but Bob headed to an empty table anyway.

"*Deux bières,*" I said to the bartender, practicing what Bob had been teaching me earlier tonight. When he looked back at me with a question I didn't understand, I turned to Bob who replied, "Amstel."

Damn language barrier.

The bartender uncapped our bottles and placed them on top of the bar while I dug out my wallet. I handed him a twenty-euro bill. He finished ringing our order in his till and was handing me my change when a high-pitch voice made me turn my head.

And there she was. The ponytailed whore. Certainly didn't look like one, though. She looked like a super-model who'd rolled out of bed and put on sweats. Big blue eyes. Blonde hair that glistened and sparkled even in the crappy lighting of this beat-up bar. I elbowed Bob.

He looked at me. "No idea how your ass can hold so much luck. Every fucking time," he said.

I handed him the two brand-new beers. "Offer her a drink and chat her up. Find out about where she works. Try to get the name of her new boss..."

3:15 a.m.

I wasted an hour of my time sitting at the bar, watching my friend make progress with the gorgeous lady. Between a couple of beers, a bottle of carbonated water, and a pack of nuts, I had run out of diversions. My patience— and my wakefulness—was wearing thin, so I decided to check up on him.

I walked over to the table and leaned close to him.

"Got something," he whispered to me. "I'll try and get more."

"I'll head home. Lucky night for you," I said in his ear. Then I straightened up and spoke louder. "You'll find your way home?"

He handed me the car keys, then gave me the thumbs up. I walked away, but just as I pushed open the front door, I turned back to my friend whose arm was wrapped around the blonde's shoulders. "Leave me a note under my door if you make it back before my appointment."

The air was crisp and cool, like a mild slap in the face that awakened me enough to safely make it back to the hotel.

11:00 a.m.

"Coffee would be fantastic," I said.

For a second I wondered if I could somehow sneak a peek at Amélie's monitor while she was preparing it, but no luck. The machine was just behind her reception desk.

Damn it.

My hand went to my pant pocket, and I felt the paper note Bob had slid under my door. The only word on it was 'Sophia.'

Is it my stewardess's name? Or maybe just last night's whore's name...

He hadn't picked up my call earlier, but I could clarify it later today when I saw him.

I returned my attention to Amélie. She was standing in front of the chromed coffee machine, pressing buttons that chimed loudly.

"Are you still taking me out tonight?" she asked with a smile.

She seemed in a much better mood today than yesterday. In fact, that annoying line between her brows had yet to appear, and she'd been smiling at me the entire time since I'd gotten here today.

"Of course. I'm a man of my word." I replied, admiring her slender figure. *Stilettos again today.*

And just then, she gave me a sly smile before stretching her arm up to adjust the position of the picture frame that hung above the coffee machine. In doing so, she exposed the lacy edge of her pantyhose where her skirt ended. *Ooh la la.* She definitely wasn't wearing those ass-covering granny hoses, and her small ass was too tightly wrapped in that fabric to hide suspenders...

And then, her arm was back down, but she didn't bother to pull down her skirt. With a clink, she placed my small coffee cup on a silver tray and came toward me.

"I saw you looking at me," she said with a wink.

I raised my right hand and smiled. "Guilty as charged. You're beautiful. It's hard *not* to look at you."

"Well, if you play your cards right, maybe I'll let you look at every—"

"Charlie?" a deep man's voice asked two feet away from me on my right.

I turned and recognized the bald lawyer I'd seen on the website. I shook his hand. "Thanks for seeing me on such short notice."

"No problem, but I only have fifteen minutes. I'm Nicholas by the way. Shall we go into my office? Amélie will bring in your coffee." He turned his attention to the receptionist. "And can you please make another one for me as well?"

I followed the man into his office, which was as impressive as my stewardess had described it. Amélie was following me, tray in hand, which she placed on the large desk in front of me, then transferred the saucer and cup to the lacquered wood surface before walking out, blurting something in French to Nicholas as she did. He replied to her in French, then turned his attention to me.

"So, why did you want to talk to me so urgently?" he asked.

I dove right in, taking full advantage of my limited time slot. "I'm here because of Gabriella Andrews and her business."

Although his poker face was pretty good, something flashed in his eyes when I mentioned her name. He stayed quiet for a solid minute. Then, he finally spoke. "I'm not following you, Charlie. Why are you here, and why are you talking to me about this woman?"

Amélie walked in with his coffee and I held off replying until she left the room.

"Please close the door on your way out," he said, in English this time.

"Oh, please cut the crap. I know she's dead. I know you two were close, and I know you were taking care of her business's legal issues. I'm not here to give you any trouble. Far from it. In fact, I'd like to apply to become a member, if it's at all possible."

He leaned back in his chair for a few seconds. "And where did you acquire this alleged information?"

"Listen, Nicholas. I know the entire business is on the gray side of things, and I'm not planning on running to the authorities with what I know. I just want to join. It's not like you have a public website, do you? I have no idea how the application process works. But I know you're involved, so I'm hoping you can tell me how to do it. Who took over after Ms. Andrews died?"

"I'm not at liberty to say anything to you. Our office doesn't represent any businesses that offer illegal services." He got up from his chair. "I'm going to ask you to leave now. I'm afraid I can't help you."

"And what about Sophia? Can you give me her contact information?"

He frowned at me, his nostrils flaring as he exhaled loudly.

I've clearly overstayed my welcome or trespassed some invisible boundary.

"Come on," I said. "Let me at least leave a business card with you. If you change your mind, you'll know where to contact me so I can send my money to become a member." I dug my wallet out and then handed him a card.

Unexpectedly, he took it and had a glance at it. "You're a pilot for a US-based airline? You don't even live here..."

"But I fly into Charles-de-Gaulle fairly regularly. I'd be willing to pay full price to access this particular business a few times per month. Think about it."

He let out yet another sigh then tossed my card into his waste basket.

What an ass.

Having never been a sore loser, I put on a fake smile and held out my hand. "Thank you for your time."

He shook my hand, then I turned around and let myself out of his office.

"That was fast," Amélie said. "You'll pick me up here?"

"Sure. What time are you off?"

"19... No, how do you say...?" she started before looking up. "7 p.m.," she said.

"I'll be here, just outside your front door. I'll let you make the reservation to your favorite place. But just so I dress the part, are we going to a casual or fancy restaurant?"

She tilted her head and winked at me. "Fancy. Let me walk you out," she said before grabbing her set of keys and leading me down the narrow staircase.

7:00 p.m.

As promised, my redhead left her office at 7 p.m. sharp.

Punctuality from a woman always surprised me. If she kept that simple promise, how would her promise to expose more of herself pan out? She'd for sure deliver on that, right?

With her looking left and right on the sidewalk across the street, I got that she hadn't spotted me yet. "Amélie!" I called out, waving at her.

She turned my way, her hand went up, and then she nodded.

I'd snatched a great parking spot just across the street from her office, but I was pretty sure that the blue and red circle meant I'd parked illegally, so I wanted to stay nearby, ready to move the car at a second's notice if needed. She crossed the busy street in the same outfit I'd seen her wear in this morning: an off-white blouse with her short black skirt... and those sheer stockings and fabulous stilettos.

A vision of her bare body wearing nothing but those heels flashed in my mind. But the sudden squealing of car brakes made the thought disappear before it'd reached my groin.

She slapped the guilty car's hood and yelled what I could only assume were some French insults at the male driver who snapped something back at her.

My inner gentleman felt a tad guilty for not having helped her cross traffic, but then again, she was a grown woman. And one with quite a character it seemed...

Finally off the street, she traded her frown for a large smile then leaned into me to kiss me once on each cheek. She smelled of pears and peaches.

"Shall we get going?" I asked.

She nodded and I led her to the passenger door of my car and opened it for her once the traffic allowed me to.

She climbed in. I watched her lean legs fold into her seated position, the top of her stockings once again visible and enticing. She placed her purse on her lap, and I closed her door before making my way around the car to the driver's seat.

"So where to?" I asked her after doing up my seat belt and starting the engine.

"Well... After the dream I had last night, I think there's only one option that will satisfy me."

"What dream?" I asked. *Women's brains made it impossible to converse in a straight line.*

Her hands left her purse and launched for my right thigh. "Let's just say you played a part in it... An important part," she said, one of her hands locked on my knee while the other slowly slid up my thigh. Then she let go of my leg just as quickly as she'd reached for it. She dug a piece of paper out of her purse and handed it to me.

"What do you think of this menu?" she asked.

Stuck in traffic that wasn't going anywhere, I had a look. The cursive handwriting read as follows:

Chez Amélie
Entrée ~ Ma chatte carotte
Plat principal ~ Ton saucisson américain
Dessert ~ Fricassé de jambes en l'air

"You know I don't speak *any* French, right?" I asked her, confused. But the title told me she wanted to go to her place. Then I spotted the word *dessert*. It had to be the menu she wanted to cook at home?

Her smile grew higher on one side of her face. Then she winked and returned one of her hands to my thigh. "I'll teach you a few words then. Drive. I'll tell you where to turn."

7:30 p.m.

My car parked, I followed her into a residential building.

We climbed a long staircase in silence, and I enjoyed every step of it, my eyes locked onto Amélie's gorgeous, tiny ass in front of me. The lines on the back of her legs sometimes distracted me from her swaying hips as she climbed, but I resisted the urge to flat out grab her—unsure why, though. It was becoming clearer and clearer that she and I shared the same goal.

Why else would a beautiful woman bring home a near stranger when I've clearly offered to put on pretenses and take her out to dinner?

Once she reached the landing for her floor, she veered toward one of the two doors and dug her keys out of her purse. A few loud clunky turns through the keyhole later, she opened her door for me.

I walked in. Other than the little bit of light that came in from the stairway, it was pitch black.

A second later, she turned on the light and pushed the door closed behind us. Then I followed her past the entrance.

I don't know what I expected exactly—perhaps a modern apartment filled with IKEA furniture or a traditional old-fashioned room with turn-of-the-century furnishings—but what occupied the room was neither. Other than a coat rack and small table where she'd just dropped her keys and purse and a mini kitchen in the far corner with two bar stools that stood below a raised counter, the apartment was bare, the blinds fully down, two other doors closed. The only other *furniture* I could see dangled from the ceiling, dead center in the room: a wide and curvy metal bar with a bunch of suspended straps and stirrups attached to it, some padded, some not. Straight below it, a pile of cushions in assorted colors.

"*Bienvenue chez moi*," she said. "Can I hang your jacket?"

I took it off and handed it to her.

After hanging it on the rack by the door, she headed straight for the contraption. She grabbed a hold of the straps, then hopped on and sat on the wide, padded one, then her feet found homes in the stirrups.

I loosened my tie and undid my top shirt button as I walked closer to her.

"First course on tonight's menu..." she started, waiting for me to make eye contact with her. "*Ma chatte*. Here's your first lesson," she said before parting her legs. Her mini skirt rode up as her trimmed red bush greeted me.

I walked to her. For a country that invented French-kissing, you'd think they'd do a bit more foreplay before getting to the point, but her pussy sounded deliciously fine to me.

"How about I get you naked first?" I asked as I positioned myself between her legs. My fingers headed toward the delicate ivory buttons of her blouse. One by one, I undid them, exposing a spaghetti-strapped, embroidered, skin-colored slip that continued under her skirt.

She tightened her legs around mine and let go of the straps before slipping out of her unbuttoned blouse and tossing it on the floor. She returned her hands to the straps of the swing and released her thigh clasp.

I reached behind the small of her back and found the zipper of her skirt. I undid it, and as a good and helpful girl, she pushed away from me, hopped out of her seated position, and then stood up. Deliciously slowly, she shimmied out of her mini-skirt before stepping out of it, letting one of her stilettos kick the unwanted item away.

Now wearing nothing but her short slip, sexy stockings, and stilettos, she stared me in the eyes, then hopped back onto the padded strap of her swing, this time resting her thighs on it and letting her ass hang behind it.

I slid my fingers between the silky fabric and her soft, white skin. I slowly made my way up her upper body, all the while placing myself between her legs and bringing her up, letting her weight rest on my thighs, her own thighs wrapped around my legs and allowing her to let go of the straps while I finally got that slip over her head.

I stepped back and watched her swing naked in front of me.

She was beautiful. The whitest of any skin tone I'd ever seen, almost blueish. The thick parts of her sheer stocking contrasted against her legs like two black piano keys. The pink nipples that crowned her small, perky breasts pointed to the ceiling.

I walked back toward her and stopped her swinging motions. I reached behind her head and my fingers found a long pin in her hair. I pulled it out and tossed it.

She shook her head, letting her long orange hair flow, and her fruity smell envelop me in the process. Her dark eyes met mine. A hand behind her delicate neck, I finally allowed myself to taste her pink lips.

Hungry wasn't strong enough of a word to describe her behavior. Famished was more like it. After nearly sucking my soul out of my mouth, she pushed me away. "Eat my pussy," she ordered.

"With pleasure," I said, kneeling on the silky cushions.

My head was at the perfect height. The sight was incredible. The smell was mysterious, musky, and inviting.

I wrapped my hands around her ankles and quickly brushed my way up her thin legs until I reached the thick band holding her stockings in place. Then I slowed to a crawl, titillating each inch of her soft, white flesh up to the fold of her legs and her red carpet. With my index finger, I traced an X through her trimmed bush, then I started brushing three fingers up and down her inviting pink pussy. I let the tip of my middle finger go in and gauge her readiness. It was unnecessary, though, since she was dripping wet. I brought my finger to my lips and licked off her juices. She tasted of a misty autumn morning by the sea.

She adjusted her position on her swing, somehow becoming horizontal in front of me; the strap she was previously sitting on now split into two, one supporting her shoulders and the other supporting her lower back. I could now open her legs as wide as I wanted, so I crammed myself as close as possible to her private, red-thatch-roofed pleasure center.

Hungry for her glistening pussy, I dove in head first.

With one hand, I squeezed her ass while my tongue tickled her small folds. I let her moans guide my mouth. I explored every bit of her pussy and tongue-fucked her while my cock wanted nothing more than a piece of the action. I tickled her. I licked her. I bit her. My tongue poked at her while my fingers rubbed her nub. She was so wet, like a flowing fountain of pussy juice. Her loud moans echoed against the unfurnished walls. I parted her folds then inserted two of my fingers inside her. I let them do what my cock desperately wanted to do to her swollen pussy. Then her thighs squeezed my head as she came in record-time. I swear she squirted in my mouth, and I enjoyed dining on her musky, salty juices. She finally yelled out something in French before releasing my head of her thigh grasp.

She sat back up in her swing and put two fingers under my chin.

"Your turn," she said. "Get up and strip for me."

I did. But with my cock ready to pounce, let's just say that I opted for efficiency instead of seduction.

"Now come and stand right here," she said, pointing to a purple cushion on the floor.

I obeyed and she repositioned herself on her swing. She first swung the device around 180 degrees, then stepped into the stretchy leg stirrups and brought them up around her legs, past her knees and up to the lower part of her thighs. Then she moved the two padded straps she'd previously used behind her back so they now crossed her hips and shoulders. Facing down, she leaned forward until she was parallel to the front. Her legs supported in the stirrups; her hips and shoulders supported by the straps; her small breasts left to hang loose, her arms free to roam wherever they wished.

And my ass is what they went for.

For a split second, I was afraid my cock would poke her in the eyes as she pulled herself toward me, but with a quick flick of her wrist, she re-aimed my erection straight into her wide-open mouth.

"God!" I said as she swallowed half of me.

I put my hands on her shoulders and pulled then pushed her entire body in front of me, as if she were a weightless super-woman giving me head mid-flight. Her warm mouth felt heavenly, her tongue twirled around my shaft. Amélie, in nothing but her lined stockings and stilettos, was quickly making me reach my point of no return. I reached for her firm butt but heard her gag reflex as my cock hit the back of her throat. Instead I reached under her and massaged her breasts as she delighted me with her tongue. Within seconds, I was done for. I exploded in her mouth, then felt the warmth of my own jism dripping on the top of my feet.

She leaned back and returned to a standing position. She stuck out her devilish tongue and licked her lower lip and chin, which glimmered from my cum.

Looking at me, she asked, "Water?"

"Sure. I'd love some," I said, my heart still pounding in my chest.

She made her way to her small fridge, opened the door, then walked back toward me with two small Perrier bottles.

Now, I know nothing about product marketing, but if someone had recorded a video of her walking toward me naked like she did, with so much hedonistic hunger in her eyes, her pussy swollen with desire, and two bottles of Perrier in hand... I'd have instantly gone and bought a truckload of this shit (or at least a whole lot of Perrier shares).

"Drink up," she ordered as her fingers grazed my abs. "I'll need you for another round shortly."

I watched her quench her thirst, debating whether I should ask her about Sophia.

Maybe I could lie my way to the truth?

"Wanna hear how I found your office?" I asked Amélie between two sips.

She raised her shoulders while downing the rest of her bottle.

"A friend of mine is a client of yours. An American woman called Sophia," I said.

She stared me down. "Sophia?" she repeated, slowly.

"Yes. Do you know her?"

She tilted her head. "Is this why you're here?" she asked me, her eyes now two thin slits.

A red alarm sounded in my head.

Shit. Bringing up another woman probably doesn't qualify as good fucking etiquette.

"No, of course not. I'm here for you, gorgeous Amélie." I moved closer and wrapped my arms around her waist.

She snaked her way out of my embrace. "Nicholas warned me about you, but I didn't want to believe him. You're on some information quest and I'm not going to play your little game. Get out!" she yelled, pointing at the door.

"I swear this isn't it. I'm here for you, baby!"

"Don't baby me! Get dressed and get out!"

The temper she'd displayed with Bob had resurfaced, now aimed at me.

Guess that meant round two wasn't going to happen.

NEXT STEPS

Sophia...

My instincts—or just hopeful thoughts?—told me she was my stewardess, now turned pimp-mistress, or whatever her official title was.

Now what? Will Nicholas reconsider my request for membership and contact me?

I doubt it. I don't think he liked me very much. Or maybe he doesn't like Americans in general?

But who cares. No point wasting my time thinking about him.

Gotta focus on what I can control...

And a trip to the Netherlands sounds like a fun experience to duplicate, hopefully with a woman as open-minded as my mysterious stewardess. And I may just find another clue that will bring me closer to her.

Sophia...

That's not enough for me to find her, but a first name is something.
Or maybe she spells it Sofia? She does speak Spanish after all… And French.
Damn, could she be smarter than me?
Nah, probably not.
I know I'll outwit her very soon in our cat and mouse game.

PART VIII

HOLLAND

THE STEWARDESS'S ENTRIES

HOLLAND

11:30 a.m.

ALEX FLIPPED a coin in the air. "Heads. You drive, but I get first dibs on men."

"As you wish." I took the key the car rental agent had been patiently holding, waiting for either of us to grab. "Thanks," I told him. "We'll bring it back in one piece in a couple of days."

He smiled and nodded, then we made our way to the compact we'd rented to travel to the southern part of the Netherlands.

Alex walked in front of me wearing her knee-length skirt and curve-hugging T-shirt. The lack of straps underneath the thin fabric of her top made it clear that a bra was an optional item for her, at least today. I'm sure the car rental guy hadn't minded at all. I'd noticed his wandering eyes here and there while we discussed the contract. Let's just say that my friend's gorgeous red hair—as bold and eye-catching as it was—hadn't been the focus of his attention.

Alex and I had both traded our uniforms for comfortable summer wear a few minutes earlier. I had opted for a spaghetti-strapped dress. And based on the bright sunlight that shone above us upon leaving the Amsterdam airport, we'd chosen wisely.

In a few hours, we'll be in Maastricht.

I was looking forward to getting out of the capital for once, past the flat lands of the north. Alex, the one flight attendant I knew who truly enjoyed camping and other outdoor activities—and the most open-minded as well—was surely the right person to accompany me on this short adventure.

Once out of the capital and on the A2 highway, Alex folded the map the rental agency had given us then stowed it in the glove compartment.

"This is so empty and orderly compared to my car," she said after clicking the compartment shut.

"You have a car?" I asked, surprised.

"Well, technically yes... But I wouldn't dare drive it anywhere far... It needs serious repairs."

I turned to look at her briefly. "Maybe you can find yourself a mechanic with benefits," I said.

She laughed. "Yeah. I should really consider that. You have one?"

"A mechanic or a car?"

"Either..."

"No. I sold mine a while back. I wasn't spending enough time in town to make it worth my insurance premiums and parking costs."

"Yeah, but you get to see the whole world instead."

Yes, I was grateful for the flat and beautiful scenery that surrounded us right now. Thousands of miles away from home. "You're totally right. We're damn lucky... Here, right now... Would you ever considering quitting this job?" I asked Alex.

"What for? It's THE perfect job! How else could you see so much of the world AND get paid for it?"

She isn't wrong.

"What if you were given a unique opportunity? What if you didn't have to do much and could still make a ton of money?"

"Like marrying a billionaire? That could be interesting for a while, but I'd get bored. I mean... One dick... for the rest of my life?"

"Yeah, that could get a bit boring. But what if this opportunity came with built-in variety?"

"Like getting my own harem of billionaires?"

A giggle left my lips. "Something like that..."

"Then I'd jump on the chance to do it. Any of my wealthy sex slaves could pay for my travels around the world if I had an urge to go somewhere. But let's face it: it ain't gonna happen. Worse odds than winning the lottery. No point in dreaming about it."

Yeah. A once in a lifetime opportunity. Should I take Nicholas's offer and settle in Paris?

But before I could think about it some more, Alex resumed her chit-chat. "So, what's up with you these days? We didn't get much of a chance to catch up on the plane."

Should I tell her?

While I trusted her with my life during work, I wasn't sure I was ready to share that secret with her. After all, Nicholas had warned me the opportunity had to remain private, and Alex did enjoy gossiping...

Better not.

I cleared my throat. "You know... The usual—"

"Did I tell you about my last guy in Boston? All talk and no cigar. I mean, he was good with his hands and his tongue, but his dick was like this," she said.

I took my eyes off of the road for a second to look at her. She was moving her pinky up in the air.

"Oh no," I said before exploding in laughter with her. "Sorry about that."

"Well, there's only so much one can do with imagination... But I do travel with toys for these rare occurrences."

"You're braver than me. I keep mine at home, safe in my top drawer. Aren't you afraid of getting stopped and searched at customs?" I glanced at her briefly. She was shaking her head.

"Could be a great ice breaker for the customs guy if he's cute. If not, then no harm done. It would probably give whoever finds it some mental material for his next solo session... God! I'm really hoping for a well-hung Dutchman this weekend. I need to make up for it... And you, did you follow my advice?"

"Guess I never thanked you for that... Let's just say that I'm on the accelerated program now," I said.

"Much better, no?"

I nodded. "Hell yeah. I had no idea my life could become that entertaining by making one tiny mindset shift."

"You're overthinking it. Glad to have helped. Buy me lunch and we'll call it even."

"Sure. And let's hope we find ourselves some handsome studs!"

"No doubt we will," she said before cranking up the volume on the radio.

4:30 p.m.

When we reached the center of Maastricht, Alex rolled down her window. A mild skunky smell wafted in the car as the heavier traffic forced us to slow to a crawl near a coffee shop.

"Hmmm," Alex said, but left it at that.

I've never seen her smoke... Come to think of it, we've never even talked *about weed. Ever.*

The traffic got moving again and she sighed. "How I'd love some of that," she finally said, breaking the silence.

"I was thinking the same." I smiled and briefly turned to look at her. Her eyes were round, one eyebrow higher than the other. I returned my eyes to the road in front of me.

"You?" she exclaimed.

"Why not?"

"First you learn to embrace my type of relationships with men... And now...

My type of occasional entertainment as well? I'm impressed with my little *protégée*. I thought the possibility of random testing would have you scared shitless."

"At first I was... Then I found a way to circumvent the results."

"Who told you?"

"Good ole Google pointed me to a helpful forum. The reviews for these cleansing kits had me adding them to my cart in no time. Have yet to be tested, though. Unsure if they'll really work, or if it's all a big marketing scam and I'll lose my job."

"For the record, they do work. At least the one I used during my last test... I came out clean."

"That's a relief." *Then again, I do have another job opportunity waiting for me if I were to fail one of those tests...*

"So, what do you say?" she asked, tapping me on the arm and bringing me back to the present moment.

"When in Rome... Let's enjoy some of the local delicacy!"

Alex clapped and let out a few high-pitch screams of joy.

Tired from the red-eye leg I'd worked hours ago, but wanting to have a good time, I wondered what was more important. "Should we do that before finding a hotel room?" I asked Alex.

"Way to go, girl! I'd say your priorities are right. There'll be lots of time to find a hotel and bike rental shop after our first stop."

4:50 p.m.

I parked the car and we backtracked on foot to the coffee shop we'd seen a few minutes earlier. For those who'd lost their sense of smell, the telltale sticker was displayed in the window.

I followed Alex in. The place wasn't as packed as I'd assumed it would be.

But then again, people do work on weekdays, and we're far away from tourist-packed Amsterdam.

"Hi. Can I get a couple of grams of whatever is popular?" Alex asked the tall blond man behind the counter.

"Do you have your resident *cart*?" he asked, rolling his R and confusing me by using the word *cart*.

But it seemed Alex was better with his accent. "A card? I thought weed cards were no longer needed?"

He shook his head. "With *de* new regulations, we can't sell to tourists. Only residents."

Upon overhearing the disappointing news, I stopped looking at the accessories and got closer to Alex at the counter. "But I read online that most places don't ask for it," I said. "Can't we just order a little weed? No questions asked?"

"Well, *dat's* true in Amsterdam and most of Holland. But here in Maastricht..." He shook his head again. "*Dey* have cracked down. Because of Belgium and Germany being so close, local law makers have different views on drug tourism. I cannot do it. Sorry."

I took a step toward the exit, but Alex didn't follow me. I turned around and saw her lean forward on the counter. She showed the cute man her biggest smile. "But isn't there a way you can make an exception for two lovely, out-of-town flight attendants?"

She stepped aside, pulled me by the elbow, then brought me closer to her. "We're only going to be here in your beautiful country for a few days..."

He looked behind Alex to the other customers. A couple got up and exited the store, leaving just two young men who couldn't be older than twenty.

"I could get in trouble..." he said.

"Come on, there's hardly anyone in your shop right now. We're not with the government. We're not going to report you." Alex looked around at the remaining customers, then lowered her voice. "These two potheads definitely don't look like they work... for anyone... let alone your government."

He let out a long sigh, looked at me, then looked at Alex again.

Maybe? I walked back to the counter. *Strength in numbers and all of that.*

But instead of using her words to push him over the edge, Alex pulled down on the stretchy fabric of her T-shirt and leaned onto the counter.

"Can I convince you to bend the rules, just this once?" she asked as she ran a couple of fingers down her exposed cleavage.

"Are you girls... a couple?" he asked, totally out of the blue.

"No," Alex said, shaking her head. "I mean, I like her, but not *that* much. We're just two single women..." Her hand went up to his face and, with one finger, she traced the outline of his bearded jaw. "Looking for a good time," she added.

He cleared his throat then licked his lower lip. "Well... Maybe," he said. "It depends on how convincing you are." He looked at me and his eyebrows went up, as if asking me to join my friend.

I undid the first two buttons of my sundress.

He leaned over the counter and lowered his voice. "Maybe I will help you, but I will need to see more than *dat,*" he said, pointing at our (still mostly covered) breasts.

The doorbell chimed again. The two young men who'd been sitting at the table behind us had left.

"Show me your tits, and I'll see what I can do," he said, this time a little louder since we were the only ones left in the shop.

I looked at Alex. She raised her shoulders. I unbuttoned the rest of my dress's delicate buttons. As if we'd practiced our timing, she pulled up her T-shirt exactly when I pulled my breasts out of my dress's built-in support. He took a good look, his tongue almost dangling out of his open mouth. Just as his hands reached toward us, the doorbell chimed again, and I covered up. Alex had done the same. I began doing up my buttons as fast as I could.

"Stefan," a deep voice said behind us. Then words were spoken in what I assumed was Dutch.

"Bram, come meet *dese* two," he said to the man that had just walked in before returning his attention to us. "He's my *broder* Bram."

My dress fully done up, I turned around. The men were obviously identical twins. Both had the same blond hair, the same beard, the same beautiful blue eyes. The only difference I could see was that the guy behind the counter wore a blue shirt, and the other one, a red shirt.

The man behind the counter—the one who'd just seen our tits—extended his hand. "My name is Stefan," he said.

We shook hands, then Alex turned around and started chatting with the newly arrived brother.

I paid for our two grams and some rolling paper while no other customers were in the store. Stash in hand, I walked over to the nearest table and was opening my baggie when Stefan called out to me. "I'm sorry, but you cannot smoke it here."

"But I thought..." I said, confused.

"I'd like to let you, but if someone comes in and sees tourists here, I'll be in really big trouble."

Alex joined in the conversation. "But we don't have a house here, not even a hotel room."

"Well..." Stefan looked at his brother. "Maybe *dat* can be solved. Bram and I live near here. Would you like to join us *dere*?"

"But what about the shop?" I asked.

He shrugged. "We own it. Locals can go elsewhere. *Dey* know where *de* other coffee shops are. I will close. You wait outside, and *den* we go to our place. How does *dat* sound?"

Everyone seemed to agree with Stefan's suggestion.

5:15 p.m.

We followed the handsome men down the street; I enjoyed staring at their tight asses in their jeans as they led the way. They probably cycled—or fucked—a lot to get such firm-looking butts. Or maybe they swam?

Their wide shoulders, their narrow hips, their long legs... Everything seemed identical. And so tempting... I could only imagine their naked bodies cutting through water in beautiful butterfly strokes.

Damn I'm horny!

"I will grab some beers and snacks and meet you in *de flat*," Bram said to Stefan. His bothering to talk to his brother in English made me feel comfortable. *How hospitable of them both.*

A few minutes later, Stefan led Alex and me up a narrow staircase. He unlocked his door and let us into their apartment.

"Make yourselves at home." He pointed to the bean bags that littered the living room, then walked over to his stereo system and cranked up some reggae before plugging in a lava lamp. "Please sit," he said. "I'll be right back."

Alex and I looked at each other. I raised my shoulders.

It had been a while since I'd last seen a bean bag...

But who am I to define what qualifies as grown-up furniture? Maybe the lovely twins are younger than I think? Maybe real living room furniture is expensive in Holland?

"Why the heck not?" I said as I threw myself on the nearest makeshift seat.

Alex moseyed around the room, looking at various paper posters that had been taped to the walls. In the process, she picked up, inspected, then put down the odd trinkets that rested on the sparse furniture. Bob Marley and cannabis leaves were definitely a recurring theme in their decor.

"Stop snooping around and sit," I said.

She raised her shoulders, then slouched on the bean bag directly opposite me, across from the tiny coffee table in the middle. On second glance, it was more of a nightstand. It had a drawer on one side, and its height would have been perfect next to a bed. I resisted the urge to pull the drawer open.

Stefan came back with a bong and sat on the bean bag in front of that drawer, between Alex and me, just as his brother entered the apartment. Bram came toward us and handed us a cold can of Heineken each, then he was off to another room, possibly to store the remaining beers in a fridge somewhere.

I cracked mine open, then clanked it against Alex's, then Stefan's.

"Cheers!" we all said.

The liquid cooled my parched throat, but I did my best not to finish it all in a few sips.

A moment later, Bram joined us in the living room and sat on one of the unoccupied bean bags across from his brother. He dropped a bowl of black licorice on the nightstand, along with a small bag of chips, unopened.

Sweet and salty snacks! I'm so hungry.

Bram picked up a couple of licorice pieces then pointed to the bowl. "Have some."

I was starving, so I did. The piece I put in my mouth was harder than I expected it to be, and its salty bitterness made me wince. But a few seconds later, I got used to the taste and began to slowly chew my way through it.

A lovely, familiar scent started to fill the room. Stefan had used his own stash to fill the bong with smoke, inhaled some, then passed the device to Alex. Soon enough, a cloud of smoke had formed above our heads.

Another round of beers was offered—and accepted, of course. A boring and long-winded conversation about the beauty of what Alex had seen to date in the Netherlands began (although her many double entendres probably went unnoticed by Bram, whose thigh Alex's hand rested on.)

I tuned her out, enjoying my increasingly potent high instead. That is until Bram opened the bag of chips; the crackling sound got my stomach's attention. "Yes, we are very lucky here in Holland," he said.

He ate a couple of chips then passed the bag to Alex. "Why did you come here instead of Amsterdam?" he asked her.

"It was her idea," she said, her hand in the bag while nodding my way.

The two handsome men now had their dilated pupils glued on me.

I raised my shoulders. "I've already visited Amsterdam a few times. It's beautiful and everything, but I think stepping outside of the capital is better if I want to see what the real Holland is like. Don't you agree?"

Stefan nodded while Bram inhaled from the bong.

It seemed like Alex couldn't care less about what I was saying. Her hand was now resting higher on Bram's thigh. Or was it Stefan's? I'd lost track of which twin had the red shirt on.

"Anyway, we're going to rent bikes and camping gear tomorrow morning and explore the countryside around here. I haven't ridden a bike in so long. Can't wait to feel the wind in my hair, inhale the fresh air while soaking in the beautiful scenery."

"Is there something we definitely have to see while we're here?" Alex asked. "We've only got two nights and two days before we fly out."

"You're looking at our country's finest right here," the twin who was closest to Alex said with a smirk, pointing at his brother and himself. He then turned to Alex and tapped on his own lap. "Have a closer inspection if you want."

She took him up on his offer, but instead of sitting on his lap, she landed flat next to him, then rolled off the bean bag onto the floor before exploding in laughter. A few seconds later, he reorganized the extra bean bags and they started making out like horny teenagers.

I was pretty high and happy. And now, with Alex's intentions out in the open —and two hot guys within reach—it looked like finding a hotel room for the night may not be something worth worrying about.

The available twin turned to me and smacked his lips onto mine before rolling on top of me. His lips tasted of salty licorice and his cologne smelled of sea salt. His hand grabbed my breasts and I let him feel his way under my sundress while I reached for his hard body. His firm buttocks didn't disappoint. I slid a hand up onto his lean, muscular back while my other hand squeezed itself between our bodies as I went for the solid bumps on his stomach. *Holy shit! Talk about a real, hard six-pack!*

As though he had read my mind, he pulled away from me for a second, then took off his T-shirt, exposing his hairless, sculpted torso. I think that's when my panties got flash flooded—or at least, that's when I noticed how drenched they were.

"I'm starving," I heard the other twin say.

And just like that, our make-out session was put on hold. My twin got up and walked over to a stack of papers on the corner of a table in the corner.

"Pizza?" he asked.

We all nodded. The high had me—and probably all of us—starving now. And not just for food. Alex licked her lips, but I'm pretty sure pizza wasn't what was on her mind either.

We smoked some more—this time from my recently purchased stash—while waiting for the pizza to arrive.

When it did, I was surprised to find it topped with lamb, but it tasted awesome.

Somehow the conversation had returned to flower fields and cycling, but after what felt like an hour of relentless talking, Alex interrupted her twin by jumping on him and kissing him half-way through his current point.

"Okay. Enough said," he said as soon as he could catch a breath.

He got up, pulled Alex by the hand, and escorted her out of the living room, leaving me alone with my twin, who didn't wait a second to kiss me.

His lips were even more succulent with the added saltiness of the pizza on them.

8:10 p.m.

Beans shifted in my twin's chair, then his hand landed on my waist before it began inching its way toward my breasts.

"My brother's going to fuck your friend real nice."

I looked at him: he was smiling, and lust sparkled in his beautiful blue eyes.

"And what are *you* going to do to me?"

His hands groped my breasts, he squeezed and massaged them through the fabric like they were Play-Doh. He locked eyes again and brought his hands to my face before replying. "It depends... What do you want?"

"Get fucked real nice...?" I asked, partly mocking him, but then again not. My sex talk in Dutch was non-existent and I wanted to fuck him so desperately.

Without a word more, he landed on my limp body. I could feel his readiness through his jeans as his lips swallowed mine, and his hands went right for my breasts again.

"Careful with the buttons!" I said, trying to squeeze my hands underneath his to undo the delicate pearl-like pieces before his strong hands would rip them off.

He got up and off from me for a second to take off his belt. I stared at his hairless chest, strong pecks, and six-pack abs... No, it was an eight-pack!

While I could have easily stared at the beautiful man in front of me for ages, I chose to take off my dress and get this party going. I flung it somewhere on the floor, but I didn't have time to remove my panties before his warm, hard body landed back on top of me.

I let my fingers run down his muscular back and my pussy warmed up even more. I swear my libido had morphed into a ticking bomb. I slid a hand between our bodies, eager to caress his abs, then went further south until I reached the waist of his jeans. His erect cock pushed itself up against the thick fabric. *Poor thing...* I managed to undo his button and zipper with a little pull of his hips, then I dove in to grab the body part that needed rescuing.

"Commando!" I said.

He moaned something, then his hands tried to pull my panties down. I lifted my ass for a second to clear the way.

Then, our fingers competed—or collaborated—in mixed confusion to get his jeans off in record time. He rolled off of me for a second before his hand fumbled through the drawer of the nightstand-turned-coffee-table.

A few seconds later, he proudly waved what he'd been looking for: a condom. *That's what they keep in there?*

Without losing a second, and before I could offer to roll it onto him, he covered his glorious appendage and leaned back against my body.

He kissed me, his twirling tongue only serving to poke at my already blazing embers of desire. I wrapped my hand around his cock and aimed it at my swollen pussy. He appeared to have gotten my message loud and clear as his mouth pulled away, then his upper body did the same. He parted my legs some more and a crooked smile appeared on his face as he stared at my pussy.

"Fuck me already!" I ordered.

And he obeyed, tenderly at first. He barely inserted the tip, then he slowly pushed the rest of his huge cock into my welcoming pussy. Every delicious inch of his impressive girth smoothly slid into me, parting my insides. His cock was the oasis my aching pussy had been longing for all day. I let a moan escape my lips, and he grunted in reply before picking up the tempo. My excitement grew to the soundtrack of our bodies meshing over the moving beans below us.

I let my hands explore his back before settling on his firm ass so I could push him deeper into me. Every now and then he grunted a few Dutch words I didn't understand. I couldn't care less about what he was saying. He could have been calling me names for all that it mattered; it wouldn't have changed how fast he was bringing me to heaven's gates.

I pulled back a bit, trying to slow down the inevitable and stretch the blissful moment we were sharing. I reached for his face, and my fingers landed on the soft beard that covered his square jaw. Our gazes met and his blue eyes had me hypnotized. While he kept pounding me, his warm and hard muscles forcing themselves against my softer body, I had to kiss his lips, my tongue had to explore his mouth. It was as though kissing him allowed me to drink up some of his youth, some of his strength. The softness of his beard against my face was delightful. It wasn't scruffy, it was just fuzzy and soft... almost silkily so.

When I started quivering, I realized I had dug my nails in his back, so I let go of him and brought my hand to my clit instead. I feverishly toyed with my pleasure center as my body convulsed out of control, taking my mind to nirvana while my soul and body rejoiced in ecstasy. Now hot, sweaty, and totally relaxed from having just come, my body turned to putty in his large hands.

But he had yet to come.

He was going on and on, strong like an insatiable Energizer bunny, ramming into me so hard I though the seams of the bag would break and beans would start pouring out.

"Turn around," he said as he got off from me.

I complied and ended up with my stomach and breasts resting on the bean bag and my hands and knees on the floor.

He moved the nightstand away then knelt behind me. His cock found its way back into my pussy, and he held on to my hips as he pounded me. I didn't know if it was the flapping noises or his incomprehensible Dutch mumbling, but he once again had me at the cusp of exploding.

"Don't stop! I'm about to come..." I said.

He thrust deeper into me for a few more seconds, then I was done for.

I let out a loud but partly muffled cry, my face in the bean bag as my limbs went limp. He was still pounding me... *Seriously? Is this man a machine?* I heard water running somewhere in the distance.

"Want some water?" he asked, pulling out of me unexpectedly.

"Sure," I said, suddenly realizing how dry my mouth was. And honestly, at that point, my pussy also deserved a short intermission.

I flipped myself around and stared at the ceiling fan that hung motionless above me while waiting for my well-hung Dutch lover to return. My high was still straddling the atmosphere even though the cloud of smoke had long dissipated.

I thought of my friend for a second, and could only imagine that these twins were identical in all ways.

I'm happy she's getting fucked by a big one this time, just like she wanted.

My fingers played with my clit as I waited for him to return. While my pussy was a little sore, my nub had proven to be more resilient... It wasn't like my excitement was going to dissipate if I didn't play with myself, but what else was I going to do?

He came back a few minutes later, a tall glass of water in hand. Seemed he'd disposed of the condom while in the kitchen. *Did he come without me noticing?* I quenched my thirst and handed the glass back to the beautiful man in front of me.

A few seconds later, we were back to where we'd been minutes ago. His glorious erect cock once again dressed for action, and me back on all fours, resting on the bean bag.

This time though, after poking his cock in me, he slid his hands under my breasts and unfolded my upper body so it rested against his warm, chiseled chest. I bent forward a bit to feel him more deeply as he rammed into me, his chest pressed against my back, his fingers pinching my nipples as his palms squished my breasts hard with every thrust. Not so hard that it was painful, but definitely harder than anyone had ever done it before.

He breathed hard behind me, an animalistic grunt that kept getting louder and coarser. I reached back and grabbed his ass with one hand while my other went between my legs in search of his balls. I cupped them, letting my arm move to his rhythm, then I pushed upward and squeezed them slightly as I pressed on that sensitive spot just behind them.

And it seemed to work. He tensed up and screamed something just as he came, filling me with his warmth, which had thankfully been held in the condom he withdrew a second later.

He slapped me on the ass and I let my body fall on the bean bag in front of me before turning around to look at him. He opened the coffee table drawer and took out a small box of tissues, which he offered to me.

"Thanks," I said after stealing a kiss from him.

I wiped myself then leaned back on the bean bag, totally spent.

He got up and walked away to dispose of the condom and my used tissues, then came back to fondle my breasts some more. This time, a little more gently. I couldn't help but run my fingers up and down his chiseled abs, then his strong pecks. That's when I noticed a brown spot near his left nipple: a small birthmark I hadn't seen before.

The oddly-timed water break...

The different, slightly more violent approach...

But exhausted and fulfilled, I couldn't care less if these guys shared everything.

9:00 a.m.

I woke up on my bean bag, still naked but with a cotton sheet on my body. The birth-marked twin was lying on his back next to me, his perfectly sculpted chest slowly rising and sinking to the rhythm of his breath.

After a quick shower and coffee, we left Bram and Stefan's apartment, eager to get breakfast, rent our bicycles, and go explore the countryside. And based on the shade of pink on Alex's cheeks, I assumed she'd enjoyed an early morning session with her twin.

I felt a little bad for no longer knowing which one was which, but I knew it didn't really matter as we likely weren't going to see them again.

Best to avoid the awkward conversation and part ways on a good note.

Following the twins' recommendations, we rented bikes and camping gear from a nearby store, then off we went, following the route the shop attendant had recommended to us.

Even though this part was hillier than the north, the ride itself wasn't difficult. But my ass hadn't ridden a bike in a while, so I was grateful for my large padded seat.

I enjoyed the fresh breeze as we cycled out of the city. We passed through several small towns, and Alex insisted we visit one of the windmills. I'd never been one for touring buildings, so I let her enjoy her visit while I found a nearby corner store and got some more water and a bottle of wine for tonight.

I was glad once we got back on the road again.

All day, fellow cyclists passed us by. Some were touring, others zooming by on their racing bikes.

We stopped at a cafe in a small village in early afternoon, ordered a sandwich and a cold beer, then returned to our saddles with an extra sandwich each to eat that night.

5:00 p.m.

When the afternoon neared its end, we decided to look for a spot where we could set up our tent and relax.

Having previously ignored the last few campground signs—and the map telling us we still had a long way to go before reaching the next one—we decided we'd just pitch our tent somewhere along the road. In a way, I liked the idea. We'd be away from larger groups and potentially loud, drunken behavior. But I knew I would miss the facilities once I had to squat in the bushes to pee.

A few minutes later, we saw the perfect spot: a beautiful patch of grass along the driveway to a farm, with a nearby group of large trees that would be perfect for our bodily needs.

We made our way along the thick bush hedges and up the driveway to the two-story white, half-timbered farmhouse, passing a smaller building that I assumed was used to store various farming equipment. We knocked and waited for someone to answer.

A man in his late forties came to the door, a tired and surprised look on his angular, sun-kissed face. He looked like he'd worked hard all his life. I let Alex take care of the conversation.

"Hello," Alex said.

"*Hallo*," he replied.

"Sorry to bother you. Do you speak English?" she asked.

He frowned. "Yes."

"My friend and I were wondering if we could set up our tent on your land, just for tonight," she said, her hand indicating our overloaded bicycles standing on their footrests in the man's driveway.

The man looked at the bikes, then Alex, then me.

I smiled but kept quiet.

He finally spoke up. "Well... This is not a request I hear every day. Is it just the two of you?"

Alex and I nodded.

"Fine, as long as you clean up before you go."

"We will, of course. Thank you, sir!"

5:30 p.m.

We returned to the spot that would be our campground for the night and began unloading our bikes.

I was working on setting up the tent when Alex called out to me.

"We forgot to refill our water," she said.

"Do you want me to cycle back to the nearest village?" I suggested, mentally trying to remember how long ago it was. *Not that far? But that last big hill...*

"Nah..." She paused for a second and we both looked toward the house. The farmer was standing outside, near his door, drinking from a cup and looking at us. "Let me ask Mr. Hot Farmer," she said, winking at me.

"Ah! So, you're into older men now?" I said, teasing her.

"He's not *that* old. And I bet his body looks fantastic." Her brows went up and her mouth rose into a slanted grin. "With his manual labor and all... I can only imagine what his back and strong arms must feel like..."

She pulled the near-empty bottles from both our bikes and headed back up the driveway to the house. "Be right back... or not," she yelled out to me.

I continued my tasks and had the tent set up, pads unrolled and sleeping bags ready to go before she got back. The tent now erect in front of me wasn't what I would describe as spacious, but we'd opted for the lightest and smallest gear since we didn't want to overload our bikes or wear huge backpacks.

I hope tonight won't prove me wrong.

Alex finally came back just as I was digging out the extra sandwiches we'd purchased at lunch and the bottle of wine I'd gotten this morning.

"Guess what?" she said.

I raised my shoulders.

"Our farmer invited us to join him for dinner. Well... Not really, but I told him we had our own food, so we'll eat what we brought and he'll cook something. Potluck-style I guess. Don't you dare touch that just yet!" She grabbed the sandwiches from my hand and put them back in one of our bikes' panniers. "We'll relax for a couple of hours, then he'll have a table set for all of us."

My growling stomach wanted to disagree, but I played along. "Should we go and help him then?"

"No, I offered. And you won't believe what I saw out back, behind the house..."

I had no idea what could have gotten her so excited. "An outhouse?" I guessed, although I had no reason to believe such a large, nice-looking house would NOT be fitted with running water and other modern amenities. I probably had my camper's hat on and the nearby bushes didn't have me so excited about the prospect.

"No, silly!" She shook her head at me. "A hot tub!"

"Really?"

Her eyes were now the size of nickels, and I swear drool was close to coming out of her mouth. "And now I officially call dibs." Her hand went up. "I kind of like Farmer John."

"John? Is that his name?"

"Nah. He's called something unpronounceable. He gave me permission to call him John instead. I'm sure you can call him that, too."

"Farmer John is all yours then." My stomach growled again. I had to do something to keep myself from biting into our sandwiches before dinner. "What shall we do now? Go for a walk?" But saying it aloud made me realize my legs needed a break. I didn't feel like walking at all.

"Do you still have some of your weed?"

"I do..."

A few minutes later, after Alex had convinced me that I'd be able to manage my hunger even after smoking a joint, we were lying with our backs on the grass, still wearing our shorts and tank tops, looking at the clouds above us. We slowly enjoyed the joint I'd rolled, our scented puffs adding a thin layer of quickly disappearing cloud around us. There was hardly a breeze at ground level although the oddly shaped clouds moved rapidly in the higher atmosphere.

"So, what else did you find out about Farmer John?" I passed her the joint.

"Nothing really. But I asked if there was a missus. He said his wife passed away last year." She paused, then a big puff came out of her lips. "The poor man has been living alone since."

I couldn't believe how easy it was for her to flirt with anyone and everyone. "And he shared all of that information with you while you were fetching water?"

"Well... You know me. One question led to another. I saw a picture of a beautiful woman in his living room, so I asked."

I took the joint she held up and I smoked some more. "Personal boundaries and privacy don't mean anything to you?"

"Sometimes. But I wanted to know if Farmer John was available for a late-night interlude... I like sleeping under the stars, but not as much as I like getting fucked by a hot guy."

"The twins didn't do it for you?"

"*My* twin you mean? That was just *one* guy. Call me greedy, but I'd like to sample a bit more of the Dutch population..."

"For the record, you did *both* of them."

She sat up. "What? Are you kidding me?"

"No. Didn't you notice they'd traded places last night?"

"What?" she asked again, this time almost shrieking.

"One had a birth mark near his left nipple. The other didn't."

She stared at me. "I don't believe it..."

I didn't budge and added a nod to emphasize my point.

"Well... I'd like to sample three instead of just two," she said, trying to inhale, but the joint was no longer lit. "Where's the lighter?"

"In the tent, just by the zipper."

And time flew by as I admired nature's incredible beauty in the shape of the clouds alone. Birds sang their last repertoire as the shades of evening skies slowly took over. My hunger had seemingly fallen to the back-burner, until it came back with a vengeance.

7:15 p.m.

As promised, Farmer John had set up a table for us on the large patio made out of interlocking stones behind his house.

On one side, close to a cluster of trees on a slight hill, two wooden swings hung, attached to a beam that had been nailed to the largest trunks. On the other side, near the table, a large hot tub presided on the backyard from the top of its elevated platform.

Unlike Alex, I hadn't seen any part of his house or his backyard to date, but it was not what I had expected for an average-looking house in the countryside.

"Nice hot tub!" I said, handing him the bottle of wine we'd brought.

"Thank you. A waste of money, I think, but my wife had insisted on getting it. Feel free to use it if you want. I keep it clean and ready for use, out of habit. Maybe we can all enjoy it after dinner?" he suggested, his eyes locked on Alex.

Her face lit up. "Wonderful idea. I'd love to!"

John invited us to sit down around the table while he went back into the house.

"Did you bring a swimsuit?" I asked Alex while our host was in the house.

"No, but I'm not planning on wearing anything in there. We're in Europe, don't be such a prude."

"No big deal, but I wouldn't want to distract him from you," I said with a large grin. "Just kidding. He's all yours. I'm pretty sure you'll get what you want."

"Let's hope so." Her eyes lit up when he came out of the house again, with three glasses held upside down by the stems in one hand and the cork-opener in the other. "Life is all about fun, isn't it?" Alex asked him.

"All about fun?" Farmer John repeated as he sat at our table.

I couldn't imagine any farmer seeing life as complete fun... "There are a lot of fields around here. What do you grow?" I asked him.

"Corn, sugar beets, and potatoes."

"We saw some miniature horses nearby. Are they yours?" Alex asked.

"No, they belong to Niek, my neighbor. I don't have animals here. I used to have a dog, but he passed away around the same time my wife did. That's all probably very boring to two beautiful women like you. Why are you in this part of Holland?"

And Alex began chit-chatting about nothing and everything while I did my best to restrain my appetite and not stuff my sandwich down in two seconds. He'd made a large bowl of a potato-based dish he'd called *Stamppot,* and I helped myself to a generous serving of it.

"That's surprisingly delicious!" I complimented him before taking another bite.

"Surprising because...?" he asked.

I pointed to my mouth as I slowly finished chewing, mentally trying to figure out how to answer his question without offending him. Although delicious for real, the dish looked like what a person would throw up right after eating potatoes, hotdogs, and green leafy vegetables. "Because most men I know do not fare well in the kitchen," I finally said.

He smiled widely, and relief washed over me. "It's very easy to make. You boil potatoes, onions, vegetables, and sausage together, then you mash it all when it's cooked."

"Ah! Well, simple and really tasty."

He poured us all more wine and the conversation moved on to another topic. Then another bottle was opened, even though all the food was long gone.

"Any chance I can use your bathroom?" I asked, my bladder about to explode.

"Yes, go ahead," he said. "On your left when you go in."

I thoroughly enjoyed the luxury of peeing indoors, then refreshed myself a bit and splashed my face with water. My hair looked messy from a day of riding my bike. I couldn't blame it on a helmet, since I hadn't worn one, but the breeze (and lying in the grass earlier) had obviously impacted my ponytail. I tied it up again, then walked back outside to find Farmer John and Alex sitting closer together. He had one hand on her arm over the table while his other, closer arm was hidden from view.

"Should we try the hot tub?" asked Alex when she saw me.

"Excellent idea," he said. "I'll take the dishes inside. Go ahead and get in."

"Do you need help?" I offered, reaching for one of the plates on the table.

He swatted my hand away. "No, no. I'll take care of it. I insist," he said.

Decent cook and not afraid of domestic chores—Farmer John's a good man!

Alex and I took off our sweaty tank tops and shorts. While I hesitated for a split second before taking off my sports bra and panties, Alex didn't, so I followed suit. I'd come a long way in getting rid of my inner prude, but I still had my moments of doubt. We walked up the steps and entered the clear but motionless water and took a seat in it, kitty-corner from each other in the four-person molded tub.

"I wonder how you make the jets go," Alex said before sitting up slightly and turning her attention to the controls.

"Shouldn't we wait for him to come back and turn it on?"

"Nah. I can figure it out." She pressed a few buttons, then lights came on, illuminating our naked bodies. A second later, a soft purring noise started and then got a little louder as the water started moving. Jets came out from seemingly everywhere. Two strong streams hit my lower back, quickly soothing away my soreness from the day's ride. I was impressed at how powerful the jets were considering their quietness.

Seemingly pleased that she had adjusted all the settings to her liking, Alex leaned back in her seat again, then pulled herself up a bit, taking her breasts out of the water and bringing her ass up to what I assumed was the jets' height.

"Now we're talking!" she said, her lips widening into a smile as she closed her eyes.

"I see you figured out how to turn it on," said Farmer John behind me.

I turned around. He was walking toward us, three folded towels in hand. A large grin had pushed away the tired expression from his face. He put down his goods at the top of the steps, then proceeded to match our birthday-suit dress code. He pulled his T-shirt over his head, exposing a very white but muscular torso, complete with abdominal muscles that could have been featured on the cover of Men's Health magazine, if only they'd been slightly more tanned, and his vertical line of dark hairs more trimmed. I looked away as he unzipped his pants, but his large, flaccid appendage caught my eyes a few seconds later when he stepped into the tub, then lowered himself on the seat next to Alex.

Her eyes met mine and, based on how wide her eyes were, I was certain we shared the same thought at that very moment. *If his cock's this big while limp, what will it turn into when he gets excited?*

"So, do you have a lot of parties here?" asked Alex.

Farmer John laughed before shaking his head. "No. Can't say that many people randomly invite themselves like you did today."

"Well... We only asked to sleep on your lawn, then you invited us back here."

He wrapped his arm around Alex's shoulders. "Even if I enjoy my simple and tranquil life, it's hard to see beautiful women like you and not want to know them better.

"Is this what you'd like? Getting to know me better?" Alex cooed as she reached for his angular jaw and brought his face closer to hers.

Then, the awkward feeling of being a third wheel started taking over. And being a third wheel in a hot tub wasn't necessarily the most comfortable environment... But then I heard something.

At first, I couldn't identify it, but as the melody repeated once more, I recognized it through the soft purring of the hot tub: my phone was ringing.

Saved by the bell, of sorts.

"I'll go and get that," I said, partly curious as to who would be calling me on this number and partly relieved to have an easy out to let them make out without me staring at them.

I got up, grabbed a towel on my way out, wrapped it around my dripping body, and then headed toward the tent.

I was grateful Farmer John's land was covered in grass and not pointy rocks that would have hurt my feet, but the day's humidity had condensed on the grass. By the time I reached my device in one of the panniers, it had gone silent. I looked at my missed calls and didn't recognize the number. I dialed it and waited.

Nothing. Just endless ringing.

I decided to give the caller a few minutes of grace, in the event he or she would try again, so I rolled myself a joint. Then, having it ready to go, I figured that I might as well smoke it under the beautiful evening sky. I unzipped the tent and pulled my mat out so I could rest on it instead of the wet grass. I lay back, put in my headset and listened to whatever Spotify wanted to play for me while I lit my ticket to the stars.

Life's so fucking great right now. Just endless possibilities, like the number of shining specks that sparkled in the sky above.

With each inhalation, any sign of remaining tension flew out of my body, heading toward the starry emptiness of the sky. The evening was so beautiful. So peaceful. Insects in the distance were doing their thing, singing their mating calls or whatever it was they did that created such beautiful nighttime noises.

A few minutes later, totally buzzed, I suddenly felt an urge to drink something. *Water?* No, I wanted wine. *I think there's some left on the table?*

I returned my mat to its rightful spot in my tent, knowing fair well that I would regret it later if I didn't do it now. I zipped the tent back up. Satisfied that my phone wouldn't ring again, I left it behind in one of my panniers then headed back to the patio the same way I'd come.

When I got there, Alex and Farmer John were in the midst of a passionate kiss so I let them have their privacy, kind of.

I poured myself the glass I craved, then went to sit in one of the swings a short distance away, after almost tripping on one of the exposed roots as I walked up the slight hill. The only light on me was that of the moon and stars above. On the other hand, Alex and Farmer John were illuminated by the underwater lights as well as the motion-activated light fixture above the back door.

I had my own private show, and my seat was perfectly positioned to see everything that was happening in that tub. Knowing Alex and her tendency toward exhibitionism—as I had found out in Toronto—I was certain she'd be totally fine with me watching them.

So I did.

I slowly sipped my wine while my toes pushed and pulled my body forward on the swing. I was already buzzed, so my slight movements were more than plenty for my mind.

With a splashing sound, Farmer John pulled Alex out of the water before sitting her down on the wooden deck that surrounded the tub. Her legs dangled against the back of the seat she had previously occupied. Then he knelt between her legs on the seat in front of her. He grabbed her generous breasts and buried his head in them, moaning loudly, the muffled sound easily reaching my ears. His balding head bobbed while his large hands squeezed her breasts together around his face as though he was trying to suffocate himself into Alex's fleshy goods. Then he pulled his head out, grabbed a handful of her right breast, then started licking it. He pinched her nipple, shaping it into a small raspberry, and she moaned while arching her back, her breasts coming closer toward him.

He slowly let go of her right breast and repeated his routine with the other before slowly licking his way down her flat ivory stomach. When he reached her belly button, she parted her legs farther apart and looked back at him again. He stepped back, then buried his face between her legs. He brought one of her legs to rest above his shoulder. Every now and then, I could see his tongue licking her clean-shaven pussy, then disappearing into her. My friend's moans were merging with those of the animal kingdom around us, getting louder and louder. Then, as though the poor man had to come up for air, his body unfolded and I got my first glimpse at his monster dick.

My hand flew to my mouth to repress my surprised gulp. It must have been a solid ten-inch stick, bigger than I had ever seen. Even bigger than the twins' cocks had been.

He reached into the pants he'd taken off earlier and dug a condom out from one of the pockets. A second later, his tool had been made weatherproof and ready for action. That was too much voyeurism for me to take in idly. I leaned down to place my empty glass on the grass near my feet, then parted my legs. With one arm holding my body steady on the swing, I started fingering myself.

Unsurprisingly, I was already dripping wet, so wet that Farmer John and Alex could have probably heard the slick movements of my fingers in and out of me if not for their own excited moans and groans over the super-quiet tub's purring noises. Somehow my towel untied itself, my parted legs having probably caused it to happen. I let the damp fabric fall as it may, and the evening air started to caress my newly exposed back, stomach, and breasts. My nipples hardened from the change in temperature, and a shiver crossed my entire body like an out-of-control tornado.

Farmer John brought the tip of his cock toward my friend's pussy.

She parted her legs wider and shook her head. "Holy shit! That's the biggest cock I've ever seen!"

A hand holding his appendage up at the threshold of Alex's pussy, he brought his other hand around her ass. "I'll be gentle, I promise," he said.

She still had one of her legs up on his shoulder, offering me the perfect vantage point. Watching his cock tease her was almost too much to bear from a distance. Its tip traced the groove between her swollen lips, not quite poking into her. My pussy ached; I wanted to feel him inside of me. My fingers, although swift and agile, paled in comparison to what I imagined he'd feel like in me.

Alex lowered her leg, partially obstructing my view. Then, the guttural roar she made as his ass moved forward a tad—probably just pushing the head of his humongous cock into her—made my heart skip a beat. Seemed the animal kingdom had also paused their soundtrack for a second.

Then she exhaled deeply and loudly twice like a Lamaze professional, then nodded at him.

"Okay. I'm ready. Give it to me. All of it."

And he pushed himself in. Her gorilla cries echoed against the nearby hills in the evening air. Her eyes rolled backward, then her entire head slammed back.

"Again!" she ordered.

He pulled out and slammed into her this time.

"Fuck, yeah!" she said. "Oh... Fuck me, Farmer John... Fuck me like there's no tomorrow."

And I watched him pound her, adding a third finger into my wet pussy. I groped my own breast with one hand, feeling even stronger ripples of desire building up inside of me.

"Wait, wait." Alex said in between two ramming sessions. "I want you to fuck me in the ass with your huge cock."

"Are you sure?" he asked.

"No, but who cares!"

He pulled out of her and rolled her onto her belly, letting her legs back down in the tub, and her ass pointed at him on the edge.

He parted her butt cheeks, then, with his other hand, brought up some of her pussy juice to her ass and let one finger in, then another, then another... A minute later, he was up to five fingers, slowly pushing in, loosening her anus, then he pulled his hand away and inserted himself into her.

Her roar made me wonder how much of it was pain vs. pleasure. Then, she turned to look his way, her eyes drunk on pleasure as each of his thrusts made her shrieks reach new heights.

When she turned her head back toward the front, our eyes met for an instant. She flinched every time he gave it to her, but her mouth stayed agape. She brought one hand under her stomach, then lifted her ass. Her eyes rolled back again as she let out a long squeal, her entire body shaking and spent. "Stop!" she begged.

He immediately pulled out of her. "Are you okay?" he asked Alex, his chest heaving up and down.

"Yeah. It's just so... big!"

"I know." He pulled his condom off, then, in a loud splash, sat himself back in the tub.

As though Alex had been reading my mind, she turned to look at me, then motioned for me to walk to them.

I left my towel behind and walked toward them, my own juices running down my right leg.

"But not all hope is lost," Alex said, now rolling unto her back, then sitting up. With a hand, she cupped her pussy, then lowered herself into the tub in front of him. She sent an inquisitive nod my way, her eyes round.

"Can I help?" I asked as I walked up the steps and joined them in the tub.

Farmer John's expression was priceless. He looked at Alex, then me, then Alex, and me again. "Really?" he finally asked.

"I'd love to feel your huge cock inside of me," I said.

"Then join us, please." He pointed to the empty seat next to Alex. I sat down, and he got up. His tool had deflated a bit from earlier, probably from Alex's request to stop, but that would likely be something easy to fix. I reached toward it, my eyes meeting his.

"Would you mind kissing her first?" he asked me.

I turned to Alex. She raised her shoulders then twisted her upper body to face me.

"You'd like that, wouldn't you?" I teased him. "Why not? Alex is beautiful."

I leaned in, put a hand behind her delicate neck, and briefly kissed her. Just a soft peck at first, but once I realized kissing my friend didn't feel weird, I started nibbling on her soft lips. I let my hand run through her red hair as my hunger for her grew. With a flick of my tongue, I parted her lips. Our breathing and excitement seemed to follow the same path toward the summit as our tongues mingled and our lips suckled. I reached for one of her gorgeous breasts under the water and gently cupped it, then my mouth departed from hers as I inched my way south, licking her ivory neck.

"Wait," she said. Her knees came up on the seat, then she pushed herself up on the edge where she sat and invited me to do the same.

I looked at Farmer John while I pulled myself out of the tub. His anaconda was now hard in the palm of his moving hand. I wanted to feel that part of him in me so badly. I reached a hand toward him, but Alex's fingers on my chin forced me to turn my head toward her.

Before I could say anything, her lips had swallowed mine again. Our breasts were now pressed against each other's. Then, out of the corner of my eye, I saw it. Inches from our faces was a cock so large it had to require a permit. Someone could lose an eye to it, if not lose themselves and be forever marked by it, comparing all future men to him.

I gently pushed Alex away from me as he moved forward between us.

We licked him. There was plenty for us to share as he was bigger than a large ear of corn—nothing any woman could fully wrap her mouth around. He tickled our tits while we did our best to suck and lick his humongous member. He tasted of chlorine, but that didn't do anything to deter my pussy's cravings.

Alex was a beautiful woman—and a fantastic kisser—but what I wanted most in the world right now was Farmer John's cock in my swollen pussy.

"It's time. I'm ready." I parted my knees.

He reached to his discarded pants again then covered himself. His dick at the ready in front of me, his hand ran a recon mission in my pussy. I moaned the instant two of his fingertips entered my wet opening.

"More!" I ordered.

Farmer John pushed another finger in me and it slid in like it was nothing. I was so horny, it was no surprise to me.

"Come on. I want the real thing..." I begged.

He licked his lips as I parted my legs wider to make room for him. He moved his hips toward me until his tip knocked on my pleasure door.

I couldn't wait a second more, so I moved my weight to my hands behind my ass, and rammed myself onto his erect cock. It took me a second to realize that the scream I'd heard was mine. In a strange mix of pain and pleasure, I felt my insides somehow accommodating his large girth, parting ways and pushing outward. I then felt Alex's boobs against my back. She had relocated to sit behind me, her legs parted around my own legs. Her hands started to caress my upper body as I forcedly silenced myself.

My gaze locked onto Farmer John's, and I slowly moved back to rest my ass on the side of the tub, some of him still in me.

"More?" he asked.

I nodded and bit my lip, knowing full well I'd want to scream when he'd filled me again. Alex's caresses soothed me as he slowly started to increase his cadence, but not his depth. I was still controlling that by angling my hips, resting my weight on both of my hands, which I had to relocate behind Alex's legs since she was cradling me. Her right hand slowly made its way to my landing strip, then to my clit. As though she knew my body as well as hers, she started flicking my pleasure button. Her lips were nibbling on the back of my neck, her other hand pinching one of my nipples. Farmer John's huge dick pushing in and out of me like a giant smooth operator was just the cherry on top.

"I'm gonna come," I said.

"Hold on... A few more seconds," he said between thrusts, just as his breathing got louder and louder.

Then, in one final, painful push, he thrust into me fully. I'd lost control of my limbs while coming and hadn't been able to pull my hips back... But the pain had been worth it. I had never come so hard in my life. Maybe it was the high, maybe it was his girth and length, but I pulsated from everywhere. And, as he slowly pulled out of me, I realized how sensitive my entire pussy had become. From the orgasm... but possibly damaged by our encounter?

A few minutes later, too exhausted to do anything else, we returned to our tent.

8:30 a.m.

The following morning, after dismantling our tent and stowing all our gear on our bikes, we kissed our farmer goodbye before saddling up again.

The trip back to town took us forever as we were both sore from riding the biggest cock we'd ever encountered.

MY XXX EXPERIENCE

HOLLAND

THE PLAN

WELL, Sophia wasn't generous with her leads this time. But here are my options:

OPTION 1: Go to Maastricht and track down the twins who own that coffee shop.

But for what purpose? I doubt she's keeping in touch since she couldn't even tell them apart when she left.
Likelihood of success: Nil.

OPTION 2: Find Farmer John.

Let's face it, I don't want to see that guy's face (or any other part of his body). I'd rather avoid proof that shows I'm not as far above the bell curve as I've always assumed I was.
Likelihood of success: Nil.

OPTION 3: Track down my stewardess based on her first name.

Since I got back from Paris with that important nugget, I haven't been able to sleep. While there's no way for me to know if she even works for my airline, it's worth a shot. I don't have access to the right people with other airlines. And maybe I'll get lucky. (And why wouldn't my streak continue?)

Likelihood of success: Low to average.

The last one is my only viable option.

And unfortunately, this means I won't go to Holland this time. As much as I like to pretend to be impulsive, I'm not. I'm a man of habits who thrives on standard operating procedures.

But maybe I'll hit the jackpot, find her, and end my quest. That would be worth so much more than sticking to my regular approach.

Bob keeps telling me I'm the luckiest guy alive. Let's see if he's right.

WHAT HAPPENED

So I greased the right wheels, bribed the right people, hired a hacker, and managed to get myself an official list of all flight attendants whose first names included Sophie, Sophia, Sofia, and even one Saufia. Whatever resembled her name, it got included on my list. I didn't want to risk missing her because of something Bob could have misheard. I got their full names, birthdates, and work history.

That was 49 of them.

Then, it was a matter of getting rid of those who didn't fit the bill physically or age-wise, although I couldn't be super precise with that last one. Facebook was a great help with this particular task, but only when my potential ladies included our common employer on their profile. I managed to get rid of a handful of blondes, a black woman, and a redhead.

A bit more unethical behavior from yours truly resulted in getting my remaining ladies' schedules, at least those who were senior enough to not fly reserve and hold their own line. My hacker worked his magic with the crew scheduler's account for that.

Then, several expensive bottles of whiskey were promised (and delivered) to a handful of my trustworthy colleagues who happened to fly the same routes as the remaining Sophias. Their sole task involved getting a selfie with that particular stewardess (or the entire crew if the solo shot was impossible). And if they couldn't deliver on that, then (and that was the least preferred option), a detailed description of what she looked like was provided.

Stalky a bit? Desperately so.

Illegal? Some parts definitely were.

But I was very careful and covered my tracks.

And it narrowed down my options to just three tall, thirty-something, curvy brunettes who required my personal attention and an in-person meeting.

But to save time and avoid extra work, I compared their schedules and aircraft qualifications with the routes my stewardess had taken in her journal. Only one match remained; it had to be my mystery woman.

My illicit activities have paid off, and I've never had such a massive hard-on before.

I found myself a seat on her next flight the minute I had narrowed it down to her.

And guess what? I'm off to fucking Amsterdam/AMS.

I can't believe it.

I'm as lucky as Bob says I am. I can stick to my regular approach. I'm still pinching myself. After months obsessing about her, I'll meet my mysterious stewardess in the flesh in just a few hours.

Wish me luck.

6:15 p.m.

As I took my seat in the third row of the airplane, I spotted her helping a family stow their bags in the overhead compartments toward the back of the plane. Saying I had butterflies in my stomach didn't cut it; a full-fledged hurricane churned within me, and my heart threatened to pierce its way out of my chest cavity.

I forcefully inhaled and exhaled deeply as I took my seat. I placed my water bottle in the seat pocket in front of me and rested my shaky hands on my lap.

This is it. Today's the day.

But the right moment still had to come. More and more people started crowding the aisle next to me, each slowly taking their assigned seat and storing their belongings away for the flight to come.

A minute after I had taken my seat, a scrawny man in a wrinkled business suit sat next to me.

"*Bonjour,*" he said.

"Hi," I replied, recognizing one of the rare French words I knew.

After sliding his briefcase at his feet, he said something to me that I didn't get.

"Sorry, I only speak English," I said.

He frowned, then pressed his service button.

The nearest flight attendant, an older brunette whose white roots were showing, responded quickly, but she was also unable to understand and help him.

She lifted her index finger in the air. "Please wait, I'll get someone else to come and talk to you in French."

A few minutes later, *she* appeared, followed by a lovely flowery smell. Her hazel eyes landed on me, then my seat mate. She smiled at both of us with her luscious lips then said something in French.

How lovely those lips were going to look when wrapped around my cock…

The businessman requested whatever it was he needed, and while he jabbered on, my eyes glanced at the name tag on her uniform: "Sophie". Her breasts, although hidden by the bulk of her uniform jacket, had to be solid Cs. Too bad X-ray vision wasn't a super-power of mine. I'd have liked to see her nipples to confirm she was indeed the one. But right when I considered speaking up, she walked away.

Probably good because I had no idea *what* I would have even said or asked.

I turned and stared at her ass as she headed toward the back of the plane. She was tall and curvy all right, pretty in a girl-next-door kind of way. Was her perfume jasmine-scented? I couldn't tell one flower scent from another, but she obviously spoke French.

Did I know her eyes were hazel? I couldn't recall that detail from her journal.

But she had to be my stewardess. She just had to.

So… now what?

I can't mess this up.

What's my next move?

She's probably going to come back with whatever the Frenchman's requested, so how am I going to charm her off her feet?

What the hell can I say?

No matter how many times I asked myself those questions, my mind always drew a blank larger than life. It was as though my smooth-talking skills had disappeared. My decades of successfully flirting with women forgotten and erased.

Where did my confidence go?

Had I jumped back to my teenage self?

In lieu of a clever pick-up line, the only thing that appeared in my mind was that hot autumn day in the neighborhood where I grew up.

I could see my own geeky self, unconfident, scrawny, long limbs, long hair. I'd been raking leaves on my neighbor's front lawn. She was so gorgeous. I can even recall what she wore on that specific day: a pair of ripped jean shorts with the white lining of the front pockets sticking out on her long, tanned thighs. Whenever she walked away from me, I would see the beautiful curves at the base of her round ass. Her old shirt had had its sleeves ripped out, half the buttons were undone, letting her ample bosom catch the last sun rays of that year's hot and humid Indian summer.

Although she always gave me a few dollars for taking care of various landscaping chores for her—like mowing the lawn, clearing eaves, or raking leaves—the real payment was seeing her body up close while she walked around or sat on her front porch. She sometimes wore a bikini or old overalls, but no matter what she had on, it always looked sexy on her.

But on that specific day in October, for raking her front lawn and bagging those dead leaves, she paid me by making a man out of me.

"When you're done, come in for some lemonade, will you?" she'd said to me before opening the squeaky screen door and walking into her house.

About five minutes later, three full bags of leaves carefully placed by the curb as she'd instructed me to, I walked up her front steps and let myself in.

"I'm done, Mrs. Thompson," I'd called out, unsure where she was. The kitchen table was bare. No freshly made pitcher of lemonade there.

"I'm in the living room."

After a few strides, I stepped into the framed opening that separated the kitchen from the living room, then I froze in place when I saw her. Mrs. Thompson was lying naked on her couch, one arm under her head. Everything I'd fantasized about for years was blatantly exposed for me to see: her large breasts, her tanned lines, her thick, untrimmed bush.

"Come here, Charles. Don't be afraid."

I remember hesitating, even though her voice had been soft and inviting.

After all, she was Mrs. Thompson, the hot divorcee my friends and I always talked about. Although I'd masturbated countless times with her in mind, seeing her naked in front of me was a different thing. Her body was even more beautiful than I had imagined. My boner had nowhere to hide, so it made its own tent out of the loose fabric of my gray sweatpants.

"I swear, I won't hurt you." Her red-hot manicured fingers were now making a come-here motion as irresistible as a mermaid's chant.

I still don't know how, but my legs somehow brought me next to her.

"Good, Charles. Now, I think you're wearing too many layers for such a hot day. Don't you think?"

I remember nodding, my mouth probably agape. I pulled my T-shirt over my head and tossed it at the edge of her glass-top coffee table.

She sat up and swung her body so her legs were now parted, directly in front of me. Her pussy—my first one ever—had me hypnotized.

So that's what it really looked like...

Then, she'd broken the spell by pulling down my pants and underwear in one fell swoop.

"My, my. What have we got here, Charles? You're certainly all grown up now."

She'd been my babysitter over a decade ago, which confused yet aroused me even more. I tried to take another step closer to her, but tripped on myself. After a short fumble, I finally managed to kick off my shoes, then remove my sweatpants and underwear from around my ankles, leaving me completely naked save for a pair of white socks with blue stripes, which obviously became my lucky socks from that day onward.

"Don't be nervous," she said as she wrapped her warm hands around my waist.

My heart pounded in my chest as I reached toward her breasts. Although I'd lied and bragged about several other first and second bases to my buddies, that was my first official feel. I didn't know *how* I was supposed to touch her. My initial light graze soon turned into a full grope. I hadn't expected her breasts to feel so fleshy, so warm, so comfortable. I kept squeezing them harder and harder, twisting them in my hand, until she covered my hands with hers and took them away from her beautiful body.

"Have you ever been with a woman, Charles?"

There was no point in lying. My lack of experience and knowledge would undoubtedly show sooner or later, so I shook my head.

"There's no shame in that. I'll show you, if you let me." Her eyes met mine and she wrapped one of her hands around my cock. "Do you want me to teach you, Charles?"

I don't recall verbally answering her, but I must have nodded or something. Come to think of it, my coming on her exposed breasts a second later may have been my only reply.

I remember apologizing profusely when she looked down at her chest, covered with streaks of my freshly squirted cum. With a finger, she traced a line through it, then brought that finger to her luscious pink lips. She'd opened her mouth slowly, then sucked my juices off from her finger while moaning.

"Let's try again, and this time, Charles, try to last a little longer... for my sake."

And I did my best.

That time, and the time after that. And the time after that.

For the rest of that afternoon, she did things to me that I'd only seen blurred through the channels we didn't get at home. And each time I came, I'd learned new things and lasted a little longer.

That's how October 15, 1992 saw the death of Charles the geek and the birth of Charlie the stud.

The following day at school, I not only got to brag to the rest of the chess club that I had lost my virginity, but I got to say that I'd lost it to Mrs. Thompson, the sexy, hot neighborhood divorcee. She was a MILF well before that term even got coined.

But right now, more than two decades later, Mrs. Thompson was nowhere to be seen.

It was just me, sitting on a crowded plane, with stupid Charles somehow having taken the controls again. I was unable to think of anything clever to say to Sophie. I drew a fucking blank. No charming remarks came to my lips. Nothing at all.

How could this be? After months spent looking for her, tracking her down, having out-of-this world sexual encounters... Had my impossible quest somehow moved my mystery stewardess up onto a pedestal?

Get your shit together, Charlie.

She's just a woman, not a goddess. A regular human being, like you, but with nice tits, a starving pussy... and sexual cravings that expand well beyond your own horizons.

7:50 a.m.

I spent the rest of the flight trying to exorcise geeky Charles and come up with a plan. But looking at the napkin onto which I'd scribbled my best lines, none of them seemed interesting, clever, or charismatic enough.

And I don't fucking know what her plans are.

I'll have to wing it, hoping that good ole Charlie will reappear, step up, and bring my macho confidence back up to snuff.

At least luck was still on my side as I managed not to lose track of her once we disembarked and cleared customs. I was even within earshot when she mentioned to one of her colleagues that she was staying at the CitizenM airport hotel.

That was all I needed for my next step. I headed there directly since I could hardly hang around any longer in close proximity to her and her colleagues without them noticing my unwelcome presence.

And luck came back to me once more. She arrived at the check-in desk just after I finished checking myself in.

"Sophie, right?" I said with a large smile, then offered my hand. "I'm Charlie."

She shook it in silence, her head tilted to the side, a slight frown on her face.

"I'm a pilot. I think we've flown together before," I said in a tone that came out more like a question than a fact.

"I don't think so," she finally said.

"Are you sure? You seem really familiar."

"Is this why you were looking at me during the flight?"

So much for what I thought had been discreet looks. "Sorry, I was just trying to place you."

Her phone buzzed, and she flipped it to look at the screen.

Afraid that my chance was going to squeeze through my fingers right there and then, I launched my best effort. "Want to grab a coffee or something?" I asked, mentally hating my lame approach while my heart started pounding in expectation.

"Hmm," she said, her eyes glued on her screen. She typed something, then finally looked up at me again.

"Well... I was supposed to be picked up by a friend, but I just got a text saying there's been a delay. I guess I have a few hours to kill now, so why not? I'll let you buy me coffee, and we can try and figure out if you actually know me from somewhere."

"Sounds fair," I said, hopeful. "I'll let you check in, and then we can meet down here in about ten minutes?"

"Better make it twenty. I want to freshen up and get out of my uniform."

9:00 a.m.

After taking my carry-on up to one of the most modern-looking, minimalist room I've seen in a long time, I went in for a quick cold shower, put on a pair of jeans and a polo shirt, and then had a good chat with myself in front of the mirror. I won't repeat my ruthless words here—I doubt I could remember everything I yelled at my reflection—but let's just say that, hands down, I would have won the World's Harshest Drill Sergeant prize.

Now completely re-invigorated and psyched, I was confident that good ole Charlie was ready to kick that wuss of a ball-less, teenage Charles out of me and play hard core. But I still had no room for errors, or else it would mean the end of it. I certainly didn't want my quest to finish in such a disappointing way.

I checked my watch: another five minutes to go. With nothing else for me to do in my room (unless I wanted to turn on the television and risk losing track of time), I headed down to the main floor.

It wasn't just my room that didn't look like the typical hotel. The entire lobby and lounge area had benefited from the same out-of-the-box thinking. Food and drinks were available 24/7 and the assortment of furniture and decorations around me felt like I was in some bizarro, wealthy man's living room filled with eclectic artwork, several bookcases serving as partitions, and interesting, contemporary artwork.

I was about to take a seat in a low, IKEA-like chair when Sophie appeared, small purse in hand and dressed in white capri pants with a light blue blouse. She'd tied her long brown hair in a ponytail. I resisted the urge to check my watch, but I believe she was right on time. *Good girl.*

I walked over to meet her halfway. I noticed she'd put on more makeup than she'd worn earlier on the plane. Her hazel eyes had somehow been highlighted more, and the curvature of her lips was even more tempting in the darker, almost burgundy shade she'd put on. So glossy and inviting...

"What are you in the mood for?" I asked.

"Coffee and... some sort of breakfast sandwich would be good."

"Let's see what they have." I pointed to the restaurant and followed her, admiring her curves from behind for just a second before returning my attention to the selection of food offered to us.

She found what she was looking for: coffee with a ham-and-cheese croissant. After the airplane breakfast—not that it had been particularly spectacular—I wasn't hungry, so I only grabbed a black coffee. I added it all to my room, then we made our way to the sitting area where we picked a small two-person table away from the other people currently enjoying their late-morning breakfasts.

After eating, Sophie pulled out her phone, a small moleskin notebook, and a pen from her purse. She checked her phone, then moved to the notebook and quickly wrote down something in it. She closed it before I could even glance at her handwriting (or see what she'd noted).

It doesn't look like the diary I have, but maybe she writes down notes in this small book and later transfers them to her diary?

"I don't want to be nosy," I said, "but can I ask what you just wrote down?"

She looked at me with a puzzled look. "Oh! Just a thought I didn't want to forget."

"Like a note-to-self?" I joked.

"Guess so. It's for something I'm writing."

God, it's definitely her.

She put her notebook and pen back in her purse. "So..." she said, her eyes wide open, "You've got my full attention now."

"I'm still trying to place you. How long have you flown with our airline?"

"Coming up on twelve years."

"Then we must have crossed paths at some point, no?"

Her phone beeped and she lifted it to read something on her screen.

"Married? Boyfriend?" The minute the words left my lips I realized my questions were too personal, too fast. "I mean, the messages you're getting. Are they from your husband or boyfriend?" I nodded toward her phone.

"No! No such man in my life, but you're almost right. The messages are from someone I've been communicating with for a while. We'll be meeting for the first time in person today. At least, we're supposed to."

"Oh. You met on a dating site?"

"Sort of..." she said.

I didn't know where to go with this line of questioning. Had I found her just in time? Just before she was about to meet another man that could be right for her? Her phone beeped again before I could ask a follow-up question.

"Damn..." she said.

"Another delay?"

"Yes." She frowned and shook her head, obviously annoyed.

"I can keep you company for a little longer if you'd like."

She looked up from her screen for a second. "Really?" she asked. "Don't you have people to meet, places to go?"

"I'm meeting you right now," I said with my largest panty-dropping smile.

"Hmmm..." Her face showed no sign of delight; her eyebrows and smile were as flat as the country we were in. *What? She's immune to my charisma?* "Is this supposed to be a 'living in the moment' kind of reply?" she finally asked.

"You could say that."

How can my mysterious stewardess be this ball-busting in real life? Did I create a fantasy not a single woman could ever live up to? Not even her?

Her face became that of a dramatic interviewer. "Seriously, why did you come to Amsterdam?"

"I'm following a trail."

"Hmmm. Detective work? Didn't you say you're a pilot?"

For a second, I saw a flash of curiosity in her eyes. "Something personal I'm looking into."

"And why aren't you looking into that thing or meeting someone if you flew all the way here?"

Careful, Charlie. "I need to figure out my next move."

"Ahh, so you're also stuck in limbo here?"

"You could say that." *Fuck, this isn't going as planned.* I looked at the bottom of my empty coffee cup. "So, what do you think? Considering our mutual limbo status, how does having another drink with me sound?"

Her shoulders went up. "Guess it'd be fine. It would probably prevent my mind from spinning into a stressful spiral of *what-ifs.*"

"Great. But I got to be honest, I don't think I can have another cup of coffee without starting to shake, so how about a cold beer?"

She raised her shoulders. "Why not?"

"Do you have time to make it into town?"

She typed a reply on her phone and waited a few seconds before answering me. "Looks like it. Terry mentioned an early flight tonight."

Terry, so that's the name of my competitor...

"It's settled then. Let's go and be tourists in Amsterdam."

10:25 a.m.

"Have you ever cycled through here?" I asked her as a few cyclists passed by us at a leisurely pace.

"Around Amsterdam? Sure. Best way to tour the city."

"No, I mean the rest of the country?"

"I've seen parts of it. Not all of it for sure."

"Did you come across... huge surprises?"

"Huge surprises?" she scrunched her face at me. "Depends on what you mean—"

Her phone beeped again and she stopped walking to read the message that had appeared on her screen.

I stopped as well, unsure what to do.

A second later she started typing away, her head shaking faster and faster. Then another beep sounded, likely signaling the arrival of another message. She shook her head again, pressed a button, and then started talking into her phone: "Just text me when you get here then. I've left the airport and I'm walking around Amsterdam."

Voice message to the mysterious Terry?

I stood still and inhaled deeply, using the opportunity to refocus.

Cat's got your tongue, Charlie? Here's your chance. She's fucking stuck with you. Can't you think of something flirty to say? Can't you come up with one single fucking line that will work on her? Wake the fuck up!

"Sorry," she said after putting her phone in her purse. "What were we talking about?"

"Can't remember. Are you flying back out tomorrow?" I asked.

"Yeah, tomorrow evening. I was supposed to explore Amsterdam with Terry today and tomorrow. At least that was the plan..."

We resumed walking, this time in silence. I had no idea what was going through her mind, but I knew I was moving on quicksand; my opportunity with Sophie was dissipating fast.

"So, you've got children?" I asked once we'd taken a seat at a table on a busy patio.

She shook her head. "Nah, I don't have the patience nor the desire to proliferate."

"But you must like practicing the art, no?" I suggested with what I intended to be lascivious eyes.

She blushed, kept quiet, and returned her attention to the menu.

There's my blushing stewardess! The speed at which her cheeks had reddened surprised me... And ignited my carnal desires faster than a gallon of gasoline would have warmed up a lit fire.

"I'll get a glass of Merlot," she finally said. "What about you? See something you like?"

I met her eyes. "Definitely."

Her cheeks flushed to an even darker shade of red. "On the menu?"

"Sure, I'll have a Heineken."

After putting in our orders, a couple of minutes lapsed into an awkward silence.

What is it about her that prevents me from being myself?

And just then, a particularly strong breeze brought along a skunky scent. *Time to bet it all on black.*

"How about trying a coffee shop after our drinks?"

"You're kidding, right? We can't go in one of those places," she said.

"There's nothing wrong with having a look." I tried to gauge her expression. Was she really offended, or was she just a good actress? I *knew* she smoked weed on a semi-regular basis. "Are you worried someone could see us and report us to the Aviation Board?"

"Duh... Yeah!"

I shrugged. "We could claim we thought it was a regular coffee shop?"

"Do it if you want, but I'm not going to go anywhere near it. I like my job too much to risk it."

I waved my hand in the air. "No worries, forget I even mentioned it." And just then, I saw the waitress appear with a tray. "Let's just enjoy our drinks."

Lifesaving timing, really. The gap between my stewardess and me widened with each passing second she stared at me with her scrunched-up face.

I lifted up my drink and offered a toast: "To the lucky ones like us who get to work in the sky."

She kept frowning at me, but nonetheless clinked her glass against my bottle. Not a word escaped her lips.

As I brought my cold beer to my lips a second later, I identified the source of the sinking feeling in my stomach.

She doesn't know who I am!

She sipped her wine in silence, her attention turned toward nearby patrons who were having a lively discussion about something or other.

Contrary to my hopes, she didn't choose me that fateful day when her journal appeared in my bag. My becoming the new (and proud) owner of her diary was just luck. Random fucking luck.

I sipped my beer, glancing at her, then taking in my surroundings while my brain tried to continue its analysis. *Because she doesn't know who I am, it makes sense for her to worry about me reporting her being in a coffee shop and getting her in trouble. After all, it had been my initial intention... until I got addicted to her and her sexual experiments.*

But my inner-jabber—combined with the lack of sleep during the previous night's red-eye flight—threatened to give me a headache, so I put an end to it all.

"Sophie," I said loudly, trying to gain her attention again from whatever she was looking at.

She turned to look at me, her expression flat, save for her raised eyebrows.

"Tell me about your worst passenger ever."

A faint smile finally appeared on her face.

Good. Not all hope is lost.

"So many to choose from. Let me think…"

She brought her glass up and took a sip. For a second, the wine moistened her luscious lips, making them look even more enticing. But then she smacked them, and they were dry again. She put her glass down and smiled at me.

"I got one. On a flight to Madrid, about three years ago, there was this one, very odd man. I mean, the guy looked like he was a hundred years old, but he was dressed like a teenager. Mind you, a teenager from a few decades earlier. He had on a black AC/DC T-shirt, ripped bleached jeans, that kind of clothing, you know?" She paused and took another sip.

"You got me intrigued. Go on," I said.

"So, it was after takeoff, but before we'd reached our cruising altitude. So the guy starts yelling—"

Her phone beeped. Again.

She picked it up from the table and, after a few seconds spent reading her screen, she recorded another voice message: "This is getting absurd. Why don't we meet at the Unicorn like we'd discussed? Ten o'clock?"

Duly noted.

She returned her phone to the table. "Sorry about that."

"No problem. So what did the guy start yelling about?"

Her phone beeped again, which drew a deep line between her brows. "I'm sorry. I gotta call Terry. This is getting ridiculous."

So I watched her get up and walk away from me, phone in hand.

She'd left her purse on the table though. The very purse that contained the small notebook she'd written in earlier today… Within seconds, if I acted quickly, I would be able to see her handwriting. I'd be able to read what she's been taking notes about…

But as I slowly moved my hand toward it on the table, I decided against it. I closed my hand into a fist and brought it back closer to my body.

That's not right. If I even want to stand a chance at getting to know her better, I have to respect her privacy.

Instead, I turned my attention to her. She stood quite a few steps away from me now, out of earshot, but I could see the phone against her ear and her arm flailing in the air.

Poor Terry. That guy may be even worse off than me! That Sophie certainly doesn't like being stood up.

I'd finished my beer by the time she came back.

Her face flushed, she emptied the remainder of her glass and said, "Sorry. I gotta go."

She grabbed her purse, and started digging around, probably for cash.

"No problem. Don't worry about the drink. It's on me."

She let out a sigh and stopped digging through her purse. "Thanks." She took a step away, then turned to me and said, "Enjoy your stay in Amsterdam."

"Same for you."

And that had been it. Probably my worst attempt at flirting with a woman on record. Disgruntled, I left more than enough money to cover my bill on the table, then headed back to my hotel room.

I had to regroup and get my game plan on if I wanted to impress her at the Unicorn tonight.

9:50 p.m.

After a long afternoon nap, I Googled the location of the Unicorn, then showed up there, dressed for success. Well, dressed in my best jeans and a sharp black shirt.

But the moment I stepped into the bar, some powerful vibe threw me off. Loud dance music made my eardrums shake, and neon light beams bounced off of various mirrored surfaces, almost blinding me in the process. The crowd was made up of young, overly-perfumed, well-manicured men and women. But mostly men.

I couldn't see Sophie just yet, but I spotted the bar and headed toward it as it seemed like the best observation point for now.

As I walked in that direction, the screen that hung above the young barman got my attention. It currently displayed an exercise video featuring five men in tiny, tight, fluorescent-colored spandex outfits. Not a single woman in that shot. Whether it was an original from the 80s or a remake in that style, the muscular men wore very little fabric. I had to look away.

Then, someone tapped me on the shoulder. I turned around and a tall, slender blond man was staring at me.

"Hi! Want to dance?" he asked as he moved his hips and arms—or at least, that's what I heard over the loud music.

"No, thanks." As I shook my head at him, it finally dawned on me.

Why is Sophie meeting that Terry guy in a gay bar? Or did I mishear the bar's name?

I turned away from the blond man—he was still looking at me, a wide smile on his lips. I turned to face the bar and dug my phone out of my pocket. A few minutes spent trying to find similar-sounding bar names proved fruitless. I looked at my watch: almost ten o'clock.

While I was definitely not hanging out in my favorite place in the world, I could stand the environment a few minutes longer. I couldn't leave without giving all I had trying to get into Sophie's pants. After all of these months...

I waved at the bartender and ordered myself a beer, then sat myself at a small table that had just become empty.

I was halfway through my drink when Sophie finally appeared, a tall, spiky-haired blonde in tow.

Did Terry cancel on her? When did she meet that woman?

Beer in hand, I walked up to them just as Sophie's woman friend left the table in direction of the bar.

Shit, wait. Terry can also be a girl's name...

"I need to talk to you," I said a couple of inches from her ears. I put my drink down in front of her.

"You? What are you doing here?" Her voice pitched high enough for me to hear it over the thump of the dance music.

I leaned in close to her right ear. "I can't stop thinking about you. Everything you wrote in your diary—"

"My diary?" She turned to face me, displaying a frown seemingly made of anger and confusion "How? When?"

I backed off, my hands in the air. "Hey, hey! Relax!" I closed the gap again so she could hear me over the loud music. "You're the one who left it in my briefcase, remember?"

She winced at me, then shook her head. "What are you talking about?"

"Canada, Mexico, Costa Rica, Los Angeles, Ireland, Thailand, France, and now here. Your entries—"

"What's wrong with you? I've never given you my diary. And I've never ever been to Thailand. You've obviously got me confused with someone else... Creep!"

"But you speak French. Your name's Sophia and you match her description to a—"

"My name's Sophie, not Sophia. I've got no idea who you're looking for, but it's obviously not me. You're a stalker. That's what you are."

The blonde woman came back to the table, two beers in hand, condensation already beading down the sides of the bottles. I didn't like that woman a bit. Something seemed off about her, and it wasn't the weird piercings that decorated her face. She eyed me down with a look of disdain, but the feeling was mutual.

"I'm Terry. Who are you?" she asked.

"Nobody," Sophie replied before turning to me. "Now get away from me or I'm calling the cops."

I waved my empty hands in front of me. "No need. I'm gonna finish my drink and leave you alone."

I grabbed the nearest bottle and walked back to my own table. I'd already taken a few steps too many to back track when I realized I'd taken the wrong bottle. The one I held was full and cold.

Fuck them. Let it be my consolation prize.

But how the fuck did I get so misled? Did she lie to me?

I returned to my previous table and sat while staring at her and that Terry woman from a distance. With each sip, I reviewed my steps, my process, my assumptions...

That was it: I'd *assumed* too many things. I'd seen what I'd wanted to see. But now, watching them together, I got annoyed. Annoyed at my own stupidity. The more I drank, the more ashamed I got. Then again, no wonder I wasn't able to flirt with her. She's a fucking lesbian.

Well fuck it, fuck her.

I got up and nearly toppled over, so I sat right back down.

Whoa. What the fuck?

I blinked hard, then reopened my eyes. The neon beams that flashed around me now had blurred edges, the floor had taken on an angle, or so it seemed... Then a wave of nausea forced me up on my feet again, so I ran to the men's room, tripping and colliding against a few people on the way, but I nonetheless reached the back of the bar. I pushed the door open and barely had time to get in the nearest stall—thankfully vacant—and I emptied my gut in a loud reverberation. The cold porcelain under my hands and the overpowering scent of bleach mixed with urinal cakes just added to my confusion.

"Are you okay?" a man's voice asked behind me.

I puked once more, then turned around. Once my blurred vision settled, I realized he was that tall blond man who'd asked me to dance earlier.

I couldn't articulate my thoughts. Words danced in my head, but my tongue was tangled and unable to move, so I just shook my head.

"Come with me, I'll help you," he said with an open palm. "I'm Frank."

I tried to grab his hand, but my vision had gotten worse. He grabbed me by the waist and lifted me up from the floor. "Do your best to stand up. I'll walk you out." He then wrapped an arm around me and guided me out of the bathroom.

Frank...

I tried to concentrate so I could remember his name while he guided me out of the bar.

The last thing I remember is seeing a cab pull over.

9:30 a.m.

I woke up in a very bright room, with sun shining in through the sheer curtains. My head and my entire face hurt. My mouth tasted of vomit.

After blinking a few times, my vision got clearer, but none of the furniture around me looked familiar. I was in a beautiful, modern-looking room alright, but it wasn't the room I'd checked in the day before in the hotel.

A clank of dishes echoed nearby.

Where the fuck am I?

I looked down at the mangled sheets. Below my naked chest, my morning erection stood proud and bare, as always. Without a clue as to where I was, how I'd gotten here, and who I'd spent the night with, I looked around the room once more for any hint. My own clothing had been piled and carefully folded on top of a large leather chair in the corner. Even my boxer briefs.

Well, that's a first.

I swung my legs out and tried to get up, but I had to sit again until the room stopped spinning. My face and jaw were super sore. On my second attempt, I managed to slowly get up and walk around the room, but no lacy bra or panties were in sight. In fact, nothing seemed out of place in this tidy bedroom, save for me and my neat little pile of clothing on the chair.

I proceeded to get dressed, but I'd only donned my underwear when I heard a knock.

"Are you awake?" asked a man's voice from behind the door.

I froze for a second, then looked at the room again. Although decorated with taste, it showed absolutely no feminine touches: no decorative throw pillows, no flowers of any kind, no shades of pink. This was a man's bedroom.

Then the name *Frank* came back to mind.

Who the fuck is Frank?

I put on my jeans and shirt before opening the door to see who that man was, but whoever had knocked no longer stood there. But I heard more clinking noises so I followed the smell of fresh coffee, which directed me toward the kitchen.

"Ha! You are awake. Good morning," said the tall blond man standing in front of the stovetop. Taller than me, but skinnier. His tousled hair made me believe he too had recently woken up.

Better not have shared the same bed...

He seemed friendly enough, although I still didn't understand or recall how I knew him or how I got here.

"What the fuck is going on? Who are you and where am I?"

"Social etiquette is obviously not your strong suit, but I can't blame you, I guess. I'm Frank, an American ex-pat," he said, letting go of the pan he was holding and extending his hand toward me.

I shook it, probably out of habit. "Charlie," I said.

"Nice to meet you officially, Charlie."

"So... Frank... Why am I here? What did you do to me?"

He shook his head, then flipped the pancake he was cooking. "Me? I was just a good Samaritan. Someone spiked your drink last night."

Spiked my drink?

That would explain the stumbling and whatever I could barely recall.

Now I remembered him asking me to dance. "And it wasn't you?"

"Pleeeaase. I understand the meaning of no."

My instinct told me he wasn't lying, but that alone didn't answer any of my many unresolved questions. "So who did?" I asked.

"Coffee?" he offered.

I shook my head; my stomach wasn't ready for coffee yet. "You have water?"

"Sure," he said before opening his fridge. "Flat or sparkling?"

"Flat's fine."

He handed me a bottle, still sealed. "I think it was that spiky-haired chick with the piercings. Although I don't believe you were the intended target. Weird friends you have."

I downed half the bottle he'd handed me and let its refreshing, cold liquid parch my thirst while the information sank in.

"But how would you know this?"

"You caught my eye last night, so I was curious about you. Watched you for a bit. I don't know the story behind that little love triangle you're involved with, but that girl with the piercings seemed to have something against you. Then—"

"Did you see her spike my beer?"

"No. I didn't. But you looked sober when I approached you earlier. A guy of your size getting that disoriented after a beer or two could only be explained by a handful of reasons. And I've unfortunately seen it before, so I knew in an instant."

"And you didn't call the police?"

"You were in no shape to stay and wait for the police to show up. Even less able to explain what had happened to you. I had no idea where you lived or if you were a tourist staying in a hotel. I wasn't going to start searching you for a hotel card key or driver's license. I figured the best option was to take you somewhere safe while you could still walk. Barely."

"Well... I guess I should thank you, then? But why the fuck did you get me naked?"

"No, that was all you. I swear I didn't touch you. You got naked all on your own. Man, I get your lack of trust here, you've obviously got something against homosexuals, but go ahead. Look in your wallet. I didn't steal anything from you."

And I did. I checked my pockets, dug my wallet out and opened it. My ID, credit cards, money... Everything was accounted for. I checked my wrist and noticed my watch was missing.

"My watch?"

"You took it off last night. Sorry, I forgot to place it with your clothes. It must still be in the living room. We can have a look later. You want breakfast?"

"Why is my face hurting so damn much?"

"You don't remember that? Go have a look at yourself in the mirror," he said, pointing toward a door down the hallway.

I walked over to the bathroom and shrieked when I saw my reflection.

Shades of purple and blue covered my right eye and upper cheek. "What the heck? Did you do that to me?" I yelled out toward the kitchen.

"To your pretty face? Never in a million years. Your big mouth got you in trouble before we got in the cab."

I walked back to the kitchen to hear the rest of his story. "What do you mean?"

"Given that you were rapidly losing it, I skipped the taxi line. One guy made a comment you didn't like, then you called him a faggot, among several other homophobic insults. You probably got what you deserved there... Especially if you consider you were leaving a gay bar. That black eye's on you. You actually had me rethink saving your ass, and I didn't want to go to the police because I didn't know if the guys you swung at were going to press charges..."

The reality of what had happened slapped me in the face just as he slid a pancake on one of the empty plates on the table. "Eat something. It'll help."

I took a seat. "Fuck... Sorry, man. And thank you for saving my ass." I poured some syrup onto the pancake then cut away my first bite.

2:15 p.m.

I figured I had to do one thing right now. I had about six hours to kill before my return flight, and I might as well use my time wisely so I could get back on the figurative horse.

So I headed down De Walden in broad daylight.

Gotta love a place where à-la-carte sex is openly and easily available, almost 24 hours a day.

After meandering for a few blocks, I spotted the right girl for me. A young brunette with curvy hips and a coy smile stood in a red window in a tiny emerald-green bikini. Her big round eyes matched her outfit. A wink was all it took to convince me to head over to her.

She opened the door, keeping her body protected and hidden by it, and she smiled at me.

"Hello. You want to come in?" she asked with an accent I couldn't place.

"Of course. You look lovely, but what will you do to me and how much will it cost?"

She eyed me up and down. "For you? Fifteen minutes: a blow job and a fuck for sixty euros."

Fair price to bring my ego back up.

I nodded, and she stepped aside to clear the door.

I walked in and inhaled her powdery perfume. She leaned in to close the door and draw the curtain. She led me up a short flight of stairs, then opened a door and invited me to step in.

The small bedroom smelled of sex and incense and was flooded with a warm, red tone that came from a couple of tall floor lamps in the corner. A washroom had been built-in without a need for partition: a small sink, toilet, and bidet occupied a corner of the room. A queen-sized bed lined with burgundy sheets reigned in front of me on a raised platform. The main wall behind the bed and the ceiling above us were covered with mirror tiles. My own discolored reflection met my eyes and I looked away.

"Pay first," she said after closing the bedroom door.

I dug out my wallet and retrieved three twenty-euro bills, which she grabbed from my hand before sending me a large smile. "Thank you."

Well aware that the clock had already started ticking, I took off my shirt and pants in record time, leaving them jumbled on the floor.

My green-eyed woman, on the other hand, wasn't in such hurry.

As I made my way to the bed where she now sat, her long legs partly folded in front of her, she pulled at the string behind her neck, slowly undoing the knot of her top. She then pulled down on one side of the strings, exposing one of her gorgeous breasts.

Standing at the foot of the bed, I reached toward her and pulled down on the other side. I let her fleshy goodness fill my hands and reinvigorate my bruised ego. After all, it was no secret—at least to me—that women and their curves were the cure to the majority of men's problems.

"What's your name?" I asked her.

"Call me Luisa."

I had the feeling that it wasn't her real name, but I didn't care. I let go of her breasts and pulled on the strings that held her bottom tied. A second later, I pulled it down and exposed her trimmed brown bush. She scooted up and sat on the edge of the bed, parting her knees to wrap her legs around mine. I liked her 'do: she'd left a small triangular welcome mat above her fully shaven pussy.

Her warm mouth went directly for my cock, engulfing my erect girth and making me forget where I was.

I let out a grunt and tilted my head back, meeting the reflection of our naked bodies on the ceiling. Her head bobbed in front of me at an irregular pace. When she pulled back to where I was barely in her mouth, I could see her breasts between us, then she blew cool air on my cock before swallowing it again. I wrapped my hands around the back of her head, her silky hair slipping between my fingers as I moved her head up and down to my preferred cadence.

Cold fingers got a hold of my balls, surprising me a little, but what she did with them more than made up for it.

My own grunts echoed in the room, her slurping sounds accompanying them as I approached my point of no-return.

"I want to come on your tits," I ordered as I let go of her head.

And she moved back on the bed to become a beautiful target, her arms holding her back up at the perfect angle for me to aim at. I wrapped my hand around my shaft and made myself come, splattering her gorgeous tits with all of my might. Pleased with my tension having finally been released, I looked up at her and that's when I noticed the void behind her gaze, an indescribable look that experienced sex workers often shared.

It was business after all.

She didn't know me from Adam.

I didn't pay her enough to care and pretend to like me.

And I was fine with that.

She got up on her knees and massaged her own breasts, letting my juices spread on her pale skin.

"You want to fuck me now?"

"Give me a minute, and I'll be ready," I said. "Turn around and get on all fours."

"Anal is more," she said to me, not budging.

"Don't worry, just regular doggy style."

She nodded. "But let me cover you up."

"Let me see your ass first."

She obeyed and got on all fours in front of me. Seeing her ripe peach winking at me like that had me ready to go again. I was putting my hands on her hips, prepared to act, but she lowered herself to the bed. She stretched out and reached to grab a condom.

She ripped it open with her teeth, then pulled it out of the wrapper, holding it in her mouth. She made her way back to me, on her knees, and then pushed the condom onto the tip of my erect cock with her mouth. Then, she unraveled it with her lips and tongue. Practiced trick or not, I was impressed.

Cock covered and more than ready to enjoy the rest of my paid interlude, I motioned for Luisa to turn around. On all fours in front of me, her ass was sublime; her pussy, inviting; her scent, intoxicating. I parted then massaged her butt cheeks, then lowered my thumbs to her warm, pink pussy. She was wet and ready.

"We don't have all day. Fuck me," she ordered.

And I obeyed, first just dipping into her, pleasantly surprised at her tightness, then I rammed the rest of my length into her warmth. I got a hold of her hips, then parted my legs a bit to lower myself and began pushing out all of my frustration, as if each thrust somehow erased my most recent mistakes. Luisa's hair fell forward, hiding her face in the reflection in the mirror in front of us and, for an instant, I saw Mrs. Thompson naked in front of me.

For a moment, I allowed myself to relive what that had been like. She'd taught me to do it doggy style. I'd gotten bad carpet burns on my knees from doing her on all fours in her living room.

Bit by bit, as I watched the beautiful woman in front of me arch her back, hearing her breasts flap against her own skin, catching a glimpse of them bouncing in the mirror in front of us, Luisa and my memories of Mrs. Thompson morphed together and finally exorcised Charles out.

And when I came in my final thrust, it was Charlie's doing. I was back. My ego healed, my hopes to find the right Sophia somehow heightened.

4:45 p.m.

"Finally got what was coming to you?" a woman's voice asked a few feet from me.

I turned slightly and recognized Sophie.

"How's Terry?" I tried to smile, but my bruised cheek made me wince instead.

"Looks painful." Her hand went up as if to touch my face, but she dropped it by her side instead. "Unsure if you deserved that. I should thank you for walking away with my beer that night. Because of you, I avoided whatever Terry was going to do to me. Steal my passport, money, kidney... who knows?"

"So it really was her who'd spiked it?"

She nodded. "And she even had the balls to try it again. But by the time she ordered me a new beer and got back to my table, I saw you stumbling away. I put two and two together and didn't touch it. I threatened to call the cops and she ran out. I suspect I'll never hear back from her. Do you want her contact info so you can report her to the cops?"

"No, but thanks for offering. A... friend helped me out. Don't know how my night would have ended if he hadn't stepped in. And sorry for how I treated you. I really thought you were someone else."

"Another woman deserves to be stalked like that?"

I let out a long sigh. "It's not like that. It's not what you think."

"Well, good luck with that," Sophie said before smiling at me and joining the rest of her crew who were already boarding the plane.

NEXT STEPS

Well, I haven't found her after all, and I definitely got my ass kicked in more ways than one.

Thank goodness there are still good people like Frank out there. No hidden agenda, no rape, no theft, nothing. Just a good person with a good heart. I respected him for that. I'm not sure I would have done the same if our roles had been reversed.

I guess I have some growing up to do. And while that black eye heals, I'll have a visual reminder of the asshole I can sometimes be.

So while I'm not back to square one, I'm nowhere closer to meeting her. But I know she doesn't work for my airline and that's something.

I could start hitting on all brunettes that wear uniforms from other airlines. My dick could go limp trying to find her...

Or I could use her unbelievable journal entries from Japan to try and narrow it down some more. The weird shit she's done—which was recorded on video—is just mind-blowing.

Those crazy Japanese game shows are just... incredible.

PART IX

JAPAN

THE STEWARDESS'S ENTRIES

JAPAN

5:05 a.m.

ALEX HANDED me a red silky envelope covered with vertical streams of Japanese characters. "Then there's this event," she said.

I accepted the document and let my fingers graze the beautiful calligraphy. "What is it?"

"It's a private function hosted by Mr. Suzuki. That man's wealthier than anyone I know. No clue what it will be about this year, but it's sure to be a blast. Our kind of fun, if you know what I mean... He invites lots of beautiful people."

"Certainly beats staying in my hotel room. What should I wear?"

Alex raised her shoulders. "I don't know, but you can't go wrong with a black evening gown."

"And how will I get there?"

"The address is inside. Just show the card to your hotel concierge or taxi driver."

I turned the envelope over and noticed the opening was on one of the small ends. I tapped it against my hand and a thick card slid out, which was also covered in characters I couldn't read or understand.

"And when is it exactly?"

"Ah! *That* I did find out. Those characters are the date and time," she said, pointing at the second line from the right. "The evening on the day you land. That should give you enough time for a solid afternoon nap, then the event starts at 9 o'clock. I guess you'll have to figure out the address first so you can plan ahead in terms of travel time from your hotel."

"Taking over your flights certainly comes with added benefits," I said. "Thanks, and good luck with your mom."

"I'm just glad you were qualified for that aircraft so I could hand you my ticket. Mr. Suzuki doesn't host events that everyone enjoys, but I know you will absolutely love it, whatever it ends up being. You'll have to tell me all about it when I see you next."

"I will."

"Okay, I gotta go now, so I can get there before her surgery."

I gave her a big hug then watched her disappear toward her departure gate.

7:45 p.m.

With the upcoming mysterious event on my mind, the past days had flown by. I really had no idea what Alex meant other than there could be some opportunities to have sex with beautiful people. Or perhaps she meant some 4:20 activities, but the latter seemed unlikely.

But now that I was in Tokyo, refreshed by my afternoon nap, I was once again day-dreaming about what would be happening in a couple of hours from now. Would it be some sort of 70s-inspired event where men put their keychains in a bowl and women randomly picked one and went home with its owner?

That could be fun.

Or maybe it would be something classier that would still involve nudity. Like a naked musical. *That's not very Japanese now, is it?*

The alarm clock by my bed indicated it was time to go.

I double-checked my makeup and outfit in the mirror. My hairdo was still looking good, with just the right number of strands cascading out of my loose chignon. I smoothed out my long black dress and got rid of a few pieces of loose threads that had somehow clung to its silky fabric.

My necklace!

I walked to my carry-on and dug it out. I'd brought a simple silver circle that hung on a delicate chain. It wasn't worth much, but its simplicity turned it into the perfect accessory in a pinch.

My black clutch under my arm, I headed out of my room and down to the reception to get myself a cab.

8:50 p.m.

The taxi slowed down as it approached a large industrial building. Had it not been for a few people spilling out of the vehicles in front of me, I'd have been worried my driver was going to murder me in an abandoned factory.

But a man in a kimono walked up to the cab as we came to a halt in front of the entrance. As he opened my door, I handed money to the driver, then stepped out of the cab.

"*Konbanwa*," said the man in the kimono as he helped me out of the vehicle.

"Good evening," I said, feeling awful for not even having bothered to learn a few Japanese phrases before coming here. But my guilt morphed into excitement as quickly as it had come.

The man pointed toward the entrance, and I joined the guests waiting to enter the building.

A short woman—also wearing a kimono—stood by the door. She first said something in Japanese, then, since I didn't understand, she asked in English: "Can I see your invitation please?"

"Here it is," I said, handing her my envelope.

"Follow the other women in front of you, to your right."

As Alex had predicted, I was surrounded by beautiful people in assorted skin tones. I saw a tall, handsome blond guy—my type down to a T—being ushered to a different part of the building toward the left.

Maybe I'll see him again later.

The women in front of me had already moved ahead, so I hurried my pace— as fast as my high heels let me—and I caught up to them as they entered a very large room. About thirty kimono-wearing staff were lined up along the front wall. In the middle of the room, chairs were paired with their own small tables, as though I'd walked into a speed-dating event.

Is this it? A speed-dating evening?

I joined the rest of the guests in the center of the room. Everyone kept quiet. I smiled at those who made eye contact with me. The silence made me feel a little ill-at-ease, adding to my existing discomfort stemming from not knowing what was going to happen this evening. I was about to talk to a black woman standing near me when one of the kimonoed staff spoke up in the microphone.

After saying something in Japanese, he added English instructions: "Please pick your assistant. He or she will help you all evening with the games." His hand pointed toward the line-up of men and women in matching outfits behind him.

Games?

Not knowing what I'd need assisting with, I picked a tall young man with a faint smile on his face. His silky black hair was parted to the side, and his long bangs cascaded in a loose loop down his ivory forehead before being tucked behind his left ear. Although long at the top, the rest of his hair was cut short at the nape. He looked like he was twenty at most.

"My name is Junichi," he said, bowing in front of me.

I bowed as well, unsure what proper Japanese etiquette called for here.

His smile got wider, and he directed me toward a set of chairs in the center of the room. "We will go through the agreement for the games. It's written in Japanese, so I will translate it for you."

"Okay," I said as he placed a questionnaire in front of me, along with a pen.

"Write your first name here and your family name here." He pointed toward specific fields on the form.

I wrote them in.

"Date of birth: year, month, day."

After I filled out the numbers he needed, he translated a series of yes/no questions having to do with my health: "Was I menstruating right now? Was I allergic to latex? Did I have sexually transmitted diseases?" The list was much longer, but those are the ones I recall.

The sound of chairs backing up on the concrete floor made me turn around during those questions. The black woman I'd nearly approached earlier had gotten up and was walking out the door. So was a tall blonde woman.

Junichi spoke up, "We have more questions to answer. If you feel uncomfortable, then you are free to leave."

My inner competitive self wanted to know if I'd stomach whatever these women were opposed to. So I let Junichi translate the next batch of questions: "Was I comfortable in front of a camera? Was I opposed to pre-marital sex? Was I open to intercourse with men? Was I comfortable with nudity? Was I okay with anal sex? Would I shave hair from certain body parts?"

"As long as you're not asking me to shave my head!" I said.

He smiled. "No, no."

"Then fine."

The first side of the questionnaire now completed, he flipped to another page. While he was fumbling with the document, I glanced around the room once more. The initial group of women had dwindled down by about a third.

On the new page sitting in front of me, a long paragraph appeared, followed by ¥10000000 and a line to sign on.

"What does this say?" I asked Junichi.

"This is the total prize amount if you win. There will also be smaller prizes for all participants. You need to sign on the dotted line."

"There's gotta be more than what you just told me," I said, worried I was signing my life away. "The paragraph almost covers the entire page."

He brought the document closer to him and translated it as he read it:

"It says that you agree to participate in the recording of a private video, along with other men and women. You also agree to partake in all of the events of this game, which may include physical contact or other activities of a sexual nature, including objectification of the body."

For the chance of winning ten million yen? What is that? Around $80,000?

"So, it will not be a public video?" I asked.

"No, it's for Mr. Suzuki and his wife. But there's a crew filming the games, so they'll see you and the other contestants, but they're not allowed to record using their own equipment.

Only one life to live! Might as well make it count. And maybe the hot blond guy will be paired with me...

I signed on the dotted line.

"Perfect," he said as he took the signed contract and pen from my hands. He stood up. "Now we'll get you prepared. Please follow me to the next room."

I got up and joined him in the preparation area, which reminded me of a very large gym locker room, complete with lockers, showers, toilets... and a whole crew of kimono-wearing Japanese men and women.

He instructed me to use the washroom and empty anything I may have in my body as this was going to be my last opportunity, then to hop in the shower.

9:15 p.m.

Even though I'd showered just hours earlier, I obeyed.

I disrobed and placed my belongings in a locker, then headed into the shower, along with about a dozen other women. Some tall, some short, some athletic, some chubby, some skinny, but all were beautiful in their own way. While walking butt-naked to the shower hadn't bothered me, I expected the open communal shower with its multiple shower heads to do the trick, but no.

My, my. How I've grown.

I no longer worried about women judging me. I was finally comfortable in my own skin. I wasn't even paying attention to those around me... That was until a woman with elaborate puffed-up hair tried to leave the shower with her 'do still dry.

A uniformed man was shaking his head at her, pointing her back toward the shower.

She put up a fuss. At least that's what I understood of her flailing arms and loud outburst in a language I didn't recognize. *Russian?*

For a few seconds, they stood there, as though dueling with their minds: the woman with her hands on her hips, the man with his arms crossed on his chest. Then, the woman's assistant, a petite Japanese woman, brought the upset contestant a large towel and escorted her away from the shower area.

Seconds later, our assistants came up to the shower entrance and yelled to us over the running water. "You must wash your hair or else you'll be expelled from the game," said Junichi.

I nodded.

The games had me too intrigued to worry about my hairdo.

After shampooing and conditioning my hair with the products provided to us, I was as clean as I could ever be. At least that was true for my body; my mind was a different story. I kept thinking about that blond man and what I'd like to do to him or have him do to me.

I walked out of the tiled area, and Junichi handed me a towel.

Once I dried myself off, I wrapped the oversized piece of plush material around me and followed Junichi to an area with more uniformed women. A few massage tables and elevated pedicure chairs had been installed here.

One of the women reached toward me and unwrapped my towel before proceeding to scrutinize my body. She asked me to sit on the massage table (Junichi translated her requests as she talked), then she inspected my armpits and my pussy. I'd gotten my hair waxed a couple of days prior, but I'd requested to keep my narrow landing strip. The woman obviously had something against it since she grabbed a manual razor and a can of shaving cream then proceeded to remove what little hair remained to differentiate my pussy from that of a pre-teen girl.

"Lean back on the table," Junichi translated after the woman spoke.

I obeyed, and the woman parted my legs, then my butt cheeks, inspecting me like cattle. I knew there was no other hair to remove. Come to think of it, I was a bit surprised that the woman had used a razor, but if they were going to be filming us, it probably made more sense than waxing, which could have left behind unsightly red bumps.

She then looked at my fingers and toes, inspecting each of my digits for the status of my red gel manicure.

She nodded, said something to Junichi, and then he translated her next request: "Please sit on the chair. She will comb your hair and tie it in a ponytail."

I followed their instructions. Then, a touch of makeup later, I was free to leave but not with just one ponytail. My hair had been parted right in the middle, and the woman had tied two ponytails with red ribbons, one on each side of my head.

Last time my hair had been done up like this was more than 25 or 30 years ago?

"We have about thirty minutes before the first game. Would you like a massage to relax?" asked Junichi.

Who turns down a free massage offer? "Of course! I'd love a massage," I said.

I followed Junichi to another area, this one populated with several tables and a handful of naked women receiving massages from their male or female assistants. Music played softly in the background, something similar in tone to Barry White, but in Japanese.

I lay down on my stomach, and Junichi began spreading a sweet-smelling lotion on my back, then my arms and legs. His fingers got a hold of one of my feet, and he began kneading my skin. Both my feet were worked on, then calves, then thighs. His slow, magical touch had me so relaxed.

Once he finished with my legs, he moved on to my shoulders and worked out the knots. His digits squeezed away the stress that had accumulated, allowing my mind to wander while my eyes were closed. I imagined the handsome blond man working on my back instead of Junichi. Each stroke and caress I received suddenly triggered a different reaction in my body. Something more instinctual, more intense, more primal.

By the time Junichi reached my lower back, I was craving hands on my ass and between my legs. Unfortunately, my wish wasn't fulfilled. Instead, he moved his attention to my fingers and arms, offering a soothing massage nonetheless.

But my mind had already been turned on; my inner fantasy world had already ignited desires that I hoped these mysterious games would fulfill.

10:45 p.m.

A loud alarm rang in the room, bringing my delightful massage and fantasies to a screeching halt before letting them crash into a figurative concrete wall.

"Time to go. The games will begin," Junichi said.

I got up and followed him. The rest of the women in the group were doing the same. With all the female contestants naked, it was easy to differentiate us from the assistants.

As we walked through various doors, then along a windy path backstage, Junichi told me more about the games. "This is how it works: We prepare for one game, then we record it live once. There's only one chance for each game, no second takes. Then, the recording stops, and we prepare for the second game. When we're ready, we record it live. We repeat the process for each game. Understood?"

I nodded. "Do they explain the rules in English?"

"I'll translate them for you," he said.

I overheard the short brunette in front of me ask a question to her assistant in an Australian accent: "How many games are there?"

"It depends on the points earned by each participant, but up to ten games," her assistant replied.

I turned to Junichi. "So, we'll be here for what... two hours?" I asked.

"No, more like all night."

11:00 p.m.

Junichi took me to the first game room. It looked pretty bare to me, except for a series of tall vertical boxes lined up against the longest wall, each with a small container in front of it. The room had no ceiling. Instead, bright lights, cameras, microphone booms, and other devices chaotically hung above us.

A loud voice boomed from an overhead speaker, first in Japanese, then in English: "Ladies, please pick a pod."

Like the other women around me, I headed toward the back wall and selected one of the tall vertical boxes.

Junichi, who had quietly followed me to the pod, walked past me. "Please step over the ledge and get in, with your back against the fabric, facing me."

The more I looked at it, the more I saw a vertical coffin, but I obeyed, stepping over the foot-high divide, and then turning around to rest my back against the soft, black, velvety fabric behind me. When I pushed my body against it, its plushness hugged me like a thick, comfortable memory-foam mattress.

Junichi opened the square box in front of the pod, which revealed a bunch of dark gray planks. He carried then slid these planks into small grooves above my pod's threshold. Each plank slowly but surely confined me into a closed box. Junichi stopped when he reached my belly button.

Just when I thought I'd been boxed in enough, I watched him head toward the box and return with one more plank, this one a little less thick than the others he'd brought. The plank also had two holes on one side.

"Watch your head, I need to bring this one in," he said.

I backed up some more into the soft mattress behind me.

He moved his hands into my pod and reached toward the top. Instead of sliding this plank into place, he hung it from two tiny hooks in front of me, way above my head. I hadn't noticed those before. The thin plank now in place, less light was coming into my pod, but I could still see three hooks at the base of the new plank, which ended just above my head. Then, as I pondered about the purpose of these hooks (and realized I was thankfully just short of touching them should I move forward), I watched him walk toward the box again. He came back with a piece of rolled fabric.

"I need to attach this to the piece above. Please close your eyes," he said.

I did while also pushing my head back as far as I could. I heard fumbling noises for a few seconds, then nothing.

"You can open your eyes again," he said.

I did and saw that a black meshing had been rolled down to around my chin, blocking more light from coming into the box, but I could still see movement in front of me.

"Step forward, please. Put your feet in the recess in front of you and bring your stomach so it's flat against the planks," Junichi said.

By stepping closer to the fabric, my eyesight improved. In fact, I could even recognize Junichi's face while he stood right in front of me. He was looking at me, focusing on my stomach and breasts, a slight frown on his face. I assumed he must have measured something with his hand as I watched him keep a specific distance between his fingers while he compared planks to his held-out hand.

He came back with another plank a few seconds later. It was about as wide as what he'd just measured.

"Please back up again."

I did.

He slid that latest plank down the front, then asked me to step forward again, his hands up in the air. "I'll touch your breasts and bring them up so they don't get squished," he said. He gently got a hold of my breasts and rested them above the plank. "Stay there, I'll move the back of the pod forward. Please tell me to stop when you feel the mattress behind you. Don't worry. It won't hurt, and I'll be right back."

I swallowed hard, then nodded.

He disappeared out of sight, walking between my pod and the next. Then, as promised, I started feeling the space shrink behind me. The soft velvet touched my ass.

"Stop," I said.

He came around to the front and looked at me.

"I need to close the space a lot more for the game to work."

I didn't like the idea, but couldn't do much about it either.

Junichi once again disappeared out of my sight, and soon enough the mattress behind me started moving forward.

"Stop!" I yelped when the planks in front of me squished my stomach.

He came back. "Push yourself back as far as you can," he said.

"I *am* as far back as I can! My stomach is against the planks. I can't move!" My heart pounded in my chest, but me trying to breathe deeper just increased my level of pain and discomfort.

"I'll move it back a little bit."

A few seconds later, after he did, I sighed in relief.

"Are you more comfortable now?" he asked when he reappeared in front of me.

"Better," I said. "Am I going to stay in this coffin for a long time?"

"No, this game will be fast. But I have one more plank to add. I need to cover the space above your breasts all the way to your nose."

"Whoa..."

"Don't worry, you'll still be able to breathe and see what's going on around you. You won't be in any danger during the game, I promise."

"Okay."

Obviously, since all the pods were one next to the other, I couldn't see the other women from my vantage point, but I could only assume they were all being prepared the same way I was. I exhaled loudly as I watched my assistant come back with one large plastic plank with U-shaped cords on two sides opposite each other. He reached around one side of my pod, then the other, which seemed to secure that last plank in place.

I'm a freaking coffin with boobs! What kind of game is this going to be?

I saw Junichi and other assistants walking out of the room holding the boxes with whatever had been left in them, then they each reappeared with rolling trays covered with goodies I couldn't quite identify from where I stood.

After rolling his tray in the center of the room, in front of my pod, Junichi headed toward me.

"The preparations are almost over. The first game will start soon. I'll be back to help you out as soon as it's over."

"Okay. Do I need to do anything during the game?"

"No, you just stand there in silence. Easy, right?"

"I guess," was all I could say, but butterflies tried to flicker in my constricted stomach.

With that, he disappeared from view again. More assistants rolled their trays in the middle of the room, and then nothing happened for a couple of minutes.

The lights suddenly got brighter and loud music from old-school porn movies started playing. It was so tacky I expected a man's voice to say, "I'm here to clean your pool."

But before I could reminisce any more about the first porn movie I'd ever seen, a loud Japanese voice with the excitement of a late-night infomercial salesman announced something. Unfortunately for me, no translation was provided.

I had absolutely no idea what was to come. A loud buzzer rang for three seconds, then a group of men ran into the room.

1, 2, 3... I counted twenty of them. All naked, with skin shades from the darkest of blacks to the whitest of whites I'd ever seen. They took their positions, lining themselves up across the room in front of the pods, in pairs.

In front of me, next to a very well endowed black man, a tall and muscular red-headed man and a slender Asian man stood, their dicks relaxed. I squinted and was surprised to see that the red-headed man packed smaller equipment than the Asian man. *So much for stereotypes, but limp dicks sometimes prove surprising. Hmm... I've never been with an Asian man before. Why is that?*

But before I could even venture a guess to my own meanderings, a loud horn sounded and the men started racing toward our row of pods. The red-headed man and the Asian man approached me nearly at the same speed.

A few seconds later, my breasts were slapped, one after the other. Then the men turned around and raced back to their starting line.

My flesh stung, and the edge of the upper plank dug in the underside of my flesh as my breasts bounced back to their previous position.

What the fuck? Is this a breast-slapping game?

I kept my eyes on both men: they had run back to the start line, then turned around and sprinted back toward me again.

Oh no... Not again. The closer they got, the more I tensed in anticipation. I closed my eyes, ready to scream if they did it again.

But before I could burst out in anger, my girls each received a kiss on the nipple, followed by a gentle squeeze.

I reopened my eyes. The men were once again sprinting away from me, but this time they stopped by the tray in the middle of the room. They came back with a small bowl and something else I couldn't quite recognize.

When they reached me again, something warm got painted on my breasts. Chocolate aroma drifted up to my nose. The red-headed man finished my right breast first. By the time the Asian man had finished my other breast, the first man had left and reappeared with a can of whipped cream in front of me. I heard the pressurized air escape and felt a cool circle being drawn around my right breast, then a tiny circle around my nipple. As both men returned to their goody tray, my Asian boob decoration lagging by a step, I noticed that they both looked up toward the center of the room, but high above.

Is there a display with instructions on what to do next?

They returned to me again, and I was unsure of what they were going to do this time. Their facial expressions were focused on the task at hand. Pearls of sweat beaded on the red-headed man's freckled forehead. The Asian man was much shorter and didn't show any signs of sweat or stress.

I, like the red-headed man, was starting to perspire inside my pod. I didn't particularly like being in my coffin-like box, but at least my breasts weren't being slapped again.

A gong sounded.

Both men bent down out of my field of vision before their wet mouth and tongue began licking and sucking on my exposed skin. Although rushed, their actions were delightful. My left breast suddenly stopped receiving its treatment; I watched the Asian man run back toward the start line. When he turned around to sprint back toward me, I saw his chocolate-, whipping-cream-, and rainbow-sprinkled cheeks.

His final move?

A twist of my nipple, which I didn't expect, nor like. He then lifted both of his hands up in the air. My other nipple got twisted and the two men double high-fived each other.

What did I get myself into?

12:00 a.m.

After we all got a chance to rinse off, then get ourselves dry, we were taken to a large rectangular room with an assortment of strange, squiggly upside-down Y-shaped boxes about four feet tall. The lower part, which inclined toward the floor, was split into two, while the upper part was more upright. Behind the latter was a door.

"Pick a pod. Open the door and sit on the stool," Junichi whispered in my ear. "More instructions will be provided shortly."

I proceeded as directed and so did the other women around me. I picked a pod near the back corner, but before I reached for the small silver door knob, I couldn't resist the urge to touch the odd-looking fabric that covered the enclosure. It was soft and bouncy, reminding me of those stress-relief rubber balls I once used.

I opened my door. The pod contained a stool with a very low back, so I stepped in, sat on the seat, but there was no room for my legs in front of me. The pod's odd Y-shape forced me to spread my legs so they could fit in the two slots that dangled down. From my seated position, I could see through a meshed screen I hadn't noticed before.

A few straggling women each entered their own pod, then a Japanese voice boomed over the speaker.

Between my legs, about six inches in front of me, an oval hole, about four inches wide and six inches high, was clearly visible.

Junichi came up behind me while the pod door was still open. "Are your legs in place?" he asked.

"I think so?"

"Looks like it," he said while poking his head above my shoulder. "Just relax. I'll lower your seat and move you forward."

He adjusted my position, then came around the front. He pressed a button, and I felt myself drop. Green light shone between my legs when the small panel lifted.

"Move forward on your seat," he ordered.

I scooched up by about an inch, blocking most of the green luminescence.

"Perfect," he said. "I'll bring you back up. Don't move."

A loud click sounded, and I was lifted up.

A few seconds later, Junichi was once again standing behind me. "You may want to warm yourself up so the game is more enjoyable." He closed the door behind me, leaving me wondering what was to come.

Soon enough, the porn soundtrack from the earlier game resumed, along with loud grunts of people fucking and coming. From the meshed window in front of me, I noticed the previously white walls of the room had turned into screens where a porn movie was being projected.

Scratch that: several porn movies.

There was one very talented young blonde handling five men at once: one fucking her in the front, one in her ass, one in her mouth, and one in each of her hands. Then to my left, there was a lone brunette playing in the shower with a purple dildo. In front of me, a tiny Asian woman was being taken in the ass by a large black man. Further to the right, a single man appeared, hot as hell. Like one of those underwear models, except he didn't have any underwear on. Just his chiseled abs, his strong, lean muscles, and his hard cock in hand. He was wanking off, staring right at the camera. Right at me, or so it seemed. I started warming myself up while focusing on him. Among the mishmash of soundtracks, I found his and tried to focus on his grunts as I touched myself, matching the speed of my finger to the cadence of his fist as it went up and down his beautiful shaft.

Then I closed my eyes and imagined his hands on my breasts and stomach as I grazed my own skin in the privacy of my pod. I took away his pretty face and replaced it with that of the handsome blond man I'd seen earlier today. I kept the rest of the porn star's body though. *Hot Blondie.* By now, my opening was slick with excitement, I'd added a second digit and could hear my own moisture echo softly in my enclosure as I fingered myself faster and faster.

Then, a horn sounded, taking me away from Fantasyland, yet again.

I reopened my eyes and took my hand away from my pussy. The same group of naked men was now coming into the room, each running toward our enclosures. I spotted red-headed man for a second, but he disappeared behind another pod. I couldn't see my handsome blond man among the crowd in my vision field. But a brown-haired man was coming my way. His chest hair was similar to what most 80s rock-band singers would have proudly shown off during live shows back in the days.

Funny how they didn't feel the need to shave chest hair...

A second later, my seat got lowered and the same green light reappeared. A cool breeze greeted my warm pussy, then pressure was applied to the rubbery surface that surrounded my exposed lips.

With a hesitant poke, the hairy man's dick parted my insides. I let out a quiet moan, glad to have warmed myself up ahead of time. Not that he was that big, but my self-entertainment had been the only foreplay here.

Then came a second thrust, this one much more powerful and confident. Then another and another. Being fucked without feeling the warmth of another person's body was odd, but I closed my eyes and played with my clit instead, pretending everything was normal, getting more and more aroused, pretending he was Blondie.

But it stopped suddenly. I opened my eyes and the hairy man was running away, his white butt and hairless back racing out of sight, leaving my pussy hanging high and wet.

Other men were doing the same. Then, a mere minute later, the walls returned to white, the music ended, and my assistant was once again talking to me behind the pod.

"This game is over. I'll raise your seat, then open your door and help you get out."

I wiped my pussy, but I didn't know what to do with my hand.

I stepped out of my pod and accepted the bathrobe Junichi handed me. I looked around at the other women and their confused faces. I must admit that my own expression was probably similar to theirs. An Indian woman started giggling nervously, then so did the Australian woman I'd heard before. She was standing a few feet away. Then the whole room joined her, myself included.

I'd seen Japanese game shows on TV before, but I couldn't say that I'd seen any of the adult-themed variety. I'd never watched them to the end because I found them so freaking confusing, so I had no idea what was in store for me and the rest of the contestants.

I could only assume I'd get my fair share of fucking tonight, and from random strangers at that.

The likelihood of anyone I knew ever watching this game show was nonexistent, but I still wondered what I'd gotten myself into.

12:40 a.m.

Our group was escorted out of the room and taken to a different area.

Calling it a *room* would have been pushing it. It was more like that secret passageway in the *maison close* I recently saw in Paris, but much wider. We were standing behind the unfinished backside of a set, probably not where the contestants would be competing.

We followed the lead assistant in a tour of sorts, walking as a group. But each time our guide came across an available slot, one woman stayed behind with her assistant while the rest of us kept going. I had no idea what the slots looked like on the other side of the set, but from where I stood, they were just body-sized recesses where we had to stand, but the wall seemed to be partly open in two spots in front of those recesses: one about a third of the way, and the other two-thirds of the height.

The third recess surprised me. Instead of being vertical like the others, it was horizontal, just off of the floor.

Then we passed another horizontal slot that required climbing up a short ladder. The black woman selected it and proceeded to go up, followed by her assistant.

We made our way around the bend, and our group slowly shrank in size as more and more contestants selected their own recess as we spotted them. We turned another corner after losing yet a few more women to more vertical and horizontal slots. I had no real incentive to rush, so I was part of the last two women who had yet to select a recess by the time we had walked around the full perimeter of the room.

Back at our starting point, the two of us were instructed to go up a ladder to the top of the room.

Once up there, I was surprised by the geometry of the ceiling. It wasn't flat as I'd expected it to be. It was more like a series of large blocks randomly piled next to each other. In fact, it made me think about what the top layer of a Tetris board would look like as a 3D game.

But Junichi took me out of my childhood memories and told me to pick a position.

I selected the next one I saw, something perpendicular to a slot the other woman had already taken.

"Rest with your face down."

I did, my arms relaxed by my side. Gravity did its thing and pulled my breasts down, away from my body. And the cooler air in the room below made me realize I had started sweating underneath the fold of my breasts. The other open area was lined up with my belly button. Other than that, it didn't feel too weird. Thankfully, the surface was well padded and very sturdy, but the two spaces where planks were missing didn't quite line up with my body.

"Lift your hips," Junichi asked of me.

I pressed my toes into the surface below me and straightened my legs, raising my entire lower body off from the padded surface. I turned to look at him.

He slid one of the padded planks up toward the hole where my breasts hung, then another.

"Lower your body again."

He was looking at my hips and the planks.

"You're aligned now. Perfect."

He walked up closer to my face. "Here's a pillow for your head, and an applicator. Insert it like you would a tampon."

"What?" I asked.

"It's not a real tampon; it's for the next game. And don't worry, it's made of clean material. It won't stay inside you for very long."

I rolled over to my side, then to my back. I sat up to perform the task he'd requested of me. While I'd grown accustomed to walking around naked for these games, I couldn't say the same about inserting a tampon in me. Real or not. It somehow felt more... personal.

As though he understood my inner conundrum, a second later, he turned around.

I parted my legs, removed the plastic cover, then brought the tip of the applicator to my pussy before pushing it in. It slid in like a normal tampon. The device in place with its super long string hanging out, I put the applicator back in the plastic cover.

"I'm done," I said, and Junichi turned around.

He took the wrapper I was holding. "Lay down in position again. Make yourself comfortable."

I obeyed, then turned my head to look at him. "Do I have to do anything?" I asked.

"No. Just stay there. Don't move and don't speak. When the game is over, you'll hear it. Then you can come back down and I'll meet you by the ladder."

He left me alone with my thoughts.

Soon porn music started playing again.

What is the fucking goal of this game? Objectification of women? Is it a cultural thing? First tit-slapping, then faceless pussy fucking—without a happy ending might I add—and now this weird boob and tampon game?

And how the fuck am I supposed to win *this game or increase the money I'll make if I don't even get to* do *anything? I'm all for new experiences, but isn't this a bit too... passive?*

A loud horn sounded, startling me a little, but I relaxed again. After all, what else was I going to do?

Hard objects began colliding with my hanging breasts. Then fingers. Then full hands grabbed me, but not in a sensual way. Fingers grazed the surface underneath my head. Slight vibrations reached my body when they were close, but it seemed they headed in all sorts of directions. Then one hand found its way to the opening around my hips. As though I was just an arcade game, these fingers felt me up, then pulled on the string like they were opening a set of blinds.

I flinched as the small device slid out of me in one fell swoop.

Then, as the porn soundtrack continued, I did my best to relax and somehow enjoy the rushed contacts I got, but when an eager hand started fingering me as though he was looking for loose change in his car's ashtray compartment, I couldn't say I enjoyed it. But at least the previous event had warmed me up, so my natural lube had made the experience a bit more bearable.

And then the porn music ended, which meant that this third game was finally over.

Thankfully.

1:20 a.m.

Junichi escorted me to the next area.

The wide room contained twenty white pods that looked like giant eggs resting on their side, each on their own platforms.

As expected, the other women and I were instructed to yet again pick a pod.

This time, I want to be front and center! There has to be some meshing again. I want to see the rest of these contestants! If they are to objectify me and the rest of the women here, I deserve to see their naked bodies up close and personal. I want to enjoy the view for once. Maybe I'll even get to see Blondie?

So, I walked to the pod closest to the line that had been painted on the floor, and Junichi followed me.

It has to be their starting point for the next game, no?

Once we reached the pod, he lifted a rounded door and told me to get in.

I climbed up the three steps leading to the pod and looked in: it was smaller than I thought it'd be. It was also much wider than it was high.

"How am I supposed to sit in this?" I asked Junichi.

"You won't be sitting. Kneel, then lean forward, with your face toward that meshing," he said, pointing away from the area I was hoping to get a good view on. "Get in fetal position."

So much for my plan.

I got into child pose, with my arms next to me, extended backward, my back rounded and relaxed. The bottom of my enclosure was actually very comfortable, once again padded with thick memory foam. A few slots enabled air to come in and out, but the view from those only covered the floor right below me. Through the meshing, I could only see the pod closest to me.

"Move back until your behind touches the pod," Junichi said.

I scooted back as far as I could, and his hands gently prompted me to realign my hips so I pointed a bit more toward the left.

"You're good. This game has an emergency stop. It involves regular sex and anal sex. If the contestant is being too violent with you, you press that big button in front of you, and he'll be disqualified. Do you understand?" he asked.

I moved my right hand toward the front, so it'd be ready, should I need to stop it.

"Don't press it unless you're sure."

"Okay, I get it."

"Good. I'll see you after the game. Warm yourself up a bit if you want." He closed the cover, and I heard him walk away.

I traced the outline of the emergency button, just in case I would have to use it, but I hoped I wouldn't. After all, I'd had anal sex before. But then again, there was the black man I'd seen earlier. Even his limp shaft was humongous. Anal sex with him could hurt.

I slid a hand between my legs and caressed myself in my darkened pod. A bit of light came in from the meshing and air slots below me, but not enough for me to see anything.

Then, while I was still busy with my warm up, the porn soundtrack began again.

A mere minute later, a panel slid open behind me.

Please don't be the black man, please don't be the black man.

First, it was a tip, and I kept praying. Then, a regular-sized cocked penetrated my pussy.

Thank you!

Gentle fingers feathered their way to my anus. Then something small poked its way past the entrance while he continued fucking my pussy. My anus closed again, although he hadn't retrieved what he'd put in. *Beads?* But for the first time in this game, I was at the mercy of a gentle lover. It almost felt normal, save for the egg pod I was restricted in.

An announcement was made in Japanese over the porn soundtrack, then the man came out of me. Whatever had been inserted in my ass was now dangling behind me. Angry shouts burst around the room in various languages. I only recognized an angry *Fuck* and *Hell no!*

What is going on?

Ten seconds later, my fuck fest resumed, and the man slowly inserted a second thing inside my ass, this one a bit bigger, but still manageable. His thrusts delighted me more and more and the added pressure from whatever he'd inserted in my ass improved the sensation. I moaned as he pushed a third, larger pearl up my ass. It made his dick feel thicker, fuller. The man behind me groaned and started pushing deeper into me. His cadence increased for a few seconds before it slowed right back down. He shouted something I didn't understand.

The unpredictable cadence of the man behind me disappointed me a little, it was smothering the inner fire that had been growing steadily in me until then.

What's going on?

Not being one who relied solely on others for pleasure, I slid a hand between my legs and toyed with my clit. Nobody said anything about penalties in this game (other than hitting the emergency button).

Maybe he saw my fingers, maybe he didn't, but he resumed a more satisfying cadence. I instantly forgave him for whatever had temporarily distracted him when he inserted the fourth bead into me. I definitely felt the large spherical shape on that one. My accompanying moan sounded loudly in my pod. As if I deserved a reward, a fifth bead got pushed into my ass. I was in heaven. The man was pounding me hard and fast now. I was on the brink as I'd never felt so full before. Just as I was about to come, my back instinctively pushed up against the top of my pod, but it was locked and I had nowhere to go.

How I wanted to feel that man's touch on my breasts, on my stomach, on my ass.

This game was both pleasant and disappointing.

Then, the beads and the man's cock retracted, much too fast for my liking, but it was no reason for pressing the emergency button. After all, he had brought me to the edge of ecstasy.

While loud moans and groans—both male and female—echoed all around the room, adding to the existing soundtrack, I continued to flick my clit until I reached climax and released the pressure that had been building up in me from the moment these games began.

I let out a long sigh of relief and cupped my hand over my throbbing pussy.

My pounding heart sounded louder than normal in the privacy of my pod, and images of the blond stranger danced in my head.

Maybe it was him behind me just now?

1:30 a.m.

"Women will now take the lead," said Junichi as he helped me out of my pod.

He'd brought with him a white, short-sleeved shirt and a red pleated skirt on a hanger. No bra, but Junichi had also carried with him huge white panties. I slipped those on first. They were so big they could almost be called granny panties, except they didn't go as high. They simply covered a lot more ass than I was used to.

Then I put on the skirt. Junichi had my measurements from before and it was no doubt a skirt that had been chosen for me. The waist fit perfectly, but I couldn't bring it lower than my belly button. Thankfully, the pleated design allowed for my ample hips but the length didn't really work for me. The lower part of my ass was hanging out.

I turned to Junichi. "Do you have a longer skirt?" I asked.

He motioned for me to spin around. "No, it's fine. That's the length we need."

I nodded and put on the shirt.

Once again, Junichi had elected the smallest size I could have fit in. My breasts pushed against the fabric, the top two buttons barely kept me in. The shirt had a red piece of fabric that followed the neckline, and I tied it into a bow, which effectively covered the buttons that threatened to pop.

To complete the outfit, I put on the pair of red stilettos he'd also brought for me.

1:45 a.m.

For the next game, we were taken to a backstage area so cold I could almost see my breath. The now familiar porn soundtrack played loudly behind the walls of the next set.

Junichi told me the rules for the game that was about to begin. "You'll run into the next room and select a column. Each has a few holes around it. Pick a hole and place your mouth on it. If the pole turns red, that means you didn't find the right hole. Pick another one and try again, until the pole turns green. Then, lick, suck, use your hands, or do whatever you want to please the man inside the column, but when the light turns yellow, you have to stop. Do you understand?"

I nodded.

"Then, once it turns yellow, run out of the room as fast as you can. It's a timed event. Clear?"

"Yeah," I said, nodding again.

"Good luck." He left me alone with the rest of the women contestants.

I rubbed my arms to warm up a little and get rid of my goosebumps. My nipples poked through my shirt but there wasn't much I could do about that. *That's probably the effect they want anyway...*

Once all the assistants had left our group, a loud Japanese voice boomed over the speaker. Then a loud buzzer sounded and we ran into the room. My breasts bounced within the confines of the shirt as I made my way toward one of the available columns. Not surprisingly, porn movies were being projected onto every available surface, including the columns.

The one I picked was about three feet wide, and around it, about six or seven black holes peppered the surface. They ranged from knee-height to shoulder-height. I picked the one directly in front of me. A second later, the background onto which the porn movie aired turned red. I moved clockwise and selected the one about hip-height. I paused in place; the column stayed red. I moved to the third one, this one very low, forcing me to kneel on the floor. I waited for a second; the surface turned green.

What now?

But before I remembered the rest of Junichi's instructions, a hard cock appeared. It was pink, with a pronounced kink toward the left, and a big vein on top. After licking its salty length and wrapping my fist around its base, I started to bob on my mystery man. I sucked and sucked, enjoying the man's warm girth in my mouth. For once, I controlled every aspect of it, and I relished in that fact: no hands to push it too deep against the back of my throat and make me gag. The tiled floor was hard on my knees, so I readjusted quickly. I took my mouth off it for a second but kept going with one hand as the other cleared a tiny rock that had somehow wedged itself under my knee cap.

A second later, my mouth was back on the man's dick, my tongue twirled around its tip while my fist went up and down his shaft. I sucked on the tip and was about to take him in deeper when the column turned yellow.

I let go of him, and he instantly retracted into his hole.

I got up and ran back the way I'd come in until I'd left the set. I joined the other three women that had already gotten out, and we waited in silence for the others to be done.

A few minutes later, once all of the female contestants had finished the current game, the porn soundtrack stopped, and our assistants came back to meet us.

Junichi walked up to me with a large Ziploc bag. "Please take off your panties and put them in here," he asked.

Can these games get any weirder?

The rest of the women were either talking to their assistants or taking off their panties.

No point questioning it.

I obeyed and slid them down my legs, seeing the large wet spot I'd left. I placed them in the bag Junichi was holding. He sealed the zipper-like opening then took the transparent bag away to God knows where.

Are panty vending machines a real thing?

2:00 a.m.

A few minutes later, our group was escorted to the next set.

Unlike the others before, the walls here weren't white, so I could only assume no porn movie would be projected during this game. This room was nearly all mirrors. But there were a few spots that weren't reflecting light: several black circles at various heights around the room, some were about one foot from the floor, others up to two and a half.

We were instructed to stand in line and Junichi approached me to whisper instructions in my ear.

"There will be a timer counting down from 10 to 0. You need to pick a hole and line yourself up in time. Then, if you're lucky, the hole will open and a man will penetrate you. If not, you'll have to run to another hole with a man behind it and line yourself up. The goal of the game is to have twenty-five full thrusts. Not twenty-four, not twenty-six. Once you have twenty-five, you run back to this line here. The event is timed."

"You mean I need to let the dick come out of me each time?"

"No, you don't have to. But for the thrusts to count, they can't be shallow. You need to touch the wall every time, then almost let the man out of you as you move forward. Do you understand?"

I nodded and he walked out of the set.

A short while later, the rest of the assistants were also gone and the porn soundtrack started airing again.

About twenty seconds passed before the Japanese announcer spoke, then a gong sounded. I started running toward one of the holes, but slowed right down because running on a mirrored surface in high heels was plain dangerous. Once I got closer to one of the black holes, I tried to see if anything was visible through it. *Nothing.*

I walked over to the next one. All were made of the same black felt fabric. They looked identical except they weren't all at the same height.

The timer on the large display in the middle of the room was still counting down: 5... 4...

I picked the nearest hole and moved my pussy down until I no longer felt the cool mirrored surface, but the soft felt instead. My feet were shoulder-width apart, nearly a foot from the wall behind me, my knees slightly bent. All in all, it wasn't uncomfortable.

1... 0.

The gong rang again and I could have sworn I heard a sliding noise right behind my ass.

Across the room from me, I saw a few unattended cocks popping into the room. The woman standing directly in front of me had a priceless expression on her face as her body jerked. Had her eyes opened any more, they surely would have rolled out of their orifices.

The woman next to me went to an available cock that had just appeared.

Should I leave and line myself up with one of them?

But just as the thought came to me, a thick shaft pushed into me slowly, confirming I did hear something before. I bent forward some more, then moved my ass away from the mirrored wall, feeling him slide out of my wet pussy. I pulled away slowly—unsure how long he was—until he nearly fell out of me. I reached between my legs to keep him at the right angle, then I pushed back until my ass flattened against the wall.

2...

I did my best to concentrate on counting thrusts as opposed to enjoying them.

3... 4...

But ignoring the sensations brewing and growing inside me was near impossible. I started counting aloud to prevent losing track.

As I tallied each delicious slide up and down the mystery pole behind me, moans echoed all around the room: some sounded a bit like cats being strangled all the way to bestial grunts.

"12... 13... 14..."

I'd settled into a rhythm now, but my body was aching to reach gratification.

"20... 21... 22..." I could feel my legs weakening.

So. "23..." *Damn.* "24..." *Close.*

I rammed my ass on the wall on the 25th thrust, and then debated whether I should put in a few more. I was so close... But women around me were already running toward the finish line and my competitive spirit kicked in, pulling me away from the wall and that wonderful mystery cock.

I can always finish myself off.

2:35 a.m.

But the next event followed immediately thereafter, leaving me no time to release my built-up desires.

Here's to hoping the next game will do the trick.

The moment we stepped into the next room, it felt like we'd entered a hot and humid jungle, except there were no trees, no animals. It was just a small, brightly illuminated room. Like fog lights, each beam coming down from the ceiling cut through the thick mist that filled the air.

Beads of condensation began trickling down my face, my back, my front, my legs. But the trickle soon made my entire skin glisten and ooze with sweat. My white shirt was now transparent and sticking to my breasts. I tried undoing a button, but it didn't do anything to cool me off. The blonde woman next to me tried to vent herself, but her shirt just clamped onto her skin as though it was a wet swimsuit.

There was no cool or dry air in this room.

Even the act of breathing became laborious, which made the room spin around me. I sat down... Or I may have fallen onto the floor instead.

A moment later, Junichi brought me a tall glass of water with ice. I let it rest on my cheeks for a second before gulping it down and nearly choking on the ice cube. Then, as if the universe had listened to my silent prayers, a large door opened, which let a burst of cooler air in, dropping the humidity levels down. Way down.

I handed my empty glass to Junichi and he left.

Over the next few minutes, the roller-coaster of climates continued, with really cold air now taking over the room. The dampness of my shirt turned it into a refreshing attribute. And it helped bring my senses back. I was now able to stand up again.

And finally, after the climate problem had sorted itself out, bringing the room to a normal and slightly cool temperature, an announcement was made in Japanese.

Junichi reappeared next to me and translated the instructions: "Pick one of the open tunnels. It will be dark. Crawl on all fours until you come across a couple of bowls on the floor. This is where you'll stop. Look up and tease those balls until the man gets hard. You're not allowed to touch his penis or they'll deduct points. You're limited to testicles, anus, and the area in between. Your tools will be your fingers, tongue, ice, and a warming gel."

"That's it?"

"It's a timed event. And you can get bonus points if you get both testicles in your mouth at once. Good luck!" he said.

I looked around and stood in front of one of the openings I now noticed. A few women were still with their assistants.

Once everyone was ready, a loud buzzer sounded. I got down on my hands and knees then entered the tunnel I'd chosen.

As expected, it was dark, but for now, I could still see a little light coming from the room I'd just left. I saw the tunnel make a left turn a few feet in front of me. My limbs went as fast as they could on the cool metal surface. Thankfully, it felt solid, not like a hanging vent that my own weight could make crash onto a floor below.

As soon as I made the corner though, I lost the faint light I previously had, forcing me to slow down and feel my way so I wouldn't bang my head on a wall. Little by little, I advanced until I finally touched a bowl. (It'd be more accurate to say that I inadvertently pushed and toppled it.) But feeling my way around, I found it again and realized it had a lid on. I brought it back next to the other bowl and remove both lids. One had cold ice cubes, the other a tube of something. It had to be the warming gel Junichi had talked about.

I looked up. Thankfully, my eyes were starting to get used to the darkness.

This part of the tunnel was much higher than the previous part. I sat down—the cool metal nearly shocked my exposed, wet pussy—and that's when I noticed something dangling above me. I reached up and my hand landed on one very long, limp dick. A loud buzzer sounded above me.

Yeah, can't touch it, but can't wait to see what he'll turn into once excited.

I reached higher until I felt the ceiling of sorts, then went looking for the man's balls. I had no idea which way he was positioned. But I soon found the clean-shaven sack hanging above me. It seemed small compared to his accompanying cock.

I folded my legs and rested my wet pussy upon my ankles.

The air was stale in the tunnel and I could smell my own arousal. I placed an ice cube in my mouth and let it melt a little, helping to cool off my urges as well. Then, with my cold tongue, I teased his balls. The temperature difference made them go up, then I grabbed them both and sucked on them. Both fit in my mouth, along with the ice cube. His dick twitched, his balls tightened and moved up some more, but I kept sucking on them until the ice was no more.

I spread warming gel on his balls with my fingers and blew on them, which made his testicles return to a more relaxed, slightly lower position. I began massaging his balls gently. I even spread some of that gel toward his anus, then got another ice cube in my mouth and repeated the process.

The man's dick grew both in girth and length. It was just beautiful... and irresistible.

I wrapped my hands around it. I wanted to feel its veins carving their unique signature onto the otherwise straight shaft.

An alarm sounded above me, but I opened my mouth as wide as I could to swallow the man's tip. There was simply nothing else that could fit. I sucked on it, my fingertips not even close to touching each other as I tried to wrap them around his girth. Red lights flashed all around me. I once again chose to ignore the alarm. I didn't care anymore. I was competitive like any other person, but I simply couldn't ignore that dick.

If I flip myself around, maybe I can push my pussy onto the tip of it?

Can I lift my hips high enough?

Worth a try.

I took my mouth away from his beautiful cock, and he disappeared instantly.

His dangling balls, his beautiful cock, all of it had retracted up past the slot in the ceiling... and the trap had closed again.

I heard Junichi's voice in the distance. "You can come back out now."

I've been cock-teased one too many times here.

My pussy now ached for real action.

My mind wanted real physical contact.

My heart... well, I couldn't care less what my heart wanted at that very moment.

3:15 a.m.

My assistant repeated the instructions again:

"Select a seat, then sit facing the front or back. When the game starts, a remote will drop from above. Use the knobs and buttons as you see fit. The goal is to come at the same time as your partner. When you reach orgasm, you must pull on the remote, as though it was a chain. You are NOT allowed to talk."

I nodded then walked in the next room. As per most of the previous games, porn was being projected on the walls, with the accompanying soundtrack blazing loudly.

This room looked near empty, save for a dozen very low, mini pyramids that were coming up from indented grooves on the floor. As I got closer, I realized they were more like mini-volcanoes, but with rounded, indented craters.

As ordered, I walked to one of the contraptions and straddled it, my bent knees positioned in the moat-like indent that surrounded it. Instantly, I realized the crater wasn't round, but oval, so I realigned myself so my pussy and ass were positioned correctly. A remote control lowered itself from above. I looked up. More strings dangled from various anchors above the set, each woman had already received their remote.

I got a hold of mine and inspected it. It had a large power button at the top, so I pressed it.

A second later, a slight breeze blew on my ass and pussy. My groin no longer rested on the previously hard surface of the crater. My legs were still anchored securely—although widely spread—on the rounded edges of the indented volcano.

Then, someone penetrated me from behind. At first, it was just something small—a finger?—then his dick, which was nice, although I would have preferred him in my pussy instead, especially after having seen that large cock in the last game. My pussy desperately craved some pumping action, and from something worth feeling.

Just as the thought crossed my mind, I had a second look at the remote. I pressed an unmarked purple button and my wish came true. *Kind of.* The dick that entered my pussy was bigger than the one in my ass. And it began vibrating. I looked down and saw a bright purple device, complete with life-like details. I wrapped my hand around the base below me and it felt soft and warm. I couldn't see who was handling it, just the person's hand.

He pulled it in and out of me in complete sync with his anal pumping action. This was the best torture in the world, and it made my entire body shiver. I knew I wouldn't be able to hold off very long. I tried to distract myself by having a third look at the remote. A brightly lit arrow flashed on the lower circular button. I moved my finger in an arc along the illuminated symbol and it reduced the intensity of the vibrations.

But even at the lowest setting, I was going to come any second. The man below me started thrusting harder, deeper. *Is he getting there too?* The intensity of his pounding had increased so much he actually pushed me off of my straddling position. I quickly re-seated myself before cranking up the speed on the vibrator. I could no longer control my body: I moaned and quivered with my eyes closed. I'd breached past the entrance and there was no turning back at this point. I quivered as I rode the wave of pleasure those games had triggered in me... then I remembered I had to do something. I reopened my eyes and I pulled on the string attached to the remote above me, and a huge bucket of icy cold water splashed down on me just as I reached the apex of my climax.

The finale would have been better without that... and if accompanied by the warm embrace of a man behind me, but it'd still been amazing.

The man pounded me a couple more times, then his warm juices exploded in my ass. A second later, he was gone, having pulled both his dick and the buzzing vibrator out of me.

I reached down between my legs and felt my pounding heartbeat through my swollen pussy. The crater had once again closed itself.

4:30 a.m.

At the end of the night, still a bit bewildered by what the special invitation had led to, but mostly pleased, I got changed back in my evening gown then slipped my participation prize in my purse: a hundred thousand yen. *Not bad!*

There hadn't been an award or closing ceremony at all.

I had no idea how points had been calculated or who had won the games. Then again, perhaps it was all a big scam, and nobody had gotten the grand prize, but at least I hadn't lost anything (assuming the video was to remain private).

Otherwise...

Heck, even if it goes public. Who cares? It was all good fun.

But as I was leaving the building, still lost in my thoughts, I spotted the handsome blond man about to get in one of the cabs that had been called for us.

"Hey, wait!" I called out as I hurried my pace toward him.

He turned to me, a confused frown on his face.

"Do you speak English?"

He shook his head. "No."

"*Français? ¿Español?*"

He shook his head again.

Is he going to be worth the trouble?

I pointed to him, then me, and then the cab.

He raised his shoulders, then nodded.

Does he think I just want to share a ride?

I stepped forward into his personal space and placed a hand on one of his hips, then looked him in the eyes, my mouth partly open.

Before I could overthink my actions, he'd planted his soft lips onto mine and wrapped his arms around my back. His ardent fervor added to my already kindled desires; I wanted to do him right there and then, but I resisted the urge and pulled back long enough to tilt my head toward the cab.

He nodded, took off his jacket, and we both slid onto the backseat.

I leaned forward to tell the cab driver my hotel address in English. The moment I was done speaking, Blondie pulled me back into his arms, and we resumed where we'd left off a few seconds earlier. *Well, almost.* He'd also taken hold of one of my breasts and his other hand had already worked its way to my knees, up my long flowing dress.

For a split second, I worried about offending the cab driver or creating some kind of cultural discomfort, but it had been too long of a night to waste my energy on that thought.

He can just look elsewhere, like toward the road ahead.

While my tongue mingled with Blondie's, my hands reached behind him. I untucked his shirt and let my hands slide up against his soft, warm back. I hadn't made out in a cab in so long, I'd forgotten how uncomfortable it was. But no matter the awkward positioning, after games that had involved too many faceless encounters, the warmth of his skin on my hands was invigorating. I couldn't wait to get the full-body experience.

And he seemed to share my eagerness.

His hand had already climbed to my thighs, which had raised the fabric of my dress as well. I parted my legs, rolling out a red-carpet invitation for his touch. His mouth pulled away from mine for a few seconds and I gently pushed on his jaw so I could meet his glance. In his steel-blue eyes flickered a hungry flame that flashed brighter than I'd ever seen.

By now, his fingers had breached the outline of my soaked thong. His soft lips zigzagged their way down from my earlobe to my chest bones, subjecting my neck to the perfect combination of sucks, licks, and gentle bites. My heart pounded hard and fast in my chest, but it was nothing compared to the throbbing going on between my legs.

Letting my head rest on the back of the car seat, I reveled in delight each time he caressed my skin with his soft, balmy kisses. I moved one of my hands to his head and let my fingers run through his thick, soft hair. He smelled of coconut and sea breeze; a deep inhalation of his cologne had me mentally transport our make-out session to the most exotic and private beach I'd ever been on...

But that's when the driver coughed loudly in his seat.

Blondie got off of me and I looked out the window. I recognized my hotel.

We're already here?

I pulled down my dress then fumbled around for my purse.

After digging out enough money for the fare and a tip, I exited the vehicle through the door that Blondie held open for me. I took the hand he offered and stepped out onto the curb.

5:00 a.m.

We rushed into the empty lobby and headed toward the elevators. One was there already; its bell dinged the instant I pressed the call button.

After stepping into the small space, I pushed my floor number, and Blondie spun me around before locking lips with me.

He'd already pinned me against one of the mirrored walls by the time the door closed. The bulge in his pants dug into my stomach when he pressed his hard body against mine. My chest heaved, and our mouths devoured each other's while his hands held mine immobile on either side of my head. In a muted clunk, my purse dropped to the carpeted floor as we sped upward.

As though a magnetic pull somehow connected our souls, my chest leaned forward. His lips headed down my cleavage while he kept me restrained. Desire and frustration mingled in my mind. I just wanted to lean into him, reach into his pants, ride his cock like it was the last one on earth.

The ding of the door sounded again when we reached my floor, so he let me go and walked out. But the fiery spark in his eyes and his loud exhalation made his intentions clear. I bent my knees to collect my fallen purse, and he offered his hand to help me up and out of the elevator.

And courteous?

I need to fuck this man right now!

I led him to my room, which was just a few doors down the left.

While I fumbled with my room card to get the green light I so desperately sought, he stood behind me, breathing deeply on the back of my neck. First, he lifted my dress up to my hips, then he pressed himself against my ass, his precious bulk poking my lower back, his hands resting on my waist, the flowing fabric of my dress piled on his forearms.

The green light finally appeared on the card reader, and I pushed open my door.

He'd slipped my dress up and over my head and arms even before the door softly closed behind us, granting us the privacy that hadn't existed earlier that night. Stepping backward in nothing but my heels and underwear, I pulled him toward my bed by his belt as I tried to undo it at the same time. He tossed his jacket toward the corner where my dress had landed a second earlier, then he undid the tiny black buttons of his white shirt.

When he exposed his chiseled chest, I pulled on his undone buckle and whipped his belt out of their loops. His waist button didn't stand a chance; it popped off its thread when I pulled on the waist of his dress pants.

A split second later, I fell backward on my bed—I'd forgotten how high it was—and Blondie landed on me, his lips munching at my neck. My hands found his zipper and undid it, setting free his manhood and drawing a huge smile on my lips.

How I love men who go commando. So fucking convenient.

He, too, had been clean shaved by those in charge of the games (or perhaps that was his regular 'do). I rolled my fingers around his girth. I admired its manly, majestic beauty for a second as he continued to pull down his pants.

Fuck. Where are my condoms when I need them?

While he fumbled with his shoes and pants, I rolled over to my side and reached into the small cosmetic bag on my nightstand. I found what I needed and unwrapped the first in the golden strip I'd brought with me.

As I attempted to roll over and reposition myself on my back, below him, he stopped me. His hands firmly on my hips, he flipped me on my stomach then pulled me back toward him; my limbs slid on the soft, silky comforter until my legs fell off of the end. He grabbed my ass, his fingers dug into my flesh as he caught me just before my knees crashed onto the floor below. He took the condom from my hand, then unrolled it on himself in record time.

A second later, he nudged my lacy thong off to the side, his fingers slid between my slick folds, and his cock thrust into me without further preamble.

Finally.

I swear a mystical creature had taken hold of my vocal cords at that point; there was no other way to explain the bestial roar that escaped my lips when my ass smacked against his warm skin. Each time he drove his hard cock deep into me, faster and faster, he took me up a few more notches. Physical nirvana was within reach. I arched my back, lifting my breasts up from the bed. I turned my head and caught a glance of him: his parted legs in a mid-squat position, his head tilted back, his mouth agape, his tongue in the corner of his lips, his grunts matching the cadence at which he was pounding me.

I let my heels find the floor below me, then straightened my legs, bringing my ass higher. He unfolded his height. Two of his digits traced a deep circle on my right butt cheek, then he cupped his hand and slapped me hard. Twice. Three times. I yelped on the fourth slap, but it morphed into a squeal as my pain merged with the blossoming orgasm that surged through my cells.

As though a perverted guardian angel had choreographed our encounter, he came into me just as my legs were about to let go. He pushed me forward in one final thrust. His warm chest landed on my back as I collapsed toward the pillows, my heart pounding, my pussy and soul finally satisfied.

9:30 a.m.

When I woke up a few hours later, Blondie had left.

No notes, no attempts at goodbye, nothing. Just a cold, empty spot on the other side of the bed.

The previous evening had proven itself to be entertaining—most certainly during its last stretch—but it hadn't fulfilled my deeper need for connection.

The games hadn't truly satisfied me, just like my self-induced orgasms had never really displayed that transcendent quality I knew to exist, even though I could count the instances I'd relished in it on only one hand. Something special, unique, almost unworldly happened when two people in love gazed into each other's eyes as they simultaneously reached their orgasmic apex.

For a few seconds, on those rare occasions, two truly could become one.

But it had been so long since I'd felt it.

In this lifetime, will I once again delight in such an exquisite, deep, and significant spiritual and physical experience?

Maybe not?

I let go of that depressing thought as I started packing my suitcase. I chose to think of something else—like last night's games, once more.

They'd mostly been about objectification. Some rich guy's perversion. I couldn't judge him for it because I wouldn't want anyone judging me for wanting what I wanted.

That being said, I had to admit that topic used to piss me off. Years ago, I'd get annoyed when a few members of an all-male construction crew whistled at a beautiful woman on the street. Now I knew my feelings had been hurt because they hadn't whistled *at me*.

When I look back in my figurative rearview mirror, seeing my path over the previous months, I think being objectified actually helped improve my struggling self-esteem.

Somehow...

Isn't it interesting how something not so good can be so useful in the big scheme of things?

But objectification had also led me to shallow, all-about-fun sex, which can be somewhat of a letdown after a while.

The more I think about it, the more I need to find something different. Something a little more meaningful, a little more compelling, a little more intimate. But I don't want to lose the progress I've made on the physical side.

There's gotta be a way, no?

But how...?

MY XXX EXPERIENCE
JAPAN

THE PLAN

CRAZY SHIT, I know! But it gets me every time. Talk about a hard night's work for my mystery stewardess.

My Japanese is non-existent, but I do know a lovely Japanese woman who recently started working with us, and I'd like to get to know her better. And maybe she can help me track down Sophia, or at least find a copy of that video.

So here are my options:

OPTION 1: Track down Mr. Suzuki.

I still don't know what airline Sophia works for (so I don't know which manifests to hunt down), but I Googled his last name, and it is the second most popular family name in all of Japan.
Likelihood of success: Nil.

OPTION 2: Find a copy of the game show.

It was obviously recorded, but no matter how hard I searched for it online, I couldn't locate a copy. During my travels, I've seen countless Asian street markets overflowing with manga porn and various ripped-off copies of movies, games, and comic books. I may be able to find a copy of that video in person.
Likelihood of success: Low to average.

OPTION 3: Track down Junichi.

I also Googled his name, thinking that if it were unique enough, I'd stand a chance to find him. But it's a very common given name for boys.
Likelihood of success: Nil.

The second option is the only viable one, and I've got an upcoming trip to Japan, so it works perfectly for me.

Now, let's hope my cute Japanese stewardess will be helpful in more ways than one.

WHAT HAPPENED

Wouldn't you know it, my plan was off to a great start.

And I didn't even have to try.

Within the first two minutes of meeting Ms. Keiki Yamamoto during the pre-flight meeting, I knew luck was once again going to be on my side.

"I heard about you," she said. "Your reputation with the female crew…"

Is this a joke? Is she part of some secret program put together by the airline to ensure I don't harass women?

"What did you hear?" I asked her in a voice low enough that she'd be the only one to hear me.

From my breast pocket to my navel, she slid a finger down my shirt. She poked her manicured nail behind my belt, pulling me in closer to her. "They say you're a well-endowed machine worth testing out." She pointed for me to lean down toward her. She whispered the rest in my ear. "I heard a test run is all women get with you. But it's a highly-recommended test run."

Well if that isn't the best compliment a man can get, I don't know what is.

"Interesting. Curious to find out first-hand?" I asked quietly, my eyes locked onto hers.

She didn't budge, but simply continued with the same daring expression in her eyes. "Maybe we can test each other when we land?"

"Possibly," was all I said, but I followed it with my winning smile and a wink.

She was putty in my hands and she knew it.

She broke eye contact and looked down.

So, it was with my mind in the gutter and high hopes of an entertaining layover that I embarked on my journey to NRT/Tokyo.

9:15 p.m.

As previously agreed, Keiki met me in the lobby of the hotel a few hours after we had checked in.

I was sipping a cold Kirin while waiting for her, hoping she'd wear something short that would expose more of her beautiful skin. But she joined me at the bar in a pair of skin-tight jeans, platform shoes, and a purple, short-sleeved turtleneck that hugged her small breasts. I offered to buy her a drink, but she turned me down, so I quickly emptied my own glass, settled my bill, and then we stepped out of the lobby to hail a taxi.

When she slid in the backseat just ahead of me, the tiny ass in her jeans still left plenty for my lazy imagination. She said something in Japanese to the cab driver before turning her attention to me. "We're going to the best night market I know. Can you tell me more about the movie you're looking for so I can help you find it?"

I told her everything I knew. No point in being sly or shy about it. I divulged every detail I'd memorized from my stewardess's description of the games.

She stroked my arm with her delicate fingers. "You're as naughty as they say you are... Will you let me watch those sex games with you?" The eyeliner she'd applied only serve to highlight the longing in her eyes.

"I'm sure that could be arranged."

I leaned in toward her, my hand on the side of her silky black hair, and I let my thumb caress her cheek. She bit her red-hot lips. As though my eyes were hypnotized by her shiny lipstick, I dove into her vanilla-scented space and kissed her. First, it was just a brush of the lips, but it evolved into something more eager, hungrier. I teased her with my tongue, and her response only served to light things up between us. My dick reacted by pushing up against the fabric of my jeans, so I readjusted, tucking the tip behind my belt for now.

We reached our destination too soon for my taste, which put an end to our friendly cab interlude. Keiki pulled away from me when the driver cleared his throat, which preceded some exchange in Japanese.

We got out, and I paid the fare once Keiki translated the amount for me.

My gorgeous, petite friend led me by the hand through a maze of smaller streets until we reached a busy night market, which had me recalibrate my definition of the word *crammed*. If she hadn't been holding my hand, I could have easily lost Keiki in the crowd here. And she was a fast walker that one... Surprisingly so, especially with her platform shoes on. I couldn't wait to see her ass out of those jeans.

Around us, the stands we passed sold everything: fresh sashimi, comic books, running shoes, cheap accessories, backpacks, noodles, loose teas and herbs, underwear, socks, puzzles, and way too many random-looking snacks to count. Smells piled on top of one another, resulting in something intriguing yet mouth-watering.

We weaved through the thick crowd and stopped at the first stand that sold movies. Among the long string of words that came out of the exchange between Keiki and the shop attendant a couple of feet away from me, I overheard Suzuki a few times. *That's a good sign, no?*

She walked back toward me. "The man says he doesn't have this particular movie, but he knows another merchant here who could arrange to find it for you."

"Do you know where the other merchant is located?"

She returned to the man and their exchange continued in Japanese. The man's hands pointed toward different directions as he spoke.

Then she was back by my side, pulling on my hand to get me going. "I know where to find it now. Let's go."

I smiled at the helpful man and followed Keiki toward my prize.

About ten minutes and three street blocks later, we paused our crowd-weaving in front of another stand that carried lots of movies and manga.

"I'll talk to the man and find out," Keiki said as she let go of my hand.

"Great, thanks. I'll stay here and browse through his selection."

The assortment of DVDs, CDs, and VCDs didn't appear to be sorted in any comprehensible manner. Interspersed together were music CDs, children's anime, Hollywood classics, and hard-core porn. I randomly picked up one of the cardboard sleeves wrapped in plastic. On it were three Japanese school girls in their uniforms, on their knees, hands tied at the wrists in front of them, their mouths wide open, tears running down their cheeks.

What the fuck is this?

I flipped the cover over to expose a naked man seen from behind, a whip dangling from one of his hands.

What?

I put it down, shaking my head. I flipped through more of the covers, until my eyes caught sight of a professional woman in a dress, half of it undone, one of her beautiful, augmented breasts fully exposed. Her smile was what I'd expect from a stock photo. I flipped the cover over. Several thumbnails competed for my attention: one of her squirting a jet out of her blurred-out pussy, another series of thumbnails next to each other where she straddled a man, staring at the camera, almost in a tutorial kind of way. Then a few more thumbnails of her ass and tits, fully exposed.

By now, Keiki had reappeared by my side. "He knows someone who knows someone... If you're willing to pay 100,000 yen, he'll find a copy for you tonight."

"What's that?" I asked her.

"Like 800 or 900 dollars?"

While I didn't expect to find my stewardess's video in a discount bin, the man's price seemed a bit steep.

"Can we tell him we'll think about it and see if other stands would have a copy?"

"I doubt anyone else would. Based on some of the people involved, you're lucky to even be granted this chance."

"What people?"

She shook her head. "Nobody you'd know."

"Okay then. Tell him I'll take it. When can he have it for me?"

She lifted her finger in the air, then returned to chat with the man who was staring at me in a way that made my spine shiver.

What's his problem?

But Keiki had already resumed talking with him, and that creepy sensation dissolved just as fast as it had appeared.

She was back by my side within a few seconds. "Give him half now, then he'll write down the address where we can pick up the copy and pay the other half. You have your computer with you to watch it?"

"Sure, I've got my laptop. Does giving him half the money now seem weird to you?"

She stared me down. "And you buying a pirated copy of a private video isn't weird? ...Or illegal?"

"Good point." I dug my wallet out and handed her ten purplish 5,000-yen bills. "Wait," I said as she was about to walk toward the man again, my money in hand. "I'll get this movie too. How much is it?" I asked her.

"The sign says 2,000 yen each."

I pulled two blue bills out of my wallet and handed them to her along with what I hoped would be an entertaining movie.

I watched the transaction happen from a distance. He wrote down something on a piece of paper and then handed it to her, with both his hands.

She came back to me and handed me my purchase wrapped in an unmarked plastic bag. She pulled on my hand again. "Come on. Let's go. We'll meet someone close to our hotel in two hours. We'll give him the rest of the money and he'll hand you what you want."

10:45 p.m.

Something somewhere had altered the vibe between Keiki and me, and I couldn't put my finger on it. Of course, the cab ride back suffered because of that mysterious thing.

We did have two hours to kill, and while I couldn't think of a better way to spend it then getting her naked and humping, I no longer thought she was in the mood for it.

"So, you're not going to tease me about my purchase?" I asked, lifting my bag in the air and hoping it would trigger a desire for some mutual fun.

She stayed silent for a while, shaking her head. "You like big breasts?" she finally asked.

"No, I'm not picky. I like ALL breasts. Small, medium, large, real, fake..."

Her lips drew a faint smile.

"I'm sure you have gorgeous breasts," I said.

"I know I do."

Is her vibe switching again?

"I'd like to see them... Just so I can fulfill that original request you had for me before we flew here."

"Are you hungry?" she asked as the driver slowed down in front of our hotel.

I dug in my jeans to retrieve my wallet. "Depends on what you have in mind..."

She insisted on paying the fare, so I let her.

"Ramen noodles okay with you?" she asked.

That damn vibe hasn't switched.

"Fine," I said, doing my best to hide my disappointment.

She walked into a busy restaurant and found two empty seats next to each other at the bar.

"What do you want?" she asked me.

I had no idea what my options even were. "I'll get the same as you."

She ordered, and then I confronted her.

"So, what's up? Did I do something wrong?"

"No. Yes. No."

Just like all women I'd ever met in my life had managed to do, she already had me confused. "Which is it? Did I do something you didn't like?"

"Not directly."

"Then what is it?"

"I'm nervous about the people we'll meet," she said.

"People? I thought you said we'd meet one person?"

"I don't know. I've never ever been in contact with those kinds of people."

"What do you mean?"

"The man who recorded that video..."

"Mr. Suzuki?" I asked.

"Shhh... Don't say his name." She looked around us, as though I'd just insulted someone important.

"But isn't it like saying Mr. Johnston or Mr. James? A name that's not particularly rare?"

"Let's call him Mr. James then. This particular, very wealthy Mr. James isn't someone you want to mess with."

"Isn't he just a regular rich guy?"

She looked around again before speaking, and when she did, her voice was so low I had to lean toward her to hear her words. "He didn't get wealthy by legal means."

"Video contraband?"

"You'd wish it was that."

I lowered my voice as well, and this time I leaned to whisper in her ear. "What is it then? Drugs? Weapons?"

She cupped her hand next to my ear to speak. "Much worse than that."

But before I could ask her more questions, our steaming bowls of noodle soup sat in front of us.

"Let's forget about it and enjoy our food," she said.

11:15 p.m.

After I paid for our meal, I double-checked my wallet to see if I had enough money for the upcoming transaction that had Keiki so worried. I definitely didn't want to make things worse by accidentally swindling the guy or guys who'd be trading with us.

"Time to go," she said, looking at the clock on the wall.

"I'm ready. Please lead the way."

She held on to my hand again as we walked around the block. And this was no sexy hand holding that promised a happy ending; this was the hand of a young girl looking to be reassured.

The more we walked, the more I psyched myself up. I'd always been a man's man and I was ready to deal with whatever man or men Mr. Suzuki would send to meet us. Cultural differences be damned.

"We're here," she said, looking up at a noodle shop that looked very similar yet different from the one we'd eaten at only minutes ago.

That's where criminals trade contraband in Japan?

"Let me go in," I said.

"That's silly. You don't even speak Japanese."

"Good point. At least let me go in with you."

"Okay," she said, nodding vehemently as we entered the noodle shop.

As I was about to whisper a question in her ear, a short, skinny man approached us and said something in Japanese.

She bowed, answered, and then nodded to me.

I took out my wallet and handed out the stash of pre-counted bills I'd located in their own compartment.

He handed me a small USB stick. Not what I expected, but hey, movies can be saved on a stick instead of a DVD. I certainly didn't want to risk offending him, so I let it slide. But what I didn't understand was why Keiki and he were still talking.

He's got his money. I've got a copy of my game show. What's the holdup here?

The man handed Keiki a small black bag. I had no idea what he was telling her, but I saw fear in her eyes.

She nodded profusely, bowed to the man, and then pulled me by the elbow as she rushed out of the restaurant.

She kept looking behind us as we hurried back to our hotel.

"What's going on?" I asked.

All I got was a shake of the head. And her head kept shaking until we made it back to the safety and privacy of my room.

11:25 p.m.

"What's going on?" I repeated as I framed her petite body between my arms, locking eyes with her. "What did he say? What did he give you?"

"Don't worry about it. It's my problem."

"No! I obviously got you involved in whatever this is. I'll help you get out of it. Tell me what I can do."

She snaked her way out of my arms, then headed to the mini-fridge. She opened it. "A drink will help. Go get us some ice, please?"

She handed me the empty plastic bucket from the top of the fridge.

"As long as you promise to stay here," I said, agreeing against my will. "I'll be right back."

I hurried down the hall, unable to find the ice machine at first, but when I walked by the staircase, I saw a sign that read "Ice machine 10th floor".

By the time my bucket was filled and I'd walked back to my door, I saw Keiki waiting outside of my room, the door barely ajar behind her.

"Don't close it! I left my room key on the desk."

She moved her index finger to her lips and then motioned for me to come closer. When I reached her, she whispered in my ear. "We'll share a drink, you'll watch your movie, then you'll call me. Once you're done with whatever this game show is, I'll need you to take me. On your bed. I'll need you to be rough, rip my clothes off, tie me up. I'll try to fight you, I'll attempt to yell. I'll pretend to not enjoy it... I may even cry, but I'll be loving every moment of it. Understood?"

This woman deserves a prize for flip-flopping.

"What? Why not now?" I asked, placing my hands on her hips and moving into her space.

"I want you to enjoy your game show first. After all, this is what you really wanted, no?"

"Yes... But who's to say you won't change your mind or fall asleep before I finish watching it?

"Don't worry, I won't. I promise."

I certainly didn't want to risk it. "Wanna watch it with me?" I asked.

"No, I've got something else to do. Call my room the moment you're done watching it.

I met her eyes and only saw truth in what she was saying.

"Why are you telling me all of this now then?"

"Because I don't want to explain what I want you to do to me just before you do it."

I guess that makes sense?

While I wasn't particularly into what she suggested, it could be hot. Especially if she was into it. Maybe those violent Japanese porn movies were actually based on real popular fetishes.

"Should we have a safe word or something?"

"Probably."

"Probably is the safe word?" I asked, confused as hell.

"No, I don't know. Think of something."

And, whether it was because I was in Japan or because I was exhausted after running around, the only word that came to mind was ridiculous. "Samurai?" I suggested.

She raised her shoulders. "Fine by me."

"But if I decide to cover your mouth so you can't scream and get us kicked out of the hotel, how will I know I've gone too far?"

She raised her shoulders again. "Don't worry. You won't."

11:35 p.m.

Keiki opened the door and took the ice bucket from my hands. "Can you make me a drink, please?" she asked.

"Sure. What's your poison?" I opened the mini-fridge.

"Whiskey on the rocks."

That woman was something. Hard to follow, but definitely *something*.

I dropped two ice cubes into one of the two glass tumblers on my desk, then dumped the contents of one mini-bottle into it before grabbing and opening a can of beer for myself. I carried her glass over to her. "Here you go, Keiki."

"Cheers," she said, clinking her glass against my can and winking at me.

She reached for the USB stick I'd left on the corner of the desk earlier.

"So, this is the game show you needed to find so badly..."

"I hope it is," I said, taking it from her hand. "Do you think they ripped us off?"

"Don't think so. Put it in your computer and see?"

I unpacked my laptop, placed it on the desk, and then turned it on. After taking a seat on the chair, I inserted the stick into one of my USB ports. I sipped my beer while the stick's red light started flashing.

A few seconds later, my computer had recognized it, and I clicked my way to the files listed on the drive. Among a bunch of extensions I didn't recognize, I saw an .mp4 file called "Sex Games".

I double-clicked it and a large window opened, showing large Japanese characters.

"What does this say?" I asked Keiki.

"Private Sex Games."

The screen had moved to something else, with lots of text.

"And this?"

"This video is private... blah blah blah, cannot be copied... You know. *That* screen."

I nodded and then the movie began with naked men running on a game show set.

"This is it!" I said.

She stood up. "Then that's my cue to get out."

"You sure you don't want to watch it with me? Maybe there are some things I'll need you to translate? Or maybe we can make things a bit more interactive?"

She tilted her head and pursed her lips. "I'm sure you'll understand all of it. I think you've got a busy evening ahead of you." She walked up to me, downed the last sip of her drink, and then kissed me. "But you MUST call me the instant you're done watching it. I want to hear all about it. You know my room number."

Her lips lingered on mine some more, my hands went up to grab her ass, but she walked away from me.

"Later," she promised with a wink.

And with that, she exited my room, her tiny rump still as enticing as ever.

I could imagine a thousand ways to reward Keiki for her helpful work tonight. She'd get my porn-Oscar-worthy performance soon enough. Violent and all, if that was what she wanted.

But what did that scrawny man tell her that had her so worried?

And I didn't know what had happened while I'd gone to fetch ice... She seemed much more relaxed when I got back.

But I killed those thoughts. I had something much more important to take care of right now: I had to work on identifying Sophia.

I walked into the bathroom, took off my clothes, and then put on the lush bathrobe the hotel had provided. A box of tissues and my carry-on size of lube in hand, I sat in front of my computer and began watching the games, the red light of my expensive USB drive still flashing.

11:50 p.m.

After a few more shots of naked men running on various sets, a quick screen transition fit for an original Batman fight scene (in Japanese) flashed on my screen. Then, two columns of five animated GIFs appeared; they reminded me of porn-site thumbnails. On the left: five limp dicks; on the right: five erect ones. The commentator said something in Japanese, then, about ten seconds later, blue diagonal lines were traced between the two columns, using the same technology a sports commentator would use to explain a play—except that limp and erect junk was matched.

What is this shit show?

After a short, erotically themed interlude that consisted of various women coming together in vocal harmony, a large headline popped onto the screen, followed by the first hint of English: *GAME 1*.

A wide shot of several male contestants standing in line served as background for whatever the Japanese commentator needed to go on about. Based on the visual symbols popping up on the screen, I could only assume he was providing instructions for this first game. The cartoon-like images reminded me of what my buddies and I used to doodle in the margins of our books when bored in high school: artful but childlike-drawings by horny boys.

At first overly circular boobs were drawn, then two stick figures were added. An arrow was drawn from one man to one boob, then a second arrow from the other man to the other boob.

The screen got wiped clean of the initial drawings, then an erection was drawn in white ink. Whoever was drawing over the screen traded his white pen for a red one, then wrapped the erect dick in a circle, then traced a diagonal line across it. *No erection allowed?*

Below it, a downward arrow and ¥10000 flashed on the screen. *Is that a penalty?*

Then a timer icon appeared. While I hadn't gotten any of what the fast-talking Japanese man had been going on about for the past couple of minutes, I believed I'd at least gotten the gist of the rules.

After another short transition with a "3... 2... 1... Go" countdown, my computer screen showed a gaggle fuck of bouncing junk as the male contestants ran in front of the camera one after the other.

Then the screen changed to a grid format once again, and with a cartoon-like sound effect, boobs popped into their spots on the grid in their oh-so-amazing glory.

Finally! Something worth staring at.

Nipples—large and small—were represented in an excellent variety of skin colors. The women's cup sizes varied as well, but two pairs were obviously man-made. There could be more, it was hard to know for sure without giving them the good squeeze they deserved.

I paused on that screen. Not for a self-indulged hand session, but because I wanted to see if I could recognize Sophia's beautiful breasts. Although I didn't have the photo of her in that wet bikini top (darn Tracy who was so protective of a stranger's privacy in Mexico), the image of her large nipples and areolae was forever etched in my mind.

Are her breasts part of that beautiful line-up?

But no matter how many times I tried to pause the movie, I couldn't get a clear enough shot to know for sure. Two of the women could match what I recalled of her beautiful breasts.

And when the camera panned out to offer an overall view of the set, I spotted an Asian man paired to compete with a muscular red-headed man. Unfortunately, the camera never showed them in any of the up-close shots. Not that it would have allowed me to see Sophia's face hidden in her dark box...

The first game lasted a total of two and a half minutes (at least based on the timer at the bottom of the screen). Two of the men received an erection penalty, one while squeezing one of the marvelous triple-D tits and the other while licking off a very perky but smallish black breast with a large nipple. A vertical line split the screen into two, then a horizontal line split each column into two rows. The commentator narrated a replay of the penalty occurring, zooming in on the men's dicks as they swelled and rose during the game.

I couldn't blame them. My own soldier had become armed and at the ready at some point during the event, but I wanted to resist the urge for now, so I'd only undone the belt of my bathrobe to let myself rise in complete freedom.

12:05 a.m.

The video cut again with a Batman-like fight-scene flicker, then another dick-matching interlude began with other contestants, one of them dead easy to guess (and immensely ego-killing). With only one black dick in the bunch, it was impossible to get its match wrong. And impossible to feel adequate in comparison to it.

When the grid faded out, the screen showed a row of male contestants again, all butt naked, dicks at rest. Some were short, others tall. Some skinny, some chubby, all with various hairiness levels... Well on their chests and heads at least. All twenty contestants' junk had been shaved to nothing.

The Japanese commentator began talking while drawing new cartoony instructions.

At first, he drew music notes, then an erect dick. Then, a stick figure with an arrow pointing to one of the strange-looking devices being shown in the background. The commentator circled a button on the screen then traded his white pen for a red one. He drew a red circle, then a stick-figure pointing toward the exit.

He traded his pen for a green one, then the word FUCK flashed on the screen followed by the number 25 and some Japanese characters. The symbols + and - appeared, with the same downward arrow and ¥10000 amount I'd seen earlier.

When the penalty disappeared from the screen, the camera panned out to get an overall view of the set. It was as though the porn industry had taken over both the games' projection and sound systems. It was so loud and exciting I had to lower the volume. While I enjoyed my porn and was not ashamed of it, I didn't want to bother those who shared walls with me. Could be a young, jet-lagged family for all I knew.

A loud buzz echoed, not unlike the starting horn at the beginning of a race, and the men hurried into the room and picked their pod as fast as they came in. The closer pods were chosen first. A few red lights appeared and those contestants left the set.

Those lucky enough to get a green light made the games a lot more interesting to me and my inner voyeur. Each pod had been fitted with a camera, which had the perfect viewing angle. At first it was one green-lit pussy on the screen, then it shrank to display a second, then a third... All shaved and exposed, like a sight for sore eyes. I paused on the screen for a second to better appreciate the view. Lips of all shapes, shades, and sizes. Some thin, some swollen, some large and droopy, some glistening wet, some barely visible. I took a screenshot of that screen so I could use it again later.

While my dick insisted I stare at those beauties a little longer, my brain knew there was a whole lot more to view. I gave myself a couple of pumps then resumed the video, my poor dick only more aroused for it.

The male contestants got busy, obstructing my view on each video thumbnail. A ticking counter appeared below each view, totaling the number of thrusts by each contestant. A few passed the magical number, but none did fewer.

Watching the pussies just after the men left was my favorite part and compelled me to resume my hand job. Too bad they didn't leave that screen on more than a few seconds, but that's why the rewind and pause buttons had been invented.

I particularly liked the one in the bottom left corner: it dripped a small stream. *Maybe a female squirter in the gang?* And the one with the red fingernails in the middle row that showed initiative to finish herself off after the guy left was also pretty inspiring for my taste.

Is this Sophia? She wrote about her red manicure, but did all contestants have red polish on?

I didn't know, but I left the screen paused there for a little while.

After all, I was only a man. And a horny one at that.

Once I'd relieved myself and taken a brief, cold shower, I was back in front of my computer, one hand on my mouse and a cold can of refreshing Sapporo in the other, ready to move on to the next game.

12:30 a.m.

After yet another round of the same dick-matching game, the video showed something I hadn't expected: a list of names along with their scores to date.

Will I see Sophia's name?

But as I made my way down through the top ten, I realized the names were not only for the male contestants, but they were also fake: John Thomas, Packer, Mr. P, Schwartz, Schlong, Rod, Peter, Jimmy, Dangler, Johnson, Dick, Willy, Wang, Mr. Winky, etc.

Whoever Mr. Suzuki was, he'd hired someone who spoke English well enough to come up with those clever names. *Does Mr. Suzuki speak English?*

Not that it mattered to me, but John Thomas was currently in the lead.

Once the score disappeared, the Japanese commentator appeared live on the set wearing night-vision goggles and a football helmet. Well... at least his voice sounded like the man who'd been talking while drawing on the screen off camera, but I didn't know for sure (nor did I care).

A camera followed him as he opened the doors leading to another game room that was pitch black. Once fully in the room with the door closed, the camera switched to infrared mode, and the commentator reappeared (kind of). His heat imprint became visible and his silhouette showed him pointing to a corner of the room, where the camera subsequently zoomed in. A woman stood there, but only two sections of her body were visible on thermal, night-vision mode. Whatever material had been used to hide the rest of her was clearly blocking her heat signature. But her breasts and hot pussy were easy to spot with their bright contours.

The camera zoomed out and slowly toured the room. Tits and pussies could be seen above, left, and right. If I died right now, that's what I'd like purgatory to look like: the kind of prison cell my soul could use to expiate my sins of the flesh... Over and over again. Even better if the women hidden in the walls and ceiling were those who'd been my best fucks in this lifetime... I shook that thought away, unsure why it had come to mind in the first place.

The camera then exited the room. Once out and back in regular light, the commentator took off his helmet and goggles, threw them to someone off the frame, then caught a small thing mid-air. The camera zoomed in on his fist: a string dangled from it.

That has to be the tampon Sophia wrote about. Come on, man! Nobody wants to see this...

But I kept looking anyway.

He pulled on the string and released his fist at the same time, showing what the string was attached to. Once again, the camera zoomed in on a very small, see-through tube that contained something cylindrical and white. The tube was smaller than my pinky. He unscrewed it and tapped the tube repeatedly against his palm until a tiny bit of rolled-up parchment paper fell out.

He unrolled it and directed the front toward the camera:

The word BONUS flashed across the screen in the same Batman-like animation.

Then I saw a number written on the minuscule scroll.

A list of bonuses appeared on the screen for a couple of seconds, then a computer-generated image replaced it. It showed a 3D representation of the room with women's bodies embedded in the walls and ceiling, a bit like what a 3D Battleship board would look like. Naked bodies were aligned either horizontally or vertically on all surfaces. But thankfully for them, none appeared to have their heads below their feet.

The screen split into two, and the left side showed contestants entering the game room with football helmets on. Unlike the commentator, the contestants didn't wear thermal goggles, but such a camera had been fitted in the room. Men were walking blind in that room, hands either reaching toward the ceiling or in front of them. They collided against each other too many times to count. In fact, it was a bit boring to watch. Although I knew Sophia was one of the women hanging from above, this dizzying fumble-in-the-dark game wasn't going to help me see more of her. And soon enough, the thermal lens footage was replaced by regular video footage showing the men exiting the room with their bonuses in hand.

After showing off the number to another camera, the computer-animated mockup of the room started showing colored bodies on the other half of the screen, probably those who'd been claimed already.

A few minutes later, that dull game had come to an end, and so had my beer. I got up and grabbed another one, hopeful that the next game would once again ignite my desires, or at least show me more of Sophia's body.

12:45 a.m.

The transitions had become predictable. A final set of dicks were matched, and the scores got tabulated once more. Willy had taken the lead, but in my books, I'd gotten at least silver. Out of the variety of ethnicities and physical statures of the contestants, I felt pretty damn proud of my own tool. Okay, not the biggest in the world, but bigger than nineteen out of twenty was a pretty fucking good way to prove what I already knew to be true.

I'm sexy and I know it.

When the camera focused on the set again, the naked men stood with their feet shoulder-width apart, their hands behind their backs, their erect dicks pointing to all angles.

These games are getting worse by the minute.

Where did the ladies go? Bring back those naked pussy cats... Show me the one I'm looking for.

A lineup of Japanese women dressed as school girls appeared out of nowhere and began tossing rings at the male contestants all the while flirting with the camera whenever it approached one of them.

Even though most men moved their hips to try and catch the rings heading their way, let's just admit the school girls' talents didn't involve, include, or have any tie whatsoever with throwing skills. But they *did* look hot in their tiny red and blue outfits.

Damn hot.

Not many rings landed around the men's dicks, and even fewer stayed there. One man with a particularly vertical erection lucked out and got a bonus: a kiss from one of the girls and a ten-thousand-yen prize.

The men walked off the stage, and the Japanese commentator started speaking fast while drawing icons on the screen, which had by now faded to black. First appeared a clock crossed out in red *(not a timed event?)*, then a cartoony ejaculating dick showed a penalty of twenty thousand yen. While the commentator wiped off his scribblings, the camera entered the set where the next game would be held: the room looked like a futuristic, minimalist, and spotless henhouse for giant mechanized chickens.

The video zoomed in on one of the egg-shaped pods for this game and the hand of whoever held the camera pressed a large button.

Ding, ding, ding!

The games once again got interesting.

There it was. In glorious high-def, smack in the middle of my monitor, a splendid, fully shaved, pink pussy. It'd materialized from the bottom up when the button had been pressed. I'd hit that magic button 24/7 if I could. In fact, to the insistence of my dick, I rewound the video a few times. And a few times more.

And then I paused.

If that view could be wrapped up and sold as virtual reality... The world as we know it would end.

And that beautiful image had me abusing myself successfully for the second time since I'd begun watching the games.

I took a screenshot of the World's Best View, and then un-paused the video to see what would be next.

A short pan a second later exposed a little more of the woman's gorgeous ass. Then, a wider pan revealed a small tray next to the egg. On it was a string of five beads—each increasing in size, up to about an inch and a half in diameter—

and a conical insert whose widest point was that of the middle bead. Both devices glistened with a thick coat of shiny lube. The camera stayed in this shot, and the commentator began drawing a dick over the pussy, then he drew an arrow pointing from the small tray to her asshole.

He went on way too long with his explanations. The rules had to be more complicated, but who cared? Certainly not me. Instead, I wrapped my hand around my shaft and concentrated on that woman's pussy while he droned on.

Then, through computer-animated ninja trickery that went well beyond my expectations for a private game show that wasn't aimed at the public, the screen showed how a woman was positioned inside the pod. The focus was on a red button in front of her face. A few lightning bolts came out of her ass, and an angry emoticon appeared over her face. Then, the animated woman pushed the button, and the camera zoomed out to show the cartoon man behind her getting crossed off in red.

What?

Then the computer animated video panned out to display a lot of those pods. With tiny popping sounds, women were superimposed to some of the pods, but not all. The animation continued, with men running into the room and choosing pods. Those who selected an empty pod were crossed off in red as well.

Oh, so being crossed off just means they're out?

Before I could wrap my head around the rules, the black screen transitioned to the male contestants getting ready, putting on condoms, and lining up in a single file.

A few seconds later, the funky porn groove began, and the doors to the game room opened. Men dashed to each select a pod, then they pressed their respective buttons. After half the pods turned bright red one after the other, some contestants left the room. Those lucky enough to have gotten a green pod stayed.

Magically, the screen changed to a tiled version of two rows of five beautiful peaches. My eyes instantly went toward the black beauty and her particularly lippy, swollen pussy at the base of the oval opening. A couple inches higher, her pink anal ring appeared within that same gap in the otherwise solid egg.

Hmmm. I sped up my pace, until a short and skinny man began fucking up my focal point—literally. His small pecker took me right out of my fantasy. I looked at the other available pussies, wondering which was Sophia's.

While I knew my stewardess had selected a pod near the entrance, I didn't know which thumbnail went with each pod. With no carpet of any kind, only skin color could guide my guess. But no matter which was hers, it was definitely a very fine, elegant specimen. The tiny pussy in the top-right corner was getting pounded vigorously, then the first bead of the device got shoved into her ass. The visible part of her green-lit pod turned red and a loud buzz aired over the porn soundtrack.

Too bad. She was pleasant to look at.

But, taking her out made the tiles rearrange themselves to fit into a three-by-three grid, which made them all bigger. Better. My imagination added in their scents, my accelerating fist their warmth, their tightness.

Tiny icons popped on the screen, showing one item for each contestant. More than half had been tagged with a cone. I leaned a bit closer to my screen, focusing on another part of the footage. One woman's folds glistened from her own juices.

But as I got back into a nice rhythm, this time looking at a slick pussy that was being treated like a proper lady with patient, gentle thrusts, a Batman-esque SURPRISE interrupted the video with a vinyl-record scratching sound.

I anxiously waited for them to be done with their long-winded Japanese explanations so I could return to my beautiful images. But when the video feed resumed, the pussies and asses were no longer the focus. Instead, the unlucky contestants who'd been expelled were returning to the set, each walking toward another male contestant.

Team work? Weren't they managing just fine on their own?

The newly returned contestants, confused looks on most of their faces, each picked up the items that the lucky contestants had not elected.

Then another SURPRISE appeared on the screen.

I had absolutely no idea what happened there, but the contestants weren't happy. I even heard one say "No fucking way" in English. That man immediately left the set. Others seemed unsure whether to stay or leave. A loud countdown appeared, seemingly forcing them to decide quickly. The top prize in yen flashed on the screen, along with a large question mark.

What do they have to decide?

But when the countdown reached zero, what happened slowly became clear to me.

The lucky contestants resumed their previous tasks, the unlucky ones took position behind them. The newly-returned unlucky contestants started pushing the device into the previously-lucky-but-definitely-not-lucky-anymore-contestants' asses.

I walked away.

And so did my erection.

Should I turn this off?

While those games now appeared to be on a downward spiral heading way past my comfort zone, they could hold important information... Maybe my stewardess's full name. And maybe I'll see her naked and recognize her. I could actually see her face for the first time.

I returned to sit on the chair at my desk, but covered my eyes with my hands and waited for this game to be over.

But when a cacophony of delighted screams—both male and female—started airing loudly, one after each other, and one on top of each other, I parted my fingers to peek at what was happening.

Not a single man looked offended anymore, save for one guy who was doing the inserting; he was grimacing. The men sandwiched between the pussies and the other men were ALL enjoying the game now. Many sandwiched men were coming right now, their mouths open, their faces almost frozen in awkward ecstasy.

Really?

I took my hands away from my face and noticed that most of them had already retrieved the devices from the women's asses. The final male-male-female threesome was just finishing up, now taking the full screen.

And as they wrapped up that game, the camera showed men fist-pumping each other. The same men who had looked so confused and offended before.

Really? Could it really feel this good?

1:05 a.m.

Although the last bit had been hard to watch, I was heftily rewarded for my patience when the next game started.

The camera zoomed onto an eclectic row of female candidates, all dressed in short skirts and white blouses, hair parted and tied in two ponytails just like my stewardess had described.

Among the group, three brunettes instantly got my attention. I took a screen capture of their faces: the strict-looking one with the luscious lips, the one with shorter hair and the button nose, and the taller one with the Mona Lisa smile.

Which one are you, Sophia?

Can her nails help me identify her?

But the nails of all three brunettes—like those of many of the contestants—had been painted in one shade of red or another. *Fuck!*

Then, as though the show had been sponsored by an old episode of Baywatch, a horn sounded, and breasts of all sizes started bouncing up and down, left and right in slow motion. A few well-endowed women restrained their movements by pressing them up and against their chest. All three brunettes had either C or D-cups.

Then, one by one, they came to a halt in front of one of the large columns. They all glued their gorgeous red lips onto the surface in front of them. Some columns turned green. As they did, a mini thumbnail of all green feeds began to appear on the screen. Dicks popped out of these openings, and within a few seconds, the lucky contestants' blow jobs were tiled onto my screen, separated into two rows of five videos.

I'd unfortunately lost track of my brunettes in the process. Red lips were hard to differentiate. But how I'd love to re-watch this game once I knew which one she was... Imagining it was my own cock she'd eagerly swallow like that. I'd let her lick it, nibble it, suck it... She could do whatever she wanted to me.

I spat in my palm and resumed stroking my own shaft, imagining her warm mouth instead of my hand.

Then the video footage showed columns turning to yellow, bringing my attention back to one specific thumbnail. After each turned yellow, the feed switched to another camera, this one within the column itself. One after the other, the male contestants came into a bucket.

Well... In the general direction of that bucket. Some redecorated the walls instead.

1:20 a.m.

Unfortunately for me, the female game transitions weren't what I'd hoped they'd be.

Mr. Suzuki could have included a pussy and tits matching game, no?

How I would have enjoyed that...

But instead, the camera showed the backstage area where one male contestant was standing in front of a window looking into a mirrored room. A few feet away from him, another man was on his knees. Then, once the camera zoomed out, another male contestant appeared within the shot. He was standing, too, but with his feet slightly below floor level.

A cartoony transition then popped on the screen. It reminded me of those Whack-a-Mole games from carnivals, except that the moles had been replaced with smiling dicks and the mallets with naked women figures bent in half.

The words "Game 6" flashed on the screen and I got to see the set from the female contestants' side of things. It all made sense now. The mirrors were one-sided, like those in police interrogation rooms, except that we weren't looking at murderers, just women lined up in their high heels, super short skirts, and white blouses.

Oh wait!

The blonde's round, naked ass dangled below the hem of her skirt. Then I spotted another one.

They've taken off their panties!

And it's with added vigor that I resumed priming my pump.

I forgave Mr. Suzuki for not including the transition I'd have loved to see the second I realized he'd placed cameras under the floor instead.

The sight was priceless. A lineup of pussies between sets of high heels. Some shier than others, some boldly exposed between parted legs. All of it to the same groovy porn beat.

I bet they didn't even know there were cameras under the floor!

So worth it!

A gong sounded, and I focused on the button-nosed brunette as she ran toward a black circle against the back wall. A loud countdown appeared on the screen. When it reached zero, the gong sounded again and the cameras switched to various new angles. I'd lost track of my brunette, but I'd gained the ideal view on all my lovely pussies.

Some got poked at. Some stayed put for a few seconds, without any action. Some left and went to a different spot, including one that left a streak of her moisture on the mirrored surface as she slid down before leaving.

Hmmm.

With one hand handling my weapon and the other fiddling with the rewind, play, and pause buttons on my keyboard, I'd say my needs were being met.

I had the best seat in the house, short of owning one of those lucky dicks that got to feel the warmth and tightness of those gorgeous pussies.

The one in the top corner tile had generous folds that parted easily when the dick behind the wall pushed through its opening. Her red fingernails made an appearance, ever so briefly, as she grabbed her ass just behind her pussy and parted herself a little. She slid down and slammed her ass flat on the mirrored wall. Then again, and again.

Come on, baby. Keep it up.

Small numbers popped on top of each of the tiles, all numbers increasing steadily, along with my excitement.

As I enjoyed matching her rhythm, another pussy took over the main shot. The large-lippy specimen was being pushed by a monster of a black dick behind her. Another camera captured her jaw as it dropped, then her eyes nearly popped out of their sockets as she reached behind her and wrapped her hands around that humongous appendage.

A Batman-esque interruption appeared again, this time Japanese characters followed by a question mark.

She spat on her hands, then spread her spit onto the tip of the cock poking at her, making it glisten. She aligned herself with the man behind the wall, her head looking between her legs. Then she faced forward as she pushed backward onto the man, barely hiding the tip of the man's tool in her pussy. The screen was now split in two. One camera focused on her heaving bosoms as she inhaled and exhaled deeply; the other on her pussy and the major deconstruction work about to happen there.

How is this even going to fit?

Then, she lowered herself more: a good two inches of him disappeared into her body. A loud cry came out of her. Then, she slowly pulled herself away, her eyes turned backwards, as though she'd passed out.

A loud alarm sounded, and the screen zoomed away from the woman in deep pain (or pleasure?) and focused on another female competitor. She was heading toward the finish line, her tits joyfully bouncing along until she reached the announcer and high-fived him.

1:35 a.m.

After showing an updated score board with fake names, the screen flashed with the words "Game 7".

The camera showed a new set—yet again—with just ten men sitting with a beer in hand, smiling at the camera. Their upper bodies were leaning back against blue beach chairs, but I had no idea what they were sitting on since their lower bodies were hidden underneath a large horizontal surface with an old-fashioned joystick on it.

As though they had read my mind, the screen shifted to a computer animation showing their sitting arrangement. It showed a man, butt naked (big surprise), with his flaccid equipment dangling between his legs through a hole in the chair. The hole wasn't big enough for the man's ass to go through, but large enough for his junk and some of his butt crack to benefit from the breeze below (or whatever the purpose of that hole was).

Night-vision cameras then showed the assortment of sacks and dicks dangling in their own thumbnails. It wasn't cold in there based on how low things dangled.

The Japanese commentator began speaking faster while drawing his rule icons.

It showed various times along with bonuses. For each additional 15 seconds, the male contestants would receive a bonus of 10,000 yen, up to 100,000 yen. Then the commentator moved the joystick, which showed a matching camera with night-vision settings. The word BONUS flashed on the screen. The commentator drew tits and wrote 10,000 yen. He then drew a pussy with the same bonus amount.

A countdown began ticking down on the screen. When it reached 0, nothing happened, except for men raising their beer bottles and cheering each other from a distance.

Beer drinking can't be what they're being timed on?

But the next footage clarified things. A horizontal line split the screen into two. The top part still showed the men resting on their chairs. Some drinking, some moving the joystick, but most doing both. The bottom section of the screen was dark green, in night-vision mode with women crawling on all fours, their bodies hot, especially their pussies, but they disappeared out of sight after turning out of the camera's angle.

Then the screen split into ten thumbnails which likely displayed what the men were controlling with their joysticks because most of the shots made me dizzy. Then some of the images started making sense. A woman, still crawling on all fours, but this time facing the camera. Her hair appeared wet, her eyes weirdly freakish-looking in that mode, but thankfully the man zoomed onto something else. The woman straightened her back and sat up. She collected her ponytails and brought them behind her back, pushing her tits forward in the process. Even in night-vision mode, her areolae were noticeable, her nipples showing concentrated heat. A loud "cha-ching" sound played and this man's thumbnail showed a 10,000 bonus.

When the first fifteen seconds had elapsed, all thumbnails showed another 10,000 bonus.

I glanced at the other thumbnails, most of them now much steadier. One showed a woman still walking toward the camera, the man zoomed onto the long crevice between her dangling breasts as they swayed in her shirt. A bonus was added to his thumbnail.

On the next one, an agile tongue tickled a sack, then the woman's mouth opened wide and she fit the entire thing in her mouth. *Like what Sophia described in her journal. Is this her mouth?*

My own equipment responded, wishing it had been the chosen sack. I wrapped my hand around it while my other hand pumped away to a great shot of a woman's pussy seen from behind. She was on all fours, her knees nearly shoulder-width apart, her skirt only covering the top of her ass; her entire crack and pussy gleamed. A line of sweat (or juices) was running down her inner thighs. That man deserved the bonus that appeared on his video stream. I also deserved a souvenir of that, so I took a screenshot.

I swear the heat of the event somehow transcended time and place and had me sweating at this very second. There was so much visual stimulation coming at me, I couldn't focus on trying to spot Sophia based on her journal entries.

Some thumbnails disappeared, making more room for the remaining ones. Another great shot grabbed my attention. This one was a close-up shot of someone's wet pussy. Her female juices had collected to form a drip which was ready to fall off any second now. *Cha-ching!*

Then a tongue licked the invisible line from a man's balls to his asshole. She pushed apart the man's cheeks and pushed the tip of her tongue into his hole. The camera was zoomed enough to show the man's dick engorge as she kept tickling his back end. A red line was drawn across the feed, and his thumbnail disappeared.

More and more thumbnails disappeared one after the other soon thereafter, and I decided to finish myself off. I rewound to that glorious ass and pussy shot and gave it my all, imagining that it was my mystery stewardess I was staring at (because it could very well have been).

1:50 a.m.

Pleased with myself, I cracked open another cold beer before resuming the rest of the games. The progress bar showed very little time remaining, so I assumed only one game was left. Sophia had described a fantastic game, and I was pretty sure it was coming up next.

When I resumed the video, it was everything I hoped it'd be... and more. So many beautiful women receiving pleasure without men being visible and ruining my fantasy.

While I knew the male contestants were fucking them from below, I imagined I was the one doing it to them. The blonde woman was arching her back so much she had to be a gymnast. I swear her head almost touched the floor. She had long let go of her remote and had decided to rip her shirt apart instead. She was fumbling with her augmented tits as her body pulsed from the pounding she was receiving from underneath the set.

Then I remembered my goal and looked at the three brunettes instead.

Which is Sophia?

The button-nosed brunette with the shorter hair was getting fucked in the pussy, not the ass. She was riding that cock like a good cowgirl, using her knees to lift and lower herself onto the man below. *Not her!*

The one with the luscious lips didn't look strict at all anymore. She looked high on her own orgasmic tsunami. *Is this Sophia?* Her entire body rocked with whatever the man below was doing to her. She was glued to her seat, so I couldn't even tell which orifices were occupied.

I found the last brunette and focused on her. Her eyes were closed, her Mona Lisa smile replaced by a slanted smirk that widened as her brow furrowed. Her mouth opened, her groans became audible over the porn soundtrack and then her eyes opened and spoke volume as to the intensity of her orgasm. She reached up for the remote and pulled on it, splashing her arched back with a mixture of water and melting ice pellets. Her now transparent shirt showcased the erect nipples I'd fantasized about for months.

Sophia...

I didn't need to see the purple vibrator being retrieved below her pussy to know she was the one. I could have recognized those beautiful breasts anywhere.

I rewound that last game and re-watched the entire thing, only paying attention to my no-longer mysterious Sophia.

She. Was. Hot.

Everything about her was perfect. She was obviously lost in her own universe while getting fucked. She moved so sensually, so instinctually. Her face and body were beautiful, but I wasn't sure if I liked her mind and thoughts more... At least the ones she put down in her diary.

She's quite something, this Sophia.

How I would have liked to be the one taking care of her right then and there.

I took a screenshot of her when she looked straight at the camera. Her traits were beautiful in a regular, pretty girl-next-door kind of way... until she smiled... or came.

When I reached the end of the video, applauses filled the air when the last woman finally came.

Then the screen went dark. No credits. Nothing.

Too bad. I'd have liked to see the contestants' names, but it was still the best 100,000 yen I'd ever spent.

My hard-on was roaring, but I restrained myself and didn't watch the entire thing right away. I could do it later.

And again and again later.

But right now, I had a promise to fulfill.

2:03 a.m.

I picked up the phone and dialed Keiki's room number.

"Hey, it's me. I finished my video."

"Great, I'll be right there."

Not even thirty seconds went by before I heard a discreet knock on my door.

I walked over, tying up my robe and doing my best to hide my erection by tucking my shaft under my belt.

Upon opening the door, she whispered to me while she slid something in my bathrobe's pocket: "Stick to the plan. When you get upset later, read that note."

Then, she walked in, leaving my mind puzzled and my cock deflated.

What the fuck?

My hand dove in my robe pocket which now contained a thick pile of folded papers.

She'd already sat on my bed and was speaking up when I turned around. "So, how were your games? Worth it?" she asked, looking at my laptop, whose monitor had turned to screen-saving mode.

"Fuck yeah!" I said, confused but playing along. "Drink?" I offered.

"Sure, I'll take another whiskey if you still have some."

I opened the fridge to see. I poured her a drink in the glass she'd left behind earlier and grabbed another beer for myself.

I walked it over to her.

She took a sip, then smiled at me with devious intent. Although I wasn't sure, I could have sworn she whispered the word "Now" at that point.

I looked at her for confirmation, and she gave me a slight nod.

Game on, then!

I drank a large sip of my beer, then placed my can on the corner of the desk before taking her drink away from her mid-sip. I pushed her shoulders back and she landed flat onto my bed, so I straddled her.

"What are you doing?" she asked.

"Taking what I want," I said. "I'm doing what I've been thinking about ever since I met you," I said unzipping her jeans and trying to pull the fabric down her legs.

Damn these things are tight. I managed to lower them enough to reach mid-thighs. *Fuck'em. They can stay there. Plenty of room for me.*

"No!" she said, reaching for the waist of her jeans and starting to undo my hard work.

But I took care of that by pulling her top off over her head. Her arms simply had to follow or they'd break.

Her turtleneck out of the way, I admired her bright yellow bra for a second and noticed it clipped in the front.

"Stop what you're doing!" she said, this time a little louder.

She had me fucking confused now. But I swear she once again nodded at me, ever so slightly. With one hand, I undid her bra and exposed her tits.

"Gorgeous breasts, like you said." My lips went for one of her small nipples while my hands pulled the straps past her arms.

"Stop!" she yelped.

"The neighbors will hear you. You gotta shut up!" I ordered.

"No, I won't keep quiet unless you make me," she said.

I untied the belt of my thick terry-cloth bathrobe and pulled it out of its loops. "That'll do. I'll have my way with you," I threatened before placing the belt in her mouth and tying it behind the back of her head.

Her eyes didn't shine with fear, just with fun.

Fuck, this is confusing.

I flipped her small body so her stomach and beautiful tits were now resting on the comforter. Doing so exposed a tattoo that began on her lower back and finished underneath her panties: cherry blossoms in shades of black, red, and pink.

Didn't expect that at all!

But seeing her in this position gave me an idea. I reached for the ends of the belt that hung behind her head and I tied her wrists behind her back.

Now free to do as I pleased in near silence (after all, she was putting on a good show with the muffled mumbling), I pulled her jeans farther down. This time, I took my sweet time, and I got them fully off, one leg at a time.

Now naked save for her yellow panties and that terry-cloth belt, I parted her legs. My fingers grazed the fabric of her underwear. Her excitement had already left a wide, dark, wet spot that I caressed. *Damn. She's really into this shit.* First I only scraped over the fabric, then I let the tip of one of my fingers glide underneath it.

Her legs closed on me when I did that, but I brought her hips to the edge of the bed and sat myself with my face right between her legs. Her scent was invigorating, inviting, and too potent to ignore.

I moved the wet fabric over to the side. She moaned through the belt, and the moans got louder when the tip of my tongue tickled the hairiest pussy I'd licked in a long time. But her musky, salty taste made it worth it.

I hated to destroy beautiful underwear, but I followed her instructions and ripped her panties right off her, revealing the rest of her gorgeous tattoo. I brought her lower body up on the bed again, my open bathrobe letting my cock free to stand gloriously over her gorgeous tattoo background.

I ditched my robe and let it fall on the floor, then walked over to my suitcase for my stash of condoms.

When I returned to the bed, Keiki had rolled herself up in a ball and was now facing the bedroom door.

Her own words echoed in my mind as I made my way around the bed to look at her. *"I may even cry, but I'll be loving every moment of it."*

Tears were indeed streaming down her face.

What the fuck? With three fingers, I tilted her chin and made eye contact with her. She winked at me.

I pulled the belt out of her mouth, to see if she would say the safety word, but no. Nothing but quiet cries came out of her lips.

This was new territory to me, but heck, she winked at me again and I knew I had to go on.

I sat her up on the bed, her hands were still tied behind her back.

"If you don't like the belt in your mouth, maybe you'd like to try this instead," I said, attempting to shove the tip of my cock in her mouth, but she shut her lips tightly.

"Then if not there, I'll have to find somewhere else for me to fuck you." I pushed her on her back again, then spread open her legs. Cat-like cries started coming out of her mouth. I shoved my index finger into her pussy. It slid in like a hot knife in butter. I added another digit. "Should I fuck you in your hairy pussy, or would you prefer it in the ass?"

Her only reply was a shake of the head.

I pulled out my fingers and used her own moisture to lube her ass. Then I pushed my pinky in.

Her cat-like noises went up in pitch and she started panting.

"Is this what you want then?"

My pinky kept tickling her ass as my mouth ripped open the condom I held with my non-dominant hand. Good thing I'd had years of practice unrolling condoms with either of my hands. A second later, I was armed and ready. I parted her legs even more, then pushed the tip of my cock into her wet pussy.

My right pinky was busy maintaining its post, but I used my left hand to turn her face toward me.

I needed to see her expression. I needed to reassure myself I was doing the right thing.

Her eyes were now red from crying, her mouth barely open, the kitty-like cries nearly silent. I brought myself up and close to her face.

"Keiki?" I whispered.

"Go," she whispered back.

"No?" I repeated louder.

She shook her head. *Fuck. What does that mean?*

"Do you want me to fuck you like a Samurai?" I asked her, hoping that my question would remind her of the safety word and she'd use it.

"No!" she said.

I rammed into her while our eyes were locked on each other's. She smiled for a split second, then resumed her kitty-like groans and cries.

This is messed-up shit.

But I'd already wasted enough time second-guessing myself. It was too fucking late for that. She was too fucking wet, and I'd given her plenty of chances to really stop me.

I rammed and rammed into her, hitting the back of her small womb as I thrust deeply into her pussy. I closed my eyes and imagined she was Sophia. Now that I could picture her face, her tits, her pussy... It wasn't long until I burst in excitement, and from the pussy contracting around my shaft as I started catching my breath again, I knew Keiki had had a good time as well.

2:25 a.m.

I grabbed my robe from the floor, put it on, untied Keiki so I could get my belt back, and then walked into the bathroom.

After cleaning myself up and splashing a bit of water on my face—coming to terms with a new threshold I'd never thought I'd pass—I went back into the room. Keiki was getting dressed. She had a big smile on her face.

"That's really what you wanted?" I asked.

"It was perfect. Thanks!" she said.

I let that wave of relief wash over me. I opened the fridge and grabbed a cold bottle of water. I lifted it up and looked at her. "Sure," she said.

I tossed it her way, then grabbed one for me as well. "Nice tattoo, by the way. Are you part of a gang?" I asked jokingly before sitting myself next to her on the bed.

"Funny you mention that..."

"What do you mean?"

"I'm not, but these men we got the video from, they're with the Japanese mafia. They've been recording you since you got back, including our little fun here, and they will have no issue releasing this video to our employer if you don't return the USB stick you got from them."

"What?"

I stared her down, giving her a chance to say she was joking. *She has to be.* But she didn't budge.

"Why would I? I paid for it fair and square."

She shook her head. "No, you only paid for the opportunity to watch it."

"What? Says who? I want to keep it."

"If you keep it, then they'll upload the video of you fucking me against my will on the internet. They can hack their way to any site, including our airline's. Wouldn't that look lovely on the home page? I'm sure it would make a big difference to your career. And mine."

Fuck. I replayed what else I'd done in my room while watching the games. *I don't want that footage out either...*

"No, you're not going to want to release that video. You're in it as well."

"Charlie, it's not *me*. It's *them*. My involvement was dictated by that man in the restaurant. He's waiting for me in the lobby. I need to return the stick and the camera very shortly. They said that if I don't cooperate with them, and if you don't give back the stick, they'll force me to report you to the police as a rapist."

"Now, that's FUCKING GREAT," I yelled, getting up.

"Hey, lower your voice and don't be mad at me. That's what I was referring to earlier," she said, her eyes going from the pocket of my robe to my eyes.

But a thick pile of papers wasn't going to help me calm down.

"How the fuck did they get a camera in here?" I inspected the room. "Where is it?"

Keiki tilted her head toward the wall near the door.

I couldn't see anything. Then I saw it. A tiny screw-like object just below a picture frame. In the middle of it, a tiny pin-sized hole with a lens. "You fucking put it there?" I asked, ripping the thing off the wall.

It wasn't attached to anything.

"How does it work? It's not connected to any wires."

Keiki was looking down, shaking her head. "The man said to just place it where it would have a good view of the bed and he ordered me to stage that little scene with you. That part of the plan was kind of fun, though. You have to admit..."

I shook my head at her.

"Did you think this through? What's to prevent them from releasing the video anyway? What's to prevent them from blackmailing us for the rest of our lives?"

"Well... I don't know. I just want this all to disappear. They've got bigger fish to fry than embarrassing us both or destroying our lives, no?"

I paced the room, inhaling and exhaling deeply.

How can the best day of my life also be the worst?

"They say bright ideas often come in the shower. Want to give it a try?" she asked, her eyes once again going from my robe pocket to my eyes.

I grabbed my cellphone and then locked myself in the bathroom. Maybe she'd written more information in those papers. And if not, maybe Google would have a fucking solution to getting out of a Japanese Mafia blackmail situation.

3:30 a.m.

After reading and re-reading her pages, I'd gotten the gist, but I wasn't any closer to a solution. She spent two paragraphs apologizing profusely before listing the facts she knew based on what the man had said:

- The camera captures audio and video with 180-degree coverage.
- The laptop must be close to the camera to receive the signal, so chances are it doesn't broadcast anything live. It probably records it onto the stick.
- Attempting to copy the game video to a hard drive will wipe your computer clean.
- If the man in the lobby doesn't receive the stick back by 4 a.m., he'll come and get it himself or track us down anywhere in the world. There's a tracking device on the stick.
- The man will check to see if I recorded the video he needed.

And the list went on about threats he'd made to Keiki and her family. It fully explained why she'd been so shaky on the walk back to the hotel.

So, I can't destroy the camera. I can't destroy the stick. I can't copy the video.

That means I can't fucking prevent them from blackmailing me and Keiki for the rest of our lives.

Can I go to the police with that? Or is it possible for the Japanese Mafia to be in cahoots with the local authorities?

Fuck. Fuck. Fuck.

And I don't understand enough about computers to get myself out of this shit.

...But I know a guy who does!

I unlocked my phone and found the contact information for the hacker who'd been so helpful to me a few weeks prior.

I couldn't really call him because I didn't know how sensitive that camera microphone was. I texted him. It was early here, but thankfully the time difference worked in my favor. He should be up.

Hey bud.

I'm in trouble.
Can you help me right now?

A couple of minutes elapsed, then I saw the three dots indicating he was typing a reply.

What's going on?

I described the situation as succinctly as I could and then waited.

Send me photos of camera and list of files on stick.

Give me a minute.

I walked into the room. Keiki was looking at me, hope in her eyes.
"Hey, would you do me a great favor?" I asked her.
She pursed her lips. "Sure, what?"
"Since I can't keep that video, I'd like to at least have a souvenir of this evening. Would you mind posing for me?"
She had a crooked smile on her face. "Okay..."
But when I instructed her to take her top off and sit right next to the camera, the light bulb lit up in her eyes.
I took two photos. One for me, with Keiki in her bra. The other for my hacker, with Keiki out of the zoomed in area.
"And how about you take that gorgeous bra off and sit right here," I said, tapping next to my laptop. "And we could take a few more?"
"Sure," she said.
The camera lens was now facing down against the desk, so it shouldn't see what I was taking pictures of, but it probably still recorded the sound.
I put in my password to get rid of the screensaver and then clicked my way to the window that showed the list of files on the USB stick. Then I took two pictures as well, their focus—and purpose—very different from one another.
"Thanks, Keiki. These photos may come handy for future solo sessions," I said before walking back into the bathroom.
I sent the two images my hacker needed and waited patiently.

Don't touch these files.
You want me to wipe the stick clean?

No, they'll check to ensure the videos are there.
Can you delete the new video file only, but not right now?
On a timer or something?

How much time do I have to code this?

I looked at the clock on my phone.

20 minutes before I have to return the stick.
Could you activate that timer in 24 hours?

OK.
I'll email you a file in 15.
Leave that stick connected when you open my email.
Double-click the attachment.
I'll take care of the rest.

3:55 a.m.

I got dressed while waiting for that precious email.

Right on time, my man delivered.

After following the instructions I received, I ejected the USB drive from my computer and gave back my most prized possession to Keiki.

"Do you want me to take it to the man downstairs?" I asked.

"I have to do it. But could you come with me, if you don't mind?"

"Of course, I'll go with you."

She placed the camera and the stick in the same black plastic bag, and then we left my room.

The elevator ride down was spent in total silence. I let Keiki walk ahead of me in the lobby. As promised, the scrawny man was patiently sitting alone, reading a newspaper. When he saw us, he got up.

Keiki handed him the same bag he'd given her hours earlier. He pointed to the empty seats in front of him and we sat down.

He pulled up a small laptop from a little pouch that had been resting next to him. He powered it up, inserted the stick, and then double-clicked on one of the files. After turning the screen so all of us would see what he was doing, a small video window popped up, showing me at the computer. He fast-forwarded until it showed the both of us on the bed. Under other circumstances, I'd have probably enjoyed watching my own performance. But not right now. Not like this.

The man then clicked on the other video file, the one I'd watched earlier. For a brief few seconds, he fast-forwarded through some of the moments I'd enjoyed hours before.

Then it was over.

He ejected the stick, closed the small laptop, packed it away along with the stick and camera, then nodded at Keiki before saying something in Japanese and leaving the hotel lobby.

A minute must have elapsed before either of us moved or said anything.

"What did he say?" I asked.

"Pleasure doing business with you."

I exhaled and prayed that the hidden file my hacker had added to the stick would work its magic as promised.

We rode the elevator up again.

"I'm fucking glad this is behind us now," I said.

"What's the solution you came up with?" she finally asked.

"When we board our flight, the latest video on that stick will self-destruct. Or, if anyone attempts to copy it elsewhere, it will also self-destruct."

"And how did you do that?"

"I know a guy."

NEXT STEPS

That Japanese layover was officially the craziest shit I'd ever gotten myself into.

But Keiki's words when we parted ways a few hours later made me feel better.

I quote: "And your reputation is well deserved. Glad to have had my test run, even though it was under strange circumstances."

I don't believe my mystery stewardess knew who was behind those games, but I'm sure glad I finally have a face that I can see when I think of her now.

And those screenshots I took?

Priceless. They've added countless details to my wet dreams.

I've got one last entry to revisit in her journal. And now that I know what she looks like, I could think of a way to track her down for real... finally.

Her Spanish layover—more like an extended vacation—was much closer to regular life than her Japanese experience, and she did make a few one-on-one connections with Spaniards that she may have wanted to maintain, so it's not too far-fetched to believe that she may still be in contact with them today.

I'm looking forward to snacking on delicious *tapas* and inexpensive Rioja wines while tracking her down.

PART X

SPAIN

THE STEWARDESS'S ENTRIES

SPAIN

2:25 p.m.

NOT ONLY WAS Spain one of my top countries, but San Sebastián, aka Donostia, was my favorite city in the whole world.

The scenery, the architecture, the beaches, the food, the people... What was *not* to love?

And those Spaniard men? Seriously, how could so many of them have drawn winning numbers from the genetic lottery? Maybe I was partial, but with geographical roots as diverse as theirs, it seemed that both men and women ranked way above the world's average looks in the land of the *tapas*. Or my attraction to the alluring Spaniards could be related to the fact that my father's ancestors had shared their genes generations ago. I'm sure Freud would explain it in a way that would make me blush, but it wouldn't shave an ounce off my excitement about the coming days.

As my plane landed in Bilbao, I wondered how many times I'd visited Donostia to date? *Six, seven... ten?* Too many to keep track of, yet still not enough for my taste.

But thankfully I'd made a few friends, which helped reduce the costs of my visits. During my last trip, I'd found the perfect apartment on Airbnb. So, this time, I re-connected with the owner and managed to bypass the site's fees by arranging to pay him cash instead. I looked forward to once again sipping a few drinks while overlooking the ocean. Best of all, the beaches and places to eat delicious *pintxos* paired with local wines were all within walking distance. I still couldn't wrap my head around the official difference between *pintxo* and *tapa—*

perhaps it was a regional vocabulary preference or a Basque word for the same thing, or maybe it had to do with the toothpicks—but the bite-sized pieces of delicious local specialties were always incredible. My mouth was watering.

I couldn't wait to see if I could uncover new ones I'd yet to try.

Both new *pintxos* and new men could satisfy my hunger.

4:45 p.m.

As promised, Eduardo met me when I got off the bus from Bilbao.

"*¡Hola amiga! ¿Qué tal tu viaje?*" My short, bearded, gray-haired friend kissed me on both cheeks, and before I could reply to his question, he surprised me by switching to English and repeating himself. "I want to practice my English with you. So, tell me. How was your trip, my friend?"

I smiled at him. "All good. I'm so happy to be here again. How have you been?" I asked.

As expected, based on his behavior during my previous visits, he grabbed my luggage from me and wheeled it to his car as he stumbled through his answer.

Chivalry is alive and well in Spain. So nice.

After putting my suitcase in his trunk, he drove me to the apartment and, through various iterations and self-correction of his answers, he shared a long list of mundane events and incidents that had happened to him and his wife since I'd last seen them. The thing that lit him up the most was the classes he'd been taking and his upcoming English exam.

"Will you come to my birthday party tonight?" he asked.

"*¿Cuántos vas a cumplir?*" I asked before catching myself. Speaking to Eduardo in English was a little weird. "Sorry. How old are you gonna be?"

"I will have fifty-two years old," he said, his eyes glued to the road in front of him.

"Happy birthday! But you'll *be*, or you'll *turn* fifty-two, not *have*, like in Spanish," I corrected him.

"Ah, yes! Thank you. I always make this mistake. So, do you want to join us? It will be my wife, my sister, and a few friends. All good people."

The traffic had come to a halt in front of us, so he turned to look at me. His smile was genuine and warm.

If the past months have taught me anything, it's that when life hands out unexpected invitations, it's best to accept them.

"I'd love to. What should I bring?"

"Nothing, just you. No gift. We'll just hang out, have some drinks and *pintxos*, and chat. Probably in English, since a few of my friends are also looking for opportunities to practice."

"Sure, sounds awesome!"

Just as we turned the corner to the street I'd be living on for the coming days, he pointed to a bar. "This is where we'll go tonight. Meet us there at around 10 p.m., okay?"

Oh yes, the Spanish eat late.

"Perfect. Should I dress up?" I asked.

"No, wear something comfortable," he said just before turning around the block.

Luckily, Eduardo spotted a place for us to park within a minute or so.

We walked to the apartment together. Eduardo rolled my suitcase behind him at his insistence, while I only had to deal with my purse. Then he carried my bag up the five flights of stairs—and for that I was really thankful. Once we reached the *izquierda* door, he pulled out the sturdy, oddly-shaped key I recognized. It was nothing like the typical keys I carried. He inserted it into its old-fashioned keyhole and spun it two full counterclockwise rotations to unlock it, then pushed open the door.

"After you," he said.

I entered my home-away-from-home with a delighted smile on my face. The exquisitely decorated apartment was just like I remembered it. The exposed beams in the living room gave it a certain anchoring quality, and the fresh-cut flowers in a vase in the center of the kitchen table were the cherry on top. The windows had been left open, letting in a lovely, warm breeze.

He handed me the keys, and I reached into my purse for my wallet. I pulled out the agreed-upon rent and gave it to him.

"Do you want a receipt?" he asked.

"No, it's fine."

"As usual, you can help yourself to any of the food in the cupboards or fridge. And feel free to read any of the books and watch any of the movies stored in the living room. Make yourself comfortable and call me if you need anything."

"Perfect. I'll probably take a nap; then I'll see you tonight at the bar."

And with that, we hugged, and he left.

10:20 p.m.

Too many instances of me standing alone, waiting for my friends to show up had taught me that Spaniards (and most of my friends in Latin America) didn't define punctuality the same way I did, especially when going for drinks or other casual events.

So, once I awoke from my nap, I took my sweet time getting ready. I showered, put on a touch of makeup, then got dressed in a black skirt, high heels, and a red top. During the process, my stomach growled a bit. I let it be. No point in ruining my appetite with the cheap snacks I'd saved from the flight.

Pintxos are going to be so much tastier (and probably healthier as well).

The breeze coming into my room convinced me I didn't need to take a jacket, so I left my apartment, headed down the stairs, and then out on the street to meet Eduardo and his friends.

As I walked toward the bar, I overheard various couples as our paths crossed. Their interdental *th* lisp instead of the regular *c* and *z* sounds made me smile. During my first visit to Spain, how I had loathed that sound! But it had grown on me like mold on cheese: its lure slowly but surely gaining ground on my heart until the Castilian lisp somehow began to sound sexy.

I reached the bar Eduardo had pointed out to me a few hours earlier and walked in; the potent garlic aroma reached my nostrils, while the loud hubbub of the patrons bounced against my eardrums. A few seconds later, I spotted him among a group of twelve that was sitting near the back. Glasses of wine and small plates covered their table, some full, some empty. Eduardo saw me, waved, and then motioned for me to join them.

As I walked their way, a man from his group got up and went to another table, then came back with an extra chair for me to sit on.

Eduardo introduced me to his friends (in English), and I made the rounds, double-kissing everyone in the group. After the introductions were over, they returned to their lively conversations. I'd already forgotten everyone's names, except for the two people sitting next to me: Virginia (Eduardo's sister) and Guillermo (the one who'd fetched me a chair). Virginia was a slender woman, and pretty much what the stereotypical Spanish woman looked like in my mind: brunette with wavy, shoulder-length hair, tanned skin, dark brown eyes, and an energetic yet sensual vibe that probably drove men crazy with desire. Guillermo, on the other hand, had blue eyes, brown hair heavily salted with strands of gray, a strong jaw, and a beautiful smile.

Is he Virginia's guy?

"So, what's good here?" I asked them both.

"Everything," Guillermo said. "But I recommend the shrimp *pintxo* and the ham sandwich in particular."

"Okay, thanks!" I said before getting up from my recently acquired seat. "I'll be right back."

I headed toward the bar, behind which stood two employees: a short, balding man with glasses and a tall, younger man with chocolate eyes, thick lips, a thin beard, and a hint of a wave in his brown hair. That younger bartender was the textbook definition of *guapo*.

I looked at the list of *crianza* wines posted on a chalkboard hung on the wall behind the bar. After picking one I remembered to be tasty, I walked up to the younger bartender and ordered myself a glass of *Torre de Oña* along with a *bocadillo de jamón ibérico*.

I returned to the table with my drink and my mini sandwich of tasty cured ham just as Guillermo was bidding his goodbyes.

"What's going on?" I asked Virginia.

"His wife called. There's a problem with his children. Nothing major, but he has to return home and deal with them."

"So, he's not your husband?" I asked her.

"Dear god, no! Nice and all, but not my type. How about you? Are you married? Single?"

I took a sip before answering. "Single. You?"

"Divorced and free again, like you. How I love my freedom!" She clinked her glass against mine. "*¡Salud!*"

We both drank a sip, then she asked, "Do you smoke?"

"Not really."

She tilted her head at my response, then dug a plastic bag out of one of the purses that were resting on the table: loose tobacco. Then she pulled out a sleeve of rolling paper.

"Do you have children?" I asked before biting into my sandwich.

She nodded. "Two, but they're adults now, thankfully. Out of my hair after all those years." She smiled as her manicured fingers dropped just the right quantity of tobacco in the crease of her tiny sheet of paper. Then she shaped it into form while keeping the paper folded in two, added a small white filter at one end, and then began the tricky rolling process. I was hypnotized by her rapid, efficient roll. One lick of her pointy tongue across the glue strip, and she was done.

"I'm stepping out to smoke on the terrace. Want to join me?"

"Sure, why not?" I swallowed the rest of my mini-sandwich, grabbed my glass and purse, and then followed her outside.

Watching her narrow hips sway as she wavered her way between the tables and finally out was just enthralling. She was like Penélope Cruz in *Woman on Top*. There was something magical about this woman, something that made me *want* to follow her, to talk to her, to learn more about her.

She picked one of the available barrels that peppered the sidewalk as makeshift tables, and I joined her.

"So, what do your children do?" I brought my glass to my lips. I was curious as to how old she really was, but I didn't want to ask since she didn't look like someone who could have grown-up children.

"They're university students. One's studying architecture in Madrid; the other's taking fine arts in Paris. I'm glad they decided to leave home." She lit her cigarette before continuing. "Plus, it gives me a reason to visit them now and then. I love to travel. What about you? Any children?"

I shook my head. "No, I never really found the right man to settle down with, so I never had any."

She snickered. "When it comes to children, finding the *right* person isn't a requirement. I was young and clueless. I married the man who got me pregnant; then we tried to make it work. It lasted about five years. Enough time to have two smaller versions of us, then he started looking elsewhere. I let him because him staying faithful was just making the both of us miserable."

"Sorry to hear." I took another sip of my drink, unsure where this conversation was heading. Parts of me wanted to hear more, but other parts didn't. The last thing I wanted to be exposed to right now was negative and depressing tales about a failed relationship.

"Oh, don't be sorry for me." She inhaled from her cigarette before blowing out a cloud of smoke off to the side. "I've got two gorgeous kids. Their dad is remarried and happy. Everyone's better off."

I drank more of my wine. "And what about you?"

"Never been freer or happier." She gave me what seemed like a genuine smile before bringing her cigarette back to her lips and emitting another puff of smoke away from me. "For once, I can have fun and live life on my own terms."

"Are you in a relationship now?" I asked before finishing my last sip.

She laughed again, a light, harmonious sound that couldn't help but make me smile. Then she squished her cigarette butt in the ashtray before replying. "I'm seeing a few people here and there." She pointed to my empty glass. "Should we get ourselves another round of drinks?"

Why not?

I nodded and followed her back inside.

When we reached the bar, she headed directly toward the cute bartender.

"JuanMa, here's your chance to improve your English. Please pour my friend and I a glass of your best *Gran Reserva*. Put it all on my tab." She turned to face me. "That *bocadillo* you had was small. Would you like to eat anything else?"

"I don't know," I said, surprised by her generosity in getting me an expensive glass of reserve wine.

"You only live once. I'm getting something else to eat. Please accompany me and eat something else as well."

I looked at the *pintxo* offerings and selected the one Guillermo had recommended earlier: a slice of baguette, a button mushroom, and a jumbo shrimp held together with a toothpick stabbing the cooked layers in place. Judging by the smell, the whole thing was drenched in garlicky goodness.

I could have sworn that Virginia winked at the cute bartender when he handed her the glasses.

"Let's go back to our seats," she said as she handed me my drink.

Pintxo and wine in hand, I led the way this time.

"So, what do you do?" I asked Virginia once we'd sat down at the table again.

"I'm an artist, a painter."

"Interesting. What kind of painting?"

"Various things, but I prefer doing oil portraits."

"Wow! I don't know any painters. Is any of your work currently on exhibit in town?" I asked.

She took a sip of her wine before answering. "Not at the moment, but I could show you photos." She put down her glass and dug in her purse to retrieve her phone.

A few seconds later, while I silently sipped my wine in anticipation, she handed me her phone. "Here's one. Swipe toward the right to see more."

"Oh, my!" The curvy woman who'd been painted out of golden, rust, red, and black strokes oozed sensuality. *How can paint strokes seen through a digital photo reach the depths of my heart?* "I can't even describe how beautiful, how poignant this painting is..." I looked up to her.

"Thank you," she said, sipping her wine with her eyes locked on my face.

Unsurprisingly, I felt my cheeks heat. *That physical reaction's* never *going to go away now, is it? Is she sending me* the *vibe? Or am I misreading the situation?*

I swiped to the next painting as a way to push those thoughts aside, at least for now. The second photo was very different, but it still had the same indescribable quality. Done in cooler aqua tones, the second painting showcased a tiny blonde woman in a lacy black undergarment and high heels, lying sideways on an unmade bed with turquoise sheets, one of her arms propping her head up. Her red lips were the only warm touch in the otherwise cold setting, but somehow it grabbed at me and pulled me in.

I flicked a finger on her screen to reach a third painting, this one of a man bearing a striking resemblance to the cute bartender, but without a beard, looking almost a decade younger. He was lying on his back, chest bare, cigarette in his mouth, held by one of his hands. The other hand held a glass of red wine. A bottle of wine on its side, a picnic basket, and roses were scattered around him on a blanket. The look in his eyes screamed passion, hunger, but also playfulness.

"Is this who I think it is?" I asked, showing Virginia the painting I was looking at, then nodding toward the bar.

She looked at her phone and smiled. "A long time ago, yes." She put her device back in her purse before I could look at more of her work.

"You're extremely talented," I said.

"Thank you!" She clinked her glass against mine.

I took a long sip of the delicious wine. "Would it be possible for me to see your paintings in person before I go?" I asked, possibly with an ulterior motive, but I wasn't sure if it was just the wine talking or my own feelings.

"Depends. How long are you staying?"

"A couple of weeks."

"Then I'm sure we could arrange that. My studio isn't in town; I paint in the mountains. I find it more inspiring, less distracting there."

"I'd love to see your studio and more of your work."

She looked down for a split second before meeting my eyes again. "Well... It's always nice to hear compliments."

"I wouldn't say it if I didn't genuinely think so."

"That much I gathered from you. Your facial expression... You must be a horrible poker player?"

I laughed at her comment. "I don't play, but I'm sure I'd be horrible at it."

JuanMa walked over to us and cleaned up the empty plates and glasses from our table.

"Do you want something else?" he asked in a sexy, strongly Spanish-accented English.

I looked at my near-empty glass. "This wine was outstanding. I'll have another, my last for tonight. And maybe an order of *albóndigas*, if you still have some?"

"Okay," JuanMa said before turning to Virginia. "And you?"

"Another glass as well and some olives, please. And add her order to my tab again," Virginia said.

"Are you sure?"

"Certain, dear. Let's just say that my art pays for more than a few bills. I can afford to buy you a few drinks and *pintxos*.

"Well, thank you." I watched JuanMa as he returned to the bar with our empty dishes. *Hmmm.* Nice ass, broad shoulders. Then, the unmistakable feeling of being stared at made me turn to look at the rest of the guests sitting at the table. My eyes met Eduardo's, then he broke contact and looked at his sister. Some secret communication was happening there, but I couldn't tell what was going on. *Siblings. Who knows what the story is between these two?*

"So, if you don't mind me asking, is Eduardo older or younger than you?" I asked while her gaze was still aimed at him.

She turned to face me, an enigmatic smile on her lips. "He's a bit older, and he really likes to pretend he's wiser than me and knows better."

Something's going on there. But thankfully, before things got too strange, JuanMa reappeared with our new drinks, her olives, and my tasty-looking Spanish meatballs.

"*¡Gracias!*" I said.

The weird energy between Virginia and her brother was still throwing me off a little, so I turned to look at him again. He was still alternating his stare between the both of us. I raised my glass toward him and said, "Happy birthday, Eduardo!"

He raised his wine and nodded. His lips slowly turned upward in a strange smile. Then the spell broke when one of Eduardo's friends tapped him on the shoulder. Eduardo got up and kissed his friend goodbye.

Well... Whatever's going on between my host and his sister isn't my business.

I turned to face Virginia again. "So, why do you have an apartment here in addition to your studio in the mountains?" I asked before bringing a small meatball to my mouth. *So tangy, tasty, and moist!*

"Different needs for different places. It can feel a bit isolated there. Life is a lot more entertaining here. Or at least, it can be... Eduardo told me it's not your first time here? Why do you keep coming back to Donostia?"

"What's not to love? I mean... Beautiful beaches within town—"

"You like the beach?" She put an olive in her mouth, her eyes locked on me the entire time while she chewed.

"I love it." I poked at my second meatball.

Her manicured fingernails picked up the pit she spat out of her red lips. "How about we meet there tomorrow?"

"Sure! I'd love that."

Virginia dug out her phone again. Let me give you my WhatsApp number. You have WhatsApp, no?"

"I do." I retrieved my phone from my purse and created a new contact with her information.

12:43 a.m.

I walked home after finishing my glass of wine, but even after climbing the five flights of stairs, I was still too wired to consider falling asleep just yet.

The culprit for that could have been my nap earlier today, or perhaps the unexpected feelings that Virginia's paintings and the handsome bartender had stirred in me. But either way, I knew I wasn't going to fall asleep anytime soon.

I nonetheless put on my lacy red slip and started my bedtime routine. I sat on my bed, my back resting on the two pillows I'd piled against the wall, and started reading a novel I'd bought in the airport store, but the story wasn't pulling me in. So, I went to the kitchen to make myself a cup of herbal tea. *Chamomile should help.*

While I waited for the water to boil, I looked at the stacks of movies that had been shelved in the living room. I traced the edge of the shelf as I scanned the titles. I recognized a few Hollywood action movies, thrillers, and cartoons for kids, and then I spotted intriguing titles I'd never heard of. But as soon as I pulled them from the shelf, their covers screamed which category they belonged in. One showed an 80s cover that featured a tall brunette in a flowing, translucent nightgown. The description made it sound more like erotica than porn. Then there was one about a weird remote that turned everyone horny and another about a group of young people enjoying a communal life in all ways possible.

The kettle whistling forced me return to the kitchen to make myself a hot drink; then I returned to the shelf that had me intrigued. Having already seen most of the films, I opted for the strange remote movie. I inserted the disc into the DVD player, closed the curtains, and then sat down to select English from the language menu.

I didn't need to look at the copyright year to know that it was either made in the 70s or early 80s. It was tacky, cheesy, and predictable, but did it ever turn me on! One of the characters even looked a little like JuanMa, but with long sideburns. I decided to turn it off after the first sex scene. I wanted to imagine another version of that story with JuanMa and me instead... And maybe Virginia, too.

I stopped the movie, ejected the disc, and then turned off the television before going to bed.

Once under the covers, I slid my hand down to my pussy and closed my eyes as my mind wandered off down a marvelous path. Convoluted and unrealistic as they were, my fantasies took many detours featuring both JuanMa and Virginia doing the nastiest things my mind could envision. My perverted imagination soon had me throwing the covers away from my body, just so the warm evening breeze on my exposed skin could make the sensations better. I pulled one of my breasts out of its lacy holder and squeezed it as hard as I thought JuanMa would if he could have me at this instant.

Even without the magic remote, he could order me to do anything to him, and I probably would, right there on the spot. Maybe he'd ask me to strip for him, or beg me to make out with Virginia in front of him. We could have sex at the bar after all the patrons had left. Or perhaps JuanMa could ask us to kiss and lick each other's bare bodies on top of that mahogany bar.

My mind didn't need any help imagining him standing there and watching us while polishing the wooden bar surface with circular motions of his rag... Or better yet, he could polish himself off a few feet away from us. Yes... He could let his erection loose in his hand; he could tame his Spanish snake as he watched me make out with Virginia. How I wanted to lick my way down her tanned skin, to taste her scent and perfume as my tongue slowly made its way down her décolletage. Maybe she'd let me rip her expensive blouse open. She'd be wearing something sexy underneath... or perhaps nothing at all.

Among the possible scenarios my mind had conjured, I preferred her wearing nothing at all. I could imagine what her toned body would look like. Her small breasts, her slender legs, her small ass...

I was so turned on, I'd created a wet spot on the bed, so I turned over to my side and imagined JuanMa lying behind me, spooning his strong body behind mine as I fell asleep, a wide grin on my face.

10:00 a.m.

The weather for this afternoon and the coming days was forecasted to be partly cloudy with a high of 30°C—with some mental juggling, I figured out that it meant 86°F.

I turned off the TV and thanked my lucky stars, since Donostia was renowned for its rainy conditions.

Today's a perfect beach day.

Considering how my mind had fantasized the night before, I was really looking forward to seeing Virginia again, so I sent her a text message.

I'm heading to the beach later today.
Want to join me?

I can at 2, after my meeting.

Great.
Which beach?

Zurriola?

Sounds good.
I'll get there before you.
I'll be lying on a towel somewhere.

OK

With lots of time to kill before the afternoon, I decided to take a walk, snap some photos, watch people in the streets, and find something fresh and delicious to eat for breakfast.

I went to a corner bakery that sold Argentinian *media-luna* croissants but in a straight, non-crescent shape. Not that I had anything against the lighter, fluffier buttery variety that originated from the country just a few miles from here, but I loved the sweeter, slightly denser version of those baked treats that were trickier to come by outside of Argentina. My stomach requested it right now. I could have French croissants later this week. Although the pastries were quite sizable, I ordered two—just in case my sweet tooth craved a treat later today.

My apartment had an Italian espresso maker, the type that held water in the bottom and required a stovetop, so I returned home to make myself a large serving that would satisfy me way more than the minuscule espresso cup I could purchase at a coffee shop around here.

Back home, sitting on my expansive balcony among a beautiful mix of potted plants—some even blossoming—I enjoyed my freshly-brewed coffee with my croissant. Each bite was as delightful as the scenery in front of me.

But it wasn't as stirring as what populated my mental screen when Virginia popped to mind once more.

1:20 p.m.

With my bikini on (covered by a loose tank top and shorts), I walked to the beach in my flip-flops. My apartment was in the older part of town, so I was closer to the other two beaches, but Zurriola was not far away. About ten to fifteen minutes at a leisurely pace and I'd be there.

The beach was fairly crowded with people of all ages, their swimwear dress code varying greatly. One man strolled along a few feet in front of me, baring it all. I knew from past visits that it wasn't a nudist beach per se, but people didn't seem to care what others wore or didn't wear. About half of the women were topless, their breasts nicely tanned like the rest of their exposed bodies.

Even after so many visits, the existence of such a beautiful beach within the city itself still had me stunned in wonder. The waves rhythmically crashed onto the sandy crescent in front of me, and the warm, salty breeze drew an irrepressible smile on my face. I watched surfers take turns tackling the waves at the farthest end for a few minutes, then decided to find myself a spot close to the concrete wall that ran parallel to the river's inlet so I could enjoy a few dips in the water without worrying about inexperienced surfers accidentally hitting me with their boards.

My perfect spot located, I spread my towel, took off my extra layers, and slathered on my SPF 30. *I'm so pale compared to the locals, but who cares?* I rested on my stomach to improve my back tan. I dug my novel out of my bag and continued reading it. The story was compelling, but not enough to compete with the hot sun that was baking my skin. Fifteen minutes in, I decided to abandon it in favor of the refreshing ocean.

I stood up and walked toward the water. Its temperature refreshed my toes but not too much. It was just right. The more steps I took, the deeper I got. But when the waves reached that sensitive midriff area, the coolness of the water made me stop in my tracks. Then, a second later, watching a wave building up and knowing very well that I'd get soaked, I opted to go for it: I dove right into the incoming swell to put an end to the uncomfortable temperature adjustment. I swam underwater for just a few seconds, then came back up for air and turned to look at the belongings I'd left behind on the beach. Other than my phone and a few Euros, what I'd carried with me wasn't worth much, so I didn't worry about people stealing them, but I nonetheless kept an eye on my bag from afar. Not that I could run and prevent a theft, but I could at least yell if someone grabbed my bag or its contents.

From here, I appreciated everything the beach had to offer: the ocean, the sun, the heat, and (my favorite) people-watching. On top of the beautiful soundtrack of waves softly crashing onto the beach, people were chatting, a couple of kids were throwing a Frisbee. A few dogs strolled around as well, their owners following them and picking up whatever treasure their four-legged friends dropped on the beach. All in all, there were countless worse ways to spend an afternoon.

Feeling refreshed and cooled, I walked back out of the water, and I returned to lie down on my towel with my book.

I'd made it through four more chapters before I heard Virginia's voice: "There you are!"

"*¡Hola! ¿Qué tal?*" I said, watching her come toward me. She wore huge sunglasses with white frames. A large purse was slung over her shoulder, and her high heels dangled from one of her manicured hands. Her hair had been pulled back into a tight bun at the crown of her head.

I got up to greet and kiss my new friend on both cheeks, careful to not let my damp bikini come in contact with her beautiful charcoal business skirt or her shimmering pearl blouse. If a dress code scale existed, her outfit fell on the opposite end of the spectrum from where my beachwear ranked.

"I'm great," she said. "I was just negotiating a deal with a local gallery. I've got my lunch break now, then I've got another meeting booked in two hours or so."

I smiled. *How I love the Spanish meal schedule. Who wouldn't want a two-hour lunch break starting in mid-afternoon? Then again, supper starts so late, they need to have a late lunch. Plus, many Spaniards finish their workdays around 7 or 8 p.m.*

"Did it go well?" I asked her as I returned to my towel.

I watched her pull out a large but thin towel from her bag. Come to think of it; it was more like an afghan.

"Yes," she said. "But I don't really want to talk about it. A little boring. Let's talk about other things." She spread her shawl-like towel next to mine, then sat on it before continuing. "So, what do you have planned during your stay here? Are you a museum person? Do you like to hike? Do you want to try some Michelin-star restaurants?"

I smiled at her enthusiasm. "Do I have to choose only one? I like most of what you just listed, and I've already done it during previous visits, but my only goal this time around is to relax, recharge, and make an important decision."

She unbuttoned her blouse as she spoke, exposing her lacy peach bra. "Hmm... It sounds like you're at a turning point? Can I ask what the decision is about?"

I looked at her and debated whether or not to share. She was busy laying her blouse flat on top of the bag she'd placed at the end of her towel.

"It's a long story and a bit complicated to explain in just two hours. Maybe some other time?"

She raised her shoulders and kept quiet for a few seconds. "So, your plan is just to enjoy the beach, read, and think..." She let her words trail as she unclasped her bra, then took it off so matter-of-factly. A second later, it was stacked on top of her blouse.

"Think, reflect, and enjoy whatever life throws at me…"

She locked eyes with me as she unzipped her skirt. "Interesting way to plan your holidays. You like flying by the seat of your pants, then?"

I tried to avoid looking at her exposed breasts, but they were just so… beautiful. Perfectly tanned. I brought my eyes up to meet hers when she unzipped her skirt. A second later, she shimmied out of it, then folded it neatly on the same pile as the rest of her clothes.

"I've already done the things I wanted to do in Donostia, but I keep coming back. I'm simply pulled by this place. I'm open to whatever new experiences it'll bring this time around…"

She lay sideways next to me, her elbow holding the weight of her head, in nothing but her tiny lacy bottom. I was pretty sure she had on expensive lingerie as opposed to a bathing suit bottom, but then again, it didn't matter.

"I'm sure we could find a few interesting ways to fill your holiday calendar then."

Am I misreading the situation? "We?"

"You know… Me, my brother, our friends. Do you have friends here?"

"Acquaintances really. Nobody I'd call a true friend."

"Then let's work on that!" She pointed at me and my bikini. "Can I ask? Don't you want to get your *tetas* exposed, get some Vitamin D? Or are you a prude?"

My inner self challenged, I sat up and immediately unclasped my top. "I'm not a prude! But I've had decades of brainwashing about what's culturally acceptable at the beach."

I looked down at my chest. My breasts hadn't seen much sun lately, and their lack of color reflected that.

She brought her hands up to partially cover her eyes.

"Gorgeous breasts, but you need to get some sun there! You're blinding me with those!"

I laughed, then grabbed my bottle of lotion and popped the top open, getting ready to apply some to my newly exposed bits when she took the bottle out of my hands.

"SPF 30? No! You need to get your *tetas* darker! Not keep them white. Give me a second."

She carefully dug into her large purse without moving the neatly folded clothes that rested on top, then retrieved a brown bottle of SPF 4 with coconut oil. She poured a small amount in her hands before rubbing them together.

"*¿Con permiso?*" she asked, her hands in the air, ready to rub the lotion on me if I gave her permission.

I nodded, and she covered all my white bits with it. Her motions were efficient, not lascivious, but they nonetheless ignited something deep within me.

"Nice *tetas*," she repeated. "Very firm. I'm jealous. Maybe that's how mine would feel if I hadn't had any children," she said, suddenly taking her hands away from mine and feeling her own breasts.

"Come on, Virginia! Your breasts are gorgeous. *You* are gorgeous from head to toe!"

"Ah, you're so kind," she said. She turned to lie on her back.

For a few minutes, silence filled the air between us. It wasn't uncomfortable, though. The gap in the conversation just made my mind wander down memory lane. Virginia was one of those people, roughly my age or more, with older kids to prove that time had gone by. My life was so different. And I couldn't imagine having raised kids over the past few years.

How quickly time flies... And how little I have to show for it...

Save for stamps in my passport and incredible life experiences...

But that train of thoughts could quickly detour toward Depressville, so I interrupted it.

"That bartender you painted..." I started as I turned on my side to look at Virginia and change my tanning position. "Is something going on between the two of you?" The moment I heard the words leave my mouth, I felt the need to qualify them. "... If it's not too nosy of me to ask."

"Not at all! If we want to become friends, then we have to talk about private stuff, no?" She turned her head to look at me and lifted her sunglasses up, resting them on her neatly pulled-back hair.

"JuanMa... He and I have been having flings on and off for years." She stopped, and her eyes looked sideways for a second. "Make that nearly two decades... He started flirting with me when I hired him to babysit. He was just a teenager, and I was married with young babies, so I never acted on it then."

"And?"

"When I officially got divorced, we finally hooked up. He'd grown up and become an adult. It was so hot. I mean... Years of pent-up sexual tension... It all finally got released, and it was... explosive."

"And since then?"

"Well... He had a serious girlfriend for a while, so we stopped seeing each other. Then he broke it off and came back to me, then off again..."

"And where does it stand between the two of you now? Are you currently on or off?"

"It's been a while since we hung out. Why do you ask?"

"He's cute."

She smiled. "Did you know he's an excellent guitar player and singer? If you want a reason to talk to him or spend time with him, you could hire him to take guitar lessons."

"I can't say that it's ever been on my to-do list, but I guess I could show up at the bar and chat him up. Assuming you're alright with me doing that?"

"Fine by me. But you know the thing about Spaniards? Especially Basque men?"

"No?"

"They wear a shield. And JuanMa's shield is particularly strong." One of her eyebrows went up as she continued. "But if you're looking for unattached fun, he could be your guy. He's very enjoyable."

"But you obviously like him, and he likes you. What's preventing you from being with him now? You're both available, no?"

"I don't know. I guess I've reached a point where I no longer think about trying to find a relationship and make it work."

Really? That's the one thing that keeps coming back to mind for me. Is there something wrong with me?

Feeling the hot sun baking my breasts, I turned to lie on my stomach again. Virginia did the same. I turned my head toward her. "Those people you paint... It's like raw emotions somehow come through your paintings. How do you do that?"

She smiled at me before answering. "Thank you. It's probably because I spend time with them. I do my best to get to know them, *really* know them."

Maybe it was due to having her near-naked body close to me, but my mind kept slipping into the gutter.

"You mean... like JuanMa?"

"Yes. I get to know some of my models... intimately."

I couldn't keep my mouth shut. I had to ask what my body wanted to know. "The women, too?"

She tipped her head to the side and paused before answering. "Yes."

Something deep within me yearned to become one of these women. And my pussy certainly knew it, as I could feel myself soaking my bikini bottom, which the hot sun had already mostly dried.

To cool that thought off—and mask a potentially embarrassing visible wet spot—I got up and headed directly to the water. "I'm going in. Do you mind keeping an eye on my things?"

"Not at all," she said.

I headed to the water, feeling a little self-conscious, feeling eyes on me. I turned my neck and saw that Virginia had moved to lie on her back again. She was propped up on her elbows, her head looking my way, but it was impossible to know if she was looking at me because of her sunglasses. I smiled at her anyway, then continued my stroll to the water line.

Having just the bottom piece of my bikini on was very useful in one way: I no longer had to worry about losing my top while diving into the oncoming waves. So I dove and dove, playing with every burst of salty water as the waves came my way. I even let myself float on my back while waiting for the next wave in one irregularly long lull. Birds flew high above in the sky, joining the sparsely located clouds. *This day's just perfect.*

Feeling refreshed enough, I swam back toward the shore. Once my feet could touch the bottom, I switched to walking, enjoying the waves splashing everywhere around me as they crashed against my skin. How I loved that sound and that feeling—well at least when waves were the size they were today.

I met Virginia's stare soon after I got my bearings as to which part of the beach I needed to return to. This time, her sunglasses were resting on the top of her head. I could see her brown eyes, and she definitely looked my way.

I lowered myself fully so I could let my hair get wet and let the pressure of the water bring it all back behind me. I stood up and squeezed the water out, from my roots to the ends, as though it were in a ponytail. The strength of the waves returning to the ocean forced me to walk in slow motion, adding to the feeling that I was a sexy Bond girl stepping out of the water. Virginia biting her lower lip while watching me certainly added to that feeling.

Am I reading things? Or am I just getting my hopes up?

But after I wavered my way around the other people, back to Virginia, she answered my own question as I bent down to pick up my towel.

"I'd love to paint you. Would you model for me?"

"Me?" I looked at Virginia. Her wide-open eyes didn't appear to kid. That would for sure be a new experience, something different and interesting to fill my holiday calendar. "Sure, I'd love to. When?" I asked.

With my towel, I patted my face dry, then soaked up the water from my hair while she replied.

"Before you go, and it will take me a few sessions to get it just right. How about you come up to the mountains and hang out with me for a few days?"

I continued drying the rest of my body. "Why not? It could be fun."

"Yes! Let's do that!" She looked at her phone and then started dressing herself up again. After she'd put on her bra, she continued. "And maybe I can even convince JuanMa to come along, if you'd like a chance to get to know him better?"

I spread my wet towel on the beach again before lying back down on it.

"Whatever you think is best. I don't know how artists work."

She slid on her silky blouse. "I wouldn't say that I have a set routine. I listen to my muse." She was back on her feet in no time, sliding her skirt back on. "No. That's not 100% right. I *do* always drink lots of wine while painting. Maybe my muse feeds on it."

I laughed. "We'll get along just fine then. What do you like to drink? I can bring some wine?"

"Don't worry about that. I've got a cellar full at the house."

A cellar full?

She carefully shook her afghan/towel to get rid of the sand, then folded it and returned it to a small plastic bag before stashing it in her sizeable over-the-shoulder purse. The only things of hers that she had not put back on were her shoes.

"So, how would I get there, and when would you want me to arrive?"

She looked intently at her phone before answering. "I've got a few things to sort out, and then I'll text you with a date and time when I can pick you up?"

"Sure. That'd be awesome. I'm really flexible."

"Then it's settled."

She blew me a kiss from her standing position. *"¡Hasta pronto!"* she said before bending down to pick up her high heels.

"Yes, see you soon," I repeated, but in English. "Enjoy the rest of your afternoon!"

She smiled, then turned away, heading toward the street behind the beach, shoes in hand. Her narrow hips swayed as her feet dug their way through the thick layer of dry sand.

I was looking forward to seeing her again.

3:55 p.m.

After soaking up enough sunshine for one day, I packed up my things and returned to my apartment, but not without stopping by a small grocery store to pick up a bottle of wine, a wedge of firm sheep cheese, and some green grapes. I walked up the stairs with my beach bag and purchases in hand, greeting other tenants as I crossed their paths.

Once in the apartment, I put my food and wine in the fridge and then showered to get rid of all the sand I'd tracked back with me. I donned a summer dress, the perfect outfit for my lazy, late-afternoon reading session on the terrace.

After preparing my snacks and bringing them outside, I was all set to enjoy what was left of daylight. The broad umbrella opened and tilted toward the table provided me, my snacks, and my bucket of ice with just the right amount of shade. I poured myself a glass of my recently purchased *Verdejo* bottle. Its dry, fruity flavor with subtle hints of lime and grapefruit didn't disappoint. It was one of my guilty pleasures when spending time in Spain. Sure, I preferred it when paired with tacos, but Spain wasn't the place for that. *Cheese and grapes should step up just fine for today.* I swallowed my first grape and proved myself right.

Intent on finishing my novel (or at least making a good dent in it), I re-opened it to the page I'd dog-eared before leaving the beach, but the author's finely crafted words didn't make much sense to me right now. I read and re-read the same page three times before giving up. I closed the book, set it on the table, and stared at my gorgeous view instead. My thoughts wandered to *What-if-land* instead of where the book was forcing them to be.

What would it be like to have Virginia paint me?

I picked up my glass and sipped it while trying to picture what her house in the mountains could look like. Come to think of it, I'd never seen any of the mountainous parts of Spain. *She must live close to here, so she probably means the Pyrenees...* But somehow, that word depicted snow caps in my mind. There weren't any of those around here (at least, not this time of year.)

I could nonetheless imagine the settings that I'd seen in the few paintings she'd shown me. Those things had to be in her house. Maybe she painted her subjects on her own bed? Or did she just add objects after the fact? *Do painters need everything to be there, ready to be incorporated into a painting? Like setting props for a photo session?*

I ate a few grapes while letting those thoughts fade away.

I could imagine her holding a paintbrush, but I've yet to see her in an outfit other than the business or semi-business outfits she wore today and the other night. There's no way she painted in those outfits. What does she wear to paint? Does she paint naked? Is this why her paintings come with intimate times?

I'd heard stories of photographers doing that while taking nude photos, but those could be a scam too. Like what had happened to Katrina and me in Los Angeles... Just another pretense... Wasn't it easy to add a layer of lies to make gullible women do what was needed of them?

Some are naïve; some are just interested in playing the part.

While I was sipping more wine, my thoughts circled back to Virginia.

Her glances felt real. A mix of interest and possibly longing? Maybe not. But definitely curiosity. Or am I just interpreting her looks as something they're not?

And JuanMa?

For a few seconds, I wondered how I would have reacted if I'd been in her shoes. What would I have done if a hot and overly confident eighteen-year-old boy had tried to seduce me while I was in my mid- or late-twenties? There were laws about such things, but I was pretty sure they'd been created to protect young girls, not young men who were into older women. Would I have been able to resist?

I picked a couple of grapes and swallowed them while imagining a younger JuanMa coming on to me.

I'd like to think my ethics and wholesome values would have kicked in. I flashed back to what my life was like back then—boring and sheltered—and I realized I probably wouldn't have put myself in a situation where this scenario could have even happened.

One thing's for sure: I've progressed lots this past year.

I let those thoughts trail off into the abyss of my mind then refilled my wine and returned to my novel.

I was half-way through my wine bottle and at the mid-point of my book when my phone beeped with a message from Virginia.

How's tomorrow?

Perfect
What should I pack?

Plan for 2-3 days.
Change of clothes.
Bring a jacket for cool nights.
Good walking shoes.

OK

Do you know the Mercado de la Bretxa in the old part?

Yes

Let's meet inside, downstairs between the market and the store, at noon?

Sure
See you then

12:00 p.m.

With my small bag of clothes and toiletries strapped over my shoulder, I walked into La Bretxa. Virginia already had a shopping cart full of large items by the time I spotted her.

"I forgot to ask. I don't know if you have any food allergies," she said after we greeted each other.

I shook my head. "No."

"Perfect. Then it's going to be easy. I already picked up the bulk of it, but I still have to get some fresh meat. How do you feel about *morcilla, chorizo, salchichón?*"

"I like them all," I said. The blood sausage (*morcilla*) had required a few tries before I decided to like it, but the red *chorizo* (when barbequed to a non-burnt crisp) and thin slices of the summer sausage they called *salchichón* had been much easier to fall in love with.

"*¿Chuletas?*"

"I love chops, too!" I said.

I followed her around the market stalls until she stopped at one of the many butchers. She put in her order for pork chops, and I watched the young, brown-haired butcher weigh a piece of meat, then cut slices with just the right thickness. With smooth and efficient knife moves, he butterflied them all in no time.

Virginia ordered some sausages as well while I walked around and looked at the offerings in the refrigerated windows that separated the butcher from us.

How I love the European markets. Among this butcher's offerings were whole rabbits, pigs' tails, and whole chickens.

"Ready to go!" Virginia said.

I walked back to her side as she moved her cart toward another merchant.

"I'll grab a few vegetables; then we'll be ready to go. Anything you crave?"

"No, I'm fine with anything. Should I buy some of this food, though?"

"No, no. Don't worry about it."

A few minutes later, we were officially done adding to the cart, after two final stops that involved buying a couple of baguettes, jars of anchovy-stuffed olives, and roasted red peppers.

I followed Virginia as she navigated her cart back toward her car. "Parking can be a little bit tricky in this town. That's why I asked for you to meet me here."

She had parked in an underground lot close to the market. *(Okay, I admit, Donostia isn't perfect, but I can deal with the annoying parking issues since I don't have a car.)*

We loaded the groceries Virginia had purchased into her trunk, returned the shopping cart, then drove back to street level, where the sun was shining brightly.

"So, where's your house?" I asked as she joined the slow-moving traffic that was heading out of town.

"In the Navarre region. We'll be there in just over an hour."

2:43 p.m.

We veered off the NA-170 in Ezkurra. "This is the last chance to buy things before we reach my village. Did you forget anything?"

"I'm good," I said, shaking my head.

A few minutes later, the road we kept driving on suddenly got narrower and much windier. So much so that it almost felt like someone's private driveway, but it was far too long for that—and it had that metal guardrail to prevent cars from falling off the side of the road. And I was glad it existed because, at times, the hillside fell sharply less than a foot from the edge of the pavement. But as Virginia swerved her car around the sinuous roads like a pro racer, I appreciated every bit of the view. Lots of farms, trees, and animals. I even saw a pitchfork resting on a tall pile of hay stacked in such a way it made me wonder if I'd traveled back in time. But considering the steepness of the slopes, modern machinery probably couldn't bale the hay here. Manual labor was perhaps the only option.

"This is it!" she said, a large smile on her red lips as we turned off the main road to enter her village. "There isn't much. A small church and one bed and breakfast. The rest are all family homes that have been passed down from generation to generation."

Virginia slowed down once we reached the concrete-paved streets that surrounded the buildings in a labyrinth of steep, narrow paths with strange intersecting angles where only small cars could pass. Certain turns were only possible if coming from one direction. Although I wasn't sure if they were one-way streets, there wasn't any room for oncoming traffic.

Gorgeous white houses randomly stacked next to each other at odd angles surrounded us. On most buildings, gray stones had been left exposed on the edges of the structures, as well as around the doors and windows. I loved the warm chestnut doors and exterior window shutters. Black metal railing decorated shallow balconies on some homes' second stories, but what I liked most were the bright red flowers in terra-cotta pots that brightened those balconies.

"Is there a small corner store or anything else where you can buy an ice cream treat or a bottle of water?" I asked as we passed by a red tractor that was parked between two buildings.

She shook her head. "No. Nothing at all. Not even a restaurant or bar, but that's why we went shopping first. And believe me, the house has more wine than we'll be able to drink." She turned to look at me, beaming. "And if we really need something and can't be bothered to drive back, then there's always a bunch of neighbors whose doors we can knock on."

That sounded like a lovely plan. I could already picture myself sitting and sipping wine while looking at the gorgeous mountains that shaped the green landscape around us.

2:55 p.m.

She parked in a small slanted area next to a three-story white home with the now familiar exposed stones along the doors, windows, and exterior corners.

"Home sweet home!" she said after turning off the ignition.

The sounds of chirping birds and the distant ring of cowbells filled the air the second I opened the car door and took in the fresh air. I hadn't seen any cows here, mostly sheep and goats, but I'd never heard of sheep or goat bells. *Are they a thing?*

"Peaceful, isn't it?"

I nodded, all smiles. "You read my mind."

"Stay here for a few minutes, so I can air out the place, and then we'll unpack the car."

I watched her unlock the low, wide wooden door on the ground floor. She had to bend down to enter (and she wasn't tall.) *Is that door five-feet high?*

"I'll be right back," she said as she entered the house.

I looked around while waiting. First, I saw Virginia open the small window right next to the door. The wooden frame squeaked as she pushed it open, then I heard her footsteps fade away. Turning around to take in my surroundings, I caught a glimpse of a curtain moving on the second story of the house in front of hers.

Nosy neighbor? Or just a vigilant one, ensuring nobody's breaking in?

A few minutes later, Virginia was outside again, but she'd traded her business-casual attire for jeans and a T-shirt. "Sorry, I wanted to get rid of the humidity. It really builds up when I'm not here for a while, so I lit a fire and opened all doors and windows to make the stench go away."

"No worries. How long have you been away?"

"This time? Probably close to three weeks."

She really did split her time between Donostia and the mountains then. "So, tell me more about this house. Have you owned it for long?"

She walked to the trunk of her car and opened it. "Let's talk about it over a glass of wine after I unpack the car. Would you mind giving me a hand?" she asked.

"Of course, I'll help." She handed me a few grocery bags, and then she grabbed a couple of large water jugs.

"Is there running water?" I asked her, wondering why she'd brought so much with her.

"Yes, *¡claro!* The water from the village's well is potable, but I don't like its taste. So, I prefer to bring my own when I come." She led the way into her home, and I followed. "But I mostly drink wine anyway," she said as she put the bottles on the kitchen table. It was a large surface made from four solid, thick planks of chestnut-colored wood. It had to be heavy. The house had a huge fireplace made of stones like those exposed on the outside of the house.

"Is this the original fireplace?" I asked.

"Yes, that's the only original thing left. That, and the foundation. The rest went up in flames around fifty years ago. At least, that's what my parents told me."

"So, whoever rebuilt it kept the original style?"

"Yes, they did a great job."

"The houses are so close; other houses must have caught fire at the same time, no?"

"That's what my parents told me. The house and land have been in our family for generations. I know everyone in this village. They've watched me and my brother grow up."

"Where are your parents now?"

"They moved to *Islas Canarias* so they could enjoy hotter weather all year long. Sometimes they come and visit, but they don't really like to fly, so Eduardo and I usually visit them instead. Come on. Let's get the rest of the stuff out of the car, so we can start relaxing and enjoying ourselves."

3:15 p.m.

I followed Virginia out of the kitchen and back to the trunk of her car, which she'd left wide open.

Once again, I saw a curtain move in a window across the street. This time it was on the ground floor, right next to the front door.

"Am I dreaming, or is someone watching us?" I asked Virginia discreetly while she retrieved more bags from her trunk.

She instantly looked at the correct house, then back to me. "Don't worry. That's Romaro, a childhood friend. He doesn't leave his house, but he keeps an eye on things. On me." She handed me the bags she'd grabbed, and I took them into the house.

"All the time?" I asked her as we were re-entering the kitchen.

"Well... a *lot* of the time. I'm his entertainment," she said before winking at me.

We made another trip, and I followed her back in again, with more goods in hands. Clueless as to what she meant, I asked half-jokingly, "You mean he watches you instead of TV?"

She placed her bags on the table and turned to face me. "That'd be one way to look at it. And not too far from reality."

One last round of bags later, we were done unloading the car, including my overnight bag, which I still held after we'd returned to the kitchen. I had no idea where to put it, since the table was overflowing with food and water.

But Virginia somehow read my mind at that point. "Oh! Let me show you to your room."

She motioned for me to follow her, so I did. We went up an open staircase to the second floor, then we walked right past two ajar doors and continued climbing. "I'll give you the grand tour later, but the bedrooms are on the top floor."

And so they were. Another flight of stairs later, she walked directly into one of the three opened doors. A double bed occupied the bulk of the space, with one night stand on its right, just below a small window, which had been opened and was currently letting in a lovely breeze.

"This will be your room. Feel free to hang your things in here," she said as she opened an armoire on the wall opposite the window. "Or leave them in your bag. Whatever. Just make yourself at home. The sheets are clean. The bathroom is next door."

"Thanks," I said before dropping my bag onto the bed.

"I have to put the perishables in the fridge. Come meet me downstairs when you're settled."

I nodded and smiled, then watched her leave the room, a part of me somehow disappointed. I couldn't quite pinpoint it.

What did I expect? A love-making fest and an invitation to share her bed? Wake up, girl. Your mind is spinning way too fast. You haven't even kissed her yet. Why the heck would she invite you to share her bedroom?

I unzipped my bag while shaking those thoughts out of my head.

Who am I kidding? All she did was invite me to model for her!

After tossing the contents of my bag around, I remembered I hadn't brought anything that required hanging: just toiletries, shorts, T-shirts, a light sweater, jeans, and underwear to last me a few days. I placed my bag with its contents in the armoire, then closed the door before walking over to the window to see what the view was like.

Gorgeous mountains.

The only house in sight from my window was across the valley, up a steep hill, probably a couple of miles away. *Now that's peaceful!*

I headed out of my room and used the bathroom next door before going downstairs to meet Virginia.

She was folding and putting away her empty grocery bags.

"Sorry about that. I'm always a bit wary of having food go bad after the drive here. I really should buy a cooler and leave it in the trunk of my car... One day. But it's all sorted now. What would you like to do now? How about a quick tour of the village?"

There were lots of other things I'd rather do, but walking around could help untangle the mess of knots that had been building up in my gut about not knowing what to expect out of this mini-getaway with a gorgeous, talented painter.

"Sounds great," I said.

Virginia proceeded to close the French doors in the living room, so I helped her. Once we were done, she grabbed her keys and pointed to the door. I exited the house, and, unsurprisingly, the curtain moved again when I stepped outside, Virginia in tow.

With the beep of a button, she activated the alarm of her car and then turned to lock the wooden door.

"Is it unsafe to leave the door open? Or are we going to be gone very long?"

"No and no. But the door could open on its own if I don't lock it, and who knows what rodent or small animal could get in. I'd rather limit my house guests to those of the human variety."

"Sounds fair." I lowered my voice before asking her, "Why does he keep looking out his window every time you pass by?"

She smirked, then replied in a hushed tone. "I think he bases his plans around mine."

I turned to look at her as we walked up an incline toward the steeple of the village's church.

"What?"

"It's complicated... I'll tell you later."

I chose to change the topic, since that one seemed to be out-of-bounds. "Have you ever had a dog? It seems like this would be a great place for a dog."

"I thought about it, but I have yet to commit. They're nice, but I just don't seem to want it enough."

"You mean owning a specific breed of dogs?"

"No, the whole commitment thing. After my divorce, and again after my kids left the house, I promised myself I would never be chained down to long-term contracts again..."

"... But you own both a house here and an apartment in the city? Aren't those long-term contracts?"

"I know. The irony. But one's just an early inheritance, and the other's a financial investment. I'm fine with those. But dogs, men, tattoos... I've successfully avoided all of these commitments, and I'm proud of it."

3:50 p.m.

We used a different route to return to her house. My mind hadn't yet wrapped itself around the mess of the street layouts, so I was surprised when she dug out her keys. But with the incline and the very few houses in the village, I was sure I would have (eventually) found my way back on my own.

Virginia unlocked the door, and I followed her to the living room. The fire she'd started earlier was still going, but not looking good. I noticed she'd hung a wet rag by it on a small drying rack. "Do you want me to add another log?" I asked.

Virginia replied from the kitchen, where she'd gone instead of joining me in the living room. "Only if you want to stay in and look at it. I just lit the one to burn off the humidity."

I raised my shoulders. I didn't care. With the day being so nice, it seemed like a waste of firewood. "What do you want to do now?" I asked.

The pop of a wine cork answered before she did. "How about we hang out on the patio for a little while?"

"Sounds great."

"Through that door over there," she said, pointing with her chin as she grabbed two wine glasses by their stems.

I unlocked the safety latch and opened the door just in time for Virginia to waltz out with our drinks. She placed the glasses and bottle on the picnic table then frowned. "Don't sit down just yet, the benches and tabletop are filthy."

"Can I help?"

"No, no. Just give me a second."

A quick trip to the house and back later, the small debris and dust had been wiped clean from the picnic table. The only thing I'd been able to do to help was lift the bottle and glasses as she wiped down the surface.

I didn't like being a lazy guest. It made me feel a little uneducated. *Hell, being near Virginia makes me... I don't know.* Feelings stirred in the pit of my stomach, but I couldn't name those sensations quite yet.

Virginia returned her cleaning supplies in the house, and I left the picnic table area to walk to the edge of the patio. A minute later, I heard the door open and close again; Virginia had reappeared outside.

"It's a wonderful view," I said to her as she stopped by the table. She filled our glasses, grabbed them, and then joined me at the edge of her patio, where the grass started. It was the same view I had from my bedroom but with the added effect of seeing the ground roll down the hills in front of me.

"I know. So much more inspiring than the city. Don't you think?" But she didn't leave enough time for me to ponder and reply. Instead, she handed me a glass. "Cheers!" she said, then we clinked.

"Cheers!" I took a sip then closed my eyes for a second, letting the wine's chocolaty flavor thrill my taste buds; the bells and chirping birds were pleasing to my ears, with their unscripted melodies.

When I reopened my eyes, I felt Virginia's gaze on me. I turned to look at her and proved my instinct to be right.

"Shall we go and sit?" she suggested.

Those ardent, sultry eyes... I pushed down the rising tide of feelings that were awakening in my gut and just nodded instead. I tried to think about something else. Anything else. The nosy neighbor came to mind.

"So, what does he look like?" I asked her, my hand pointing toward his house, which we couldn't see from where we sat on the patio.

"Romaro? Most would describe him as a skinny, scrawny man with very, very pale skin because he never goes outside."

"Never? How do you know what he looks like then?"

"I grew up with him." She smiled and paused before continuing. "Heck, I'm the one who taught him that girls had different body parts than boys. But that was a long time ago. Before his motorcycle accident... His brain never fully recovered from that. Now he's stuck somewhere in his youth, but his body is that of a man."

"So, he's... mentally disabled?" I asked.

"Well, he's not like a regular guy. His brain injury had permanent effects. He looks like an adult, but since he's always been deaf as well, he doesn't sound like one. And he does not act like one."

"Aren't you scared of him?"

"Why would I be scared? He's the kindest soul I know. It's not his fault... Well, I don't know if the accident was his fault or not, but I will not hold prejudices against him because of what that accident did to him. He's a good person, but he's stuck in a strange situation."

"How old is he now?"

"Early forties. He's lucky to still be alive, but he's never been the same since. His brother takes care of him. He told me that their family's attempts at re-introducing him to social situations failed miserably. Since Romaro doesn't seem to miss those anyway, they've let the issue slide."

"Do you go and talk to him?"

"Yes, but we don't really... communicate. Not much anyway. I use what little sign language I remember learning as a kid, and if he wants to say something that's important, he writes it down for me. But it's an arduous process. Body language and facial expression are what I go with."

"What does he do all day?"

"Not much. He watches TV, and, like I said, he keeps an eye on me."

She took hold of the bottle and topped up both of our glasses.

I paused for a second, overwhelmed by gratitude for not having to deal with such difficult circumstances. *My life's so easy. Sitting here, next to a gorgeous, talented painter, drinking tasty wine. Rolling hills, peaceful countryside... I have nothing to complain about.*

"Your lawn," I said, nodding toward the slanted green land that quickly descended out of sight within the low rock walls that likely served as property lines. "How hard is it to mow?"

"Mow?"

"How do you keep it so short? Do you have a lawnmower?" I asked.

From her lips escaped a delightful cacophony of untamed, warm, and light noises that cascaded onto one another. Her laughter was so ... honest. "No, none of those noisy machines. One of my neighbors brings in his herd of goats on a regular basis. They eat, my lawn stays under control. It's a win-win."

"But wouldn't they... hmm... shit all over the place?"

She shook her head at me. If it weren't for the warmth in her eyes, I could have taken offense. "That's called fertilizer, my dear. You didn't grow up in the countryside, did you?"

"You got me there." I took another sip of the wine to hide my embarrassment, but my cheeks were feeling hot. Looking at the house, I tried to figure out which window was mine, and I spotted only two windows on the third floor. My room was in a corner, so it had to be the left one.

"That's the room I'm staying in, right?" I asked, pointing at it. She looked up and nodded. But there was only one more window on that wall, which could only be that of the bathroom next door. "Don't you have windows in your bedroom?" I asked, still looking at the house.

"I have one, but it looks over the village. I forgot. I still haven't given you the tour. Do you want to do that now?"

"I'd love to see your studio," I replied.

"Let's do that."

She got up and once again topped up our drinks. I followed her back inside the house, glass in hand, careful to not spill its delicious content.

After showing me the half-bathroom on the ground floor, and a trap door in the living room floor that led down to the wine cellar, she walked up to the second floor again. I followed her. This time, we went in the first door. From the room oozed a weird mix of paint, perfume, and something else I didn't quite recognize, the unusual odor fell to the bottom of my concerns once I saw the contents of her studio.

"It's so big," I said.

"I had an architect come in and put a support beam so I could take down the wall and join the two bedrooms on this floor. I'm happy with how it turned out. It gives me much more space to play with."

Paintings of all sizes and colors surrounded me. Two large windows let in plenty of natural light. In front of me, an oversized wooden easel on wheels held a vast canvas on which warm earth tones had been laid. It looked like the background to something that was yet to come.

"Work in progress," Virginia said.

I moved my attention to some of the other paintings that leaned against the walls, some small ones rested on one of the two large wooden buffet pieces with multiple drawers, while larger ones stood angled on the paint-splattered concrete floor. A few empty wine bottles sprinkled the floor here and there. There was a large portrait near me, but the strokes were distracting from up close. I took a step back, which made them all make sense.

"A man from the village," she said.

"Great work."

I walked away from it to explore the rest of Virginia's studio. In the middle of the room stood a chaise draped in a white sheet, but this one wasn't splattered in paint. I let my fingers run on the fabric as I walked by it, its silkiness surprising me a little. I placed my wine glass on the corner of the nearest piece of furniture and approached a pile of paintings that were leaning against the wall.

"May I?" I asked Virginia.

"Of course," she said, sipping her wine.

The one that rested on top of the pile was a three-by-four-foot representation of a brunette posing topless, her left arm holding her long hair up on top of her head, while her other hand was caressing one of her breasts. Her chin was up, her eyes were closed, but her pouting mouth told a story of lust and hunger. It wasn't as colorful as some of the other paintings in the room, but somehow, the fewer colors it showed made it very powerful.

"This is so raw and beautiful," I said.

"Thank you," Virginia said behind me.

I moved the beautiful woman on top of the next pile so I could have a look at the one that was stacked behind it. It was much broader, almost five feet wide, but not very tall. I took a few steps back to better appreciate it. The model was nude, lying sideways, and... she looked like Virginia.

"Is this you?" I asked, turning around to look at her.

"An attempt at a self-portrait," she said. "I don't like it."

She walked away. At first I thought she was leaving the room, but she headed toward the large window instead, where sheer curtains moved to the breeze's whims.

The painting pulled me back in, as though my eyes were magnetically attracted to it. I soaked in the magnificent representation Virginia had made of herself. Her brown hair flowed down, wavy and untamed, hiding the arm that was supporting her head. She'd painted her other hand stretched out toward something out of reach. Her legs were slightly bent, as though she was just relaxing, but the dip of her waist made her gorgeous curves too enticing. She'd painted her pussy bare and inviting.

And that gorgeous woman was right here, in the same room as me.

I turned to look at her again. She was looking down at her watch instead of her beautiful piece of work.

"There's something wrong with it, but I can't quite fix it," she said. "I should burn it. Or save the canvas and paint over it."

"What do you mean? It's beautiful!" I said.

"No. No need to protect my feelings. I know this one isn't good."

"You're the artist, but I honestly *love* it, just the way it is. It's a gorgeous representation of you. It's a little bit... darker than the others, but that doesn't take away anything. It's amazing."

"Hmmm. Darker? ... Maybe it's just the way I see myself."

"You're stunning... and so talented," I said, walking toward her.

She looked down at her feet instead of at me. I lifted her chin, forcing her gaze to meet mine. Just a few inches separated our bodies, our faces. Even without heels, I was much taller than her. Virginia was a petite woman, but her presence was anything but.

What's that, flickering in her dark chocolate eyes? Distraction? Fear? Self-judgment?

Impossible for me to know. But deep within me screamed a yearning I could no longer keep quiet. My heart pounded in my chest as I brought a hand to her cheek. The scent of cigarettes lingered around her, blending in with her citrusy perfume. Ever so slowly, I leaned down and brought my lips to hers, doing what I'd wanted to do since the first moment I laid eyes on her: I kissed her.

An electrifying current passed between us the moment our lips touched. At first, she stayed still, which didn't help quiet the flutters in my stomach, but she began responding to my kiss. Then, just as suddenly as she'd started, she pulled back.

"No," she said, her head shaking, backing away from me.

"I'm sorry," I said.

Fuck! What did I just do?

She shook her head. "Don't be."

4:00 p.m.

What now?

I followed her out of the studio and down the stairs.

Shit, I really messed up. I'm not even getting the rest of the house tour. Is she going to tell me to pack my things and go?

The silence was awkward, but I didn't know how to fill it. Instead, my cheeks were heating up; my brain was going into overdrive.

Way to go. First prize in misreading body signals!

My mind cycled through potential conversation subjects to try and recover from my unwanted move, but the weather wouldn't cut it right now.

The moment I stepped off the final step and reached the main floor, Virginia took my glass away from my hands and brought it to the kitchen table, along with hers.

I don't even get to finish my drink?

Fuck. How could I have blundered so badly?

"I'm so sorry," I repeated. "Can we pretend it didn't happen?"

She was shaking her head, walking toward me as though she had some serious business to attend to. But when her hands got a hold of my face, when her lips met mine, she proved in no gentle, soft, or tender terms that my worries didn't belong here.

Her mouth devoured mine. Her tongue forced my lips to open. Before I knew it, my entire body had been ignited, and my hands were roaming all over her. In what looked like a confused waltz, she pushed me against the back of the entrance door; then she continued kissing me as if her existence depended on it.

And she stole my breath away... while she confused me even more. I wanted nothing more than to see where her passionate kiss would lead us, but I retracted from her and stared into her eyes.

"First, you turn me down. Then... this? What's happening here?" I asked.

She sighed, then brushed my cheek with the back of her fingers. "No, I just meant that upstairs was not the place or time for that."

I shook my head at her, forcedly ignoring the effect her closeness had on me. "I don't understand. Is your studio a no-kissing zone?"

She bit her lips. "It's complicated. Come. Let's sit down, and I'll explain." She pulled on my hand, and I followed. A few steps later, she grabbed our wine glasses from the table and motioned for me to join her in the living room.

"Remember what I said about Romaro?"

"Yeah, he's like a security system. He keeps an eye on your house, on you."

She shook her head. "No. Well... Yes. I'm sure he'd text his brother for help if he saw something odd, but he keeps an eye on me... in a different way."

"What do you mean?"

She swallowed a large gulp of her wine. "Romaro gets an excellent view of my studio and my bedroom from his house. A few years ago, I discovered that he's got ... a whole collection of me."

"A collection?"

"Hundreds of photos, hours of videos... He's quite gifted, but what he does is illegal."

Taken aback, I downed the rest of my wine. "Why don't you report him?"

"He's not hurting anyone. If taking photos of me keeps him entertained and happy, I want him to do it. And he's too much of a good soul to go and sell them online. He's like a young boy, trapped in a man's body, but 4 p.m. is never a good time. I can't paint anyone around that time. I can't kiss anyone. I can't kiss you even if my entire body wants it so bad that it hurts."

I shook my head. "You're confusing me."

"As long as what Romaro sees from his windows stays private between the two of us, then I'm good. But daily, at around 4 p.m., he gets deliveries, or his uncle visits, or sometimes other people show up. I want to make sure they don't find him staring at me or filming me when they arrive. It's a small village. I'm impressed our little secret isn't out yet."

"But what about getting frosted windows, or even curtains?" I asked her.

She smiled at me. "That was my initial thought, but I didn't want to change the light coming into my studio. I like it the way it is. And as for curtains... I installed them and started using them, but then I stopped. It affected the light... and a little part of me didn't mind knowing that he could be watching me. Somehow, thinking about him lurking and getting excited by it... I don't know. For some reason, knowing he was there, watching... It turned me on, so I gave in. He's as innocent as a fly. If nobody catches him masturbating while looking into my windows, nobody will know there's even something to see here. No other neighbor can peer into my home the way he can.

"But the villagers know you're a painter."

"Of course, they do."

"And they know the kinds of paintings you do?"

"Probably."

"So, you don't think they've put two and two together?"

"There's no reason for them to believe I have sex with my models. I don't scream out loud. I don't kiss them in public. I don't even hold hands with them." Virginia looked at my empty glass. "More wine?"

I nodded in silence, still processing what she'd just told me.

She got up, took my glass, and then headed back toward the kitchen.

"So, Romaro has no girlfriend? No wife?" I asked her when she was pouring our refills.

Virginia shook her head. "No mother or sister either. No female presence in his life. Maybe that's why I have a soft spot for him. He was a friend before that awful accident. He was cute. I mean, he still is, but he's got some mental issues now. He can't leave his house. He won't even walk out his front door and come here. Everything he needs comes to him at the same time daily. His visitors don't stay long. Most of them just come in for a quick check to see if he needs something or if anything's changed."

After returning to the living room and handing me my glass, Virginia sat down next to me, but a safe distance away.

"Why do I feel like there's something you're not telling me?" I asked.

With a coy, slanted, and intriguing smile, she eyed me down, then finally spoke. "You're open-minded?"

"I like to think that I am," I said, bringing my glass to my lips while my neurons fired in all sorts of directions in an attempt to guess at what she was about to tell me.

"A few years ago—maybe a year after I found out about what he'd been doing —I decided that I would offer him some home entertainment. I knew for a fact that he didn't get any action. I mean... I can see who comes in and out of his house. The poor man had to have urges driving him mad, no?"

Not having seen that twist coming but thrilled to hear more, I sipped my wine quietly while watching her eyes spark with joy as she continued her story.

"As far as I know, I'm the only woman he's ever touched," she said. "Or maybe he had sex before his accident, but if he did, he must have forgotten all about it. His brother told me that the doctor had explained it to him like the universe had taken away a whole chunk of his life, of his memories. Today, Romaro's an odd character, but not a dangerous one."

She paused her story and drank in silence.

I didn't want to interrupt her, so I just smiled.

"So, that's why I decided to get rid of my thick curtains and have an open-window policy, so Romaro can peek if he feels like it. And, to be clear, I always ask my nude models if they are fine with him watching. If not, I rearrange the room and have them pose elsewhere. So, that's the long version of why I turned you down earlier. And I'm sorry about that."

I took a sip, swallowed, and smiled at her. "Do you still pay him doctor's visits?" Although half-joke, the idea somehow turned me on.

"Don't you find it a little sad?" she asked, but it must have been rhetorical, since she continued before I could reply. "No, it didn't come out right. I don't want you to think that I pity him. It's not that. Far from it. But doesn't a man deserve to feel the touch of a woman? Not being able to leave his house doesn't negate him that right, does it?"

Maybe it was the honesty pouring out of her eyes, or maybe it was the way her lips moved as she spoke, but Virginia had me hypnotized, and I agreed with her.

"Variety is the spice of life, and unfortunately, I can't offer him that. I'm just one person," she said.

I moved closer to her on the couch and gently brushed my lips against hers. "I don't know if it's you, or what you just said, or your way of thinking, but I'm so turned on right now." I leaned down to kiss her neck, but she pushed me away, gently.

"Wait, there's more I need to tell you."

"What?" I looked at her, and something in her eyes made me add more space between us.

"If you're about to describe your house visits to me, then be warned that I won't be able to control myself," I said.

She smiled at me, a full grin that caused tiny wrinkles to appear around the corners of her eyes. "Well, Romaro *is* a good man. Always at the ready. You could hang a jacket on his cock. Feel free to go and visit him if you want. I'm sure he'd appreciate getting to know you. I know I'd appreciate getting to know you, too..."

But her eyes didn't reflect any temptation to take any action on the idea she'd just voiced.

I know that pause.

"But..." I said.

She's driving me crazy, acting like a weathercock.

"As much as I'd love to do more than paint you right now, I've yet to pin your essence down. This may seem a bit strange to hear this aloud, but I need to get to know my models really well. That's the only way I can make their personality come out of the painting. I'm not yet solid on who you are deep inside, and I find that the best way to strengthen that essence, to force it out of you—out of any model—is to deprive them of something they want."

"Deprive me of what I want?"

"Don't worry. I'm not a beast. You can have all the food and drinks you want. You'll be safe under my roof. All your basic physical needs will be met, but I need to make you crave something. Withdrawing sex is the most powerful way for me to achieve my goal."

I didn't think twice about my next move.

"Wait here," I said before rushing upstairs to my room.

I looked through my bag and dug out my diary. Everything she could possibly need to know about me was written in painstaking details. If she didn't like it, then too bad, but it would save me the trouble of having to deal with the growing feelings inside me.

If she liked it, then she'd know a lot more than anyone's ever known about me. And then we could get on with getting to know each other better.

I rushed back downstairs, and when it came time to hand it to her, I hesitated for a split second before doing it.

For relationships to work, there needs to be trust.

"Here, I want you to read this."

"What is it?"

"Details about me, my life, stories about significant events that have happened to me and have made me who I am today."

"Why?"

"Expressing my feelings aloud is difficult. I can do it through physical affection or the written word. Since you're preventing me from doing the former, I want you to read it."

"Are you sure?"

"Yes," I said, going for my glass of wine and gulping it down. "And you'll see what decision I'm here to make."

4:30 p.m.

Disappointed with the cards Virginia had thrown on the table, I'd nonetheless come to terms with what was to come.

Delayed gratification was not any worse than having to eat dessert last, once all the vegetables had been eaten. Though how I loved to eat dessert first from time to time...

But her house, her rules.

"So, what do you want to do now?" I asked, doing my best to think about anything except what kept popping up in my mind when I looked at Virginia.

She looked at her watch. "We're in the clear now. Let's use the last few hours of light in the studio."

Here goes nothing.

She refilled both of our glasses then grabbed another full bottle of wine before going upstairs.

Once we'd stepped back in the studio, I waited for her to instruct me on what to do.

"Just sit on the chaise."

"Dressed like this?" I asked, looking down at my jeans and T-shirt.

"Yes, that's fine. I'm just going to sketch your portrait for now."

So I did. I sat on the silky sheet that covered the chaise, feeling awkwardly aware of not knowing how to sit anymore.

Fortunately (or not?) she seemed to spot my discomfort.

"Just make yourself comfortable and turn your face to look my way," Virginia said.

I obeyed.

She leaned her back against the wall, a large pad of paper in one hand and a piece of charcoal in the other. She did look like an artist in her old T-shirt that slid off one of her shoulders. There was no bra strap there. To avoid increasing my already blazing libido, I didn't want to stare, but I was pretty sure she didn't have a bra on. Her nipples were poking through.

"Did you know I used to live in that apartment you're renting?" she asked.

Grateful she'd come up with a good topic, I replied after letting out a quiet sigh of relief. "No, I thought it was Eduardo's apartment."

"Well, it is now. Kind of. We own most units in the building. Over the years, we bought them as they became available, and if we could afford them, obviously. But Eduardo took over managing the rental units."

"Why is that? Was it taking too much time away from your art?"

"Hmm... Yes, but there were other reasons, too."

Is this what the weird sibling vibe had been all about?

"Okay, this is going to sound weird, but the other night, your brother was looking at us—at you—really strangely. Do these other reasons have anything to do with his behavior at the bar?"

"Good observation skills. I hadn't realized he was that obvious. You guessed right."

"You don't have to explain, but... I'm curious." *And I need to think about something other than having you naked next to me.*

"I used to oversee the interaction with renters when I was in town. But I made Eduardo very happy the day I decided to turn the family home into my painting studio."

"I'm not following. He didn't like you helping out with the rentals?"

"At first, he loved it. But on one... no, make that *two* occasions, I crossed that invisible line he said I shouldn't have crossed."

I looked at her in silence, tilting my head, unsure what she was talking about, but hoping she'd go on to fill in the gaps.

She was moving her right hand quickly on the paper pad, a slight frown on her face.

"Long story. But one of the tenants, a gorgeous Italian man, flirted with me when I checked him in. Then again, he did the same any chance he got. He'd find reasons to call me and get me to come over to the apartment to look at something... A leaky faucet, a creaky door, help with the TV... Anyway, one thing led to another, and I slept with him. But I think it was more than just sex. The man invited me out to dinner, and Eduardo saw the two of us at a restaurant. The Italian may have had his tongue down my throat at that very moment, so my brother wasn't impressed..."

"But why would he care?"

She stopped moving and dropped her pad for a second, her eyes looking up to the side, as though she had to think about it. "Being professional? Getting good reviews? It's not like I encouraged him to have sex with me instead of paying rent! It was mutual, natural, far from planned. I pushed him away a couple of times before I gave in. He was just too hot to ignore."

When she was done speaking, she brought up her pad again and resumed her movements on the paper, scratching and wiping with the tips of her fingers.

"So, what did Eduardo do?" I asked, still curious.

"What big brothers do. He yelled at me, made me feel bad for my behavior, then decided I would no longer handle any male guests. He would handle all of those himself... But since he was still working full-time at his other job, he still needed my help. So instead of splitting the tasks by units like we were doing, he made the call to split them based on guests. I'd get women and some of the couples. He'd take all solo males and the other half of the couples."

"How did you react?"

"Hmm... I was offended at first. It's not like I'd thrown myself at the man... But in a way, I was also very relieved. I didn't particularly like it when tenants dictated my schedule. Their check-in and check-out times made it hard for me to get into my creative groove. He made my life easier when he made that call."

"Okay... What's the other occasion?"

"A woman from Barcelona. I hadn't come out with my bisexuality yet. Eduardo walked up on us kissing in the staircase. Once again, I hadn't done anything. It was her who'd made a move on me. And she was gorgeous..."

"Did he react right then and there?"

"No, of course not. He's not one to make a scene in public. The following day, I called him, knowing fair well that he'd think I'd once again done something way out of line... So, after an angry exchange, he decided to handle all interactions with tenants unless there was a big emergency where he needed my help."

"And how do you feel about that?"

"I was annoyed at first, but a couple of days into it, I flipped my position. I'm happy things turned out this way. Now I get to spend more time here, less time waiting around for guests to arrive, less time cleaning apartments, making beds, cleaning sheets and towels. The whole Airbnb thing falls in my 'avoiding commitment' category."

She sipped her wine then returned to her paper pad, her hand flying on the sheet, the light rubbing sounds filled the air for a few minutes while I absorbed what she'd just told me.

About thirty minutes passed in near silence while she sketched me. Her mind (or at least her fingers) seemed focused on the task at hand. Her eyes kept bouncing from her sheet of paper to me while my own eyes took in her beauty.

Untouchable beauty... at least for now.

Her lips, her long flowing hair, her eyes... even with that little line that appeared from time to time as she scratched up her paper pad. I let my eyes drop down to her delicate shoulder that was exposed through the wide neck of her T-shirt. How I so desperately wanted to plant a thousand kisses on it. How I wanted to lift that shirt off completely, then caress her breasts...

But other than wetting my panties, this train of thoughts wasn't doing me any good. I looked out the large window instead, hoping the intermittent breeze would help cool off my urges.

A few minutes later, I saw movement in the house across the road. From where I sat at the opposite end of the room, I couldn't quite see what was happening, but I could see a silhouette moving in the window. *Romaro?*

"Your neighbor... How could he have hours of video of you without anybody else being aware of it? All of the people that visit him?"

"A while back, his uncle gave him a video camera, one of the old bulky ones. Then the following year, he got him a digital converter, so he could copy the footage and burn it to a disc. I once saw his collection. There are two parts to it. It started out as mostly bird filming. And I think that's what his uncle saw and made him so happy. That's probably what everybody thinks he's been recording on all the tapes and DVDs he has at home. Nobody wants to watch hours upon hours of chirping birds on tape. They're everywhere here.

"So, my guess is that everyone has already sat with him through a few hours of those tapes. If he ever mentions watching another one, they'll probably turn him down. I know I did until he insisted and I reluctantly agreed. That's when he showed me a video of me with a woman I was painting. I stormed out. I couldn't believe he had done that. It felt as though he'd violated my personal space... But then again, he hadn't done anything with the videos, only used them for himself. So, after I clarified with him that these special videos of me should *never* be shown to anyone else, not his uncle, not the delivery man, not anyone, I agreed to let him record more of them."

"And how can you be certain?"

"We shook on it, and that means a lot from him."

10:30 p.m.

Having taken kissing and sex off the menu left very little for us to do in a small village that didn't have a bar or a restaurant to go to and hang out at night, so we agreed just to chill and read.

Virginia sat on the comfy chair with her back resting against one arm and her legs folded over the other, the back of the chair to her left, my diary resting against her lap while I lay on the couch, pillows propping my head up, my novel in hands.

"Hmmm," she said before flipping a page with one hand, then taking a sip of her glass from the other hand.

"What?"

Her gaze met mine, and a crooked smile appeared on her face. "Very interesting..."

Now she had me puzzled. "Something in particular?"

"Yes and no. Little details. Not necessarily what I expected of you."

I began regretting my decision to let her read my diary. *Is there something I've written that she shouldn't see at all?* "Good or bad?" I decided to ask to quiet my mind, or at least prevent it from spinning out of control into freaking-out territory.

"All good, believe me. I'm not going to judge you for anything I read in here. Some personal stuff, obviously, and everyone has their own journey to go through."

"Any of it helping you capture my essence?" I asked, hopeful.

"It's helping for sure."

I tried to guess where she was, based on the thickness of pages before and after her current location, but it appeared as though she randomly flicked through sections of it as opposed to reading it from front to back.

10:20 a.m.

The following morning, Virginia handed me back my diary, and I spent about an hour transcribing my latest thoughts and recollections from the past day and evening, which didn't help to tame my horniness.

While parts of me expected her to finally let us move on because my journal would have made her understand my 'essence,' I wasn't granted that pleasure. Instead, all she said was, "Thank you for trusting me enough to let me read it."

Yeah. You're welcome.

And now, after a tasty breakfast and enough coffee to wake a bear out of hibernation, she'd upped the ante with the first official session of her painting me naked on the chaise, one arm propped above my head, my legs comfortably angled to remain in the position for a while.

But the uncomfortable—if not painful—part wasn't my posture. It was looking at Virginia and not being able to touch her. I swear she must have chosen her outfit to extract my essence by ways of mental punishment and hormonal castration.

She had put on a pair of worn-out overalls, oversized, with a few small blotches of paint here and there. The cut of the garment itself wouldn't have been particularly flattering on anyone, especially someone like her, with such a delicate figure, but she'd also not worn a shirt or a bra underneath the thick denim fabric, and the legs had been ripped just below the crotch. The results? The exposed sides of her breasts around the edges of the front panel were killing me, and the bottom only let me dream about what was hidden just a few inches above where the fabric ended. Sure, her nipples were hidden, but barely. Her outfit was so big that when she moved sideways at times, the curvature of her lower back appeared unobstructed, making me want to jump from my chaise and touch her, caress her, follow her beautiful curves... Every bone and cell in my body wanted to do her already.

"Smile at me," she said, a focused look in her eyes when I met her gaze a second later.

I did, and she smiled back, placing a hand in her back pocket, which pulled the fabric down a bit, exposing her hip bone on that side. *No panties either.*

She's naked underneath it all. My pussy twitched, and my legs jerked when I felt my wetness starting to drip down my skin.

"Virginia, you're killing me with your outfit. You look so fucking hot... I just want to walk over there and... take you, kiss you, touch you..."

"Keep that thought in mind. I promise it won't be much longer."

I brought a hand down to my pussy, trying to cup it and avoid making a mess of the sheet I sat on. "I'm about to explode here..."

"I'm sorry, but I swear it will be worth it. I'll give you the release you crave. Very soon."

I bit my lips before running my only solution by her. "Is it okay if I touch myself while you paint me?"

"By all means! But so you know, there won't be any contact between the two of us... At least, not until I finally pin your spirit down."

9:15 a.m.

We spent two more days and nights like that, with me pining for her, watching her tease me and not being able to act on it.

I'd reached a personal record in the number of times I'd masturbated in such a short period. And about half of those sessions had been in front of her. In front of Romaro's camera.

And she hadn't touched me either, just like she'd promised. Half of me felt like a depraved person who needed counseling, but the other half—the horny part—was totally fine with it. And Virginia made me feel better about my solo sessions on the chaise when she started touching herself as well while painting me.

One moment in particular would forever be etched in my mind. She was holding her paintbrush and grabbing one of her breasts with the same hand and then brought down her other hand through the side of her overalls down to her groin. Through the movements underneath the jean fabric, she obviously teased her clit, and I was pretty sure she'd also fingered herself. Although there hadn't been any physical contact between the two of us, we'd managed to come within a minute or so of each other.

Then her phone rang downstairs, ruining my momentary bliss.

She ignored it, returning her paintbrush to the canvas while one hand still stayed hidden by her pussy. But then it rang again and again, which forced her to shake her head, swear, then leave the room to get it.

Next thing I knew, she was putting an end to our painting session for the day.

"I have to go back into town. Eduardo's stuck in Madrid with his wife, and there's someone who decided to check-in earlier than she was supposed to. If I leave now, I'll make it just in time."

"Okay..."

"I'm sorry about this. Please do as you wish, keep yourself busy, read, eat, go for a walk, drink, whatever. I'll be back as soon as I can."

9:30 a.m.

Alone and naked in the studio, I looked outside. The sky was peppered with puffy clouds of varying shades of gray, but it also showed large chunks of clear, bright blue.

A bit of fresh air won't hurt, and it will certainly get my mind out of the gutter.

I went to my room and got dressed in Bermuda shorts, hiking shoes, and a long-sleeved white T-shirt. I grabbed the spare key that Virginia had left for me by the door and headed out. After locking the door, I turned around and wasn't surprised to see the curtain move in Romaro's window. I smiled his way, unsure if he could see me, then I walked up the small incline toward the church.

While lost in thought, I continued to follow the road well after I'd left the confines of the village. It was peaceful. It was beautiful. It was just what I needed right now. The chirping birds and the animal bells... It was heavenly. There was a breeze, but nothing too strong. Somewhere in the distance, I started hearing a babbling creek. It took me a few minutes, but I finally saw it, way down, running almost parallel to the road. The small brook curved its way down there, below the trees, and it called to me. I don't know why, but I wanted to soak my toes in it.

I looked down past the metal guard to estimate the difficulty of hiking all the way down, then making my way back up. At this point in the road, the slope was too steep for me to do it safely, but, as I kept walking, I finally spotted a section of the hill that was not as steep. In fact, it seemed like a path down to the creek had already been carved through the bushes and foliage and patted down, possibly by animals or humans.

I'm going for it.

I climbed over the rail, then carefully made my way down. About ten minutes later, I reached the stream. I found myself a large rock to sit on, then took off my shoes and socks, then went to stand in the shallow water. The water was cool and refreshing: the perfect medium to ground myself in paradise at that very moment. I stared at the clear water for a few minutes, wondering if I'd see tiny fish swim by my submerged feet, but I didn't see anything. So, I closed my eyes and breathed in deeply.

So relaxing.

Until a mosquito bit me behind the knee. Then another.

Argh. Time to get out of here.

I returned to the large rock where I'd left my shoes and did my best to dry my feet before donning my socks, but the mosquitos had seemingly followed me to my sitting spot, so I opted for speed instead of comfort.

A minute later, both shoes were laced up, and I started my ascent back to the road just as thunder started roaring nearby.

When I reached the road, the sky opened up, and gallon after gallon of rain began pouring out, as though the ocean had relocated to the sky and urgently needed to return home.

I began running toward the village, regretting not having worn a sports bra. My shirt and shorts were clinging to my skin, and my breasts ached from bouncing in my lacy underwire bra, but I nonetheless made it back to Virginia's home, out of breath and exhausted. But no matter how many times my hands dug in my pockets, I couldn't find the spare key I knew I'd taken with me. I checked the door, even though I remembered locking it.

Still locked, obviously.

Shit, shit, shit! Where did I lose the key?

I looked around me, but the heavy rain prevented me from seeing too far from me. The key wasn't here. *Shit.* It probably fell out of my pocket when I walked down to the creek. *Shit.* I'm not running back there to try and find it now.

I looked up, but there was nowhere to hide and stay protected from the rain.

Maybe I can get in the house from the back?

I walked around the house, hoping that one of the doors or windows would have been left open, but none of those on the ground floor were. I returned to the front door just as I remembered the nosy neighbor. He never left his house, so he *had* to be home right now.

I crossed the road and saw the now familiar movement in the window by the door.

I knocked, then remembered he was deaf so I pressed the doorbell, imagining that perhaps there was a light or some visual signal that he'd see on the inside. The door opened by about a foot a second later, but nobody was visible in the doorway.

"*¿Hola?*" I said aloud as I walked in, then turned around.

A tall, skinny man with dark brown hair was closing the door behind me, instantly blocking the rain and bringing down the noise level. His doe eyes popped on the palest skin I'd ever seen. He just stood next to the door, staring at me in his Real Madrid shirt and leisure pants, which were currently barely disguising his erection.

Virginia wasn't kidding.

I wiped my face, getting water out of my eyes and taking a better look at the kind soul who'd opened the door for me, saving me from the deluge and my own stupidity of having lost the house key. His eyes were locked on me as he stood immobile.

"*¡Gracias!*" I said before moving my hands up and down my arms, trying to warm myself up. "*¿Tiene una toalla?*" I asked, hoping he'd read my lips and have a towel I could use.

He nodded profusely, then left and returned ten seconds later with a large towel in hand. But instead of handing it to me, he opened it wide and wrapped it (and himself) around my wet body. The warmth of his limbs didn't do much to reduce my increasing shivers. His erection poked into my back, and one of his hands held both ends of the towel while the other hand patted me dry. Patting soon turned into full-on grabbing, with his hand handling my breasts like they were bags of candy. Virginia's description of him as a kind soul echoed in my mind, so I turned to look him in the eyes.

But all my body wanted was more warmth. I shivered from head to toe; my teeth had even begun clacking. He let go of my body and motioned for me to follow him, so I did, holding my towel around me. We walked into the next room, which had a large fire burning in the chimney. He sat down on one of the cushions that topped a large cowhide, then he tapped on another cushion next to his, inviting me to sit down.

I did, all the while rubbing my arms, letting the heat of the fire warm me up. Slowly. After squinting at me, he got up, left, then came back again, another towel in hand. I handed him the wet one, then reached for the dry towel he held, but he pulled it away, pointing at my wet clothes.

It does make sense to get rid of the wet clothes if I want to warm up faster. Or is it just a ploy for him to see me naked? I was too cold to give a damn, and his erection had disappeared. So, in between shakes, I managed to pull my shirt over my head. It clung to my skin, but at least the fire was right there, throwing its powerful heat my way. Then I pushed down my shorts and noticed how much dirt had accumulated on the backs of my calves, probably while I was running back. I undid my hiking shoes so I could take my shorts and socks off. I once again reached toward the dry towel Romaro was holding, but he motioned for my underwear.

At this point... Might as well.

I reached behind my back and unclasped my bra, then pulled the straps of wet fabric down and away from my arms and body, then slid down my panties, which couldn't do anything but turn into a rain-drenched roll of pink material.

Finally, he handed me the towel I so dearly wanted, which exposed his rising erection.

After stepping away from me for a few minutes, he came back with a cup of steaming liquid in his hands, his hard-on still roaring in his leisure pants.

I could smell the sweetness of the chocolate from where I stood. But when he handed me the cup, I was surprised to see it topped with a few colorful sprinkles, the kind that bakers tossed on top of cupcakes.

A child in a man's body.

His smile was genuine when he handed me the cup. He blew on it, as though to warn me it was hot.

"*¡Gracias!*" I said while I reached up to get the cup he was lowering for me.

He sat down next to me again, and we both stayed quiet while I slowly drank the warming liquid. A solid ten minutes of silence must have gone by with the two of us sitting and staring at the fire. A few times, he poked at it or added a log, but otherwise, he stayed still. My body had finally warmed back up to its regular temperature, or at least, it felt like it had. My shivers had subsided. Outside, the rain still poured, adding to the relaxing soundtrack of the fire that only my ears got to enjoy.

Being deaf must be hard: missing out on all the pleasant little sounds I take for granted.

Every now and then, between sips, I glanced down at his pants to see if his soldier had lowered to an at-ease position. And it finally did, just as I finished the last delicious drip of the super sweet hot chocolate he'd made for me.

I handed him my cup, and in doing so, my towel, which had previously held up just fine with a minor tuck of the corner around it, fell and exposed my breasts. His eyes instantly went for them, and his hands went up. And so did his cock.

Yet he surprised me. He didn't reach for my breasts; he went for the towel instead. But I wrapped my hands around his wrists and brought his pale fingers to my exposed chest instead. The look in his eyes was priceless. It was as though I'd handed him the most gigantic stuffed animal at the fair.

He kneaded me with a mixture of awkward motions, but I let him. His curiosity was genuine, his touch inexperienced. Virginia hadn't been kidding. I placed a finger on the tip of his chin to try and get his attention, and he looked up at me, his mouth agape. In Spanish, I silently asked him if he wanted to get naked. He apparently read lips very well, as not a full second went by before he'd taken off his shoes, then brought his pants and white underwear down past his ankles. He'd kept his socks and T-shirt on, though. But it was his bare erection that got my attention.

I brought my hand toward it and didn't even have a chance to fully wrap my fist around his shaft before he exploded in a quiver that shook his whole body.

He looked down at the mess he'd made, then reached for the pants he'd just taken off, covering himself up with the bunched fabric.

"*Todo bien,*" I said uselessly, since he hadn't looked my way, so he'd not seen my lips voice that it was alright.

With a couple of fingers, I turned his face so I could meet his eyes again. He looked down, so I tilted his chin up until he looked at me as I smiled tenderly.

I uttered a few comforting words as I once again took his hands to my body. When I brought his right fingers to my pussy, his eyes got round, as though he'd just seen a lion. I parted my legs and gave him a full view of everything I had to offer. And that did the trick to bring him back in business.

I moved my head toward his, then got a hold of his neck, gently guiding him to kiss me. Then, as though the man inside him had mysteriously awoken, he stopped acting like an embarrassed little boy, and his mouth swallowed my lips... But not before he awkwardly banged his teeth against mine.

He deserves to feel like a man. He deserves my guiding touch to happiness.

I let him kiss me like he meant it. Then his hungry lips left mine as he slowly made his way toward my breasts, leaving a hickey or two where he suckled a little too long.

Child-man or not, I wasn't going to risk getting pregnant out of this, so I opted for the thing I thought would be worth his while. I guided him to lie on his back, with his head resting on one of the cushions we had been sitting on. Then, straddling him, with my knees on either side of him, I got a hold of one of his arms and made my way up to his face, holding his hand. Then I brought his hand to my pussy. My eyes locked onto his, I stuck out my tongue and wiggled it, hoping he'd get the gist.

And he did.

I let my groans echo loudly. I knew he wouldn't be able to hear them, but I thought that maybe, if I were loud enough, they could vibrate through my body, and he could know how much pleasure he was giving me.

Romaro was clumsy but deserved an A+ for effort. Despite his inexperienced moves, he was slowly bringing me to my desired destination, but reaching my own orgasm wasn't my goal here. I wanted him to have a great time as well, so I brought my hips up and made eye contact with him. Then, with my index held up in the air, I made a circling motion. I didn't know if he understood what I was about to do, but I did it anyway. I carefully repositioned my knees, so I was now facing his feet, my pussy still over his mouth, then I folded my body at the hips and moved my head toward his erection.

I heard a strange grunt coming from him, but a second later, he was pulling my hips closer to his face and returned to his duty. So, I leaned forward, got a hold of his shaft, then gently brought my lips to the tip of it. He tasted salty from having just come minutes earlier.

And I swear, not two full licks along his shaft later, he came onto my face, splattering me with his musky seed.

Romaro needs some practice to extend his endurance.

He'd retracted his mouth from my pussy by the time he'd jerked underneath me, and a loud noise had come out of his mouth. After wiping my face the best I could (thankfully, I hadn't gotten any in my eyes), I got off of him and repositioned myself to lie next to him, my face close to his.

And that was when the rain finally stopped, along with the loud soundtrack it had been making while it was bouncing hard on the streets and window panes. Disappointment (or maybe shame?) shone through Romaro's brown eyes. I once again smiled dearly at him. *"Vale, vale. ¡Todo bien!"* I said, hoping he'd be reassured that he was doing well.

I leaned back on him again, this time letting my entire body hover on top of his small frame. I lifted his T-shirt so he could feel my breasts against his chest, and the poke in my stomach told me the boy-man miracle was already back in business.

My wet hair traced its way down his stomach; then I took him in my mouth after briefly kissing the tip of his cock. I tightly wrapped my lips around his shaft, and I began bobbing up and down.

There's no way he'll come in record time again, is there?

But there was no guarantee, so I gave him all I had, letting him tap against the back of my throat as I took him in fully. My wet tongue swirled around his cock as though it was following the red line of a spinning barbershop sign.

Soon enough, he came once more, but this time, I caught all of it in my mouth while he squeezed my breasts. He'd already made enough of a mess on his cowhide. As he moaned, a weird sound escaped his lips again.

That's also when I heard the roar of an engine coming around the corner and stopping. *Virginia's back.* Although I would have liked to have Romaro take me past the threshold of pleasure, I counted it as one more sign from destiny. Virginia's wish to make my essence the strongest it could be had been granted. It was even more potent than it had been when she left earlier today.

Stronger essence… I'm just the horniest I've ever been. And maybe now she'll be able to capture 'it' so we can finally have sex.

I got up and off from Romaro, and he got up, too. We both started getting dressed again, as though he'd read my mind. (Or maybe he was just following my physical cues.)

I put on my wet shirt, shorts, and shoes then grabbed my knotted panties, socks, and bra, placed them in a bag that Romaro graciously handed me.

I walked over to his front door, with him in tow. I hugged him, then kissed him on the cheek before letting myself out and crossing the short distance to Virginia's door. It was locked again, but at least I knew she was inside.

So, I knocked and waited, my body hesitant about whether or not to start shivering again.

2:50 p.m.

Virginia opened the door, a curious look on her face. "Ha! There you are!" She took in my wet hair and clothes before clearing the doorway for me to come in. "Looks like you got caught in the rain... Where did you go?"

After kicking off my water-soaked shoes, I walked toward the fireplace so I could hang my drenched bra, panties, and socks. "I headed out for a walk, but then I got caught in the rain, and..." I turned to face her after I was done hanging my underwear. "Don't be mad at me... I lost your house key! I was locked out."

"So where did you go if you didn't have a key?" But as the words left her lips, a smile began to draw on her face. "And why did you take off your underwear?"

"Your neighbor rescued me from the torrential pour," I said.

"...And?"

I felt my skin blush. "Well... He was very sweet to me, and I felt that... considering..."

"Considering?"

"Considering how kindly you talked about him..."

"And..." she said, tilting her head.

"... And with his rocking erection..."

She walked closer to me, one eyebrow raised and a twinkle in her eyes. "And?"

"And considering how much of a tease you've been to me... Essence-seeking or what not... I ... We found a way to entertain ourselves while it was raining outside."

She wrapped her arms around my back and smacked her lips onto mine. "I knew it! You're a kind soul who understands what I do, and you're willing to help!"

"Help?"

"Doing your part. You don't know how much this turns me on right now."

But no words were needed. The ardor of Virginia's kiss, and the hands that reached and peeled my shirt off were enough.

"I think we're ready to release that tension between us." She pulled me by the hand.

"Can't we stay here? By the fire?" I asked.

"We could... Or we could go upstairs and give him a good show... Your pick."

A second later, I made up my mind and followed her upstairs, riding the blossoming wave of excitement about our upcoming semi-private session.

3:00 p.m.

When Virginia pushed open her bedroom door, my eyes landed on a large painting of a younger JuanMa; it reigned above her headboard. On the next wall, the large window which faced Romaro's house was wide open. I walked up to it and saw a tripod stationed in his house, dead center in his window, aimed at Virginia's room, but the neighbor wasn't there; no camera or equipment was attached to the tripod either.

"Don't worry, he'll be up and filming us in no time," Virginia said. "I know him. He's probably checking the other window right now."

Or cleaning up the mess he made on the cowhide.

I took off my wet shorts, and Virginia pushed me onto her bed, even though our dress code was far from equivalent. But as she approached me on all fours, like a business-attired tigress coming for her prey, my heart began pounding in my chest. When she reached me, I started undoing the delicate buttons of the silky blouse she'd put on before heading into town earlier today.

Once I was done, she helped me take it off of her, exposing a sexy bronze bra. I lowered the zipper on the side of her pencil skirt, then slid my hands underneath the smooth lining, feeling the warmth of her soft skin along her narrow hips. My arms helped push down her skirt, but she took care of removing it entirely, soon kicking it off to the floor with her bare feet.

She was gorgeous, mesmerizing, stunning. The woman had put a spell on me, and the lacy bronze fabric that barely covered her hot body only served to make me want her more. She straddled me then stretched and lowered herself so her chest rested on top of mine. Her lips went for my mouth as though that was where they belonged. Her hands had taken hold of my face, so I closed my eyes and followed her lead, enjoying every flick of her tongue, every bite of her lips. I just let my fingers graze the soft skin of her back and of her sides as our mouths devoured each other's. Her body swayed on top of mine, my breasts rubbing against her bra, my groin wanting nothing more than some action— sooner rather than later.

Then she let one of her hands slide down from my face, down past my neck and my collarbone, to finally stop on one of my breasts. Its mere presence there made me realize my chest was heaving. I reached behind her back and unclasped her bra before peeling down the straps from her shoulders and letting them slide off down her arms. As though we were on the same wavelength, she instinctively pulled her arms back to allow me to finish my task before her hands returned to their previous positions, but I wanted more.

And I wanted it now.

I rolled and flipped her small body. She landed softly on the bed, a foot or so off from where we were a second prior, but with me on top. When I made eye contact with her, a hungry look flickered in her sultry brown eyes. I stood on my knees, towering over her beautiful body so I could take off her bronze thong.

But then I reconsidered. Virginia had made me wait for days, I could—and I would—tease her for at least a few minutes.

I lowered my face to her belly button, then began tracing a wet line with the tip of my tongue, all the way to the top of her panties. Then I began blowing my warm breath over the fabric of her thong, warming her pussy, but not directly. I let my fingers follow the intricate lines in the lacy design, knowing fair well that I was driving her mad.

At least, it'd drive me mad if she did this to me.

Varying the pressure of my digits, I followed every exquisite curve over her most sensitive areas. At times, I lingered and pushed the tips of my fingers as far into her folds as the fabric would let me. She'd already moistened her thong well through the material, and I brought my mouth to her wet spot, tasting her unique shade of muskiness, albeit indirectly. And her flavor and scent were heavenly. I pointed my tongue and let it glide up and down over the wet fabric. Her hips began heaving and swaying as moans started to escape her lips. I started sucking on her underwear over her clit before finally allowing myself to slide one finger under the fabric.

"Come on," she said. "Stop teasing me!"

But I decided to continue doing just that. I let my finger barely touch the contour of her outer lip on one side. I went up and down about a dozen times, slowly, while I began eating her through the fabric of her soaked thong.

"Please!" she begged.

Okay, enough is enough.

I slid two fingers on either side of her hips, then slowly peeled her thong down toward me, exposing her bare pussy. I briefly bent down to brush it with a kiss then unfolded my body again so I could take her panties off fully.

Now rid of all unnecessary undergarment, we only had to enjoy ourselves, and I was looking forward to releasing that tension. I parted her legs and nestled my face by her beautiful pussy, but she reached down and pulled on my hair, gently.

"Come up here," she begged.

I let my body glide up against hers, then moved my ass up so my knee could rub against her wet groin as our lips once again met in a ravenous kiss. I got a hold of her small breasts, massaging them, letting her nipples peak in my palms as the motions of her hips made it clear she had begun aiming at her finish line. I dropped one of my hands to replace my knee and began fingering her, slow at first, but her hand joined mine, and she started rubbing her clit, her soft moans whispering in my ears as I looked down at her pussy.

"I'm close," she said.

I lowered myself between her legs again and nibbled on her lips, my tongue intermittently penetrating her as I sucked on her opening.

Her moans grew louder, her right leg began shaking against my side, and I felt her insides clenching against my tongue as she let out a final groan.

"Come here," she ordered, and I brushed my body against hers as I did.

I took a good look at Virginia. With her hair spread out around her face like that, on her gray satin sheets, a wide grin on her face, my heart skipped a beat in my chest. "You're so gorgeous," I said before cuddling sideways in the open arms she was offering me.

"No, you are."

Inhaling deeply, a sense of overwhelming joy filled my gut as Virginia's citrusy perfume entered my lungs. She tightened her embrace around me, squishing my breasts together as she spooned me from behind. Then, one of her hands began caressing my side before she lowered it to my hips, then to my pussy. Her fingertips circled my swollen lips as she murmured sweet Spanish nothings in my ears. If I hadn't been turned on before, I was about to erupt now. I parted my thighs, letting my upper leg rest on my foot, opening myself up to her soft touch.

She began massaging me by pressing two fingers against her thumb on the other side of my folds. She repeated the gentle pressure from the top of one lip to the bottom, then the other. My nerve endings were simmering; I was on the brink of explosion. So, when she finally dipped her fingers in my opening, gently tapping against my sweet spot, it only took a few seconds before she triggered my orgasm.

And it was just the first of many to come.

3:50 p.m.

Exhausted, but in the best of ways, I let my head hang at the foot of the bed, completely satisfied and finally freed from the spell of arousal she'd had me under from the moment I first met her.

Well, not entirely free, but the spell had lost the strength of its hold for now. I suspected it would soon reappear and grow on me until I had sex with her again.

Virginia was just that kind of woman; she held that sort of epicurean power over people. *Or at least over me.*

As I lifted my head and then the rest of my body to sit in front of her, facing her headboard, I had a look at the painting that hung above her.

"Something's still going on between the two of you... Or else you wouldn't keep JuanMa's painting on your wall, no?"

She tilted her face up, looking at it from beneath it, then shook her head. "As I told you before, it's on and off, but I can't seem to let go of his painting. There's nothing that prevents you from going for him. I'm serious."

I came and lay next to her, cradling her in my arms. Then she continued. "In fact, why don't I arrange for him to come up here? Would you like that?" she asked, turning her head around to meet my eyes.

"Here?"

"Yes, here. You. Me. Him. What do you say?"

My body responded by sending a shiver up and down my spine. I debated with the idea for a few seconds in my mind. Virginia didn't seem like one to ask trick questions that backfired if I didn't select the correct answer. She seemed honest, nothing like some of the manipulative people I'd met before.

"Sure... It could be fun," I said, watching the smile appear on her face.

She got out of bed. "I'll go get my phone."

And with that, she left her room. I watched her beautiful bare ass stroll away from me, then I closed my eyes and smiled.

How fucking awesome is this going to be!

8:05 a.m.

Realizing that the end of my stay in Spain was approaching faster than I wanted it to, I rolled over to the nightstand to grab my phone so that I could check my calendar. But I was determined to enjoy every remaining minute of it. Virginia was certainly making it easy to do now, allowing me to share her bed, her body, her time.

I flipped the sheets away from my naked body, then got out of bed. The cold floor greeted my feet and sent a slight shiver through me, so I hurried to my room to find myself some clothes to wear. But when I dug through the bag I'd brought, I realized I'd run out of clean clothes. I hadn't expected to stay here so many days, after all.

So, I headed downstairs, where a delicious aroma of sweet onions and eggs emanated from. I wrapped my arms around Virginia, who was standing in front of the stove preparing breakfast.

"I didn't bring enough clothes with me. I don't have anything clean to wear. Is there any chance I could do laundry?" I asked her.

"Sure, or you can borrow some of my clothes if you want. Go and help yourself to whatever's in my wardrobe upstairs. We can do a batch of laundry later, or if you need detergent to hand wash certain items, it's in the vanity upstairs."

"Cool," I said. "Do you need help with breakfast?" I asked her as she put the finishing touches on her fluffy potato, onion, and egg tortilla.

"No, it's all good. Go and get dressed. JuanMa should arrive any minute now."

I started climbing the stairs when she yelled a few more words at me. "Not that we would mind if you stayed naked."

"Funny!" I said as I continued to climb my way back to her room.

Free to roam through the clothes in her wardrobe, I took my time, but soon came to realize that most of her stuff wouldn't fit me. She was merely built on a smaller frame than I was, and my breasts were also larger. But I finally found a pair of black yoga pants and a light pink T-shirt that would stretch enough to accommodate my upper body. It featured a faint design of a target, and it would be perfect for me to wear while washing my clothes. I slid the top and pants on without any underwear, since my first task was to hand wash all my soiled undies in the bathroom.

By the time I had hung all my delicates in the shower upstairs and run back down to the kitchen, Virginia was done cooking and was setting the table for the three of us.

As though timed flawlessly, the roar of an engine got louder, then it stopped. A knock echoed in the house, and Virginia headed to the door to let in her guest.

"*¡Hola*, JuanMa!" Virginia said before kissing him on both cheeks.

"*¡Hola, hermosa!*" he said before noticing me walking up to the door.

"And you remember my friend, right?" Virginia said to JuanMa before turning to wink at me.

I walked up to him and greeted him with the customary double kiss.

"Yes, of course," he said. "Good morning." He then turned to Virginia. "I'm going to get a few things out of my car."

"Do you need help?" I offered.

"No, thank you."

About five minutes later, he'd unloaded everything he'd brought, including his guitar and a case of wine. *Yes, a case,* which made me feel like a bad guest. I hadn't brought anything (except for my expectations).

"I'm sorry I didn't bring anything," I said to Virginia as I watched him move the bottles he'd brought down to the cellar.

"Don't worry about it. I invited you! There was no need to bring anything. Now JuanMa's picky about his wine. That's why he brought his own bottles."

"You're planning on drinking that much?" I asked him, jokingly.

"Better to have too much than not enough, plus we'll share. These bottles will be gone in no time."

A few minutes later, the three of us sat at the kitchen table and began eating the delicious tortilla that Virginia had prepared, accompanied by some roasted red peppers and *serano* ham.

"Delicious, as always," JuanMa said after eating his first bite of the fluffy egg dish.

I cleaned up my plate in no time then got up to make more coffee. When it was ready, I turned to JuanMa and Virginia, asking them if they wanted more.

"Not for me," he said.

"No, I'm good as well," Virginia replied.

"Then it's all mine," I said, happy to be the only real coffee addict in the house.

"Isn't that your shirt?" JuanMa asked Virginia, his head nodding toward me.

"Yes—" she said.

"Laundry day. She was kind enough to let me borrow it," I said, feeling a little odd.

"I think it looks much better on her. What do you think?" she asked him.

He stared at my breasts for a second, and I looked down at myself, noticing my nipples poking through the thin fabric, but also realizing that I could totally see the dark circles of my areolae. I hadn't realized I was showing through, since I hadn't bothered to look at myself in the mirror after getting dressed. I felt blood rushing to my cheeks.

"It looks good on you, Virginia, but I have to say that she... rocks that shirt... I mean..." His eyebrows went up, then he tilted his head slightly. "I feel bad for the thin fabric, but then again..."

And as though I wasn't embarrassed enough already, Virginia cupped a full feel of my left breast.

"She's got beautiful breasts, and I'll gladly let her stretch all my shirts if that means I get to see them and touch them like that." She got up to poke a gentle kiss on my lips, then dropped her hand from my breast and returned to sit and finish the rest of her breakfast as though nothing had just happened.

A little confused and taken off-kilter, I sat and sipped my coffee in silence, staring at the table, unsure where things were heading from here. I'd had threesomes before, but I'd never been in this awkward position of not knowing if that was where we were heading. I didn't know what Virginia had told JuanMa. I didn't know if that was even part of his plans. But he was apparently interested in the goods I was inadvertently showing off right now. Each sip of coffee seemed to fuel my discomfort about not knowing what was to come.

Though, come to think of it... What man would turn down a threesome with two women, one of whom he's been sleeping with on and off for years?

...The type of man who's in a committed relationship with someone else, that's who.

But he wouldn't be here right now if that were the case, right?

My head was beginning to ache from over-thinking this situation. I continued sipping my coffee in silence instead. *It's way too early for a fuck fest to start anyway.*

And then I watched JuanMa pull out a small baggie whose scent spilled into the room the moment he opened it.

That would be good for my nerves right now. And perfect to get us over the awkward beginning, bridge the gap of discomfort, and bring our actions into the realm of the less socially acceptable, but more thoroughly enjoyable.

He began talking to Virginia about his upcoming gig in town while he rolled a couple of joints.

"Are you going to smoke this early in the morning?" Virginia asked him, a slight frown on her face as he licked the second one.

"Maybe, maybe not," he said, his eyes on her.

An uncomfortable pause occurred as they stared at each other.

"Could you wait until... After...?" she asked.

"Of course, *cariño*," he said.

Virginia exhaled loudly then got up, pushing her chair back along the concrete floor. "Good! Let's go and sit in the living room," Virginia said, holding out her hand toward me.

I got to my feet, clasped her hand, and followed her gorgeous little ass toward the lit fireplace. JuanMa followed us, then stopped to touch the pink bra I'd hung by the fireplace days ago, after I'd been caught in the rain with Romaro. It was long dry, but would require hand-washing as well, to get rid of the smoke scent that likely permeated it now.

Shit, I forgot to wash those.

"Yours?" he said, turning to look at me. He even gave me a full up and down scan then paused on my breasts again before meeting my gaze.

My heart changed gears, doubling its cadence just as quickly as my skin heated up. And then he started approaching me, which made my breathing stop. *So, this is really going to happen? Just like that? No preamble? And sober?*

While my mind zoned in on the handsome man that was quickly entering my personal space, I lost track of Virginia. Then, as JuanMa's spicy cologne reached my nostrils, his tall body mere inches away from mine, he raised a hand and brought it to my cheek, his finger grazing down until he found my jaw bone, which he then traced down to my chin.

I felt my mouth open. My shallow breathing was hardly present, but it seemed my heart was throwing itself against my rib cage. Then he leaned toward me and pressed his soft lips against mine just as my breasts were being grabbed from behind. Startled a bit for a split second, I realized it was Virginia who'd just wrapped herself around behind me, and was now bringing her hands underneath the fabric of my borrowed shirt. JuanMa's insistent tongue brought my focus back to the handsome man in front of me. I let my arms fly up to wrap themselves around his strong back; his muscles begged for attention underneath the soft plaid shirt he wore.

Virginia lifted my top from behind, letting the fabric rest above my now exposed breasts. She massaged one of them while her other hand quickly headed down the front of my yoga pants.

JuanMa got a hold of my other breast, and his growing erection poked at my stomach, telling me he was enjoying this. I brought one of my hands between us and began to undo the pearl snaps of his shirt. One after the other, I released them, their faint sound only serving to turn me on even more. A few seconds later, I flipped away one side of his shirt and slid my hand down his chest. It wasn't hairless, but he was far from being the hairiest man I'd touched. A few hairs peppered his pecks, and a dark line began just below his belly button. How I wanted to see what lay at the end of that trail...

Virginia's digits had begun sliding up and down my wet slit while her other hand was now twisting my nipple gently. She kissed the back of my neck, her soft and warm breaths making shivers race throughout my entire body. JuanMa's mouth had moved down to the front of my neck, and his hands got busy peeling off his top layer.

Shirtless, he pulled back from me long enough to get a hold of my rolled-up shirt, and then he lifted it above my head.

Virginia appeared to be of the same mind as she retrieved her hand from my pants, and then pushed them down my legs. A second later, she guided my ankles out of the garment while JuanMa returned to me, his hands on the small of my back at first, then he brought one down to my ass and brought me closer to him. His scent was invigorating and hypnotizing. From the corner of my eyes, I saw Virginia relocate behind JuanMa, her hands coming between him and me to undo his belt, then his jeans. While his lips reconnected with mine, I closed my eyes and let my desires and his actions guide me. I could hear his belt buckle clinking as his pants were taken off, probably by Virginia, since JuanMa's hands were still pleasantly groping me.

Next thing I knew, he was pushing me toward the couch.

"Sit on the edge of it, with your legs spread open," he ordered.

Hypnotized by his sexy voice, I obeyed with my eyes now open and was able to see that Virginia had gotten him fully naked. His impressive cock was at the ready in front of him, my no-longer-hidden treasure shining at the end of his line of pubic hair.

My chest heaved in anticipation of feeling him inside me, feeling his hard body against mine, and once again feeling his strong hands on my skin. But Virginia, who was still fully dressed in her skirt and blouse, turned him around and claimed his mouth. His hands went for her face at first, then he lowered them to her shirt and began undoing the delicate buttons. One of her hands had wrapped itself around his shaft, the other on his ass. My attention was divided between the two of them and their actions, but it only served to double my hunger. Once her buttons were all undone, he pulled the silky fabric out of her skirt and tossed it toward the large chair next to the couch. Then he slid down the zipper on the side of her skirt, and a couple of seconds later, it also got tossed aside, although Virginia's feet had done that.

With the hot pair making out in front of me, him fully naked and her in just her black lacy bra and thong, my system was revved up and ready for action. I didn't know where things would go from here, but I enjoyed watching them kiss in front of me while she began giving him a hand job. I moved one of my hands to my right breast and let my other stroke my pussy, my legs still parted at the edge of the couch.

Then, as I was getting myself into a rhythm, enjoying the view and cranking up my own arousal, JuanMa slapped Virginia on the ass and, in Spanish, told her to get her gorgeous ass next to mine on the couch.

And with a beaming smile, she did. First, she brought her lips to mine, just leaning toward my face, but then she knelt next to me on the couch, but farther back, in between the back cushions and my body. And the gorgeous Spaniard walked toward us, a longing look in his eyes, but my glance quickly abandoned his beautiful eyes in favor of his even more glorious shaft.

He bent down to grab a pillow, then moved the coffee table off to the side and tossed his pillow in front of me before sitting down on it, his long legs extended off to one side. His hands dug into the back of my thighs as he pulled my entire body closer to the edge of the couch, bringing my pussy closer to his face, to his mouth. With Virginia massaging my breasts and kissing the back of my neck and shoulders and JuanMa moving in to eat my pussy, I closed my eyes, eager to relish the pleasant sensations that had already begun to deluge over my body.

My moans and whimpers accompanied the crackling sounds of the fire a few feet in front of us. JuanMa's slurping sounds—or perhaps it was just those of my own wetness and excitement—added to the mix, then Virginia whispered naughty things in my ear, all in Spanish, with her interdental lisp. My level of excitement had never been higher, and JuanMa began adding a finger then two to the mix, I knew I wasn't going to last much longer, though I would have done anything to make my current state last forever. I realized I'd been selfish enough, my own hands having done nothing but keep me balanced on the edge of the couch. I could have taken care of Virginia's pussy instead. I twisted my upper body sideways toward her, leaving my pussy in JuanMa's very skillful hands and tongue, then Virginia relocated next to me.

I slid my palm into the front of her thong, letting my middle finger go directly down her slippery slit while I brought her upper body close to me with my other hand and arm. My mouth devoured hers as she continued to massage my breasts and I stroked her. But the incoming shivers that jerked my lower body told me I was just seconds from exploding, so I let go of her side as my back arched and my entire body started convulsing in uncontrollable shakes. My breathing was jagged, my moans coarse, my mind in an altered state of ecstasy. I then remembered my hand in Virginia's pussy and realized I'd been forcing my fingers into her while my entire body was pulsing. I opened my eyes and met hers while I was still shaking. Now overly sensitive, I gently pushed away the head of the gorgeous man who'd made me come in the best post-breakfast delight I'd ever had.

But, of course, my two lovers also deserved their happy endings, so as soon as enough blood made its way back to my brain, I focused on them again with one hand covering my pussy, feeling my heartbeat slowly returning to normal.

JuanMa now stood in front of a seated Virginia, his dick staring her right in the eyes while her glare was aimed upward toward his face. Her mouth agape, she brought his cock to her lips, her tongue circling his already glistening tip. I moved to reposition myself behind Virginia, my still-throbbing pussy resting against her ass, my legs dangling on either side of her, then I slid my hand back in her thong and resumed fingering her, but the undergarment made it a little hard. Since taking it off right now would interrupt their activities, I opted to gently pull the fabric down and push the front to the side, using both my hands to make it happen. The hand that held her lacy fabric aside also parted her folds while I brought my other hand to my mouth for a second, so I could spit on it and give me more lubrication with which to play. She was wet, but most of it had soaked into the lining of her panties.

And Virginia began striking JuanMa's clean-shaven sack as she continued bobbing onto his glorious cock. All the while, I teased her pussy. Every now and then, I caressed her breasts, pulling one out of its lacy holder, but leaving the bra tied up behind her to perk them up some more. Her small nipple peaked in one of my hands as I continued to finger her with the other. While her mouth was overflowing with JuanMa's manhood, it didn't prevent her from moaning here and there. And based on the goosebumps that began to cover her soft skin and her own body beginning to spasm against mine, I knew she was about to come. I returned my second hand to her pussy, this time rubbing her clit the way she'd shown me she preferred it as she came, her insides tightening rhythmically around my fingers. One of her hands grabbed hold of my knee, squeezing it just as her moans—muffled by the fabulous cock still pushing in and out of her mouth—morphed into a long, pleased sigh.

And as though the mere sight of her coming in front of him had been the cue he was waiting for, JuanMa gave one last push into Virginia's mouth, but then brought his hips backward a tad. Whether it was his own reflex or out of respect for Virginia—I'd never know—but the look they shared as she licked her lower lip, getting the last drip of him after he'd pulled out and she'd swallowed it all was priceless.

The three of us were still heavily breathing, sweaty, and horny—at least I was still horny—JuanMa dropped his naked body next to us on the couch.

He turned to Virginia and asked, "Now?"

"Sure. If you want to."

I had no idea what that had been about, but when he got up, went to the kitchen, and then returned with one of his joints and a lighter, I understood.

Virginia got up and walked away. "I'll be back," she said, heading toward the kitchen.

JuanMa sat on the sheep hide in front of the fire and lit his joint.

I pulled a few tissues from the box in the corner and dried myself up a bit, even though I knew the faucet that'd been opened by those two gorgeous Spaniards was going to have me dripping wet for the foreseeable future.

The moment it reached my nostrils, the smell pulled me in. I tossed my tissues into the burning fire and joined him on the hide before he could turn around and offer it to me. So, he passed it with a smile, probably happy to have me on his team.

What was up with Virginia earlier? Does she not like pot?

When she walked back to us with a large pitcher of water and glasses, then stole the joint from JuanMa's hands, she answered my question without speaking.

The three of us lay on our backs as we passed the joint back and forth. I was the meat in a spaced-out sandwich of Spanish bread. As smoke from our joint rose above us, clouding our view of the exposed wooden beams in the ceiling, my high got stronger. But it wasn't a downer high; it was one that wired me. By the time we finished the first joint, I had closed my eyes and let my right hand reach toward JuanMa, first finding his hip, then his limp equipment. I began teasing it with the tips of my fingers while I let my left hand wander over onto Virginia's soft skin, this time going for her breasts, which were still hidden under her bra.

As though she'd read my mind, I felt her body fold into a seated position. I opened my eyes, one hand still touching JuanMa's growing excitement while I watched Virginia take off her bra, then her panties.

Naked, she offered me a hand and helped me up, then did the same to JuanMa.

"Let's head upstairs. My bed is much more comfortable," she said.

3:45 p.m.

After our sex marathon, aware that 4 p.m. was quickly approaching, we all agreed to give our private parts a well-deserved intermission and our lungs a chance to breathe some fresh air.

And since JuanMa had offered to barbecue us a feast, then take his guitar and play some of his latest songs, it was a no-brainer. We got ourselves dressed again—I'd once again put on my borrowed shirt and yoga pants, Virginia had opted for a short flowing dress, and JuanMa had put his plaid shirt and jeans back on—then we headed out into Virginia's backyard.

She uncorked one of the bottles JuanMa'd brought and then joined me at the table while our lover-boy got the charcoal ready. After handing him his glass, she whispered something in his ear, he turned around, and they both smiled at me.

"What's going on?" I asked.

"Nothing," Virginia said before winking, then walking my way. She sat on the opposite side of the table from me.

"Did I do something?" I asked her, partly worried, but mostly curious about the secret they'd just shared, possibly at my expense.

"What do you mean?"

"What was that just now?" A tiny part of me felt left-out, so I added, "I can't be part of your secret club?"

"Oh, that's just it," she said, winking again. "You're part of our secret club now. And as to what you *did*? You know *everything* you did. And it's *all* good, believe me."

And when she finished airing those words, something probed my parted legs under the table.

My body jerked, my hand went directly for the intruder, but after realizing it was Virginia's bare foot, I let it be. After all, it was her house, and if she wanted to play footsie with me outside, in her backyard, where a neighbor could potentially walk by and see us, then it was her decision.

I smiled at her, moved my ass a little closer, and brought out my chest, all the while leaning my head back to look at the sky, listening to the church bells echoing against the green hills that surrounded us.

How I could get used to spending time with her. And with JuanMa, of course, I thought, bringing my gaze back to earth and looking at the tall man stoking coals and moving a fan to increase the intensity of their shade of red. *What an ass he has...*

"And you're wondering if you did something wrong..." she repeated, bringing my attention back to her. She was shaking her head while her toes kept tickling the fabric of my pants. I could feel myself drenching the fabric over my groin, my lips were still swollen and hypersensitive, and the random movements of her toes made me twitch in all the right places.

I started sipping my wine, and then Virginia took away her foot and headed back in the house for a few minutes. She came back with a small speaker, which she set at the end of the table. A few seconds later, she was looking at the screen of her phone, and Spanish pop hits began playing softly from the speaker.

"If you're not going to sing for us, I'll put on some music, then," Virginia said, stretching her arm out to pinch his ass.

She sat in front of me once again. From the way she was positioned, her hands resting on her knees, I could tell her legs were parted wide.

Is this an invitation? Only one way to find out.

I kicked off my flip-flop and brought my right foot to her groin. As though she'd expected my move, her hands came up to hold my ankle, and then she lifted the fabric of her skirt over my foot. My toes tickled her bare, wet folds, and she smiled at me.

Without breaking eye-contact with me, she began to speak to our lover-boy. "JuanMa, did you know I'm painting our new friend?"

"No," he said from the barbecue area. "Can I see it?"

"It's still a work in progress," she said, arching her back a little. Her body began to sway to the thrills my toes were likely inducing in her. "But when I'm done, if she likes it, then I'll let you see it," she finished. Her chest was now heaving more noticeably, and she was pushing her hips forward, rocking her pelvis against my toes.

"When do you think you'll be done?" I asked her.

"It depends on how busy you keep me," she said. "... With other ... activities." Without breaking the spell she had me under with her sultry eyes, she moved her hand down her skirt and pulled my foot closer to her, forcing my big toe to enter her while wrapping the rest of my toes in her fingers.

Feeling out of balance (and running out of leeway for movement), I lowered my body a tad, and I did so without breaking our gaze.

She yanked on my leg repeatedly, which altered her breathing, her chest no longer discreet in its heaving, her erect nipples now boldly poking through the fabric of her bra and shirt. Then, as her body jerked its first full-body wave, she broke eye contact with me and just pulsated, her other hand reaching toward her collarbone, a muffled moan escaping her lips as her face scrunched up in a muted orgasmic expression.

That's when I turned to look at JuanMa. His eyes were on Virginia, and the erection in his jeans was as discreet as her moans had been. I looked around to the neighbors' yards and fortunately didn't see anyone standing there.

"So much for taking a break," JuanMa said to Virginia.

After inhaling deeply, she reopened her eyes, sent me a big smile, then turned to spit out a smug one-liner to JuanMa in Spanish. Then she added, in English, "Would you be kind enough to refill our glasses?"

"Of course," he said before heading to the house.

I don't want this mountain getaway to end. Ever.

As he poured wine into our glasses, he said, "I'd do anything for you two beautiful ladies."

He returned to his barbecuing duties, and Virginia started to brag about how talented he was.

"Come on, JuanMa, play us a song?" she begged.

"I'm just about done grilling here. I don't want things to burn—"

A loud ring sounded from the pocket of his jeans. He retrieved his phone, looked at the number, then answered it. A few seconds later, an anxious expression on his face, he headed down the slope a little to continue his phone conversation in private. Virginia turned down the volume on the speaker.

When he walked back to us a couple of minutes later, he was shaking his head.

"I have to head back into town," he said.

"Why?" Virginia asked.

"Work."

Virginia furrowed her brows. "I thought you said they'd given you the night off?"

"The other bartender got into an accident. He's okay, but he can't make it back into town tonight, so I must fill in for him. Can't wait till I can quit that job and become a full-time musician," he said.

He finished the last sip of his wine. I was pretty sure he'd only had a couple of glasses maximum, but he said he was going to make himself a cup of coffee, then pack up and head out in about thirty minutes.

"Then you've got time for at least one song," I said, begging him.

He looked at me, pursing his lips. "Okay, but just one song. And I need to get the meat off the grill first." He went inside to grab an empty plate and his guitar.

After moving the assortment of sausages onto a plate, which he handed to Virginia, he sat on a stool and ensured his guitar chords were all tuned correctly, then he began strumming something catchy, but Virginia stopped him.

"JuanMa, please. If you're only going to play one, can you sing my song?"

"Of course," he said.

And instead of strumming, his fingers began dancing on the chords. His left hand moved up and down, while his right fingers picked at the chords one by one, but quickly, which reminded me of flamenco, but a little slower.

Then, when his dusky voice began singing, adding to his already beautiful guitar melody, the floodgates opened in my groin. I swear, there had to be a special, hidden, hormonal compartment that got triggered by sounds, and only when it was a particular tone or frequency.

I remained mesmerized, and it was only when Virginia began clapping that I was able to come out of my stupor. I joined her claps and got up.

"Now, that was just breathtaking," I said. "I want to hear more!"

"Maybe some other time. I have to pack up and head back to Donostia now."

And he entered the house again, leaving Virginia and me alone.

"Incredible, no?" she asked.

I was shaking my head. "Amazing."

We chit-chatted some more while our lover-boy ran up and down the stairs, picking up his things and putting them in his car.

Then he popped outside to say he was ready to leave.

"Sad to see you go," I told him while hugging him.

"Believe me. I'd rather stay here and have fun than go back to work, but if I don't..."

Virginia got up and said, "I'll walk you out."

They headed to the front door, which put an end to the threesome part of my Spanish getaway.

But based on the look in Virginia's eyes when she returned, we were far from done with enjoying each other's presence.

1:40 a.m.

I woke up in the middle of the night, opened my eyes, and saw Virginia lying peacefully on the bed, curled up in a C, facing me, about a foot away from me. Her brown hair covered her pillowcase, giving her a semblance of a halo.

Virginia...

She'd grown on me way too fast, and even though I'd done everything to prevent my head from going into a relationship-seeking mode, I kept thinking of ways to stretch this out. She had a daughter in Paris. Maybe I could see her again if I took the job? But then, if she came to visit her daughter, she wouldn't have time to have a fuck fest with me... That would be weird.

Or maybe the painting still in progress was the one reason I could stay in touch after this trip. Like she'd said, she'd have to show it to me once it was completed. Considering I only had less than two full days left in Spain, chances were that she wouldn't be done before I had to go.

I watched her chest move as she quietly inhaled and exhaled. So peaceful. So beautiful. So angelic-looking when she slept.

But this whole year has been about getting away from needing a relationship. Why am I craving one right now? Wouldn't it be like starting over or back-tracking? Or am I looking at this wrong? Who's to say that I'm not meant for a semi-permanent relationship with someone? And maybe a relationship with a woman would be better than one with a man?

And that mind of yours is spinning out of control... Again.

She made it very clear that she doesn't want any commitment, and you're already making plans that rely on the two of you being an item.

Seriously.

Get it together, girl!

Breathe, let her live, and just see where it goes from here.

9:05 a.m.

I picked up my phone and read the message that had made it beep.

"Eduardo's asking me what time I want to check out tomorrow," I relayed to Virginia as she sat down next to me with our breakfast plates.

"We can head into town whenever you want. I don't have meetings or anything scheduled for tomorrow."

I raised my shoulders. "I've already packed most of my things. I just need to bring back what I have here, then meet up with your brother to do the checkout. So, what should I tell him?"

"Does he know where you are now?" she asked.

I shook my head. "I know the story there. I didn't want to make things weird."

She finished chewing the piece of toast she'd put in her mouth then got up. "Don't worry. Let me call him right now." And she took her phone and stepped out of my ears' reach.

I had finished half my plate by the time she returned to the kitchen.

"It's sorted," she said. "I'll drive you home and take care of your checkout. He was just worried that he wouldn't have time to check you out and clean the apartment before he heads out of town. I told him I'd take care of it. But he insisted on beginning the cleanup while you're here with me anyway."

"Okay, so you're not in trouble?"

"No. He just thinks that you're here to model for me. He doesn't need to know about the rest."

10:40 a.m.

I packed what little items I'd left out in the apartment while waiting for Virginia to return after she found a parking spot. In doing so, I looked at the objects around me with a new set of eyes. It was Virginia who'd decorated it when she used to live here. The choice of wall colors was warm—like her personality—and the eclectic selection of exotic souvenirs she'd likely brought back from her multiple trips abroad was intriguing—like her spirit.

Did a more important purpose bring me here?

Why did Virginia appear into my life?

There were old photo frames and lots of smaller paintings. As I looked at them more closely, I recognized the same pseudonym with which she signed the bottom right corners of her paintings, but the pieces in this apartment didn't stir in me the same emotions I'd felt while looking at the larger ones at her house.

Probably some of her earlier works?

Then again, maybe I'm just imagining things.

Is this what's happening here?

Am I infatuated with her so much that I can't see clearly?

This apartment felt so comfortable, and maybe that was why I liked Virginia so much. We shared a lot in common, at least in terms of how to decorate an apartment, taste in books, movies, men, and, as I'd learned over the past week, how to please each other's body.

10:50 a.m.

With my suitcase packed and ready by the door, I was double-checking every drawer to ensure I hadn't forgotten anything when Virginia knocked on the apartment door.

"Come in!" I yelled from the bedroom before walking back into the living room to meet her.

"My old place..." she said. "It's been a while since I've been in here." She looked at the items hanging on the walls and resting on the shelves. "Did I tell you about this movie?" Virginia asked, sliding out the DVD about the woman discovering her sexuality.

"No, what's special about it?"

She flipped the cover in her hands, and a nostalgic smile appeared on her lips. "It changed my life."

How I enjoyed watching her beautiful face express old memories.

I am so going to miss her.

"In what way?" I asked, heading toward her, then wrapping my arms around her small frame from behind.

She rested her head against my shoulder. "It made me understand who I was, what I craved. I know... Maybe it's not 'appropriate'," she said with air quotes. "My brother told me to remove my personal items. I did. Most of them, but I left those few videos behind. If a guest's life can be transformed by one of these movies as much as this one has transformed mine, it deserves to be watched. I don't care what the other guests think about it."

She turned to face me while staying in my arms,

"Global sexual enlightenment," I said, smiling at her, tracing her jaw with a finger. "Sounds like a social cause worth supporting."

She double-tapped me on the chest. Her expression had turned a little stern, probably the business façade she used when meeting with galleries. "Seriously. Short of making a sex-tape myself, I don't know how else to help people break their limiting beliefs about themselves. We are all sexual beings! We need to act as such!"

"Why don't you?" I asked rhetorically. "We both know the bulk of the work's already done."

One corner of her lips curled up, and a spark shone from the depths of her eyes. "Why don't I…" But she was nodding, and her smile had grown full. "You have the best ideas sometimes," she said before getting on her toes to kiss me.

And of course, kisses from Virginia had side-effects. Her ardor was contagious, her passion, incendiary. Next thing I knew, she was spinning me then pushing me back toward the bedroom.

A few steps later, she tossed me onto the bed, her body on top of mine, her hands already taking off my shirt before her mouth swallowed my lips again.

Between kisses, I yelped, "But Eduardo's… already changed… the sheets… and made the bed… for the next guest!"

"Don't worry about the damn sheets. We can mangle them all we want. There's a washing machine."

11:20 a.m.

I pulled out my diary one last time while sitting in bed, with Virginia lying next to me, half-naked and rosy-cheeked from our speedy encounter that still had my heart pounding in my chest and my pussy pulsating in post-orgasmic contractions.

"Do you want me to drive you to the Bilbao airport?" she asked, a genuine smile on her luscious lips as she began doing up the buttons of her shirt.

"That would be amazing, but you can just drop me off at the bus station in town. The airport's a long ways away…"

"I may want to enjoy your company a little while longer…" She sat up in bed, then placed her hand on my folded knee, her fingers tracing little circles that tickled my skin. "What do you say?"

I smiled and raised my eyebrows at her last question. "Okay, give me a minute to finish my thought," I said before darkening what remained of this last page:

Writing down my thoughts about my recent life experiences has helped me untangle my values and desires. I think I've come to understand myself and my needs a little better—albeit not completely, my thoughts often contradict each other—but one thing is for sure: when I think of the future, there's only one clear path for me.

I know what I have to do now.

MY XXX EXPERIENCE

SPAIN

THE PLAN

"I KNOW what I have to do now."

This line has been driving me crazy. What did she mean?

Was she referring to getting that ride to the airport?

Was she referring to the job in Paris? Or Virginia? Or JuanMa?

Or did she mean dropping the journal in some guy's briefcase? And if so, did she already have me selected? Or was it random?

Or did her words have an entirely different meaning?

I can't read this woman's mind, but that's no surprise. At her core, she's got to be just like all the other women I've met. Men being from Mars and women from Venus bullshit. But I'd sure like to give a decent try at understanding her if she'd let me. She'd be worth getting to know. How I'd love to understand what goes on in her head. (And of course, I'd like to get to know her physically as well. That goes without saying.)

While she mentioned that her father's family was Spanish, it doesn't mean anything that will help me track her down today. She could have been talking about *several* generations ago, like when the Spaniards conquered the Mayans. Or maybe her ancestors moved to any of the South or Central American countries in the past century. Or perhaps she holds a European passport. I don't know, but I'm so freaking close to finding her.

Here are the approaches I could tackle during my last sprint to the finish line:

OPTION 1: Track down Virginia.

I don't know her last name, but she's a pretty successful oil painter. Visiting art galleries in San Sebastián and asking around may be enough for me to do that. But the problem is that her signature wouldn't be "Virginia." I don't know what pseudonym she uses for her paintings. But the descriptions of her pieces may be enough? Or I could also try and find Virginia's house in a small Navarre village. Maybe the few hints at directions that Sophia left in her journal would be enough, but there's no guarantee I'd show up while she's there. She also has an apartment in San Sebastián, and she visits her children in Paris and Madrid. I don't think I'd be able to communicate with the nosy neighbor either.

Likelihood of success: Low to average.

OPTION 2: Look for a bartender named JuanMa.

This would involve locating the right bar. Other than being within walking distance of the beach and around the corner from her apartment, I don't know much. Based on a map I found online, most of the old town is close to the beach. And there are lots of *pintxo* bars. And I don't know *where* the apartment she stayed at is located.

Likelihood of success: Slim to none.

OPTION 3: Find Eduardo using his Airbnb listings.

It sounds like Eduardo is the only one who handles the siblings' Airbnb listings now, so spending hours scouring through listings may be worth it at this point because I know her first name and what she looks like. Chances are she'll have left a review. That's what friends do, right? If her profile name makes sense and if the photo of the reviewer looks like what I found out she looks like in Japan, then I'll know which apartment she stayed at.

Likelihood of success: Average.

Let's hope Eduardo will be open to sharing Sophia's last name with me... Or his sister's contact information?

A FRIEND'S HELP

After spending an entire day and a half scouring through Airbnb listings, my eyes had gone dry and red from staring at my monitor, and I had yet to find the correct apartment. I had gone through the reviews and owner information for all the listings that had shown up among my search results. Even though I carefully read every single one that could potentially match Sophia's description, nothing fit.

I closed my laptop. For a few minutes, I considered posting an online job, asking for help from one of those virtual assistants I kept hearing about. But I had no idea how to go about doing that, so I decided to leave it for now, but take my laptop with me to ask Bob after the game.

He'd invited me over to watch it on his big-screen TV, and the wings Stacy always cooks made it worth the drive to his house to see it. The Red Sox were going to get smashed by my Yankees. I just knew it, and I was so looking forward to it. The televised game was scheduled to start shortly, so I packed up my laptop, and just in case, I also took along Sophia's diary—to be fair, I hardly went anywhere without it nowadays.

After picking up a 24-pack of cold beers from a nearby store, I rang Bob's doorbell just as the red door opened in front of me. A tall, young, brown-haired man I'd never seen before looked as surprised as I was when he almost walked into me.

"Hi. Sorry. Bye," he said, then pushed past me and headed down the driveway and onto the street.

I turned back to face the door, which was still open, and Bob invited me in.

"Who was that?" I asked Bob while watching Stacy run up the stairs behind him in nothing but a long T-shirt, her long legs disappearing quickly as she reached the upper floor.

"Hey, Charlie," she yelled from upstairs. "I'll be right down."

I opted to wait until she returned instead of yelling to greet her from here. So, I followed Bob into the house and dropped my laptop case on the arm of the couch as we made our way to the kitchen.

"Him? No one you know," Bob said, turning to face me, then looking down at the beers I was carrying. "Good. You brought some. I was gonna call and ask you to pick some up."

"You know me. Baseball requires beer. And a lot of it." As I watched him open the fridge and make room for all but three of the cans I'd just brought, I caught on to what had just happened. I pointed my thumb back toward the door. "Fuck. Was that one of *them*?"

"What?" Bob asked, handing me a can, along with one of the three cold beer mugs he'd just taken out of the freezer.

"One of your... things," I said. My eyes tried to meet his, but he was focusing on pouring a perfect headless beer in his mug. "You and Stacy... You... had him over, didn't you? I arrived just after you finished... your fuck fest."

While he'd already shared with me that they sometimes had the *Devil's three-way*, it was one thing to hear it while staking out a whorehouse in Paris, and another to catch the guilty parties immediately after the act right here in my corner of the world.

I swallowed hard. Well, I tried to, but the knot in my throat was blocking the path that this specific thought needed to clear to enter my system. I took a large sip of my beer instead. Half of the can to be exact.

I'm grateful I didn't arrive any earlier.

"Charlie," he said before shushing me and lowering his voice. "Stacy doesn't know I told you."

I finished the rest of my beer on the spot. "Hand me another, will you?" I asked Bob.

"Still not getting it?" he said with a tone I heard as a tad condescending.

"Not my thing. Nothing against the other variety, though. Quite the opposite."

He shook his head at me while grabbing another can from the fridge. "I get it, but you're so stubborn and close-minded. One little try could change your world."

"Don't you fucking go there." I tilted my mug and poured the second serving of golden liquid into it.

Bob headed toward the living room with two beers in hand—one for him and one for Stacy—and I followed him. "All I'm saying is—and I'll leave it at that— our nation's greatest enemy isn't outside our borders, it's buried inside the random values that were drilled into our heads by people with good intentions. It took me a while to get past the fear of experimenting with it, but I realized it was just that. The fear of the unknown. There's nothing *bad* or *evil* about it."

"Whatever," I said, shaking my head to get rid of the pretend wisdom he'd just spilled. "Hey, aren't you going to Costa Rica soon?"

"Yeah. Gotta pack my bags after the game. We're flying early tomorrow morning."

"Going to ... enjoy Henrietta then?"

"There would be worse ways to spend time down there. She's something... What's up with the laptop?" he asked, pointing to the bag I'd dropped on the couch a few minutes earlier.

"Some research I'm doing. Boring as hell, but I'm stuck. I figured I'd ask you after the game, just to see if you can work your magic and help me out."

"Of course, but later. The fun's about to start," he said, grabbing the remote to enable the surround sound and turn up the volume. "Stacy! Get your gorgeous ass down here. It's about to start!" he yelled toward the stairs.

A couple of minutes later, she joined us in the living room, her wet hair tied in a ponytail, her Yankees shirt topping a pair of fitted jeans.

"Hey Charlie, nice of you to come and join us for the game," she said, kissing me on the cheek and hugging me. Her freshly showered look didn't take away any of her natural beauty, and a random inappropriate thought crossed my mind as I watched her take a seat on the opposite end of the couch, closest to her husband.

If only Bob hadn't told me that she'd wanted me to take part in their extra-marital menagerie program. While I would never dare go out of line with that piece of information, a tiny part of me was curious. Very curious indeed. But as flawed and weak as I was, I'd managed to shut down any bubbling fantasies that involved my best friend's wife.

And thankfully, the presenters got my full attention when the game began, allowing me to remain faithful to my own set of ethics.

———

Once the game was over, my stomach still satisfied from the tasty sweet and sour wings Stacy had fed us throughout the game, Charlie offered to help me out. I took out my laptop and explained how I'd gone about searching for that mystery apartment I so desperately wanted to find.

"I think I know why you can't find it. Can you run that search again, the same way you did it before?"

I started typing "San Sebastián" in the location bar, and after about five letters, I selected the full location offered by the site's auto-fill feature (with the accent on the A and Spain appearing next to the city name), I selected random dates, and then added one guest.

"That's it there," he said. "You're messing up your own search."

"What?"

"Leave the dates blank. The apartment is probably booked during those dates, so that's why it doesn't appear."

I flipped my palm up. "Are you kidding me?"

"Try it and see if it makes a difference."

So I went back to the previous page and ran the search as he'd recommended it.

Boom. Loads of new results suddenly appeared. Pages and pages more.

"See?"

"Thanks, man. Now it looks like I've got two more days' worth of work just to go through them all. Do you know if there's a way to look for apartments based on the name of the owner?"

Bob scratched his right temple, looking off to the side, then he looked at my computer screen.

"You can click on the name of a host and see all of their other listings, but I don't think you can *search* for it."

"Okay. Thanks for your help."

"So, what now?"

"I guess I'll go through every one of those listings one by one."

"What? That's ridiculous. Come on. Tell me *everything* you know about it—

don't hold out any important detail—I'm sure I can find it for you way faster than that."

So I did. I dug out my precious diary, then scanned through Sophia's entries from Spain, relaying every word she used that had anything to do with the apartment in terms of location or description. While I was doing that, he handled my laptop, changing a few advanced settings for my search and narrowing down the search area on the map.

By the time I closed the brown-leather diary and placed it back into my laptop case, he yelled out a scream. "Got it! Who's the king? I'm the king!"

"What the fuck?" I asked, repositioning myself behind him to view the screen.

The apartment he'd found did feature wooden beams in the ceiling and large potted plants on a balcony overlooking the ocean. I scrolled down to see the rest of the listing. When I read the part about the host, my hopes crashed.

"No, man. The owner's name is Eduardo. Not Lalo."

He shook his head, ridiculously gleaming from his partly inebriated smile. "Lalo *is* Eduardo, Charlie. Look it up. Common Spanish nickname."

"What?" I did trust my friend, but I checked anyway. *What kind of messed up name shortening is that?* But Google confirmed it; it was true.

I returned to the detailed listing for the apartment, then began going through the reviews it had gotten. I loaded quite a few, and then a few more. I scrolled through them, paying attention to the reviewers' photos and names. Then I saw a review from Sof81. *The avatar for this person? An image of half of her beautiful face.* I would have recognized that Mona Lisa smile anywhere. The profile picture had been taken up close, close enough for me to see the amazing variety of colors in her hazel irises.

"This is it! Love you, man!"

I hugged Bob so hard I began to feel awkward once the initial exaltation of finding the correct listing wore off.

I turned to look at the listing again, but it was unavailable for months.

Can she be back in this apartment right now?

"So, it's booked," I told Bob. "Can you show me how to find the other listings by the same host? There should be a bunch in the same building."

And a few minutes later, thanks to Bob's help, I secured my apartment in San Sebastián.

Now, the rest was up to me, but there was no way I'd let her slip by me this time.

WHAT HAPPENED

After many attempts at composing a message to Eduardo asking for more information about Sof81, I gave up. I couldn't come up with a way that didn't sound creepy.

Instead, I decided that feet on the ground and a face-to-face meeting with him during check-in or check-out would be a better environment for the odd line of questioning I had in mind.

So, I found myself seats on flights all the way to BIO/Bilbao that matched my Airbnb booking. According to Google, San Sebastián was just a bus or taxi ride away from there.

If San Sebastián was my Sophia's favorite place on earth, I couldn't wait to experience it for myself and find out what the big deal was all about.

3:15 p.m.

On the cab ride from Bilbao to my Airbnb, I kept imagining what Sophia's life looked like right now.

Was she still seeing Virginia? Was she living full-time in Paris, or was she still traveling? Could she be staying in the top-floor apartment in the same building I was going to right now? Could I randomly run into either her or Virginia while visiting her favorite city on earth?

Even though Bob kept saying I was the luckiest man he knew, wishing for any of these things felt like I was asking the universe for a little too much.

So, I stopped dreaming and instead rehearsed the line of questioning I had prepared for Eduardo in my head while my cab went through the mountainous scenery.

But by the time we reached the city's outer limits, which looked much larger than I had imagined in my mind, I reconsidered my poorly planned approach.

After all, it had been one question too many that had gotten me in trouble with Amélie in Paris. And being too persistent with my goals (and making too many assumptions) had gotten me in trouble in Amsterdam. And being too fucking foolish to think that my actions in seeking a copy of a private video couldn't have negative repercussions had gotten Keiki and me in trouble in Tokyo.

This time, I had to think it through. I had to act cool. Asking Eduardo directly about either Sophia or Virginia would be equivalent to stepping into a fully-armed bear trap. And I didn't want to get Virginia in trouble either. For all I knew, she could still be part of Sophia's life. Since Virginia had already had problems with her brother because of her inappropriate relationships (inappropriate at least according to his views), if I were to insinuate that something had gone on between Sophia and his sister, I could be shooting myself in the foot.

No. Everything I'd prepared wouldn't work (or was too likely to backfire on me).

Fuck.

As Eduardo and I had agreed, I texted him that I was near the apartment when I saw the ocean in the distance as our cab rode at the top of a hill as we made our way deeper into traffic.

"¿Cuantos minutos más?" I asked the cab driver, hoping to give Eduardo a more exact arrival time.

"Quince, más o menos," he replied.

I told Eduardo that I'd arrive in about 15 minutes. Good thing I'd brushed up on my Spanish before the trip.

A second later, he sent me the thumbs-up symbol.

I spent that entire 15 minutes thinking about my options.

When the cab driver dropped me off, I still hadn't come up with anything. I nonetheless paid the man, grabbed my small leather bag, slipped the strap over my shoulder, and then did the same with my laptop case.

A silver-haired man walked up to me as the cab drove away.

"Charlie?" he asked.

"Yes," I said, extending my hand to preemptively avoid the culturally appropriate double-kiss greeting.

"Eduardo. Nice to meet you. Do you need help with your bags?" he asked.

"No. I'm good, thanks."

He proceeded to show me how to unlock the main front door, then we walked up to the third floor, crossing paths with a gorgeous, tall blonde on the way. I smiled at her, and she quietly nodded, a faint smile on her lips.

Once Eduardo and I reached my apartment, he unlocked the door and invited me to go in. It was much roomier than I had expected it to be from the photos, and it smelled of freshly-used cleaning products.

Eduardo gave me the grand tour in two minutes flat, and we returned to the living room, where I'd left my bags.

"I put some papers and information here if you want to find activities to occupy your time while in Donostia."

And that was when the perfect opening popped in my head.

"You know what? I like art. Paintings. I heard there are quite a few local artists who are worth following. Would you have any recommendations for me?"

He tilted his head, as though weighing his options.

"What kind do you like? Landscape? Portrait? Abstract? Modern?"

"Anything featuring people, the female shape in particular."

"Ah! Then you should visit some art galleries." He walked to the pile of colored pamphlets that covered the coffee table, then found one that he handed me. "You will like this one. Also, I don't see information about it here, but there's a monstrous modern building called Kursaal by *Playa Zurriola*. You can't miss it. Starting tomorrow, there's a new exhibition that you will enjoy. I know one of the artists featured, and her style is exactly what you like."

"Thanks so much!" I said, smiling at the pamphlet I held but mostly proud of myself for having elicited the exact answer I needed without being explicit. *Well, at least I hope he meant his sister.*

"And if you have any questions during your stay, please text me, and I'll do my best to help." He headed to the door and bid his goodbyes as he let himself out.

Fucking Charlie. You are *the luckiest son of a bitch alive!*

4:03 p.m.

While he hadn't said it outright, my gut told me Eduardo was talking about his sister. But since I didn't know her artist name, and because several more would also be featured there, I had to figure out what her painting pseudonym was.

As such, walking by that Kursaal building (and the beach) seemed like a great way to spend the rest of my afternoon, and I could also grab some of those tasty *pintxos* while out, since my stomach had been grumbling for some time now.

I looked at the map Eduardo had left among the pile of flyers on the table and figured out my bearings before heading out.

After fifteen minutes of strolling through gorgeous old European streets packed with tourists and locals, I came out of the old part of town and reached the river. From there, I spotted the Kursaal building Eduardo had mentioned. Its modern lines and large cube-shape clashed with the delicate lines of the 19th-century buildings I'd been surrounded with since leaving my apartment. But then again, the ocean was right there, drawing my eyes away from that building.

The sound of the waves crashing onto the sidewalk that lined the river got louder the closer I got to the ugly building. Well... it wasn't ugly. It would have looked great in New York City. It was just out of place and time here. But perhaps that was the whole point.

I walked in through the glass doors at the front of the building and found myself lost and confused as to where to go. There was no way the art exhibition could occupy this entire building. It was just too big of a structure for that. But my eyes soon found a line of tellers where a few people were waiting, possibly to purchase tickets for something or other. Before entering the building, I had seen a long series of posters that decorated the outside entrance, so more than one event took place here.

That's when I spotted a set of holders that each contained colorful sheets of paper, so I walked toward that area. A few seconds later, I spotted one trifold pamphlet that featured photos of paintings and sculptures along with several paragraphs of text. On the front cover, below the exhibition name, appeared dates in large bold letters. I smiled at my correctly-dated treasure, grabbed a copy, and then headed out of the entrance hall the same way I'd gotten in.

Let's just find a place to read this with a cold drink in hand.

I decided to keep the same bearing and walk along the boardwalk that followed the beach. While there were quite a few sunbathers, it wasn't as crowded as I'd expected it to be. But then again, the afternoon was coming to an end, and today was a workday. I could see a terrace just a few hundred feet away, with people enjoying drinks while overlooking the sandy crescent. *Exactly what I'm looking for.*

A few minutes later, seated and a cold *caña* of beer in my hand, I took out my prized pamphlet and began reading it. At first, I was confused. The number of Ks and Xs that appeared in the first paragraph told me I wasn't reading Spanish. *Was this available in more than one language? Did I pick up the wrong version?* But then, I flipped it open and saw that the following paragraph was in Spanish. A second later, on another panel, I found an English translation. *Great.*

My small *caña* didn't last long. I didn't know what the word meant exactly, but it seemed to be equivalent to about half a pint of beer, so I ordered myself one more and told the waiter to keep them coming while I resumed reading my pamphlet:

"The Kubo Hall Kursaal Convention Center is proud to present *The Human Experience*, a selection of paintings and sculptures by local Basque artists who explore the physical form in this unique exhibition limited to 21st-century art. By bringing together over 50 works by more than a dozen artists, this short-term exhibition shines the spotlight on local artists who have represented their experience of the human form through colorful modern lines, subtle and powerful portraits, time-trusted as well as innovative media, from simplistic to the most lascivious representations of partial or full human forms, in small or large scale. Artists include Julio Zubiri Esquivel, Julietta Arostegui Muñoz, Valentina, Pedro Juarez Domingo, David Nieto, Rodrigo Hernandez Aragon, Santiago Castillon Jardi, Juana Massó Ballos, Aarón Crespi, Eliseo Uriz, Juanita Vive Roda, Pau Palomas, Alberto Sauleda Morato, Abrahán Farreros, Mara Rojas, and Berengária Peri."

And it went on with the dates and hours during which the paintings and sculptures could be enjoyed, with a little extra tidbit that delighted me:

"Join us on opening night for a meet and greet with our local artists."

It appeared I had my job cut out for me. I mean... There was a little bit of research needed, and my phone wasn't the best device to do it on. But since I had a beautiful soundtrack of crashing waves, a view of half-naked women sunbathing nearby, and an unlimited supply of cold beer coming to me, rushing home to run my searches on a larger monitor seemed rather pointless.

I skipped the obviously male first names and started with the female artists. It turned out that a lot of them had a web presence, but sometimes in that weird Basque language with Xs and Ks. But thankfully, browsing through their art portfolio was more than enough to allow me to determine if they were Virginia.

And, just as my fourth *caña* arrived, this time accompanied by the small order of fries I'd requested, I found her.

Valentina.

Like Madonna (and most strippers I'd encountered), she'd somehow decided to forego the use of a last name and used a one-name-only pseudonym. While the idea sounded a bit self-absorbed, who was I to judge? Maybe there was already a famous artist with her name? Who's to say what went through her head when she picked Valentina?

But her paintings did elicit a reaction in my brain and between my legs. I readjusted my sitting position while I began eating a fry or two, letting my mind cool off a bit. I allowed my eyes to scan the patrons around me for a few seconds, mostly couples or small groups of friends who were chatting and laughing.

I returned my attention to my phone, which still featured the large painting of a beautiful, bare vulva, but it was far from clinical. The shades of pink, burnt orange, red, and other colors I couldn't name gave the image on my phone the impression that it was coming out of my screen. Through some shadow-trickery effect—or however she did it—she made me want to touch my screen. I shook my head, realizing that anyone could potentially see what I was staring at, and then continued swiping through her portfolio.

The next painting featured a naked woman lying on her front, her curvy ass decorated above by two dimples that invited some attention. Her blonde hair had been spread over her shoulders, her head tilted to face out, her eyes and facial expression asking the viewer to do nasty things to her (or at least think about them.)

Shit, she's talented.

While I was no real art enthusiast, I could easily picture myself buying some of her pieces and hanging them in my bedroom, in my bathroom. Possibly even in my living room.

When my cock twitched again in my pants, telling me that perhaps I should stop looking at her art while sitting in public like that, I tapped my way to the about page.

And what I saw there made me smile.

9:40 p.m.

After a half-day surf lesson and a bit of erring down various streets at random (that's how I came across a neat plaza and a beautiful, ornate church), I returned home and began psyching myself up for the evening to come.

Good thing I nearly always traveled with a suit or business-casual attire—although my best outfit only consisted of a pair of flat-front, black pants, dress shoes, and a light-blue, long-sleeved shirt that brought out my eyes (at least that's how the sales lady had sold it to me.) I shaved again, just to look my best, splashed a tad of cologne on, and then headed out with high hopes.

I took my sweet time walking over to the Kursaal building. The evening was warm, and the last thing I wanted was to show up with sweat stains under my armpits. I mentally rehearsed a few lines for the gorgeous Virginia. I had no idea she was *that* kind of woman, and I couldn't wait to meet her in person. Her about-page photo had been... enthralling to say the least, and I may have beaten myself off thinking about her in the shower earlier tonight.

So, when I finally reached the modern building I'd seen the day before, I got myself a ticket and a copy of the small catalog of art pieces on display before walking into the reasonably spacious room called *Kubo-Kutxa*. The brochure said it was 1,000 m², and I couldn't tell off-the-cuff what that was in square feet exactly, but it looked like the size of a baseball diamond. In addition to the paintings that hung on the walls and extra partitions that had been added, several sizable sculptures and other pieces of art dotted the floor. As the title of the exhibition had indicated, all of them were about the human form. Some sculptures featured certain muscles in specific sports situations, including a full-size soccer player kicking a ball and another man playing some sort of racket sport that wasn't tennis or badminton. But I wasn't here for the 3D pieces, so I moved along quickly.

I knew I'd found her section when I recognized that very vivid vulva canvas. And was it ever powerful in person! The five-by-seven-foot painting had me hypnotized. For a brief second (or maybe it was a full minute or two), I wondered which lovely lady owned such a pleasing pussy. Had Sophia kindly posed for this painting? Or could it be a self-portrait of the most exciting variety?

And, most importantly, would it fit on my bedroom wall?

I consulted the catalog I'd gotten earlier and saw a price tag that would require some thinking. It wasn't out of my financial reach, but it was out of my pre-determined impulse-shopping range.

I decided to move along to the next painting. My dick twitched in my pants as my brain appreciated the powerful, beautiful representation of a female form in front of me. It wasn't a painting of Virginia or Sophia, but the blonde model was sitting naked in an empty bathtub, one arm folded behind her head, and the other loosely hung over her body. Her fingers were extended to partially hide her pussy, but made it obvious what she was doing to it. Her body was entrancing, but it wasn't just her generous breasts or her curves that inebriated my senses. It wasn't the way the delightful and powerful strokes had hit the canvas either. What agitated my dick once again was imagining that woman naked while Virginia was painting her. Envisioning the way Virginia had made the gorgeous model repress her sexual desires until she'd captured her essence.

And captured it she had.

The sex that must have followed at that point had to have been nothing short of phenomenal. But that last thought was too much. I had to look away from the canvas or risk tenting my pants.

At that point, I took a break from appreciating Virginia's paintings and scanned the room instead, hoping to see the lascivious and extremely talented painter in the flesh.

Many guests walked around the room, and it wasn't necessarily easy to differentiate an artist from one of the potential customers, but when my eyes landed on the petite woman in the sexy black dress with a tiny name tag pinned to her chest, I recognized her from her About page. Her hair cascaded in thick waves down past her shoulders, her olive skin had been kissed by the sun, her smile as she currently listened to the couple talking to her was hypnotizing... But when I heard her laughter echo all the way to my ears, I was hooked. It had to be the most delightful sound I'd heard this year.

I made my way toward her, slowly, hoping the couple would soon walk away and clear my path. But they didn't. I stood a couple of feet away, overhearing a conversation that didn't sound like Spanish. That weird language with the Xs and Ks, whose name Google had told me was *Euskera*. It had to be that.

Sexy, smart, talented, speaks at least three languages fluently. Virginia seemed like the whole package... And she was my ticket to Sophia, an equally good, if not even better, woman. Now I wanted them both. At the same time or not. But right here, standing so close to Virginia, I couldn't deny my urges. All I could do was order my dick to stand at ease and try to think of anything but having her naked under me. But she was killing me. Watching her red lips move as she spoke words I didn't understand was like throwing gasoline on a fire. I had to walk away, at least for now.

I headed out of the display room and followed signs until I found the men's bathrooms. Empty. Good. I splashed cold water on my face—careful not to get any on my shirt—then debated whether or not I should beat off quickly to release some pressure, but the door opened, and an elderly gentleman walked in, making me decide against it.

I could power my way through this. I'd done it before, and I could do it again.

After drying my face and hands, I headed back to the room, this time intent on talking to her. She'd already moved away from the couple she was talking to earlier and was now chatting with a tall brown-haired man, this time in Spanish. The lisp that Sophia liked so much was grating on my nerves, but coming from her beautiful mouth, I couldn't hold it against her. She spoke so fast. My rusty Spanish wasn't keeping up, but I stood patiently. A minute later, the man must have felt my waiting to talk to the artist—or perhaps he was just done saying whatever he needed to say—and I got my opportunity to step up and finally meet Virginia.

"*Buenas noches,*" she said to me.

"Good evening," I said with a slight head nod. For a split second, a tiny line appeared between her brows, and then it was gone.

"Welcome to the exhibition," she continued before smiling wide at me. "Where are you from?"

"New York," I replied.

"I can't say that I've seen many international tourists tonight. What brings you here?" she asked, but there was something odd in her expression again. That line once again reappeared on her forehead, and she took a full up and down look at me. "I'm Valentina, one of the artists in this exhibit," she said offering her hand.

"Nice to meet you, Valentina... or should I say 'Virginia'?" I asked, lowering my voice on the last part so as to not divulge her real identity to the world. I knew I was gambling with my tactic, but as long as she didn't get mad, I figured it was my fastest route to talking about Sophia. She'd have to ask where I'd heard that from, and I could mention that we shared a common friend called Sophia. Easy peasy.

But my words didn't have the effect I'd expected. Instead, she pulled her hand away as though I'd just hurt her. And before I could continue speaking and introduce myself, she spoke: "You're Charlie, aren't you?"

I hadn't seen that coming.

Not in any of my rehearsed conversations had I ever considered she'd know who I was.

The next ten seconds were spent in total silence as we exchanged confused looks. Then a woman walked up to us and started speaking to Virginia, ending our brief conversation.

10:30 p.m.

How the heck did she know who I was?

Was it something I'd said to Eduardo? I mentally revisited what I'd told the man. No, I'd been super careful. There was no way.

Then how?

I mindlessly walked around the rest of the room for what must have been a solid thirty minutes. No matter... I simply couldn't understand how she knew who I was.

After returning to her section, my eyes glanced at the thickening crowd, hoping to find her so I could ask her plain and simple. There was no point torturing myself. I had no clue what was going on here.

But I couldn't see her.

Then someone grabbed my elbow, and I turned around, surprised to see Virginia next to me.

"There's a small bar across the road from here, on the corner. It's called *Ondarra*. Meet me there in an hour."

I nodded, and she walked away.

12:05 a.m.

I was sitting alone at my table listening to the surf in the background and watching intermittent traffic go by on the avenue right in front of me when she appeared out of nowhere. I imagined she'd just walked on the sidewalk like a regular person, but I was so lost in my thoughts that I hadn't realized the hour had already gone by.

"So, you're the American who's been tracking down Sophia," she said as she took a seat on the empty chair I'd saved for her.

"How do you even know about me?" I asked.

"Paris. You left your business card with the lawyer, and then you tried to get information from that poor secretary." She shook her head, a partial smile on her face.

I let that information sink in for a while. So, Maître Lancelot *did* tell Sophia about me then. He'd kept my card, even though he'd pretended to toss it while I was there...

"Why are you trying to find her?" she asked me before turning to the waiter who'd just dropped drinks at a nearby table. She asked him for a beer in Spanish.

I waited until she looked at me again before answering. "Her diary. After reading it, I couldn't just leave it at that. I needed to meet her."

"You needed to fuck her," she said, her face stern, her eyes unrelentingly locked onto mine as though she was trying to pull the truth out of me through my pupils.

I stayed silent for half a minute while I maintained her stare, but a nearby honking car made me look away.

"Yes. Of course, I've thought about that."

"And this is all you want?" she asked.

I raised my shoulders and frowned at her. "What do you want me to say here? I'm not planning on asking for her hand in marriage."

"I didn't peg you for the kind."

"What does that even mean? And why do you care?" I asked.

Her beer arrived, which gave me a chance to realize I was not helping my case here. I ordered another drink for myself, then inhaled deeply before approaching it differently.

"Sorry. I still don't understand what's going on here. If you know about me, that means you're still in touch with Sophia. Are you a serious item now?" I asked.

She tilted her head. "It's complicated."

"But you're still in her life?"

"Yes, of course."

"What do you want me to say? After months of obsessing about this woman, after tracking her down and nearly getting myself in deep trouble a few times, I deserve to meet her."

"I may be able to share her contact information, but only if you prove yourself worthy."

"Worthy?" I asked, wondering if this was just a coy way for her to invite me to her bed for a test run, but there was no spark in her eyes, no body movement to support that theory. Her arms were crossed over her chest, her lips slightly pursed.

"So, tell me then. What will it take for you to believe I'm worthy? What do I need to do to prove I'm good enough to meet her? Can't she make her own opinions of me?"

"For a start, tell me what you want from her."

"What I *want* from her?"

This conversation was booby-trapped. I had to carefully consider what I was going to say next. Thankfully, she spoke again first.

"You just want to fuck her and discard her like the others?" she asked.

"Like the others? What others? Who have you been talking to?"

"I know you. I've heard of your reputation."

An irrepressible smile drew on my lips. "Do tell me more."

"You're a self-absorbed ass, but a good fuck."

"Ouch, and thank you."

Then we both stared at each other in silence for at least a minute. Two people estimating the competition, or perhaps just trying to look for common grounds.

"Listen," I started. "A few months ago, I would have given my first-born just to get a chance to see—"

"To fuck her," she interrupted.

"Alright. Granted. But I don't think fucking her once will get her out of my head, though. Her words, her stories, her private thoughts. Reading those things can't help but..." I exhaled loudly while my mind tried to form a complete sentence. "A part of me feels... somewhat... attached to her." And as the words left my lips, I realized they weren't a lie, although I'd never thought of it before. "She's a gorgeous woman, and I think she's the real deal."

"You're right about that," she said, uncrossing her arms and reaching for her beer. "I'm sure you would have stopped your quest by now if you thought she was ugly or uninteresting. But aren't you just a world-class player trying to get as many notches on your belt as possible?"

Her slanted eyebrows and the color of her cheeks screamed danger.

"Don't be so quick to judge me. I've got layers."

"A real onion, you are."

She drank more of her beer, and the waiter arrived with mine.

After thanking him and taking a good swig of my drink, I resumed our passive-aggressive turf war. "There's more to me than what you seem to think."

"Sure. There's the homophobic layer. There's the misogynistic one—"

"Now, hold your horses. I don't hate women. Far from it. I'm the biggest fan of the female form."

She shook her head. "My point exactly. The female *form*. To you, women are just objects. They're things you fuck, they're nothing but walking pussies."

I refrained from smiling, but the imagery she'd put on my mental screen was priceless. Then I realized that this very thought was proving her point.

"I guess I tend to see women this way, but that doesn't mean I don't see them as more than that. The German Chancellor for example. I don't want to fuck her—the idea of it made me wince—but I admire her qualities as a political leader."

"Go on..." She brought her glass to her lips, and that little line appeared between her brows again.

"Artists. There are lots of very talented singers and actors out there... But they're not helping their case or my case here. I'm not the one who ordered them to wear next to nothing."

"But you appreciate the sight of them—"

"What living-breathing man wouldn't?"

She raised her brows, probably in agreement with me. After all, I knew she also enjoyed the female form in all its glory.

"Don't tell me you've never used people," I said between two sips.

"Used them?" she asked.

"I know you have sex with your models when you paint them."

"I don't sleep with all my models. Only those with whom I shared a special connection, so that's not using them. What's the purpose of life if not enjoying the corporeal pleasures with others who have that little something special?"

"Exactly what I'm saying."

"No. There's a difference. An important one at that."

"What difference?"

"I always go all in. I'm not in it for a quick fix."

"Can't it be both? I'm always all in. My mind is 100% with the person I'm fucking at the time I'm doing it. And yes, it can sometimes happen quickly. No point in stretching the moment with uncomfortable conversation afterward."

"That's where you don't even understand me. You'll never understand Sophia either."

I took in a few deep breaths. "Then please explain it to me in layman's terms so it can pierce my thick skull. I'm obviously not getting your point."

"From what I've heard about you, you see life as a series of one-night stands. Would you agree with that?"

I reflected on her words for a second or two. "Pretty much."

"Sophia and I don't see it this way."

"No, that's where you're wrong. I read her diary. She's had sex with *several* people with no intentions of getting to know them better."

"That was then, but it's not where she's at now."

"What changed?"

"She figured out what she wanted."

"And what is that now? Does she want to settle down and have kids? I thought she wasn't into the regular program. Long-term monogamy isn't her thing."

"No. That hasn't changed, but she wants a certain level of commitment. I don't believe you even know the meaning of that word."

Now she was plain insulting me. "I've worked with the same employer for nearly two decades. I can commit."

But before I could come up with more examples, something clicked in my head.

"But how come you know so much about me?" I asked.

"People talk. Sophia and I talk. A lot. What do you think we do when we're together? Or is your alpha-male brain picturing us going down on each other 24/7?"

Although the image was worth picturing, now was not the time. And maybe it was proving her previous point again. And in a frighteningly accurate way.

"But I don't get where you got your information. What was there to talk about?"

"In Paris, you freaked Nicholas out. You scared him, Sophia, and me. He was afraid you'd expose the illicit business. Sophia couldn't believe her plan had worked so well, and then she came to realize it could backfire in her face. So she freaked out."

Too many questions mentally arose from what she'd just said, but I had to prioritize. "And what were *you* scared about?"

She finished her beer before answering. "That you'd steal her from me."

As much as I wanted to learn more about Sophia's plan—whatever that meant—I knew a critical detail would surface if I kept at it.

"So..." I prompted.

"So, I hired a detective to track you down and learn more about you."

I restrained myself and resisted the impulse to scream at her. Instead, I paused and quietly asked: "You did what?"

She repeated herself, her eyes wide open, her stare glued onto me, then she turned to the waiter and ordered us another round.

"Since when? For how long? Am I still being spied on?" I looked around, half-expecting to see a man in a trench coat hiding behind a newspaper.

"Relax, Charlie."

I turned to look at her again. "You want me to relax after hearing what you just said."

"It only lasted a couple of weeks. A little in New York, and in Amsterdam a short while ago."

I looked at the table while I tried to recollect what the investigator could have possibly seen.

"I'll spare you the trouble. He overheard your homophobic rant before you got in a cab... with a man."

The black-eye that had ensued had stayed with me long enough to know what she was talking about. "I'd been drugged. But that's no excuse. I acted like an ass, and I now see the errors of my ways there. The guy who helped me out, he was nice. Whatever slurs escaped my lips then, I can assure you I'd never say or think again." Upon hearing my own words aloud, I was relieved to realize I meant them.

Our next round of drinks arrived just in time. It gave me time to rethink her accusations that I was misogynistic. Did I do something wrong while in Amsterdam, trying to get into the pants of the wrong Sophie?

"Okay, Charlie. Maybe you're not as much of an ass as I assumed you were. And I can think of one excellent way to know for sure." The corners of her lips went up a tad, but not enough to qualify as a smile. She nonetheless raised her glass toward mine and offered a cheer. "To Sophia," she said.

"To Sophia," I repeated as our raised glasses clinked against one another.

She took a sip, then voiced words I didn't see coming. "Here's to you meeting her in the near future."

There was nothing more I wanted in the world right now, but somehow, it felt like a trap.

"But what's in it for you?" I asked her. "Wouldn't me meeting her risk ruining whatever thing you have going on with her?"

"Quite possibly. But I know something's missing in her life. I want to make her happy, and I'll do whatever it takes for that to happen. If that means helping you meet her in the flesh, I will do it. But first, you still have to prove to me that you're worthy."

"You still haven't told me what I'm supposed to do to prove it to you. And I need to ask. The plan you talked about, Sophia's plan. What was it?"

A frown reappeared on her face. "You'll have to figure that one out for yourself. I thought you already knew, but if you can't do that, I'm afraid you're not worthy."

Insulting my intelligence wasn't something I took lightly. I'd admit I wasn't the smartest man alive, but I was far from the stupidest. "Let me guess. It wasn't random."

"What?" she asked.

"The diary ending up in my briefcase."

"Go on..."

"She picked me," I said.

She nodded and brought her beer to her lips.

"Now... I don't know if she knew me. I certainly don't remember meeting her... And she's obviously someone I'd remember meeting."

Her expression remained flat. No clues as to whether the theory I'd just voiced was correct or not.

"But I know I'm her type down to a T. She likes tall blond men, pilots in particular."

She nodded again.

But I couldn't yet connect the rest of the dots.

"Did you find it yet?" she asked.

"What?" That woman kept confusing me with her erratic conversational segues.

"I can only assume you're following every little hint or clue she's left in her diary. That's the only way you were able to get so close to finding her. That's the only way you tracked *me* down. So, did you find the clue here in Donostia?"

I racked my brain with her words.

"What clue?"

"Maybe *clue* isn't the most appropriate word. More like a souvenir."

"The painting of her. Did you finish it?"

"No and yes. That's not what I was referring to, and yes, it's finished. Maybe you'll see it one day... Maybe soon."

As though something I'd said or done had somehow swayed her to become my ally, she surprised me with the suggestion she made after finishing her glass: "If you're not smart enough to figure out what we did, then you don't deserve to meet her in person. Find the souvenir, and then I'll show you the painting."

And with that, she got up.

"But how will I get in touch with you again?"

She grabbed a pen from her purse, then scribbled her number on a napkin she pulled from the dispenser on our table.

Three seconds later, I watched her narrow hips sway away while I tried to pull myself together and understand what had just transpired here.

8:30 a.m.

After waking up from a restless night, I made myself a cup of coffee, then sat down to re-read Sophia's diary for the nth time, intent on pinpointing what it was that she'd left behind in the apartment. An apartment which I, unfortunately, didn't have access to right now. Asking Eduardo to let me in would be plain irresponsible, and possibly detrimental to Virginia and Sophia. The latter I wanted to avoid at all costs.

What was it? Did she leave another diary behind?

After closing my leather-bound treasure, still clueless as to where she would have left that other diary, I decided to go and take another surf lesson.

Since I was at a dead-end, how else was I going to occupy my day?

About two hours later, as I paddled my way toward the incoming waves, my conscious mind focusing on the physical motions I needed to go through, my subconscious screamed at me.

There can't be another diary. The last pages of the one I have were written at the end of her Spanish stay.

I had to forget about that.

Virginia wouldn't provide me the help I needed until I proved to be smart enough to find that stupid clue—or souvenir.

Why don't I just go and kindly ask whoever lives there now?

6:00 p.m.

I walked up to the fifth floor and knocked on the *izquierda* door.

No answer. No noise. No movement.

I checked the doorknob.

Locked.

As much as I wanted to go in, breaking and entering wasn't an acceptable option (plus, I didn't have the skills to crack a lock.) Instead, I walked back down to my apartment and wrote a note.

I went through quite a few drafts before I had it ready, but thirty minutes later, I was once again at that door, knocking and hopeful the tenant had since returned.

When nobody came to answer, I slid my folded sheet of paper under the door. As it swooshed against the floor and disappeared from sight, it dawned on me that my plan didn't make much sense. I'd written my note in English. What if the person didn't speak it? I was in Spain, after all.

Shit!

But I left it, since I couldn't retrieve it easily. Too much *MacGyvering* for a stupid piece of paper.

My phone number was on there. If I lucked out with a helpful person who spoke English, then I could wait while enjoying a drink at the bar.

Hey, come to think of it, maybe I can try and find the young bartender and corner him for some information instead. Maybe JuanMa knows what the souvenir is.

Out on the streets, I wandered for a while, unsure which corner bar he worked at. I went around my block a few times, then picked one of the two I thought could potentially match Sophia's description.

The second I opened the door and walked in, a strong garlic aroma overpowered me. The place was reasonably quiet. No loud music, just the background noise of the random chit-chat of a handful of couples and a small group of older gentlemen.

I sat my ass at the bar and considered ordering myself a cold *caña*, but the tiny beer serving wasn't what I wanted right now. Trying some of those inexpensive Spanish wines and tasty *pintxos* sounded like a much better plan.

"*¿Quiere tomar algo?*" asked the bartender, who looked well into his sixties. His hair was in the final transition from salt and pepper to white, but his eyebrows were still brown, with a few long straggly white hairs in the mix.

"*Una copa de vino tinto,*" I said.

"*¿Joven, crianza o reserva?*"

In Spanish, I requested clarification about what the first two were. Based on his reply and their respective prices, I opted for the *crianza*, which offered the best value for my wallet and taste buds. Although a tad more expensive than the default young red wines (what he'd called *joven*), those with the *crianza* classification had been aged for a couple of years, including a year in a cask before being bottled.

He pointed to a list of *crianzas* written in chalk on a blackboard behind him. Since none of the names rang a bell, I asked him to pick one for me.

"*¿Y quiere algo de comer?*" he asked as he poured a generous serving of burgundy wine in front of me.

I looked at the offerings under the glass display nearby and picked some small oval, battered balls in a bowl. I had no idea what they were, but trying something new sounded good.

He re-heated them in a microwave, then put the small dish in front of me with a toothpick and a tiny bowl of peach-colored dip. Judging by the words he used when he deposited my food down in front of me, I gathered that these bite-sized things were called *croquetas*.

I first rinsed my palate with wine before dipping my first *croqueta* into the dip, then taking my first bite. The other half of the oval-shaped *pintxo* that hung from my toothpick didn't look like anything I'd ever seen, but the flavors partied in my mouth. It was as though someone had taken a small chunk of ham, dipped it in a thick white béchamel sauce, rolled the lump in breadcrumbs, and then fried the whole thing. Tasty. And addictive. I quickly ate up the other half of my first *croqueta*, then devoured the entire contents of my bowl.

I ordered myself another serving while I sipped my wine and pondered my options, but I took my phone out of my pocket, just to make sure I hadn't failed to hear it ring. *No missed calls.* I left it right in front of me as I continued to enjoy my hearty *crianza*.

When I received my second order of *croquetas*, I slowly savored them as if they were the most deliciously fluffy, light, moist, creamy, and tasty ham appetizers I'd ever eaten because I was pretty sure they were.

By the time my glass was down to one last sip, a new person had come in behind the bar. He had longish brown hair and a beard. He kissed the other bartender on both cheeks, then put on a green apron that looked exactly like the one his older coworker wore. *It has to be him.* I didn't have an ounce of gay in me, but I had to admit that he was on the handsome side. He looked like he could have been created by merging the DNA of Antonio Banderas with that of Ricky Martin.

I turned to look at the patrons. All female eyeballs were on him. One of the women was licking her lips while watching him, but her actions could have been caused by the food she was eating. *Or not. Who knows?*

Part of me had been hoping I'd walked into the wrong bar, or that he wouldn't show up, just so I wouldn't have to ask him the awkward questions I needed to ask to find that souvenir Sophia had left behind. But yet, there he was.

How do I broach the—

My phone began vibrating and ringing loudly. An unknown number appeared on the screen. I swiped to answer, brought the device to my ear, and heard a female voice with a strong accent. "You leave note under my door."

"Hi! Thanks for calling. Are you home right now? Could I come over and talk to you?"

"Yes. You live in building?"

"Yes, I rent one of the apartments below yours. I can be there in five minutes?"

"Okay."

As though my lucky star had returned to its alignment, things were once again looking up. I waved a twenty-euro note in the air, and it got the attention of the older bartender, who gave me a head nod.

As soon as my bill was settled, I hurried out of the bar and down the street.

7:05 p.m.

After double-stepping my way up to the top floor, I paused for half a minute to let my breathing slow down.

Don't want to ruin it right here by looking like a crazy person.

Once my heartbeat had returned to normal, I knocked on the mystery woman's door.

When it opened, I was surprised to see the tall blonde I'd crossed paths with on the stairs the day I checked in. Her flowery perfume overflowed into the stairway. Her hair was pulled in a ponytail that sat very high on her head, her blue eyes decorated with thick dark lines, and her inflated lips colored in a bright shade of magenta.

"Hello, I'm the one who left you a note," I said with a genuine smile.

"I saw you before. Come in."

Must be Russian.

I walked into the apartment I recognized from the Airbnb photos I'd seen online. Eclectic art decorated the walls, and brown leather furniture filled most of the space where the woman was going. I followed her. It was hard not to stare at her ass in her tiny shorts. Her blouse ended about two inches above where the waist of her shorts started, leaving a nice gap that showed two small dimples on her lower back.

I brought my stare back up just as she turned around to look at me.

"Yes, I remember seeing you before as well. It would be hard *not* to notice someone as beautiful as you," I said, smothering her with way too much schmooze. I knew girls who looked like her got it all the time. While my best lines were often those that insulted them a little, I didn't want to risk it here. I needed to stick with my time-proven—and slightly boring—lines and compliments.

She pointed to the couch, and I took a seat.

"Thank you. Do you want water? Coffee?"

"Hmm... Water would be good," I said, then I noticed the lone half-empty glass of wine on the coffee table. "But if you're drinking wine, I could join you," I added.

"Okay." She left for a few seconds, then came back with an empty glass, which she filled generously before handing it to me. "Here. Tell me what you need."

Here goes my big fat lie.

"I used to live in this apartment, and it holds a strong... emotional... and sentimental value to me. I'm about to leave town in a couple of days, so I just wanted to check and see if the person who was living here would let me spend a few minutes in the apartment, just so I could remember some of those happy times."

"You strange man," she said.

Fair, it wasn't my best lie ever.

"So, thank you for letting me come in. I really appreciate the opportunity to be here again." I scanned the apartment, hoping the souvenir would jump at me, but no luck. I returned my attention to my host. "What do you do? Are you on vacation?"

She raised her shoulders. A second later, she took a sip, and then replied. "This and that."

I lifted an eyebrow at her but didn't probe.

"You work for government?" she asked, her face stern.

"No, I'm a pilot for a US-based airline."

A smile appeared on her pale face. "Good. Then, I tell you what I do." She leaned closer to me and shoved her manicured hand directly onto my groin. "I make men happy. You want to be happy?"

She'd flipped that switch so fast that I almost spat my wine when the unexpected grope occurred.

Paying to have sex with an attractive woman seems like an entirely viable way to spend more time in the apartment. More time for me to uncover what the souvenir is. And I could totally do this Russian piece of ass.

After agreeing on a price, she got up and efficiently stripped down to nothing right there on the spot. Her svelte body was just perfect. Surgically enhanced perhaps—no, that was a certainty. It was perfect, like those Photoshopped images on magazine covers. Her breasts lived in the 38D neighborhood, but no natural drooping there, everything overly perky and firm-looking. Her pale skin didn't display any tan lines at all, her belly button had been tagged with a long, thin silver rod, and her pussy was clean-shaven, leaving me to assume she was a real blonde, but there was no way to know for sure. Her eyebrows could have been dyed for all I knew.

"Bedroom or here?" she asked, one hand on her hip while the other pointed to a door behind her.

I had no idea if the clue would be in the bedroom, but it was my best-timed excuse for going in, so I lifted her gorgeous naked body up in my arms and brought her to the bed.

Once I unloaded her gently out of my arms and onto the mattress, I took off my clothes, her agile hands helping the process along. But I did spend a few seconds to take in the room and its decorations during the process: a dresser topped by a vase filled with fresh flowers, a handful of unlit candles, and two paintings—signed by Valentina of course. While Virginia's art was delightful and the salacious models aroused me, nothing here qualified as a souvenir worth my while.

By now, my Russian friend had already brought my pants and boxer-briefs down to my ankles. I stepped out of my shoes, then took off every layer of clothing, including my socks, of course.

"Tell me what you want," she ordered as she covered my cock with latex.

"Get on all fours on the bed. Your fine ass pointing toward me."

And she did, exposing her pussy and augmented ass in the best viewing angle possible. I groped her beautiful curves. Out of habit, my legs and hands instinctively lined everything up, and next thing I registered was her warmth as I slowly began to thrust into her experienced money-making pussy. She readjusted her position, curving her white back toward the right, then the left before settling her head and shoulders down on the mattress.

The flapping of my flesh against her round ass soon became rhythmic. With my hands holding on to her hips, there wasn't much thinking or planning required, and the woman I really wanted to fuck wasn't the one on her knees in front of me, so I closed my eyes.

How I wanted to do that to Sophia instead. Or Virginia...

I could imagine Virginia folded in front of me here. By concentrating enough, I could even smell her perfume. I could hear her voice. The moans of the woman in front of me could easily be hers. Her voice began airing in my head. First, I imagined her talking dirty to me, then begging me, but then the real words she'd voiced in our exchange last night came to mind. I did my best to push her words away, trying to think of her body instead.

With each thrust, the more I banged against the woman in front of me, the more the sounds we made morphed into something else when my head processed them. They somehow changed into those of a boxing glove hitting an empty punching bag. Leather against leather, but with nothing to absorb the shock. No substance. The warmth of the Russian woman somehow stopped registering in my head. The moans she'd started making somehow blocked from my ears for now. My mind was on autopilot; my cock was leading the show. I didn't know if Virginia's earlier words were to blame, but I opened my eyes, and for the first time in my life, I saw what I was doing.

The firm buttocks of the woman folded in front of me were beautiful, but they did nothing to fill the void that had appeared out of nowhere. Like a boxer stripped of an opponent, I suddenly lost my bearings. *I don't even know her name!*

I continued pounding her, budding anger beginning to mix with my inner confusion, speeding up the unavoidable.

Sure, she was a paid prostitute, her name wasn't consequential (and I'm sure she'd have given me a false one if I'd asked), but what scared me most was that I'd been here, in this exact position, too many times to count. With women whose jobs weren't in the sex trade. And I'd treated them exactly the same.

I have been using and objectifying women... All this time... All these years.

Is sex... my figurative, emotional punching bag?

While the Russian woman in front of me looked perfect—and pounding her ranked way up on my pleasure scale—it didn't do anything to nudge my happiness needle. And as I grunted my way past my finish line, for the first time in my life, my orgasm felt hollow. It still felt damn good—of course—but it also came with a generous side-dish of unexpected confusion. I could only guess I hadn't made her come. Sure, she'd made some noises while my mind was elsewhere, but I hadn't paid attention to her. I'd been selfish.

Fucking her (and spending money to do it) had only been a one-sided pleasure.

Nothing more. Nothing less.

But why was I so upset at myself right now? She was a paid prostitute.

I pulled out of her and stayed quiet, lost in my thoughts. She got up from the bed and returned to the living room. A few minutes later, after getting myself cleaned up and dressed, I joined the Russian woman in the living room. She'd already put her clothes back on and had even had time to light a cigarette.

She stood by the window, turning to the street to exhale the smoke she'd breathed in.

I dug my wallet out and retrieved the correct amount before walking it over to her. While I was walking back toward the door, with half my mind focused on sliding my wallet back in my pocket, the other half noticed the row of movies above the television. Then I remembered what Sophia had written about. I stepped closer so I could read the titles, letting my finger run along the edge of the shelf as I moved through the selection of action, thriller, and comedy movies... until I spotted those I was looking for.

I pulled out one particular case, and its cover featured a woman in a flowing nightgown, the one about a woman exploring her sexuality. Maybe watching it could help soothe whatever my mind had uncovered minutes earlier. But when I turned around to look at the Russian woman, she was watching me, her head tilted to one side.

Thinking fast, I realized I had two options. I could somehow steal it: I could pretend that I'd forgotten something in the bedroom, and ask her to fetch it for me while I slid the case under my shirt. Or I could just ask to borrow it. Feeling as though my karma was in debt, I opted for honesty-ish.

"I'd forgotten about this movie. Any chance you'd let me borrow it, and I'll return it tomorrow?" I asked her. "And sorry, what's your name?"

"Andrea," she said. "Sure. You can borrow whatever movie."

"Thanks, Andrea. Thanks for letting me in, for letting me borrow this... and for the entertainment." I smiled at her, then opened the door and stepped out.

A minute later, down a couple of flights of stairs, I unlocked my apartment door and caught a glance of myself in the mirror. I didn't like what I saw. I couldn't even bear to look at my reflection right now. So, I dropped the DVD on the table, then headed right back out.

I had to do something to change my mood, to get me out of this uncomfortable funk, to get rid of this realization my mind had stumbled upon at the worst of times. Thankfully, I knew just the thing that could help me right now.

I needed a cigarette.

7:50 p.m.

I stepped into one of the red and yellow government-run shops that sold souvenirs, postcards, stamps, and tobacco products to get myself a pack along with a lighter. I resisted the urge to open it right then, hoping that some magical, earth-shattering realization would come to me before I unsealed the pack and turned back to my previous addiction, so I walked instead.

I didn't know where I was heading, but my feet led the way; traffic lights dictated if I'd go around a corner or cross a street. I followed the green lights. The nearby traffic kept me distracted from the thoughts I didn't want to face, but deep down, I knew I had to.

A few minutes later, I found myself walking along the water on *Pasealeku Berria*, the road that curved around Mount Urgull. I sat on one of the empty benches overlooking the sea. Powerful waves crashed onto rocks and man-made blocks a few feet below the edge of the road in front of me, at times sending some post-crash sprinkle my way. *The universe's way to spit in my face.*

I hesitated once the filter sat between my lips, but old habits kicked in automatically. Next thing I knew, I was lighting it up and taking a deep inhale of the very substance I'd previously had so much trouble quitting.

"Fuck this shit," I mumbled to myself.

Usually I was good at compartmentalizing information, thoughts, and feelings. *What's wrong with me here? Why can't I push aside the realization that I've been a dick all these years?*

The question probably held its own answer.

But why couldn't I simply go back to my previous way of thinking?

With each inhalation of nicotine, I tried to let go of my thoughts, but instead, I was pelted by memories. Memories of various women I'd fucked. Women I'd never called back. Women I'd treated like objects. Women I'd treated like shit.

The memories battered my brain with the same intensity as the waves pounded the rocks a few feet in front of me, at the base of the protective wall onto which this road had been built. While this structure had been constructed to withstand forces of nature, it appeared my mind couldn't even stand the truth. My attitude had been a protective veil. Once lifted, it could no longer be lowered, no matter how much I wanted it to.

You can't know what you don't know that you don't know.

But now I knew, and I was fucked.

Virginia, why did you have to say that?

Why did you ruin a perfectly good thing?

Or was it Andrea? Was it just the flapping noises? What did it? Could I repeat the experience and somehow undo what had just happened?

Closing my eyes, I hoped the marine air could cleanse me from my sins, or somehow dissipate the awful feelings that clouded my brain.

But it didn't.

I reached for the pack and lit up a second cigarette instead. This time, I forcefully pushed away any thoughts that tried to reach me. I just concentrated on the sensation of the hot smoke slowly burning its way down my throat, into my lungs. My head recognized the slight high I hadn't had in a while. How I'd missed that feeling...

I must have sat on the bench for nearly two hours. Well past sunset, and well past the end of my pack. Whatever light buzz I may have had from my two glasses of wine was long gone. All I had left was just my sad old self, and I'd have to face my life moving forward with a giant ball and chain that would forever be attached to me.

No matter how much I shook my head, no matter how much I swore under my breath, no matter how much I wished the thoughts away, I was now stuck with them. Branded with shame. A scar on my self-esteem.

I got up and headed toward the lit skyline in front of me. A red, white, and green Basque flag flew high in the evening breeze, perched on the side of the hill, lit up by a flood light. For some self-battering reason—or perhaps to try and wake up from this nightmare—I walked as close to the edge of the road as possible, my left hand touching the railing that prevented people from falling down the wall and crashing to their deaths, or at least suffering severe injuries if they ever landed below. The waves had gained strength, or perhaps the tide was coming in, but spray intermittently splashed me, and I let it.

A cold, salty slap in the face from Mother Nature. Payback from all the women I'd hurt. And I deserved every bit of it.

Needless to say, I quickly became a wet mess, inside and out. The man tending the shop where I stopped to get another pack of cigarettes gave me a strange look, but he accepted my money nonetheless and sold me the solace I craved.

I headed up the stairs to my apartment and into the bathroom. After tossing my wet clothes in the sink, I got into a warm shower. I remember standing immobile under the dense stream for a long time. I was unsure how long, though, and a few tears may or may not have joined the running water.

I could not recall ever being that down on myself. If I could no longer be that Charlie, who the fuck was I going to be? I wasn't going to let Charles the geek come back in charge. Was there a way to balance my macho pride with more respect for women? With my self-confidence now devoid of its very foundations, what the fuck was I going to do?

I swore aloud, until all my anger had left my system.

Then I shut off the water and got out. The mirror was coated with condensation, so I wiped a small area to dare look myself in the eyes. I still didn't recognize the man that gazed back.

After toweling myself off, I walked to my opened suitcase in my bedroom to find something dry to wear. My plaid pajama bottoms and a white cotton undershirt donned, I paced the bedroom for a while. Then I went for the only relief I could find: the pack of cigarettes.

Sitting on the small balcony with an ashtray, a lighter, and my stupid problems, I stared outside. A few people passed by, enjoying their evening walk. But six cigarettes later, I hadn't made an ounce of progress.

I put out my latest cigarette, then returned to the living room. Picking up the DVD I'd borrowed hours ago from Andrea, I carefully read the description on the back of the cover. My Spanish wasn't good enough to understand all of it, but it did seem intriguing. It couldn't be worse than sitting in my stew of negativity, so I took the DVD over to the player that rested on the shelves below the flat screen in the living room.

But when I opened the case, an extra disc fell out. One disc was still securely clasped within the case, its label matching the name of the movie, but the one that had fallen out had no stamp on it. Just the name of the writable DVD brand I'd often seen sold in large packs back in the day.

Holy shit! That's the souvenir!

And this time, no crappy VCR would swallow and destroy it. No Japanese mafia would come after me.

11:03 p.m.

The disc contained several short sequences, all accessible from the main menu, all time-stamped with dates from over a year ago.

I started at the beginning. The first few short recordings featured Virginia painting Sophia in what I could only assume was Virginia's studio in the mountains. Virginia's long hair had been pulled into a ponytail at the very top of her head, and she wore the sexiest coveralls ever made. Sophia's description of the outfit didn't even come close to how hot she looked. The camera's angle only gave me back and side views of her barely-covered toned and tanned body as she moved around her canvas.

But when the camera zoomed out to include more of Sophia, a loud moan escaped my lips. My Sophia was lying sideways on the chaise, butt naked, smiling at Virginia. Her lips started moving, but I couldn't hear anything. Grabbing the remote, I tried to increase the volume but soon realized there was none. The two of them appeared to be chatting about something funny, both smiling and laughing. Sophia had me enthralled. The way her breasts fell and moved naturally as she laughed and repositioned herself. The way her entire face brightened when she smiled. She wasn't one of those who only smiled from the lips. Her whole face brightened with emotions.

Virginia began walking toward Sophia, then the video ended abruptly, taking me back to the main menu.

Without hesitation, I began watching the second recording, which consisted more or less of the same, but with less laughter this time. Virginia was painting Sophia, sometimes walking up to her to readjust the way she held her head, the way her hair fell, or the angle her long legs took as she rested them one on top of the other, bent at the knees.

The third video was more along the lines of what I was hoping to see. It was one of the solo sessions Sophia had written about. Watching a woman masturbate was a rare treat and made me feel as though I'd been granted god-like privileges over something that generally occurred behind closed doors or curtains. Sophia's eyes were closed, her face relaxed, and her Mona Lisa smile more or less static, save for the corners of her mouth pinching upward at times.

She lay sideways, facing Virginia. One of Sophia's hands cupped her left breast, massaging its shape with the outer fingers while her thumb and middle finger pinched her nipple. Her other hand moved slowly between her legs, her index and middle fingers bent as she slid them between her folds, just below a narrow landing strip. Then she readjusted her position and rested on her back, making the motions of her chest much more noticeable as she inhaled and exhaled. She'd kept one leg folded, but the one closest to the camera was lying flat, offering Virginia (and the cameraman and me) the perfect viewing angle.

Although there was no sound on this video either, the mere motions of her heaving breasts made me feel like I could hear the ravenous, sexy moans coming from her lips. The hand between her legs began moving faster, then her other digits left her gorgeous breasts and headed southward as well, joining the others. The zoom left a bit to be desired, but I believe one hand was pulling her skin taut while she began to make circling motions with her other hand, toying with her clit. While she continued playing with the intimate toys Mother Nature had given her at birth—with her movements increasing in both scale and speed—her back began arching away from the chaise. The leg that had previously lain flat and immobile started twitching, her toes curling erratically. Her stomach began shaking, and her face scrunched as her lips parted from each other. During her final set of convulsions, which rocked her entire body and made both of her nipples harden into thick pins, she turned her face to look at Virginia, her mouth agape, her eyes seemingly heavy with unspoken feelings.

It was safe to say that my own soldier had enjoyed the show. I even surprised myself with how heavy my breathing had become. I had yet to touch myself, and was unsure why. But maybe knowing how many more videos existed on this disc was partly to blame. Perhaps I was saving myself for what I hoped had been engraved onto this unexpected treasure.

When Sophia brought her hands back to her chest, rubbing one hand up and down over her heart as her chest slowly reduced its scope of motions, the video ended and took me back to the main screen.

And as though my horny prayers had been heard, the following clip began halfway through the action I had been imagining ever since I first read Sophia's Spanish entries. Sophia's and Virginia's bare bodies lay against each other, limbs intertwined over a large bed covered in gray sheets. This video was set in a different room, with a curtain sometimes flapping up and to the side, hiding some of the action. Unfortunately, the viewing angle into Virginia's bedroom wasn't as enticing as the one looking into her studio. But maybe the narrower field of vision somehow added some mystique to the whole shebang. The flowing curtains sometimes obstructed my spying on their lovemaking, but it also made it feel more realistic.

The sight was too much for my poor cock. I pulled down my pajama bottoms, spat in my hand, and then began taking care of myself as I watched the two most gorgeous women I'd ever set eyes on devour each other's bodies. Although inaccurate, it's the only way I could have described their actions. Their feverish, unstoppable, repressed emotions finally exploded into their newfound freedom. Their hands were groping at each other's flesh, their mouths nibbling, licking, biting, and devouring every bit of exposed skin, from their heads to their toes. And how they lingered over their erogenous zones. I came before they even started going down on each other, my other hand doing its best to catch my mess, but failing miserably.

Since I wasn't home, I got up, paused my video on a particularly exciting scene that involved Sophia having just pulled Virginia's body toward the edge of the bed and positioning her face right in her pussy—how lucky was that—then I immediately headed to the bathroom to fetch a box of tissues. While in the bathroom, I figured I might as well grab my travel-sized bottle of lube because making myself sore from watching these two beauties was a definite possibility.

A few minutes later, my mess cleaned, I once again sat down on the couch, which I'd covered with my bedsheets, knowing fair well that another spillage of my seed would be imminent the minute I resumed the best homemade porn I'd ever seen.

And when I pressed play again, my favorite ladies didn't disappoint.

An hour later, they were still at it, making love to each other slowly, passionately, and intently. Now that was very different from any porn I'd ever seen, and from any action I'd personally taken part in. It made me wonder if they both favored tantric sex (or if what I was looking at qualified as that. Mr. Google could undoubtedly enlighten me later once the video ended).

And after coming for the third time while enjoying my entertainment, my stomach grumbled. I once again paused the video and headed to the fridge to pick up and reheat some of the leftover pasta I'd cooked earlier today. Stomach satisfied, I resumed the footage as this specific video ended.

Back at the main menu, I selected the next one in line and was surprised to see a third person in this video. I recognized the handsome bartender as he carried Virginia into the bedroom. Both were naked. His erection stood proud underneath her ass as he held her petite body in his arms, then gently dropped her on the bed. *Déjà vu*, I thought, revisiting how I'd brought Andrea into her bedroom hours earlier, but then the *déjà vu* ended sharply. Sophia soon joined them on the bed, and as much as I didn't want to stare at JuanMa, I had to do it. The way he stood, sat, touched them, talked to them—not that I could hear what he was saying, as there was still no sound—but his lips moved. A lot. And there was lots of smiling and giggling involved.

My threesomes had been the complete opposite: just a series of motions and positions that had brought me the pleasure I wanted. And based on the moans and groans of the ladies, I could only assume that I had also granted them the orgasms they had sought, but I was no longer sure of it. What JuanMa and the ladies displayed on video... For the first time in my life, I began to understand. Now *that* was intimacy.

And with the passing hours, their passionate love-making somehow turned into an educational movie for me, but without anyone needing to narrate what was going on.

What was wrong here? Or was it finally right?

If I hadn't had that awful realization earlier today, would this video have had the same effect on me?

Would I wake up tomorrow having completely snapped out of it?

But my soldier once again took control of my brain the minute JuanMa stepped out of the room, leaving my two gorgeous beauties alone to munch on each other's pussies in the most beautiful 69 I could have ever dreamt about. Virginia was sitting on Sophia's face while my no-longer-mysterious stewardess lay on her back. But a few seconds later, Virginia folded her tanned body over Sophia's, bringing her face down to caress Sophia's most intimate parts. They tenderly continued their actions, even as JuanMa came back into the room with a tray of food in his hands. Neither him nor the food distracted the beautiful ladies in the least. At some point, Virginia suddenly brought her upper body vertical in what I could only assume was a powerful orgasm. Her entire body shivered. She grabbed her small breasts, arched her neck, and her mouth went agape as she frowned the most beautiful orgasmic expression.

At this point, JuanMa knelt at the foot of the bed, near where Sophia's pussy rested and he dove head first between her legs, soon allowing her to reach pleasure peaks similar to those Virginia had reached just seconds ago, at least based on her physical response.

And the video ended.

When I returned to the main menu, I sadly realized that this one had been the last bit of footage on the disc.

I took out my laptop and decided to make a copy of it on my hard-drive. Just in case. I'd learned my freaking lesson too many times. There was a limit to the number of video problems I was willing to face, and I'd long exceeded it over the past few months.

While the files were being copied, I dug out Sophia's diary again and re-read the section where she'd hinted at this video. I couldn't keep it for myself. The women had intended to spread their message, and I wasn't going to stop them. It was a beautiful message after all.

Once my priceless souvenir had been safely copied to my computer, I returned the disc to its case and placed it by the door, intent on returning it to Andrea the following day, as promised.

As I lay in bed, about to fall into the arms of Morpheus, I thought about the differences I'd seen between the women and their ménage with JuanMa. All hot as hell, but the loving kindness exchanged between the women had been much stronger. And there was something more nurturing in the way JuanMa made love to the two most beautiful women I'd seen in recent years.

That was it. He wasn't just fucking them like I wanted to fuck them. He was making love to them in a more patient, sensuous kind of way.

That I could do. I could learn and improve there.

While it wasn't the complete solution for not acting like a dick anymore, it was a small step I was most willing to make.

And just like pro athletes reviewed tapes of their games to improve, I swore to myself that I would watch and re-watch their lovemaking fest. I had to be honest with myself and acknowledge that I'd learned a thing or two from JuanMa during my initial viewing. A few moves of his were worth adding to my own (already quite diverse) repertoire.

Who's to say what else I could pick up from a more thorough review of it?

9:30 a.m.

The following morning, I sent Virginia a photo of the unlabeled DVD with the caption: "I found it."

It took precisely thirty-eight minutes of agonizing doubts before the double checkmarks turned blue, indicating she'd seen my WhatsApp message.

OK.

I'm a woman of my word.

I'll show you the painting.

But before I started typing any of the questions that popped into mind, I saw the triple dots indicating she was typing something else, so I waited.

A minute later, an address appeared, followed by a tiny map with a location pinned in the center of it.

Meet me at 2:30 this afternoon.

I sent her the thumbs-up emoticon as a smile drew on my face.

2:30 p.m.

Without giving me time to identify myself, Virginia buzzed me in from the intercom in the entrance of her building.

I walked up the stairs until I reached the *derecha* apartment on the sixth floor. After knocking lightly, I waited in silence until the door opened and Virginia appeared, wearing business attire that consisted of a form-fitting, well-tailored burgundy skirt and jacket. Where the flaps of her well-fitted jacket crossed, her décolletage dipped invitingly low, making me believe there was no other layer of clothing under there, save for perhaps one of those push-up bras that misled men like me and got us acting all sorts of crazy.

Since I didn't know where we stood on the friendship scale—her behavior the last time we'd met had left me more confused than anything—I didn't know what to expect in terms of greetings. But when she saluted me with the double-cheeked kiss, I figured we were off to a good start.

"You look great," I said, hoping the honest compliment would help keep us on good terms.

"Thank you. Please come in," she said before closing the door behind me.

I ambled, unsure where to go, but soon realized there weren't many options. The short hallway opened into a small but well-furnished living room that was surrounded by a few closed doors and another short passageway that disappeared around a bend.

"Nice-looking place," I told her as she joined me in the room. "Is this one of your paintings as well?" From where I stood, I couldn't make out the signature, since a massive abstract statue of something curvy blocked the lower right corner where she'd signed all the other paintings of hers I'd seen.

"This one isn't. It was a gift from a painter friend, but I don't believe you're here to admire my living room decor. You want to see her?"

For a brief second, my hopes rushed upward, and then I realized it was near impossible she meant Sophia. She was probably just referring to the painting of her.

"Of course," I said, nodding.

She turned to face a few doors to our left and opened the first one. "This way," she said.

Virginia walked in, and I followed her into the spacious bedroom, which was generously illuminated by sunlight coming in from the large window on one side. It smelled of citrusy fruit and something else, but the mysterious odor was soon forgotten when I looked above the bed. There reigned a wide horizontal oil painting of a naked woman, but it wasn't any woman. It was Sophia. *My* Sophia. *Virginia's* Sophia, in all of her curvaceous, lascivious, and naked glory. And her Mona Lisa smile... Virginia had captured it perfectly. While I was sure it wouldn't compare to how I'd feel upon meeting her in the flesh, I could only assume it was a close second. As though a tsunami of repressed urges had suddenly crashed onto me, I paused and nearly choked. I'd somehow forgotten how to breathe.

Once blood flow and thoughts started reaching my brain again, I unfroze and asked Virginia the first thing that came to mind: "When did you finish it?"

"A few days after she left Spain from that trip."

"It's fabulous," I said. "You're an amazing painter."

She smiled. "Thank you, but I think the model played a big part in how this one turned out."

The odd scent kept tickling my nose as I continued staring at the woman who'd been haunting my dreams for more than a year. *Could it be Sophia's perfume?*

"When was she here last?" I asked.

She inhaled and exhaled loudly before answering. "A while ago."

I turned to face her. Now, that was an odd answer. The only thing I could conclude from her words and her facial expression was that Virginia and Sophia might not be *that* serious of an item anymore.

"Is that so?" I said, hopeful that she'd spill a few interesting details, but she stayed quiet and instead walked out of her bedroom.

I followed and joined her in the living room.

"What now?" I asked. "Do I get to meet her?"

She anchored her fists onto her narrow hips, with her elbows out, as though trying to make herself look more important. Or more impatient. "I'm afraid I can't make it that easy for you. I stand to lose a fair bit here. I'm not sure I want to risk it based on your reputation."

"Stop it with my reputation already. People can change. Whatever odious thing you think is integral to my personality... People change."

"No, they don't."

"Let me prove it to you then."

She eyed me up and down but kept quiet.

"I get the impression you're keeping something from me." Since she remained silent, I decided to bet it all on black. "Because you're a woman of your word, you can't guarantee I'll be able to meet her. That's why. When was the last time you spoke with her?"

Her eyelids closed for a few seconds before she reopened them, raised her chin, and answered. "It's none of your business."

"So, it's been a while..."

She once again exhaled loudly.

"The two of you argued over something. God knows what. But..."

While my mind continued spinning to scan for various scenarios, she kept quiet, her eyes darting at me, as though she dared me to say something specific.

"I get it. You broke up. But you're still in love with her."

She shook her head, this time vehemently. In her eyes flashed an urgent emotion. *Anger?*

"Okay. Maybe not broken up, but on a break?" I suggested.

Although her poker face had been relatively good—or at least inconclusive—to date, seeing her throat move as she swallowed around the knot my guess had caused gave her away.

"That's it. What you said the other night... And the reason why you're even talking to me in the first place..."

"I need water," she said before walking into the short hallway behind the couch. "Do you want any?" she yelled from whatever room she'd stepped into, out of sight.

"Sure," I yelled back, then decided to follow her. If she'd retreated into a different room to quench her thirst or to hide her emotions, I didn't know, but I didn't want to risk missing out on what was happening if it was the latter.

And I'd made the right guess. I walked in on her sniffling and wiping her nose.

Shit.

"Listen..." I said.

She turned away from me and raised her hand as though she wanted me to leave her alone, but I opted for the opposite approach. I wrapped my arms around her and squeezed her tight, rocking her slightly as her erratic breathing pulsed through my body. At first, she tensed up, then, as I gently rubbed one of her shoulder blades through the fabric of her suit, she turned to mush in my arms.

"It's okay," I whispered in her ear, letting her citrusy perfume envelop me as surges of tears ebbed and flowed out of her, shaking her entire tiny frame in my arms.

3:10 p.m.

After her emotions had wound down, we sat on the couch next to each other, and she opened up to me, spilling some details about their last argument. Without context, it was hard for me to make sense of what she was saying, but I listened and nodded nonetheless. When she finished speaking, I waited for a full minute before saying anything, just to ensure she was done.

"I get what you're saying," I said, although the statement wasn't 100% true. "But very few things are final in this world. Save for death..."

She finally looked up from her knees, where she'd been staring for the best part of the past fifteen minutes. Her eyes met mine with hope spilling out of them. "But how can I fix it?"

"I wasn't there, but from what you just told me, it sounds like you love each other. From that, you can achieve almost anything." While my words sounded foreign coming from my mouth, I'd seen my parents do crazy things to each other when my mother was still alive. I still had faint memories of them arguing. A lot. But they always forgave each other and moved on. "You keep telling me that I need to prove to you that I'm worthy. Is this because she asked you to do the same?" I asked.

One of her eyebrows lifted, but she stayed quiet. I let her silence expand into minutes, most of them uncomfortable, but I pushed through it with all my might. As though she was replaying some memories in her head, her expression kept changing. Her face became the outward projection of whatever her mind was running through, changing from that of a fearful little girl to that of an angry woman, all the while never misplacing her sensuality for too long. Watching her expression as she did so, I'd just redefined the word *intrigue*.

"Okay. I think I know what I need to do," she finally said.

"Good?" I said, half-statement, half-question. Figuring that asking for Sophia's contact information right now was a dick move, I stayed quiet. But oh, did I want to ask. I was staring at the finish line, yet it remained out-of-reach, as though I was running on a treadmill and someone was dangling a carrot just inches from my mouth.

"When are you leaving?" she asked, bringing my hopes up.

"Tomorrow."

The weight of my single-word answer had turned her shy smile into a frown again.

"Hmm..."

"Is my departure date related to your plan?" I asked.

"Maybe you can help. But not if you're leaving tomorrow."

"I'm planning on leaving Spain tomorrow evening so that I can be ready for my flight out of Heathrow in two days."

"That's not enough time," she said before exhaling loudly. "I need at least two full days, ideally three."

"Let me think if there's a way around," I said.

This was it. My single opportunity to prove to her that I was worthy. But skipping work was something I'd never done before. I'd never called in sick without having a doctor ground me first. I'd never let the airline down. Not once in nearly two decades with them. Thinking about my upcoming routes, I had to see if I could find a solution that would not get me in trouble or leave our passengers on the lurch. How I hated personnel who allowed their circumstances to mess up everyone else's plans, but now I stood on new ground, really considering doing so for the first time in my career.

But there was a first for everything. And this seemed to be particularly true during this trip to Spain.

While airlines typically kept a few pilots ready to step in should any of us call in sick, the policy didn't cover all airports. I knew for a fact that our airline didn't have extra personnel at the ready in LHR since it was an overseas hub. Too cost-prohibitive or something. And whoever would take over my flight would have to make it there well before then.

I pulled out my phone and flipped through my calendar.

Then I looked at the time and did some mental math.

Bob. He was qualified for these flights. If he found out now, he could get there in time. But he was also enjoying a holiday with his wife... and Henrietta.

I scratched my head. *Fuck.* If our roles were reversed, would I be willing to step up for him and shorten my time off? *For Bob? In a heartbeat.*

I flipped through my contacts and found his Costa Rican number. I stood up and walked toward the window as the international ring tone echoed in my ear.

Stacy picked up on the fifth ring. After greeting her, I asked to speak to Bob, but she said he was out in town.

"When do you expect him back?" I asked.

"Shortly. In an hour or so?" Stacy said.

"Please tell him to send me a message on Facebook when he gets home. I'll call him back right away. I've got an emergency, and I need his help."

4:00 p.m.

"It's sorted. I can stay here two more days. Three max," I told Virginia over the phone.

"That's fantastic." Her voice alone told me she was beaming right now.

"Well, the work component has been sorted, but I haven't spoken to Eduardo to see if I could extend my stay in his apartment."

"Oh, don't worry about that. You won't need it."

"So, will you tell me what your plan consists of then?"

"Pack up your bags. Everything, as if you were checking out now, and I'll come and pick you up in about an hour. You'll find out soon enough."

6:00 p.m.

While my inner machismo craved driving instead of being driven, I had to admit that Virginia maneuvered the curves of these mountainous roads quite well. Probably nearly as well as I would have.

But a sudden surge of adrenaline came over me as she avoided a crate that fell off the truck we'd been tailing. She honked and yelled something I didn't understand as she sped up and passed the driver.

Sharp reflexes and smooth recovery. Could she be a better driver than me?

Once my heartbeat had returned to normal, I broke the silence that had been weighing heavily since we left town.

"So, what's the plan? Are you going to fill me in?"

She turned to look at me briefly before returning her eyes to the road and answering my question. "All you need to worry about is being at your best. Show me that you're a decent human being, that you're not the misogynist I believe you to be."

"What? How is that a plan?"

"There are other components to it, of course. But all you need to worry about is that. Do your best to charm me as though I were Sophia. Think you can do that?"

I cleared my throat as the notion made my dick twitch in my pants in pre-emptive approval. "You *want* me to turn on the Charlie charms and impress you?"

"Yes. Crank it up as high as you can."

I stared at her in silence for a few seconds, digesting what she'd just said. "To be 100% clear, you're not talking about my platonic charms, are you?"

She snapped her neck at me, her eyes round. "Is that the approach you'd take with Sophia?"

"Hell no."

"Then pull out all your stunts. Make me fall in love with you. But always respect me. Don't escalate things faster than I'm ready for them. That's all you have to do."

I grinned while watching the way the setting daylight embellished the hills around us. "Looking forward to it then. Somehow, I'd gotten the vibe that I wasn't your type." Or maybe Virginia's insecurities about the whole Sophia thing could have triggered some mixed signals. Or perhaps it was my newly found revelation that messed with my mind, but I kept those thoughts to myself.

She giggled. "My type? You're probably right. I normally like my men tall, dark, and handsome, but I can settle for two out of three."

7:00 p.m.

And from the moment Virginia turned off her engine, I became the best version of myself I'd ever been. No way was I going to let anything screw up my chances of meeting Sophia in person, especially my own flaws. I was so close now. I was all for showing off my good side, especially when hot Virginia had given me the green light to crank it up.

I did notice the curtains move in the house across the road, but I knew that whole story, so I ignored it. Instead, I gentlemanly unloaded every single bag that Virginia had loaded up in her trunk. Mostly groceries, but there were other boxes and things as well. After placing the last bag on the kitchen table, she began unpacking what she'd brought.

"Would you like me to light a fire?" I offered.

"That would be great, thanks," she said with a smile.

While I did so, I noticed the photos on the mantel. There was one of Virginia, JuanMa, and Sophia that had been taken outside. Possibly even here, but since the night sky had already blanketed the scenery, I couldn't tell. Tomorrow morning would come soon enough for me to find out.

Fire lit, I walked back to the kitchen to see if I could be of service to my gorgeous host.

"Could you walk down to the cellar and grab a bottle of wine?"

"Of course. Where is it?"

She pointed to a trap door in the floor of the living room.

"Any kind in particular?" I asked as I lifted the door and was greeted by brisker air.

"Maybe *Banda Azul?* Red wine—it has a blue stripe on the bottle."

I walked down the wooden steps, and a short metal chain brushed my forehead. *A light.*

After pulling on the chord, the whole room lit up. Spacier than I had expected, yet not high enough for me to stand without bending my neck, the room contained hundreds of wine bottles. All were stored horizontally in slots, in groups that were ten bottles wide and thirty bottles high.

After pulling a few bottles at random from the group on my left—all of them being white wine—I figured the bottles had been sorted by wine types, or at least color. I moved to the opposite wall, which held three of those storage units. Sure, the racks weren't full, but a little mental math told me the bottle count was closer to a thousand. *Won't run out anytime soon!*

"Look on the right, second batch," Virginia yelled from the kitchen.

And a minute later, I did find a few of those bottles. I carried one up with me, turned off the light, and then lowered the trap door back down slowly and quietly.

"Here you are. Shall I open it?" I asked as I placed the bottle on the kitchen table, which had already been cleared of all the bags I'd unloaded earlier.

"Please do." She opened a drawer, retrieved a corkscrew, and then handed it to me. "Do you like red wine?"

"I do," I said as I warmed the plastic sleeve with my hand and then pulled it away from the bottle.

Virginia looked at me with a strange expression on her face, that tiny line once again appearing between her brows.

"Much nicer than cutting it," I said, feeling a need to explain myself. I pushed the tip of the screw into the now exposed cork, and, a few seconds later, a light pop echoed in the kitchen.

Virginia had already grabbed two glasses and brought them to me. After pouring us both a generous serving, I raised my glass and offered a toast. "Here's to getting to know each other," I said.

She repeated my toast and clinked her glass against mine. After we both took a sip—the round flavor in my mouth surprising me with a chocolaty undertone—her head nodded toward the stairs near the front door.

"Want to get the grand tour?"

Over the next twenty minutes or so, she showed me everything there was to see. The highlight was, of course, her studio, filled with more of her paintings. That woman was genuinely talented. No art had ever affected me like that before. It was like she had somehow refined the brush strokes so that once the image she created was viewed and captured by my irises, it sent a direct signal to my groin. And that message made me want to do things to Virginia. Nasty things, but also delightful things... But not right now. I had to play it cool. I had to charm her off her feet, and that required time. And lots of attention.

She also showed me her bedroom, then mine, clarifying any doubts I may have had.

"I'm going to change into something more comfortable. Meet you downstairs," she suggested. "Make yourself at home. Feel free to do or grab anything you want. Help yourself to some food, whatever you need."

And so I returned downstairs and sat on the couch, staring at the flickering flames for a solid twenty minutes. I'd already refilled my glass. Twice. *What is taking her so long?*

My rumbling stomach told me I should probably eat something to soak up that wine.

After a quick inspection of the cupboards and fridge, I found all the ingredients I needed to make myself a sandwich: baguette, Spanish ham, mustard, and cheese. I was cutting my snack in half when Virginia reappeared downstairs, wearing yoga pants and a loose, slanted T-shirt whose stretched neck exposed one of her shoulders. Seeing that little bit of her in the flesh brought to mind flashbacks of her naked body recorded on that DVD, but I suppressed the thought for now.

"Sorry, I had to make a few phone calls," she said, a smile appearing on her face when she saw what was on my plate.

"Would you like a sandwich?" I offered.

"Hmmm. I could eat something."

"Try this one. I don't know how you like your sandwiches. I can make another kind. I saw other things in there. Tomatoes, eggs—"

But she'd already taken a bite and was smiling. "This one's good!"

"Then take it, I'll make another one for me."

And so I did, my stomach grumbled in disagreement, but that was the only gentlemanly option.

By the time I'd made a second sandwich and joined her on the couch, she'd already eaten hers. She poured herself another glass of wine, finishing the bottle.

"Should I get another one?" I offered.

"That would be lovely."

My second excursion into the low-ceiling cellar was much faster, but not fast enough to save my sandwich from her hungry hands. She'd already eaten half of it!

"Sorry," she said. "I was starving. And you make good sandwiches."

I looked at her with a smile. A part of me wondered if she was doing this to test me or to push my buttons—which could be a possibility, considering her full plan was still unknown to me—but the bulk of me became even more turned on by that little piece of a woman... My dick had met quite a few women who weren't afraid of eating, and its conclusion—to which my brain agreed—was that hunger for food almost always corroborated with ravenousness in bed.

"Help yourself to the rest of it if you want," I said as I walked back to the kitchen to get the corkscrew... and to make myself yet another sandwich, I realized as I looked up and saw her chewing the rest of my snack.

When I returned to the living room with the wine and my third attempt at a sandwich—which I was now ready to guard with my life—Virginia had moved to the fire, adding a log and moving the coals around. Her tiny round ass was pointed my way in her yoga pants, and my dick started stirring a little. I couldn't peel my eyes off it, but thankfully, she soon finished her task and sat herself down, preventing a full-fledged erection from happening in my pants.

"Tell me about yourself. Your family," I said before biting into my sandwich.

And a flood of words began spilling out of her mouth. She was fascinating to watch tell stories about herself, her kids, Eduardo and his kids, and even her parents... Expressive, her face lit up when she recounted happy or funny moments. To be fair, I had trouble paying attention to her words. As she gesticulated, her arms made use of the entire space around her, her T-shirt moved, allowing me to see a bit more around her naked shoulder, and it was driving me mad. Mad with desire. Mad with urges. So, I let her speak, mentally ordering my dick to keep calm and focusing on keeping both our glasses full as she talked and we drank.

"And what about you? Tell me about your family."

I took a sip before speaking, trying to formulate an answer. I didn't usually talk about my family much. "Well, my mom died when I was still a boy. My dad's still alive. I don't see him much."

"Sorry about your mom. Do you have brothers and sisters?"

"No, I was an only child."

"How was your parents' relationship while your mother was still alive?"

"Lively and dramatic, but they were very much in love. Very happy."

"And can I ask how she died?"

"Car accident. She lost control on black ice, spun, and slid until her car collided with a tree, driver's side first. The paramedics said she'd likely died on impact. Her body had been too damaged to have an open casket at the funeral."

"That's tough. I'm so sorry."

Silence weighed between us as my mind traveled back in time, remembering that day as if it had been yesterday, except that I was still just a boy. That was the first time I'd worn a jacket and tie. My dad had asked one of his sisters to help take care of me while he 'got better.' At least, that's how he had phrased it. With 20/20 hindsight now, I think he just needed alone time to process the information. To deal with the fact that the love of his life was gone. To come up with a plan as to how he was going to continue raising me on his own.

When my aunt brought me back to my family home, that was when the second phase of my childhood began. My father, having never been able to cook or wash anything in the house, had come up with a solution. He'd gotten a woman to help. As a child, the nuances of what was going on went unnoticed for quite a while, but what I did realize was that these women never stayed long. It seemed that we got a new 'maid' every week or so. I didn't mind. I got to try a lot of different types of food since they all cooked differently. Some of them let me help them, some didn't.

I learned how to remove tough stains by hand, I learned how to use the machine to wash clothes, and I even learned to cook a few basic meals while surrounded by the endless supply of women that came and went through our home until I finally left town.

A few years into the charade, as my teenage hormones kicked in, I figured out the women weren't actual maids. They were just women my dad was hooking up with, trying to fill the void left behind by my mother.

Is this where I picked up my behavior? Shit. I swallowed hard. *How stupid am I to have missed that for what...? Thirty years or so...?*

"Fuck," I said aloud.

"What's wrong?" Virginia asked.

"Sorry, nothing." I shook my head. All this time, I'd associated my father's built-in happiness with his lifestyle when, in reality, the only time he'd been truly blissful was when he was with my mother, not after she'd died.

I downed what was left of my glass and got up. I needed something to do, something to take my mind away from this other realization.

I opted for adding another log to the fire and stoking it. I poked at it hard, as though the charcoal I massacred with my tool represented my own stupid self. *All these years. Believing that? How stupid are you, Charlie?*

When a flying piece of charcoal scorched my arm, I stopped poking. I placed the safety grill back in front of the fire and returned to the couch a few feet away from Virginia. She stared at me for a few seconds.

"Is everything alright?" she finally asked.

I nodded. "I'll be fine."

6:50 a.m.

After a night of tossing and turning, peppered with disturbing memories of the various women who had temporarily taken on the role of my mother—more like my father's pussy of the week—I rolled out of bed, intent on not letting a bad night's sleep ruin my chances at wooing Virginia in the most respectful manner possible.

I headed downstairs to make myself a cup of coffee and clear my mind. The house was silent; Virginia was probably still sleeping. Once I figured out how to work the gas stove, I brewed myself a hefty serving of a strong, bitter cup of joe.

Steamy beverage in hand, I unlocked one of the French doors that surrounded the living room where we'd hung out the evening before and walked out onto the patio at the back. I lit a cigarette from the pack I'd brought with me and was about to fall back into a mental funk when I heard bells out in the distance. At first, it was just the sounds of small ones that echoed around the green hills that rolled sharply in all directions, attached to whatever animals I couldn't see. Then, seven loud chimes rang from the village's church steeple. Birds chirped along, adding to the melody.

I inhaled deeply and relaxed.

New day. Let's make it a good one.

I sipped my coffee while exploring her backyard, still in my pajamas. I saw a few wildflowers growing against the stone wall that delineated the boundaries of her property and thought of the perfect idea to charm Virginia this morning. Once I finished my cigarette, squishing its butt into the barbecue, I knew what I had to do. Carefully avoiding the prickly bits of their stems, I picked a few colorful flowers to make a little bouquet, shook off the small bugs that had found themselves a home among the petals and buds, and then took them inside. It only took me a minute to find a suitable receptacle for a make-do vase (a tall and narrow glass). A quick inspection of the fridge later, I fired up the stove again. I had no idea what she usually ate, but who didn't like breakfast in bed? That would surely earn me some bonus points.

Thirty minutes later, after making myself a simple plate of scrambled eggs, I had a full breakfast ready for my host: a tomato-and-mushroom omelet with half an avocado (sliced) and a serving of home-made hash browns, along with a cup of coffee. I had no idea how she drank it, so I poured a little bit of milk into a small glass and found a little packet of sugar. Looking through her kitchen cupboards, I didn't see a serving tray, but I did find a large cutting board, which would work for my purposes. Placing my hot items and my mini bouquet of flowers on it, I carefully walked up to Virginia's bedroom.

I put my ear against the door, just to check if she was awake, but I didn't hear anything, so I rapped gently, and her voice chimed instantly from behind the door.

"Come in!" she said.

Balancing the makeshift tray on one knee, I released one of my hands so I could turn the doorknob, then I stood in the doorway with her breakfast.

"Good morning!" I said.

Virginia was sitting on her bed, her back resting against her headboard, reading glasses on her nose, a hard-cover book in her hands. While her legs were hidden underneath the sheets, her bare shoulders and arms hinted at what I was able to confirm the second she dropped her book to her lap. She was naked. Her gorgeous, tanned small breasts were hanging out in the morning light, nipples erect, probably from the cool breeze coming in through the open window. Her hips were also visible, no panty lines in sight.

I paused in the doorframe, unsure if the gentleman I aimed to be should walk into the world's most delightful trap.

"Can I come in?" I asked.

"Of course, please do!"

The sight of her was a little too much for my poor cock, which had taken the liberty of stretching itself out, along with the fabric of my pajamas. Thankfully, though, I believe the board I held hid my status, at least temporarily. The mere seconds needed to walk the tray over to her wouldn't be enough to tame myself, no matter what horrific sights I tried thinking of.

"Smells good," she said, her face beaming as I approached the bed.

I couldn't help but imagine those lips of hers around my cock right now, which wasn't helping my case, so I started speaking instead, spilling the first appropriate words that came to mind.

"Hope you like it. I didn't know what you normally ate for breakfast, so I made a few of my favorite things, since you had all of the ingredients here."

"You weren't lying. You can cook." Her eyes had lost the judgmental or condescending spark I'd seen when we spoke a few days before. "Please put it down on the nightstand. Smells delicious. Did you make some for yourself as well?" she asked.

"I ate while in the kitchen."

"Ah," was all she said.

I hesitated once I reached her nightstand. Although conscious of my inappropriate erection, I had no other options. So, I decided to not care anymore. I put her breakfast down on the wooden surface, which exposed my tented pajama bottoms as I moved back.

She did a double-take, then met my gaze. "Thank you, you can leave now," she said before flipping the cover off her lower body, exposing herself to me as she turned to sit on the edge of the bed, her hand going for the steaming cup of coffee I'd made for her.

"I'll come and meet you downstairs once I'm done my breakfast," she said with a twinkle in her eyes.

I bet her plan involves playing that essence-capturing game on me.

That was why I left her room, closing the door behind me. But instead of heading downstairs as she had suggested, I walked into the bathroom next door and took an interactive warm then cold shower to get her gorgeous naked body out of my mind.

At least for now.

9:10 p.m.

I spent the rest of my day being a perfect gentleman—well mostly. At least I didn't flaunt another erection in her face.

As we occupied ourselves with various platonic activities, Virginia kept dancing on that fine line between her flirtatious and guarded side, never giving me the clear go-ahead my cock and my mind wanted to hear, but I had to say I was having a grand time hanging out with her. We went for a walk; we watched a movie; we talked (well she did most of the talking—I listened).

But I did slip a little while we were cooking dinner together, and it only served to stoke the embers of my animal desires. She was making a sauce for pasta, adding spices ad hoc, without measuring them, tasting as she went along, letting the sauce simmer, and allowing the flavors to develop. I was busy cutting up bread when she offered for me to try it.

"I think it's just about right. What do you think?" She stood and brought a wooden spoon close to my mouth. The steamy red sauce it was covered with was speckled with tiny pieces of vegetables.

I blew on it, confident I'd burn my mouth if I didn't. When I finally tasted her sauce, flavors exploded on my tongue, with garlic and tomato taking the starring role, but the blend of flavors supporting them was also just perfect.

"Hmm. Tasty!" I said, looking at her and noticing a little bit of tomato sauce that had stained the corner of her lips. Without thinking, I brought my thumb to brush it away, but touching her face in such an intimate manner proved a little too much for the moment. Whether she felt it as well or not, I didn't know, but the second I did make contact with her soft skin, an energizing connection was triggered in my mind. She parted her lips ever so slightly. I met her gaze briefly. She lowered her eyelids, so I bent down and brought my lips to hers, finally letting myself taste a bit of the prize I was hoping to get out of this plan, whatever it was.

And did her lips ever taste good: a fountain of garlic and forbidden desire, which for a few seconds flowed both ways as our lips feasted on each other's, as our tongues mingled, as our bodies pressed themselves against one another to add more fervor to our kiss.

But she slid a hand on my chest and pushed me away.

"No. We can't. Not right now." Yet something in her eyes told me she wanted me as much as I wanted her, and that was enough for now. It took a couple of minutes before I could convince my dick, though.

Fortunately, she changed the topic. "I'll get started on the pasta now."

"Do you need my help with anything else?" I asked, and I honestly mainly referred to the kitchen. My mind had already come up with five or six lines I could have used here, but I kept them to myself. *The lady said no.*

"No, I'll be fine. The table is already set."

"Then maybe I'll have a smoke out back. Would it be alright?" I asked.

"Of course."

8:05 a.m.

When I got up, I headed downstairs, intent on making myself a strong cup of coffee so I could energize my mind against the barrage of tricky situations I knew would arise. But once I got downstairs, I felt a breeze coming in from the living room and noticed a set of doors were open. I walked toward them, wondering if we'd forgotten to close them last night, but I saw Virginia sitting on the patio, a book in hand, a cup of something resting on the table in front of her. Although I had enjoyed seeing her read naked in bed, it was probably better for the neighbors (and my cock) that she had decided to don some clothes for this morning's reading session.

"Good morning," I said.

"Morning." She lifted her eyes away from her book for a second and smiled. "There's coffee on the stove if you want some."

"Thanks!"

After pouring myself a cup, I went for my pack of cigarettes, which I'd left on the kitchen table last night. *Empty. Shit.* I walked out and joined Virginia out back.

"I ran out of cigarettes. Is there a shop nearby?" I asked her.

"No. Sorry, but you can help yourself to some of my tobacco," she said before pointing towards the house. "My purse should be somewhere in the kitchen."

Yeah... Sophia did write about the lack of shops in the village. How could I forget?

I headed inside the house and brought back her purse, feeling it was best not to go and dive into her bag without supervision. Women's handbags were mysteries to me, filled with things I was better off not knowing about.

"Oh, you could have looked through it," she said, but she nonetheless dipped her hand into her purse and then pulled out the plastic wrapper that contained loose tobacco. Then, she retrieved a sleeve of paper and a pack of filters.

"Here you go," she said, tossing the items on the table.

"Hmm..." I opened the bag of tobacco. In all my previous years as a smoker,

I'd never once seen—let alone used—loose tobacco. So, I had no idea how to go about rolling a decent cigarette. I glanced up and noticed Virginia staring at me.

"You know how to roll?" she asked.

The macho façade I'd typically use to hide my ignorance didn't stand a chance here. She'd find out in seconds and would see me as a liar as well. "I'm afraid I don't."

"Then let me show you how."

About fifteen minutes later, I'd managed to roll myself half-a-dozen, slightly misshaped cigarettes. Getting the tiny little filter to stay put by rolling the paper tighter around that end proved to be the most challenging part for me, but I'd enjoyed learning a new skill, no matter how useful it could prove to be later.

I should really stop smoking now. It was such a bad habit... But I nonetheless lit up and let the nicotine soothe my bruised ego, calm my nerves, and take my mind away from the thought of fucking Virginia.

5:20 p.m.

At the end of the afternoon on my second full day hanging out with Virginia (possibly the longest time I'd ever been on such good behavior and so damn horny I wanted to fuck anything and everything, but I only had my own hands to release the pressure), something unexpected happened.

Virginia was sitting across the table from me. We were in the midst of a card game she'd taught me that used weird-looking playing cards. Forget about diamonds, hearts, spades, and clubs. Her deck only contained 40 cards, and it was split into cups, coins, clubs, and swords. When I first saw them, I thought they were tarot cards.

But getting back to my point, Virginia suddenly spoke up. "So, I have to say... You surprised me, Charlie."

I cocked my head and waited in silence.

"You've proven me wrong. I think you may be worthy of her."

I locked eyes with Virginia before getting my hopes up. There was no evil plan lurking behind her gaze, no obvious trap.

"Glad to hear. So, what now?"

"Thanks to you, I have a good-enough reason to call her back."

"When are you going to call her?"

Instead of answering, she got up and headed back in the house. A minute later, she joined me on the patio again, her phone already against her ear, a radiant smile illuminating her face, her eyes glistening with hope.

"I was wrong, Sophia. Charlie's not who I thought he was."

My ears perked up at her mentioning my name, but I couldn't hear the other side of the conversation.

Virginia hummed and nodded her way through the next minute, seemingly agreeing with what Sophia was going on about.

"You want me to test the goods for you?" Her smile couldn't have been more alluring, nor the signal to my dick stronger.

"But it's just the two of us here," she said. Another thirty seconds went by. "Yes... That could work. I'll call and see if it can be arranged before he has to leave." And then she laughed. "We'll see about that!"

She looked at me as she continued humming her way through the conversation.

"I understand. I'll make it happen, and I'll be in touch again." She hung up.

I began extracting myself out of the picnic table bench, ready to take her, but her raised hand stopped me in my tracks.

"Stay here. I'll be right back."

5:45 p.m.

Instead of coming back to the patio, I heard her yell my name from the house, but it wasn't an urgent call. It was melodious and stretched out, like a siren's call trying to lure me closer to her.

Following the sound of her voice, I walked back into the house and found her at the bottom of the stairs, near the entrance door. Her devious smile and the way her hips tilted to one side already had me game for whatever she wanted.

"Care to come up?" she asked while unbuttoning the top few buttons of her shirt.

Before I could reply, she began running up the stairs, and I followed. If this was how she was going to play it, I was all for it. By the time we'd reached the top floor, my heart beating fast from sprinting up behind Virginia, we'd both shed our shirts. She leaned against her closed door for a second, letting me finally catch up to her. Her chest was heaving from the dash up here, making her small breasts move in her beautiful bra. I placed my hands on the door on either side of her head, my arms framing her body and preventing her from darting away from me.

Her perfume enveloped me, but another scent came along for the ride, one that spoke directly to my cock. I invaded her personal space, lowering my head and closing the gap between us until my lips touched hers. Just a brief kiss was all I gave her, but she responded by biting my lower lip and then undoing my belt. "Let's go in," she said in a sultry voice.

We both reached for the doorknob at the same time and opened the door. Virginia ran toward the bed, half-giggling, then kicked off her shoes. I sauntered instead, taking in my surroundings, pacing the room, and coming up with my game plan. So many scenarios involving Virginia had populated my dreams and daytime fantasies in recent days. *Which one should I go with?*

In the corner of my eyes, the curtain swayed in the breeze, bringing my attention to it. I looked toward it, then through the open window past it. The pale, dark-haired, and skinny neighbor I'd read so much about stood behind a tripod, the camera aimed at the room.

So that's what this is about. A video interview. Fine. I'll show Sophia what she can get.

And that was the last time the thought of the neighbor or his camera entered my mind.

I turned my attention to Virginia, who'd relocated to the center of her bed, her bottom half already freed of her skirt. All that was left on her gorgeous olive skin were the tiny lacy bits of her undergarment. Her legs were stretched out in front of her, save for one bent knee, her elbows held her upper body at an angle, and her chest still heaved heavily. She bit her lips while looking my way, her eyes possibly glued on my abs, or maybe a few inches lower, where the fabric of my shorts was being tested.

I kicked off my shoes, then took off my socks before unbuttoning my shorts and tossing them aside. Now wearing nothing but my gray boxer briefs—which seemed like the appropriate dress code here—I jumped onto the bed to join Virginia. Her hands reached my chest before I even made contact with her.

I laid her down on her back and lay atop of her, my knees preventing my weight from squishing her petite frame. Staring in her wandering eyes for a second, I knew we were in for a fun time ahead.

Take it slow, Charlie. Take it slow.

I let the back of my fingers flirt with her cheeks, then her neck, then her collarbone. Her warm breath caressed the side of my face as I looked down at her breasts. Barely brushing the outline of the place where her flesh met the lace, my movements triggered Virginia to arch her back, to get more pressure out of my digits. But I didn't let her. Instead, I lowered my head and dotted that area with light kisses, breathing and licking her soft, warm skin, but never intruding upon the boundaries of her underwear. For now. I had to tease the hell out of her, just as much as she'd teased the hell out of me for two solid days.

Delayed gratification.

It would be good for both of us this time.

I let my mouth head south once I reached the space between her breasts. Slowly licking a sinuous line down her flat stomach, I found my way to her navel, then to her panty line. Her scent was intoxicating. My cock twitched as though it was sending Morse code to my brain, ordering me to get in there already, but I ignored its order.

For a couple of seconds, I dipped my fingertips under the sides of her thong, on her hips, which resulted in a loud moan from Virginia's lips, but I pulled them out and left her panties be for now. I blew hot air over the small piece of fabric that covered her pussy, then brought my tongue to the soaking-wet material. Even through it, I could taste her musky arousal. It was potent and undeniable, like a billboard announcing the obvious. Her hips jerked sideways beneath it while she continued moaning.

But I ignored her.

I continued lowering myself, this time parting her legs and letting my lips and tongue work their way down the inside of one thigh. Slowly. I kept going down her leg. Once I reached her toes, I sat up on my ankles and looked at her. Her chest was still heaving, her eyes sultry and demanding, her legs parted and inviting.

"I'm begging you..." she said.

"Tell me what you want."

"You know what I want."

"You'll get it soon enough. I'll make it worth your while," I said before picking up her other foot and bringing it up to my mouth. I began kissing it, then slowly worked my way up her other leg as I lowered it back down.

By the time I licked my way up her inner thigh, her fingers had already grabbed the sides of her panties, and she was lifting her ass off the bed and rolling them off, exposing her clean-shaven pussy.

As much as I wanted to tease her forever, the sight of it convinced me to help her get out of the ridiculously small bit of fabric.

A few seconds later, I'd freed both her legs and my mouth returned to her groin, attracted to it like a moth to a flame. For a brief second, she looked familiar. No two women were alike when it came to their southern lips, but I honestly believed I'd seen her up close before. Then I remembered the painting. *A self-portrait of the best variety.*

But no matter how talented she was—there was no doubt she was gifted, and I'd seen the painting up close—it was nowhere near the experience of smelling her, of tasting her.

As I let my tongue trace her folds, my taste buds got to enjoy every flavor, every mystery she had to offer. And I savored every little bit. My fingers joined the party, one hand working her left inner thigh while the other parted and massaged her folds, giving me better visuals. Her open pussy glistened for me, and my tongue went for it, darting ever so briefly into her to get a better taste, to see how much she was turned on. Even if her wetness hadn't told me so, her incessant groans spoke for her desires. Ebbing and flowing, the sounds coming out of her mouth were intoxicating as I continued to explore her womanhood with my entire mouth.

Coming up for air for just a few seconds, I saw that her clit had already swollen, and I pulled its hood before diving back down, focusing on it with my mouth while I gently inserted a finger into her pussy. Her moans intensified, and her hips began jerking, moving my playground as though an earthquake was going through her. I added a second finger and then used my thumb to rub her clit.

"Oh, Charlie..."

My fingers sped up, and my mouth swallowed her clit, teasing it as she crossed her finish line, moaning loudly as her insides clenched against my fingers, as I continued licking her quivering pussy.

I left my digits in her for a few seconds longer, enjoying feeling how hard she'd come, but my cock twitched again, feeling abandoned. I pulled my fingers out of her, then brought them to my mouth. She was finger-licking good. Much more so than the famous fast-food chain. I sat on my ankles, between her parted legs as I continued cleaning my fingers in the best way possible. She watched me lick her juices off my digits, and she smiled. I'd missed seeing her orgasmic expression. But there's always a second chance, and I could start working on it right away.

But before I could lean back down and kiss her, she sat up and reached for my waistband. Precum had left a small wet spot where my tip pushed against the comfortable fabric. She expertly stretched and pulled it down without making my dick bend at an uncomfortable angle. Seconds later, in my birthday suit and ready to pounce on her, she once again threw a wrench in my plan by bringing her mouth to it. And I supported this, with one minor modification.

"Hold on," I said as I got up from the bed and onto my feet.

She came to the edge of the mattress and then swung her legs out around me, her knees folding where the mattress ended. I was the perfect height for her and her bed. Comfort for both parties. And when her mouth swallowed me, my brain shut off. It had closed shop until further notice as I let tsunami-like sensations sweep through my body one after the other.

I cradled her head, letting my fingers massage her scalp as I followed her lead, allowing her to control the cadence with which she was taking me up the elevator toward O-town. One thing was obvious: it wouldn't take long.

I reluctantly pushed her away for a second to let me regroup and go down a few notches on my excitement scale. Bending down to kiss her, I could taste my own saltiness in her mouth. Then I took her body to the center of the bed and lay against her one more time. The warmth of our bodies touching each other wasn't helping me cool down.

"Do you have protection?" I asked her.

She nodded, then reached for her nightstand. A few seconds later, the game was back on—my dick covered and eager to do what it did best. I wanted to take her, but not from behind. I shook the memory of Andrea out of my head. I needed to stare into her eyes as I made love to the woman who loved my Sophia. It was too soon for me to feel anything for Virginia, save for an incredible amount of lust and admiration.

So we lay sideways, facing each other. I lifted her upper leg and brought it up, folding her knee to rest past my hip, then instinctively lined myself up with her wet opening. Pulling her ass toward me, I slowly inched my way into her.

Her eyes closed as she tilted her head back, her lips parted to let out a long, satisfied grunt as I pushed deeper into her pussy. Her warm exhalation caressed my face as I watched a smile grow on her lips before she reopened her eyes.

"Can you take more in?" I asked her once our gazes mingled again.

"Yes!" she whispered.

And I continued parting her insides until I felt her body jerk a bit. Her round eyes told a tale of part surprise, part pleasure, and I took it as a sign to pull back out a bit. She folded one arm under her head and let her other hand roam along my side and my back, at times drawing me closer to her, which only made me resume my thrusting motions, this time a little faster, but still not allowing myself to ram my full length into her. Virginia was a petite woman after all. But maybe once I'd warmed her up some more...

I tilted my hips, changing my angle just a tad, and then really grabbed hold of her firm ass, squeezing it as I increased my cadence some more. With my other arm useless under my side, I decided to swallow Virginia's mouth in kisses instead. And did she ever respond to that! As though we were teenagers, our tongues did their expressive French dance. But I wanted more. I needed more.

Rolling Virginia onto her back, I freed my other arm. I pulled out of her for a second, just to sit on my ankles, between her parted legs. Then I brought her hips up onto my slanted lap. Her sultry eyes and flushed cheeks were my focus as I aligned my dick and began pulling her light body up and down. A line appeared between her brows, but before I could ask if I was hurting her somehow, she used her arms to push her back off from the sheets, raising herself to a seated position on me. Wrapping her arms around my back, she began riding me, her small perky breasts now within view and reach, so I let her. But my own gratification was soon approaching, and I needed to slow it down a bit, so I grabbed Virginia by the waist and slowed down her rhythm.

"I'm close," I said, looking into her eyes.

"Me too," she responded, nodding.

Her brows began moving, and I took it as a sign she wasn't lying. So, I took control of the next dozen thrusts, which resulted in her showing me her orgasmic stare for just a few seconds before she arched her back and leaned away from me, facing the ceiling instead. I gave her a couple more thrusts before I exploded into her.

She lowered her shoulders to the bed, leaving her hips attached to mine. We stayed like this for a minute or so, my dick comfortable in her pulsating pussy as I caught my breath again. My eyes danced on her beautiful naked body while I reveled in the moment. From her slightly outie belly button to her gorgeous brown hair spread around her face on the sheets, Virginia was genuinely beautiful, inside and out.

Feeling that odd sense that someone was watching me, I remembered the neighbor. I turned to look out the window. He was still there, behind the camera.

I aced that interview.

6:30 p.m.

Needless to say, my stomach had become ravenous once Virginia and I left her bedroom. And I also craved a cigarette.

Standing outside in her backyard, we shared mindless chatter and kept our hands off of each other, but my mind couldn't stop picturing her naked.

When she put out her cigarette, she said, "I have to go and talk to Romaro. I'll be back shortly."

"Should I make us some sandwiches for when you get back?"

"That'd be lovely," she said with a squeeze of my hand. "Could you also light up another fire? It feels a little cool down here."

So, I returned to the kitchen once I finished my smoke and got to work. After preparing more than one for each of us (I'd learned my lesson), I was opening a bottle of wine when Virginia returned from her neighbor's with a DVD in hand.

"I just need to email Sophia, and then I'll be back down."

She rushed upstairs. Ten minutes later, she was back on the ground floor and found me sitting outside at the picnic table in front of a small mountain of sandwich pieces, a bottle of wine, and two wine glasses.

"Sorry, the file was quite large. It's still uploading to Dropbox, but I share a folder with her. She'll have access to the file once it's in the cloud."

"And then...?" I asked, hopeful the video indeed served as an interview, although she had never said those words aloud.

"And then Sophia will be in touch, with good news, I think." She winked at me and raised her glass. "I'm sure of it. To Sophia!" she said.

I repeated her toast and added, "And us."

"To Sophia and us."

And a warm sensation swirled in my gut when I heard Virginia say those words.

We ate in near silence. I forcefully slowed my pacing, wanting to do nothing more but swallow everything whole. But this was a nice day. Everything was nearly perfect right now. And meeting Sophia was indeed within reach now, thanks to the gorgeous woman sitting in front of me. Watching her devour her food only made me want her again. And again.

I let that thought dissipate by swallowing a generous sip of wine, but it resurfaced. I pushed it down with the final bite of my sandwich. It still resurfaced.

"I need to have you again," I said, breaking the silence. "Dessert?"

She smiled at me. "So no longer a one-test-run man, either?"

"With you? Who could stop after the first one?"

Her tongue followed her teeth in her closed mouth, probably clearing whatever food might have gotten stuck, but my mind jumped to something else I'd like that tongue of hers to do. Then I thought of what I wanted my tongue to lick right now.

Once she finished both her food and drink, I spoke again.

"Let's go back inside. I know of a great way to pass the time while we wait for Sophia to receive your file."

"Sounds like a good idea."

I carried the empty dishes back into the house, and she carried the wine, refilling her glass instead of putting it in the sink.

"What do you have in mind?" she asked before dipping her lips into the red liquid.

"I want to eat your pussy again. I want you to sit on my face—"

"Charlie!"

"What?" I asked.

She closed her eyes for three seconds and reopened them. "I like your plan, but I don't like the way you phrased it. Can you be a little less... rude?" she asked.

"Hmmm. Sorry. I didn't realize it was rude..."

She tilted her head. "Maybe not rude, but less... direct and crude?"

I closed the gap between us and wrapped my arms around her waist. Between kisses, I rephrased my demand. "Could I... please... kiss... your sweet skin... your gorgeous body... all of it... and I mean *all* of it... for dessert? Pretty please?"

With a slanted smile and her sultry eyes, she replied. "Now, what woman could turn you down after such a lovely request?" She grabbed my hand and brought me to the living room. She stopped in front of the fireplace.

"Here okay?"

"Hell, yes!" I began unbuttoning her shirt while she reciprocated with mine. A couple of minutes later, both of us in our birthday suits, we moved to the cushions she'd laid on top of the hide. Already hard for the past few minutes, I had to convince my cock that this one was not for him. I focused on her mouth at first, but slowly worked my kissing path down to my dessert. But I didn't want to eat her like that. I turned to lie on my back, resting my head on a pillow, then ordered her to come to me with my fingers.

"Come and let me taste you again," I said, careful with my words.

On her knees, she approached me, then parted her legs over my face.

"A bit lower, please."

And my stretched-out tongue soon got what I wanted. Having a face-full of Virginia's gorgeous, tasty pussy was the perfect way to finish my meal. I closed my eyes to fully revel in her flavor, her scent. My hands groped her small ass as I munched on her, enjoying her taste of arousal. I could feel her hips beginning to sway, I opened my eyes for a second to take in the sight, and decided to keep them open. She massaged her breasts, looking up. For a fleeting second, I wondered if she imagined Sophia eating her out instead of me, but then I decided not to care. I was the one enjoying her right now.

When she brought one of her hands down, her moans grew loud. I watched her toy with her clit when, somewhere in the distance, a phone rang.

It was Virginia's ringtone, not mine.

She stopped moving, and her face turned toward the source of the noise. Her hips, hands, and entire body had frozen, even though I was still at it. At her.

"It can wait," she finally said, shaking her head and resuming her motions.

It must have taken her a solid minute before her moaning reached the stage she'd achieved earlier, but I didn't care. Eating her was paradise on earth. I'd pay to do it longer if I had to.

But her legs soon began quivering around my head, her groans turned to a pleading, happy, soft whimper, and her insides started convulsing around my tongue, my entire mouth feeling, tasting, and sensing her orgasm. I sucked on her clit, but she brought her hand to stop me after a few seconds.

"That was just ... lovely, Charlie. Thank you." Then she lifted one knee and got off of my face.

I could feel her wet juices and the results of my own sloppy work running down my cheeks, my neck. But that had been sloppy in a good way. Her scent had even dripped into my nose. With a hand, I wiped my face, getting a concentrated whiff of her even though she'd already stepped away to fetch her phone.

She screamed with joy a second later.

"I gotta call Sophia back right now." I sat up, and she knelt next to me, her phone against her ear.

"Hola cariño," Virginia said into the handset.

I so wanted to hear Sophia's voice, but there was no way I was going to do anything that could risk ruining the odds of me meeting her now, so I let things fall as they may.

About a minute elapsed before Virginia spoke again, but her smile only kept growing with each passing second. "Okay, let me ask him," she said before covering the phone.

She turned to me. "When are you leaving and what flights are you catching?"

"Tomorrow morning, flying out of Bilbao to Madrid, then an afternoon flight to Heathrow."

She repeated my words to Sophia, then turned to me again: "Do you have your flight numbers?"

Through the same (inefficient) process, she relayed my information to

Sophia. *Patience, Charlie. You'll hear her voice soon enough. You'll get to talk to her fast enough.*

"Yes, I can drive him there," she said, but her eyes were on me, as though asking me if I'd like that.

I nodded.

She smiled in return.

A few minutes of humming and nodding passed, then her entire face lit up. "Perfect. I'll let him know."

What?

I was more excited than a kid on Christmas morning.

A message from Sophia. What the hell is it?

But Virginia continued her conversation, testing my patience. "And when will I see you again?" she asked.

I had no idea what Sophia told her, but ecstasy was the only way to describe her facial expression.

"I can't wait... *Te quiero*... Bye," she said, then hung up.

She wrapped her arms around me and kissed me with even more fervor than she'd already displayed earlier today. I didn't even think that would have been possible.

Although I wanted to dwell in her embrace, I also needed to know what Sophia had to tell me, so I gently pulled out of her kiss.

"What did she say?"

"You helped me fix it. Thank you, Charlie."

I frowned at her reply. "I'm glad to have helped, I'm very happy for you, but what did she say about me? Do I get to meet her?"

"Oh! Yes, sorry." She stretched her body to place her phone on the coffee table.

"So?"

"Yes! Tomorrow. She'll meet you at the Madrid airport."

Fucking A! Finally!

So I rolled on top of Virginia, eager to show my gratitude by leading her up toward the best orgasm she'd ever gotten. Well, at least I would do my very, very best. The rest was up to her.

And based on the efficiency of her move when she twisted her legs around mine and managed to put me on my back in one fell swoop, I knew from the way she sat on my hips that I was also going to be in for a wild ride.

11:15 a.m.

How I loathed not being in control.

Sitting at a coffee shop about a hundred feet from my departure gate at the Madrid airport, I sipped my Americano while looking at the beams and roof arches above me; their color-coded design was helpful in directing travelers to the appropriate sections of the airport.

There was no point in walking around and trying to find her. We could be walking circles around each other. She knew my flight number. She'd have to come to me. That was the only way.

But that also meant she'd have a flight to catch, otherwise she wouldn't be able to find me here. So no happy ending for me today. As the realization dawned on me, disappointment surged to my heart, but a little part of me was also okay with it. I couldn't wait to see her, to hear her voice, to meet her and discover whether or not there'd be chemistry between us.

"Charlie?" said a voice as smooth as Bourbon behind me.

I turned around and saw her, standing right there, in a perfectly-tailored gray skirt suit that highlighted her sumptuous curves.

Sophia. In the flesh.

A single button closed her jacket at the waist, and the vast opening between her lapels made plenty of room for her generous breasts to fill the silky black layer she wore underneath.

My heart palpitated in a syncopated dance. My breathing stopped for a few seconds.

I swallowed hard, pushing my anxiety aside. "Sophia. Finally."

"Mind if I take a seat?" she asked, her hand already on the back of the empty stool next to me.

I nodded, unable to speak.

As she sat, her perfume swooped over me. She turned to face me, and my eyes temporarily darted to the cleavage line that rose from her black top, then I brought them back up to her eyes. Her gorgeous, intriguing eyes that held too many colors to be accurately described with one word. Then her Mona Lisa smile... Her luscious lips were sending me an invitation to be kissed.

"We don't have much time," she said, snapping me right back to reality. She moved a large black leather purse up onto her lap, then withdrew a large manila envelope from it. Placing it on the counter in front of her, she then slid it toward me, but kept her hand on it, as though I wasn't yet permitted to have whatever it contained.

"What is it?" I asked.

"It's the least you deserve considering your adamant efforts in tracking me down."

Too many questions fought in my head, and I spurted out the one that'd been stuck in an endless loop for months. "Why did you do it? Why me?"

"I'm sure your reputation is not unknown to you. Plus, I'd already decided to quit my job, so it didn't matter if you were going to use my words against me with the airline. But I figured your obsession with sex would win. I wanted to find a handsome, smart, and interesting guy to play with on an intermittent basis. I figured if I found someone who enjoyed the chase, that man may find it worth his while. I guessed right. Well, mostly."

"Now what?"

"Things got complicated..."

Her sentence hung heavily between us, as though more needed to be said.

"But..." I offered.

From the corner of my eyes, I saw people get up and line up to board at my departure gate. But I stayed put. I needed to hear what she had to say.

"It would be awfully mean of me to end it here, without a happy ending for either of us," she said.

"Mean? No. But damn right disappointing."

"I'm certain Virginia took good care of you. And it looked like you took good care of her." Her eyes sparkled with an indescribable sensuality. "Thank you for that." She'd nodded once with her last comment, and then she lifted her hand from the manila envelope. "Take this."

I grabbed it and felt its weight. *Lots of paper.*

"I brought you something you wanted. Going through the process should occupy you while I get things sorted out on my end."

"The process?"

"Open it."

I did, and I slipped all its content out on the counter. There was a single-page of double-sided, hand-writing—I recognized her hand-writing—and a thick pile of papers held together by one of those black paper clips. I flipped through the pages, but none of it made sense.

"It's in French, sorry. There's no reason to have our application forms translated into English. But if you're interested in becoming a member for real, then you'll have to learn it anyway, or else you won't be able to communicate with our staff."

Really? An application for her maison close *in Paris?*

"By the time you're done with those, you'll know how to contact me, and we'll take it from there."

"Take it from there?"

"If you want to start courting me."

"What?" And then Virginia's words came back to me. *She's changed. She wants a certain level of commitment.*

She shook her head. "I thought... Virginia gave me the impression she'd told you about me. About the past year."

"She did... But why don't you clarify it for me?" I asked.

"I love Virginia. She loves me. But there's something missing. I think it's a man. Maybe someone like you. Virginia obviously likes you enough, but I don't know you. You may feel as though you know me, but what you've read in my diary were my thoughts as I got to know myself a little better. I don't recall what

I wrote exactly, but I can think of a few things I'd do differently if I had a chance to relive the past year."

"Such as?"

"I really don't have time for this now—"

Sophia was interrupted by an announcement made for my flight. "Final boarding call—"

"You really have to go now." She stood up from her seat, and I did the same. "Have a safe flight, and see you around, Charlie," she said before leaning in to kiss me on the cheek, but I put my hand on the side of her neck and turned her head to face me so I could swallow her luscious lips instead. She tasted of strawberries and cream, and butterflies fought in the pit of my stomach as the world around me stopped. An electrical current passed through my veins when she kissed me back. I wasn't a sole player here. Her tongue interwove itself with mine as a year's worth of urges surged through my mind, through my heart, through my body. I wrapped my arms around her back, pressing her body against mine as though I could soak her essence in and somehow merge my soul with hers.

But before long, she pulled away.

"You gotta go," she said as a woman's voice paged me by name to report to my gate for the final boarding call. She stepped away from me, a smile on her lips. "See you soon."

Her parting words had been more of a question than a promise, but I didn't have time to overanalyze it.

I slipped the envelope into my briefcase then dashed to my departure gate.

EPILOGUE

AFTER A YEAR of random international vacations and short getaways that each fueled my obsession toward my mysterious stewardess, I finally found her: Sophia Andrews Vasquez. (She signed her full name at the bottom of her handwritten letter.)

Her real identity is no longer mysterious, but what happened to her in the past year is still unknown to me.

Sophia, a former stewardess, now turned *pimptress* (or whatever she calls herself), who'd relocated from God-knows-where to Paris.

Out of curiosity, I contacted my guy who could access airline records in his dubious ways. She did work for *my* airline! But she'd quit before I ran my search for all Sophias. That's why I didn't find her then. Damn timing.

Isn't life just a series of poorly- and well-timed events? Had she dropped her diary in my briefcase two years earlier, there's no knowing whether or not I'd have played along. Or if I'd have given up after only getting a kiss out of her at the end of this (partial) journey.

But—call it wisdom, brain malfunction, or self-discovery—the realizations I came to terms with while in Spain have changed me. It's too early to say if it was for better or worse, but right now, my mind's at peace with the idea of courting Sophia. My dick disagrees, of course, but my heart sides with my head. Two out of three, so I gotta roll with it.

Ever since kissing her at the airport, my dreams have been centered around her even more than they've already been. Sophia deserves my full attention. What I felt when our lips touched was nothing short of breathtakingly magical.

A mysterious, magnetic pull that somehow connected my soul to hers. And I'll have to use my innate charm and learn an entirely new language to conquer her, but she's worth it. And knowing that the gorgeous and talented Virginia is part of the deal... Well, that's just priceless.

I like a good challenge.

Bring it!

And it seemed the universe heard my call.

A couple of weeks ago, following the instructions she'd left in her hand-written letter, I mailed her a diary of my own, in which I described my adventures as I crisscrossed the globe to track her down. It seemed like a fair request. And it should help her get to know me better. At least I hope so.

And this morning, the mailman gave me a (very premature) Christmas present: another beautiful brown leather journal along with a black moleskin notebook. When I opened the brown diary, I recognized the handwriting, but the words were new. The black one had to be Virginia's. Parts were written in Spanish, parts in English.

Their journals may very well hold the keys to their hearts. But if not, they will surely turn me on and enrich my sexual life through fantasies, new ideas, experiences, or good ole hand pumping action.

I'm sure you understand that I have much better things to do right now than to continue writing my thoughts down on paper. I gotta learn French and fill out my application to Sophia's very special establishment. And I've got not just one but two diaries to read and fantasize about.

Look for me again in a few months. By then, I should be able to report back on what I've learned about Sophia's and Virginia's experiences over the past year (and finally understand the 'complications' they both referred to.)

Women...

But at least I won't have to try and read their minds. Their convoluted thoughts should hopefully untangle themselves and become easier to follow and understand as I decipher their handwriting.

And I certainly hope to cross paths with Virginia and Sophia again in the very near future.

How I crave both of them now.

I'm hopeful that I'll find a way to court them and finally have the sensuous threesome that has occupied half of my mental bandwidth for the past days and weeks.

Yours truly,

Capt. Charlie
Undisclosed Airline

P.S. If you want to read her hand-written letter, you can download a copy for free here: http://smpratt.com/dear-charlie

SEASON TWO IS AVAILABLE!

The story continues in another episodic novel called *The Diary Obsession*.

ABOUT THE AUTHOR

S.M. Pratt is a single woman looking for more than love. Before the world changed, she used to lead a nomadic lifestyle. Fun adventures and unique cultural experiences were always at the top of her agenda, no matter the country she happened to be visiting. She thrived on traveling the world on her own, learning new languages, and living in the moment.

Her unstoppable wanderlust and international experiences inspired her ongoing episodic saga, which starts with The Stewardess's Diary (first season) and continues with The Diary Obsession (second season). S.M. Pratt's exciting tales feature characters exploring their sexuality, living outside societal norms, and enjoying polyamorous relationships (mostly of the FFM variety).

Visit https://smpratt.com to learn more about her and her books. You can also download a free erotic story when you subscribe to her mailing list.

BONUS CONTENT

Letter to Charlie

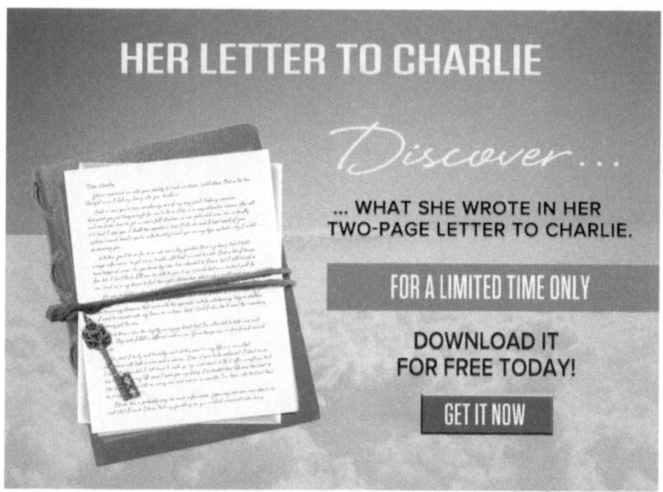

Subscribe to my newsletter and receive a free copy of the two-page letter the stewardess wrote to Charlie:

https://smpratt.com/dear-charlie

AUTHOR'S NOTES
JANUARY 2018

Are you curious as to how this series came to be and what inspired it?

You may have read the "official" version on various websites where I sell my books, but if you keep reading, you'll get the "unabridged" version.

The "official" version:

The idea for *The Stewardess's Diary* came to me while traveling. I was re-reading Helen Fielding's *Bridget Jones's Diary* at the time, and I liked how it read, the humor, the characters... So, I decided to present my story in the same format (a diary) and include similar tropes (a woman who struggles with her love life, a good-looking boss who sleeps around, and humor), but I also wanted to add a bit of mystery and include some sizzling sex scenes. So that's how the idea for the book came about, but then I decided to turn it into "an episodic novel" so I could publish each part separately, to get readers to follow along while I wrote the next episode.

The "unabridged" version:

What I wrote above is true, but there's a lot more to it. As a single woman who travels a lot and loves to immerse herself in different environments, I couldn't help but write these stories. The specific event that triggered the whole concept occurred while I was living in Costa Rica. Having just finished a book under a different pen name, I was looking for another story idea. I'd found one and written about ten chapters into an action/adventure story when I got distracted with the concept behind *The Stewardess's Diary*. To be more accurate, I became obsessed with it. I'd wake up in the middle of the night to write down a few notes.

It all started with a man.

I vividly remember swimming naked in a pool under the stars with him. We didn't speak the same language. There were cultural barriers, awkward situations, unreciprocated feelings, too much alcohol, some recreational substances, even a few shamanic ceremonies. But I'm getting ahead of myself. (Those happened in different countries, months later.) Other than one very entertaining evening with that guy, nothing came of it except for this book series.

A few months later, while living in Argentina and enjoying a friends-with-benefits relationship with another man (good ole "Netflix" plans), I decided to publish the first three installments of the story. I had no idea where the characters were headed, though.

The larger picture came to me while I was living in Colombia, writing the seventh installment. My research into French laws regarding prostitution opened up my story for the second season. I knew how the first season had to end at that point, but I couldn't quite wrap my mind around how it was going to work.

Then, almost a year later, while in Mexico, as I worked through the tenth installment, trying to wrap all my loose ends, I realized Virginia would play a much larger role than I had initially anticipated. But that's something you'll learn more about when you start reading the sequel.

So how much truth is there to these stories?

A few details are anchored in or were taken from my real life, but otherwise, it's all fiction.

For those who joined my reader group a while back, you should know that I am not (and never was) a flight attendant. I am a veteran of online dating, culture hopping, and making friends. I've traveled miles and miles on planes and spent countless hours in airports, bus stations, and train stations. I have a few pilot and flight attendant friends and a very vivid imagination when it comes to finding love or sexual opportunities in strange places.

But if you're reading this section of the book, I'm pretty sure you're curious about other aspects of my stories. You want the "juicy tidbits," and I can't blame you.

So here it goes.

The following details were inspired by my life. It doesn't mean that the rest wasn't. The following tidbits were not necessarily portrayed accurately either. They were just the seeds I used as part of my creative process.

Part One: Canada

Several years ago, I went on a camping trip through the Northwestern US and Western Canada with my then boyfriend. He was my last official romantic relationship to survive long enough to be granted a title (even though it lasted less than a year). I loved him, but the feelings weren't mutual. When we broke up, he assured me that he hadn't cheated on me, but I could never shut down my suspicions. (I'm not the jealous type, so this was a weird situation for me.) And if any cheating had occurred, it wouldn't have been while camping. Anyway, I still love and miss the guy. I wish him love and happiness from the bottom of my heart as I do my best to meet new people and find my own path to happiness.

Part Two: Mexico

I've always loved being in or around the water. And as of the time of writing this, I'm currently living in Mexico (not in Cancun but nearby). The two blondes, pirates, and coast guard do not exist in real life, but some odd tidbits here and there came from my time in Costa Rica. I have several gay/bisexual/lesbian friends (including a couple of older blonde women). Did I subconsciously wonder what they were like in their younger years? Who knows...

Part Three: Costa Rica

I lived in one Costa Rican town for five months. My experience in that country was a happy daze. It did bring me out of my shell (a lot). The weird stuff I experienced first-hand... This is where I swam naked in a pool with a guy I had a major crush on. (And for the record, there's nothing like floating around and staring at the stars in the middle of the night.) I also went skinny dipping at night in the ocean, just diving into the oncoming waves by myself. Did I mention how much I love water?

While I didn't take surf lessons, a stranger on the beach did offer a free massage while I was there. (Yeah, I know... This should have raised a red flag in my mind.) But I'll spare you the details and say that his fingers went places they shouldn't have gone. My Spanish wasn't that great then. Anyway, I don't want to rethink about this incident any more than I have to. I ended up washing the lousy memory away with a few beers that night and then turned it into something else in my story. FYI, I never got in trouble with the local police. I'm a good girl (and I'm pretty lucky).

Part Four: USA

I honestly don't know what triggered the idea behind this story. Do I watch too much porn? Or too many movies with Owen Wilson? Ah, the mysterious things my creative muse whispers in my ears...

Part Five: Ireland

This one was definitely inspired by a porn movie I watched while staying in an Airbnb in Spain (more on that later). I've been to Ireland before, but it was a long time ago. There's nothing like a pint of freshly-poured Guinness (both watching it settle and drinking it). I want to go back and live there one day.

Oh, and (as far as I know) the redacted castle doesn't exist.

Part Six: Thailand

I was a little hesitant before hitting publish on this one. I wasn't sure how people would react. I've visited Thailand a couple of times, and I've always been impressed by the warmth and friendliness of its people. While there, I did encounter quite a few situations where I didn't know if a person was a man or a woman. Sometimes I suffer from spurts of insomnia, so I use those bits of extra time to wonder about things. Things like how difficult life would be for someone who feels trapped in a body that isn't theirs. I admire people who have the courage and determination to go through a sex-change procedure (and then deal with the sucky consequences—let's be honest, a large majority of people are too close-minded to even understand the situation). I'm all for LGBTQ pride. We *all* deserve to be happy.

Part Seven: France

Oh... this one. I'll be honest and admit to blacking out a few times in my life. I do drink a fair bit at times. But somehow, I've always made it home safely, so I'm very grateful for that.

I was dumped by email by the first man I ever loved for real. It took me around ten or fifteen years to get over him. But thanks to that man, I developed a love for traveling. While we were dating, I'd fly to meet him somewhere or vice-versa. I was young, stupidly happy, innocent, and hopeful. Things didn't turn out the way I thought they would, but it's all good. I also wish him love and happiness, wherever he is in the world now.

And the part about an aunt owning a whorehouse is all fiction. As far as I know, I do not have any relatives in France, and—unless someone's been really great at keeping secrets—I do not have any relatives who run businesses in any way associated with the sex trade industry.

Part Eight: Holland

This is all made up. I once had a crush on a twin when I was around 15 or 16. I always wondered if identical twins took advantage of their genes to double up on their sex life. And I (allegedly) enjoy weed. After a few experiences with various shamans over the years, I'll admit that I'll always favor nature's own medicines over any pharmaceutical ones. (Of course, modern medicine has its place, and I was grateful for the availability of surgery and painkillers when I broke my ankle a few months back.)

Part Nine: Japan

Yeah... way out there, I know. While lost in a haze in Costa Rica, the game show events kept popping up in my mind. The bare-bones version of this Japanese episode helped determine what later became the structure of her journal + his journal because I wanted to show the captain's reaction to the games, so he somehow needed to get his hands on a copy of the games. And you know the rest.

Part Ten: Spain

The first season ends where my current nomadic phase of life started. I still shake my head at my former, very innocent self. I first went to Spain because I thought it would be the safest place for me to travel alone while immersing myself in Spanish. It turns out that the Spaniards speak way faster than the rest of the Spanish-speaking world (and they have that lisp). So, while Spain is my favorite country on earth, I'd probably start with Peru if I had to redo this whole language-learning-through-immersion thing. (Regarding Spanish dialects, I found Peruvian Spanish to be most neutral and easiest to pick up and understand.)

The city I used in the book isn't accurate, but many details are. (And, for the record, San Sebastián is my favorite city on earth.) I met a guy there whose family owned a house in a small village in Navarra. My descriptions of the scenery, food, and other non-identifying details are accurate based on my recollection of them. Virginia and Eduardo are fictitious, but my Airbnb host (in the other city I went to--sorry, I'm keeping this a secret) was super friendly. She did leave a lot of her belongings in her living room and mentioned that I could read/watch whatever I wanted. There were three porn movies in her collection: a seventies one with a remote, one about a woman discovering her sexuality, and one with a castle where the owner would peek at everything that happened. (Thinking back now, I guess that last movie also inspired parts of episode seven...)

Hope these author's notes were interesting to read and gave you a glimpse of what went through my mind as I wrote the first season of what will hopefully turn into a very long series.

Join my reader group if you'd like to hear more:
https://smpratt.com

www.ingramcontent.com/pod-product-compliance
Lightning Source LLC
Chambersburg PA
CBHW050841210726
48290CB00004B/1034

* 9 7 8 1 9 8 8 6 3 9 6 0 4 *